KAROO MOON

KAROO MOON
OLIVE SCHREINER

Undine
The Story of an African Farm
From Man to Man

EDITED BY T S EMSLIE

STONEWALL BOOKS

'*Look, there is General Jackson's brigade, standing behind you like a stone wall*'

2004

Undine was first published in 1928
The Story of An African Farm was first published in 1883
From Man to Man was first published in 1927

© *Karoo Moon* Stonewall Books 2004

TRADE PAPERBACK EDITION: ISBN 0-620-31843-0
HARDBACK EDITION: ISBN 0-620-32132-6

COVER BY MICHAEL PETTIT AND ADBUL AMIEN
SET BY ADBUL AMIEN
PRINTED AND BOUND IN THE REPUBLIC OF SOUTH AFRICA
BY CREDA COMMUNICATIONS

STONEWALL BOOKS
52 MAIN ROAD • ST JAMES • CAPE TOWN • 7945
SOUTH AFRICA

Distributed in Southern Africa by Book Promotions
P O Box 5 • Plumstead • 7800 • South Africa
Tel: 021-706-0949 • Fax: 021-706-0940
email: orders@bookpro.co.za
and in the United Kingdom by Central Books
99 Wallis Road • London • E9 5LN • England
Tel: 020-8986-4854 • Fax: 020-8533-5821
email: orders@centralbooks.com

*For the free spirit nurtured
on the illimitable veld*

OLIVE EMILIE ALBERTINA SCHREINER
1855–1920

CONTENTS

Introduction *ix*

Undine *1*

The Story of an African Farm *179*
Author's Preface *181*
Introduction by S C Cronwright-Schreiner *185*

From Man to Man *397*

List of subscribers *705*

INTRODUCTION

In the introduction to his book *Only an Anguish to Live Here–Olive Schreiner and the Anglo-Boer War*, Karel Schoeman says the following:

'By 1899 Olive Schreiner was probably the best known South African besides Cecil Rhodes and President Kruger, and as likely as not the only South African woman who was known outside the confines of her own country, her fame being based largely on a single novel, *The Story of an African Farm*, which had appeared in 1883. During the mounting tension of the preceding decade, she had moreover begun to achieve increasing fame as an eloquent and impassioned defender of the Boer people and their cause, and her opinions were eagerly sought by the world press.'

This introduction is but a brief summary of the external facts of Olive Schreiner's life, mainly prior to publication of *The Story of an African Farm*, to assist readers of *Karoo Moon* to judge for themselves the extent of the literary accomplishment of her three 'African farm' novels.

Olive's father, Gottlob Schreiner, was born in Germany on 6 August 1814. Following in his father's footsteps, he set out to become a cobbler; but at the age of eighteen adopted a different course and enrolled at the mission house of the Basle Missionary Society. In his early twenties he went for further training to Islington College in London, where he met and fell in love with Rebecca Lyndall, a 'Methodist Calvinist' minister's daughter. They were married on 7 November 1837, and in February 1838 Gottlob and Rebecca Schreiner arrived at the Cape Colony under the auspices of the London Missionary Society.

In 1846 Gottlob Schreiner joined the Wesleyan Missionary Society, and on 24 March 1855 Olive Emilie Albertina Schreiner, sixth of the surviving Schreiner children, was born on the Wesleyan mission station at Wittebergen, near present-day Herschel in the northern mountains of the Eastern Cape. She was named after her deceased brothers, Oliver, Emile and Albert, and as a child she was known as Emilie, or Emily – sometimes Emmy – until at the age of fifteen she eschewed the name Emilie in favour of Olive. Two younger brothers, William, who later became Prime Minister of the Cape Colony, and Cameron, who died in infancy, were also born at Wittebergen, where Olive spent the first six years of her life.

In 1860 the Schreiners moved to Healdtown, near Fort Beaufort, travelling by ox-wagon for about five weeks. This and a journey to attend the Wesleyan annual general meeting in Queenstown in October 1859 were the two long ox-wagon trips undertaken by Olive during her childhood.

In 1865 Gottlob Schreiner found himself in the position of being obliged to resign from the Wesleyan Missionary Society (for reasons linked to his private commercial transactions, albeit that there was no dishonesty involved), and he obtained a plot at Balfour in the Kat River Settlement and attempted to make a living by running a shop. This and other efforts to support his family culminated in his bankruptcy in 1866.

In 1868, after two years of penury and financial stress, Olive and, later the same year, her younger brother Will joined their elder brother and sister, Theo and Ettie, in Cradock, where Theo was a school principal. This was the thirteen-year-old Olive's first experience of the Karoo.

Towards the end of 1870 Theo and Ettie Schreiner went to the Diamond Fields and Olive, whose relationship with her sister Ettie was not an easy one, left Cradock at the age of fifteen for stays with various friends and well-disposed acquaintances in the Eastern Cape, unable to live with her parents due to their precarious financial position. She travelled *via* Burgersdorp to Avoca (Orpens), to Kraai River, to Hermon in Basutoland and, again *via* Burgersdorp, to Dordrecht.

In 1872 Olive travelled *via* Queenstown to her parents' home at Hertzog, joined Theo and Ettie at New Rush (later Kimberley), and in 1873 travelled through Beaufort West to Fraserburg to join her two married sisters, Katie Findlay and Alice Hemming. She stayed with the latter and in 1874, after three months in Fraserburg, travelled with the Hemmings to Cape Town, whence she sailed on the *Edinburgh Castle* to Port Elizabeth, and from there *via* Grahamstown to Hertzog. The same year she travelled through Bedford and Cradock to Colesberg, where she began service as governess to the children of the Weakley family.

In March 1875 Olive moved to the Cradock district to teach on the farm of Mr Stoffel Fouché, Klein Gannahoek, at a salary of £30 a year, and there, in February 1876, she completed her first book, *Undine*, and wrote a considerable part of *The Story of an African Farm*. In May 1876 Olive again changed her employment, joining the Martin family on their farm Ratelhoek in the Tarka district, at the same salary. She later described her time at Ratelhoek with the Martins as 'the quietest and best' of her life. Her father Gottlob died in August 1876, and in December of the same year she travelled through Tarkastad and Queenstown to visit her mother at Seymour. In 1877 Olive again visited her mother, travelling through Cradock and Fort Beaufort, and returning *via* Queenstown; and in January 1878 she once more visited her mother at Seymour, returning *via* Queenstown, where she fell ill. In the winter of 1878 Olive was seriously ill. In December that year she made her first unambiguous reference to *The Story of an African Farm*.

In March 1879 Olive left Ratelhoek because of her ill-health, the house there being badly situated for her asthma, and she moved to Gannahoek in the district of Cradock, where she stayed with the Cawoods. After a few months she again visited her mother at Seymour, then travelled *via* Healdtown and Fort Beaufort to Cradock.

In August 1879 Olive arrived at the farm Leliekloof in the district of Cradock as a teacher, again employed by the Fouché family (who had moved there from Klein Gannahoek), at a higher salary. Here she completed *The Story of an African Farm*, which in 1880 found its way through intermediaries to the Edinburgh publisher David Douglas, who returned it with the comment that it showed considerable talent but needed to be shortened for publication.

In February 1881 Olive travelled *via* Cookhouse to Grahamstown to take leave of her mother, and in March she sailed from Port Elizabeth for England, where she arrived on 30 March 1881, met by her brothers Fred and Will. She intended to qualify as a nurse in Edinburgh, but her asthma, which had plagued her for some years and continued to do so for the rest of her life, forced her to drop out after just a few days; and she never fulfilled her medical ambitions.

Thus *Undine*, *The Story of an African Farm* and parts of *From Man to Man*, which was in fact begun before *The Story of an African Farm*, were written during Olive's itinerant youth, against the background of an almost total lack of formal education, separation from family, financial hardship and ill-health. Perhaps the Karoo isolation of this formidable, intelligent, passionate, freethinking young woman was, paradoxically, the key to her hunger for books, her literary ambition and her intellectual sophistication. Her husband, Cron Cronwright-Schreiner, later said:

'She had never had schooling worth anything to her: all that she knew was from intercourse with her cultured mother and from her insatiable thirst for knowledge and reading, worked upon by her precocious and penetrating intellect.'

Those interested in reading further about Olive Schreiner's life up to the time of her first departure for England are referred to Karel Schoeman's excellent *Olive Schreiner, A Woman in South Africa, 1855-1881*. Writing in 1992, Schoeman said:

'While much is still being written and published about Olive Schreiner seventy years after her death, the greater part of these writings is theoretical, and she is all too often used merely to illustrate the social or political views of the authors. In South Africa, where greater subtlety and a wider range might reasonably be expected in Schreiner studies, the position is not much different: while there are a number of individuals in English-speaking academic circles who are regarded as Schreiner experts, and this title is jealously guarded, it has on the whole not been associated with much profound research, and has, for that matter, often been awarded on somewhat flimsy grounds.'

Olive took the revised manuscript of *The Story of an African Farm* with her to England, and was almost in despair as one publisher after another rejected it. Eventually Chapman & Hall accepted it and it was published in January 1883 to instant acclaim. Cron Cronwright-Schreiner wrote as follows:

'The author's name was given simply as "Ralph Iron", and there was no dedication or preface. This edition brought Olive £18 2s 11d. In July 1883, a second edition was published. This was in one volume and contained a short preface as well as the dedication to Mrs John Brown. The author's name, in brackets beneath the original pen-name "Ralph Iron", appeared in the 1887 edition. Olive used to tell with amusement how surprised Mr Chapman was when, having asked "Ralph Iron Esq" to call, a small, shy, girlish-looking young woman was ushered in, instead of the big, powerful man expected.'

Olive became instantly famous as soon as her identity was revealed.
Karel Schoeman comments on her first period in England as follows:

'The grandiose plans and aspirations she had formed on her remote farms could never be squared with reality, and she soon abandoned the attempt. She never again had fixed employment, practised a profession, or earned a regular income; instead, she drifted along on her royalties, some journalistic work, and the support of her family. Despite fame, intense friendships, fervid polemics and hectic activity, the years abroad were, all in all, a time of loneliness and physical suffering, of restless wandering from one boarding house or private hotel to another, one city to another, one country to another, in quest of health, happiness and peace of mind.'

On her return to South Africa in 1889 Olive Schreiner, by then a household name, lived for a time at Matjiesfontein. In 1892, on a visit to her friends the Cawoods at Gannahoek, she met their neighbour, Samuel Cron Cronwright. After another brief visit to England, Olive returned and in February 1894, at the age of thirty-eight, she married Cron in Middelburg. The Cronwright-Schreiners, as they chose to be called, settled for a time on the farm Krantz Plaats near Cradock in the Karoo. In 1895 Olive gave birth to a baby girl who lived for less than a day.

Although she published no other novels during her lifetime, Olive became prominent in her own right as a political commentator, polemicist and feminist. She and her husband Cron were outspoken in their support for the Boers during the Anglo-Boer War (1899-1902), and she endured a long period under martial law in Hanover in the Karoo. Writing about the Boers, Olive Schreiner said:

'For five years I lived among them as a teacher on their farms, sometimes among the more cultured, and sometimes among the more primitive but not one whit less lovable and intelligent, class. Sometimes for eighteen months I did not see an English face and was brought into the closest mental contact with them which is possible – the mental contact between teacher and taught. Watching them in all the vicissitudes of life, from birth to marriage and death, I learnt to love the

Boer, but more, I learnt to admire him. I learnt that in the African Boer we have one of the most intellectually virile and dominant races the world has seen; a people who beneath a calm and almost stolid surface hide the intensest passions and the most indomitable resolutions.'

Her stance during the Anglo-Boer War brought her into conflict with family and friends, but Emily Hobhouse, who did so much to improve the situation of Boer women and children in the concentration camps during the war, and elsewhere thereafter, met her at Hanover in 1902, and wrote as follows:

'It is hard for my unskilled pen to find words to describe your South African Olive. One gained breadth and grandeur from her. She gave me the illimitable feeling of the veld.'

In 1914 Olive Schreiner returned to England, where she stayed until 1920, leaving (just three weeks after being joined by her husband) in order to return to the Cape to die. She died in Cape Town on 12 December 1920. When Cron returned from Europe some months later, he obtained permission to have her body exhumed from the Schreiner family plot in Maitland cemetery, and arranged for her re-interment atop Buffelskop near Cradock in the Karoo, along with the remains of their baby daughter and those of a pet dog, Nita.

Olive Schreiner wrote and rewrote *From Man to Man* right up until her death. This was the book she cherished most and which, in fact, she never finished. It is nevertheless a satisfying work, and her settings are vivid and sensual – city as well as country, Rondebosch as well as Karoo, and some sharp English scenes. The essay-like passages, of which there are several, are rich, varied and inventive.

Olive's use of words such as 'kaffir' and 'nigger' was not intended to have the perjorative connotation it would have today, and readers who find themselves affronted by this should consider, with humility, how the attitudes of today might appear in a hundred years' time; they should also bear in mind that Olive Schreiner went on to become the champion not only of women's rights but also of the rights of black and disenfranchised people at the time of the South African Convention in 1910. Indeed, in *From Man to Man*, in one of the essay-like passages, one of her characters contemplates an imaginary form of *apartheid* (the building of a wall across Africa, with white people on one side and black people on the other) and rapidly rejects this notion. Inevitably, though, her work portrays nineteenth century attitudes despite her own unconventional views.

I wish to acknowledge the role in this publication of Dr Peter Knox-Shaw, who suggested that the out-of-print *Undine* was worthy of re-publication, a suggestion that culminated in this somewhat more substantial trilogy.

Slight editorial changes have been made to certain old-fashioned words, for example *velskoen* instead of *velschoen*, *Afrikaner* instead of *Africander*, *Karoo* instead of *Karroo*, *today* instead of *to-day*; other words such as *kopje* have been retained as being wonderfully evocative of the era in which the novels are set. No change of substance has been made, in keeping with the overall object of this publication, *Karoo Moon* – to enable readers to experience Olive Schreiner's three novels as a trilogy, the works speaking for themselves. Each novel contains strongly autobiographical elements; together they have wonderful breadth and, apart from their intrinsic worth as novels, give us interesting glimpses of nineteenth century life in the eastern and western Cape, as well as valuable insights into the personality of South Africa's first novelist to achieve international acclaim.

T S Emslie

Matjiesfontein
12 April 2004

Undine

by
Olive Schreiner

Contents

1 A Queer Little Child 5
2 Undine's Jottings 19
3 The Man with the Mouth 27
4 Going to Chapel 30
5 A Sunny Afternoon and a Wild Night 435
6 Greenwood 37
7 Lovers 42
8 Beautiful Snow 55
9 Trodden Snow 66
10 Melted Snow 70
11 A Clever Little Man and a Poor Little Fool 75
12 Sold Her Love 78
13 A Very Wicked Woman 85
14 On Board Ship to South Africa 88
15 In an Ox Wagon 104
16 New Rush 116
17 Little Irons 134
18 Little Irons and a Digger 147
19 Albert Blair 159
20 Alone with the Stars 169

CHAPTER ONE

A Queer Little Child

Karoo, red sand, great mounds of round iron stones, and bushes never very beautiful to look at and now almost burned into the ground by the blazing summer's sun. An old Dutch farmhouse built of the brightest red brick to match the ground and stones; an old stone wall broken down here and there at irregular intervals, as if to allow for the ready ingress and egress of the hundred enterprising goats, whose delight it is daily to regale themselves on the deformed peach trees and leafless cabbage stalks which the enclosure contains; an old tent-wagon, whose tent and floor have long gone the way of all flesh – wood flesh – into the fire; an ancient willow tree, which stands vainly trying to reflect itself in a small pond of thick red fluid, and under which may at all times be seen a couple of dirty and benighted ducks, who there disport themselves under the happy delusion of its being water.

All these parts compose a picture in which, when looked at by daylight, it were hard work to find the slightest trace of beauty; but tonight, penetrated in every nook and corner by the cold white light of an almost full moon, there is a strange weird beauty, a beauty which the veriest sheep-souled Boer that ever smoked pipe or wore *velskoen*, might feel if he had but one ray of light left in him.

It was a silent night. Even the great dogs had crept to sleep under the old tent-wagon, and nothing living or moving was to be seen except a small child and a smaller ape who were perched in one of the gaps of the stone wall.

There they had sat for the last hour, never moving but very busy cogitating, if one might judge from the grave expression of both faces. Likely the smaller pondered on the dire injustice of tying him up all day and giving him orange peel in place of orange pulp, and uncracked almonds, which all the world knew he could not break. His thoughts might have been the most profoundly philosophical, however, if judged by the appearance of his small black countenance – abstruse inquiries into the nature, origin, and destiny of the moon, whose course he was following with his eyes hardly less grave and earnest than the large brown pair above him.

He was wrapped up in the end of the small blue pinafore which the child had on, the only parts visible being the small wizard-like face and a small black hand, with which he held his chin and every now and then raised for a soft sympathetic pat of the little white hand that served as chin-rest to the white, dark-eyed face above him. The child might have been ten years old, but she looked much less as she sat there, perched on the top of a large round stone with her thin little legs drawn up under her in a queer little fashion of her own.

'Socrates,' she said, presently. The monkey turned his soft brown eyes and fixed them full on hers.

'I wish we knew,' said the child.

Socrates gave a long sigh in answer and turned the gaze of his great sad eyes back to the slowly moving moon.

'Come to prayers, come to prayers,' shouted a stentorian voice from one of the back windows, and Socrates's reflections for that night were ended. He was tied up to his stand; and with a kiss on the crown of his little grey head the owner of the blue pinafore left him and went into the house.

The house, as we have said, was Dutch, built in the true Dutch style, with one large front room, from which opened six or eight cabin-like apartments to serve as bedrooms; and with that indispensable of all Dutch farmhouses overhead – a great loft.

In the front room were two large glass cupboards let into the wall, which in the days of their old Dutch proprietor had been wont to contain dolls, earthenware, and all the wealth and glory of the household, and which even now, in spite of their being filled with books, had an uncomfortably Dutch appearance. The room was well furnished, and lighted by a great lamp standing on the centre-table. Before it, with an open Bible and Prayer Book, sat the farmer: an English Africander with nothing worthy of remark about him, if it were not the unusually fine development of his tall muscular figure and the unusually large amount of yellow hair upon his face. There were five others in the room – his wife, a delicate, refined, fair little woman who reclined on the sofa – his son, handsome and bright-eyed, and now home for the holidays – and two little Dutch girls, grey-eyed, yellow-haired, pudding-faced, who were here to share with his step-daughter the instruction of the very stiff and upright individual who sat on a chair near the door. This individual wore three curls on each side of her head and carried a large wart on the tip of her chin.

'Late for prayers again, Undine,' she said, as the owner of the little blue pinafore slipped in at the door and took her way to the nearest seat.

No one else took any notice of her entrance, and the chapter being finished they knelt down to pray. Undine did not listen to the prayer but to the great red clock overhead, that was ticking away such solemn words, the child thought, as she bent below it:

'Another week gone, another day gone. What have you done? We never come back, we moments; we fly, but we never return, never, never, tick, tick. What have you done with us? If you do the best you can with all the rest of us, you can never bring one of us back, never, never, tick, tick.'

Undine tried to listen to the prayer, but the old clock's voice was louder.

'Tick, tick,' cried the inexorable old clock, 'what good have you ever done? How are you better able to die now than you were last week? You are nearer death, but are you ready, ready, ready, tick, tick, tick?'

Undine tried to listen to the prayer again, and she caught these words: 'Thousands, O Lord, are going to destruction every moment.'

'Yes, yes, yes,' said the clock, 'tick, tick, hell, hell, going, going, going, thousands, thousands, thousands, tick, tick, tick, tick.'

She could kneel there while the old clock told only of her own sins and fate, but now – when every tick talked of half the world, for whom there was no help, no hope, who were going, going, going – she felt as though she were being suffocated and the walls and roof were throbbing and coming down on her. She leaped up from her knees, and was recalled to a sense of things present only by being very sharply pulled onto them again. Fortunately the prayer was almost ended, and when they rose there were at once so many human voices trying to make themselves heard that the voice of the old wooden prophet was quickly drowned.

'Undine, my dear, I really must report your conduct to your mamma; it really is most reprehensible,' said the stiff and upright individual. 'You surely have time enough in which to run about; you might forget your play and worship God, when you come *here*. Your mamma thinks so. Do you not?'

The lady thus appealed to not only fully endorsed the opinion, but also, on hearing the nature of the offence, ordained that henceforth the offender's seat should be in the centre of the room, beside her stepfather, and so to speak under the eye of the assembly. This was intended as a direful chastisement, but the child's thoughts were still occupied with the ominous tickings of the old clock, and she would have cared nothing just then if they had sentenced her to sit next some savage king of Timbuctoo who makes his meals off little girls. She stood there before them, with the end of the blue pinafore twisted round one small arm which the other was nursing and patting as tenderly as if it had been Socrates.

'Really, Undine, you are the hardest child to manage. There is no need to put on that look of proud indifference; go to bed at once and let me see no more of you tonight,' said her mother; and the child took up her light and went. Soon she had put it out and crept into bed, but she could not forget the old clock; and how dark the room was! Perfect, boundless, endless darkness it might be, for anything she could see; like that silent darkness which surrounds poor lost souls and is all the answer they get when they cry aloud to God. She pulled the cover over her head and buried it under the pillows; but whoever has tried these means of dodging disagreeable thoughts knows how signally they always fail. She found this out; for by and by a small white face showed itself above the blankets and a pair of troubled eyes looked out into the surrounding darkness.

'Dear God! Great God!' cried the little child, covering her face with both hands, 'You who are so very happy and great and strong, who can do all things, O dear God! Save them. They are going, going, forever, forever, O God! God!'

She lay still for some minutes and then burst forth again, this time in a perfect agony: 'O God! Great God! Save just one soul tonight because I pray. I know that I am wicked and will never be saved, but I pray with faith; save, oh save one soul, for my prayer. Great God! God! God!'

She sat up and buried her face in both her trembling hands. What was the use of her praying – she who did not love God, who could not believe, who could never be saved? How easy it was to understand how the great Son of God could come down to die for souls. The child felt that night as though she, too, could have died to save only a few, a few souls from the great company of the God-hated who were passing over the edge to darkness. How many had gone since she came into that room tonight! How many through the long dim ages of the past! The old Greeks and Romans, and the wild millions of Asia; and how many would pass over long after she had taken her place in the great company and vanished into sin and woe forever! Before and behind her seemed to stretch a chain of endless pain and anguish.

After a time she lay down and tried to close her eyes and drop asleep; but now it seemed as if already she had passed into that unknown land, prepared by God for the souls at whom he laughs. In Dante's hell there were fire and fellowship, earth and pain, but in hers there was nothing so merciful or so material. She seemed in a wide void in which there was only endless space and blackness, and she had not even two hands, the one of which might touch the other and in touching find fellowship; and when she cried aloud her voice fell dead upon the air. There was only emptiness, and black space, above, around, below, and she was one alone. Oh, how the silence ached! One throb of pain, one touch, one sound, how blessed they would be.

An indescribable terror seized the child. Such must be death, eternal death, the death of the wicked, changeless and everlasting as the throne of the God who made it. She crept out of bed trembling and lay down on the cold mud floor; that at least was hard and solid, and it seemed to calm her. She pressed her face onto it, and a few burning tears fell on it; then she lay as still as though she were asleep. How comforting it was, that solid earth; but it was dead and cold, and she would like the touch of something warmer; so after a time she got up and, noiselessly opening the door, stood in the large front room. It was dark and quite still but for the ticking of the old clock and the sound of her own breath. She stood for a minute listening; then she crept on till her fingers touched a door at the far end of the room. After a little pressure it opened, and she went in. There were two beds in the room, both occupied, and she kneeled down at the foot of the nearest and stretched out her hand. It came in contact with what she was in search of – a small foot, soft and warm and full of life. She held it for some moments in both hands, and then, afraid of waking the sleeper, rose to go, noiselessly and softly as she had come.

How the owner of the foot – one of the grey-eyed, cheese-faced little Dutch girls – would have wondered and been mystified, could she have watched the proceedings of her little white-nightgowned visitor, who, feeling her way softly by chairs and tables, soon found herself again in her own room.

She was comforted, but not sufficiently; so she drew from between the mattresses on her bed a small brown New Testament. Pressing it close to her side with one little arm, with the other she dragged a large wooden chair to the window; and with its aid, and that of a stool, climbed up into the window seat. Pushing her hand through a broken pane, she sent the heavy wooden shutter flying back on its hinges. A flood of white moonlight fell into the room, and the face of the moon herself looked in – on the little tumbled bed and the whitewashed walls and the mite of a thing, with its little white nightgown and bare feet perched up in the window.

The mite of a thing closed her eyes tight and opened her book, turning the leaves over and over again, and at last brought down a small finger upon one of them. She opened her eyes and stooped down to read by the moonlight the words on which it had already alighted; they were these: 'Which was the son of Melchi, which was the son of Addi, which was the son of Cosam, which was the son of Elmodam, which was the son of Er.'

She closed the book and sat looking at the cover in silence, with very much the expression of Socrates when lost in the contemplation of a nut he had vainly endeavoured to crack. Faith is strong, however, and reason weak, at ten years; so the brown comforter was opened again; and, after the fashion of the Apostles and good men of old, Providence was appealed to.

This time the words were these – 'Strive to enter in at the straight gate, for many I say unto you shall seek to enter in, and shall not be able.'

She did not close the book this time but sat looking at its open pages with her eyebrows slightly bent; then she caught the book up tightly in one hand and flung it from her with such force that it left the story of its journey written in a large brown dent on the whitewashed wall opposite. She threw her head down on the window seat and cried long and bitterly; but by and by, when she grew quieter, she sat up and pressed her little burning cheek against the window pane. How calm and still the outside world was; so far removed from all passion and strife, damnation, fire and brimstone; so strong, so self-contained. How peacefully the great round stones lay resting on each other. Through that subtle sympathy which binds together all things, and to stumps and rocks gives a speech which even we can understand, the night spoke to the little child the sweet words of comfort which she had looked for in vain in the brown Testament. She left off thinking and only sat and listened, and the sweet night wind blew in through the broken pane and touched her softly, till the weary eyelids closed and the little head found rest once more on the window seat.

Of course Undine was late next morning, late even for Sunday morning. Socrates, in despair of ever getting his breakfast, sat disconsolate on the top of his box, making believe to eat his tail, and every now and then raising his hands to his head and slowly rubbing them across his forehead, as if still suffering from the effect of too much moonlight thought.

It was going to be a sweltering day; even now it gave one an unpleasant sensation to look at the little hills of red round stones scattered here and there and acting the part of great reflectors; as though man and herb were not desiccated and burnt red enough without their help. Indoors the blue flies buzzed. In spite of the soothing effect of more than half-closed shutters, all sat down to breakfast feeling mortally aggrieved, though hardly knowing in what respect, and, according to their several dispositions, desiring to have it out with someone or lapsing into silence.

When Undine came to the table she was met with the usual: 'Late again, my dear; surely going to bed when *you* do, you *might* get up a little earlier. It is this sleeping so much that makes you so incurably stupid. Sannie and Annie were up hours ago,' said the governess, casting an approving glance at the two little maidens opposite, who by their earnest patronage of mutton chops and fat were incontrovertibly proving their Africander origin.

'They went to bed much later than you and were up earlier, and have done their hair much better than you,' continued her instructress, whose ideas were so truly correct, femine, and orthodox, that they might all have been placed in an ordinary breakfast saucer and left there forever, without the least fear of their ever running over.

The meal being ended, the farmer went out to bully the herdsmen for not having let the sheep out earlier, and to saunter about till the heat should drive him in; while his wife hied to the nether regions, where bitter and clamorous war was being waged between Hendrik and Gobalee as to the possession of the sheep's-head-and-feet. The two little Dutch girls stood in the kitchen doorway, and for once the dawning of a light, which if it had arisen might have been called animation, shone in their placid countenances as they drank in every word and even now and then inserted one.

Undine collected some bits of bread, took half a green *mielie*[1] and a cup of water, and, putting on her great brown *kappie*, went out to visit Socrates in the yard. He was glad of the contents of cup and plate, but quickly satisfied himself and began playing with his mielie, now throwing it from him with disdain and gazing up into the sky with an air of deep abstraction, as though completely unconscious of its existence, then seizing it up, taking a bite and hugging it to him, with an expression of earnestness so comical it might have set a Methodist parson laughing on his way to class meeting. Undine did not laugh; she sat down on the ground beside him and looked at him, wondering if he really felt so happy, or only played so wildly because his heart was heavy. She wondered if he ever wished to be anything in the wide world but himself, and yet didn't see anything that he liked better; wondered if he ever longed to die, and yet wished never to die, and nothing in the world ever to die; wondered if it made him feel queer to look up at that little white fleecy cloud in the blue sky overhead; wondered what the little cloud meant and how it came there and why it came there, and why anything was where it was, and why the world was the world, and the sun the sun, and she, she; and why ... She could not wonder any more,

---

1 The *mielies* ('corn') being on the cob.

for two strong hands were shaking her so that the little white cloud, Socrates, the blue sky and red earth, were all jumbled up together.

'Do you wish to ruin your complexion completely, you wicked child, that you sit here staring up into the sky as if you had never seen it before and were bereft of all your senses? Get your *kappie* from that ape and come into the house at once.'

For Mr Socrates had possessed himself of the large brown *kappie* and seemed in no hurry to restore it. Finds are keeps according to the code, and it was only after a world of persuasion had been lavished upon him that he very gingerly descended from his box and, with an air of melancholy resignation and a touch of condescension, delivered it to its owner. Then he sat gravely following with his eyes the little blue pinafore and brown *kappie* as they vanished into the house, and, there being nothing left worth his looking at, he then clambered up into his box to take a doze.

The sheep's-head-and-feet quarrel had been settled, and when Undine entered the front room she found the two little Dutch girls demurely seated on two chairs with their hymn books in their hands, learning their Sunday lessons. Undine, too, got her hymn book down from the shelf, but instead of following the virtuous example before her, she placed her book on the floor, laid herself across a chair, and in this very highly unorthodox position had just composed herself to learn, when she was asked if she had not yet rested enough and were going to sleep again. Of course there was nothing for it but to sit up and learn away steadily till the hour arrived at which, every Sunday morning, the three scholars were marched off into a side room to receive such religious instruction as was suited to their limited capacities and tender years. The first part of the program, which consisted in the recitation of lessons, was soon over. Then Bibles were produced. The little brown Testament was not one of them – false friend it might sometimes be, but friend for all that, and not to be brought out for common eyes to gaze on.

The stiff and upright individual sat in a large armchair, and before her the two little Dutch girls on high-backed *riem*-bottomed chairs, while Undine took possession of a green wagon-chest that stood near the door.

The chapter chosen for their perusal and consideration was the twenty-fifth of Matthew, and when it was concluded each was in turn required to ask some question bearing on its contents. The eldest of the Dutch girls – on whom the heat, the darkness of the room, and the exertion of spelling out the long English words had had an almost stupefying effect – sat for some moments gazing at the face of her oracle with an expression of hopeless vacancy. At length a happy thought occurred to her: Were the virgins men or women? The mental effort required for the birth of this question seemed so completely to have exhausted all her powers of mind as to make it highly probable that the reply of the oracle was lost upon her and that she remained forever in total ignorance on the momentous subject of her inquiry.

It was now the turn of number two, who, with astonishing brightness, asked if the bridesmaids wore white muslin dresses and carried eau-de-Cologne bottles in their pockets. This searcher after the truth having been satisfied, it was Undine's turn to inquire and learn. But that young lady sat upon the green box, noiselessly tapping it with her heels and fixing on the skin carpet that attention which should have been bestowed on her worthy instructress.

'Well, Undine, my dear, what have you to ask?'

'I understand that chapter,' said Undine, without raising her eyes to the face of her interlocutor.

'You do, my dear! Well, then I suppose we had better reverse the order of things and I will question you. What was the oil which was generally burnt on all such occasions in the East?'

'I don't know,' said Undine, very composedly.

'I thought that you understood everything that this chapter contained. I very soon find that you do not. You are woefully ignorant, my dear,' said the teacher.

'I did not notice that there was anything said about the kinds of oil,' responded Undine; 'otherwise I should not have said that I understood it.'

The questioner was fairly at her wits' end, but she shifted her ground. 'What does the thirty-first verse speak of, my dear?'

'The judgment of the world,' said Undine.

'And what does he say to the good people on his right and the bad on his left hand?'

'He says to the good people, "Come, you blessed, inherit the kingdom prepared for you from the foundation of the world"; and to the others, "Go, you cursed, into everlasting fire".'

'And what lesson does this teach us, my dear?'

'That God has prepared a heaven for the people he means to save and a hell for the people he means to burn,' said Undine, very gravely, never raising her eyes from the carpet on which they rested.

There was a pause; then came the remark: 'Hardly the right way of putting it, my dear. It teaches you that you should be a very good little girl, so that when you die God may take you to heaven and not send you to hell to burn forever and ever.'

'I would much sooner be wicked and go to hell than be good only because I was afraid of going there,' said Undine, now raising her eyes from the carpet and fixing them on the horror-stricken countenance of her instructress.

'Undine!' gasped forth that unfortunate individual. 'Undine, what *do* you mean? You were always an evil and wicked child, but you grow viler every day.'

'Yes,' said Undine, getting off the box, with a face alternately as red as the sprigs on her little print dress and as pale as her little white pinafore – 'yes, I don't want to go to heaven, and, if God wants to, he can send me to hell and I will never again ask him not to, *never*. I know I'm very wicked, but I'm not half so wicked or so cruel as he is. Nothing is, not even the devil. The devil is glad when we go to hell, but he did not make us on purpose to send us there, and he did not make hell, and he did not make himself, and I'm sorry for him. I believe he tries to be good and God won't let him, that's what I believe,' said Undine, who, with her wild dark eyes and clenched hands, looked more like some spirit who had just arrived from the regions of which she spoke than a carefully-brought-up Christian receiving her Sunday lesson.

If she had been Medusa her gaze could not more completely have paralysed her opponent, who sat there as if turned into stone; while the two little pudding-faces looked from one to the other with wild astonishment in their big grey eyes.

Undine clasped her little hands behind her and walked slowly out of the room.

It was the first time that she had ever given utterance to the evil thoughts with which her small and, as she believed, devil-ridden soul was haunted; they were fiendishly evil thoughts, all of them, she knew; but, if they were hers, why should she not give them utterance?

Her little heart swelled so it well nigh suffocated her, but it was with a sense of freedom and strength that she was pacing up and down her little room, when she heard the key turn in the door.

It was pleasant enough to think of having a day all to herself with no fear of interruption and no company but her books; but to think of that clink of the key and know that, wishing it or not, she was a prisoner, made her stamp her feet upon the ground as she walked up and down and to rebel in her bitter little heart against all powers, human and divine.

The world was not the place for her, she was feeling persuaded; she was not fit for it. Why then had she been made so bad, and put into it? It was no use saying she ought to be good; she couldn't. The devil did not come to other people and make them think such thoughts as he made her. She felt herself very much aggrieved by these attacks from the infernal regions, and presently became very wrathful. Then reaction set in and she grew sleepy. Lying down upon the floor, she was soon sound asleep, dreaming of the glorious time when she would be a woman and would know everything and be loved by everyone, and when she would be free.

The ringing of the dinner bell wakened her; and, finding that nothing in the shape of food was sent her, she kneeled down before her little bookshelf in search of refreshment of another order. There were delicious fairy tales – *Arabian Nights* whose old torn pages seemed to emit an odour of myrrh and roses caught from the gardens of Bagdad – Hans Andersen's beautiful song in prose about the mermaid and the young prince – but these and others were of course not to be looked at. It would have hurt the child's conscience as much to have read a fairy tale on Sunday as to have told a lie; one of the crimes which always came to haunt her in the dark watchful hours of the night was her having read, on one never-to-be-forgotten Sunday afternoon, a part of that story of *The Mermaid and the Prince*.

So Undine, rebel though she was, touched not, looked not, at the wicked thing, but from its hiding-place behind the other books brought forth a large, dull-coloured, leather-bound volume.

It was *A Careful and strict Enquiry into the Modern Prevailing Notions of the Freedom of Will, which is supposed to be essential to Moral Agency, Virtue and Vice, Reward and Punishment, Praise and Blame,* by Jonathan Edwards, AB. They would have laughed at her for reading such an old man's book and one with so grandiloquent and lengthy a title, so it was always stowed safely away behind the others where there was no fear of its being discovered by prying eyes. The faded ribbon placemarker had already found its way into the middle of the book, and the child was soon deeply absorbed in sections eight, nine and ten of section two, in part three. She did not get through more than these, for each sentence was found so pregnant with profound and misty thoughts that she was obliged to read it carefully, and often re-read it, before it could be dismissed.

There was a strange contrast between the little reader and her great brown book as she sat there on the floor on that Sunday afternoon. The child so warm, with the wild blood dancing in every vein, looking out so eagerly into the world, so ready to give and take – the book so old, so dead, with the life thoughts of another generation petrified in its old yellow leaves, now probably being read for the last time.

The book had belonged to her own father, who, much to the grief of his father, had turned aside from the paths of truth and Arminianism, to the ways of Calvinism and error, and in those evil ways had died.

About three o'clock the key turned and one of the little Dutch girls put her face in at the door.

'You can come out when you like,' she said. Undine did not even raise her eyes from the book, determining to show that she by no means objected to being made a prisoner in her own room; and she would in all probability have remained where she was until called to tea, had she not suddenly remembered Socrates. Of course pride must be swallowed and his wants attended to; so with an air of extreme indifference she made her way through the front room and, having got a mug of water and thrown a large damp towel over the brown *kappie*, went out into the yard.

She found Socrates lying on the floor of his box, quite exhausted with the heat and very glad to get under the shade of the damp towel. Loosening him from the stand, she carried him down to the little dam, where, under the scant shade of the willow tree, her brother Frank lay reclining on his back. He had thrown open his jacket and waistcoat, more from force of habit than from reason, one would think; for the wind, like the breath from an oven, seemed, in place of cooling, to blight and desiccate all it touched. He was a fine specimen of an English Africander, tall and broad, with a fair handsome face, though rather sleepy-looking just now as he lay with his legs raised against the trunk of the old tree and his hat pulled half over his eyes. With one hand he kept it there while with the other he picked up small bits of baked earth wherewith to pelt the miserable ducks who, red, dirty, and hot, were endeavouring to swim in diluted mud by way of improving their condition.

Undine sat down close to the trunk of the tree, for that cast a small shadow if the branches did not; and for some minutes nothing was said.

'Had him that time,' muttered Frank at last, as a more than usually lucky hit caught the old drake in the eye.

'I wonder why you do that,' said Undine; 'everything is miserable in the whole world.'

The only response to this observation was another throw, but presently he said, 'So you've been in the wars today, little woman, eh?'

Undine made no reply, but stroked Socrates softly the wrong way.

'Too bad to make you go without your dinner, little woman, wasn't it?'

'I don't mind that one bit,' said Undine, 'but I wish I had never been born. I'm miserable, and nobody loves me.'

'Why, I do, and we all of us do, though you are such a queer little coon,' answered Frank lazily.

'Yes, that's just it,' said Undine, gravely tying Socrates's tail into a knot as she spoke, much to that gentleman's dissatisfaction. 'Yes, that's just it; you only care about me because I'm your sister; you call me queer and strange; you don't like me one bit – only Socrates.'

'Well, that is good. How do you know that Socrates likes *you*, and not the bread and butter you bring him?' asked Frank.

'I know he likes me,' answered Undine, very indignantly. 'Can't I see it? Don't I know it? When we sit together of an evening, I can feel he is thinking just what I am, and when I talk to him he understands me. That is what I hate,' said Undine, twisting at the tail more vigorously than ever; 'people don't know anything about it, and they say he hasn't got a soul. How do *they* know, I should like to know? If only people would not talk till they knew, I think the world would be a much nicer place.'

Frank said nothing, but laughed, and directed a bit of mud straight at the tip of Socrates's black nose, who merely opened his eyes and closed them again very solemnly.

'I wish I were one of those ducks,' remarked Undine, presently.

'I don't; they look hot,' said Frank; 'and I thought you said, just now, everything in the whole world was miserable.'

'Yes, but not so very miserable because they don't think; at least, perhaps they do; but they've no Bibles, you see, and I don't think the devil ever tempts them. It would not be worth his trouble, they are so small.'

'If he paid visits only on account of size, I expect you would not see much of him,' said her brother, with an amused expression on his face. 'Are Bibles your great trouble?'

'Yes,' said Undine, unhesitatingly. 'Sometimes I feel quite good, and I am sitting and reading, and I come to something that is quite different from what it was somewhere else. Then the devil makes me think, How can two things that say the opposite both be true? And then I feel wicked and I can't go on reading any more. Sometimes, too, when I'm praying and I feel as though I loved God very much, I remember all at once how it says in the Bible that he never forgives anyone for nothing, but always makes someone suffer pain first; and I remember all the other cruel things it tells about him; and then I hate him, and for a long time I can't pray again.'

'Oh dear!' she said after a little pause. 'I wish the world belonged to me. I would make it much better; I would let all the devils out of hell and love them and make them good, so there would be no one to tempt the people any more. Did you ever feel so wicked as I do when you were little like me?' asked Undine, looking earnestly at him, as though with the vague hope that his answer might be in the affirmative.

'No, I should rather think not,' was the answer.

'I used to make little clay oxen and train kids in an old box and enjoy myself; that is what I used to do when I was your age.'

Undine heaved a little weary sigh and looked at the ducks. 'I wonder if there are any people in the world who feel like I do and who have such wicked thoughts,' she said at last.

'Of course there are, and much wickeder, too; there are people who don't believe the Bible is true, or anything else, and they write books also.'

'Do they?' said Undine. 'I wish I could read them. Have you ever?'

'No,' said Frank; 'it's too much bother; but I will, when I'm a man;' and pulling his hat lower over his eyes, he either made believe to do so or really went to sleep.

Undine did not go away, but sat at his feet, nursing Socrates and watching the ducks, till the *kopjes* began to cast long shadows and the fast-cooling air told that sunset was not far off.

By and by the back door of the house opened and the whole family appeared equipped for their Sunday evening walk – all, with the exception of the smallest Dutch girl, who, complaining of a headache, was left to keep Undine company.

'Take care of everything; get into no mischief; and above all remember that it is Sunday,' were the parting injunctions which they received as the group, which now included Frank, moved off.

The two children stood still watching them till they passed out of sight. Then Undine, after crying and praying half the night, and reading Edwards and meditating half the day, began to discover that she was neither anchorite nor saint, but only a very young animal with much wild blood in its young veins that needed circulating. It may have been the evening's cool that made her conscious of this, for it seemed to have an inebriating effect upon Socrates, who leaped, grinned, and turned somersets in a manner truly astonishing.

'I wonder,' said Undine, 'if Socrates and I were to run a race, which of us would beat'; and without waiting for a reply, she set about testing the matter at once. With one end of his chain held firmly in her hand they set off, but had not gone thirty paces when it had slipped out and Socrates, chain and all, was making his way to the nearest *kopje*, with jingling, screeching and leaping, much to the mingled horror and delight of his little pursuer. The delight soon vanished, however, for, the *kopje* reached, Mr Socrates felt himself quite in his own element, and absolutely refused to be cozened by soft words or specious promises. Seating himself on the top of a large round stone, he would very leisurely stretch out his legs, scratch himself, and then look up into the blue sky with an air of melancholy abstraction; this till his breathless pursuer was within half a foot of him; then, with a whirl, a cry, and a somerset, off to another and more inaccessible stone, round which his little pursuer might dance and beseech in vain, leaping to catch the tip of the chain he left hanging almost within reach of her fingers. It is uncertain how long this game might have continued had not the idea entered Socrates's small head that more fun might be got from scampering over the roofs at home than by remaining where he was.

Accordingly, he was off like an arrow, while Undine followed him breathlessly, minus one shoe and with more rents in her garments than could well be counted. Arrived at the house, she found the exemplary Sannie standing exactly where and as she had left her; except that she had placed one finger in her mouth and partly turned her head to look at Socrates, who was now on the roof of the house, busily occupied in pulling out thatch and working away with the greatest dispatch and precision.

Undine quickly saw that, if this were allowed to go on for many minutes, he would have worked his way into the loft and perhaps to a bloody death as the reward of his evil deeds.

What was to be done? She looked at the little Dutch girl in despair; the little Dutch girl looked at her.

'He is naughty,' said that little maiden at length, and then slowly replaced the finger she had taken out of her small mouth. Undine turned away in disgust; there was no help to be got from her, and nothing for it but to climb the roof herself and capture him.

With much difficulty a long ladder was brought which reached just to the top of the wall; and this was soon mounted. Once there, how to get on to the ridge was the question; for at every touch the old thatch crumbled away by handfuls, and she had not crawled many inches before it seemed inevitable that she should soon find herself deposited among the skins in the loft or with the thatch upon the ground.

'You will fall down and die,' said the little Dutch girl, very deliberately, as she watched Undine's perilous ascent with almost as much interest as Socrates, who had now taken his seat on one of the gables, and with his chin resting on his hand was contemplating her movements most attentively.

Undine took no notice of either, but continued to climb, doing more harm at every move than Socrates in twenty. The ridge was gained at last, after infinite trouble, but not so Socrates. He waited till her fingers touched his tail; and then, with that appendage cocked high in air, walked off very quietly to the other gable, where he ensconced himself far more comfortably than his little pursuer found it possible to do at hers. There was no getting down again, for the first step down would have been on the ground; there was nothing to be done but sit still and wait. Consequently the appalling and shocking spectacle which met the eyes of the upper powers, on their return home, was Undine, shoeless, *kappie*less and torn, seated on the ridge and holding on with one arm to the gable, while at the other end Socrates, with clanking chain and tail in air, was dancing a true devil's quadrille. Never were worthy parents and instructors, on their return from a quiet Sabbath ramble, met by so horrific and wrath-rousing a sight.

A second ladder was quickly got and Undine safely deposited upon the ground, where she was instantly marched off into the house to answer for her evil conduct.

'How did you get into this plight, you wicked, wicked little girl?' said her mother.

Undine stood with her hands crossed and her eyes fixed on the one little white toe that had forced its way out of the stocking.

'I did not mean to,' she said, feeling very contrite and not a little ashamed of herself.

'Did not mean to! Of course not! You never mean to do anything that you do. The wind loosened Socrates and blew you both up onto the roof of the house! Of course it did; we all know that it did.'

Undine felt very much inclined to say that she was sorry and was not going to do so any more; then she remembered that saying so might make her punishment less, so she stood still and looked down at her toe.

The lean and lanky individual now struck in her note.

'Undine, my dear Undine,' she said in a very low and subdued voice, 'if you continue this course of action, what will become of your immortal soul? What will become of it?'

This was too much for Undine who had stood still to receive her bullying, filled with contrition and repentance; it raised all the evil in her nature. 'I know I'm wicked and I don't care, and I don't care what becomes of my soul, and I'm not afraid of anything,' said Undine, lifting up her face and throwing back her long tangled hair defiantly.

'Was there ever in this world so evil disposed and ungodly a child?' said her spiritual guide, shaking her head solemnly. 'Go to bed, Undine; go to bed; I shall say no more to you.'

'Goodnight,' said Undine and she walked off to her room with almost a smile upon her face. But once there and alone, she flung her tired little body across the foot of the bed and cried bitterly.

'Oh, I wish I was dead! I wish I was dead! There is nobody like me, and nobody loves me. Oh, I wish I was dead!' And at last, without undressing, she fell asleep.

CHAPTER TWO

Undine's Jottings

It was a bright summer afternoon, just three weeks after my arrival in England. We were expecting visitors, and Aunt Margaret and I had taken our needlework out among the rose trees in the garden.

My brother Frank lolled beside us on the grass, pulling flowers to pieces and showering the leaves over Aunt Margaret's golden hair and white dress. He had changed in the three years that had passed since last I saw him, and had grown noble and handsome enough, I thought, even to possess the beautiful woman on whom his eyes were resting. In my estimation no one else was worthy to own her; certainly not my grandfather, whom I could not learn to like. He reminded me, when I first saw him, of the ox hides so often seen lying near the little dam at home, which had once been damp but by dint of lying in the sun had been reduced to a stone-like mass of wrinkles and lines; and he was so tall and thin. For a long time I never could see him rise from his seat without having recalled to my mind the image of an earthworm creeping out of the ground, which unfolds and unfolds itself to unimagined lengths. He had more resemblance to the skin than to the earthworm, however; for he was mentally as ossified and incapable of growth as any ox hide under the sun. Only in connection with Aunt Margaret did there seem a trace of softness in his nature, and it could not be otherwise. Nature gives to few persons to have the influence of sunshine on all they touch – silently softening, warming, melting it – and she was one. I worshipped her; for in those days I had not eaten of the tree of knowledge, and worshipped and thought perfect all I loved.

I did not care for my grandmother nor yet dislike her. She was a weak, nervous little old woman, who had had all the soul pressed out of her long ago, and whose trembling little hands I never saw at rest for an instant, except she were asleep.

On that summer afternoon we three sat there, feeling very happy. They because they were together, and I because the roses were beautiful and the sky blue and they glad. The work had dropped from my hands and I had just got into a delicious dream, in which rosebuds, princes and spirits were largely concerned, when Frank tossed a great white rosebud into my face.

'At your old work again,' he said, laughing. 'You've no idea,' turning to Aunt Margaret, 'what evil thoughts are always fermenting in that little innocent-looking head. It's my decided opinion that in a pre-state of existence she was a Buddhist philosopher, or something else equally disagreeable and full of contemplations, and at her rebirth she did not become quite rejuvenised or lose all her old habits;

otherwise I can't account for her,' said Frank, turning round onto his back, while Aunt Margaret and I laughed.

'It's all very well to laugh,' he continued, 'but she is awfully bad, much worse that I am. She is only a little girl and she has not any right to have thoughts at all. It's all very well for *me* to think that it's a hard state of affairs when a poor fellow has to be called into existence for the purpose of being sent to fire and brimstone; but it does not do for her; it's highly improper, *highly*,' said Frank, rolling round onto his face again.

Aunt Margaret opened her big blue eyes and looked at me. I had been so shy and said so little since I came there, that I think they all thought me a particularly childish child; and I was glad of it. I was young, but I had learnt a little worldly wisdom – enough to tell me that, if a man is unfortunate enough to have ideas of his own, he had best keep them to himself. I was tired of being called queer and strange and odd, and all those other epithets which I had so learned to hate; and here was Frank dragging all my weaknesses out into the sunshine that the old names might be branded on me again. What I should have said I don't know, but at that moment, greatly to my joy, our expected guests arrived. They consisted of a parson, his wife, an old young lady, and a certain Jonathan Barnacles, whose wife had been a cousin to my father. All these had come to assist in the stirring up of the deadened consciences of my grandfather's congregation.

From behind our wall of roses we could, without being seen, observe and criticise them as they walked up the long garden path.

The advance was led by the Rev Joseph Goodman and his portly spouse, both tall, both fat: she decidedly good-looking, with large brown eyes and a Roman nose; he, decidedly greasy and with a dirty white choker. I was struck dumb with horror at the way in which the good lady turned her head from side to side, evidently bent, as I thought, on discovering our whereabouts, but, as I afterwards learnt, merely from a long-acquired habit and a wish to overlook no one.

Close at their heels was a little angular figure, dressed in a very fashionable and juvenile manner, whose head and face were completely enveloped in a blue gauze veil. Frank said she had taken to attending revivals and staying to prayer meetings only since the arrival in their circuit of a young assistant preacher whose mother she was old enough to be.

The rear was brought up by Jonathan Barnacles, Esq, at whom I looked with more interest; for, after the Dutch fashion, might he not be called a relation of mine? He was a lean, bony man of about two-and-forty, with large calm blue eyes, lanky and scanty hair and beard, and an enormous mouth – a mouth that seemed forever hungering and seeking after something. I wished he were no connection of mine when I looked at it, little child though I was. Looked at from the lip upwards, he might have been an angel; looked at from the lip downwards, he might have been a devil. He was dressed then – and I never, in all the years I knew him, saw him in anything else, except on Sundays – in a rusty brown jacket and a pair of dark green-and-blue-plaid trousers. To me those trousers have become so a part of the man that I can never see any like them without being unpleasantly reminded of him.

As soon as the visitors had gone into the house Aunt Margaret rose to follow them, and Frank and I were left alone. He asked me if I were going to the revival meeting that evening. 'You had better,' he said; 'it's great fun. I always do: I take my notebook and pencil; one hears things worth remembering sometimes. Beside, you'll get into hot water if you don't go, and pretend to be edified, too. There are just three grand crimes according to your grandfather's creed – to give expression to an idea that has not been propounded at least one hundred times before you were born; to believe in the possible salvation of a Roman Catholic; and to absent yourself from a little heaven below:

"I have been there, and still would go,
'Tis like a little heaven below ——"'

hummed Frank as he rose to go into the house, where he would no doubt look up his 'Golden Light', as he nicknamed Aunt Margaret.

I went to the revival meeting that evening, for I had never been to one before. Aunt Margaret and I started some time after the others, so we had a pleasant long walk all to ourselves. Frank, in spite of the sage advice of the morning, did not go. I suppose, having got what he wanted, he did not care whether he pleased my grandfather or not, and could not make up his mind to leave an easy chair and cigar for 'those purgatorial Methodist planks', as he irreverently called the straight-backed pews in my grandfather's chapel.

We walked on in silence at first through the quiet twilight. At last I said: 'Do they do you good, Aunt Margaret?'

'I don't know that they ever did,' she said, hesitating a little, 'but Christ does show himself wonderfully sometimes; and I feel, if only one soul is saved, it must be God's own work and I must help it. Think, if only one soul be saved from endless pain and sin, what a glorious work.'

The twilight gave me boldness, so I said, 'I wish you could feel as I do, that our Father will let nothing he had made be lost forever. As long as I believe as you do I could not love him, nor serve him; but since I have left off looking to the Bible, and listen to what he says in my soul, I love him and I am happy.'

'I wish you could make me think so too,' she said, 'but I know it is wrong even to say so. If once we listen to our own hearts and use our reason, we go away from God. Yet do you know, if someone whom I loved very much were to die not loving Christ, I think — I am sure, I should go mad, quite mad. It is so terrible that you cannot pray for them, that you cannot do anything for them when once they are gone. We must pray for them now, now,' she said, with a passionate earnestness that astonished me; she was so bright and placid generally.

I looked up into her face, and I fancied there were tears in her eyes, but I could hardly tell, for it was so dark. I knew of whom she was thinking, and long after I remembered her words.

The chapel was dimly lighted. Only round the pulpit there were two or three candles, whose light served to make clearly visible the three principal actors in the scene about to be performed.

In front of the pulpit stood Cousin Jonathan, and when he spoke I could look at nothing but that mouth, that dreadful mouth, that seemed to have a horrible fascination for me. On his right he was supported by the Rev Joseph Goodman, who stood with eyes turned heavenwards and fat hands folded meekly across his greasy and distended waistcoat. On his left stood my grandfather, his cold hard eye engaged in critically examining the scattered occupants of the different pews.

The proceedings were opened by the singing of a hymn, in which the torments awaiting all mankind, except that infinitesimal portion who are believers in Christ, were set forth vividly, and in no bad verse. That being ended, my grandfather engaged in prayer. The prayer was very much in the same key as the hymn had been, but a little bolder and weaker. When it was ended Brother Vickers prayed. He was one of those who most frequently called Frank's notebook into requisition; and if my grandfather's way of treating fire and brimstone was cool and calm, so certainly was not his. The good man fairly worked himself into a profuse perspiration and dragged away at the pew-back before us with both hands and with such fervent energy that I momentarily expected to see him fly, pew-back and all, against my head.

Brother Vickers's prayer ended, another hymn was sung, and then Brother Jones was called upon.

Some men must think the Almighty very ignorant, for they never kneel down to speak to him without feeling themselves called upon to explain to him the whole plan of salvation, creation, and damnation: subjects on which, one might almost suppose, he would be better informed than themselves. Brother Jones was one of these. It may have been that my mood was not very charitable that evening, but it certainly seemed to me that, in place of praying to any other being, he was laying out for his own personal edification and satisfaction the whole circle of his theological knowledge.

When we rose from our knees, before cousin Jonathan gave out the next hymn, Mr Goodman came forward and told us that, if the spirit of God had touched any of our hearts during the preceding prayers, we were requested to come up.

'Do come up, dear friends, *do* come up,' he said. The hymn finished, the spirit still remaining inactive and no one having accepted the invitation, it was repeated a second time, more urgently than at first.

'Do come up, dear friends, *do* come up. While Brother Stiles engages in prayer, do come up.'

Brother Stiles began, Brother Stiles ended; no one moved.

Before Brother Stubbles engaged, the invitation was again renewed: 'The time is young, dear friends. Will no one begin? Will no one come up?'

No one would; so Brother Stubbles began. Between every verse of the hymn that followed Mr Goodman continued to ask, at last almost with tears, if no one would come up, if no one would lead the way. 'Do come, do come,' he cried, as he moved both hands unctuously to and fro; and my heart was touched with pity for the unfortunate man. I looked round the chapel anxiously to see if there was no sign of an upward movement, but could discover none.

Brother Snappers, who prayed next, seemed to have been moved in the same way, for he scolded quite rabidly: If there were any there that evening (and he knew there were such) whose hearts God had touched, let them be beware! If they refused to accept the invitation, if they refused to come up, that night, that very moment, the spirit of God might leave them; and that day year, or that day month, or that day week, nay, by that time tomorrow, they might be in that place from which there would be no coming up forever. He did not say so, but he left one the impression that he would not have many tears to weep if such *were* the case.

Brother Goodman himself prayed next, a rambling, meandering sort of prayer, which would have been just as suitable at a funeral, a coronation, or a wedding.

Then Cousin Jonathan, after a last vain appeal, closed the meeting with a prayer; and that prayer, sweet, tender and earnest, seemed strangely out of harmony with the rest of the evening's proceedings. 'Twas like entering a silent sunny cove after being tossed among black breakers. He prayed for those who had not yet felt the love of Christ, that to them it might speak with its glorious power, till at length, perfect in purity, they might become but the living reflection of that unfathomable love. Perfect purity, perfect truth; through every sentence the yearning for it breathed; and when we rose from our knees and I looked up into his face, I could not see that the mouth was always craving something; I looked only at the serene eyes and brow.

When the meeting was over we all walked home rather silently, for it had been a failure to all of us. As for myself, I had made up my mind, even in spite of Cousin Jonathan's beautiful prayer, never to attend another; never, come what would. On our way home the Goodmans turned in to have a chat at Brother Vickers's, Frank and Aunt Margaret went for a stroll on the beach, and when we got to the house my grandfather and Cousin Jonathan took themselves off to the study. There was nothing else to be done, so I curled myself up at one end of the great parlour sofa with Wolf's fairy tales. I still enjoyed them as much as I had done when I was eight years old, though I had such an old, old-womanish feeling sometimes.

Presently my grandmother and Miss Mell came in and sat down at the other end of the room. I think they soon forgot my presence; Miss Mell kept up a constant flow of talk, while my poor nervous little grandmother put in a timid little yes or no when she thought it required, and pulled away at the fringe of her crochet wrapper. She was old and not beautiful, but she looked so beside Miss Mell who sat opposite her in her juvenile dress, with her wrinkles and her sharp nose and chin, over which the skin was drawn so tightly that a little more would surely have caused it to crack. At first I was too much engrossed by my book to pay any attention to what they said; but when my tale was ended I sat and listened.

'A pity she praises up those great fat girls so,' Miss Mell was just saying of Mrs Goodman. 'They are the ugliest girls in the village, but she can't see it. She has a very good opinion of herself, too,' continued Miss Mell, seeing that my grandmother gave no response; 'and she imagines there is no other minister's wife to be compared with her, and *I* know that she takes good *care* never to go where there is any infectious disease, and ——'

Here the door opened and Mrs Goodman's face, with its beaming smile, presented itself. 'Did you think I was very long gone, dear?' she said to Miss Mell; and, kissing my grandmother affectionately, added, 'It was a shame to leave you, but the dear good creatures would have it so, and I came back to you just as soon as I could, dear, just as soon.' She seated herself close to my grandmother and, taking one of her hands, proceeded to pat, smooth, and caress it during the whole of the conversation which ensued.

'What were you talking about, dears, when I came in? I am sure it was something *very* entertaing; Miss Mell's conversation always is so entertaining. As Sarah Jane said to me yesterday afternoon: "Oh, Ma! There comes Miss Mell. Shall we not have a nice afternoon!" And we had a *pleasant* time. Had we not, my dear?'

'Very. Did I tell you that Alice Brown had come back?' asked Miss Mell.

'No, dear, you did not; but when I was up at Mrs Barnacles's this morning she told me of it, and that she has grown into such a beautiful girl! Is it true?'

'Beautiful!' said Miss Mell, with a sharpening in her voice that made it very fit company for her nose. 'I should beg to be excused from such beauty! She's as large as an elephant and a great deal coarser, and as for her forest of hair – the best thing she could do with it would be to cut it off; it's as black and coarse as a horse's tail!'

'I don't know what she *looks* like,' said Mrs Goodman, shaking her head, 'but she's been very badly brought up.'

'Brought up!' interrupted Miss Mell. 'Why, she has not been brought up at all. They were the lowest people in the place till they got this money left them, the lowest and the poorest; and she is the worst of them. Did you every hear of that affair with young Mr Blair?'

'No, my dear, I heard nothing,' said Mrs Goodman, in her great interest for a moment forgetting to caress my grandmother's hand.

'It's about two years ago now,' said Miss Mell. 'Mr Albert Blair was swimming in the great pool near Brown's house and got cramp. He called for help, and the girl (she was then about fifteen) happened to hear him. You will hardly credit it, but in place of going for someone, she actually had the immodesty to tear off her own clothes and leap in; and, as if that were not enough, she actually carried him in her arms up to their house. You may believe me, for I had it all on the best authority; my servant was very intimate with the Browns in those days, and she told me all about it. She said, too, that he sent her ever so many presents afterwards, and thought nothing of stopping to speak with her in the streets – the brazen-faced creature.'

'Is it possible, my dear!' said Mrs Goodman. 'How wanting in modesty and self-respect! How very shocking!'

'It's not the worst thing we shall hear of her, mark my words,' said Miss Mell, with a gleam of intense satisfaction in her grey eyes as she gave utterance to this prediction; which, considering its nature, was by no means unlikely of fulfilment.

'Ah! This is a sad, sad, wicked world,' said Mrs Goodman, gazing fixedly at the wall opposite and shaking her head slowly. 'As I said to Sarah Jane only this morning, if once we depend on our own weak selves how miserably we shall fail, fail, fail!'

Miss Mell, not perceiving the exact bearing of these remarks on the subject in hand, sat still; but my grandmother uttered a timid, 'Yes.'

'Ah! You may well say yes, dear. I have had a dreadful blow this evening. Oh, it is a wicked, wicked world in which we live. If my dear girls had not given their hearts to Christ, I should tremble for them, yes, even for them'; and the tears that had been gathering in the good woman's eyes rolled slowly down her cheeks.

'What have you heard?' said Miss Mell, who already scented something good.

'Oh, you know all about it, no doubt, dear – about Dr Harper, who I always thought such a dear, good man, and Mrs Harvey.'

'Dr Harper and Mrs Harvey! I've heard nothing,' said Miss Mell.

'You don't *say* so, my dear! I'm *so* grieved I said *one* word about it. I made sure you knew it *all*. You know I never talk about such things, never, never; but, oh! it is the saddest, *saddest* thing I've heard for a long, long time; though I always knew that that Mrs Harvey was not a good woman. I said so long ago – at the time she left our chapel for the church. Mrs Lovedy was nursing her when her first boy was born, and she told me things, dear, dreadful things; she said ...' and there followed the relation, in minutest detail, of things such as I had not even dreamed of, whose hideous shadow had never yet been thrown across my young life. From my lonely African home I had brought an ignorance of evil (and of that which, holy and pure in itself, man's folly has made so) that might have been thought strange in a child of six years. Much that had been cause of vague speculation and wonder was made clear to me that night, and I was wretched; for, alas! is it not the old, old story – that the tree of knowledge is the tree of pain, and that, 'In the day wherein thou eatest thou shalt surely die' stand written on every fruit of the wonderful tree?

The gentlemen came in after a time to say goodnight, and I slipped off the sofa and went to my own little room, for I did not feel in the mood to be spoken to by anyone.

When I got there, it somehow seemed that all was changed; nothing looked as it used to look; the very light did not produce its old effect when it shone on the white bed curtains; and my beautiful bunch of roses told quite a different tale from that which it had whispered in the morning. I felt sour and bitter, and I took the poor bunch I had gathered with such care and flung it out of the window; then I partly undressed and sat down upon the floor and set my candle down opposite me. It did me good to look at its wicked red flame flicker and flare. Before that night I had often felt sympathy with my candle; but then it had seemed to me a poor soul always striving to grow higher, and never succeeding; now it looked red and bad, like the new world that had been opened to me. This was a wretched earth, and perhaps, after all, there was a place of endless sin and therefore of endless pain; it would only be the world a little more worldly, I thought.

Aunt Margaret came in to wish me goodnight just then; she had a crimson wrapper over her head, so I knew she had just returned from the beach. She looked more beautiful than ever and happier than I had ever seen her; but she seemed to have changed, just like the roses and the light.

'I thought I should find you in bed,' she said, stooping down over me. 'Which are you studying – your little bare toes or the candle?'

'Neither,' I said; 'but I wish I was not a woman. I hate women; they are horrible and disgusting, and I wish I had never been born rather than to be one.'

'Why, darling, what is the matter now?' I am very glad I am a woman; it is so sweet'; and a soft smile played round her mouth as she spoke.

'Did you like the revival meeting this evening?' she asked me after a pause.

'No. It was horrible. I am never going to another,' I answered, briefly.

'Oh yes, you will. You will make papa so angry if you do not.'

'I can't help it,' I answered. 'There are some places that make one wicked, and it's not right to go to them. I feel tonight as if everyone in the world were a hypocrite, and I shall be one too, if I go to these places just for the sake of pleasing some one else – as bad as Miss Mell and Mrs Goodman.'

'You are tired tonight, darling; tomorrow things will look brighter to your poor little eyes. You have sat up too late. Goodnight, sweet;' and she went out and I was left alone with my red light. I soon got chilly and sleepy and crept into bed.

I remember that day because, first, on it the joy and peace I had lived in for two years began to break; because on it I first entered the shadow of that cloud in whose darkness I was to walk for years, hoping nothing, believing nothing, trusting nothing.

CHAPTER THREE

The Man with the Mouth

As Aunt Margaret had said, things looked brighter in the morning – the beautiful morning that throws its veil of misty light over the great ugly truths which, in all their hideous nakedness, have stood staring us in the eyes and riding us on the breast all night.

Undine, as soon as she was dressed, ran down to the beach; there the tiny waves danced laughing on the sides of the big ones, which in their turn chased and overtook one another, tossing their heads high into the sunny air and turning to white foam, or making a mad dash for the land and dying away in laughing ripples on the sand.

On such a morning, on this side of twenty, with no ghosts to haunt one and come in between the happy sunshine and the eyes, who would not forget that there are such things as revival meetings, and good people who always say one thing and mean another, and jealous old maids and unfaithful wives, and dry hippopotamus-hide-like old men? Who would not forget that underneath this green, laughing, merry old world lies fire and brimstone, into which a fall from any rock may send one in a moment? Undine forgot this and everything, and grew at last as wild as the dancing waves. She had brought poor George Macdonald with her for company, but now she threw him down upon the sand, where the waves caught him and made fine sport of his *Unspoken Sermons* and almost ran away with them; while she leapt from rock to rock, and finally pulled off her shoes and stockings, the better to keep her footing and capture the queer little beings which every wave left behind it in the rocky hollows.

She was very busily securing an extraordinary little monster, with a multiplicity of tails and feelers, and, with her head some two feet lower than her feet, was in no small danger of having an unexpected bath in the shallow pool, when she heard a voice at her elbow.

Rising to her feet with some difficulty and throwing back the wild hair from her eyes, she saw, standing beside her, none other than the man with the green-plaid trousers and the mouth – Cousin Jonathan.

He asked what she was looking for; and when he understood very soon captured the queer little fish.

The presence of a second person had in an instant taken all the exhilaration and life out of the morning and brought her back to the disagreeable human world, in which wild hair, wet clothes, and bare feet were terribly disgraceful things. She felt conscience-stricken and looked down into the little pool, wishing she were one of the little fishes swimming there.

Cousin Jonathan held out the fish he had just caught with one hand; in the other he had poor George Macdonald, looking almost as wet and disreputable as its mistress.

'I find your name in this book, so I suppose you must have dropped it,' he said as he gave it to her. 'The waves were very nearly stealing it, as I fear they may you one of these days, if you continue such a very zealous little naturalist.'

'I'm not a naturalist; I don't know anything about fishes or about anything else,' stammered Undine, hardly knowing what she said.

Cousin Jonathan smiled, not an unpleasant smile of ridicule, but one of quiet amusement.

'They say, when we know our own deficiencies they are half rectified. You would like to know all about a strange little fellow like this, would you not?'

'I would like to know something about him,' she answered, the kind, quiet manner of her companion already beginning to set her at her ease. 'When I was at home I used to try and learn a little about plants and insects, but I never had anyone to help me and I had not the right books.'

'Perhaps I could help you a little,' he said; 'at least I am sure I could, with books; but if you do not wish to study them, what makes you take such trouble to catch them?'

'I don't know,' said Undine, 'but I never see anything beautiful without wanting to have it, especially if it's very hard to get. It's not beautiful now,' she said, turning over the poor little fish in her hand.

'I never can see some beautiful things without wishing for them,' he said, and when he spoke those words he spoke the truth.

He helped her over the rocks, with that respectful kindness with which even little children like to be treated; and, when they reached the beach, sat down beside her and let his talk wander on, from a description of the nature and habits of the little creature in her hand to that wonderland which the microscope makes visible; and Undine sat and listened till she forgot his mouth and forgot even her own bare toes.

'We must go home to breakfast,' he said at last, and Undine went in search of her shoes and stockings. Cousin Jonathan never forgot when it was time for a meal.

On their walk home he changed the conversation and tried to draw her out; for the study of character pleased him, and he felt attracted by the queer, babyish, womanish creature. She was an orphan, too, and almost friendless, and he pitied her. Moreover, had she not looked lovely as she stood there on the rocks with the hot blood in her cheeks and her exquisite little feet clinging to the rough stones. Cousin Jonathan liked beautiful things – of the feminine gender.

Undine as she trotted beside him had little idea that he or anyone else could see anything in her to admire; but with a woman's quick perception she felt intuitively that whatever she might say, it was all right, it would be well received; and accordingly her ideas and words flowed forth in such a stream as would have astonished anyone who knew her as the shy awkward child in whose throat even yes and no seemed usually to stick.

Undine passed the day almost entirely in Cousin Jonathan's society. Aunt Margaret was busy, and when she had time to spare was with Frank, who was returning to college the next day. In the evening Cousin Jonathan left, for his wife was an invalid and he could never be from home long. At parting he told Undine that he would send her books and that, in return, she was to write and tell him what she thought of them. When he walked down the garden path, she stood looking after him and feeling almost as though an old friend were going.

CHAPTER FOUR

Going to Chapel

Every house has its smoky chimney, its draughty room, its creaky door; every life its own haunting shadows; and every state of life its own small troubles. It may be, when we arrive in a new place or enter upon altered circumstances, the sky is all serenely blue above us; but 'tis never long before the discovering eye perceives the tiny cloud – the cloud on the horizon, at first no bigger than a man's hand, which, growing greater and never quite dissolving, hangs over us, forever ready to rain sorrows on our heads. The direction from which her storms were to arise was soon made clear to Undine. After Cousin Jonathan left she took her work and sat down at one end of the pantry dresser where Aunt Margaret was busy making cakes for tea. Every now and then Aunt Margaret looked down at Undine and wondered what was knitting her brow and making her little hands work away with such desperate energy.

Undine herself could hardly have traced the gyration of the thoughts that were tossing in her own small head, but the result was an unalterable determination that she would go to chapel no more. It was her duty, yet she could not go, she thought; and wondered wearily if she were always to be afflicted with senses of duty driving her into paths where no one else would or could walk.

The Goodmans and Miss Mell had been asked out to tea, so there were none but the family round the table that evening.

'You must make haste,' said Mr Roch, 'and get your tea done; the meeting begins in three-quarters of an hour.'

'You must take care to wrap yourself up warmly,' said the grandmother; 'you are not accustomed to our climate yet.'

'I am not going,' said Undine.

'What do you say?' asked her grandmother, in whose throat the words stuck so fast that not even Frank, who sat next her, could hear them.

'I am not going to the meeting this evening,' she answered, staring very hard at her plate as she spoke.

'Do you feel ill tonight, dear? You look very pale,' said Aunt Margaret.

'I am quite well, thank you; but I would rather not go tonight.'

'I wish all my household to be there,' said the dried hide, straightening and elongating himself in his seat.

'Perhaps she wishes to stay with Frank, as it is the last evening,' said the poor nervous little grandmother in an apologetic little whisper.

'Frank is going with Margaret,' said the dried hide, with is leathery, intonationless voice. It sounded so terrible to Undine and filled her with such tremblings, that the brown Wesleys and Fletchers in the little bookcase behind her grandfather seemed to go up to the ceiling and come slowly down to the floor, and she wondered if everyone in the room could not hear her heart beat.

'I would rather not go, I don't mind staying alone at all,' she said at last.

'Why do you not wish to go?' said her grandfather, fixing his cold eyes upon her.

'I don't think it is – I mean – I don't get any good from going, and, I – would – rather – stay – please.' Her voice had almost died away as she spoke the last words.

'Why do you not wish to go?' repeated her grandfather in his usual calm voice.

The blood came back to Undine's cheek, and with it her spirit rose.

'Because it would be wicked of me,' she said, and then, feeling that anything would be better than the silence that ensured, she went on, 'I can't go and pretend to be serving God when all ...'

'Be silent,' said her grandfather. 'Little children who act in this manner should be whipped and taught how to behave themselves. It is a pity you are not a few years younger, Undine.'

The child looked up at him, with eyes almost blinded by rage and hatred, and trembling in every limb; then suddenly there came to her a thought – the thought of One who bore all things in meekness, wrongs in silence, who returned cruelty with acts of mercy, and the hatred of evil with the love of a god. Through long years of ceaseless dreaming he had become to her no vague shadowy existence of the long past, but a present living reality, ever aiding and ever sympathising, to whose influence were ascribed all her higher thought and better feeling, no matter from what source they arose. She thought of him, and no answer rose to her lips; and in place of fury only a cold fainting at her heart was left. She sat here so quietly, breaking up into little bits the bread in her plate, that Frank, remembering the Undine of the old African days, gazed at her in astonishment, expecting an outburst. None came; and when her grandfather rose from the table and told her to get ready she quietly went to obey him.

'Conquered,' thought the old man as he put his coat on in the hall; but perhaps he would hardly have thought so could he have seen what was passing in the heart of the conquered. 'It is very hard and bitter to have to go after all this, but because it is bitter it must be right to go just this once, at least as a punishment to myself.' So she reasoned as she walked beside him on the way to the little Methodist chapel.

The meeting passed for Undine very much as the last had done; only that this evening, on the seat in front of her, sat a tall, gaunt old woman in a black bonnet who from time to time pushed and pulled at the shoulder of the sallow girl who sat next her, in an endeavour to drive her up to the rails every time the invitation was uttered afresh.

'I don't want to go,' the poor creature whispered, drawing back; and she would,

Undine thought, have kept her ground had it not been for Mrs Goodman, who, leaning over the back of the bench, whispered loudly in her ear, 'Go up, my dear; go up.'

The girl looked round with a startled expression. It seemed as though all things, above, around, below, were combining to send her 'up'. The poor preacher calling from the rails, the prayers hurling anathemas at those who did not accept the invitation, the hand of her companion persistently applying physical force in the direction of salvation, the mysterious voice from the gloomy depths behind urging her upwards: these were forces which she had not strength to resist, and rising slowly she went up.

Undine wondered what she found to tell him when Mr Goodman's greasy head was bent down over her.

She was the only fruit that evening, but as they walked home Mrs Goodman expressed her joy that the blessed work of Christ had begun and that she had been the humble instrumentality in his hands for beginning it.

'A word in season, my dear Mrs Jones, a word in season; let us be thankful when the dear Lord allows us to speak a word in season, allows us poor weak voices to speak a word for him.'

Mrs Jones, whose road lay in the same direction, was accompanying them part of the way. She fully acquiesced, and at parting begged Mrs Goodman to come and spend the next day with her. Mrs Goodman was deeply grieved, but the next day they were returning to Greenwood; she would not see more of her dear Mrs Jones. That lady was, in her turn, deeply grieved at hearing this, and bargained that Sarah Jane and Elizabeth Ann should be sent over to spend a week with her.

Mrs Goodman said there was no one in the world with whom she would so gladly have her treasures as her dearest, oldest, friend, and they should surely come. Mrs Goodman's dearest always was the person whom she happened to be addressing at the moment.

They parted with an affectionate embrace, and Mrs Goodman was still wiping her cheek from the traces of Mrs Jones's rather moist salutation when she remarked: 'What a dear, good creature Mrs Jones is! What a pity she should think so much of her dress at her age; and oh, the adornments of the outer man, what are they, my dear Miss Mell, what are they?'

'Yes, indeed,' said Miss Mell, 'yes, indeed.'

'And her poor husband, my dear,' continued Mrs Goodman, 'he can't stand it, my dear, he can't stand it. Did you notice the really *su*perb silk she had on – really *su*perb.'

'I don't think it was silk; it was alpaca,' said Miss Mell.

'Alpaca, my dear! You are quite mistaken. She sat close to the rails, and I was looking at it from the time she came in till we went out, and what a lovely brown it was.'

'I think you are mistaken about the silk,' said Miss Mell, determined not to yield her point.

'I know it's silk, my dear,' replied Mrs Goodman. 'We were in the middle of the first prayer when she came in, and I heard the rustle of the silk as soon as ever she opened the door. I thought, "Whoever is that!" So I just looked up as she went by.'

'Well, it might be,' said Miss Mell. 'I know she is as extravagant as she is stingy.'

'Yes, it's a great pity; she is such a dear, good creature,' said Mrs Goodman, with much earnestness; 'it is a sad, sad pity she should be so close: the fly, the fly in the pot of ointment, my dear. Ah! that fly!' And so the good souls continued their conversation all the way home.

Arrived there, Undine ran away to her own little room, tonight to study not her candle, but the little brown Testament. She sat reading a little and dreaming a great deal till she had worked herself into a state of beatific felicity; and in this state Aunt Margaret found her when half an hour after she entered the room.

'What is making you so happy?' she asked.

'You look like one of the little angels I used to dream about long ago.'

'Nothing,' answered Undine, the golden light fading as quickly from her face as it was from her heart. Heaven on earth is only found in perfect solitude, whether by saint or by poet; and 'tis only a step from the heights of the celestial mountains to the depths of the valleys below.

When Aunt Margaret had left her she began slowly to pull off her boots; and it seemed as though the thought of last night, mingled with today's bitter feelings, all came back to her.

She could just catch the sound of her grandfather's voice as it rose in prayer from the room below; and as she sat there listening, the old hobgoblins of doubt who had been silent for so many months began their dance over her once more. They asked the old unanswerable questions, and new ones, more unanswerable still; and dared even to lay profane hands on the words that had just been transporting her into the seventh heaven.

When, however, the prayer below was ended and she had got into bed, she put these suggestions of the evil one from her. She had been reading too much, she had been thinking too much, she had been turning her eyes away from Christ. For a whole month she would touch no book but His word and think no more, and so resolving she fell asleep.

The cloud, the little cloud, at first no larger than a man's hand, waxed greater as the months went by – grew in the end to be so thick and heavy that at last even Aunt Margaret's sunshine was absorbed by it.

Undine went quietly to chapel Sunday after Sunday; and a meek, sweet, quiet child she was, they all said even if rather dull and stupid. They little knew how those still eyes made food of their every action; how forever they were being hung in the balances and dismissed to have that unchanging 'Tekel' written up against them in her mind.

She kept her resolution, and except when at her lessons allowed no book to tempt her but her little brown Testament; that she pored over daily for hours, just as she had done in her little whitewashed sanctum at home.

Was the Testament most to blame, or the inherent wickedness of her own small heart, or the good women with whom she came in contact in her grandfather's house who, when not in chapel or talking of their neighbours, were thanking the Lord that they were not as their sisters in the mire?

Whichever it might be, at the end of three months this small heathen in a Christian land had made up her mind to go no more to chapel, had come to the conclusion that neither prayer meetings nor their cousins, the class meetings, were the gates of the Golden City, but rather the entrances to that other way that, beginning with a short circumbendibus, at last leads one straight to the gates of the city whose walls are of groans and whose pavements of sighs.

Having now a very decided hankering after that Golden City and a very decided impression that she was bound for it, it could not but be that she should eschew those entrances. She did not believe that at the gates of the Golden City stands a great winged angel:

'How old are you?' he asks of the applicant for entrance.

'Thirteen years.'

'Have you always tried to do as your conscience told you? But, no, stay. Had you no one who gave you bread and butter and shoes?'

'Yes.'

'Oh, then they kept your conscience. If you only tried to obey them – Well and faithfully done, enter into joy, and sit down on a throne.'

This was what she did not believe; and so one Sunday morning she came downstairs with a laggard step and slow.

When she got to the door of the breakfast room she ran back again, to pray one prayer more, for it was a terrible mountain she had to cross that morning.

The window of the breakfast room was wide open and the morning light forced its way in, gilding for once the brown Wesleys and Fletchers in the bookshelf, and playing over the little bunch of flowers Aunt Margaret had put beside her plate. She ate little, and before breakfast was half over had strewed the carpet with the leaves of her broken flowers.

Aunt Margaret wondered what was wrong with her little niece, and made vain conjectures; while Undine kept repeating to herself the nice little speech she had prepared to make to her grandfather, which she had even taken the trouble to write down the night before by way of strengthening her memory. She would tell him that she could not go to chapel, because it did her harm; but she would tell it him so humbly and in such terms that even he must forgive her.

But alas for human plans! Every time she essayed to begin, the words stuck fast in her throat; the precious moments sped and breakfast was over without one syllable of her carefully prepared little oration's having got further than the region of her heart, where it lay, heavy as lead.

When, however, her grandfather had risen to go, and had passed out into the passage, she also rose quickly and, standing in the doorway, said, 'Grandfather.'

He turned round slowly and fixed his cold eyes on her.

'What is the matter?' he asked.

Seek of the dumb an answer, and you will as easily find it as Undine the words of her precious and laboriously concocted little speech. They had hopelessly vanished and gone, and in their place came only these – 'I am not going to chapel.'

'I thought I had given you clearly to understand, Undine, on a previous occasion, that I wished you always to go. I allow no disregard of my wishes in this house.' So saying, he turned round to enter his study, but Undine passed him quickly and stood in the doorway before him.

'I am not going,' she said. 'It is a wicked cruel world in which one human being has power over another, but you cannot make me do what I think is wrong; and if I go to chapel just because I fear you I shall be a hypocrite like all the others who go there; and I will not. All people who love Christ should keep away from such places, which only bring disgrace and shame upon his name. If he came to earth today he would denounce them as he did the Pharisees and priests in his day. It's all a mockery and an empty show, and I shall never go again, never, never.'

Her words followed one another in a quick incoherent stream while she pounded away vigorously with one little hand in the palm of the other, till both were furiously red. Her grandfather stood silently looking down at her. In his heart horror and wonder largely mingled with hatred were moving, but his face told nothing. For one moment he felt a wish to strike her, but she scared him, as she had often done her old opponents, by her wild earnestness. He looked at her again, and then, without making an effort to enter his study, walked out the front door, conquered for the first time in his life; conquered by a little child.

And Undine, the conqueror? Alas! Has not the victor's fate been, from the beginning, to lie down and weep? She went out into the garden and dropped down onto the soft green turf among the rose trees.

The sweet Sunday bells were ringing loud; through the clear morning air their music came to her, sounding strangely soft and sweet now that she knew they would never summon her again. For all others they were calling, but they had no word for her; she was one alone, without kinship or fellowship among men – so she said in her bitterness. Had she been born with a curse over her head? Would it be so wherever she might go, that her hand should be against every man, and every man's hand against hers? Or was she really so much worse than others that, wherever she might go, love and sympathy would be denied her? Would she have to walk on alone, alone, unloved, misunderstood, right on to the end?

She was sobbing and digging away with her toes into the soft earth when Aunt Margaret came and kneeled down beside her.

'Go away,' said Undine, fiercely. 'I am alone. *Leave* me alone.'

'Undine darling, what have I done to you? What has anyone done to you? Undine, you say you love Christ and are trying to be his child. Don't you think you were wrong to speak as you did just now?'

Undine threw from her the soft hand that was caressing her hair, and said, though more gently, 'Please go away'; and Aunt Margaret rose and left her.

Long after, Undine thought, with tears bitterer that those she then shed, of the hand she had thrown from her that morning; but they were bitter enough to the little child – the little child, who had not yet found out, as we all must sooner or later, that the path through life in which each soul must tread is single; that no two walk abreast; that where one soul stands, never has stood, and never shall stand, another; but that each man's life and struggle is a mystery, incomprehensible and forever hid from every heart but his own.

CHAPTER FIVE

A Sunny Afternoon and a Wild Night

It was summer again; a dreamy, hazy, delicious summer afternoon. Three sat upon the brown of a small grassy hillock near the beach – Frank, Undine and Aunt Margaret.

The grass was rich with great golden-eyed flowers, and he picked them as he lay there, to fasten in the golden hair of the woman he loved – long silky yellow hair that hung about her, soft and fleecy as the small white cloud that lay dreaming far away to seaward.

Undine, sitting a little apart with her book, looked up ever and again to watch them; they were pleasant to look at as the blue sky overhead or the green grass and shimmering light below. Every now and then she caught a word of their conversation; they were making little plans for the spending of the long good years that were coming to them, when they two should be always together. At last they called to her: 'What shall the colour of the study curtains be – red, green, or yellow?'

'Blue,' said Undine – 'blue, just the colour of the sea where it lies at rest, far away.'

'No, no; not that colour,' Aunt Margaret answered, quickly. 'I never did so before, but this afternoon I hate it. Every time I look up and see it, I hate it.'

'Look at that cloud,' said Undine; 'when we came 'twas a tiny speck we could hardly see, and now 'tis like a great fairy snow-ship in the sky.' Then a silence fell on all three; but by and by Frank fastened more golden flowers in the yellow hair, and Aunt Margaret's merry laugh was heard mingling with the rippling of the waves and the hum of the brown insects in the grass. Undine sat looking at the picture before her, all green and gold. Surely it must be that in such a world life and love are alone realities, and death and pain are but the fevered dreams of our own minds.

There were withered flowers lying among the grass stalks; there were heavy shadows growing in the valleys; the fairy ship was growing darker every moment and would come with the storm wind and the hellish grin of the lightning, to plough up the smooth face of the sunny sea before morning, but they saw none of those things and sat there smiling in the sunlight.

'Delilah, you are bewitching me,' said Frank at last, as he sprang up from the grass on which he had been lying with his head in her lap. 'I promised to be at Leeford tonight; must be there, in fact.'

'It's too late now,' said Aunt Margaret, shading her eyes with her hand to look at the sinking sun; 'if you walk ever so fast you cannot get there before dark.'

'I shall not walk; I shall hire a boat in the village and two boys, and shall be back again by ten o'clock.'

'It is the last evening, Frank,' she said, turning her bright childish face up to his, 'the last for four whole weeks. Be sure you come back.'

He stooped over her and whispered softly for a moment, and then with a goodbye to Undine sprang down the green slope and over the rocks along the beach.

Just as he was passing out of sight he paused for an instant to look back at them and call out, 'Only till ten o'clock, you know, only till ten o'clock.'

The two left rose to go home then.

'Shall I pull the flowers out of your hair?' asked Undine.

'No; I leave them there; I feel like only a little child tonight. Oh, Undine, I hope you will one day be as happy as I am.'

She had reason to be happy, Undine thought; in a few months more he would have finished his studies and was to settle as doctor in Greenwood, and they were to be married; reason enough, but so had most women. How glorious it would be when she, too, was one!

Later on in the evening Undine kneeled in the seaward window of Aunt Margaret's room. Aunt Margaret stood behind her with her arms twined round her, and both were looking into the darkness. Except the flash of the distant lightning, nothing was to be seen, nothing to be heard but the faint roll of the thunder and the roar of night wind as it flung the mountains of water it had created against the cliffs or hurried them madly over the rocks.

'It is no use looking out any longer; he will not come tonight, Golden,' said Undine, using, as she often did, his pet name.

'No, no, you do not know him as I do. He would do anything rather than disappoint me,' she answered.

'But the boys, the boys,' said Undine; 'they would never venture out on a night like this.'

'Then he would come alone.' The words were said in a calm, measured voice utterly unlike her own; and Undine looked up at the white face above her and out at the darkness, and shuddered.

'What time is it?' Aunt Margaret said at last.

'I don't think it's very late,' said Undine, with a piteous attempt at a smile that faded instantly when she had left the room and was making her way through the sleeping house.

As she stood before the great clock in the hall it struck the hours slowly; and then the solemn ticking was renewed. She thought of the things it might once have spoken to her, concerning the bright brown face that had looked back at them from the rocks – the rocks where now the wild water was foaming in the darkness – and was glad that it could speak them no more.

When she got back to the room, Aunt Margaret was kneeling at the side of the chair on which the candle stood, with her two beautiful hands clasped over her head.

'It is just twelve,' whispered Undine as she sat down beside her. 'He will not come tonight; it is too late.'

'Too late, too late!' Aunt Margaret hissed the words from between her clinched teeth. 'I never prayed for him as I ought, I never kept on praying till I felt God's answer, and now I can do nothing more for him, nothing more. It is what I deserve, it is God's punishment on me for loving a man who mocked His name, who had no faith in Christ; but, Undine, Undine, heaven will be no heaven to me if he is not there. I would give my soul so willingly to reclaim his; I could bear all for him. Pray, Undine, pray. I cannot.'

And Undine prayed – prayed as we pray for that which we are losing, for that for which we fear the day of prayer has almost ended.

'Talk, Undine, talk,' said Aunt Margaret. 'If you are quiet I cannot bear it.' And Undine talked on, the words of her own sweet dreamy faith – talked on till Aunt Margaret fell asleep with her head in the child's lap. Then at last Undine leaned her forehead against the chair, and slept also.

When she awoke next morning the world was laughing, the sky all blue with not one tell-tale cloud, the hills all green and glittering in the morning light, and the blue sea beyond them rippling in the sunshine, with a smile like the dimpled smile of a beautiful wicked woman after she has broken hearts and sucked the sweetness out of human lives.

Undine, before she was well awake, smiled back at the picture that laughed back at her through the open window; then wondered what this heavy weight about her heart might mean, and remembered all.

Had he come? Where was Aunt Margaret? Glancing round the room, she hurried out to look for her. As she passed her grandfather's door he opened it and called to her:

'Do you know who went out at the front door last night and left it open? I felt the cold wind blowing in, and had to go down and close it, about four o'clock.'

He felt pretty sure the culprit stood before him; no one else in the house was given to wandering out at night, and in the dark. It would only be of a piece with all her other eccentricities, which had at last brought him to the conclusion that the child whom he thoroughly detested, yet could not get rid of, was not quite in her right mind.

She gave him no answer to his question, but asked hurriedly, 'Has he come?' And seeing from his face that he did not know, she passed on.

Where was Aunt Margaret! Not in the garden, not in the house. Soon everyone was in full search of her except her father, who went into his study to prepare next Sunday's sermon.

She had angered him last night by asking him to send someone over to Leeford to hear if Frank had left. He hated his future son-in-law with a hatred only less perfect than that which he felt for his little granddaughter. A freethinking child of the devil, he had more than once called him to Aunt Margaret, and he would never have had her had it not been that from his mother he had inherited something.

Gold is like charity; it covers a multitude of sins; it maketh a cloak wherein even freethinking may array itself, and its nakedness shall not appear.

Two hours later he came out of his study with a troubled look. His wife had been to tell him that Margaret was nowhere to be found, and that one of the boys had returned from Leeford. Frank with the other had started in the boat at eight o'clock the night before, hoping to reach home before the storm broke.

If there was one thing in the world the dried-hide loved, it was his daughter; and in the search that followed no one looked so anxiously or so earnestly as he.

He had refused to send anyone last night, and she had gone herself, he thought; and so thinking he set out on the road she must have taken. Undine went to search where she knew Aunt Margaret's own heart would have taken her – to the little green hillock where the yellow flowers he had picked lay withered here and there, where she could see the rocks on which he had stood to wish his last goodbye and the placid sunny sea which murmurs on so softly, telling no tales of the beauty and the strength it has devoured.

Undine could not bear to stay near it and hurried back to the house and the dear old rose-filled garden.

Her grandmother met her at the door, crying and wringing her poor weak hands: 'Oh, he is dead! Poor Frank is dead! They have found his body, and the boys that were with him. And my darling, my poor darling, where is she? It will kill her! It will kill her!'

Undine did not stay to mingle tears with her, but passed from room to room like one in a dream, searching where yet she did not hope to find; with the restless moving water ever before her eyes as she wearily closed and opened door after door.

The door of her own room stood half open, but she only glanced in, and was just leaving it when her ear caught a sound from the corner near the window. There, with the sunlight streaming full over its yellow hair, crouched a naked human figure. The knees were drawn up till the chin rested on them, and one arm was clasped tight round them; the other was stretched out, and one finger pointed to a crack in the boards. The eyebrows were drawn down till the eyes were hardly visible, but they opened slightly every time the mouth twitched nervously to one side or the other.

Undine stood motionless in the doorway and watched it. Had sorrow touched her reason? Was she mad? Or was that really what she looked for – that thing with the faded yellow flowers in its hair?

'Ha-ha-ha!'

'Twas a hellish laugh that filled the room and rang out across the rose trees in the garden. The finger was till pointing to the crack along the boards.

'Ha-ha-ha! There they come – one, two, three; there they come – the devils that have got his soul, hundreds of them, thousands of them. That is the door they took him down, there. I asked God to take me instead, but He would not, and now they have got me too. He used to say there was no God, and no hell, but God will show him now. Ha-ha-ha! How they come! Little devils – one, two, three!'

Undine uttered a low cry and dropped down onto her knees beside her.

The yellow thing, with its faded flowers, crouched down lower, crouched till its chin rested on the floor, and its half-closed eyes glanced furtively now on this side, now on that. Then springing to its feet, with a cry, it seized Undine with both hands and bore her to the ground. Kneeling on her and putting its lips close to her ear, it hissed forth: 'I know you, who you are. You look like Undine; but you are the devil; the devil to whom God gave his soul. I know, I know. You left his body lying there upon the beach, and you tore it with your cruel hands that I might not know it when I found it lying there in the grey dawn; but I knew it, I knew it.' She fixed her teeth in Undine's arm and clasped her to her breast until Undine's cries were smothered and she became unconscious. When those who had heard them entered the room, Undine lay upon the floor insensible, and in the far corner crouched a thing that licked its red lips and cried exultingly as it pointed at her: 'I have killed the devil! I have killed the devil! Ha ha-ha!'

A week after, and Cousin Barnacles had taken Undine to his house in Greenwood.

It is not time which makes old men and women of us. Undine's childhood lay buried in the grave upon the hillside where a form which the sea had given up was laid, and in a dark strong house far off where a mad woman grew wilder still if they showed her a Bible or a yellow flower.

Ignorant of the world, shy, childish in her manners, yet for her childhood was forever of the past. She would never again dance with naked feet among the rocks and wonder how, in the world of green and gold, men ever sigh and pray for rest beneath its crust. For her, henceforth, the merry laughing children would be you, and grave-eyed men and women, we and us.

CHAPTER SIX

Greenwood

It was a white lifeless face that Cousin Jonathan brought with him to Greenwood. So ghastly and pale that even Mrs Goodman and Miss Mell, if they were not moved to pity, could not find it in their hearts to exercise their tongues upon it.

All day Undine used to wander in the old wood that lay between Cousin Jonathan's house and the village; used to wander there when the dried leaves were falling down in showers and piling themselves up in little grave-like heaps at the roots of the great trees; used to look at them and fancy, with a kind of apathetic pleasure, that, when the spring came with all its young green, she, like the leaves, would have vanished away. She thought her heart was broken. Perhaps it was; but she did not know that hearts are only Time's china cups – china cups which the old father is forever throwing hither and thither, cracking and smashing in his wild reckless way, and then carefully picking up and cementing so cleverly that the old scar does not even show. They may ring a little dead if you strike them – but that is all.

Not knowing this, Undine wondered at herself when she found out that she intended to live, and to grow strong, and pretty too.

Then the women in the village began to say malicious things, and to find out that she was stupid and conceited and unchildlike; but she cared nothing for what they said, and read her books and curled herself up to dream for hours among the roots of her favourite old tree by the little bridge in the woods. At first they were sad, unearthly dreams, but when the year grew older and the golden colour came creeping over the hills, it crept into her dreams also; and she would sit there smiling and glad; then she would wonder at herself and go home slowly, thinking of the dark lonely house and the Goldenlight that was buried there forever.

Cousin Jonathan tried to cheer her, buying books for her, a horse, dresses and trinkets, and everything wherewith man seeks to comfort and delight the heart of womankind. But, as his wife remarked to Miss Mell, he might as well have saved his money and spared himself the trouble: she never showed the least pleasure at receiving his prettiest gifts, except it happened to be a book that pleased her, and then it was only in a staid, old-womanish way.

Three years had passed by, and Undine the child had changed into Undine the woman – pretty, very pretty, even Miss Mell was obliged to allow that, 'for those who like that style of beauty'. But she was stupid, terribly stupid and old-fashioned. All her female acquaintances were agreed on this point. The most ravishing dress could not win even a glance, the most delicious piece of scandal the least attention. No little party or picnic, however heart-subduing in person or purse the gentlemen who were to be there, could ever awaken in her the faintest enthusiasm. People left off having anything to do with her at last.

'I'm terribly anxious about her,' Mrs Barnacles would say. 'It's not that she is old; she is a mere child; but I don't see what's to make her change; and if no one ever sees her, who's to marry her?' Mrs Barnacles was a yellow-faced big-nosed invalid, who passed her life on a sofa and was apt to take a dyspeptic view of things. 'She has need of all her good looks, if she is to go off; men don't take readily to those queer, dull sorts of girls; and with those idiotic ideas of hers, on religious matters, too, half the men would not have her as a gift.'

'Of course they would not,' Miss Mell would here strike in; 'and I believe it's all put on too – her not going to chapel and all the rest of it – just to be peculiar. It's all nonsense. What does she know about such things? For clever learned men it's all very well, but a stupid child like her ought to be well whipped and fed on bread and water for six months; that would take the nonsense out of her better than anything else.'

'Yes,' Mrs Barnacles would assent, 'for men it's all very well, as you say; but a woman, and one who lives on charity, ought to keep them to herself if she has ideas of that unwomanly kind.'

She used to tell Undine all this, to her face, sometimes: 'Go to chapel and give up reading those nonsensical books, and act like other people even if you don't think like them. It won't answer, it won't answer at all; and you had better give up all this sort of thing before it's too late. You'll repent it if you don't.'

Then Undine, half bitter, half indifferent, would get away from her to the dear old world of inanimate nature, which never calls us queer and strange or advises us to wear a mask. It was well for her that she cared for that at least, for dark loveless times had fallen on her, and she cared for nothing else. Cousin Jonathan was good to her, did all in his power for her, but she liked him less as the years went on. She had never loved him, and the intellectual help which he had been able to give her ceased to be a bond between them when she had reached his ground and even passed beyond him. So now Cousin Jonathan shared the fate common to all lovers, and gave out his gold, such as it was, for dust.

One afternoon late in the summer Undine sat half buried among the long grass at the foot of her old tree. Mill's *Political Economy*, with its face turned to the ground, lay at her feet, while a little black beetle scudded hither and thither among its pages, all unnoticed. Her hands were busily employed in picking off small bits of dried bark from the trunk of the old tree; while her thoughts were in the same key, and as sweet and impossible of fulfilment, as ever were little Ellie's when she sat alone 'mid the beeches in the meadow.

It may be true that the man who has never dreamed with his eyes open never can know what disappointment means; but it is also true that he never knows what heaven is like. Undine's stay there was not of long duration, for by and by Cousin Jonathan came sauntering through the woods in search of her.

She was so enwrapped in her own thoughts that she did not notice his presence till his hand had been passed softly over her hair.

'Where are your thoughts wandering?' he asked as he seated himself softly beside her on one of the great knotted roots of the old tree which had forced its way out of the ground.

'Nowhere,' Undine answered wearily.

'That is the answer you always make me now,' he said, very gravely; 'you don't make a friend of me now as you used to, Undine.'

'Because I can't. There never was much sympathy between us on any subject; there is none now.'

'It is you who do not understand me,' he answered, passing his fingers softly through her hair and letting his hand rest on the back of her neck.

There was something in the action, simple as it was, that she did not like; and a feeling of disgust came, as it had often done lately when he kissed or caressed his little daughter, as he called her.

She threw his hand from her as she would a toad's claw, and sprang lightly to her feet.

'What is the matter?' he asked, looking up at her with his serene blue eyes; and Undine felt ashamed of her ingratitude and foolishness.

'Nothing is the matter,' she answered, laughing, 'only I am not quite so old as you and believe in perpetual motion.'

Standing on tiptoe, she caught one of the overhanging boughs and swayed herself gently backwards and forwards. Cousin Jonathan thought, as he looked at her, that never, even on that first day when he saw her standing with her little naked feet upon the rocks, had she looked so deliciously lovely: as round, as downy and inviting as any golden peach that ever schoolboy eyes looked at and, looking, thirsted for, because it was unattainable.

'How dared you intrude upon me in my private residence!' she said, still laughing. 'Is it not enough to make me disagreeable? Why don't you wait till I invite you?'

'I should have to wait a long time, I fear,' he replied, still looking at her.

'Perhaps so, but death may make me more agreeable and sociable; and, as I am sure to die long before you, when you hear that I have departed this life you may come and hold converse with my spirit under this tree. I mean to haunt it, if the old monster does not quite dissolve me into nothingness.' She rattled on thus, not knowing what to say and not wishing to be silent.

'You have a queer mind,' said Cousin Jonathan. 'As surely as you seem to be in one of your merry moods, you drag in some grim and ghostly thing to spoil it all. I don't believe you know what it is to be gladly happy.'

'Perhaps not. I know that when I was a child and used to romp most wildly and do mad things that none of the others dared, it was just because I was not happy. Whenever my thoughts and miseries were too great for me, I used to let off steam by doing something terribly naughty; and when I had been lying awake all night under my bed, in the greatest agony about my sins and other people's, I used to get up and have the most desperate of romps all by myself. I remember one day, when I was only seven years old, having the story of Cain and Abel for my Sunday lesson. It made a great impression on me. If God accepted Abel's sacrifice not because of its value but because of his faith, why, if I only had faith, should not fire come down from heaven upon my sacrifice at Wilge Kloof.[1] I could think of nothing else for days, and so I waited till one day when I was very hungry and there was very nice meat for dinner. I thought the sacrifice must be one that had cost me something; so I would not touch a mouthful, but saved the nice little chop that was put on my plate till dinner was done and everyone had gone to take their siesta. It was a broiling day, but I went out to the shady side of the house and collected twelve little flat stones and piled them up neatly in a square heap; then I put my meat down on them and knelt down to pray. I trembled with ecstatic joy when the prayer was finished, for I felt sure that, when I looked up, the flames would have descended and devoured my fatty chop. I was almost afraid to raise my eyes. When I looked up and saw the chop lying just as I had left it, I felt astonished, but my faith was not at all shaken, and I set to work again, praying with all my might. I looked up again after a long time, thinking I would see the chop and perhaps the stones themselves, like Elijah, licked up by the heavenly fire; but it was just as I had left it, only the sun had made the fat melt a little and run down the stones. I kept on praying till the people in the house began to stir, and then I threw down the altar and gave the chop to the dogs, and felt ever so wicked and miserable as I walked up and down in the shade of the house. I knew I had prayed with faith, and I thought the only reason why the fire had not come was because God hated me, as he had done Cain. By and by I sent down to walk by the *kraals*, and saw one of the Kaffir girls fetching cattle dung to smear the floor of the house with. I thought smearing must be delightful work, and I could not bear to think about my poor altar and my chop any more; so I found a hard flat piece of ground at the back of the *kraal*, fetched some water in a broken oil can, and mixed up the water with the dung nicely, just as I had seen the black girls do. I worked so hard that in half an hour I had smeared a place the size of a room, and my clothes and face too. I was just beginning to feel quite better and as though I did not care so much that my offering had been rejected, when someone came and caught me in the middle of my dirt and happiness, and I was perched up on the top of a great box till bedtime.'

Undine paused to take a breath at the end of this long relation. She did not care much for Cousin Jonathan's company nowadays, and the fear that he would feel it and be pained made her very voluble generally.

---

1 Wilge Kloof – pronounced Vilgerkloof. Wilge means willow.

45

'You have changed strangely since those old days,' he said. 'I don't think you are troubled with too much faith now; you believe in nothing under the sun.'

'That only proves what I said just now,' she answered. 'You don't understand me. I believe more truly in some things than you do.'

'In what, for instance?'

'Oh, in more than one. You said yesterday that there was no such thing as a love that must live while the soul lives; that wrong or neglect *can* change the love that can be felt but once in a lifetime for one human being and which is the best of earthly things. You pooh-poohed it and called it dreaming, not reasoning. I merely return the compliment.'

Cousin Jonathan did not like this enthusiastic speech, and smiled a sneering sort of smile. Beautiful men and women can afford to sneer; Cousin Jonathans cannot, and he looked grotesquely ugly as he did so.

'With your magnificent intellect and your profound reasoning faculties whereby you profess to test everything, one might almost expect you to show a somewhat deeper knowledge of life and human nature. But after all you are only a child, and will grow wiser, when you have seen more of the world, than to believe that love can live without hope or return, any more than a body without food or air.'

Undine hated to be told she was but a child and had no knowledge of the world, because there was so much of truth in the assertion. The little man knew this and therefore he told her so, for he felt angry with her that afternoon, though he hardly knew why and his blue eyes never showed it.

'You read all manner of trash and sentimentality till your mind is completely enervated; you came down here this afternoon to read some of Mrs Browning's poetry and effete nonsense, I have no doubt.'

'There lies what I have been reading,' she said, pointing to where Mill still lay upon the ground. 'There is nothing very sentimental in that, I fancy.'

'You are likely to get just as much good from this style of reading as from the other,' he replied as he picked up the book.

'You are difficult to please, my old father,' she said as she caught the bough again and rocked herself gracefully to and fro.

Difficult to please! Of course he was. There was one thing in the world that would have pleased him, and that thing he could not have. The little man felt, as he sat there among the long grass, with his mild angel eyes and his seeking mouth, as though he could have killed her, for he knew that she would never love him. She hung as far from his reach as the rose that hangs on the topmost branch of a bush is from the worm that creeps up and down on the rotten leaves below. He hated her, and yet he loved her with a love that had grown with her opening beauty and her softening figure, as the worm grows while the rose but swells. It is a long way from the dirt to the rose; but may it not be climbed?

Was he asking himself this question as he sat looking at her? Undine thought he looked ugly and strangely out of place among the dreamy flowering grasses on which were dancing the sunbeams which had made their way through the thick foliage. The little brook that murmured all the more sweetly, because almost buried out of sight – he could not understand what it was saying, and why had he come to disturb her quiet? Her conscience was just beginning to give her the most unpleasant twinges for thinking so ungratefully of one who had done more for her than any other being, when steps and voices coming over the bridge made her look round. There were two gentlemen crossing it, and Cousin Jonathan rose to his feet and went to meet them. He introduced them to Undine as the Mr Blairs, father and son. There must have been at least thirty years' difference in their ages, yet as far as form and feature went there was a strong resemblance between them. Both were short and very broadly built, with round noses, round faces, blue eyes, scant beard, and sandy-coloured hair; but here the resemblance ended. In place of a painfully flexible and sensitive mouth, and eyes more soft and melting than a woman's, the father had thick, firm, pressed lips that told of a strong animal nature and an iron will, while the eyes above were so cold and dead that the great stone in his breast-pin gave out more light and warmth than they did.

The path through the woods allowed only of two abreast; Undine had what half the girls of Greenwood would have given their little fingers to gain, a long walk and a *tête-à-tête* with Mr Henry Blair.

'Are you fond of reading?' he asked her, noticing the book in her hands. When a man opens conversation by this remark you may make pretty sure of one of three things – he wants education, he thinks you a fool, or he is one himself. Undine decided at a glance that neither of the first two was the case, and that consequently the last must be.

'At times,' she answered him, in a very indifferent voice. Books were her meat and drink, her friends and lovers, but she was not going to tell him so.

'You have Mill's *Political Economy* here, I see,' he remarked. 'I am just going through his works with very great pleasure. They are beautiful, are they not?'

'Very,' said Undine, smiling inwardly.

Her companion then went on to state how he delighted in reading, how he spent his whole time in it. There was no work of note in English, French, German or Greek that she could mention, which he had not read. He liked philosophy, he revelled in poetry, he studied history, he worshipped science. He was a wonderful man, with a brain crammed as full of facts and ideas as a brain could be; and yet not one of them had ever been able to reach him. Just the backboneless, warm-hearted, weak character which nature had given him he had, and would have to the end of his days. 'Tis small use trying to graft an orange tree on to a Coonie.[2] If you have no thought of your own, those of other men will find nothing to which they can fasten themselves;

---

2 The 'c' is a click. Coonie is a tree (shrub).

and you will have to carry them about with you – if carry them you will – much as you do your rings and your gloves, rightfully or wrongfully yours, as the case may be; but always outside of you, and never part of you.

So Undine walked beside her companion, with his black-blue woman's eyes and his soft voice, feeling a kindly contempt for him, in spite of his infinite superiority to herself in knowledge and acquirements of every kind.

'What do you think of them?' said Cousin Jonathan, when after a somewhat lengthy call their visitors had taken their departure.

'Nothing,' said Undine. 'The son has not a bone in his whole composition, and the father is all bone, or something harder.'

Cousin Jonathan smiled, not displeased to hear her express her disapprobation of other men.

'I wonder if you ever did meet *anyone* whom you approved of,' he remarked, smoothing her soft hair.

'You are quite right with regard to the father, however; he is not troubled with too much tenderness of heart. The first time he married it was to a lady of very good family, whom he married just on account of her blood. He led her a very fine life, and when she died at the end of two years he married a woman who was immensely rich and whom he liked still less and treated still worse. She left him all her money when she died; but I believe he hates her son, who was here this afternoon, just because he is hers. I never saw them together before.'

'Has he any other children?' asked Undine.

'Yes, Albert, his eldest. In my pedagogue days, before I married Mrs Barnacles, he was my pupil. He is here now, and is sure to call and see me in a day or two.'

Albert Blair! Yes, that was the name of the man Miss Mell had talked about as having been saved by a girl from drowning. Albert Blair – yes, that was the name; then she took up her book and thought no more about it.

Next morning Undine rose early and took her morning walk onto the little hill that lay behind Cousin Jonathan's house. The grass was still heavy with the great glittering dewdrops, and the fresh clean air reminded her of the mornings in her old African home when she used to get up early and go to pray behind the little *kopje*. There it was so still and beautiful that it was easy to pray and to believe in God's love. She wondered if the dew lying on the English grass were really as lovely as the great drops that used to stand trembling on the bushes and silvery ice-plants among the stones of the *kopje*. Her thoughts went back to those old days – not longingly, for there hung over the memory of her childhood little of that free gladness which to most men causes it to lie behind them, a land of light and song, to be looked back at across the thirsty steppes of life with vain longing and some regret. She had looked out onto the world with eyes too grave and earnest ever since the time when, a little child of six years, she had kissed the leaves and cried among the thorn bushes, because when chopped down and burnt they would die forever. She had found griefs and mysteries where other children see only playthings, and had passed a tearful solitary childhood in a home of love and plenty. There was no wish for their return in the eyes that looked back to those days; but they had about them that subtle charm which death alone gives to men or times. With all its intense solitude, its tears and doubts and bitter prayers, there had been hours of happiness in her childish life, hours when the heavens had seemed to open and the angels of God had descended, and ascended from the earth.

Her thoughts wandered on from those old days to the first year of her life in England, to the glad love that had lived before her and which had been so suddenly put out.

The impression those days had made upon her, extinguishing all hope, all faith, all trust, had somewhat faded, but a strange deadness seemed to have settled down upon her; and, with an intellect vigorous and alive, it seemed as though all emotional vitality had died within her.

Cousin Jonathan had said, 'You believe in nothing.' He might with as much truth have added, 'and love nothing.' Not Cousin Jonathan's extinction or disappearance into fire and brimstone, or that of anyone else, would now have cost her one tear; and even for herself she had but a kind of apathetic indifference. In a way, it might be, she loved her books and nature; but her feeling for Spencer's *First Principles* was not like the love which had poured itself out in hot kisses on the leaves and cover of her little brown Testament.

It was the sense of this coldness and deadness that made the days of passion and feeling look so beautiful to her now, and that almost brought the long-stranger tears into her eyes as she looked down on the glittering dew and thought of those early mornings behind the *kopje*. Agony, anything, would be better than this dreadful coldness and indifference. Would it never end, never break? If only I could love something, she thought, as she passed slowly over the wet grass. To love something, to believe in something, to worship something, even if that something were only herself – to look at something with eyes other than those of calm indifference – it would be worth sleepless nights of tears and prayer.

She walked on with her eyes fixed on the ground, and was surprised when she looked up to find herself at the top of the hill. It was not a very stirring or striking scene that lay before her, but calm and bright. At the foot of the little hill on which she stood lay Cousin Jonathan's house, and beyond that the little wood in which grew her old tree. The white houses of the village were visible on the other side of it, and beyond that again the large mansion of the Blairs with its roof glittering in the sunshine. Not a soul was to be seen except at the edge of the wood, where a man and a woman were standing. It looked as thought the woman's head were resting on his arm, but they soon parted; he turned back among the trees, while the woman took the little path that led straight up the hill. Undine sat down, listlessly watching her as she came nearer; then she saw it was not a face she knew or had ever seen before in Greenwood. 'Twas a young face like those that sometimes haunted Undine's waking dreams and made her wish she were a painter, to fix them everlastingly on canvas. The woman was of more than middle height, with a magnificently developed yet graceful figure; her features were regular and almost of a Jewish cast, while her long curled eyelashes drooped over cheeks as dark and brilliantly coloured as the rare hothouse flowers she wore in her bosom. Undine looked at her as she passed, filled with genuine admiration, but the woman seemed quite unconscious of her presence. She loves someone, and she is happy, thought Undine; if I could love I would be happy too.

When she sat doing her needlework in Mrs Barnacles's room that morning, she asked her who the beautiful stranger was; for that lady was kept well informed in the doings and saying of all Greenwood by the indefatigable Miss Mell.

'You must mean Alice Brown, I think,' said Mrs Barnacles, after a moment's consideration; 'they say she is growing more and more beautiful. It's very queer, but whenever the Blairs are here, she is. Generally she lives with her grandmother.'

'I should like to know her,' said Undine.

'Oh, they are only common people,' said Mrs Barnacles. 'We don't associate with them.'

That afternoon Harry Blair put in his appearance. As a rule he was careless enough about his dress to be mistaken for the greatest genius living; but on that afternoon he had arrayed himself with punctilious care, and had come to invite Cousin Jonathan and Undine to look as some fine pictures which had just arrived. Undine had said she was fond of pictures, and these were really beautiful.

Of course she could not refuse to go; and Cousin Jonathan went, for he followed her steps as smoke follows a train.

George Blair was a rich man, and no miser; a man who valued his money only for the status it gave him in the eyes of his fellow men and the ease and luxury it might bring him. The erection and adornment of this house at Greenwood had been the employment and delight of the last twelve years. He would pay away hundreds of pounds for a picture or a statue that was said to be good, though he was about as well able to understand the one or the other as would have been one of the thoroughbreds that stood in his stable.

It was the first time Undine had been in the house, for during the three years she had been in Greenwood the owner had been travelling abroad. It was aristocratic to travel on the Continent, therefore he went. He had married his first wife because she knew who her great-grandfather was. He would have sold his own soul to be thought refined and of blue blood, but he never succeeded in producing the desired impression.

Perhaps it was the sense that where he so deplorably failed his eldest son was by gift of nature pre-eminently successful, that gave rise to the feeling of dislike he entertained for him. This, if not so strong as the feeling with which he regarded his younger son, was to say the least unfatherly.

It half amused, half disgusted Undine to see the little bloated, leaden-eyed creature standing among the elegancies and beauties which his money had bought, talking of *my* pictures. My pictures! As if anything with a trace of beauty could ever belong to him. He might lay out his money for them; and if they were pictures they might hang on his walls, if they were women (a luxury in which he still largely indulged) he might dress them richly and buy their smiles and obedience; but possess them – never! The flesh-incrusted soul that looked out through the hard blue eyes in their setting of red fat would know nothing of the possession of that which had beauty. Undine thought as she looked at him how unenviable was the fate of both women and pictures. But she soon forgot him before a large oil painting. It represented a battlefield. Horses and riders, dying and dead, lay around in wild confusion, while in the foreground, stretched out upon a heap of the slain, lay the figure of a man gorgeously clad in the knightly costume of the olden days. His plumed helmet lay at his side, filled with blood; and the beautiful face, so faultless in feature, so pitilessly hard in expression, was turned upward to the dark evening sky. At his feet, clasping them with both hands while it crouched upon the ground, was the figure of a woman, its delicate and voluptuous development being hardly concealed by the coarse, scanty clothing it wore. On the face there was a wild look almost of joy, though the lines about the mouth were those of speechless agony.

'You seem fascinated by this picture,' said Harry Blair, gently, as he stood behind her. 'It is my favourite also, but I confess I like it only because of the woman's face; I can make nothing out of it.'

'It seems to me to tell its own story,' answered Undine, speaking softly, as though more to herself than to him. 'He was a noble, high-blooded lord, and she a poor serf, with only her soul and beautiful body to give him. He hardly cared to take them, though it was for nothing; and now, in the hour of death, she has followed him and found him lying dead; and she is crouching at his feet in agony because he is gone, and in wild joy because he is hers alone now, hers and no other's, if only that she may lie at his feet and die there.'

'A very desirable fate, certainly,' said a voice behind her that was far too melodious and well modulated to be that of either Harry Blair or Cousin Jonathan, whom they had left in the next room.

Undine looked round quickly from her slaughtered knight and passion-filled maiden to behold, standing behind her, that 'piece of divine perfection' as his lady admirers were wont to call him – Mr Albert Blair.

He was a man of somewhat more than six feet in height, with a lithe graceful figure and a head of beautiful yellow-brown curls. His moustaches, of the same colour, were so delicately curled that one felt surprised to see the firm powerful lips under them. His features were delicately chiselled, and from the regular white teeth to the small round ear there was neither fault nor flaw to be found in him, unless it were his eyes. They were of a pale cold blue, and would not have been small had he not habitually kept the lids more than half closed. There was nothing lost by that proceeding certainly, for when now and then on rare occasions he lifted them, the gleam shot forth was as icy and chilling as a moonbeam falling on a glacier. It was one of these that fell on Undine as she looked round, and it instantly froze her. She knew without looking at him that the cold light was falling on the small rent in her glove and on her ruffled hair which she had not smoothed before coming out.

There are some men and women in whose society we instantly feel a sublime indifference as to the cut of a coat, the dust on our sleeve, or the sit of our necktie; while where are others who, the moment we see them, set us running over all the flaws and defects in costume and person, from the want of blacking on our boots to the broken nail on our forefinger. There are men and women in whose presence we seem to be released from ourselves and to be possessed of ideas and powers of expression which till then we never dreamed of; while others seem to shrivel us up and leave us standing without an idea or a correct word in all our vocabulary on which we can lay hands. One of these latter was Albert Blair.

Everyone on whom the cold beam fell felt awkward, ill-dressed, and ignorant. Elegant dandies felt in his presence that their whiskers were too long, the set of their coats execrable, and their way of handling a cane simply clownish and disgraceful. Ladies, however well contented they had been with their own appearance the moment before, discovered that their dress was all in shocking taste, their knuckles were too large and their sleeves too short, when the blue eyes were turned upon them. And Undine in the hour that followed thought of nothing but her split glove and ruffled hair and, while she stared at the pictures, saw as little of their meaning as did the Piece-of-perfection who walked at her side, with his deferential manner and his disagreeable eyes, passing commonplace conventional remarks upon all they looked at.

It was a great relief to her to get away from him into the fresh evening air, and walk down the green lane between Cousin Jonathan and Harry Blair.

An hour or two later that young gentleman was seated in the smoking-room, with Mrs Browning's *Portuguese Sonnets* open before him. His feet were drawn up under his chair, his elbows rested on the table, his head was stretched forward, and his great eyes fixed on vacancy. His brother Albert was at the other end of the room, reclining in an easy chair with his legs stretched over another. His glass, lamp, an elegant cigar-stand, and a pile of blue papers lay at his side on a small round table.

Presently he took the cigar from between his lips and, throwing down the last of the blue papers, said with one of his graceful inimitable little yawns: 'You seem to find your book singularly entertaining this evening. You have not looked at it once in the last half hour.'

His brother started, and answered quickly, 'Quite as entertaining as those everlasting blue papers of yours'; and then added, after a pause, 'Don't you think Miss Bock is very like the woman in that picture?'

'What woman, and what picture? You should *try* and be a *little* more explicit if you wish for an answer,' said Albert Blair, now really closing his eyes and puffing the blue smoke softly through his lips.

'Of course – I mean the picture we were looking at when you came up this afternoon,' responded his brother, in a tone that very clearly showed how unwelcome that coming up had been.

'Yes, possibly there is a resemblance; but your divinity has not nearly such a delicate hand; and a good hand ranks next to a good figure,' retorted his brother, calmly.

Harry looked fire and lightning at him, and the Piece-of-perfection, who had a strange aptitude for seeing things without opening or at least appearing to open his eyes, said, as he puffed away serenely: 'There is no occasion to excite yourself about what I say, my dear fellow. She is a very pretty little girl, an uncommonly pretty little girl; beats Lady Edith and her sister hollow; only rather too careless about her dress, and a little peculiar in her manner, that's all.'

To think of comparing her to Lady Edith, a die-away beauty with no more soul in her than a fly, and to speak of her with that cool air of superiority, was a crime on his brother's part which put into poor Harry's hand a strong inclination to send Mrs Browning in her red morocco binding among his brother's curls.

Other books had been so sent for smaller offences in their boyish days, and the sender had been invariably knocked over and coolly kicked out of the room. He was not one of those to whom experience teaches much, still on this occasion he was wise enough to take himself out of the way of temptation; and making his way into the garden he paced up and down the paths in the moonlight. Surely that thing of grace and beauty which in two days had filled the whole circle of his existence – surely it was now in like manner wandering up and down under the dark trees around Cousin Jonathan's house. For had she not said in answer to his question that she loved walking alone and in the moonlight?

Now as it happened, on this particular evening Undine sat beside a little table darning Cousin Jonathan's stockings, listening and laughing at extracts from the daily papers and *Punch*, which the little man read aloud to her as he lay on the sofa.

When she stood up to put her work away he asked her what she thought of Mr Blair number three.

'Think of him?' she answered. 'He is only an equally proportioned mixture of ice and iron. With all his deference and politeness, he would freeze one or crush one to atoms with as little compunction as a fly, if one happened to stand in his path. I don't like his brother, I dislike the father, and I detest him,' said Undine, as she threw the last stocking into the basket and thought of her torn glove. She sat down to mend it when she got to her room.

'What a contemptible little wretch I am becoming!' she thought when she had finished it, 'to allow such trivialities to break into my real life and drive out higher thought. Am I no better than other women after all? I've no heart; if I lose my head what is to become of me?' She felt weary of herself and disgusted, and she could not now lie down on the floor and pray, till in an agony or an ecstasy, she should forget herself. She had taken the first bite at the forbidden fruit, and could see that the terrors which had haunted her were but the inevitable creations of the human mind, as it looked out in its ignorance on this world of suffering and wrong – could see that the visions which had entranced her were but the dreams of the human soul in its craving after happiness and truth. So much she saw; but saw no farther. Inevitably as to the soul in its search after its highest truth there comes a time of agony and of blood, so too there comes a time of deadness and of cold. The old life has been cut down to the roots, the new life has not yet arisen. So, too, in our childish vision of hell, we stand alone in a world of darkness and silence till the world around us and even we ourselves seem to become mere mocking shadows. Yet, could we know it, it is but the silence that comes before the dawning; it is but the darkness that comes before the day breaks; it is but the land of glittering glaciers that lies between us and the celestial city. And what if we should perish alone in its mist and cold? Better to die frozen, striving for the glorious golden city of God, up yonder – better than here, in the land of Egypt, with the flesh pots and the onions, the leeks and the garlic.

That evening, while Undine sat mending her glove, Albert Blair still leaned back in his chair, sipped his glass, and smoked with his half-closed eyes, making calculations and thinking hard all the while.

Unknown to his father and without capital, he was speculating, as he himself would have allowed, in a rather wild and reckless manner. These speculations had for him the same irresistible fascination that the gaming table had for many, and only through their help, if ever, could he hope to free himself from his father's control – unless he should marry a rich wife; and to Albert Blair's proud palate a wife's bread would have tasted yet more bitter than a father's.

'Still, I must keep Lady Edith well in hand. If these speculations should fail, it must come to marrying her. She dresses in good taste and is in perfect style – but I would rather it were her sister,' he soliloquised.

CHAPTER SEVEN

Lovers

There be loves many and gods many; and happy the man whose god and love are one – happy for the time being; most miserable of mortals when the time of revelation comes and at one stroke both god and lover crumble into dust.

Harry's love for Undine had sprung into life, full grown and omnipotent, on that first afternoon when he met her in the woods; and if from that time it could not be said to have grown stronger, it had certainly grown larger, until at last the whole world animate and inanimate, intellectual and moral, was for him but one being, imaged and reflected in a thousand ways. Women's dresses and faces had a new meaning for him; for, though standing afar off, were they not like to hers? And the little wild forest flowers that she loved, were they not emblems of her, as they nodded their innocent white heads at one another? In the books that he read, he paused only when he came to some sentence that might have been hers; and all that was beautiful and sweet sang back her name to him. Dark days came for his well-worn Bible, and for Beecher's *Life Thoughts* and a score of brethren who had been his daily study. *She* never read them; and they were thrown contemptuously onto a lower shelf, to lie there till the wheel of time should have turned.

'Why do you always change the topic when our conversation turns to religious subjects?' Harry asked Undine one day, some four months after their first meeting, as he sat in the low bow-window in front of Cousin Jonathan's house, with his feet resting on the gravelled path outside.

Undine stood behind him, mending a great rent in her dress, made as they had been rambling in the wood together in search of the wild flowers which now, tied into a great bunch, he held in his hand.

'Religion is like love,' answered Undine. 'It flourishes best in silence, and is to be felt, not spoken of.'

'I don't mean merely what one may call emotional religious subjects,' he answered, looking up into her face with his great pleading woman's eyes. 'You were arguing last night with Mrs Barnacles about the right or wrong of committing suicide. You never talk with *me* about such things; your conversation with me is always about the smallest trivialities, such as you talk of to Miss Mell.'

The dark eyes above him looked down on him with that half-pitying, half-scornful look that was so often in them when they rested on him.

'You must be contented with what you get,' she said.

'But you give me so very little.'

There was something very piteous in the words and in the face that looked up at her which would have cut sore against the hearts of many women; but she cared nothing, only said: 'I give light where I get it. When you enlighten my spiritual darkness, I shall try and do as much for yours.'

She had a contemptuous pity for the great boy, with his manly years and his crammed brain, and his passionate love that had made him follow her about for the last four months and serve her like a dog.

'If a bird is only fitted to live among the marshes and reeds in the valley, why tempt it after you to the cold high rocks where the eagle finds a glorious life in the clear cold air?' So Undine said to him, and so thinking, she made no attempt to lead her poor wild duck to the heights for which nature had never fitted him, and where he must die of frost and starvation.

His ideas as to what her views might be were not very clear, but he had a vague notion that she believed in nothing; accordingly he had convinced himself that he also believed in nothing and he had not a little disgusted and very much astonished her by informing her, as he scraped up and down with his boots on the gravel, that he was an infidel, an atheist beside whom Hume was orthodox and Voltaire a credulous believer.

'I am sorry to hear it,' was Undine's brief reply.

'Why should you be sorry that I resemble you?' he asked.

'I was not aware that you did so,' she answered. 'Will you please tell me the name of that little purple flower? I wish I had all at my finger ends that you have.'

He told her the name of the flower and sat twirling the bunch round in his hands.

Undine stooped down for it when the rent in her dress was mended.

'I wish you would choose out one flower and give it to me,' he said, never removing his gaze from her face. 'May I have one?'

'Of course you may,' said Undine, carelessly holding out the bunch. 'They are very pretty; choose which you like.'

'I care nothing about it unless *you* give it me,' he answered, in a deep passionate voice that always angered her.

'There,' she said, pulling out a great gaudy dandelion, which in spite of his disapproval she had persisted in putting in the bunch.

'How long the shades are growing. I really must go and get tea ready. I'm very discourteous to dismiss you in this way, am I not?' said his angel, and with a laugh fluttered out at the back door.

'What a poor fool I am!' he said to himself as he sat in the window, looking at the gaudy flower in his hand and feeling a strong inclination to throw it down on the ground and tread on it. In the end, however, he fastened it carefully in his button-hole and walked home moodily through the wood; for, is it not written on the iron leaf:

'Who drinks of Cupid's nectar cup
Loves downwards, and not up:
He who loves of Gods and men
Shall not by the same be loved again.'

It was not often the case (and it showed the discretion of all parties that it was not) that they were alone together, the three Blairs, father and sons. On this evening, however, all three sat in the smoking-room and all three were smoking; for had not Undine said that 'A man who does not smoke is as bad as a woman that swears'. It was purgatory before that time to Harry Blair, but he stuck to his pipe with the resolution of a martyr.

There was a blazing fire in the grate, and at one side of it sat Albert Blair; while before it lay a great curly brown-and-white dog with his nose resting on his master's foot.

'You are leaving for London tomorrow, are you not?' he asked his father, who sat on the opposite side of the fire.

'Yes,' was the short rejoinder.

'Be back at the beginning of summer?'

'Perhaps so. Depends on circumstances.'

'When are you taking yourself off?'

'Don't know.'

The master of the dog had more than one attraction in Greenwood, and a lady who must be kept in hand close by; so, though the place was wretchedly dull, he was in no hurry to leave it.

'There is no need to ask when you go,' said the father, turning with one of his most sinister smiles to his youngest son. 'We all know you are booked for Greenwood till a certain individual, despairing of a richer morsel, shall consent to swallow you.'

Harry Blair threw down his pipe, emptying its contents on his trousers and the carpet; and drawing himself up and making a tremendous effort to look dignified and serene, after the manner of his elder brother, he said with trembling lips: 'I must beg of you to say no more upon a subject upon which you are in total and absolute ignorance.'

His father laughed, one of his coarse brutal laughs; Albert leaned down to stroke Prince's head and went on curling his moustaches.

'As to my being in total ignorance,' said the father, 'I know nearly as much of your little beauty as you do yourself, and infinitely more about woman in general, I fancy. She would think no more of throwing you overboard, along with her books and her flowers, if by doing so she could gain a few thousand a year, than I do of knocking the ashes off the end of my cigar.'

Harry Blair rose to his feet, knocking over the tumbler that stood at his elbow. His hot blood, which in schoolboy days had gained for him the highly appropriate sobriquet of 'Fire Brain', was now fairly roused.

'If any man but my father had dared to speak those words,' he said with tremendous passion, 'I would have knocked them down his throat; as it is, I will only prove to you that they are a lie, a cowardly dastardly lie.'

His father spoke with a quiet sneer: 'You surely forget in whose house you are standing, whose money it is that causes women to look at you! Go and tell your beautiful Undine that your father has turned you out of his house, that you have not a penny in the world, nor the wits to make one; go and tell her that your father would rather see his money rolling in the gutter than that a penny of it should ever come to you. Go and tell her that, and see what her answer will be! Go, go at once.'

There was no passion in the words; they were calmly, sneeringly spoken, as words are that have been lying on the tongue for years, ready for use.

Albert Blair sat lazily looking into the fire. He had known it would come to this some day, and he was glad; it gave him a better chance.

When he looked up his brother had left the room, and his father, sitting opposite him, was puffing away vigorously.

'The young dog!' he said after a pause. 'He has all his mother's damned impertinence, and he shall learn a lesson or two yet before he dies. Young dog!'

Albert made no remark and a long silence followed, suddenly broken, greatly to his surprise, by a long-continued, deep chuckling laugh proceeding from his father. The Piece-of-perfection for once fairly opened his eyes and stared at him. His respected senior was not generally given to mirth, even of the demoniac order.

'I'll do it,' he chuckled, 'I'll do it.' And then, seeming to remember himself, he rose, kicked the dog, and took his departure, leaving his son in undivided possession of the fire and his own meditations.

The next morning was cold and stinging and Undine half repented that she had not stayed at home, as Cousin Jonathan wished, in place of going for her morning walk.

She was just turning homeward when, hearing a step beside her, she looked round, and saw, to her great astonishment, no less a personage than Mr George Blair, looking redder than usual and almost out of breath.

'I heard this was you favourite early walk,' he began, after wishing her good morning; 'and I have walked myself almost out of breath, fearing I might miss you. I have long wished for an opportunity of seeing you in private, and at last I have it.'

A pause followed, Undine ransacking her brain to discover some possible cause for *his* desiring a private interview with her.

'I trust,' he began again, 'that you will not be much surprised at what I am about to say. I trust – I feel in fact convinced – that you have understood what the attraction has been which has led me so often to your cousin's house. Though so much your senior in years, I trust, my dear Miss Bock, that you will believe me when I assure you that the affection which I offer you is as ardent and as sincere as that which any younger man might give you, and that, with the will, I have also the power to surround my wife – and such, if you will permit me, I would make you – with everything which can induce to happiness. I cannot ask, I would not desire, an immediate answer. It is of course only right that you should first seek the advice of your friends; but will you not give me some hope, however faint it may be?'

He paused to take breath at the end of his pedantic little oration, while Undine turned on him a face in which nothing but blank astonishment was written; it changed to one of disgust as her eyes rested on the little red-faced creature. He saw the look and had expected to see it. He had had, as he said, great experience in woman, and knew that the handsome penniless young lover must hope to carry the day by storm or not at all, that time and reflection are fatal to his success; while the man of fifty, with his bloated face and bags of money, has nothing but these to rely on; and they work for him more surely when he is absent than present.

He took no notice of the look she gave him, but it made him swear in the fatty depths of his inmost heart that, come what would, he should yet have her as his wife. He drew the little scarlet cloak that was slipping back lightly over her shoulder, and fastened it with a brooch formed of diamond-studded flowers which he drew from his pocket.

'Pray do not,' she said, as she wrenched it loose and held it out to him as though it had been a creature which stung her hand. 'You do me a great honour,' she said; 'but it is quite impossible, quite.'

The old man peered out at her from his rolls of fat, and before turning to leave her said, 'Then I had best wish you good morning; but before I do so may I beg of you, my dear Miss Bock, to remember that if ever you should change your mind (and we never know what the future may bring us), I shall not have changed. I leave for London tomorrow,' he continued; 'and unless you should write to me, having altered your mind, as I sincerely hope you may do, it may be long before we meet again. Goodbye, Miss Bock.' And without waiting for her reply he turned away and trotted down the lane. Undine stood to watch him as he rolled out of sight.

'His wife!' She laughed a merry, mocking laugh. 'His wife!'

The idea of being any man's wife, of bearing any man's children, was absurd enough to her, to whom a lover was only a reality of the imagination, to be adored, worshipped, and endowed with every perfection mental and physical, but not to be seen, clothed in flesh and blood; just as we dream of heaven, but would laugh to scorn the man who offered to show it us.

Her merry mocking laugh would have sounded almost as derisive had it been Albert Blair, the son and graceful Apollo, instead of George Blair, the father, old and coarse.

'Money,' she said. 'What is money?' And kicked with her little foot a rotten stick which lay in her path as contemptuously as she had just thrown from her the wealth that a word might have made hers.

Aye, gold and love, what are they? The great gods that rule us! Gold, god of the body with its lusts and its clay; love, god of the soul with its fire and its passions. As long as a human being lives shall they, too, not live and struggle and strive for the mastery? – the one ruling over the young and fresh, the other stealing his kingdom from him when he grows old and wrinkled?

'Money! What is money?' said Undine, derisively, for she had seen no deeper into life than love songs and dreams could take her; and she wrapped the little scarlet cloak about her and went home light of heart and singing.

She found a letter waiting for her on her bedroom table, but took off her things and stood warming her hands at the fire before opening it.

'Only from poor Harry Blair, about some book or flower,' she said. 'Poor' falls naturally before some names; it did before his.

She opened the letter and threw the wrapper into the fire, where it flamed up and turned to ashes, like a young heart devoured by that cruel merciless old God of Love.

At first as she read she looked a little puzzled, then angry, then amused, and finally with a mingling of all three upon her face sat down before the fire with the three great blue sheets in her lap.

It was as passionate an appeal as ever was penned by arrow-smitten man.

For her sake he had given up all – fortune, friends, rank – without a thought and without a regret. She alone could give him that for which alone he longed, that which alone could make him happy. Would she refuse him? No, she could not, would not; he felt sure of that. Nothing else was dear to him on earth, nothing else did he desire. So it ran on. It might be years, he said, before he could make her his wife, but all he yearned to know was that her heart was his, her head, her soul.

When Undine got thus far the disgust she felt got into her fingers, which sent the two sheets she had finished into the fire after the wrapper.

'The father asked for my body and offered me gold in return; *he* asks my soul, spirit *and* body, and has nothing in the universe to give but a pair of great staring woman's eyes, and a soft brain, crammed to bursting and without a particle of sense in it.' So she said to herself, as she sat tearing up the last page, still unread, and letting the fragments fall in a blue shower at her feet.

Well was it for the hapless penman that he could not see this and was not where he longed to be – lying at her feet; better wandering the woods where now and then, as the wind swayed the leafless branches, he would catch a glimpse of the house which held her.

She had just finished writing him a few very cool and careless lines in answer, when the breakfast bell rang.

'I will say nothing about it to Cousin Jonathan. It must make a man feel wretchedly small to find that another knows his love has been thrown back at him. And I suppose it is a kind of love they both have for me,' she thought as she rose to go.

Passing out at the door, she caught sight of her own face in the little glass that hung on the opposite wall, and for the first time that morning a womanly, or in justice let us say a human, feeling of pleasure came to her.

It is so nice to be desired by others, so nice to be beautiful.

When she entered the breakfast-room Cousin Jonathan was standing with his back to the fire, dressed in his everlasting salt-and-pepper coat and plaid trousers.

'I'm a little wretch,' she thought as she looked at him. 'Here is a man who has been more than a father to me, and yet whenever I look at him I detest him. And two men have told me this morning that they loved me, and I feel no sorrow that I can't return it as a true-hearted woman would. I'm a heartless creature and horribly hard, there's no doubt of it.'

'You are late this morning,' said Cousin Jonathan. 'I suppose you have been writing your answer.'

'To whom?' asked Undine.

'The letter you received was given me to bring. I know all about it,' replied Cousin Jonathan, smiling. He felt no trepidation as to what her answer might be; for, if there was one thing which the little man had studied in the last three years, it was the character of the pink-and-white thing before him. He understood her better than anyone else had ever done, in many ways. He knew of that power of passion that lay dead and unawakened beneath the cold, feelingless shell; and he knew as surely that the day would come when it would be called into wild life, not by his hand or that of any Harry Blair, with woman's eyes and soft trusting nature.

'You have still got your red cloak on; I always like you best in it,' he said, as he drew her to him to receive the morning kiss he had given her ever since she came to him.

Undine turned quickly from him and sat down to pour out his tea.

'Where is Cousin Jane this morning?' she asked.

'She is feeling worse than usual and has just sent for the doctor,' he answered as he drew his chair near to the table and to her. 'What answer are you going to give a certain individual?' he asked her, after a pause.

'There is only one answer I could give him,' she replied, shortly, as she passed Cousin Jonathan's tea.

'And he gave up everything for you! His father has vowed to have nothing more to do with him; and now all the world will say that you did not marry him because he had no prospects.'

Undine laughed her little scornful laugh.

'All the tongues on earth may clamour; they cannot hurt me,' she answered.

When breakfast was over she dispatched the note, as cold and killing a missive as ever carried destruction to aerial castle. She did not love him, never could; would never care to be any man's wife; hoped they would always be good friends; hoped he would find someone to make him happy and love him; so the note ended.

All the morning she sat with Mrs Barnacles who was really very ill; but when the afternoon came, bringing Miss Mell and Mrs Goodman, she felt free to take her book and cloak and wander out.

'Twas cheerless and wintry enough, but the air was pleasant and fresh after the close room, and her book engrossed her attention.

Presently she heard voices, but did not look up until she found herself close to Albert Blair. There was no one with him but his dog, so she concluded he must have been speaking to it.

Master and dog made a pretty picture as they stood on a raised bank, with the leaden sky and leafless trees for a background. Both looked so strong and placid, so perfect after their types.

The half-closed eyes caught sight of her in a moment, and their owner came forward to meet her. He made some graceful remarks concerning the weather, inquired after her cousin; and they paused as they walked beneath the very trees where poor Harry had wandered in the morning.

'Here, sir! Here!' he called to the dog, who bounded out of the little path in search of some imaginary game. The dog came slowly back and rubbed his head against his master's knee, who stooped down to stroke his head.

'How absolutely that dog obeys you,' said Undine, feeling as she always did in the presence of the Piece-of-perfection, at a loss for an idea.

'I make most things which belong to me do that,' he answered, quietly; and as she glanced up at the firm lips beneath the delicate golden moustache she felt it must be so.

How nice it must be to have something you must obey, something you cannot help obeying, whether you wish or not! I never have, she thought.

'Have you had that dog long?' she asked.

'About two years, and he never leaves me; sleeps at the door of my room every night.'

'You would miss him now if you were to lose him,' said Undine, thinking of Socrates.

'Perhaps so,' he replied, carelessly curling the tip of his moustache; 'he is an exquisite animal. I have been offered fifty pounds for him, but would not let him go for four times that sum.' Again he stooped and touched the dog's head, who walked close beside him, proud and pleased.

Undine, walking at the other side, envied him.

'Will you allow me the pleasure of carrying your book? It is rather too large a one for you,' he said, noticing the ponderous volume under her arm.

Taking if from her, he glanced at the title, and Undine saw the satirical lines at the corner of his mouth and eyes grow deeper; but he only said in his blandest tone, 'Rather stiff reading, I should imagine,' and stooped to loosen a dry branch that had caught in her skirt.

Undine wished the book buried under the highest pile of leaves that ever wind collected and left there to rot; though only half an hour before she had been so absorbed by it that Greenwood and the vanities of the present life were banished from her mind.

In the presence of all other men and woman she could walk erect. Why in this man's presence was she bowed down wishing only to do and say what he might approve? Others might ridicule her dress, her manners, her tastes, and she would cling to them with the greater tenacity; but if a line deepened round *this* man's mouth, she would have given untold treasure to be able to alter or disclaim them.

She was glad when the walk was over – as she always was to get out of his society – and yet, when she was alone before the fire, she took the great book and quietly tore out the leaves one by one and watched them wither and shrivel in the flames.

'I must be going mad,' she said. 'What makes me do this, and take such pleasure in doing it?'

Going mad! – of course she was, as we most of us go once in our lives and, thank the gods, not more than once.

Cousin Jonathan was sitting with his wife upstairs; and when it grew dark Undine built up the fire, blew out the light, and lay down on the sofa.

Presently down the passage came Cousin Jonathan on the way to his study; quietly, for Cousin Jonathan's footfalls were never heard. As he passed he looked in at the door. The red coals cast a ruddy glow over the little room, and the chairs and tables cast long flickering shadows on the brown wall. On the sofa in the corner opposite the fire *she* lay, just visible in her white dress, with arms clasped over her head and dark eyes fixed on the firelight: not seeing *it*, but only a tall figure with a rough dog at its side standing on a leaf-strewn bank, with the wintry sky and barren trees for setting.

Long the little figure in its brown coat and plaid trousers stood watching in the doorway; at last it entered and kneeled down softly beside her.

He had loved her so long, he had loved her so passionately, with the best love his nature could give; and tonight this love spoke itself in words as vehement and startling as the passion itself had been long restrained and covered over.

She started up and threw him from her, and, quivering with rage, stood before him.

Still on his knees at her feet, the little man caught her hand and glanced up at the face above him. Even in the dim firelight, the look of intense loathing it wore was visible. It brought him back to reason.

Dropping the hand, filled with insufferable shame, he crawled from the room almost on hands and knees, as thought to hide him in the ground. As he shuffled through the doorway he dropped one green slipper on the mat.

Undine stood as one in a dream and watched the little figure in its plaid trousers and brown coat as it glided swiftly from the room, to pass out of her sight forever.

For the little man, in his green plaid, with his angel eyes and beautiful prayers, she was to see no more, though from afar off his shadow might fall on and darken her.

As she passed out at the door she drew up her skirts, lest in passing they might touch the shoe that lay there.

''Tis a pretty little thing,' soliloquised Albert Blair as he walked home though the wood the same evening; 'a pretty little thing, and if she were trained might be good for something. She would not care to be any man's wife, she tells my poor fool of a brother. Well, if these affairs of mine turn out well and I am able to indulge a fancy, who knows? How should you like a certain little eccentricity for a mistress, Prince?' he said, touching with the tips of his fingers the dog's head. 'Whether I ever let things go as far as that or not, I may see what I can do with her. Ha, ha! How wrathful the poor boy would be, and the old one too, for I think *he* had his thoughts of her.' And Albert Blair smiled his quiet smile. He had but one smile for friend or foe, for prince and beggar, which meant nothing, told nothing, showed nothing.

The next morning, when Undine had fallen into her troubled sleep, Mrs Barnacles's maid came to rouse her.

Cousin Jonathan had been obliged to leave on some unexpected and most important business and might be gone for weeks. He had started before daybreak, and his wife was terribly cut up at his having left her when she was so ill. She seemed worse and wanted to see Undine at once, the girl said.

When Undine entered the room she found the poor invalid in tears. 'It was so cruel of him to go away like this,' she said, sobbing; 'he knows how that hateful Miss Mell and Mrs Goodman will talk and say he cares nothing for me, to go away and leave me when I am so ill, and yet he does it.'

Undine tried to console her and felt she could not tell her, as she had determined, that in a few hours she also would leave.

In her cold way she felt pity for the poor woman whose husband cared as little for her as she did for him, who loved nothing, had no friends, and lived in the constant fear and dread of Goodman, Mell, & Co.

'I was thinking,' Undine said, 'of going to stay with my grandmother. Since my grandfather's death she lives alone and has often asked me to come to her; but I will not leave you till you are better.'

So all that day Undine sat at her bedside.

'Why *don't* you take a book and read? You could turn up a corner of the blind,' said Mrs Barnacles.

'I don't care to read today, thank you,' said Undine.

'Why, what on earth has come to you?' said the invalid.

Later on the servant entered, to say that Mr Albert Blair had called to know how her cousin was.

'Tell him she is no better,' answered Undine.

'But he wanted to see Miss Bock herself,' said the girl.

Undine rose and went downstairs.

He was leaning against the mantelpiece in the parlour when she entered, and his dog lay at his feet.

She looked ill and pale, but he had never liked her aspect so well as he did at that moment.

'Your cousin is seriously ill, I hear,' he said as he came forward to meet her; 'and you look as though you had not found much rest last night.'

There was a kindly feeling in the words but none in the tone or in the face that looked down at her, only bland politeness.

'I had not to sit up last night; Mr Barnacles left only early this morning,' answered Undine.

'So I heard just now. Wouldn't you allow me to send someone to sleep here? You have no man about the place, and it is a long way to the village to the doctor.'

'No, thank you,' said Undine, wondering to find in him such thoughtful kindness. 'You are very good, but we require no one.'

'I am sure you will feel very lonely. Won't you let me leave Prince to keep you company?' He noticed that she had stooped to caress the dog.

'He would not stay,' said Undine, smiling.

'He will do just as I tell him,' said his master, touching the dog with his foot. 'Here Prince, lie down!'

The dog lay down again on the rug, but watched his master with anxious eyes as he turned to leave; and was only kept from following him by another stern, 'Lie down!'

'Poor old fellow! It's very cruel of me to keep you,' said Undine, kneeling down beside him after his master had gone, and burying her face in his rough curls.

'I'm very cruel, but I am so lonely, and I love nothing, nothing at all. I thought I loved my books and nature, but now I find I don't care anything, even for them. O Prince, I wish I were you! I don't want to be loved; I only want to love something.'

The dog looked up at her with his loving, trustful eyes and tried to lick her face, till she buried it again in his neck.

Albert Blair called again the next day and every day in the dreary two weeks that followed, but he never stayed more than a few minutes, and sometimes did not even come in, only wanting to hear how the invalid was.

Undine as she sat before the fire, not caring to read or work, counted the slow hours as they passed, for they brought his coming nearer.

Prince stayed with her always. She had thought never to love another animal again when Socrates died; but our hearts are often larger than our wills, and the great curly dog had grown to be almost what the brown-eyed monkey had been to her in other days.

CHAPTER EIGHT

Beautiful Snow

It was a cold wintry afternoon and the white snow clouds were lying low and heavy. Undine, after many almost sleepless nights, crept down to the little parlour and had a fire made there, the first that had been made since Cousin Jonathan left.

Miss Mell, now her friend was getting better, had offered to come and sit up with her; and Undine, as she nestled down in the great armchair, looked forward to a long evening of drowsy rest. Prince lay sleeping before her with his head at her feet, and she, half dozing, watched the little sparks as they fluttered up the chimney. So short, so warm, so bright; how pleasant the life of a spark must be!

'You seem to find something very absorbing in the contemplation of the fire this evening,' said a voice beside her; and Prince, wide awake in an instant, leaped up to greet his master.

'You quite startled me,' she said. 'I did not think you would come tonight; it is getting almost dark.'

'Yes; we have the promise of a heavy fall of snow,' he said, as he seated himself in an armchair on the other side of the fire.

'You can have no idea what a charming picture this room makes, coming in from the cold outside,' he continued, trying at the same time to repulse Prince, who in a transport of joy had put a paw on each shoulder.

'You must take him home with you tonight,' said Undine. 'I am not going to be so cruel as to keep him here any longer; and you must miss him.'

'No, I never miss him. You had better keep him if he is any pleasure to you,' answered the Piece-of-perfection, stretching out one delicate white hand to the dancing flame.

After a short silence he said, 'Do you never wish to return to Africa?'

'No,' she replied. 'I know no one there. My stepfather has remarried. But I should like to see the old farm and my little monkey's grave again.'

He was leaning back now with his face in the shadow; she could not see the lines she dreaded at the corners of his mouth, so she answered, 'Yes, he was the best friend I had.'

Another pause followed; then he said, more abruptly than was his wont, 'I have a favour to ask of you, Miss Bock.'

'You rather puzzle me,' she said. 'I never feel sure I understand you, and I do most men. At times I form an opinion of you, at times another, but I never feel sure that

I am right. I wish you could satisfy my curiosity and explain to me how it is you come to have such extraordinary views and manners.'

'Why do you not put some other word in the place of "extraordinary" – say, "pernicious", "reprehensible"? That is what you really think,' she replied, using a freer speech with him than ever before, for in the firelight the bands of speech are loosed and the tongues of men and women do wonders.

He never paid her compliments or spoke to her as he would to another woman, so he answered quietly, 'Those words would be almost too strong; say, unwomanly.'

Another making this remark would have been answered by a contemptuous silence; or at best she would have launched out into a denunciation of that singular injustice which cramps and dwarfs a woman's mind, making it an unpardonable offence against her womanhood to entertain a thought or give utterance to an idea that has not been repeated and re-echoed till it is as stale and unpalatable as a last year's loaf. Tonight she only said: 'Why are they unwomanly? What is your idea of what a woman ought to be?'

'You are asking me a question hard to answer,' he replied, looking with his half-closed eyes into the fire. 'A woman to be womanly should have nothing striking or peculiar about her; she should shun all extremes in manners and modes of expression; she should have no strong views on any question, especially when they differ from those of her surroundings; she should not be too reserved in her manners, and still less too affable and undignified. There is between all extremes a happy mediate, and there a woman should always be found. Men may turn to one side or the other; woman never must.'

Undine said nothing when he ended. She could not help it; she had been born with strong and determined ideas on every subject, sub-and super-lunar, and not one step of her sixteen years' journey had she walked in the happy mediate road. It was too late to change now. They had told her that the day would come when she would repent having done nothing to try to conform herself, at least outwardly, to the views of others; and she did repent it as she sat there that evening. She would have parted with all that was highest and best in herself to become a little less Undine, a little more like anyone else. Who was this man, what was he, that he should make her grovel so? she asked herself.

'You have not yet answered me,' said the Piece-of-perfection, again stretching out his delicate hands to the blaze. 'Are you going to satisfy my curiosity?'

It seemed so strangely delightful to do something at his request, and yet she seemed to have nothing to tell, nothing that she could tell *him*; and she said so.

'Nothing! And you have lived for sixteen years and in two continents, and certainly are not troubled with lack of ideas. You must excuse me, however. I have no right to press you in this way.'

Undine sat leaning forward with her arms folded on her knees, looking into the bright flame that threw its light full upon her, and began, awkwardly and stupidly enough at first, to tell of the old African days – awkwardly and stupidly enough till she forgot the presence of the man who was leaning back in the shade on the other side of the fire and watching her with his cold blue eyes. Then she saw only Socrates and her governess, and the little Dutch girls, and the old red farmhouse in the Karoo – saw the little round-stone *kopjes*, with their milk bushes and red sand, and was again the little child among them all, with the child's thoughts and longings.

Albert Blair sat and listened without the shade of a sneer upon his lips.

Most men have their moments of insanity, which belie and are at variance with all the days and years of the past and will find no successor in the future, moments when their thoughts and feelings are opposed to all they have ever deemed rational, right or possible.

Such moments came for the first time and the last to the Piece-of-perfection as he sat listening to Undine in the firelight.

A pity, nay, a passionate sympathy, filled his heart for her; for one moment he forgot that the soul which troubled itself further than to find and eat the bread and honey of this life was the soul of a fool – forgot that the only right of a woman is the right of the rose – to simle and be, not to think and live.

Forgetting all this, bewitched, befooled, infatuated, he stretched out his hand to the little figure opposite him.

'Your life has been lonely; no one has understood you; you may have had no one to guide you,' he said, speaking for the first time and in a voice strangely sweet and unlike his own. 'Will you let me be your friend and take care of you?'

She sat and looked at him as one in a dream.

'Come to me, darling,' he said, holding out his hand to her.

Still she sat and looked at him; then he drew her softly to his arms, and she nestled close to him.

She did not kiss him or speak: only clung to him and rested with her arms round his neck and her head on his shoulder.

If she lay there for hours or moments, she did not know; it was enough to be there.

'Why do you lie so quietly, darling? Why do you not tell me that you love me?' he said, turning her face round to his.

It seemed to break her rest, and she only answered him by putting her hand softly on his cheek.

'Are you not going to kiss me, my little girl?' he asked again, lightly bringing his lips down to hers and kissing them.

She kissed him and then buried her face in his shoulder.

'Did you ever care about anyone before you loved me? Did you, darling?' he asked her, running his fingers through her hair.

What was the past? What was the future? The present was enough. She answered: 'No.'

'You could talk so well a little time ago, and now you can hardly get out one little "no". Tell me that you love me, my little girl.'

'I love you more than anything, more than everything,' she said, holding his face between her two hands and putting her cheek softly against his; then she nestled close to him again.

'Are you happy now?'

'Yes.'

'How astonished everyone will be when they hear who is going to be my little wife,' said the Piece-of-perfection as he thought with infinite satisfaction of the discomforture of his father and brother, also of Lady Edith and others of his worshippers. How would she look among them all? Beautiful? His wife must shine and eclipse all women. Men must envy him his wife, as they did his dogs and his horses. Would it be so with this little girl?

'Undine, I want you to do something for me,' he said, after a long pause. 'I know you will do whatever I tell you. Will you not?'

'Yes,' she said, creeping very close to him.

'You must not spend so much time over your books as you have done. I would rather you left them alone altogether. You must give two or three hours a day to your music, and learn dancing. I want my wife to be deficient in nothing. Do you hear?'

It was the cold Piece-of-perfection with the half-closed eyes that spoke these words, not the lover of half an hour ago, and they struck Undine a little chill; but she only whispered in his ear that she would do all he told her.

'Why do you tremble so, my little darling?' he said, as he stood her down on the hearth rug. 'I must go now, but I will come again early tomorrow. How cold your little hands are. Warm them by the fire and then go to bed. Now you belong to me, I don't want you to have dark rings round your eyes, as though you had sat up all night. My wife must be always bright and beautiful, you know. Goodnight, darling.' So he left her.

Undine kneeled down before the low window and drew back the blind to watch him as he passed down the garden path.

The snow had fallen, the clouds had gone, and the full moon poured down her light on a white glittering world – so white, so pure, so calm. Even the iron paling had its coat of crystal, and the dark evergreens that grew beside the window were bent beneath their load. As far as the eye could reach stretched the silent white snow; only down the little garden path there were his footmarks in it.

CHAPTER NINE

Trodden Snow

'Undine,' said the Piece-of-perfection the next day, as he stood in the doorway putting on his greatcoat, preparatory to taking his departure; 'did that little old cousin of yours never try to make love to you?'

'No,' said Undine.

She hated him so, it would have given her such infinite satisfaction to have injured him; yet at the same time it seemed the height of meanness to speak against him – the man who had befriended her. The untruth seemed, in the darkness and confusion of the moment, higher than the truth, and it passed from her lips to bring forth the poisoned fruit which the lie bears, be it spoken for God's glory or the salvation of the soul.

She would have retracted it almost in the same breath, but he answered quickly, 'I am glad to hear it; I have a greater respect for my old pedagogue than for almost any man I know, but I had an idea from the way he sometimes spoke of you that he cared rather more for you than a second cousin's husband generally does. I am glad it was fancy. I will come again this evening and take you for a walk.' And he was gone.

He was gone, and the untrue word was gone also. She stood in the hall and buried her face in both hands, utterly humiliated. She had told a lie, and told it to *him*. In other days her sorrow would have been that anything could have tempted her so to demean herself. Now it was all swallowed up in this – it was to him.

She ran out through the little garden with nothing on her head and the sleet and snow falling thick upon her. He was just entering the wood. She paused when she had almost reached him at the thought of the cold light that would fall on her when she presented herself before him in such plight – paused, then turned slowly back to the house.

Evil times had fallen on her, and she asked no more, 'It is right?' but only, 'Will he think it right?'

'This afternoon I will tell him,' she said, as she walked, damp and chilly, up the garden path. 'I wish he had never asked me.'

It seemed so evil to speak against the man she hated, worse to leave things as they were; yet neither on that afternoon nor on any of the days that followed could she look up into the cold half-closed eyes and say, 'I told you a lie.'

The words were always on her tongue, always in her heart; but the white face with its wonderful crushing influence over her kept them unspoken.

'I will tell him tomorrow, some day when he loves me better, when he understands me, when I am his little wife,' she would say to herself, whenever he had just left her. But a silent though not less abiding conviction was with her that the day never would come when he would know her better. Her one hour of light had passed that night in the little fire-lit parlour; henceforth, strive as she might to annihilate herself and be only what the man might choose, he would never come near her, they would never meet.

'I am afraid I made a great fool of myself,' soliloquised the Piece-of-perfection, as he walked alone one sharp frosty evening. 'No other woman ever made me lose my head, but I do believe the little creature bewitched me that night with her sentimental talk. She loves me, I can do anything with her, I shall make something of her in time; but I was a great fool.'

'What are you doing here?' he asked, coming suddenly upon the subject of his thoughts as she stood below her old tree, wrapped in her little red cloak, with Prince at her side.

The dog rubbed his head against his master's foot; the human dog crept nearer him.

'You know I do not like your wandering about alone,' he said, in the cold, unlover-like tone in which he had always spoken to her except on that first evening.

'I would not have come if I had thought you would not like me to,' she said, glancing up into his face.

'I want you to go to church tomorrow,' was his next and rather abrupt remark. 'Your cousin is better; you will be able to go, will you not? You will have to go some day; I would rather you began now.'

'Yes, I can go,' she answered after a moment's pause.

''Tis a matter of supreme indifference to me,' continued the Piece-of-perfection, 'what you choose to believe; but you must do nothing to make yourself peculiar. There is nothing so hateful in a woman as eccentricity of any description.'

Undine had now heard this remark so often that she had no new reply to make to it, and walked on in silence.

'Were you very busy this morning, Undine?'

'No, not at all,' she said. 'Why do you ask me?'

'Because your glove is torn, and I was thinking you might have had some very important matters to attend to which prevented your mending it; but you have a weakness for torn gloves, I fancy.'

'You will never see me with one again,' she said, pulling it off quickly.

'I hope not,' he answered, quietly. 'There are few things which I admire less than a slovenly woman. If a woman cares to retain the affection of those about her, she will always be particular as to her dress.'

'So that others might love her dress, not herself,' said Undine.

'I will care for my wife just as long as she gives me reason to be proud of her,' he replied, coolly.

'Just as you do for your horses and your dog?'

'Yes; I believe I care for that dog as well as for most things; but if he became disobedient or vicious, I should care nothing more about him.'

He spoke gravely; Undine knew he meant what he said; and the life that lay before her seemed to look almost as cheerless and icy as the white frosty world that lay stretched out before her eyes. But, she resolved, I will be all he wishes me; he shall be proud of me, prouder than of all his dogs and horses, she thought, as she clenched and loosened the fingers of her little gloveless hand.

'What causes you always to move your hand in that extraordinary manner whenever you are angry?' It is not very pretty, I can assure you.'

'I am not angry; I was only thinking.'

'What?'

'That I will try and be everything you wish. Do you believe me?'

'If I did not believe that you would try and that you would also succeed, I would not care to make you my wife,' he replied. 'You are a clever little woman and can do anything you wish.'

And Undine felt more exultant at these equivocal words of praise than Lady Edith at his most honeyed compliments.

For some time after that they walked on in silence, only the sound of their footsteps on the hard frozen ground breaking the stillness.

At last she said, very suddenly and very hurriedly: 'You know that if ever, at any moment, at any time, you change and would rather not marry me, if it were the very day before our wedding – you must feel quite free – you must tell me so – it will be all right.'

'Are you changing your mind already?' he asked, glancing down at her.

'No, I shall never change,' she answered.

'Nor am I in the habit of retracing my steps, either; but it is certainly better, if one does repent, to do so before it is too late.'

They said no more till they got to the gate of the garden.

'Are you not going to come in and see my cousin today? She is up,' said Undine, and while he sat in Mrs Barnacles's little sittingroom she ran upstairs.

There was an ominous pulling about the corners of her mouth but she knew if she gave way to it her eyes would be red and swollen in two minutes; so she tore off her hat and cloak and, changing her dress, spent at least five minutes in arranging a black-and-red bow in her hair and a few more on her dress. It took her a long time before she was satisfied with her appearance; then she went downstairs.

He was satisfied with it, too, though she could not tell it from his face. Poor little fool! How she did love him! And he felt a kind of pity for her.

It was growing dark and the red lamp in the hall was already lighted when he rose to go. He had wished her goodnight, and she was turning to go upstairs when he called her back softly. He uttered her name twice and drew her tenderly to him when she came to his side.

'Be sure you practise this evening; you are my own little darling,' he said, and pressed a long kiss on her lips. 'Don't sit up too late, and look as pretty and as sweet when I come tomorrow as you do now. Goodnight, my little girl.' And again the firm stern lips with their soft golden moustaches were pressed against hers as he folded her close to him.

It was late the next morning when Undine rose; for it is very pleasant, when one has delicious visions, to be dreaming and dozing in bed on a winter's morning. And her visions were sweet, sweet – though, God knows, they were childish and small enough. She would do her hair so; she would dress herself so; she would go to church; she would do this; she would do that. He would kiss her, he would kiss her, as he kissed her last night.

She was sitting on her bedside, as she had been sitting for the last five minutes, with one stocking half on and the other in her hand, when the maid knocked at the door and passed her in a letter.

The hand was his, and it was the first she had ever got from him: she tore it open quickly. It ran:

My dear little girl! I have just heard that my immediate presence in London is indispensable. 'Tis a matter of business and I can't delay. I have a note from Mr Barnacles in which he tells me that he has been ill, but returns to Greenwood on Monday. As you intend leaving for your grandmother's as soon as he does so, I suppose I shall not find you here when I return. I shall try to run down and see my little girl as soon as I am able.

Yours most affectionately,
A Blair

She threw herself down among the pillows, and after half an hour rose slowly to begin her packing. When it was done she went to Mrs Barnacles's room, to tell her that she was leaving that evening.

'It's just another of her freaks,' said that lady to Miss Mell, who came to spend the afternoon with her. 'No one could have been more kindly treated than she had been here; quite spoiled in fact. There is no telling what she will take into her head next. I wish her grandmother joy of her, I'm sure.'

'Don't you think Harry Blair's going away so suddenly, without making her an offer, may have something to do with it?' said Miss Mell, looking enormously sharp and green about the eyes.

'I am sure from what I have seen that she could have had him at any time she chose, but – you will not mention it to anyone, I know – his father has quarrelled with him and will have nothing more to do with him.'

'Ah, I understand now,' said Miss Mell; 'that will have put my lady out just a little in her pretty little game. A poor penniless boy is not much of a catch. It serves her right. I always thought it shameful, the way she used to walk about everywhere with him quite alone. I wonder she had not more regard for her character than to act as she did. *I* would die sooner than be on such intimate terms with a man to whom I was not engaged; and even then I think a modest reticence *so* becoming in a woman.' And Miss Mell drew herself up stiffly in her chair and drew down the corners of her mouth.

'Well, anyhow,' said Mrs Barnacles, sipping her tea, 'I do wish her grandmother joy of her. There is something one can't help liking about the girl, but she is so peculiar and eccentric I shall be glad to have her off my hands.'

'Don't you think she is trying it on in another direction?' inquired Miss Mell, with that wrinkling about the mouth which was all she had to show for a smile.

'I don't think she tries it on in any direction; that is just what I complain of,' replied Mrs Barnacles. 'From what I know, I am sure she could have had old Blair if she had chosen. He is much older than she is, but a penniless girl can't be too fastidious, and he is terribly rich.'

'As to her not trying it on, I don't know about that,' said Miss Mell; 'I don't think she would have said no, if he had given her a chance of saying yes, but perhaps she has higher game in her eye. What do you think someone comes here once and sometimes twice a day for?'

'Oh, he is polite to all women; his attentions mean nothing. He will look higher when he chooses a wife,' said Mrs Barnacles. Miss Mell smiled a far-seeing smile and broke her cake.

While they sat talking of her in the little parlour, Undine was standing for the last time under her old tree in the wood. It was leafless and bare now, and great white icicles hung from its branches. The little stream was silent and noiseless.

Next summer the green leaves would break forth on it and the little brook would run laughing past, whispering to the long grasses and white forest flowers, and among its knotted swollen roots the bright-backed beetles and busy ants would run; but she would rest no more among them. 'Goodbye old tree,' she said, breaking off a bit of its dry frosty bark. 'Goodbye, my friend, my dear old friend. I have had such beautiful dreams beneath you; I have had such happy thoughts. They will never come to me any more; my higher life is dead, quite dead; I love only him and I must serve him now. Goodbye.'

CHAPTER TEN

Melted Snow

How white, how white and dazzling, that road upon the hillside lay! All day she sat at the window, watching it. In the dusk, when no other eye could mark it, she saw it winding in the dimness. All night in her dreams it lay before her, in its white aching emptiness.

How slowly the chill weeks crawled over her – two, four, six, eight. Still she watched it till the colour faded from her cheeks and the bright restless light grew strong in her eyes. Her old grandmother would lay her work aside and, standing behind her, would stroke her hair softly with her old withered hands and say, 'You are not well my child; you are lonely; the place is too quiet for you; a young life like yours should not be buried away here.'

And Undine would answer nothing, and sit watching, only she knew for what.

The snow had vanished and the road lay, a white chalky line between the brown fields; only now and then a farmer's cart or a labourer from the next village would pass along it.

'Why do you never sit by the fire? It is so cold and cheerless at the window, and there is nothing to be seen,' the old woman would say. But still she sat there, looking out and stitching away always at delicate white muslins with pink bows and dreamy blue and white stuffs, which the old woman thought made her look like an angel when she tried them on.

'The child has changed,' she would say to herself, as she sat knitting and dozing in the firelight. 'She never reads now and thinks only of dress and music; but I suppose it is natural; the young will be young.'

The winter went early that year, and the first signs of spring were showing themselves. Undine did not count the days any more; she did not reason or ask herself any questions; she only waited, waited.

One day she saw a boy coming down the road. It was quite midday and the sun was shining with an almost summer-like warmth. She sat there with her hands folded in her lap, looking at him yet not seeing him till he came up to the open window and put a letter in her hand.

She started up and passed out through the next room, where her grandmother sat knitting in the sunshine of the open door.

'What is it? What has happened?' asked the old woman; but Undine only hurried past her with the letter pressed tight in both hands against her breast.

Through the long leafless garden she passed, where the soft buds were just beginning to swell under the brown bark, through the rough uneven meadow beyond, and sat down at the side of the little cozy river that crept slowly between its muddy reedy banks. She sat long looking at the paper in her hands, with its great red seal; then she tore it open.

What that letter said she never could remember; but she knew, when she had read it, that the dream of her life had vanished, to return no more.

She put the letter whole into her mouth and chewed it fine between her grinding teeth; then she sat still and watched a tiny white feather that lay upon the muddy water bobbing up and down, up and down. Her mind seemed a perfect vacancy but for the thought of that little white feather. She wondered if it would be caught by nodding leaves of the reeds that dipped in the water, or whether it would be stranded on the oozy bank – looked at the little white feather and wondered, and ground the letter fine, fine, between her teeth.

Then, a sudden wild impulse seized her. She must rise – she must run – she must flee – she must go – somewhere, anywhere.

With nothing on her head, sinking ankle deep in the soft mud, she broke through the reeds and bushes and climbed up the steep bank with hands and feet. She did not pause an instant, but ran on to the rugged hill with its winding sheep tracks and sharp stones, climbed it, and ran on among the trees and rocks that lay scattered on its summit. She did not seem able to get further; again and yet again she thought she found herself in the same place; and every time she looked up at the great red sun it seemed a great, laughing, cruel human eye, looking down at her from the clear blue sky.

It was on her, on her, wherever she went, that great blood-red eye, and the great brown hill opposite with its white chalk road was like a leering human face that laughed at her, jeered at her, mocked at her; and the stones, and the trees – they had all a hidden sneer about them. 'Fool! fool! fool!' they cried. And the blue cloudless sky overhead was so hard and pitiless, like a righteous human soul which has no mercy for the erring. 'O sky, blue cloudless sky, have pity, have pity on me!' she cried in her madness; and she threw herself down and lay on a great flat stone in the footpath. Gazing up into the sky's blue depths, she looked straight at the dazzling sun with an unnatural strength of sight.

They drove her madder, madder, the sky, the sun, the earth; till she writhed in her pain, like a trodden worm, on the ground and stones. Then the old feeling came over her again, and she rose up and ran. Her sight seemed to grow dim and blurred at last, and she stumbled and fell again and yet again over the stones and stumps. Bruised, bleeding, she felt nothing, only knew she must run on, on.

Her grandmother looked out anxiously for her all day, and when it was growing dark that evening, saw her walking slowly up the little garden path, with her head drooping on her breast and her arms hanging heavily at either side.

'Where have you been, my child?' she said, coming out to meet her. 'Are you not bitterly cold?'

'No,' said Undine, wearily; and when they entered the little parlour with its cheerful lamp and firelight her grandmother noticed that the bright anxious light she was accustomed to see in her eyes had vanished.

'You look ill, my child?' she said, resting her nervous old hand softly on her arm.

'I am not ill,' Undine said, 'only tired. No, I am not hungry; I only want to rest. I am tired, very tired. I want no light, thank you. Goodnight.'

CHAPTER ELEVEN

A Clever Little Man and a Poor Little Fool

If the ploughboy knew how the worm suffers that writhes beneath his foot, surely he would not crush it. If we saw the work of the cruel word, surely we should not utter it. If we could see the light of a life vanish and die out, surely we would be loath to extinguish it. But we never can see, never know, never watch these things; therefore blighting, cursing, and inflicting suffering, we go on our way rejoicing.

Albert Blair was not a cruel man. A man of high principle, the world said. A man to whom no one in trouble ever appealed in vain for help. A man who never gave his horse or dog a blow more than was necessary – a good master, a good man, as the world goes. Yet he felt no sorrow for the young life he had crushed. It had to be done, and he did it – as he beat his dog or discharged his servant when necessary.

He had meant to write to her from London, but important affairs occupied his attention; his speculations were coming to a bad end – he had no time to think of her.

'I will run down and see her when I go back to Greenwood,' he said. ''Tis a pity, as things seem to be turning out, that I ever let the poor little thing make such a fool of me, but it can't be helped now.'

Lady Edith with her thousands would have mended matters at once, but what was the use of thinking about her?

The first night after his arrival at Greenwood, Cousin Jonathan came to see him. The little man had heard, on his return, of the frequent visits which had been paid during his absence. Passion has eyes, as far-seeing in the dark as love's, and he knew both visitor and visited so well that he soon came to certain very definite conclusions on the matter of these visits. He knew well that a hundred Harry Blairs were not so to be dreaded as one Piece-of-perfection, with his cold eyes and iron will.

It would be hard to say whether the little man started from home that evening with any particularly fiendish purpose in his head, but his heart was fed on by the green-eyed monster and his weak legs trembled and quaked beneath him as he thought of what *might* be – of what she might have told. Perhaps the reception from his sometime pupil would be a summary dismissal from a boot point. At any day all Greenwood might know that, in place of Jonathan Barnacles the saint, the holy man, and the blessed man of God, they had been bowing down at the shrine of a poor sinner, a man of like passions with themselves. For with the exception of one or two benighted individuals, Cousin Jonathan stood highest of the high in the estimation of the Greenwood world. 'He is so pure, so calm, so transparent. If there were more Christians like him, all the world would soon become Christian,' one of his admirers was wont to say, when expatiating on his transcendent virtues.

It is a cruel thing they do, who fasten on a man too high a character. 'Tis a small hobgoblin on his shoulder, forever pushing and poking him into the wrong paths, leading more straight along the devil's road than gold, wine, or women. Having committed one action out of keeping with it, he must sin on eternally to make a grave wherein to hide that action.

Cousin Jonathan felt sick at heart as any girl when he knocked at the door and was ushered into the presence of the Piece-of-perfection, who met him just as usual, made him take an armchair, and offered him a cigar.

'You have been ill?' was one of his first remarks, noticing the pale face and troubled look in the usually serene eyes of the little man.

Cousin Jonathan declared he was in perfect health, in the best of spirits; and, after a few more remarks had passed, began to express his gratitude for the kind attention shown to his wife and Miss Bock during his absence.

'It was exceedingly kind of you,' he continued, rubbing his hands together as nervously as it was possible for such a very unnervous little animal to do.

'It is quite unnecessary, I assure you,' said the Piece-of-perfection, knocking the ashes from the top of his cigar into the delicate china stand. 'You will understand that it is so when I tell you, as perhaps I should have done sooner, that in all probability, e'er very long, Miss Brock will become my wife.'

The little man had a wonderful command over his features, and showed at this announcement no more feeling than that amount of surprise which it was to be expected he would experience.

'You really must excuse me,' said Cousin Jonathan; 'but I am amazed, astonished; it is so very, so altogether, unexpected. I – you really must excuse me, but I was under the impression that, if ever I had the honour of looking upon any member of your family as the future husband of my charge, it would be another.'

'I do not imagine Miss Bock ever had any very great regard for my poor brother,' he replied contemptuously, curling the corner of his delicate moustache between his finger and thumb.

'Has she not told you? But of course she will have told you more than even I know,' said Cousin Jonathan.

'On what subject?' asked Albert Blair, closing his eyes closer than usual and playing with Prince's ears.

'About this affair with your brother; but of course it is all passed now, and I wish you both every blessing, every happiness,' said Cousin Jonathan, apparently very much affected.

'I always understood from Miss Bock that she was perfectly indifferent to my brother, in fact rather repelled than favoured his addresses. I imagine you must have misunderstood her.'

'Oh, yes, and there can be nothing gained by speaking now over things that are past and gone,' said Cousin Jonathan; 'and I cannot tell you how grateful, how relieved, I feel to think that the dear child will be in your care. When she seemed so devotedly attached to your brother, of course I did not like to interfere, but it was, I can assure you – it was a cause of great anxiety to me. If she were my own daughter, I could not feel a greater regard for her welfare; and she is so peculiar, so eccentric, that with all her noble qualities and rich and vigorous intellect she has never been able to get on anywhere.'

The Piece-of-perfection sat passive, so Cousin Jonathan went on.

'It may seem, and I fear was, very selfish on my part, but I could not help feeling less concerned at your brother's trouble and departure than I should otherwise have been. It seemed wholly to change her mind, and as things have turned out I am thankful, how thankful I cannot tell you. He was very sincerely attached to her, but he would never had submitted to her tastes and ideas, as it would be absolutely necessary he should if they were to live together. But that is all past now and I cannot tell you how relieved, how thankful, I feel. I have loved her as if she were my own,' said Cousin Jonathan, screwing up the corners of his eyes till they began to look watery.

A long pause followed, then the Piece-of-perfection said, 'Perhaps I ought to explain to you that what exists between myself and Miss Bock is not a definite engagement. It is an understanding which either party may bring to an end at any time he or she should wish to do so, and it might be just as well to say nothing on the subject till matters are more definitely arranged.'

'Certainly, certainly, if you wish it,' said Cousin Jonathan; 'but I do hope that matters will soon, very soon, be in that condition. I have often feared that she might be tempted for the sake of wealth and position to give herself away to a man who was utterly unworthy of her. She is so young, and therefore it is only natural that she should desire such things, and having also been brought up in circumstances of almost more than poverty, they necessarily appear all the more alluring to her.'

'I understand that Miss Bock's family, though not wealthy, was a very respectable one. Take another cigar; yours has gone out,' said Albert Blair, passing his case.

'Oh, I know nothing, nothing whatever, against the character of any of her relations. Her father was a connection of my own, and as far as I am aware his family are all well to do. Of her mother I know nothing. He made a great mistake in marrying her, I believe. She was some woman he picked up in London and who married as her second husband some low farmer at the Cape. Her grandfather got her home when her mother died, but she could not get on with them; they did not seem to understand the dear child's little peculiarities and could not appreciate her.'

It would not take more faith and prayer to obtain pardon for one lie than for twenty; and Cousin Jonathan, having told one, found that lies flow as easily as truths if only one is used to them. Cousin Jonathan held great faith in ghosts, but nowadays dead people do not rise out of their graves and come to avenge themselves, be they ever so slandered; and 'tis safe talking in an English smoking-room of an African farmer between whom and yourself there are some thousand miles of sea and a hundred of still more separating Karoo. Her mother had been the only daughter of a wealthy London merchant and had been disinherited for marrying beneath her; but does not every man who finds a wife pick her up, and had not her mother taken as her second husband a Cape farmer? He had only spoken the truth judiciously, of course, *very* judiciously, but only the truth.

'I feel so sure,' he continued, 'that you of all men will be able to overlook any small deficiencies in the dear child, when you consider all the adverse circumstances with which she has had to contend. There is something so original and strong, so noble, in her character, that if she were only a little more open she would be almost perfect in my estimate. Not that I mean,' said the little man, apparently recollecting himself and speaking with great earnestness – 'not that I mean to say she is not quite truthful, but she is sometimes not quite – so open, as one might expect to find her. Her nature is, I believe, a *thoroughly* truthful one in *every* respect, and it is only the effect of early mismanagement. And are we not,' said Cousin Jonathan, falling into his preaching voice, 'are we not all of us formed during the first few years of our lives? What is done then, can it ever be undone, ever?'

He seemed lost in thought for some moments, then he said suddenly: 'But it is all right now; I feel so rejoiced to think that for the future she will be shielded and cared for better than I could care for her. I have felt very anxious about her lately, very anxious; I could not see clearly where the path of duty lay with regard to her.'

'You're a very devil of wickedness or a poor fool of a saint,' thought the Piece-of-perfection as he leaned back in his chair with the lamplight falling full on the inscrutable white face, the lines of which Cousin Jonathan was vainly trying to decipher.

'I may tell Mrs Barnacles, of – of the understanding, may I not?' he said. 'She has been much grieved at Undine's sudden freak of leaving us; and I cannot myself understand how the idea came into her head, unless she thought we were imposing on her by leaving her alone with an invalid on her hands. She never told you if that was her reason for leaving us, I suppose?' inquired the little man, casting a quick furtive glance at the face of his companion.

'No; she told me she was leaving because she was weary of the place and wished for change. You are surely not leaving yet?' for Cousin Jonathan had risen to take his departure.

If you wish to ruin a man's character, if you wish to have your revenge on an enemy, if you wish to blight a man's life because you have done him an injury, be sparing with your words. It is the small drop that falls in between the wine and sugar that poisons the cup.

So Cousin Jonathan, having eyes as far-seeing as they were blue and saintly, discovered that it was quite impossible for him to remain any longer, much as he wished to do so. There was a special prayer meeting in his house that night, and his presence there was indispensable.

People remarked, as they walked home after the meeting, that never before had he prayed with the eloquence and earnestness of that evening for perfect purity, for perfect truth; truth that might challenge, not the dull eye of the world, but the deep-seeing, perceiving eye of conscience; truth in thought, truth in word, truth in deed, God-like truth, he prayed for with passionate fervour. And let he who will sneer and raise the ever-ready cry of hypocrite. Through a long life free of temptation he had in the main been pure and truthful, as those about him deemed him; but the hour of his trial had come and he had fallen, as the son of the morning fell, to rise no more.

The greatest devil among us has his white spots, and the purest saint has ink-black stains which will be clearly visible if he do not keep his white clothing too tight about him.

When his visitor had left him, Albert Blair paced slowly up and down the room. Was the little man a fool, or a devil? He turned the matter over and over in his mind as he passed slowly from one end to the other, with Prince following close at his heels.

The poison took its full effect, and early the next morning he started for London. 'I will write when there,' he said. 'The little schemer quite deserves to be kept waiting, and it gives her more time to forget me. They may say what they like, but I do believe the little devil likes me or at least my prospects.'

'I don't know what's come over Miss Undine,' said Nancy, her grandmother's maid, as she stood chatting with her lover over the gate one evening. 'When she come first, why, there she'd sit from morning till night, stitch, stitch, stitch, at them lovely white dresses, and staring out of that there window. If we'd not 'a' made her come and eat, I believe she'd just 'a' starved. Well, all of a sudden, just four weeks gone, I went upstairs to make her bed, thinking as how of course she had been up and out hours; and there she was a-sitting on the floor in the middle of the room, never been in bed the whole blessed night, though one could see as she'd been a-laying on it, her dresses and ribbons and all her nice things that she'd been a-working at lying in a pile that high before her.'

'"Nancy," says she, sort of strange and quiet like, "you can take all these things."'

'"Lor'! Miss Undine," says I, "what do you mean?"'

'"You can have them," says she; "and if you don't want them you can burn them," says she so quiet like, and walks out of the room with her arms a-hanging down at each side of her – like *this* – and her head a-lying sort of loose like on her chest, as though she'd gone and got her neck broken; and, Lor'! her back was bent as double as an old woman's. I never see anything like it, 'cept when my poor brother Jim got shot in the side by them horrid poachers and came back the night afore he died, looking just like that.'

'And did you get the dresses?' asked her lover.

'Course I did,' said Nancy, 'and other things too. And Miss Undine she just goes on walking about in that 'ere sort of a way. Lor'! and she is queer sometimes; she takes a cloth and begins rubbing down the chairs and things in the parlour. "I can do that Miss Undine," says I.'

'"No, I like to do it," says she, and there she sits a-rubbing at one leg of a chair for five minutes or more, like as if she was in a dream like.'

'"Don't you think that chair is pretty well about polished down now, Miss Undine?" says I.'

'"Yes," she says, and goes on to another. And, Lor' bless me, if she don't go and lie down under them trees in the garden for a whole blessed day sometimes, as still as a corpse. She is just that deep with blossoms when I come to call her in of an evening; and if I did not, why I do believe she would lie there till the morning,' said the puzzled Nancy, emphatically.

It was not only Nancy who was puzzled. Her grandmother would watch her wonderingly as for hours she would sit under the great tree that grew before the cottage, gazing vacantly at the soft early grass and the budding hedges. It was no use asking if she were ill; she would only answer, 'No, I am well – only tired – rather tired.'

'The flowers of last year, when their stalks grew hollow and empty, fell to the ground, to give place and food to the fresh green shoots of this year; then why must we live on, when we are tired, so tired?' she would ask herself. Sometimes she got out the little wooden box where she kept her papers – little songs and allegories, fairy tales and half-written essays. They had lifted her up to heaven when she wrote them; now they were bits of blue paper, scribbled over and blotted, and she would put them away listlessly without ever looking at them.

One night, in the middle of the night, she woke up. Generally she went to sleep early, and slept heavily till morning, but tonight she woke and lay still, listening to the wind as it moaned around the house. Then before her eyes lay the little river, with its muddy banks, and the great trees knocking their bare branches together over it, and the brown still pool where the little feather had nodded up and down, up and down, on that afternoon.

It had moved very restlessly, but deep down, at the bottom of the pool, it was very still and restful. The mocking sun with his jeering blood-red eye could never look through to see what lay there.

She was tired, so tired; so she got up slowly and drew on her clothes in the dark. She was turning mechanically to feel for her little crimson cloak that hung behind the door, when, 'Why should I spoil it?' she thought. So without wrapping anything around her, she went out into the night wind and the darkness, through the long garden, over the uneven field. She stood at last beside the muddy pool. Overhead the leafless branches rattled their dry joints together, and through the rifts in the cloudy sky a few stray stars cast their uncertain reflection on the water.

It seemed so still and quiet, it seemed to lure her to itself.

'I cannot help it – it is not cowardly – I am too tired – so tired. He does not want me any more. There is nothing in the world, and I am so weary,' she whispered under her breath, as though excusing herself to some unseen judge.

'I shall never trouble him any more, down there.' She pressed closer to the muddy edge and stood looking down into the water. Then, sudden and unbidden, a thought came to her, as may have come the angel's touch to the lone prophet when in the wilderness beneath the juniper tree he laid him down to die.

Might I not serve him!

How or in what way, who could say? But life is very long, and the wheel turns strangely. How could she tell that he would never need her!

The prophet of old ate of the angel's bread and went forty days and forty nights in the strength of that meal; she also ate of angel's meat, the only food which the heavens now yield us, and went forty times forty in the strength thereof.

Back to the house she turned slowly; and no one ever knew how nearly she had found rest and quiet on that windy night.

What a small thing it is sometimes that makes life's kiss sweeter than death's to us – the light in a pair of blue eyes – a little applause for a picture we have put on canvas – a few comprehenders for a song we have written – the knowledge that our name means something when scrawled on the bit of paper which we call a cheque. These mean life for some of us. Take these out of life, and what an unbearable weight it becomes. We walk about in this rich teeming world as through an empty, howling wilderness; and if we do not fear to meet with something more wearying on the other side, how we seek to get out of it by way of a muddy pool, a bullet, or a few drops of arsenic.

'Tis very strange, very ridiculous, quite incomprehensible, no doubt; but some really do require something more to reward them for the trouble of living than black cloth, roast beef, and the power to use them.

CHAPTER 12

Sold Her Love

The summer had come and the little cottage looked like a monster nosegay in its sheath of climbing roses. In the great tree that stood before the door the birds had built their nests and sang there all day long, and the blossoms in the garden had turned to fruit and the tender green leaves had grown dark and strong.

Undine had sat below them, working a little, dozing a little, all day. She was glad the blossoms were gone, for their smell made her heart heavy.

'Lor'! Miss Undine, you'll catch your death of cold; the dew's a-falling already, and there's a gentleman in the parlour a-wanting to see you,' said the good Nancy, bursting with desire to give an account of the visitor's appearance, with her ideas thereon appended.

Undine, however, asked no questions, but, rising, walked towards the house.

The little parlour was almost dark when she entered it, and the man was sitting with his back to the window. Instantly she recognized the bald crown and tuft of hair belonging to George Blair.

'This is indeed a great and unexpected pleasure,' he said, rising and taking her hand into his own fat and flabby palm, 'a great and most unexpected pleasure. I have been in the neighbourhood for some days, engaged in inspecting a large estate I have just purchased, and it was by the merest chance that I heard of your being here.'

Then he launched forth into strong and vehement denunciations against the roads and inns of the neighbourhood, directing his remarks principally to her grandmother. At last the old lady rose to order candles, and Undine and her visitor were left alone.

'Have you been to Greenwood lately?' she inquired.

'Not since the autumn.' Then, after a moment's pause, 'I have been hoping continually to hear from you since that time, but have been always disappointed hitherto.'

This remark eliciting no response, he went on, drawing his chair a little nearer to hers.

'I trust I need hardly tell you, my dear Miss Bock, that in the months that have passed *I* have not changed in my feelings or wishes. What I then asked, I still most earnestly and truly desire.'

The timely entrance at this moment of Nancy, bearing candles, saved Undine from the necessity of making him any reply. She asked him where his sons were.

'I know nothing of Master Harry's whereabouts,' he replied; 'and as for his brother, I *will* know nothing. He has gone in for all manner of mad speculations without my knowledge or advice, and of course has got into trouble and expects my help now. He shall not have it, though. I shall have as little to do with him as with his brother for the future. If he wants help he may go to his aristocratic relations, who, if they were sold up, blue blood and all, could not raise the sum he wants. *I* could let him have the money and never miss it,' said the old man, very complacently, 'but he has seen the shine of my cash for the last time, I can assure him.'

A fat, disagreeable-looking old man, her grandmother, though not generally very discerning or critical, thought him, when she re-entered the room at the end of his speech.

Undine soon made an excuse for leaving them and went out at the front door and stood before the house. The evening air was cool and balmy and the smell of the cluster roses that covered the cottage was sweet, but she only dragged a bunch from its stem and crushed it in her hand till the thorns pierced it. The time had come, and come so soon, when she could serve him. Once or twice she paced up and down the length of the house; then she re-entered the little parlour.

She asked her grandmother to leave them alone for a few moments; and the old man looked at her in some astonishment as she stood before him pale and eager. Surely she was beautiful, this woman, with a beauty deeper than that of form and colour; and if she were so fair in her rough, careless dress, what should she not look like in the velvet and damask he might give her!

She crushed the flower in her hand till the blood fell in a crimson drop on her crumpled white dress; and, standing straight before him, said: 'You asked me once long ago to become your wife. I told you then that it could never be; but I am willing now if you will give me what I want.' There was something so strange in her manner and look that the old man, not knowing how to answer, sat still, and she went on.

'If you will settle on me, before our marriage, fifty thousand pounds in cash, to be mine absolutely, to do exactly as I please with, then I will marry you as soon as you wish. I do not love you, but I will be a good wife to you.'

She looked at him and the old man looked at her. Many women had sold themselves to him before that night, but not the most abandoned in a more open and barefaced manner than this: 'I do not love you, but you will have no reason to repent marrying me if you are willing to do so on my terms.'

He hesitated for a moment, but his mind was soon made up. That she should consent to marry him for anything except his money he had never dreamed, and, whether the bargain was expressed in words or tacitly understood, where was the difference? So he answered her.

'Not only what you ask, but everything I have, shall be yours; though of course if you wish it, an arrangement such as that which you mention shall be made.'

He stayed a little longer, and when he had kissed his wife that was to be, upon the lips, he left her.

They were pretty lips and he did not repent his bargain when he thought it over at leisure. They had answered him scornfully once; he might do what he would with them now. His son had coveted them once, but gold had won when youth and learning had failed.

So it must always be, he thought, as he rolled his fat joints into bed. Youth and learning and love, they are all convertible into terms of cash, and have their equivalents.

CHAPTER THIRTEEN

A Very Wicked Woman

A few weeks after the night of the bargain two notices appeared in the same paper. The first informed the world that on a certain day George Blair Esq and Undine Bock had become, till death should part them, bone of one bone and flesh of one flesh, by a holy and inscrutable mystery, two in one and one in two.

The second notice asserted that the like wonderful and miraculous though oft-repeated process had taken place between Mr Albert Blair and Lady Edith Mountjoy.

'Did I not say so?' said Miss Mell, excitingly, as, seated beside Mrs Barnacles's sofa with the paper in her hands, she read the two notices. 'She was not half the poor little fool you all thought her; she understood her game when she let the son slip to catch the father; she knew where the meat lay.'

'She has a nice nest of it,' continued Miss Mell. 'The old man is too stout and apoplectic to last long, and the sons are both in his bad books, where you may be sure she will take good care to keep them. She is an innocent little creature, only likes her books and her flowers, but she knows a thing or two. We shall have her here after a few years,' continued the poor little woman, 'a widow with her thousands, cutting a dash and riding roughshod over our heads.'

She felt it was an unjust world this, in which one woman wins all the cakes and bon-bons and another nothing more than dry bread and weak tea.

An hour or two later Cousin Jonathan, sitting in his study, read them also, and as he read his heart grew lighter. It had been heavy, strangely heavy, of late.

'She could never have cared for him or she could not have done this,' he muttered. 'To marry for money and so soon: she could never have cared for him.' And with these words the little man was wont to quiet unpleasant stirrings for months and years to come.

Albert Blair, taking up the paper to see his own notice, read what stood above it.

'What a merciful escape I have had!' he exclaimed, and for once the imperturbable calm that reigned within him was almost disturbed. It is never pleasant to find yourself a dupe where you thought yourself adored, and a fool where you thought yourself wise; and what small pity he had felt for the little girl who loved him was changed into loathing for the woman who had fooled him. From that moment his flickering faith in women died and he held his father's creed – the creed that all women have their value in coins, though some mount high.

In a poor half-furnished room the owner of the woman's eyes and the crammed head sat beside a bare deal table. Before him lay an open newspaper.

'There is nothing worth loving, nothing true, nothing noble in the world,' he cried, bitterly, and buried his face in the paper before him. When he raised it, it was wet with tears. She was not only as all women are, but lower than many: to sell herself, with her youth and talents, to an old and evil man for his money and lands.

'O God, my God!' he cried in bitterness of soul, covering his face with both hands, 'and this is the woman who I have allowed to come in between my soul and Thee.'

In a richly furnished apartment, enveloped in a soft cloud of white lace and delicate azure ribbons, sat Undine Blair. Diamonds glittered in her hair and her little jewelled fingers strayed listlessly over the leaves of the paper before her. Around her on every side lay a profusion of those things in which a woman's soul delights – the bon-bons and cakes that the Miss Mells of this world sigh for.

She was sitting waiting for dinner and the arrival of her husband, and ran her eye carelessly over the sheet before her. There, below the notice of her own sale, stood that other notice. She read it and a burning mist gathered in her eyes. From her ears and neck she tore jewels that hung there and threw them on the ground at her feet. Signs of her servitude, worn for his sake, there had been a sweetness in their very bitterness. Now they were accursed – burning into her very sleep; she trod upon them with her foot. For nothing, all for nothing; he had no need of her. Poor childish fool, to think that ever he could stand in need of her or of her sacrifice.

'Dinner is ready and my master is waiting,' said a servant who a few moments later came to call her.

'Say I am ill today and cannot come,' she answered, and when the door closed behind him sank back in the chair and covered her dry throbbing eyeballs with her hot hands. She ground her teeth in futile rage and helplessness. Parched and very bitter was her soul that night.

Truly, a very fiend's had been the voice that had called her back to life from the muddy, reed-edged pool, called her back to life to pass from evil on to evil.

A soft pulpy hand rested on her bare shoulder and her husband spoke to her.

'Is my little pet ill this evening? What is the matter with her?'

She threw his hand from her with passion through which involuntary disgust was clearly visible, and, eluding the hand with which he strove to detain her, passed quickly from him.

'What do you mean by this?' cried the little man, and stood staring at the closed door by which she had vanished. His astonishment was great. In the three weeks of his married life she had taken all his caresses, submitted to all his wishes, as absolutely as though subdued by the most slavish passion. As an automaton is guided by the hand of its master, his will had moved hers, and of desire or inclination of her own she had seemed devoid.

Was his honeymoon to end so soon? Were his self-congratulations to end in this?

Had he really puchased a scourge and a termagant in his fair young wife? As soon as he could leave the delights of the table, had he not hurried upstairs really concerned at the indisposition of his precious new treasure – puffing and red with wine, soup, and exertion? Had he not entered the room to caress and fondle her? And was he to be met so? Had he played the fool in his old days? he asked himself. For the first time in his long life he thought he had fallen into a bad speculation, but he changed his mind as time passed on. In the months that followed the scene of that evening was never repeated. She grew quieter, colder, but more passive and submissive every week. Whether it were to sit by his side, to have her lips kissed, to wear a particular dress, to attend a certain ball, the obedience she gave him was equally absolute, unquestioning, and lifeless.

He had paid his price for her faithfully, she realised, and it was not his fault if the thousands he had given her were of as little service as a handful of gravel from his paths. She had bartered her life for his gold and she must give it.

In the autumn they went to the seaside. The restless murmuring of the water stirred up old memories which she would fain have left buried; but he wished to be there and she said nothing. The winter and spring they spent in London; when the summer came they went to his new estate.

'I shall never be able to live in Greenwood,' she said. And he paid deference to the one wish she had expressed.

'You never ask me to do anything for you,' he said one day. 'Ask me for something.' And she, obedient in this as in all else, asked him to buy the little rose-covered cottage in which her grandmother lived. The gift came too late to profit the one for whom it was intended; for in the winter her grandmother died.

If she felt the loss, no one could tell, for she showed no feeling on that or any subject. During the summer their house was filled with guests of many kinds, not because either host or hostess had many friends or was well liked, but because there was good shooting, good living and good company to be had there. All admired the young wife and pronounced her lovely – even women. They had as little reason to feel jealous of her as of the silent statues that adorned her rooms.

'She is a cold, dull, heartless little creature in whom nothing can awaken the faintest spark of womanly emotion,' said one who considered himself pre-eminently endowed with those charms of appearance and manner which cause disturbance in the hearts of women, and who, through a long morning ramble, had been vainly endeavouring to exercise his charms upon her. For him, for all, there was one constant smile that went no higher than the lips, and that had no meaning save when a little scorn showed itself. Cold, heartless, and surely money-loving must be one who could marry an old, bloated and apoplectic little man who had only gold with which to varnish himself and cake over his deficiencies.

'She dresses well and knows how to make herself look beautiful, but that is the only thing she has sense enough to understand,' said the women. But none of them accused her of vanity. She was too supremely indifferent as to the impression she made on others.

No one offended her, no one cared for her: not her inferiors in spite of her lavish generosity to them. Her kindest actions were done in an indifferent, feelingless manner that made it as impossible to feel thankful for them as to the rain for falling or the wind for blowing.

Nancy, being now without employment, came one day to see if Undine would take her into her service. 'And, Lor'!' said she, when giving an account of all that had passed to her lover that evening. 'I did not know Miss Undine: she's grown so beautiful and dresses so grand; it kind of took my breath away to look at her. Then I just remembered how she used to lie under them old trees in the garden and rub down them chairs, and so I says, "Miss Undine – Mrs Blair I mean – I hope you'll be so good as to forgive me for making so bold, but I'm out of work now and I thought perhaps as how you'd be so good as to let me get some work, if as how you have any to give."'

'"Aren't you married yet?" says she, a-looking straight at the book in her hand.'

'"Lor'! Mrs Blair, no," says I. "I've not got anything to get married with," says I.'

'"If you had that little cottage my grandmother used to live in, I suppose you could do well," says she; "it's got a large garden."'

'"Lor! mum," says I, "we could never have a house like that; it's worlds too grand for the likes of us."'

'"Well," says she, "if you think it would help you, you can go and live in it for nothing," says she, "and I'll see that you get work whenever you want it."'

'"Lor'! Mrs Blair, you don't mean it, mum!" says I.'

'"Yes, you can go in as soon as you like," says she; "but the housekeeper asked me to let a woman stay in the little shed outside the garden; you must not trouble her," says she, and goes on reading as though there weren't no one in the room. My head was all of a-whirl like, so I just says thank you, mum, and walks out of the room.'

A few days after Nancy's visit Undine made her morning ramble a longer one than usual. She was alone, and a solitary walk was a pleasure she had rarely enjoyed since her marriage. Mile after mile she wandered on till she found herself near to the little rose-covered cottage, very silent and desolate now with its flower-clothed walls and its closed shutters. She did not enter the garden, but passed round to the front of the house, thinking to rest on the bench beneath the great tree that grew before the door. The spot was occupied, however, and she stood at a little distance, watching its occupant who, not aware of her presence, was stitching quickly at the blue work she held in her hands. She was an erect, tall, well-proportioned woman with lustrous black eyes and glistening black hair.

She had been very beautiful once, thought Undine, more beautiful than I. But the young face was worn now and there were lines of suffering round the dark eyes and curved lips. Something hard, almost repellent, was in the expression of the face she bent over her work, but the look vanished when she paused for an instant in her work to throw down a bunch of green leaves at the baby that lay before her on the soft short grass, a pink-and-white thing with blue eyes and yellow hair. She smiled a soft, glad smile, and Undine felt sure it was not the first time she had looked at that face and smile, though where and when she had looked at them she could not tell. The woman was raggedly clothed, not even cleanly; the child was spotless, and neither in colour nor in features bore any resemblance to her.

She was just resuming her work when she noticed Undine and rose from her seat as the little silk-clad lady approached.

'Do not rise,' said Undine; 'the bench is large enough for us both.'

She felt attracted by her, not because of her neglected beauty, not by the vague impression that they had met before, but by a look in the dark eyes which drew her, as a look sometimes will in the face of some passenger in a crowd or a woman behind a counter. We may never speak, have no communication, but we feel that we have come near to one who is of our own flesh and blood.

'Do you live here all alone?' asked the silken-clad little beauty as she took her seat beside her rag-clad sister, who, if she remembered meeting her before, did not show it and stitched on quickly with downcast eyes.

'No. I have him,' answered the woman, looking down at the nine-months-old baby at her feet. 'Having him, how can I be lonely? How can I want anything?' the look said; then she hurried on with her work again.

'Do you not feel very lonely, living here so far from all other houses?' asked Undine after a moment's pause.

'No,' said the woman, shortly. 'I like it.'

Then Undine sat quietly watching the large, soft, brown hands that had evidently not been accustomed to hard work, the proud erect figure, the defiant sullen face, and the pink-and-white thing that laughed at their feet. She was a woman who had come no one knew from where, with only a baby, and her story was not difficult to read. Her neighbours read it after their fashion and called her a wicked woman, a very wicked woman.

When Undine had rested a few minutes longer she rose to go, but first she kneeled down on the grass where the baby lay.

'One kiss, for the sake of your bonny blue eyes,' she said.

As she walked slowly past the garden hedge she came to the shed where mother and child lived. 'Twas a miserable tumbledown place, yet Undine, as she passed it, envied them.

'I am not alone, for I have him, the child of love,' the eyes had said; and Undine with her empty heart, and the knowledge that she, too, soon would be mother of a child, not the child of love, but of loathing – Undine with her riches and her good name envied the dark woman her disgrace, her baby, and her rags.

'Where have you been all day? Not climbing the hills and over-exerting yourself,

I hope?' said her fat little proprietor as he met her in the door on her return; and for the rest of that day she was never free of him; neither on many days that followed did she find an opportunity for repeating that morning's walk.

The anniversary of their wedding day came. They had given a grand dinner, but the guests had departed early, and her husband, having indulged a little more freely than usual in that which makes heavy the heart of man, had fallen asleep on the sofa in his dressing room. She stood at the low open window of her room, looking out into the oppressive night. There was that heavy stillness in the air that precedes the bursting of a great storm.

'You may go. I shall not need you tonight,' she said to her maid; and when she had withdrawn, Undine threw a great shawl over her head and stepped out of the window, still dressed in black velvet and wearing on her neck the pearls that had made her the envy of many women that night.

She walked on quickly, not caring which path she took and pressing her foot hard on the ground at every step. It had caused a greater strain than usual that evening to wear, without once dropping it for a moment, that mask of smiles that she wore till the lines in her cheeks grew stiff and hurt.

As she walked on, the lines of an old song she had liked ran through her head:

> 'Behind no prison gate,' she said,
> 'That slurs the sunshine half a mile,
> Are captives so uncomforted
> As souls behind a smile.'

'God's pity let us pray,' she said.

Thinking of nothing, with these lines running, running thought her head, she walked while the sky grew dark and yet darker. Presently gusts of wind came hurrying past her, and then the great storm whose forerunners they had been overtook her. Fiercely the wind shook the branches of the trees over her head, and the large drops fell heavily through them. She was too far from home to think of returning, but she knew her grandmother's cottage would not be far off. She would go and sit in the little porch till the worst was over, she thought, and walked on slowly while the fast-falling rain made its way through her shawl and drenched her to the skin.

As she passed near the broken shed she noticed light coming through its small crooked window and through the crevices and cracks in its old stone walls. When she passed the window she paused for a moment and looked in. Most of the panes of glass were gone, their place being supplied by strips of pasted paper, but through the two squares that still remained she could clearly see all that the hovel contained. In one corner stood a small stretcher which was now unoccupied, for on a small stool before the fire, with her back turned to the window, sat the woman, her head stooping low over the baby she held close to her. Before the window stood a small table in which a tallow candle fixed in a broken brass candlestick was flickering and flaring. In the hearth the smouldering fire was almost extinguished by the rain which came down through the chimney, and the drops which made their way through the roof gathered themselves together in pools on the uneven floor.

It was a strange reversal in the order of things – the honoured wife of the rich man in her velvets and jewels standing out in the night storm and gazing in with envious eyes at the home where poverty and shame had taken their abode.

There came a hush in the storm and Undine could hear the woman was murmuring to the child as she bent over it. The first words she did not hear, but some came to her through the crevices and holes in the crazy window frame: 'My child, my little child, you will not leave me, you will not forsake me. You are all, all I have.' Then there came words Undine did not catch, and then again: 'If you will only stay with me, I will live for you, work for you, starve for you; you shall be rich and clever one day. I am not cruel to want to keep you. You must not die, you cannot die, my little baby. I loved you so before you lived. You are all I have of him. You must not die and leave me, my baby, my little baby.'

Then the mad storm came back howling after its rest, and the words were lost. Uncertain whether to enter or to go on to the cottage, Undine paused for an instant, then knocked at the door. There was no response and she laid her hand on the broken latch. The crazy door, opening, let her in, with a flood of rain and a gust of wind that almost extinguished the quickly melting candle.

'I hope I have not frightened you,' she said, when she had fastened it once more. 'I have been overtaken in the storm.'

The woman made no answer, but looked up at her with dull, lustreless eyes; then, recognising her visitor, she said, 'You liked my baby; you were the only one who ever kissed him. He is dying now.' She said the last words slowly and distinctly in a harsh whisper, and then looked down at the little figure wrapped in a great shawl that lay upon her knee.

Undine kneeled down beside her. She would have spoken words of comfort, but when her eyes fell on the little face, even by the uncertain light of the flickering candle and fire, she saw that death's hand was on the baby and the little life of love and shame would soon be ended.

In silence she kneeled by them, holding in her white jewelled fingers the tiny cold hand that rested on the shawl, while her long velvet train was curled up in one of the pools on the floor.

There was no word spoken in the hut for a long time. The storm shook the loose walls in its fury, the great raindrops killed the smouldering fire, and the two women sat watching in silence for the coming of the awful stranger.

At last there came a sudden hush in the storm. No sound was heard but the slow falling of the raindrops as they dripped from the roof into the puddles on the floor, and the candle flickered no more but burnt up straight and steady. Then the little child heaved a long weary sigh, and the clasp of the little hand relaxed, and the closed eyes partly opened, and they knew that death had been with them.

The mother sat as one who dreams, looking down at that which lay upon her knees, and their breathing sounded loud in the stillness.

At last she rose suddenly and, dropping the child heavily into Undine's arms, turned towards the door.

At that instant the storm came back, loud and fierce after its rest. She went out into it and to the darkness, and in the hut Undine sat with the dead child on her knee.

The light fell full on the little face with its half-closed eyes that looked so strangely old and stern now with the shadow of death upon them.

As she looked down at it she seemed to see, not the face of the little snow-white baby, but that other face that haunted her day and night – the face that she would never forget, that came in between her eyes and the sunny grass and flowers when they smiled upon her.

Was she not to look into the face of a dead child without seeing it even there, also?

It was like madness, she thought, and drew from beneath the small chin a white handkerchief that lay folded there, to cover from her sight the strange white face.

As she opened and spread it out, her eyes fell on a name beautifully worked on one corner. She read it and then sat thinking. After a long time she raised the little baby very gently and held it close to her. *His* dead baby. For she knew now that it was no madness that showed her the old haunting face in the features of the little child.

She knew now where she had seen that woman's face before, with its lustrous eyes and brilliant tints; remembered now the old hints and stories which she had regarded as lies but which tonight came back to her as truths. And she saw it all – the deep love of years, giving all things, denying nothing, pouring itself out at the feet of that stern strong man to whom it was only a thing to be sued, drawn upon, and, when no longer needed, trodden on and forgotten.

His little baby! Cared nothing for – loathed, perhaps – but what a difference. *His* little baby still. If she had only known it while the warm blood ran in the lips that struck her cold and chill when she pressed them now. If she had only known it sooner.

She gathered it up in her arms and moved the pearls aside that it might lie close, close against her soft warm breast – close, as though she would have given of her life to bring it back.

Then she laid it down once more and sat looking at it, and when the candle fell into its socket she still sat holding it, and the grey dawn when it looked in still found her sitting here.

The storm had gone, and when the sun arose the earth was green and laughing. The fresh morning wind helped the green branches to shake off the glittering drops that still hung on them, the flowers opened their eyes by thousands, the warming earth sent up a delicious smell, and the heavy grasses raised their wet heads and the tender plants shot out of the moist ground through every crack.

The storm had gone; only here and there a strong bough hung broken, or a great tree lay upon its side, whispering of last night's work. For nature keeps her secrets well and hides away from the sunshine the things which she does in darkness.

Yes, well she keeps her secrets!

When the curious morning sunbeams forced their way through the tall reeds and matted boughs that grew over the muddy pool, they saw nothing, they knew nothing; *they* could not tell what it was that lay across the old rotten trunk deep under the thick still water, with its brown hair buried in the mud. They did not know it, and the small birds did not know it, or how were it possible they should sing in the branches overhead such joyous lies? 'Life is sweet,' they said. 'Life is sweet, and love is long; it lasts all summer time.'

'Tell me all about it, Nancy,' said her lover as he conducted her home through the quiet fields that evening.

'So I will,' said Nancy, 'but Lor' bless me if I know where to begin, there's been so much a-happening today.'

'Begin at the beginning,' was her lover's very sage advice, which Nancy followed.

'Well, this morning, afore ever the sun got up, I went to the cottage to have a look at them shutters which we forgot to shut after we had been a-cleaning up last night and which I thought as how the wind would have blown off. Well, just as I goes past the little shed outside the garden, what should I see but Mrs Blair a-standing in the door as large as life, and a great shawl over her head and all.

'"Good-morning," says I, wondering how she comed there at this time of day.'

'"Nancy," says she, "there's a little child dead in here. I wish you'd call your mother and come and see to it, and see to the mother, too."'

'"Where is the mother?" says I, looking in.'

'"I don't know," says she, and walks off.'

'What do you think she came there for?' asked her lover, curiously.

'Lor'! I don't know,' responded Nancy. 'Nobody can't give no reason for her goings-on. I wouldn't be in no ways surprised to hear she'd been and gone and drunk poison, or gone up in a balloon, or been a-doing anything unlike other folks.'

'Well, I went and called mother and we seed to the baby: and the prettiest fattest little thing I ever seed it was.'

'Mother says, "Nancy," says she, "look in that there little box under the bed and see if you can't find no clothes for it. The woman don't seem to be a-coming yet."'

'"Yes," says I, and pulls out the box. The thing was locked, but, Lor'! it was so rotten, afore you'd touched it was broken open, and there weren't much in it, neether – just a pair of baby's clothes and the beautifullest little box that ever I see;

and, Lor'! I do believe it's real gold and writing all over the top, and mother and I, we spelt out, Alice Brown and something about a drowning, but the other words were a sight too long.'

'And what was in the box?' asked her lover.

'Money?' said Nancy. 'No. I just opened it afore I thought, and what do you think I seed in it? Why, the likeness of the beautifullest young man I ever set eyes on in all my born days. The man on the hairpin box ain't nothing to him, nothing. Curly hair and moustaches just the same, but a sight more handsome.'

'Was that all?' said her companion, not feeling in any way entertained by the raptures of his lady love over the pictured perfection.

'Yes, that was all,' said Nancy, "cept a couple of bits of cigars, half burnt out, and an old glove a sight too big for her I should say, though she is pretty considerable big.'

'What did she say when she came back and found you'd been a rummaging all her things?'

'Comed back! She *never* comed back,' said Nancy, 'and it's my belief she never will neither. She's come from nowheres and she's gone to nowheres. She thinks as how other folks can see to its burying, but it's always the way with the likes of her. Women that do the sort of thing she's been a-doing of, they never have no natural feeling,' said the virtuous Nancy. And her lover agreed with her.

'Did you tell Mrs Blair about her never coming back?' inquired the swain.

'Well, that's what I'm just a-coming to,' said Nancy. 'At four o'clock I says, "Mother," says I, "hadn't I better be going down to Mrs Blair's just for to tell her that the woman hasn't come?"'

'"I was just a-thinking so," says mother. So off I went. When I gets there, "Can't I see the mistress?" says I.'

'"Don't you know?" says he.'

'"Know what?" says I.'

'"That she's a-dying, and the baby, too." says he.'

'"Baby," says I. "Lor'! you don't mean it."'

'"Yes," says the housemaid, a-coming up, "she was took ill this morning, and the baby ain't much bigger nor your hand and more like a rat nor a baby."'

'Well, afore I could say anything in comes the nurse.'

'"How's Mrs Blair?" says I.'

'"She's pretty near gone," says the nurse, "but she's asking after somebody. I can't hear the name very clear, but I think it's Nancy Grey."'

'"If it is," says I, "here I am," and so she takes me upstairs.'

'The room was so dark I could see nothing at first, but, Lor'! when I did it was awful sad to see her a-lying there so white and dead like. She didn't take no notice of me, so after I waited a bit she said as how I had best come out. And I was just a-going out at the door when the nurse brings her baby for to put it by her side.'

'"Take it away, take it away!" she cries out, quite strong like, and then I comed out.'

'And what are you going to do with the other baby?' inquired Nancy's lover.

'Have it buried, to be sure,' said Nancy. 'Mr Blair, he'll pay for it if she's dead.'

But Undine did not die. And the baby lived, a puny shrivelled thing, but still it lived. One Sunday afternoon, four weeks later, they carried her from her bed to a sofa, wrapped in a richly embroidered dressing gown and a great shawl. Near her, in its white-and-blue-satin-covered cradle, they laid her baby.

Why would they always bring that thing into her sight and keep it near her? Was it not enough that its little weak cry had rung loud in her ears when she was insensible to every other sound and had made her lose all love of life, all wish to keep it, even more than the kisses of its father had done.

For every few hours the little man would steal softly into the room on tiptoe, with his hands open and his fingers stretched out, and, breathing very hard, would come up to her bedside to see how matters stood. When the death scale seemed to be going down he was seriously concerned, and refused to find consolation in devilled turkey, allowing the gravy on his plate to congeal there several times before he touched it, an event wholly unprecedented in the past. Now, however, he could sip his wine at ease and smoke his cigar in tranquillity, for the doctors had pronounced her out of danger and the baby still lived. True, it looked as though the first ball coming its way must inevitably bowl it out of the game, but a baby is not very much. Babies are plentiful, and he had his wife and would have another baby someday.

On this Sunday afternoon he sat dozing peacefully in his chair, and the nurse sat by his wife.

'I think I shall sleep. I don't want to be disturbed,' said Undine; and the nurse, not unwilling to take the hint, rose and left her. The room was very cool and still. A soft light came in through the dark-green curtains. She lay on the soft pillows with her face resting on her thin hand, and looked at the baby, a mere speck of red amid the blue and white. Her baby and his, therefore she hated it. Her baby – she looked at it, and then lay thinking.

It was strange to know its life had sprung from hers. Strange to have hung another tiny wheel in the great world machine that grinds on so mysteriously with its ever-jarring, never-resting wheels flying round forever. And what did it all mean? What were they all, really – that little life – the purple violets – the dark-green curtains – herself lying there and thinking? Were they all nothing, dreams, shadows? Or something? And, if something, O God! What?

It was the old question she had asked so often when she stood, a little child, looking at the dry Karoo bushes on the old farm; and it met, as then, the old oppressive silence for an answer – silence like the hush which comes when we sit by the seashore on a dark night and hold our breaths to hear the great restless waters running up and down.

Presently she moved her hand quickly across her eyes, and then rose slowly and moved with trembling steps to the cradle-side.

'Poor little soul,' she said and stooped down over it, 'life is too wonderful to hate in. Poor little soul, we are all too nearly bound for hating'; and she took the baby to her. When her husband came in half an hour later he was surprised to find his child in her arms and a bunch of soft violets clasped in its tiny hand.

'Why do you do that?' he asked as he sat down beside her.

'Because I am going to call her Violet,' his wife answered, and looked up at him with a smile so bright and unlike her own that it made him feel uncomfortable for a moment. Surely she was not going to die.

But after that day he often saw it, and others saw it also. The very servants whispered that their mistress had changed strangely; and surely it was the coming of the baby that had changed her, they said, speaking like the little children who fancy that the swallows bring the summer.

In the long bright days that followed she would have an armchair put out under the great trees on the other side of the lawn, and would sit there all day with the child in her arms, drinking in the sunny beauty of grass and sky, as though birds sang to her what others could not hear.

Sometimes she read in those still sweet days; and books, which to her had so long been meaningless and dumb, had again voice and life. Whether they were the hot words of a passion filled heart singing to appease its own intolerable hunger, or the calm record of things long past, or the exact statement of some savant concerning a flower he had dissected, there was life in them all and music. To her they were as food to one who wakes hungry after a long dark dream.

Oh, the beauty of those days, the glory of the brown that rested on the hilltops, the brightness that hung over the cut stones of the house walls!

So sweet was that first draught of a new life that she had no eye to mark shadows, and did not notice, as all others did, that the life of the little child was growing weaker and fainter as the autumn days drew near. She knew so little of children that its slow growth did not trouble her; it knew her, and would open its dark eyes and lie smiling up at her for long times together, as they sat out in the sunshine.

'My little friend,' she used to call it softly, and whisper *all* to it of things which could not have been spoken in any other ear.

'My little friend, who loves me.'

'Someone ought to tell her; she does not dream of it,' they all said. 'She will wake up some morning and find the child lying dead in her arms.' The doctor said so, her husband said so, they all said so; yet no one cared to tell her.

At last one evening, when the sun was almost setting, the old doctor went out to look for her. He found her sitting on the grass with the baby on her lap, bathed in the rich regretful sunset light that warmed the soft tints of the flowers in the little wreath she had wound around the child's head. He looked down at the little face below the wreath, and wondered that love could look at it without reading it. He asked her very gently how it was.

Undine only smiled softly for an answer, and said, as she stuck tiny leaves of grass among the flowers: 'She is so fond of flowers, and does not tear them to pieces as other children do. She holds them so carefully in her hand and turns them round and looks at them. We don't give babies credit for half wisdom enough,' she said.

'It is growing very thin,' said the doctor, taking its small clenched fist into his hand, 'very thin.'

'Not thinner than it was,' said Undine; 'and when next summer comes we will go to the sea; it will soon be strong and well then.'

'That is a long time to wait,' said the doctor, gravely. 'Many things may have happened before next summer.'

Undine looked up into his grave face, and down at the little one with its crown of flowers. After a long pause she said, 'What do you mean?' And he knew she had read what was written there.

It was not needful to say much more. He soon left her sitting in the sunlight. 'Oh, my little friend,' she said; 'is it to be always so? Are we only to lift our heads above the water to be pushed down again? Do we only rise up because, if we did not, we could not be flung down to earth? Is light only sent to make the darkness visible?'

She sat there till the last glow had faded from the hilltops and the grass on which they sat began to grow damp and cold.

'My little friend, I am very cruel to wish to keep you. Would life have more of happiness for you than it has had for me? – a little gladness out of colours and lights; a little sweetness out of dreams; one hour of bliss looking at footmarks in the white snow? Is that enough to make it worth keeping? Oh, my little friend, it will be better to go. You have made a little brightness. There is nothing better waiting for you if you stay.'

'Not in bed yet?' said her husband when, returning late the next evening from a dinner he had been attending in the neighbouring town, he found his wife still up and sitting on a low chair with the child on her knees. 'You might as well have gone with me if you meant to sit up so late. You will never get your roses back if you go on in this way.'

'I cannot go to bed tonight,' she said, quietly, smoothing softly the crumples in the child's little nightdress. 'It is very ill.'

'Ill? What's the matter?' he said, peering down into its face for a moment. 'It looks just as usual to me. I suppose that fool of a doctor has been frightening you.'

'No; he says there is no cause to be anxious just tonight, but I can see more than he can.'

'Oh, we all know you can see through a wall, but it would be more sensible of you to go to bed and rest,' responded her master, sullenly, as he turned away and left the room.

'Would not touch the baby at first, or have it brought near her; goes and makes a fool of herself over it now,' he grumbled. 'Couldn't see that it was ill, and thinks it's dying now. She's a queer composition.'

It was a warm night for that time of year, and Undine had opened the great doors and windows on both sides of the room to let in the air. Yet the lamp that hung overhead burnt steadily and threw down its unwavering steady light over mother and child. On the mantlepiece the bronze clock ticked regularly, but the breathing of the child was so low it could not be heard.

Perhaps she was very foolish, after all; the doctor must know best; and she looked down inquiringly. There was just the faintest smile about the little mouth and the hands were crossed loosely on the little breast. As she looked the smile passed slowly and the child opened wide its eyes and fixed them on the lamp overhead – those large, unearthly deep brown eyes.

Undine would not move for fear of disturbing it, but the baby turned its head round slowly, and looked up into her face with those great calm eyes. Did they speak to her or did she only fancy it? Those dark awful eyes of her own little child. There was no dread, there was no questioning in them, but a calm, solemn light.

Undine looked deep, deep into them. She did not hear the clock strike or know how the moments passed, till the white lids dropped slowly. There was no sigh, there was no change, but when she laid her hand upon its breast she knew that the baby was dead.

She rose up and carried its body to the large white bed, and laid it down just as it was with its peacefully crossed hands. Then she dropped down on her knees beside it with her forehead on the ground, and the dead was not more motionless that the living.

The next morning when her husband, having been roused early and told of his child's death, went out in search of Undine, he found her sitting in the sunshine on the dewy grass.

'It is dead,' she said, looking up at him with a calm, cloudless face, as though she had said, 'It is asleep.' He wondered, for how should he understand the love she bore her child, the passionless love, loving it in spite of its being hers? The baby I love, because it is mine; the woman I cling to against my reason – I must hear them, see them, touch them, or be devoured by a senseless gnawing; but the friend whose soul has reached mine, the thing I have loved for what it taught me, I let them pass without a tear, for my part of them remains with me, and for the rest, let it go.

'You have heard the news, of course,' said Miss Mell one morning before she had entered Mrs Barnacles's room. She was very much out of breath, for she was growing asthmatic of late. 'Harry Blair has come. I saw him myself half an hour ago, and he says his father is dead. Did you ever hear of such a thing? Some people *are* lucky,' said Miss Mell with energy.

'Why, I don't think he will get much. Did his father leave him anything?'

'Leave him anything! Of course he didn't. You may be sure she would take good care of that. I can see it now just as well as if it were past – how she'll come here lording it over everybody and marrying a big swell before the year's out. With all her money and her bold, free manners, men are sure to be taken by her. I am sure she has no good looks to talk of, but they are such fools they never see it. They are so easily taken in.'

'Even if they are, I don't wonder that you never managed to do it,' thought Mrs Barnacles; but she only replied: 'I don't know anything about her. I've never heard her mentioned since her baby died two years ago. I've never had but two notes from her since she left. Gratitude was and never will be one of Undine Blair's virtues.'

Mrs Barnacles refrained from making any further animadversions on the character of her connection; for it struck her that should Miss Mell's prognostications be verified, it would be just as well to have a smile for the young heiress and get the benefit of some of the fruit and game that would be plentiful at Blair House. Indeed, it would be rather pleasant than otherwise to have all Greenwood ridden over the head by a connection of hers, provided only that she were not included in the everybody.

Miss Mell, whose aversion for Undine was of the same nature as that of a cat for water, or a Kaffir for work, quite irrepressible, inherent and inextinguishable, continued to express her opinion of the character of her natural enemy with asperity that might not be rivalled. She was just remarking on the perfidy of her behaviour towards Harry Blair, when Cousin Jonathan's mild blue eyes looked in at the door.

'Do come in, Mr Barnacles. You've heard the news, no doubt; perhaps you've seen Mr Blair?'

'Yes, he called on me as soon as he arrived. He was on the Continent when he got the news of his father's illness, and came to find him dead.'

'Poor fellow! Did he really expect to get anything?' said Miss Mell, in a voice expressive of infinite scorn at his credulity.

'No; he was astonished when he got home to find that the property was to be divided equally between the two brothers. He had no idea of any such thing.'

'So the old man left her nothing?' said Miss Mell.

'No,' assured Cousin Jonathan; 'he left her everything, but she's gone off, nobody knows where, and has left an order that everything is to be divided between them. Harry Blair has come here to enquire whether I know anything about her.'

'I should say the best thing would be to let her alone,' said Miss Mell; 'she has evidently got some nice little game of her own to play.' But Miss Mell was discomfited. Hitherto her abhorrence of that red-cheeked, scheming affectation had been of a groundless kind, accountable only on the hypothesis of natural antipathies. Other girls as pretty did not arouse the latent feline propensity of her nature in anything like the same degree; it would not have given her half the infinite satisfaction to efface *their* beauty with thumb and finger nails that she would have had in operating on the cheeks of the scheming affectation. But now, to be proved a daughter of Belial, a false prophetess, by Undine obstinately refusing to commit the evil prophesied of her: was it not just cause for bitterness?

Saints made perfect forgive such injuries, but not a wrinkled woman on the rotten side of forty, with no money or intellect to keep the wine of life from turning sour in her bottle.

She sat there wishing Undine might be gone to the devil, as Alice Brown had gone in verification of her prophecy of six years before. She did not stay long, however, and found it hard work to change the expression of her countenance to one of serene affability as she passed young Mr Dunstables in the street.

After she had gone, Cousin Jonathan sat down to smoke and read a sermon. It was a good cigar, but it hadn't any flavour; it was a nice sermon, original, by Henry Ward Beecher, but he didn't like it. He had not felt so many nasty twinges since he had read a certain marriage notice in the papers years before. 'I am growing too studious,' he said; 'my nerves are debilitated, seriously debilitated. I must take a tonic. I must take a walk.'

Exercise is good for debility of many kinds, and he came home feeling better.

While he was walking in a desperate hurry with flying arms up the hill, Harry Blair was wandering in a desultory manner among the trees below. Cousin Jonathan was more light of heart than he had been for many a brown day.

'She was not so evil as they thought her, not so mercenary,' he said, and rejoiced.

CHAPTER FOURTEEN

On Board Ship to South Africa

On that Wednesday morning the cause of the violent exercise of the former and the joy of the latter was standing on board a steamer bound for South Africa.
Undine was leaning over the side of the ship and turning back no wistful look to the fast receding English shores. Like a great impassioned living creature whose burning, striving heart impels it to wander on forever, the steamer passed over the blue, breezy, swelling sea, leaving its track of foaming bubbles to dance and die in sunshine. The wild free seabirds, as they dipped their wings into the water and spread them out in the morning light, were glad and full of life.

It was such rest to stand and watch them, it was long before she turned her eyes to the little world on deck. There was motion enough there also, and happiness too for all that might be seen; but Undine looked back longingly at her seabirds as they floated over the water, as though it might be pleasanter to be among them than among the wiser fowls that trotted on the deck.

Near her were sitting two Afrikaner girls who had been sent home for their education, and who were returning sublimely ignorant of everything in general and their own deficiencies in particular, to make a grand sensation in their little up-country town, to be worshipped and sought after by the sterner sex and woefully traduced and servilely copied by the gentler, who would for a short time look up to them as Young Lady's Journals in the flesh and worthy of all imitation from their collars to their walk.

Further off there was a portly dame wearing the stiffest of black silks with the stiffest of necks, who could by no conceivable effort bring her eyes lower than the great gold rings that adorned her short fingers, and who devoutly believed this ball had been launched into space and continued suspended there to serve as a floor whereon might be placed her well-shod feet. Long ago she had done her own ironing, and her own washing too at a pinch when no Kaffir maid was to be got, but her husband had been a lucky emigrant and those days were forgotten now. Her husband, who sat not far from her, looked as though the rolling of the ship were considerably more than he could stand and fervently wished himself in old Africa again: old Africa, to which he would return smaller and wiser after his travels, the truth having been revealed to him during his wanderings that the world has greater things than a British settler. To his wife no revelation had been made, for the darkness that surrounds the female soul is dense.

A little to the right of this couple was standing a pimply young missionary, biting his nails and staring very hard at a very pretty blonde who was going to the Cape to be married and who filled his bosom with those gentle stirrings to which the sacerdotal breast is strangely prone. She looked not at him but from under her black silk hat her dove's eyes glanced softly at a group of young Englishmen, birds of a feather, who stood together smoking and chatting. A fish in the hand is worth six at the hook, and more than one bride has come out to her beloved to find herself unwanted; so, if there were any golden fish on board, it might be as well to angle for them. The young gentlemen on whom her eyes were resting now were small game, however – puny, white-faced young Londoners, 'raw Englishmen' they would be called out in the Colony, where they would no doubt go into stores as clerks or become petty diamond-buyers at the Fields. There were one or two German Jews on deck, smoking cigars and sunning themselves, some going out for the first time and some returning to the Cape: not the little snivelling, weasel-like creatures who come out third class and, as soon as they land, supply themselves with a wagon and a couple of mules and become *smouses*,[1] hawking false jewellery and damaged clothing among the Dutch farmers, and growing rich on it; but gentlemen Jews, with their polite foreign manners and their fascinating broken English, who will make you swear round is square and sell you to the devil before your face, and you shall never know it; who will squeeze you to pulp to get your last shilling today, and tomorrow, when your wife is starving and no Christian will help her, will give her ten.

There were men and women of all shapes and qualities to be seen, but nothing so pleasing as two little children with pretty faces who stood near to her. Innocent blue eyes and pink-and-white dimpled faces were surrounded by a maze of fine yellow hair. Presently a very diminutive and equally ugly terrier with a white body and little yellow ears came up, and received from the foot of the smaller of the two an astonishingly lusty kick.

'Oh, Lily, how can you!' said her sister. 'It belongs to that lady in the black-silk dress.'

'No, it doesn't, or I would not have kicked it,' responded the little one; 'it belongs to that woman with the plaited hair and the old grey frock.'

'Oh, then it's all right,' answered the elder, complacently.

Undine stooped down to caress the shabby little creature whom the world ill used because its mistress had not a chin or a silk dress. Even in a morsel of humanity not three feet high, with a baby face and golden curls, must one find the world, the flesh, and the devil full grown?

She looked away from them to the woman with the plaited hair and the grey dress. She was shabby, dreadfully shabby. Her grey skirt had been turned not only inside out but upside down; her loose cloth jacket had once been black but was now brown,

---

1 *Smous* – hawker, peddler.

and, to judge from its cut, was the last relic of a long-deceased fashion. On her head she wore a great round hat ornamented round the crown by a piece of brown lace which must have been young when the jacket was black. Her black gloves were three sizes too large for her and yet did not conceal the knobbly condition of her long thin hands. She had a weak, nervous mouth and sat on the edge of the bench, as though hardly sure she had a right to be there at all. Her hands were crossed in her lap and her eyes looked out across the water. Immense wonderful steel-grey eyes that were strangely out of keeping with the wrinkled wizened face in which they were set.

'I wonder who that woman in the grey dress is,' said a gentleman standing in earshot of Undine to his companion, a military man who boasted an immense pair of moustaches and a most elegant drawl.

'Woman in grey dress? I saw one just now. Deuced pretty little thing. Tried to get up a conversation; couldn't. Best-looking thing on board.'

'Then she's not the woman I mean,' responded his companion. 'She's not your style, would not exactly attract you, but she has marvellous eyes.'

'Who has?' inquired that captain's pretty sister, coming up at that moment. Possessing a pair of eyes as remarkable for their brilliancy as the shabby woman's were for their shadowy deepness, she thought the remark referred to none other than herself.

'I can't say that I admire your taste,' she said when the owner of the grey eyes had been pointed out to her. 'A living song they are you say? You who have so much of the poet's blood should really try and translate them into something intelligible to us poor mortals who see nothing in her but a piece of very shabby gentility. You poets should not absorb all the light that falls on you without reflecting a ray on us.'

'I'm afraid it takes more to make a poet than nature has poured into my mould,' he answered, laughing lightly, as he offered her his arm and walked off with the graceful black-eyed beauty. Undine thought his dancing blue eyes as pleasant to look at as the rippling waves, and stood watching as he passed to and fro, now stopping to throw bon-bons to the children or stooping to stroke the yellow-and-white terrier they had kicked, then standing to chat with a lady or raising his hat and turning his face against the breeze to let it toss and play with his brown curls. A boy he seemed in his perfect enjoyment of life in spite of his rich brown beard, the only glad childish thing on board. Undine's eyes followed him and she forgot the shabby woman till she went down to her cabin and found that she was to be her companion there.

It was better than having the captain's pretty sister or any of the gay butterflies on board; and truly better she found it when, lying down in her berth, she did not rise from it for weeks. The strain under which she had lived for years, the excitement of the last few weeks, had told on her, and now when it was all past she broke down utterly. After a few days she was well enough to lie still and enjoy the quiet rest, but was weak enough to feel grateful for the silent constant attention of her companion, who sat beside her night and day.

'You are very good to me, very good,' said Undine one day, when the woman sat bathing her head with vinegar and water. 'You do everything for me so much better than the stewardess can.'

'I ought to be able to,' said the woman in a low, nervous voice. 'I have been nursing for twelve years. I do nothing else.'

All day Undine's occupation was to lie and watch her, for she never went on deck but sat there sewing at innumerable little white shirts and petticoats, with those great marvellous grey eyes which always seemed looking beyond the object on which they were fixed to something far away.

She might have been any age between twenty and forty, for in spite of the wrinkles in her sallow face there was something more of a girl than the woman about her.

She never spoke unless spoken to, till one day Undine had scribbled half a dozen lines of rhyme in which she told what she felt when there had been rain in the night and she went out to see the roses knocking their faces together and sending down a second shower into the face of the moist sweet earth. She was looking radiantly happy, for it is as thrilling as a lover's hot kiss to have fixed on paper something that has looked beautiful to us.

'Are you going to someone?' asked the woman suddenly.

'Going to someone?' repeated Undine inquiringly.

'Yes. I beg your pardon,' said the woman, seeming terribly abashed and speaking more nervously than usual. 'I hope you will forgive me. But I meant – you looked so happy – and I – I thought you must be going to someone.'

'No, I have no one to go to,' said Undine. 'Are you going to friends?'

'Yes,' said the woman.

Undine leaned back wearily on her pillows. So it was only she who was utterly alone; even this queer grey woman had friends.

'Where are the friends you are going to?' she asked presently.

The woman waited for a long time, then she said, suddenly, 'I have one; I am going to him.' And then, after a short pause, 'He is dead.' And a smile as sad as the last red light that burns on the highest crag of a mountain passed over the worn face and the great grey eyes.

Undine asked no more questions. Some great sorrow has shaken her reason, she thought.

The next day the woman sat at her interminable sewing and Undine, who lay reading, felt as a generous child does who is eating something sweet and cannot understand that it would be less sweet to another. 'Would you like me to read aloud to you a little?' You must grow so tired of sitting here always and sewing,' she said.

'Thank you,' said the woman in a tone that was as far away as the look in her eyes. 'Long ago I used to like books; they said it was that made me so stupid.'

'How could that be?' asked Undine, resting her cheek on her hand and looking at her.

'I don't know, but I never could learn, and I used to sit in the window in the moonlight reading the books I liked; and they said it was that made me so stupid; but I don't think it was; I would have been stupid anyhow.'

Then she remembered the work which had dropped from her hands while she spoke and she stitched on faster than ever.

'Reading makes no one stupid. They must be strange to say so,' said Undine.

'I don't know. You see, I could only remember poems and tales, I couldn't do sums or remember the tables; I was very stupid, but I understood some of *them*; Shelley was the name of one man I used to like, but I did not understand him; I only felt sorry for him. It was wicked, I know, but I used to wish I could have seen him. I used to like him.' She spoke this in the low tone peculiar to her, and more as though she were speaking to herself than to anyone else.

'I don't think he was wicked,' said Undine. 'It is so long ago, perhaps I have forgotten.'

'I don't know, but I thought he and his wife went away from each other, and I thought he loved another woman; but I forget.'

'He did love another woman, but I don't think that that's any reason for not liking him. It's always right to love, love as much as we can, and as long as we can, and as strong as we can,' said Undine, emphatically, raising herself on her elbow and watching the busy fingers as they moved to and fro.

The exertion tired her, so presently she lay down again, forgot all about the book, and was following her roving fancies, when the woman laid her hand softly on her arm.

'Do you really believe it?' she said. 'Say it again.'

'Say what?' asked Undine, looking into the grey eyes which for the first time were really looking at her.

'That it is not wrong,' she whispered.

'Not wrong to do what? Not wrong to love? How can it be? It is not wrong to feel warm or to feel strong, and we can as little help loving as feeling either.'

'But if it hurts other people,' said the woman slowly.

'Then it must be silent as the dead are, who they say live, yet we never hear them.'

The woman sat with her hands folded in her lap. Undine lay and watched her wonderingly.

Suddenly, with the abruptness which was at all times common to her, she drew from her bosom an old gold locket that was tied to a black-velvet string, and put it into Undine's hand.

'Look at it,' she said. 'I never felt so before – but I would like to tell you. I never felt so before – but I would like to tell.'

Like to tell! Yes, we all like it. It is not only the purple dove in the deep shade of the bush, it is not only the poet in his rhapsodies, talking to stones and trees, but the coldest hardest sinner among us who passes through life without giving a sign. We all like to tell, but, alas! too often find no comprehender, and walk through life dumb and mute with our burden.

Undine opened the old gold locket. In it there was the face of a young girl, a pretty, weak, sensitive face, with a setting of abundant brown curls and great, timid, fawn-like eyes.

Opposite was the face of a man – a dark, handsome, sensual face with bold black eyes.

Undine lay looking at the pictures, while the woman talked on in a low dreamy voice, so softly that at times she could hardly hear her.

'I was always stupid,' she said. 'I think that must have been the reason why no one ever loved me. They sent me to school when I was quite a little child to see if it would do me any good, but I used to get so frightened I could never remember when we had to come up and say our lessons, and so I always stayed in the classes with the little girls. I think they used to like me, the very little ones; I could dress their dolls and even help them with their lessons a little. You see, I was not stupid to them, but to the big girls and they could not bear me, but they used to let me darn their stockings for them and, when any of them got into a scrape, then they used to come to me and say, "Don't say it's not you if the teachers ask, because you are sure not to get a prize anyhow." And I used to say yes, because I thought it would make them love me; but it never did, it only made the teachers hate me. One of them I thought liked me, she always talked so softly to me; but one day when I was shut up all alone in the dark room that opened out of the schoolroom, I heard some of the teachers talking. I think they had forgotten me and I heard them say I was the stupidest girl in the school and that they could not think how she could like me. "I do not like her," she said, "I feel sorry for her, she is such a poor thing; but there is not a girl in the school I care less about." Then I lay down and cried. I had been so happy when I thought she loved me, and when I came out the girls all laughed at me because I had been crying, and said I was afraid of the dark; and I was not afraid at all, I liked it, but I did so want someone to help me, someone bigger and cleverer than I was.

'Afterwards, when I grew a great girl, I left off trying to make people love me, because it was no use.

'I used to get away from the others whenever I had time and sit and read all by myself. I had not many books, only some books of poetry and a tale called *The Wide Wide World*, and some other little books that I forget, but I read them over and over till I could repeat them by heart. I don't know how it was I could remember such things and not my lessons. I know I tried to learn them, but somehow I never could.

'When I was grown and wore long dresses my mother died, and my father a little time after, so I had to go away from school, and I had nothing and no one to go to except one aunt. She had a beautiful little house close to the sea, with a balcony and a flower garden in front, with little white gravelled paths, and she and her three little children lived there alone. I thought I would be so happy there and make her love me, and I thought I would not read my books any more, because they said it was that made me so stupid that no one could like me.

'When I came there she gave me a pretty little green-and-white room all to myself, and she told me I should only have to teach the eldest two children and help her a little with her needlework; but I would make her love me if I worked very hard and tried to do everything I could for her. So I used to get up very early and help the nurse to dress the children and the cook to get the breakfast, and I used to work all day and late in the evening. When the children were in bed I used to get out the needlework; and when she used to ask me if I was not tired yet, I used to say no, though sometimes I was so tired when I went up to my room I used just to lie across the foot of my bed and cry for tiredness till I went to sleep. I knew it was very wicked of me, but somehow it seemed as though she would like me better if I said I was never tired. After a little time she sent the nurse away and I had to go and sleep with the children and look after them all day and take them for walks, and she never asked me if I was tired any more, however late I sat working. You see it was all my own fault. She believed what I told her, but it seemed so hard that she should not care about me a little bit. If she had sometimes looked at me as she looked at the children, I don't think I should ever have felt tired.

'At last one day she told me she was expecting visitors; a friend of hers and her husband and child were coming to board with us for six months, because she was very delicate and wanted to be near the sea.

'I was half sorry and half glad when I heard it. It would give me more work, but then I always fancied, before I saw people, that perhaps they would like me and not find me so dull as all the others had. By and by they came. She was a pretty woman and used to sit in the parlour all day, making wax flowers and baskets. My aunt used to sit and talk with her, but she never took any notice of me, even when I put fresh flowers on her table or brought her pretty seaweeds for her baskets; and her husband I was very frightened of. I could not bear him. He used to sit in an armchair on the balcony just before the schoolroom window all day, and I used to feel as if I could not teach the children anything, especially when he looked in. I was so afraid of him, I wondered how anyone could love him, till one day when I saw him sitting there with his little girl on his knee. Her head was on his shoulder and both arms were about her, and he looked down at her with such a look in his face, and he was so strong, that I ran away to my room that the children might not see me. For I could not help crying; I wished so I was that little girl.

'After that, early in the mornings, when I used to walk on the beach with the children and his little girl, he would often meet us when he was coming back from his bathe and stand and talk to his little girl and sometimes to me. I wondered he did not mind being seen talking to me by the other gentlemen who went past us, because I always had my aunt's baby and looked like a nurse girl. I thought it was very kind of him, but I did not like him and I was afraid of him. I went round another way when I saw him coming. He always talked so kindly to me. He said my arms were not strong enough to carry such a big baby, and he asked me if I was not tired. No one else ever did.

'One day he had brought a beautiful painting of a woman and hung it up in the parlour. I was passing the door with a cup of arrowroot for the baby, when he called me to come in and look at it. It was a very pretty picture.

'"Do you know whey I brought it?" he said. "Because it was like you."

'I could not think how anyone could think such a beautiful face was like mine, so I looked at the picture again. Then I felt him take my hand softly in both his, and when I looked up into his face it seemed to have just the look that had been there when he looked at his little girl.

'I pulled my hands out of his and ran away to the children's room and knelt down by my bed and cried. I was so happy. I never thought anyone would look at me like that, and all the day I was so glad; I never felt tired or miserable. In the evening two or three gentlemen came to play whist with him, and my aunt told me to make some eggflip for them. He had showed me how to make them before and I could make them very nicely, but this evening he came into the dinning room just as I had finished, because he said he was afraid I would not do it right. We were all alone, and as he went out of the room he put his arm so softly round me and kissed my mouth. It seemed as if there were a great river running past my ears, and I sat down and put my head on the table. I did not think there was any wrong in it; I did not think at all. It was all so strange, and I was so happy. I did not think that day or for many days after. I had no time to think. You see, I was working, working all the time with the children or at housework, from early in the morning when all the other people were in bed till late in the evening, and at night I was so tired I could not undress. I went to sleep in my clothes. I only know that I was happy. They say when people are idle and have nothing to do they sin, but I think people do more sins when they have no time to think, because you can love without time, you see. One Sunday evening I had time to think. They had all gone to church and the little ones I was taking care of were asleep, and I could sit at the foot of the bed and think. I saw that his love for me was not like his love for his little girl, else why did he never kiss me when even the children were by? There must be something wrong in it. So I thought I would ask him to go away very soon. I did not love him; I hardly knew if I liked him, except just when I was talking to him; but I knew it would be very hard to lose him. You see, nothing else had ever loved me like that.

'Just as I was thinking so, I saw him standing in the door. He had gone with the others to church; I don't know how it was he came back. He came into the room and stooped down over me and asked me what I was thinking of. Then I told him, and he said I was a foolish little girl and told me there was nothing wrong in his loving me; he said some kinds of love between men and women were wrong, of course, but he only loved me as if I were his little girl. I was his little sunshine, he said, and he did not show his love to me before others because his wife was so queer; she did not like him to have a friend, even a man, though she did not care for him at all, he said. He had never had anyone to love him and he longed so to have someone who cared for him utterly; he asked me if I would not. Then I felt as if I had been quite wrong to think it was not right to love him, and when he asked me to kiss him I did, though I never had before. Then I loved him better, and I felt quite glad and happy till the next day. I was dusting the parlour, and I heard his wife talking to him in the other room.

'"I'm not a fool, or quite blind either," she said. "I understand your small games by this time. I know very well why you bought that picture, and the meaning of your pleasant looks. Oh, yes, I am not such a fool as you take me for, nor she, either, with her flowers and her seaweeds and her pretty innocent face."

'I went out of the room then, because I did not want to hear more; but suddenly, I don't know why, the thought came to me that they were talking about me. I asked him that evening, and he said: "You must not mind her; she would be jealous of your aunt if you were not here. It is only her nature." I felt very unhappy after that whenever I had time to think and was alone, but when I was near him I was quite happy, and I got to love his little child so. I had it near me all day long, but I could not bear to see him play with it. I did not feel jealous of anything else, but when I used to see him kiss her, I got a sick feeling at my heart. He always called me his little girl and his little sunshine when we were alone, and at last it seemed to me as if he were the only real thing in the world; all the other people seemed like dreams. I liked so to go and put his room neat; it was so nice to touch the brushes he used every morning and to fold up his clothes and put them away, and it was so nice to touch his greatcoat when I passed through the hall. One day I picked up a torn likeness of his on the floor, and I put it in my mother's locket by mine, and that was nice, too.

'One afternoon, when all the others were out on the beach and I was left at home to get tea ready, he came in. I was kneeling on the pantry dresser, filling a glass pot with jam, when I looked round and saw him standing behind me. He came up and lifted me down in his arms and carried me into the dinning room. Then he sat down with me in the great armchair and held me very close to him, and asked me if I loved him, utterly, better than anything else in the world. When I said yes, he put his face down close to mine and said very softly. "Then you must come away with me, far away, to another land where you and I can be alone with each other till we die, and we will make each other happy, so happy." He told me he loved nothing in the world but me; and when I looked up at him it seemed as thought his eyelids were wet. I lay quite still for a minute and then I tried to jump up and run away, but he did not let me go.

'"How can you leave your wife and your little child?" I asked him, and then I crept close to him again and told him that I loved him. I don't know what else I said; I don't think I even knew then.

'But after that day I loved him with another kind of love, not like the love I loved him with before; and I could not bear to be in the same room with him when there were other people, because it seemed as though they must see in my face how much I loved him. And every day he begged me to go away with him, but I always said, "No, no, no." It would have been wrong of me to go, but I did not care about that, I was so wicked; I could not bear that he should be selfish and leave his wife and his little child. If he had asked me to do anything I would have done it, I would not have cared; but I did not like him to be wicked.

'So many weeks went on and sometimes I used to get miserable and ask him to go away. Then he used to hold me in his arms and kiss me, and I forgot everything. You see, I was working, working all the day and at night I was tired, so tired. Sometimes when I was with the children on the beach in the morning I was so sleepy that I went to sleep sitting on the sand.

'At last one day they all went away to see a great show in the next town. They went for two or three days, and I was left to take care of the house. It seemed so dreadful to have to think of being there alone for two whole days and never seeing him once. I cried, and in the afternoon I fell asleep on the sofa wrapped in his greatcoat, and did not wake till next morning. Then I put the house in order and got a great heap of his stockings to darn. When I went to bed that night I was not very tired.

'I lay thinking and thinking, and I cannot tell how it was, I seemed to see so suddenly all at once how wicked I had been, and how wicked I had made him. It was just like being in hell to think of it all. I felt as if I should go mad, and at last I got up and lit the candle and sat down and wrote to him. I don't know just what I wrote, but I know that I told him I had been very wicked; it had been all one great lie; I had tried to look and act as thought I did not care for him, and I had made him do wrong. I told him I would never speak to him again or touch his hand, and that I would go away, but I would always love him. I must have said something more, for I wrote many sheets, but I don't know what it was. Perhaps it was the same thing over and over.

'It seemed to me as thought the morning would never come and I would go mad before it came. He had called me his little angel and his sunshine and I had been like a devil to him, making him sin, and now it was done and could never be undone.

'The next day they came. I thought he had got tired of me, for when he came in the dinning room where I was standing he hardly said goodday to me or looked at me. He took the letter from my hand and we never were together again. I told my aunt that evening that I was going away. She was very angry and said I was mad and very ungrateful, but that she would be glad when I was gone. Then I went into the nursery and wrote to the teacher of the school I had been to, and asked her if she would let me come and teach the little ones. I would not want money if only she would let me come at once. When I had done I sat thinking and it seemed to me as though I must go and tell his wife everything; it was sin, nothing else mattered, and it seemed as though if we told everything that it would be less. So I got up, but when I got to the door of her room I thought how angry he would be and so I went back. By and by, I went again; but now the light was out, and when I stood close by the door I could hear her breathing and his. I listened for a little time and then I went back again to my room. The next morning when I looked out at the window I saw him walking on the road that led to the beach, and I never saw him any more. I got an answer from my old teacher and I started that day, but I did not stay with her long. Perhaps I was very foolish, but it seemed to me as though, if I worked very hard all my life for other people and at work I did not like, it might make it right for him a little bit. I was very foolish, but I could not help thinking it would be of use, a little use. I always hated so to see blood and people that were in pain; so I got them to let me help in a great hospital, and I learnt to be a nurse. I used to feel faint at first, and as though I wanted to run away when I saw anything dreadful, but I used to think it was helping, and then I felt strong. I never heard of him any more, I thought he was tired of me before I went away, and that he would soon forget me. I thought so for twelve years and I never heard his name. But the other night I was sitting up with another old nurse. She was telling about a gentleman with whom she had gone out to South Africa. I was stirring the gruel before the fire and I did not listen to what she said till I heard a name; it was his name. Then I asked her to tell me all she could about him. She told me that he had some disease and the doctors said he must take a long voyage; but it did him no good. At last when they got to a little town in Africa they saw that he was dying. He did not like his wife to come near him or do anything for him, and all the day and all the night he lay groaning. At last one night just before the light came they saw that he was going. He lay quite still, but at last he opened his eyes and looked all round the room.

'"Come to me, come to me," he said.

'They asked him if he wanted his wife, but he said, "No, no; my darling, my little sunshine, once, just once, darling." He did not say anything more. And so now I am going to him,' said the grey woman, very quietly.

When Undine turned to put the locket in her hand, tears were in her own eyes; but on the woman's face was only that strange smile, sadder than any tears.

The voyage was almost ended. That night they would be in Table Bay.

Undine sat with her companion on the deck.

'Do you stay here or go on to Algoa Bay?'[2] she asked her.

'I must stay here,' the woman answered. 'I must earn money to take me on. I never worked for money before.'

'It is not very hard to live without it,' said Undine.

'No, I never wanted it till now,' said the woman, 'and a lady whom I had taken

---

2 Port Elizabeth.

care of paid my passage and my dog's. I don't know what made her so kind to me.'

A little while after, Undine got up and went down to their cabin. She got her little bag from under her pillow and took out her purse. It was not heavy; there were only ten pounds in it, the price of a brooch her grandmother had left her. She counted out five and quickly pulled out the small black portmanteau that contained the woman's work and slipped them into it; then she went up on deck again.

The woman was gone, and she sat there by herself watching the captain's pretty sister as she walked up and down with her hand on the arm of the handsome boy-man. He was not chatting with the other ladies this morning, nor playing with the children, but he carried her great white hat in his hand and looked down at the little black head beside him.

CHAPTER FIFTEEN

In an Ox Wagon

'Gold! What is Gold?' So we ask scornfully in the days of our ignorance. 'Gold! What is Gold?' We ask it derisively.

King Gold sits on his throne and laughs secure, for well he knows that sooner or later, if he withholds his cold light, the proud knee will bend and the stubborn hands will rise and the old prayer of humanity will come from the derisive lips:

'Oh, Gold, thou art King and Lord; if not the God, yet a God forever, in whose hands lie health oftentimes, and joy oftentimes, and the desire of the heart and of the eyes. Pour down upon us the light of thy countenance we beseech thee, O Lord!'

But the God of Gold is growing old and deaf now, like the other gods, and he often lets our prayers rise and die unanswered.

'Gold! What is Gold?'

Undine had asked it and laughed her glad mocking laugh in the frosty lane years before. She had thought it with a bitter heart and envy, as she looked in at the broken window of the wicked woman who had her baby. She had asked it of herself, when two months before she had thrown it from her and made up her mind to wander free over the world and enjoy life and learn. And she was wandering free and learning, but the enjoyment was still yet on the hills before. Yet she had not bowed her knee to King Gold – only thought that a purse heavier, a little heavier, were an improvement.

She was walking through the streets of Port Elizabeth, her head bent down to preserve her eyes from the rain of sand and fine stones that fell on the flat roofs with a sound as dismal and disheartening as the fall of sand on a coffin lid.

She had sat in the hotel till she thought it was better to go out and face it than sit there listening to its dreary music. Moreover, no work or any other good thing would find her while she sat there, and her money was surely taking wing at the rate of twelve-and-sixpence a day; so she went out into the street to escape the tap-tapping and to seek her fortune.

Africa, as it appeared in that desolate and sand-smitten seaport, was not the Africa of her memory. The old Africa with its great grass and Karoo flats and rough rock-crowned mountains, unridden and un-man-defiled old Africa, was little like the sand-smothered town in which she stood, which might have been in any country in Europe but for the ragged niggers slouching about the streets and the dark, dirty, half-clothed fish-boys who dragged their wares along with tails draggling in the sand.

One thing was certain, here she would not stay; though how to get away remained as yet an unsolved problem. One of her pounds was already gone, and four pounds take one nowhere in a country where all locomotion is at the expenses of muscle and sinew. She was attracted, like all others who were near enough to feel its influence, by the great magnet that draws to itself all who are good-for-nothing vagabonds, wanderers, or homeless – the Diamond Fields.[1] Three hundred miles of bush flat and Karoo are not to be bridged over by four pounds, however. Cobb and Co,[2] as it tore past her as she laboured up the street, made thicker, if it were possible, the thick cloud of dust around her; but it was not for beggars with four pounds to enter its red swollen body or perch on its crowded roof. Presently she stopped to take breath in front of a large store, before which was standing an ox wagon with a long span of red oxen. She stood resting and considering what was next to be done.

Why should a woman not break through conventional restraints that enervate her mind and dwarf her body, and enjoy a wild, free, true life, as a man may? – wander the green world over by the help of hands and feet, and lead a free rough life in bondage to no man? – forget the old morbid loves and longings? – live and enjoy and learn as much as may before the silence comes?

So she had asked herself on the first morning of her freedom, the morning after her husband's death, as she lay back in the velvet armchair of her boudoir while the maid stood behind her combing out her hair.

Now she had broken through conventional restraints and was free – free to feel that a woman is a poor thing carrying in herself the bands that bind her. Now she was free, but how to extract enjoyment from the present state of things was more than she could accomplish at that instant; and how long would she be able to maintain herself without getting under someone's thumb?

If she had been a man she might have thrown off her jacket and set to work instantly, carrying the endless iron buckets and coils of rope and wire with which the wagon beside which she stood was being laden. She might have made enough in half an hour to pay for a bed at one of the lower hotels, might have wandered about the town, seen something of life, and enjoyed herself in a manner. As it was, being only a woman and a fine little lady with the scent not yet out of her hair nor the softness rubbed from her hands, she stood there in the street, feeling very weak, bodily, after her illness, and mentally, after her long life of servitude and dependence – very weak and very heartsick.

Two men passed her carrying a large packing case, and even through the dust that descended before them her eyes could distinguish the 'New Rush Diamond Fields'[3]

---

1 Kimberley. The distance is 485 miles.
2 The line of horsedrawn coaches.
3 The Kimberley mine of 'the Diamond Fields' was, on discovery in 1871, called 'Colesberg Kopje', then 'New Rush', before the town was officially named Kimberley in 1873.

that was painted in great black letters on its lid. She stood still a moment to consider, and then stepped up to the back of the wagon, on the back of which a small tent was fixed. Between a gap in the closed sails a woman's *kappie* was visible. Undine raised one corner of the flap and looked in.

The part of the wagon occupied by the tent was not more than six feet square and was one great bed covered by a *velkombers*[4] on which were seated the owner of the *kappie* and two fat children. The former held in her arms a great baby whose clothes she pulled quickly down to hide its not over-delicate feet. It was a shrewd, bright face that was concealed by the *kappie*, the face of a woman of about thirty-two, which would not have been without its claims to beauty had it not been for the marvellous display of stumps made visible whenever her thin sharp lips moved. She was dressed in a black-and-white print, as was the fat and dirty baby at her breast. The two children were busy wrangling over a brown paper of sweets which their father had just thrown in for them, but they stopped as soon as the strange face presented itself under the sail.

'Is this wagon going to the Diamond Fields?' inquired Undine, while the woman, not best pleased at being found in her wagon trim by a stranger, was busy pulling down her sleeves. She answered in the affirmative graciously enough, but stared curiously at the intruder and wondered what could bring a lady to the back of her wagon on such a day with such a question.

'Do you know what the owner of the wagon would charge for taking a passenger to the Fields?' Undine asked again, with no hope that the contents of her purse would be sufficient, but thinking hurriedly that her shawl and one or two good clothes might bring her something.

'The wagon belongs to my husband,' answered the woman, 'and I'm sure he can't take anyone. You see, there is me and the three children, and the tent is small, and I could not undertake to care for anyone else. I would rather try and get someone to help me.'

'I would do all I could to assist you,' said Undine, 'and I have very little luggage. If you could make it convenient to take me I would pay for four pounds and should not mind doing anything.'

The woman looked at her *very* shrewdly now. There was nothing visible except a pretty pale face and a little black velvet hat, but they were scrutinised closely. She could not quite make up her mind, so resolved to solve this difficulty as she did many others by finding what view her husband took of the matter. She poked her head out in front, between the tent and a great box, and hailed him.

Mr Snappercaps, a huge sluggish English Africander, with mild light eyes and a red beard, approached, and she proceeded to inform him of the offer.

---

4 Skin rug.

'You don't mean to take her, do you? You don't know what sort of a character she may be,' said Mr Snappercaps. 'If she's dressed up it does not say much for her that she's knocking about by herself and wants to go to the Fields. Is she married?'

'I suppose she can mind the children just as well if she's married or unmarried,' said Mrs Snappercaps, 'but you never think *I* need any help.'

'I don't expect it's much help you'll get from her, but do as you like,' he said, and walked off to his work. His wife drew her head in, and, it being evident that he was decidedly opposed to her accepting the offer, all hesitation on the subject was at once put an end to.

After plying her with half a dozen questions, Mrs Snappercaps informed her that, if she would have her box there and be ready to start in fifteen minutes, she might come.

The tone and manner in which this information was conveyed contrasted somewhat sharply with that of ten minutes before; but when first the little black hat made its appearance she could not tell that its owner was not possessed of a phaeton and a score of silk dresses; now she was wiser, and acted accordingly.

In the middle of the afternoon a day or two after, the great buck wagon, with its long span of red oxen and heavy freight of wires and buckets, was creeping slowly along the sandy road. It was a sweltering day, and the small oven-like tent at the back of the wagon was buzzing and alive with little black flies of every shape and a pair of droning bluebottles.

The oxen, reluctant as they were to lift their weary feet only to put them down again on the burning road, and leisurely as they ploughed up the heavy sand with the great wagon wheels, yet raised a cloud of the finest dust which, covering hands and face and clothes with a thick red coat, seemed to enter the very windpipe. Undine was seated at the extreme edge of the wagon, Mrs Snappercaps having declared that under any other state of affairs she could not possibly find room to extend herself. She lay now with her arms and legs stretched out, her head on one pillow and another on her face to keep off the dust. Very fast asleep she was, if judged by the periodical snorts that at regular intervals proceeded from beneath it; but in truth very wide awake, with a small cylindrical curve made in the pillow straight from her eyes to the little black hat, now fast changing to a reddish brown.

Ferinando Shakespeare and Algernon Sidney were fast asleep, the former with the piece of fat mutton still between his lips which he had been engaged in consuming when overpowered by the heat and the motion of the wagon. It attracted to his countenance a score of black flies and one of the bluebottles, making it, if possible, a more interesting scene of animal activity than that of Master Algernon Sidney, whose infant charms were totally concealed by a coating of syrup, coffee, sand and flies.

The baby, otherwise Master John Wesley, was not asleep, however, but awake and endeavouring with furious kicks and struggles to precipitate himself into the road, or at the best on to the 'trap'.⁵ It seemed hardly impossible that he would ultimately succeed, for he was fat and powerful and there was not much strength in the 'bits of paws' that held him – 'bits of paws' being Mrs Snappercaps's designation for those useful appendages in the object of her scrutiny.

The baby was dirty, astonishingly dirty, several days of ox-wagon dirt having accumulated on him. Mrs Snappercaps saw this, and saw that someone else hated dirt, was always washing her hands and trying to rub the grease spots off her clothes; and so, by way of bringing down the things that are mighty and do exalt themselves exceedingly, Mrs Snappercaps ordained that no ablution should be performed on the person of Master John Wesley, and, moreover, that except when absolutely necessary, he should never be out of the 'bits of paws' for a moment.

Now also Mrs Snappercaps was desirous of ascertaining whether her employee would, when thinking herself unobserved, maintain that serene urbanity of manner which irritated and exasperated her yet more than her constant ablutions and her good English. Would she still keep her leg curved in that most awkward posture, to prevent if from touching Ferdinando Shakespeare's face? Would she yet do her best to keep the baby from bumping its head against the bottle bag, though it was clearly to be seen that she loathed it to the tops of her fingers?

To discover all this Mrs Snappercaps snored and breathed hard and looked out from under the pillow, only to see that, as far as any desired result was concerned, she might as well have saved herself the trouble. Ferdinando Shakespeare's face was not pressed nor the baby allowed to knock its head.

She was just about to throw off the pillow and declare that she didn't know when she had had such a sound sleep, when Mr Snappercaps, who was engaged in putting a new lash to his whip, dropped behind the wagon.

He was a great, good-hearted fellow, though he *was* fond of a glass of brandy and water when in pleasant company; so, when he looked up and saw the pale little woman endeavouring to manage his great baby and sitting on the very edge of the wagon and looking worn out and weary, his good nature and his ignorance led him up to the back of the wagon, and he said, 'Expect you're pretty near done up; not used to riding in an ox wagon and minding babies.'

These were the first words he had ever addressed to her, and, his conversational resources being exhausted by them and his whip being needed, he stepped out in front to try it on the backs of his oxen.

Mrs Snappercaps threw the pillow off her face, sat up and rubbed her eyes. John W had screamed himself stiff by this time, so she took him and, having pacified him, proceeded to loosen the comb-and-brush bag and, putting its not very delicate contents into the 'bits of paws', remarked that there was nothing so wretched as

---

5 The little movable stepladder at the back.

having nothing to do and that Undine had better clean them. 'It's miserable to have nothing to do,' said Mrs Snappercaps, asserting a fact the truth of which she had had ample opportunity for verifying during the last few days, during which the sum of her own labours had been to eat, sleep, and slap the children. Truly, Mrs Snappercaps had underestimated her own ability and womanliness when she imagined she might fail to extract her bread-and-meals' worth of labour from her passenger. Not that she was a hard woman, or a cruel one. Mrs Snappercaps was looked upon among her female acquaintances as an exceptionally kind-hearted and generous woman, better than the run of themselves, and no doubt they were right. She shut her eyes and ran away screaming if she heard they were going to kill a sheep; and she used to call Mr Snappercaps a cruel beast when he lashed his sticking[6] oxen – except she were very anxious to get on, when she sat still in the wagon and thought he did not cut half deep enough.

No, she was not a hard woman, only a woman, and she envied her white-handed soft-voiced little dependent as one feminine thing envies another. She was the daughter of a Lower Albany farmer who had sent her to a Grahamstown boarding-school, where Miss Sarah Jane had taught her to play the piano and make slippers and caps and use long dictionary words without the slightest idea of their meaning, and long words that are not found in any dictionary and whose meaning was known only to herself. When she went home was regarded by her elder sisters with mingled awe and envy and by her mother with unfeigned admiration. She reigned supreme, and only in her own mind was there a dim perception that, after all the money that had been expended on her, she was not quite the lady, not quite the genuine article.

Her mother never let her make bread or salt the meat, her sisters ironed her petticoats, and her father gave her an extra pound whenever they went into town, yet she ended by marrying Will Snappercaps, who rode transport and was the son of a neighbour. When she met in the street any of her old school-fellows who had since married attorneys or merchants, they always looked up into the sky, onto the ground, or at the houses, at anything but the particular spot of earth on which she stood. They were out of her reach, that upper ten who talked good English, dressed in taste, and went to balls; she could never retaliate on them. But now, good fortune had put into her hands one of the order, soft-voiced, white-handed, and refined as any of them, and for many stiff bows and for many clear cuts Mrs Snappercaps had to indemnify herself. Her heart rejoiced as the heart of a homeopathic quack might do who held under his thumb a licensed practitioner. Mrs Snappercaps's faith in the efficacy of vicarious atonement was not stronger than in other uncultivated minds, so she did not allow her joy to express itself clearly in her own mind, but it was there all the time as she sat on that sweltering afternoon watching the 'bits of paws' at their

---

6 When the wagon 'sticks fast' (in mud or deep sand, for instance), it is said to be 'sticking'.

comb-cleaning. She was certain, she remarked inwardly, that there was something wrong about her; there always was about people who were so agreeable and never got out of temper, never got savage with the flies, never were ruffled or put out by the jolts or the grouty[7] coffee or any of the innumerable evils attendant on an ox-wagon journey. And then, to be sure, as her husband had remarked, would a woman who was good for anything be knocking about in that way by herself? No, there was no doubt of it, she was a bad character, a very bad character; and her own – Mrs Snappercaps's – great goodness of heart had prompted her to do a very foolish thing in taking her. If she were not a sinner, where did she come by that diamond ring? If she had friends of the right sort, rich enough to give it her, would they not have looked after her? And a nice story this was about her husband being dead and her having no relations. Mrs Snappercaps was not a child and she was not born yesterday; no not she!

'You had better leave the combs alone,' she said; 'you don't seem to understand it; you sprang a tooth again without cleaning it. If a thing is not well done I would rather it wasn't done at all.' With which remark, the combs being now fully cleaned, Mrs Snappercaps seized them and the brushes and with great energy put them into the bag and hung them up; while Undine, her hands empty for the first time that day, sat watching the deep oscillating track of the wagon-wheels in the red sand.

After a time Mrs Snappercaps found the heat and closeness becoming something really unbearable, and she was about to direct Undine to loosen the front clap by way of producing a current of air when that individual proceeded on her own responsibility to roll it up. Mrs Snappercaps instantly discovered that her neck was stiff, that she had neuralgia in all the teeth on one side of her head, both of which complaints would be infinitely aggravated by such a proceeding; so the clap was carefully fastened down again, and Mrs Snappercaps endured suffocation for the rest of the afternoon with a martyr's fortitude.

But even Mrs Snappercaps must sometimes really sleep, and so it came to pass that night that she and her three children were snoring in chorus, while Mr Snappercaps plodded along at the side of his oxen, calling out to them every now and then drowsily as they stepped on steadily in the cool night air.

Up above the still stars glittered and gave out just light enough to make visible the great round clumps of bush through which they passed.

Undine crouched down in her corner at the back of the wagon and listened to the tink, tink of the tin coffee pot and mug that were tied to the roof and the tom, tom of the great iron kettle and gridiron that were fastened on the trap, and the creak, creak of the wagon. She could rest her head on the wooden blackboard and look out and feel herself again a little child, Socrates curled close in her arms. Frank's clear

---

7 Full of coarsely ground coffee grains.

light-hearted whistle came from the front box, her mother's voice sang the evening hymn as they rode home in the starlight from the town, and the loves and passions of her womanhood looked strange and unreal to her in the creaking wagon, under the light of her childhood's stars – the still, unchanging stars that shine on unaltered while our poor little systems go to ruin and desolation – the silent stars that can hold so many memories, which but for them would be forgotten, that we sometimes dread to look up at their white, faraway lights, for fear of hearing whispers and feeling the touch of fingers that can bring only coldness now.

Yes, the old faiths and old loves, they are written up there; and when we have put them from us and buried them deep, the night sky gives them all back to us.

About eleven the wagon stopped, and Mrs Snappercaps, by no means in the best of humours after being roused from her slumbers, allowed Undine and Mr Snappercaps to spread a skin counterpane at the side of the wagon and make as comfortable a seat as might be with half a dozen pillows against the hind wheel. Here she bestowed herself and her baby, while Undine took out of the back box the coffee, bread and ribs of mutton that were to form their repast.

Mr Snappercaps, worn out with his day's work, flung himself down at full length on that part of the counterpane which his wife had not appropriated, and in five seconds was sound asleep. Undine, when all was finished, sauntered off to a little distance among the bushes, where she could have a good view of the wagon as it showed in the light of the blazing fire.

It looked picturesque enough, the great red wagon with its little white tent and rows of iron buckets that glittered in the firelight. A little further on the tired oxen were dimly visible, lying down just where the yokes had been taken off their necks, too weary to look for food. Even Mrs Snappercaps, as she sat in her spotted print and white *kappie* hushing her baby, added to the scene; and her husband also, lying close to the fire with his hat drawn down and his head resting on his crossed shirt-sleeved arms. Among the bushes, a little to the right, the driver and leader had made their fire. The driver, a great heavy Basuto, lay in his master's fashion on the ground; the leader, a sprightly little Hottentot, sat watching the meat on the roaster with his wicked little black eyes. He had a more than usually apish appearance as he sat there with his knees drawn up to his chin.

After some time, when the meat was ready and the coffee made, Undine returned to the wagon.

'I thought you were inside,' said Mrs Snappercaps.

'No,' said Undine, 'I was walking about.'

'Walking about?' said Mrs Snappercaps. 'What on earth for?'

'It looks so nice at a little distance, the wagon and the fire,' said Undine.

Mrs Snappercaps gave her long flexible lips a little screw.

'I should think you had seen enough of ox wagons and fires by this time,' she said, and looked upon this proceeding as an additional proof of the badness of her employee's character; though why she did so she could not easily have explained to herself. She could hardly fancy that Undine had made love to the green bushes, or galavanted with the dry stumps even in the dark. But Mrs Snappercaps was unable to assign any reason for her walking off in the dark, and the story about the beauty of the wagon was on the face of it a lie; and, as there must incontrovertibly have been *some* reason, she felt sincerely persuaded it must have been a bad one.

Undine's wandering about in the dark proved her a bad woman; and that being proved, one did her no injustice in suspecting her of evil, even though there might be no harm in her wandering about.

Mrs Snappercaps's logic was conclusive, so she gave the coffee pot an energetic shake as she poured out Undine's basin, by way of winning her disapproval. She could hardly drink her own cup when she saw with what apparent unconsciousness and exasperating indifference the contents of the basin were drunk, grounds and all. 'All put on. What a hypocrite! That's the worst part of her,' thought Mrs Snappercaps, as with her stumps she tried to masticate a piece of tough mutton. 'It's worse than her immorality; I could get over that. Thinks she looks beautiful now, with her head on her hand, staring into the fire, and her hair flying about like a mad thing's.'

Whether she thought so or not, great good Mr Snappercaps, as he sat drinking his coffee, thought she looked tired and sad, and felt sorry for her, as he did for his Hottentot leader when he thought he was overworked.

When he had finished he rolled himself up in his blanket under the wagon.

'There's no use to tie the oxen,' he said to his driver. 'They are too tired to stray tonight.'

The morning came and brought woe to him who had trusted to the weariness of his oxen's legs, and double woe to him who hoped to recover them through those of his Hottentot.

The oxen had vanished and Jan was sent to look for them. He had followed on their spoor[8] for a little distance, when it suddenly came to his recollection that he had not had his sleep out. Accordingly, he ensconced himself snugly under a large stone, and in three minutes was wandering amid quids of tobacco as large as himself and brandy the very fumes of which made him merry.

From these visions he did not return till the sun, now inclining to the west, had burnt him out of his hole, when he rose and instantly retraced his steps. He appeared before the wagon with a limp and an air of extreme dejection. He had searched up hill and down *kloof*, but had seen no trace of them, and he rubbed his weary feet with his right hand as he spoke.

Mr Snappercaps saw there was nothing for it but to give him a good feed and himself to set off on the search.

---

8 Footprints

'The poor devil of a Hottentot must be tired,' he remarked.

Mrs Snappercaps smiled a mingled smile of pity and contempt. She was not a child, and she was not born yesterday, and she was up to Hottentots at least.

Mr Snappercaps returned late that night after a fruitless search; and neither on that day nor on the next nor on several after that was there any sign of the oxen. It was weary work, waiting there day after day. Sunday morning came. It was six days since they had decamped – six days of endurance of half the plagues of Egypt: six days of flies; six days of water red as blood, alive with monstrosities of every shape; six days of being devoured by red ants if one sought for shade under the bushes; six days passed in the care and company of three wretched, screaming, sun-oppressed children.

They had wellnigh exhausted everyone's patience and had made Mrs Snappercaps very desirous of improving others, and very virtuous. Her desire to improve others was made manifest by the copious corrections she administered to the Masters Ferdinando Shakespeare and Algernon Sidney; her virtue, by the petty but constant mortification of the flesh which she caused to be felt by the immoral person whom chance had placed in her hands.

On this Sunday morning Mrs Snappercaps woke early and poked her head softly out at the back of the wagon to take, unperceived, a survey of her antagonist's proceedings. That individual, in happy unconsciousness, sat on the trap just below her, reading a small shabby book.

'A Bible, no doubt,' soliloquised Mrs Snappercaps, as she drew her head softly back into the wagon. 'I could get over anything else, but her pretending to be religious – it's too much.'

She prepared a nice little homily to be delivered at breakfast-time on the duty of serving God in secret and unseen; and when she had finished lacing her boots, she poked her head cautiously out again.

On a second and closer inspection the book appeared to be no Bible, but, judging from its long words and dry look, she concluded it to be a volume of sermons. It was not so good as if it had been the Bible, but still, if judiciously modified, the homily might still be delivered with great effect.

At this moment Mr Snappercaps, who had been to the top of the mountain to see if any signs of the men or oxen were visible, returned.

'Having a read?' he said, wishing to say something kindly but not exactly knowing how.

'Yes,' said Undine, smiling and closing her book.

'No going to church today,' he said again. 'I don't mind it. I'm used to it. But I expect it won't seem like Sunday to you without.'

Undine made no answer, so, wishing to be very agreeable, he continued: 'What church do *you* belong to? Now *I* like the Methodists.'

'I belong to no church,' said Undine as she climbed off the trap and, slipping the unfortunate book, cause of many sorrows, into her pocket, proceeded to make the fire.

Now, making a fire seemed a particularly easy and pleasant occupation when watching a nimble little nigger throw a dozen sticks on one another and in half a minute produce a blaze big enough to roast a lamb by; but when once the sticks were in her own hands it seemed a very different matter. Surely they must be wet or of the wrong kind; for after she had expended a whole box of matches, two Grahamstown *Journals*, and all her breath in trying to blow them into flame, they remained as obstinately cold as though there were no combustibility about them.

Undine, having blown herself red and dizzy, was about to give up in despair when Mr Snappercaps's good nature brought him to the rescue. He handled the sticks with as much science as his own Hottentot could have shown, and in no time produced a roaring blaze.

Mrs Snappercaps from her spy point in the wagon saw all that passed and, perceiving a weak point in the enemy, she proceeded to place her artillery accordingly.

Presently the baby cried. Undine climbed up into the wagon and took him, but he was not easily pacified. 'Of course he cries, and he will cry till you take the hard thing out of your pocket,' said Mrs Snappercaps; 'it hurts his leg.' Undine took the book out; Mrs Snappercaps took it up.

'"Spencer's *First Principles*." Who wrote these sermons?' asked Mrs Snappercaps.

'Spencer,' said Undine.

'Spencer, of course; I know that,' said Mrs Snappercaps, perceiving for the first time that Spencer was the name of the author and not of the book. 'Of course I know his name's Spencer, but who is he? What is he? What does he believe?'

'I shall be glad to lend you the book,' said Undine, 'if you care to read it.'

'Not unless I know who he was,' said Mrs Snappercaps, combing the hair down over her eyes.

'What church does he belong to?'

'None,' said Undine.

'None! No church!' cried Mrs Snappercaps.

'What church do you belong to?'

'To no church,' said Undine, quietly.

'To no church, *no* church! But of course you don't mean to say you never go to chapel anywhere.'

'It's a long time since I went,' said Undine.

'Why, surely you're not a Roman Catholic, are you?' asked Mrs Snappercaps, putting down the comb and brush and dividing the hair that hung over her face with both hands.

'No,' said Undine, and prepared to follow Ferdinando Shakespeare, who had just descended from the wagon. But her interlocutor scented a rat and was not to be thus eluded. 'You must be *something*; everybody is *something*,' continued Mrs Snappercaps, fixing her dark eyes on her antagonist to make her words more impressive. 'You *must* be something; nobodby's *nothing*. You aren't a Unitrinitarian nor anything of *that* sort, are you?'

Undine very gravely disclaimed all knowledge of or participation in the errors of so deluded and extraordinary a body as the Unitrinitarians; but Mrs Snappercaps was not satisfied.

'Well, what are you, then?' she asked. 'You are not an atheist, or a deatheist, like Shakespeare or Votter or that wicked Bishop Colso who lives at Delagoa Bay, are you? You believe the Bible, don't you?'

'Ferdinando will be getting into the fire,' said Undine, quietly slipping down onto the trap, and showing her astonished catechiser that there really were limits to what she would endure in return for her bread and meat.

At night, a corner not big enough for a rat to crouch in; grouty coffee; meat which John Wesley had mauled; work to which the amen was never said: – all these she accepted with smiling indifference; but Mrs Snappercaps had spoken with a woman's own shrewdness when she remarked that it was those very agreeable quiet people who have the devil's will and spirit in them in spite of all their softness.

'There is no need to rush away in a rage,' she continued, speaking very rapidly and her lips becoming very moist. Undine, who stood leaning against the trap with the baby in her arms, might have edged in some answer, but Mrs Snappercaps's speech was as voluble as it was energetic and carried all before it.

'Of course you'll try to get away, of course you don't like to speak about it, when you know it's true. If it wasn't true, wouldn't you be glad to disown it, wouldn't you be glad to disclaim it, when charged with it? If that book you've got in your pocket was not some monotheistical nonsense, would you read it alone on the sly, in secret when there was no eye to see you? Oh! no! no! I wonder you are not afraid to say such dreadful, terrible things lest the God you don't believe in should strike you dead. I wonder that you weren't afraid, when the wagon went over the bridge, that God would break it down and let you tumble into the water. I wonder you weren't. If it wasn't – if it wasn't that I want to act like a Christian by you, I would not let my oxen take you one step further. How do *I* know how you may divert my poor innocent little children. Give me the baby!' said Mrs Snappercaps. Undine gave it, with all the more alacrity as Algernon Sidney had just fallen over the pole, to the great damage of his skin and nose.

At breakfast Mrs Snappercaps maintained a rigid silence; she ate with a purpose and drank copiously and with energy, and her husband clearly perceived that evil was approaching. He picked his chop and drank his coffee in silent uneasiness, though in what direction the storm would burst he could form no conjecture.

Breakfast being ended, Mrs Snappercaps climbed into the wagon, and after some trouble produced from one of the lowest boxes a great red Bible and a copy of

Wesley's hymns with great shinning clasps. Armed with these weapons, she again descended, and took her seat on a campstool that stood against the back wheel on the shady side of the wagon. Her husband, having already assumed his favourite posture, lay at full length on the ground, with his head resting on his arms.

'Mr Snapperacps, do you intend to listen?' said his wife.

'Listen to what?' asked Mr Snappercaps, looking up sleepily.

'To the word of God,' responded Mrs Snappercaps. When the question was converted into these terms it was impossible to reply in the negative, so he picked himself up and, leaning back against the front wheel, pulled his hat low over his eyes and wondered what on earth this new turn of affairs portended. Six years he had been married, and never yet had she used such instruments for administering to him the reward of his numerous transgressions; but today he felt a vague yet strong conviction that the books were to become the instruments of his correction for some as yet unknown dereliction from the path of duty. To Undine, who sat on the ground nursing the baby, she said, '*You*, no doubt, will not wish to remain; you may go. I compel no one to stay,' she continued. 'The worship and the love of God flow from the inner mind, from the outer soul – it must be free – it must be like the rays of heaven. I compel *no one* to stay.'

'If you have no objection, I shall remain,' said Undine, who felt no inclination to leave the shade of the wagon and march off into the broiling sun with Master John Wesley in her arms.

Mrs Snappercaps now seized Masters Algernon Sidney and Ferdinando Shakespeare, and seating them with great force very flat on the ground on each side of her proceeded to loosen the clasps of her Wesley's hymns. Having given out in the most approved style the whole of Hymn 1, she proceeded to sing it with great energy. Mr Snappercaps pulled the hat yet lower over his eyes and reckoned out for the hundred and fiftieth time how much he was losing by this delay with the oxen. Nor were the rest of the audience very attentive. Ferdinando Shakespeare was engaged in counting his fingers, Algernon Sidney in catching the ants that ran up his legs, while Undine sat wondering for how long a time John Wesley might be counted upon to remain quiet. That young gentleman sat motionless, with a finger hooked in his mouth, staring with wide-open eyes and rapt attention at the marvellous display of maternal stumps made visible on Mrs Snappercaps's upper and lower jaws during her vocal effort.

The last verse having at last been reached, Mrs Snappercaps put the hymnbook down on the ground exactly in front of her with great precision, and proceeded to open the red book. From its pages she made a careful and apt selection of passages applicable, she deemed, to the case of at least one of her hearers. These she read with much emphasis and many a long and ominous pause; denunciations against Pharisees, hypocrites and unbelievers she delivered with equal fervour and point. Having brought this part of the proceeding to a termination, she went on to part two of the programme. This consisted in reading the eleventh and twelfth chapters of the second book of Samuel, wherein is recorded how the amorous King of Israel walked on his roof at evening tide and beheld the limbs of the beautiful wife of Uriah the Hittite; how for love of them he caused the faithful soldier to meet his death before the walls at Rabbah; how the wife of Uriah the Hittite, when she heard that her husband was dead, mourned for him many days, and when the days of her mourning were ended went to the arms of the king.

Mrs Snappercaps had just reached this point in the very appropriate narrative she had selected, when John Wesley, no longer entertained by the dental display, made the most emphatic demonstrations of disapproval and obliged his nurse to carry him off.

Mrs Snappercaps now turned one eye on her husband, otherwise King David, and beheld him, much to her wrath, either pretending to be or really fast asleep. Preferring to act upon the assumption that he was pretending, she addressed him thus, but in a tone loud enough to awaken him, however far gone in the land of dreams:

'Thank you, Mr Snappercaps, thank you, but I'm not quite such a child as you fancy me, no, not by a long, long way.'

Mr Snappercaps opened his eyes.

'No, I'm not a child! I was not born yesterday! You are no more sleeping than I am, Mr Snappercaps; but I wonder, yes, I *do* wonder that you can act as you do. I wonder you can act so. You can sit there still, you can listen, when even that vile, lowly, venomous outcast felt it; she could not sit still and hear it; she had to get up and go away; but you, you have no more heart than a stone, than a Kaffir, than an adamantine. When David heard the voice of the Prophet *he* repented, but you, you have no faith, no pity, no affection. Ho-o-o! Ho-o-o! Ho-o-o!'

This latter sound was as the whistling of the wind through a keyhole, produced by drawing her lips into the smallest possible circle and moving her head to and fro.

It was her way when she reached climax and language failed her, and Mr Snappercaps was accustomed to it; but waking suddenly he felt confused, and looked out over the still Sunday landscape, the clear blue sky, the hazy brown hills clothed with clumps of dark green bush, looked out and wondered whether he were still asleep, whether Sarah Jane had taken leave of her senses, or whether he had.

'Oh, it's very nice to put on that innocent look,' said Sarah Jane. 'Very nice, so nice; but it won't do with me, no it won't. You think I've not seen it, do you? I've never heard you call my baby heavy, have I? I never saw you go down on your knees to blow the fire for her. I was asleep, fast asleep, of course, in the wagon. Oh yes – no, don't speak, don't try and deny it; it's no use, William, it's *no* use. It's not once, it's not twice; it's four times: it's *four* times that I've seen you with these eyes turn the chops over to find a raw one because she said she liked them raw. I saw it once' – Mrs Snappercaps's tone was now low and subdued – 'I saw it once, and I kept still. I said, "I'll see if he does it again, and you did it again, and you did it *again*. No, don't speak; I don't wish you to take more guilt upon your guilty soul. That puffadder,[9] that ringkals[10] has caused you to do sins enough without adding any more to them. Oh, William! William! How can you? How can you? How can you?'

'I don't know what you are talking about, Sarah Jane. You've gone mad,' said her husband, staring stupidly at her.

'That's right, Mr Snappercaps; say I'm mad, send me to Robben Island,[11] slaughter me, murder me, as David did Uriah. There'll be no one to trouble you then. But you shan't, no, you shan't; for the sake of my children I mean to live.' So saying, she raised the Masters Ferdinando and Algernon from the ground, with each arm and with as much energy as she had seated them.

'The man who stabs my body I can forgive,' said Mrs Snappercaps; 'but the man who runs a sword into your *soul* – no-o-o! no-o-o!'

'Oh, damn it all, Sarah Jane!' said Mr Snappercaps, rising, 'what confounded nonsense you do talk!'

'Curse and swear, Mr Snappercaps, curse and swear; that's right. They cursed the prophets and apostles, but it didn't hurt them. You can't deny what I've said; you know it's true; you love her, you know you do!'

'Oh, hang it! Damn it! Confound it all!' said Mr Snappercaps. 'I wish the woman would go to blazes, to the devil.'

'There is no need to wish that,' responded Mrs Snappercaps; 'every step that your oxen take they are bringing her nearer to him. What do you think she's going to the Fields for, if it's not to go to him?

'Oh, don't try and defend yourself any more, William,' seeing he was about to speak; 'don't, don't.'

'Look here, Sarah Jane,' said her husband as he turned to go away, 'if you give me any more of this nonsense I'll put the woman down at the first hotel we come to.'

'No, you won't,' said Mrs Snappercaps, who had no intention of losing her drudge, and he well knew it. 'No, you won't. Vile as she is, I'll act to her as a Christian should. I've said I would take her to the Fields, and I shall take her there.'

'Didn't know Christians took folks to the devil,' said Mr Snappercaps under his breath, as he walked off in the direction of the muddy *kloof* from which they got their water, to seek for a sleeping-place under some brush.

It was near evening, and as he had not returned, Mrs Snappercaps, after dozing all day in the wagon, descended to resume her old seat on the campstool, and took her baby. Undine, now her arms were free, sat with the children at the side of the road, making houses in the sand for them.

---

9 A snake.
10 A snake, one of the cobras.
11 Where lunatics used to be kept.

As mischance would have it, Master Ferdinando Shakespeare bethought him at this moment of getting a mug of water from the iron bucket that stood under the wagon, the better to moisten their sand. Stumbling over the *disselboom*[12] with the mug in his hand, its contents were deposited on his person, drenching his begrimed white pinafore.

'That is what comes of playing on a Sunday,' said his mother. 'You wicked little boys! Leave that sand alone.'

'It was my fault; I began the play,' said Undine.

'Well, I wish you would take his pinafore and wring it out; and if you have his, it would not be more trouble to take Algernon Sidney's and the baby's and given them a rub,' said Mrs Snappercaps, loosening the pinafore as she spoke.

Undine rolled them up with a piece of soap, and was just starting off in the direction of the *kloof* when Mrs Snappercaps, speaking in a high shrill voice, detained her.

'Oh yes, do go to him, go at once. I don't wish to hinder you, not at all. Go to him! Go! Go!'

'Go to whom?' asked Undine, looking round in blank astonishment, for she had been out of earshot when the little encounter of the morning took place, and imagined that Mr Snappercaps had gone in search of his oxen.

'Oh, you *sweet* little thing!' said Mrs Snappercaps. '*You* don't know that he is over at the *kloof*, do you? You never sit with your head stuck on your hand staring at the fire, just to try and look sentimental and make him feel sorry for you. *You* never do, do you? You would not do such a thing! And you never pretended you could not make a fire on purpose to get him to come and help you! And you don't get up early,' continued Mrs Snappercaps, speaking very rapidly, with the solitary canine, the only complete tooth she boasted, looking very strangely like a fang; 'you don't get up in the grey dawn and sit on the trap and try and look melancholy till he comes to talk with you. You would not think of doing such a thing! I'm glad to see you don't deny it; you can't,' said Mrs Snappercaps, rocking herself and her baby energetically to and fro.

The true state of affairs now dawned on Undine, who stood irresolute with the soap and pinafores in her hand, half inclined to laugh, half to enter a protest.

It ended in her doing neither, but asking very quietly whether Mrs Snappercaps could tell her in which *kloof* she would find the little fountain the driver had discovered that morning.

This cool manner of receiving her attack brought yellow spots to the corners of Mrs Snappercaps's mouth. Her only reply was a passionate and often repeated injunction to go to him, go to him, go, go, at once.

---

12 Pole of the wagon.

In direct opposition to these kindly instructions, Undine walked off through the bush in the direction of a small *kloof* where, instead of the great clumps of elephants-food and coonie[13] with which the hills were covered, a thin line of forest trees showed, at least sometimes, the presence of water.

The sun was almost setting; his rays made the great round clumps cast long oval shadows and the busy red and black ants were hurrying home with their last load of sticks. Undine killed many of them as she walked on quickly, and her heart was not very light as she passed in and out among the bushes. She had worked till she felt as though she had no head left, and no soul, and the golden glory of the sky and the still beauty of the bush said nothing to her. In her ears rang the yells of a baby; with its weight her arms ached, and her whole body too, she was wretched; she was finding out that there are aches other than those of the heart, and weariness unutterable that is not of the spirit. May a man's soul be tapped out through his muscle? Are there things more enervating and destructive to its life than being the idle plaything of a rich man? Is it crueller pain to be pricked by a woman's pins than lashed by a great affliction? When we labour like brutes, do our hearts become like theirs, till to eat and have rest becomes all our ambition?

The busy ants as they hurried home had no answer for her question, nor the still green bushes. Only one feathery outstretched arm of wild asparagus caught at her dress as she passed by and tore it, because she would not stay to loosen it, but hurried on angrily, petulantly. She was tired, she was wretched, she was disappointed.

To rush the world over seeking for happiness is a fool's work. Is it also a fool's to look for a life which, however hard and rough, shall be high and noble, a life worth living?

From being the useless plaything of a man, from dressing and eating and lounging on sofas, to nursing another woman's children, to making another woman's bed! Will life's changes be always so, shall we never get any higher? Oh, the things of life are very little, and the soul is great.

She walked on till, just as the sun set, she reached the little *kloof* and, forcing her way through the rocks and trees, came to the bed of the mountain torrent. She clambered down its steep bank and leaped onto the smooth white sand that lined its bottom. Then she paused to take breath and leaned against one of the great dark boulders that lay about on every hand. Long years ago the rushing torrent had torn them down from their home on the mountainside, but they lay very quiet and unmovable now on their bed of white sand. Over one of them, a little higher up in the bed of the torrent, a tiny stream of water trickled. The drops as they fell down slowly on the face of the flat stones below had the soft silver sound of faraway evening bells, and everything else was very silent. The silver band of water as it crept

---

13 Hardy shrubs.

through the sand made no sound, and the long low tremulous bank of maiden-hair fern, though it heaved and swayed to and fro in the stillness, made no sound. High on the western bank of the stream against the white dreamy evening sky, the branches of the oliven[14] trees were visible, with pale, quivering, up-pointed leaves. All the dark trees around lay glittering and motionless, but the air stirred those pale green upward-pointing leaves till they shook against the still white night sky; and on Undine, as she stood looking up at it, a great hush came and a great joy; for heaven is not a long way off, nor the beautiful for which we thirst. She dropped the pinafores she held in her hand and knelt down on the smooth white sand, and when she rose, just above the treetops the first star was shining.

She washed out the pinafores and then walked back with them to the wagon.

Mrs Snappercaps wondered that she sang so softly to the baby as she put it to sleep and sat half smiling in the firelight with only the remnants of their supper before her.

'She's a fool and out of her senses,' said Mrs Snappercaps as she leaned back against the wheel, munching the last biscuit.

Aye, and a fool sees more than a wise man, sometimes.

---

14 Wild olive.

CHAPTER SIXTEEN

New Rush

Every grace must come to an end, so philosophises the hungry child; and even the dominion of a Mrs Snappercaps has a limit and a termination. She and her little soul and her little tortures may shut out all the great varied world for a little time; she may seem to engulf everything for a little time, till all above, around, below is Mrs Snappercaps and her babies; but land must be gained at last, if it be only the land of death.

For Mr Snappercaps that land might be the only one in which his poor good old soul should find refuge; but Undine's deliverance came near at hand when the white tents of Du Toit's Pan[1] came in sight, gathered like a flock of white birds round their monster sandheap.

The next evening, free and emancipated, she stood before a store in New Rush, where Mr Snappercaps had just unloaded his wires and buckets. She felt very strong and very free as she stood there, with her box at her side and two shillings in her pocket, and watched the wagon roll slowly up the street and out of sight.

It was glorious to be alone again. Alone, though the street was so thronged with the streaming crowd of niggers and diggers returning home from the work that they kicked up the red sand into a lurid cloud over their heads – stark-naked savages from the interior, with their bent spindle legs and their big-jawed foreheadless monkey-faces, who, though they were going home to fire and meals, could hardly get out of their habitual crawl – colonial niggers half dressed, not half civilised, and with some hundred per cent more of evil in their black countenances than in those of their wilder brethren – great muscular fellows, almost taller and stronger than their masters, the white diggers, who formed a thin sprinkling in the crowd and who, in spite of the thick dust that enveloped them, might be distinguished by their more quick and energetic movements.

Undine stood watching the crowd as it rolled past, till the sound of someone closing the window just behind her made her look round. A very swell nigger with a real gold chain and a black cloth suit was putting up the bars.

He was a gentleman who made his living principally at night, but he found it useful to have some ostensible employment which might serve to account for his gold chain and black cloth, if ever he found himself in the close hand of the law.

---

1 Now a suburb of Kimberley.

She asked whether she might leave her box there till the morning.

'No,' was the prompt rejoinder, 'not if you don't give me a shilling.'

She gave it, for it was impossible to carry it with her or yet to leave it there in the street. She saw it safely deposited in the store, and then walked off in search of a bed of some kind, nothing doubting but that her shilling would gain her a resting-place, if it were only a little square of hard ground in the corner of a tent.

She went to a greasy-looking yellow canvas house with some kind of sign over it, in front of which half a dozen men were lounging. In the house there was only one woman, very gaudily dressed and very florid, whose eyes Undine imagined saw right through her pocket and purse and beheld the one poor shilling that lay there in solitude. She wished herself out in the street again, but it was too late now.

'Can I get a bed here for tonight?' she asked.

'She's a bad one,' thought the woman, who, being one herself, ought certainly to have judged rightly.

'You can get a bed for four and six,' she said; and Undine with her shilling made a very speedy exit.

Out in the street once more, she plodded on through the wilderness of canvas, past round tents, square tents, torn tents, and whole tents; past canvas houses and wooden houses and iron houses, and nondescripts. There were places enough and people enough, but just no place for her. The fresh night breeze as it crept among the tents struck her chill and made her feel cold and heavy to her heart. She was now in the poorest and most wretched part of the camp which lay around the Circus, and was walking on slowly when an empty scotch cart, coming home from the Kop[2] and tearing down the street in the gathering darkness, caused her to step quickly out of its road and almost into a small open tent.

It was hardly dark yet but there was a candle alight in it, and at a great packing case a dark bright-eyed Malay woman stood ironing white shirts. On another case close at her side, a heap of articles, still waiting to be done, lay piled. There was little else in the room except a torn red curtain covered with lions, which marked off the sleeping-place. On the floor sprawled the woman's brood, forming a motley forest of dusky arms and legs. She was so engrossed in her work that she did not notice the intruder's presence till she had wished her good evening, then she looked up quickly and curiously.

'Could you tell me where I could get lodgings for tonight?' inquired Undine when her salutation had been returned.

'No, not in this part of the Camp,' said the woman; then eyeing her sharply, 'Have yer been long in New Rush?'

'No,' replied Undine. 'I arrived this evening.' A pause followed, then Undine said:

---

2 Colesberg Kopje, later the Kimberley Diamond Mine.

'Perhaps you would be so kind as to tell me where I might be able to get work. I should be very much obliged to you if you could.'

'Work?' said the woman. 'There's work enough if there were only hands to do it. What sort of work do yer want?'

'Ironing – any kind of work,' said Undine. 'I don't care what.'

The woman looked at the great pile of ironing on the case beside her. She must get it done that night though she stood over it till morning. So she said:

'If yer can iron, yer can come in and help me get these things done and stay here tonight, but I can't give yer a bed; we've only one and that's only sacks.'

So Undine stepped into the tent, to pass her first night at New Rush in ironing gentlemen's pocket handkerchiefs and nightshirts, leaving the other shirts for the more experienced iron of Mrs Snods, which glided over them with marvellous rapidity and ease, leaving no singe or crease in its track. By and by the noise and squalling of the children ceased as one by one they fell asleep on the ground or crept off to the sacks; only the eldest, whose occupation it was to carry the irons in and out, remained awake. He was an over-worked, under-grown boy of about nine years, with a very solemn face and a pair of squinting bead-like eyes that were always trying to see each other across his nose. He wore a narrow-brimmed crownless hat, from the top of which his curly black hair rose in a great bunch; the tattered remains of a red tancord jacket and trousers covered his body; on his feet he carried a solitary boot, whose sole was loose and, at every step, flapped solemnly as he passed in and out with the irons. When not so occupied he stood bolt upright before the packing case, with his hands clasped in front of him, slowly twirling his thumbs, always in the same direction and always very regularly.

About twelve the last shirt was finished, and Undine, half asleep, crept into one of the great packing cases and slept soundly till morning. When she awoke she found the woman already busy putting fresh clothes into starch, and Tommy just starting off with last night's work. It was agreed that Undine was to remain there that day, and in consideration of her assistance was to get food and a bed in the packing case that night. Before setting to work, however, she started off in search of her box. It was a real New Rush morning. The fresh air seemed thrilling with a life that even in the close man-defiled camp it could not be robbed of; it crept among the tents and houses and brought back for the moment the rose to the sunburnt sallow faces of the dirty children, and made Undine feel brave and able to face anything. She was almost sorry when, after wandering about for a little while, she discovered the store at which her box had been left. Before it stood a digger examining some picks that had been placed outside and a couple of naked niggers who were gazing affectionately at a row of guns. In the doorway leaned the swell nigger with his legs crossed, playing with his watch chain.

'I've come for the box I left here yesterday evening,' said Undine. The nigger pointed with his thumb over his shoulder.

'There it is,' he said.

Undine went in and saw it standing against the counter.

'Is there anyone here I could get to carry it?' she asked. 'It's not very heavy.'

'No,' said the nigger.

'Can't you? It's not very far,' she said, holding out the shilling.

He took it without making any reply, and spreading out his white handkerchief upon his shoulder to prevent the nap from rubbing off his coat, he raised the trunk.

Undine led the way; he followed close behind; but they had not gone very far when the sound of his loudly creaking boots suddenly ceased, and looking round she was astonished to behold her box deposited in the middle of the street, and the tall black form of the nigger disappearing round the corner.

'This is not the place; you have made a mistake,' she said.

The nigger was not a man of many words, so he merely screwed up one eye very tight and opened the other very wide, and walked off. Undine went back to her box and stood by it, looking at the passers by, but none were available for her purpose. There were troops of niggers going to work at the Kop, and sharp little diamond-buyers going to look for the worm,³ and busy diggers in a desperate hurry, with their sleeves rolled up above their elbows. To none of them could she apply. At last a good stupid-looking Kaffir made his appearance. He had no bucket or pick and seemed to have nothing to do, and though he stared stupidly at her English and broken Dutch, he soon comprehended the meaning of the scarf she held out to him; and the trunk was shouldered once more, Undine taking care to walk behind him. When she reached the tent Tommy had just returned with three loaves of bread, and the solitary knife of which the establishment boasted not being forthcoming, Undine opened her box and produced a handsome silver-mounted penknife. The bright black eyes of the Malay woman marked it eagerly, and marked also the rich red shawl that covered the contents of the box. She watched the knife as it cut the bread and watched it as it went back into the box, and then began ironing again. Presently she called to Tommy to come out with her to the back of the tent and help her chop some wood. Tommy went, but there was no sound of chopping, nor, when they came in a few minutes after, was there any wood to be seen.

Undine, who was busy ironing, never noticed this; something in one of the children's faces had reminded her of what lay in a little English grave far over the water.

The woman began ironing, too, but presently she stopped and, leaning both elbows on the table and fixing her bright eyes on her companion's face, she said:

'I've been thinking that perhaps yer'd like rather to get work on yer own account; if yer *would*, why, I knows a Mr MacCuligan who pays well, he does, and he's not

---

3 That the 'early birds' were out to catch.

over-particular neither. I would not give him up, but, yer see, I've got more work than I can manage, as 'tis. You see, everybody knows me, that's the thing; they know what I'm a *honest* woman, would not touch a button. It's the character as brings the work. If nobody knows yer, why, yer won't get a shirt to iron,' said the woman, still fixing her bright eyes on Undine's face.

Undine wondered, if that were the case, how anyone ever came to be known, but she answered that, until she got irons and a place of her own and knew something of ironing, it was useless for her to think of taking work.

'Oh, yer could use some of my irons; I've got a lot yer see; and wood and such like yer could pay for, yer know, and Mr MacCuligan *he* don't care how his shirts are neither.'

Somehow Undine did not take vastly to this idea of doing Mr MacCuligan's ironing, but she felt touched by the woman's kindness; she cold not pain her by refusing to take advantage of it.

It was very hard to be a stranger at the Fields, the woman said; she had known what it was; but when once a person got known, why, there was more work than they had hands for.

'It's an awful paying thing, ironing is,' said the woman, 'awful paying. It's as good as having a claim in New Rush Kop, it is'; and when she saw Undine cast a glance round the empty tattered tent she added quickly:

'To yer it would be, of course, I mean. I've got so many brats, what I makes goes.'

After a little more conversation it was decided that Undine, with Tommy for a guide, should set off to Mr MacCuligan's to fetch the ironing.

'It's a long way,' said the woman, 'and perhaps yer'll think it round about, but the ways in this Field *is* round about. Tommy, he knows the way to Mr MacCuligan's well, he does. Don't yer, Tommy?'

Tommy nodded his head very confidently and was soon pattering along the road in front of Undine, the flying sole of his boot flapping up and down at every step.

They turned in the direction of the West End, and Undine, as she trudged behind him, tried to be profoundly philosophical and to place before herself very clearly her own advanced ideas on the subject of labour.

How superficial were the general ideas on the subject. Is not all work, if it be earnestly done, noble and ennobling? Is not all labour worship, be it only scraping a carrot or ironing a shirt? No longer would she be bound be prejudice, but, leading a life based on reason, she would enjoy the greatness of the man who labours.

They had now reached the West End, that most desolate wilderness of gravel-heaps[4] and tents, the tents for the most part not arranged with any attempt at order

---

4 The 'debris' heaps – the residue after the diamonds have been washed and sifted from the diamondiferous earth in which they occur.

but forming acute and obtuse angles of every degree. They with their gravel-heaps are pervaded by a melancholy air of decayed greatness. To Undine it seemed a more desolate spot than the most barren plain of the Karoo as they wandered in and out among the gravel-heaps on which the blazing sun was now pouring down dazzling light – blue gravel-heaps and yellow gravel-heaps, new gravel-heaps beside tents, old gravel-heaps, where once, in better days, tents had been. Up them and down them, over them and round them, before them and behind them, their course was like that of the wind which goeth to the south, and turneth to the north, and whirleth continually.

'Are you sure this is the right road?' she inquired of her dilapidated little guide, who was trotting on steadily before her.

'It's the way,' he answered confidently, turning his head but not his body, and with both eyes still fixed most solemnly on his nose; 'it's the way.' So Undine plodded on.

'Why, I thought we passed this tent with the barrel before it a little while ago! Are we not almost at Mr MacCuligan's yet?' she asked again after a little time.

'It's the way,' said Tommy, shaking his head confidently three or four times, but not even looking round; and soon they found themselves in the Circular Road.

The Road was lively and busy enough, and the glare of the sun on the white road was almost blinding. A scotch cart drawn by a wretched mule and containing a huge barrel of water rattled past them. It leaked, and some ragged little savages, one white and the rest black, were clinging to the cart with their mouths wide open and upturned to catch the drops as they fell.

'Where can I get a drink of water?' inquired Undine of her guide, the bright drops making her more thirsty than ever.

'You can buy some at the well,' was Tommy's answer.

Buy some! Undine walked on and tried to forget she was thirsty, and wondered what the charm of these strange Fields might be that drew all to them.

'If we're not near Mr MacCuligan's yet,' said Undine, 'I think I shall turn back. I can't go on any more.' She was growing dizzy from the fierce heat of the sun, and the white tents seemed to throb before her, and the burning sand into which they sank ankle-deep at each step blistered her feet.

'It's the way, but yer don't get there if yer don't keep on,' said Tommy, looking back over his shoulder but never pausing for an instant.

Undine, fixing her eyes on the flapping sole of his shoe, followed on.

They were in the best part of the Camp now, where tents were scarce and pretty little canvas houses with verandas and reed fences lined the road on every side.

Before one of these Tommy stopped.

'There's Mr MacCuligan's,' he said, 'and I'll run round to the back and see if he's in.'

While Undine stood waiting for his return, she leaned against the reed fence of the house that stood at her right and looked over into the enclosure. There was a new canvas house with a pretty veranda, at the ends of which hung great Venetian blinds to keep off the sun and wind. On the veranda were some green garden benches and two large cane armchairs. In one of them sat a lady, a delicate milk-white thing dressed in pale blue, with rippling gold hair that was simply gathered into a knot at the back of her small head. Undine looked at her breathlessly. Women as beautiful, more beautiful, she had often seen, but none had ever looked to her as that woman did, contrasted with the coarse clay she had looked at for so many weeks, and contrasted with the boiling, toiling, sandy, grimy world around them. The lady's white slender hands were crossed softly over the gamboge cover of the novel that lay in her lap, and she leaned back with closed eyes, looking like some fairy queen whom a strange chance had transported into the land of dust and diamonds. Undine leaned long against the fence, watching her till she slowly opened her eyes and looked up. They were straight-out-looking, cloudless baby-blue eyes; there was not much expression in them when they fixed themselves on the head and battered hat that showed themselves over her fence; but Undine limped away quickly and looked down at her own 'bits of paws', already brown and rough, and at her own dust-begrimed garments, and felt a little ashamed of them. What are fine clothes, and a fine skin? Well, nothing, just nothing, when you come to reason about them, and just everything when you come to look at them.

Undine limped away as quickly as might be to the back of Mr MacCuligan's compound, but when there she was astonished to find no opening by which Tommy could have gained an entrance to make his inquiries, and no Tommy was to be seen. The fence was very high, but, mounting on a gravel heap that lay against it, she was able to look over. A coolie was squatting in the shade, cleaning a pair of boots. Undine inquired whether he had seen anything of her guide and whether the compound were Mr MacCuligan's. To both these questions the coolie replied by shaking his head and staring. Did he know where Mr MacCuligan lived? The coolie shook his head again. Didn't live in that part of the Camp. Didn't know him if he did.

Undine dropped down on the ground in the shade of the high fence and held her throbbing head between her hands. She tried to think, but before she knew she had dropped into a heavy sleep.

When she awoke it was almost evening and the cool breeze was blowing in her face. She felt better after her sleep, though her feet were still blistered and her legs trembled a little. She made her way back into the street, and after not many inquiries found herself once more in the neighbourhood of the Circus, and was soon in sight of the iron[5] canteen, that she knew stood next the tent she was in search of.

When she stood before it, Undine raised her hand to her forehead, for surely the

---

5 Corrugated iron.

terrible heat of the day had touched her reason. She looked and looked again. There was the iron canteen on this side; there was the shoemaker's tent on the other; but the tent she looked for and the box she came for were nowhere to be seen. A good-natured man who stood at the door of the canteen noticed her bewilderment and called out: 'If you're looking for the Malay woman who used to take in ironing, she's shifted early this morning. If she's got work of yours there's not much chance of your seeing it again, I'm afraid. She was a bad lot,' said the man, stepping back into his house to serve a customer.

It took her a moment fairly to understand her situation, and then she soon persuaded herself that it was a most fortunate occurrence that had befallen her and freed her from her possessions. Were they not more trouble than they were worth? And had not experience taught her a lesson which, as that biter dame teaches nothing for nothing, left her nothing to complain of?

She began slowly to retrace her steps, thinking the while that she clearly perceived where her mistake had been. She had allowed her pride to keep her from her own class, from the white-handed, silver-voiced people of refinement and polish – that was the only reason why she had fared so ill.

With that cool veranda and its milk-white blossom in her eyes, she pressed on through the now crowded and busy evening streets till she came in sight of it once more.

Just as she had sat there in the morning, the lady sat there now, only that she had now a pure white dress, and in place of the gamboge-covered book she held now a small china cup. A few rays of the setting sun had found their way under the veranda and played on the rippling hair till it glittered like burnished gold.

When Undine's dusty figure and battered hat appeared before her, she raised her clear blue baby-eyes from her teacup and looked at her – looked very straight, and said: 'What do you want? Work? Yes, I have plenty of work.'

Undine's eyes followed her tall graceful figure as it moved into the house.

She returned in a moment with a small child's garment in her hand and held it out.

'You can take this first,' she said. 'If it is well made I will give you two shillings for making it – if it is well made,' she said in a clear measured voice, and, without giving the dusty little figure before her a second glance, sank down into her chair and resumed her teacup.

Undine hesitated and spoke again, for work, without needle or thimble or cotton to do it with, would be small help.

'I will give you needles and cotton, if you wish it,' the lady said, 'but not a thimble. I never do that; and sixpence must be taken off the needle and cotton.'

The little reed gate closed behind Undine, and soon she was again threading her way thought the crowded streets – crowded with home-goers. They were all going to a place of their own; even the naked Mahoras[6] had a pot of mielie[7] pap and a skin waiting for them; but she wandered on till she found herself at the entrance of the Kop they had just deserted. She sat down to rest on the side of one of the mountains of gravel between which the road passed, and, when the camp below was aglow with evening lights, and the noise and stir in its tents and streets became louder and stronger, she rose up and walked into the Kop in the bright moonlight. It was like entering the city of the dead in the land of the living, so quiet it was, so well did the high-piled gravel heaps keep out all sound of the seething noisy world around. Not a sound, not a movement. She walked to the edge of the reef and looked down into the crater. The thousand wires that crossed it, glistening in the moonlight, formed a weird, shinny, mist-like veil over the black depths beneath. Very dark, very deep it lay all round the edge, but, high towering into the bright moonlight, rose the unworked centre. She crouched down at the foot of the staging and sat looking at it. In the magic of the moonlight it was a giant castle, a castle of the olden knightly days; you might swear, as you gazed on it, that you saw the shadows of its castellated battlements, and the endless turrets that overcrowned it: a giant castle, lulled to sleep and bound in silence for a thousand years by the word of some enchanter. You might gaze until you almost saw the ivy clinging to its yellow crumbling walls, till you almost saw the figures of brave knights and lovely ladies, whom the death-like sleep had overtaken as they wandered on the castle terraces, till the motionless horse and the small arched window and the mighty dragon resting in the gateway were all visible.

Undine, as she crouched beneath the staging, looking at that silent moonlight wonderworld, forgot she was hungry and forgot she was weary, and, when she grew drowsy, dropped asleep on the ground with her head resting on her work.

The next morning the turning of the wheel[8] overhead aroused her. It was hardly light, but the Kop wakes early, and there were many men at work already among the staging. None of them seemed to notice her, and she got up feeling a little stiff and a little cold. There was nothing of beauty about the scene before her now; *that* had gone with the moonlight. It was nothing now but a great oval hole in the ground where worshippers of King Gold burrow and scrape and scratch, all in his service.

Very dull, and very prosaic now – unless indeed one had happened to be so high mounted above earth that all things fell into perspective, when even Colesberg Kop with its grovelling and grasping might, like niggers and bluebottle flies and rouge pots have a charm, a beauty of its own.

But Undine was not high mounted nor was her soul inclined to soar that morning; rather to grovel very pitiably. She was cold, she was stiff, she was hungry,

---

6 Natives.
7 Pap of ground maize.
8 A haulage wheel on the rim of the mine.

and she held the creed of the hungry – that ideas are delusion and sentiments a snare, that the way of the world is the wise way and leads to bread and butter, and that all ways which lead elsewhere are inventions of the devil and must be foresaken. She made her way into Main Street, and as she turned the corner she saw a great naked nigger devouring a huge lump of mielie-meal pap which he held in both hands as he passed down the street on his way to work. She thought him the happiest soul she had passed that morning as she walked on looking for a place where she might sit down and work.

No such presented itself till she found herself free of tents and houses on the long low grassy ridge that separated New Rush from Du Toit's Pan. There she sat down, screened by the low scraggy bushes, and began to work.

She stitched as one stitches who stitches for bread, but the calico was stiff, and without a thimble the needle hardly went through, and it made long stitches and little ones, and worked a small hole in her finger which stained the work with little drops of blood. Yet she worked away, without pausing, for an hour, then she sat still for a moment and lay down upon the ground.

It was so strong and drawing, that earth; she stretched out both her hands and clung to it as she used when a little child, as we can cling only when we are weary and heartsick and lonely, as we must cling to something if it be only a tree stump or a stone, feeling as if we were not then so forsaken.

It was a bright warm morning, but she was cold from hunger, and underneath the ground it must be warm, so warm. The earth, the dear old earth that has been mother to us all and must cover us all again sooner or later – it would be so easy to drop asleep upon it, so much better than to go on living with nothing worth living for.

'I will die,' she thought. 'Why should I go on like a fool, labouring and striving to keep a life that is worthless? I will lie still and die.'

She turned her face round and looked at the grass on which she lay. Mingled with it were tiny blue and red bells and a bright creeper with yellow flowers. The sunshine came through the low bushes and danced on their golden faces, and up above the bushes she could see the clear blue sky.

It is not *all dark*, it is not *all* evil in this life; while the sky hangs overhead and the many-tinted earth lies at our feet, there will always be what is beautiful, always be what makes life worth the battle; and her heart grew strong again. Very empty life may be, very useless, but worth having while there is sunshine.

Hour after hour Undine sat there stitching, and the work became more stained and the stitches bigger and her hands trembled more. At last by midday it was finished. She rolled it up and sought her way back to the canvas house with its cool veranda and green Venetian blinds. The lady was inside and opened the door, looking as fresh and fleecy-white as she had done the day before. She took the work from Undine and examined it carefully.

'I don't take such work,' she said, raising her round baby-blue eyes to Undine's face. 'You must take it back and unpick it carefully and wash it, or if you wish you can leave it here; but of course I can't pay you for it. It is for a bazaar and should have been kept very clean.'

They were so pitiless, those baby-blue eyes.

Undine felt the tears starting to her own; so without giving any answer she turned round quickly and went out again to the hot sandy street.

As bad as a beggar! Crying for sixpence! Faugh! She hated herself.

She had undertaken to do the work, she had done it badly, she had got what she deserved. Besides, was it not for a bazaar that was to pay for a church? There should be no stains or long stitches in work intended for such purpose. She was in fault, no one else.

'Old clothes bought here,' was written in large letters on a piece of battered cardboard that hung at the door of a little wooden house. Undine noticed it and went in. She had nothing to sell but a fine white handkerchief, for which the woman gave her sixpence, which at the next shop she exchanged for a drink of water and a small piece of bread, such a small piece. When she sat down on the shady side of some gravel heaps that lay behind the houses, she held it in her hand and sat looking at it for a long time before she began to eat. She had felt so hungry in the morning, she could have made friends with the naked Kaffir for the sake of his mielie-meal pap; and now she sat there with a lump of bread in her hands and could hardly eat it. Slowly breaking off little bits of crust here and there, she got through half, and with the remainder still in her hand laid her head drowsily on the gravel and for half an hour lay there almost sleeping, but hearing always the rumbling of the carts as they passed in the street. When she aroused herself she felt gnawingly hungry and very glad of the bread, which she still ate very slowly to make it go the farther.

Not far from her, crouching on the ground with his head between his paws, was a great brown dog; surely the leanest and lankiest that walked New Rush. While she had slept he had crouched there, watching the piece of bread in her hand, and now with half-closed eyes he looked at it still.

Undine looked at it too and then at him, and then took another bite, and then looked at him again, and then at the bread in her lap; and feeling sure that if she waited it would not be there much longer, she took it up and threw it from her straight into the hungry jaws that were opened wide to receive it.

Almost without a gulp it was gone, and, resuming his old posture, the dog waited for more, but none came. Picking up the crumbs that lay in her lap, she rose to go. The dog sprang up too, and, sidling nearer to her, proceeded to perform around her a grotesque dance, at every step of which the sharp bones threatened to protrude through the brown skin.

When she walked away he tried to follow her, but she drove him from her again and again. 'Go away,' she said. 'Go away. Do not follow me. If you do I shall learn to love you, and I am tired; I have had pain enough.'

The afternoon light was beginning to grow old and yellow when Undine, passing among the tents at the North Side, was attracted by a small figure seated on the ground between two tents. 'Twas a child of it might be twelve years. She was leaning back against an old box, with her naked feet stretched out in front of her, and the afternoon sun looked full into her face and on the great shock of red hair that hung around it. Everyone else Undine had passed had seemed so hard at work and so engrossed, even the little children in their play and the women in their talk; but here sat someone alone and doing nothing except gazing down at the half of an old iron three-legged pot which she held in her lap.

Undine came near her.

'What have you got there?' she asked, softly.

The girl raised her head quickly and looked up. It was a broad freckled face with very little forehead, and that little wrinkled and knit in every direction, with a great heavy mouth and a pair of clear grey eyes.

Before she answered Undine she fixed them on her, and then said in a low, sullen tone, 'Looking at my plant.'

Undine stooped down and saw, surely enough, growing in the broken pot, the tiniest of rose slips not half an inch high and crowned with two tiny green leaves.

'Do you like flowers?' Undine asked.

'Yes.'

For a moment the sullen look vanished and a smile that parted the heavy lips showed a set of dazzling white teeth; then it settled down on the child's face again and she looked at her pot.

'It's the first flower I have seen growing here,' said Undine, touching it softly with her finger.

'A gentleman threw it away one day. It had a withered rose on it then; but I put a white bottle over it, and I hold it in the sun all day, and now it's growing, you see.' She touched its little leaves softly and caressingly with her finger as she spoke.

'Don't you get very tired of sitting still with it all day?' asked Undine.

A very black look came over the child's face as she answered shortly, 'I can't walk; my back's hurt.'

'And so you sit here alone all day nursing your flower.'

'Mostly, but sometimes the woman who stops with father don't always go out. I wish she always did. When mother was here she always stayed in, but she's dead,' said the child. There was infinite satisfaction in the tone in which the last three words were uttered.

'Have you been long unable to walk?' said Undine, laying her hand softly on the red head.

'Since she beat me the night before she died.' She spoke more sullenly than ever and twitched her little brown toes backwards and forwards.

'What do you do to try and get better?'

'Nothing,' said the child. 'One of those gentleman that go about with the little black bags and the sugar pills, he stopped and talked to me one day and he gave me something to rub with, but I can't rub it and there is no one can.'

'Can't I rub it for you?'

The child looked up half suspiciously, and then her eyes brightened a little.

'It's in the tent, and Mary Jones would be angry if anyone went in when she's gone out. Do you live far from here?'

'I don't live anywhere,' said Undine. 'I am looking for work.'

The child scrutinised her from head to foot, with the shrewd suspicious old woman's look that the faces of Field children so soon learn to wear. Then she said:

'What kind of work?'

'Anything – ironing.' She would have added, 'Needlework,' but a short experience had made her very wise, and she knew that a man's dog is an animal more enviable than a woman's friend if so be the one is mistress and the other maid. Needlework must be done for women, ironing might be for men, so she decided in favour of the ironing.

Her red-headed little companion meditated for a time, then she said, "Mary Jones has lots of ironing in the tent, and she always drinks too much to do it. If you stay till she comes I think she'll let you get some.'

So Undine sat down on the ground beside her and waited.

CHAPTER SEVENTEEN

Little Irons

Six months after, Undine stood in her own little tent, sorting and piling into heaps the ironing she had just finished. 'Twas a New Rush winter's morning; in the blue sky there was not a cloud, and if it was cold and numbing in the inside of tents and on the shady side of gravel-heaps, out in the sunshine it was warm and genial.

She was hurrying to get into it, and truly to impartial eyes there was nothing very alluring in the interior of the little tent. 'Twas a small palace, six feet by eight, and held three packing cases. The largest was a table, covered over with shirts. The second was a bed; it had low sides which lay flat on the ground and served to keep off the wind which at night blew in chill under the skirting. The smallest had a kind of tick; it was a desk and general repository. It did not lock, but that mattered less, as its only contents were paper scribbled over and clothes that would not have paid a Kaffir the time it took to steal them. It was an empty place, and cheerless it would have looked to other eyes; but to Undine not a yellow water stain in the canvas nor a mark in the cracked poles, nor a knot in the rough cases but had its own story, and a pleasant familiar face showed itself in each of them. Even the old black bottle stood in the corner made home, more home. She might have changed it now for a candlestick, but so many pleasant thoughts hung round its old black neck that the bottle kept its ground.

Placing on a tray one of the piles of ironing, and putting on the huge white *kappie* which had replaced the battered silk hat and very much added to the respectability of the ironing woman, she went out into the sunshine, buttoning down the door after her.

The tent stood in a quiet corner of the Camp on the outskirts of the North End. The only very near neighbours were a family of Dutch Boers who camped on the right. On all other sides it was surrounded by low gravel-heaps, among which the tent nestled like a white bird in a yellow nest, as Undine said when describing it to her little broken-backed friend.

She went to visit her this morning before taking her work to its destination, and found her basking in the warmth at the back of the tent, a veritable Diogenes, with only her head and shoulders sticking out of the great tub in which she had ensconced herself.

In answer to her visitor's look of inquiry, she said, 'The ground's so wet I can't lie on it, and in here it's so nice. I can rock from side to side. Just see!' And she put the tub in motion, leaning heavily first on one elbow and then on the other.

'And the rose?'

'Oh, it's all right, but it seems as though spring would never come,' said the girl, touching with her thick little forefinger the still leafless and brown slip that stood in the side of the old three-legged pot.

'You only stayed such a little while yesterday, you must not go soon today,' she said; and Undine put down her tray and sat down on the ground beside her.

'I can't stay very long today,' she said. 'I must try and find the owner of those shirts. Three months ago they were brought me, and no one has every called for them; I am afraid the person to whom they belong might be poor and need them, they are so fine and so old and worn.'

'He's waited so long, he won't mind waiting a little longer,' said the girl, resting her head in her companion's lap and looking up into her face with her clear grey eyes.

'Tell me what you wrote about last night,' she said.

Undine's hand rested on the same great shock of wild red hair, and the broad freckled face that looked up at hers was the same that six months before she had seen for the first time; yet it resembled that face only as a face awake resembles the same face asleep. It was like a dark room into which the sunshine had looked.

'I did not write anything,' said Undine, as she passed her finger tenderly along the lines in the low forehead; 'I was so tired I went to sleep with the pen in my hand, and when I woke the candle had quite burnt out.'

'And have you not anything to tell me?'

'No. I have been so busy all the morning.'

'And can't you think while you work?'

'Sometimes, not often; but yesterday evening, when I was putting the collars into starch, a little story came to me that seemed beautiful then, though it does not now. Shall I tell it you?'

The child nodded; and Undine, running her fingers through and through her coarse hair, began:

'A mother was lying on her bed, dying, and at her side was a very little baby. The people who stood round her thought she knew nothing, saw nothing; and truly she saw none of them. She felt only the touch of the little baby's fingers upon her breast, but she saw what no one else could see – in the far end of the room were two, drawing balls from a box which had no bottom; and Death's balls were the pure white and Life's were the blood red.

'Death was very tall and calm and his face was smooth and white, like a face cut of marble; his eyelids were half closed and in the eyes beneath them lay the shadows of wonderful dreams. Round him was a mantle of many cold grey tints, and his wings were folded close against his side.

'A ball was drawn, and it was Death's white ball; so the mother knew that she must go to him; but when they were going to draw again, she prayed and said: "Stay!

Stay! O Death; give Life my child!" For she feared him, he was so still and cold, and they were strange wonderful dreams that wandered beneath his eyelids.

'And Life said, "Let the mother see what we have to give it, and she shall decide who is to have the child."

'And Death bowed his head slowly.

'Now Life was very beautiful; her hair was like the yellow glory of the sunset, and her limbs were strong and soft and round, and her breast was as white as an open lily. Her cheeks were red, so red that the tear traces could hardly be seen on them, and her white dazzling wings were always quivering and expanded, yet they never raised her or took her from the earth. She was very lovely, and the bright robe she wore was of spotless tender green, the colour of the first shoots on the white-thorn tree; only here and there, where it turned up a little, the lining showed it was red and had clots on as though it had been dipped in blood. She was very beautiful; but when the mother looked at her forehead, knit with thought and pain, and at her large wide-open eyes through which the light and darkness chased each other endlessly, she feared her also.

'Life spoke first, and her voice was like the singing of the birds in spring-time, and the murmuring of the crowd in a great city, and the weeping of a lonely woman at a graveside, all strangely blended.

'"Look in my eyes," she said, "and see what I have to give"; and the mother looked.

'In the streets of a great city rolled the carriage of a rich man, and the mud from its wheels sprang up into the faces of two who were poor and hungry and stood at the corner of the street talking.

'"Whose carriage is that?" asked the one.

'"The man who rides in it is the richest and most fortunate man in all this city," answered the other. "From his boyhood upwards all that his hand has touched has turned to gold. Misfortune has never crossed him. His very dogs live longer than another's and die easier deaths. We were friends once in our youth, but now he counts his gold by millions, and I have nothing but a starving wife."

'"And why do you not go to him for help?"

'"Because how should he pity me who has never known want, and how should he remember me who has entertained lords and princes?" But still when they parted the poor man turned his steps towards the house of the great.

'"If I had but half that one of his horses eats I would be happy," he thought.

'The fortunate man was walking in his garden. He was very fat, and the only walk he ever took was up and down its gravel paths. The air was rich with the scent of the flowers, and the light of the afternoon sun made the drops of the leaping fountain sparkle more brightly than the diamonds on his finger. A small bird was bathing itself in the water.

'"Now," said the rich man, "if it were not too much trouble, and the shot worth more than the fruit it eats, I would kill that bird."

'Then he thought of the grand dinner he was to give the next day, and how his beautiful daughter was to marry one of the great lords who would be there.

'Then he thought how they all envied him his grand old mansion and his priceless horses; then he looked up and saw the poor man standing between him and the sun. He did not know him, for it is very hard to remember people who are so shabby, and so he asked him who he was. The poor man told his story, and when he had finished went back out of that beautiful garden sorry that he had entered it.

'Then the rich man walked up and down again and basked in the sunshine. It was a man's own fault if he had trouble and was poor and friendless, for the world was a good world. There was no help for him but in the grave, the poor man had said, and the fortunate man thought, as he walked up and down, what a very great fool he must be. It was such a nice pleasant world this, with its great red sun warming one on a chilly afternoon all for nothing, and ripening one's fruit and vegetables and asking for no pay. It was such a nice pleasant world this, with such a nice pleasant sea, over which pleasant ships could bring pleasant wines and turtles from other pleasant lands. He moistened his lips when he thought of another disagreeable dark place that the man had spoken of, where there were great cobwebs which were not round old bottles and living things that we not gay horses. That was the place he did not like to think of; it made the sweat stand in great drops on his red neck. Life had been so good to him; she had given him all the sweet and kept back all the bitter; she had brought no tear to his eye since he had been old enough to tell a sixpence from a penny; it would be hard to leave her now, when all men envied him. So he pulled out his watch with its setting of jewels and wondered when the dinner hour would come, and tried to forget that other hour. And at last the dinner hour came, with its guests and its laughter and its wine. And at last that other hour came also – the only hour of which we are all sure; and the fortunate man, who had never suffered and never wept and never pitied, went to the place he feared where the living things and cobwebs were. Nobody missed him, nobody wanted him back again – not his pretty daughter, for she had all his money.

'Now, when the mother saw all this, she would have given the child to Death, for she said, "It were as well he had died a baby."

'But Life prevented her: "I have other things to give," she said.

'And the mother looked. It was a garden again, a wild neglected garden where the flowers and creepers grew rank and free in each other's arms, and beauty was not measured out. At the root of a great tree, almost enfolded and hidden by the shrubs that grew around it, stood a man. His face was young and one to be pitied by the old and wise, for it was very glad and full of hope. In his arms, pressed close to him, was a woman, and not one of the flowers had a face so fair as hers; but, deep in her eyes, crept a look like the look which crept in the eyes of the serpent in that First Garden long ago. They were sweet long kisses; and the words she spoke to him were sweet, the sweet old words of love and faith which women speak to men; and he believed her.

'His heart grew very strong and great through the mighty love that came to him, and their life path lay before him in a mist of light and beauty. Truly God's world was good, and the life He gave great and beautiful, and only the pure and true of heart were worthy of it. So he thought; and looked in the eyes of the woman he loved, and pressed his lips to hers, and drew her closer to him, for he never saw the serpent's look that glided in them.

'But the day came, at last, when he did see it – when she looked into his face and laughed, and he knew that when he pressed the woman he loved to his heart it was only the grey old father of lies he had held. Now, life being for him that woman and that woman being evil, he became evil too. For the sake of what he had once loved, he deceived all women, and drank and cursed, and gained gold by evil, and spent it in sin; and men said that, wherever he passed, you might trace him by the ruin and evil he left behind. Yet they envied him, for the women loved him, and where other men would have starved he made gold. He might eat of the fruit of the earth and satisfy himself: its gold, its wine, or its women – they were all free to him who had no conscience to restrain and no faith in a higher power.

'The woman he had once loved was told of him – how the devil befriended his own, how he sinned and came to no evil, and enjoyed life as other men could not.

'Then she said, softly: "It was well that I deceived him, very well"; but in her inmost heart she feared to meet him, and when she knew that he was dead the world seemed larger to her and her breath came lighter.

'"I have that to give," said Life.

'"And I have sleep," said Death.

'And the mother would have given the child to him, but Life said: "I have yet other things to give"; and again she looked.

'There was a street with great and noble houses, and out at the door of one of them came a young man. His shoulders were bent and, as he walked, his eyes were fixed upon the ground; only once he looked up at the great houses at his side and saw the faces of two soft women looking out of a large window. Then he clenched the fingers of the hand that hung at his side till the nails went into the flesh, and clenched his teeth and swore under his breath a bitter oath.

''Twas a strange presumptuous oath for a man to swear who wore brown threadbare clothes out at elbow and boots that were split and who lived in a garret; for he swore that the day should come when those rich men should ask him to their tables and he would refuse to come, when those white proud women whom he cursed in his bitterness should covet a smile or a word from him, when the world should know him and call him great. This he swore and went home to his garret.

'It was a dreary empty place where the sunlight never entered and where dry bread was eaten and where nothing pleasant ever came except only a young girl with hard work-worn hands. She was the landlord's daughter, and she crept in every day to rub the dust off the rotten table and turn the straw mattress and carry out the ashes, if there were any. In the long evening, when to save light he would sit there thinking in the dark, she would sit there too, close beside him with her hard little hand in his, just as she had done when he came there three years before. She had been a child then; she was a woman now; but it made no difference to her.

'One evening she did not come, and he sat there alone, thinking, thinking. The room was very quiet, but there was a great war raging in the man's heart. At last he brought his hand down on the table and swore between his clenched teeth, as he had sworn that day before the rich men's houses.

'"She will not help me in my work," he said; "she and her children will be a weight on me, dragging me down. If I stay here it will conquer me. I must leave her, I must leave her, for she cannot help me."

'So in the grey dawn of the winter morning he stood in the door of his room, ready to leave it for the last time. She was labouring up the stairs with a great heap of coals in her arms.

'"These are for you," she said, her breath coming quick with pleasure: "the lodger belowstairs gave them to me. See, how many!"

'There were burning drops under his eyelids, but he let her pass into the room; then he said, "I am going away."

'She looked up into his face, for his voice sounded strange, but it was too dark to see him.

'"Will you stay long?" she asked.

'"Then he told her he was going away forever, that he would never come again; and he shut the door behind him very quickly for fear he might turn back. Quickly he shut it, but it was not quick enough, for he heard the coals fall on the floor, and a low short cry that followed him out into the street and on and on into the long years that followed.

'Years came, years went; his hair grew whiter; his shoulders stooped lower yet; and alone and in bitterness he laboured on.

'"Oh, you rich and noble," he said, "you who think no more of me than of the dogs in your kennels; when you vanish and your names are as forgotten as theirs I shall live on, my name shall be immortal!" And then he pressed his lips together and worked on.

'And at last it came. The world called him great; it wrote of him in its papers; men talked of him on the street, and women in their houses. The children learned to lisp his name; rich men asked him to their dinners; noblewomen came to visit him, only that they might say that they had seen him.

'He was very great, and his fame was very great, and his riches were very great; but he was old with work and his life was done.

'"Put me in my great chair beside the fire," he said to his servants, "and leave me. You say I am dying – why should you stay for that? You cannot help me." So they went out and left him.

'Nodding, dozing in the firelight, he looked up and saw before him, sitting in a velvet armchair, an old man with a cap of crimson and a silver silken tassel that was shaking in the firelight. 'Twas the phantom of himself who sat there, nodding in the golden firelight.

'"You have been fortunate," said the phantom; "you have succeeded as few men in the world succeed. You are very rich, and all men pray for riches."

'"I never cared for gold," said the great man. "Of what use is it to me, alone? Once ..."

'He had grown a little deaf of late, and now he could hear less; there was often a low short cry ringing in his ears.

'"Fools pray for gold," he said, "not wise men."

'The phantom nodded. "In your youth," he said, "you swore you would be great and that the high and noble should receive you into their houses, fair women should covert your notice and proud men your visits. You have gained all that; surely you are blessed. It is true you have paid something for it – a little – some pleasure, the rest of a few thousand nights, the woman you loved – but what is that! Many pay all that and die in a garret, or on a dung-heap. You are blessed!"

'"If that were all, then better never have been born," said the great man, bitterly. "They write of me in their papers; I never read their praises now. My house is better – why should I go to theirs! Fair women come to see me – what are fair women to me! They only disturb me with their childish chatter; and sometimes, if they have blue eyes – Ha! If that were all, better to have died a baby."

'The phantom leaned his hands upon his knees and leered across the firelight.

'"What has it been for then? All this battling, all this striving, all this heartache? Surely it has not been for nothing?"

'"No," said the great man; "it has not been for nothing. The man who looks for happiness in this life is a fool. I live for the future. *I* would be immortal. Immortal!"

'The phantom leaned back in his armchair and laughed till the silvered tassel of his red cap trembled again in the firelight!

'"Immortal! I thought you were a great man, yet you juggle with this word immortal, like the rest of your kind. What do *you* mean by it now? That your name shall live after you are dead? Well, if that is all you seek, you shall have it. They will give you a grand funeral, and write of you in papers bordered deep with black, and for a few days, a very few, everyone will speak of you. But there will be no woman to wear one flower the less in her hair, and no man to drink one glass less of wine, because you died that morning. You are a great man, a very great man, so perhaps they will raise a statue of you, and for a few hundred years, now and then, someone will speak of you, oftenest in praise at first, oftenest in blame at last; for to men of the new ideas and the new light the great men of old look very small. Immortal! Ha! Ha! Who are you? What are you?" laughed the phantom. "A paltry two thousand years has dimmed the radiance of her redeemers and prophets; how long do you think earth will remember you?"

'The phantom laughed again and looked into the fire: "That coal that is burning there: Five million years ago or so it was a great tree growing in the green old forests. Perhaps it thought it was to be immortalised – immortalised into coal. And so it was, for five million years; but in five minutes it will be ashes now. In five million years where will you be? – Immortal – Ha! Ha! Ha!" laughed the phantom. "Fool! Fool! Fool!"

'With his hands clasped over his face and his head bowed down to his knees, the old man sat.

'"Oh, my life," he cried, "my life! I have given it, I have given it, and I have gained nothing."

'Three days later the great man died, and the noble and the great followed him to his grave, and they wrote of him in their papers. They said, "Weep, weep, for a great man is dead; weep, weep!" But for all that, no one wept. Only one half-starved man who lived alone in the garret where he laboured and toiled, he wept for envy, for he said, "Why should he have all the good, I all the evil?"

'Then Life dropped his lids for a moment.

'"And I have rest," said Death.

'And the mother would have given him her child, but Life said: "Look again, once more"; and the mother looked for the last time.

'It was four o'clock in the morning, and beside a table, with his forehead resting in his two hands, a man was sitting. The candle was almost burnt out, and soon it would be time for him to go out to his day's work; for all day he stood behind a counter, selling yards of print and muslin to the ladies that came in.

'The other clerks called him fool; if they had known how his nights were spent they would have called him so more often. When their day's work was over they went out to amuse themselves, but he only shut himself up in his room and walked up and down and prayed and wrote himself half mad before the morning came.

'It was well there was no living thing to see him but the little brown mouse that looked out of its hole and wished it could have nibbled at the candle. But the candle stood safe and did nothing but devour the bits of paper scribbled over with songs that were always being put to her. She had just devoured two great blue pages, on which was much of such hot talk as comes from young pens at four o'clock in the morning.

'She would get no more, however, for the pen was lying under the table, and the man looked very disconsolate as he sat beside it.

'If he had written anything just now, it would have been: "Yes, I'm a great fool, as they say. Let us eat and drink, for tomorrow we die. Let us do as the sheep do; they only are wise. Beauty is an angel that no man ever caught; truth is a deception that changes to falsehood while you finger it. We are shadows among shadows. Why be so in earnest? Why make oneself so hot about it all? Why strive and pray and make so great a bluster? Life isn't worth is. Something, nothing, here, gone; let us make the best of it, wear the nicest clothes, eat the nicest meat, and love the easiest love, and believe what comes to hand; tread on, steady and safe, step by step, in the narrow sandy path our fathers cleared from stones and bushes long ago. If this cannot be, why, curse life and die – it is the best thing left."

'So he thought then, for he was weary, and threw himself down on his bed. Perhaps he slept, but his eyes were heavy and red the next morning as he stood behind the counter, selling ribbons and prints.

'So this poor clerk went on, month after month, praying and writing all night and measuring off dresses by the yard all day; but at last it happened that one of his dreams took a human shape, and a pair of clear still eyes looked into his life and made him richer than the great princes of the Golden Isles, whose houses and whose shoes are covered with jewels. It was true, as men speak, that the eyes belonged not to him but to a woman who was nothing to him – a woman who was high above him and who would surely be carried, some day, to another man's home. Yet when he was beside her she spoke to him kindly, and in her face he found the beauty in her mind, the truth he dreamed of. He knew that she was his though she did not love him, for he loved her, and no one could ever take her from him, not she herself.

'He heard at last that she was going to be married, and then he left the town and went far, far away, and for a little time there was a heavy aching at his heart all day as he stood behind the counter or sat alone in his silent room. But at last the aching went, and there was only gladness left. He had not her body, it was true, but her beautiful soul was living somewhere and it was true and real, and the earth was never again quite empty for him.

'The years passed on, and they still called him a fool, for he made no money. He never stayed long enough in any place, but wandered on from town to town and land to land, just when the longing seized him. Sometimes a child's face, or a reach of sea beach, or the charm of snow-crowned mountains made him pause a little, but having got all they had to give, he wandered on again.

'He made no money and no friends, this poor fool of a clerk. Only sometimes, when pain or sorrow would draw people to him, they would enter his life for a little time; but when they were comforted they would go out of it again, and he would go on with his wanderings and sing his songs and smile and love the beautiful green old earth.

'Sometimes his songs were sad, but oftener they were glad, for it did not take much to make him happy – a little stream of sunlight breaking in through the goods within the window, or the shadows which the trees cast as he passed below them on his way to work or to lie on the grass on Sunday morning and watch the rippling in the pool of water; that was enough to make life sweet to him – so sweet that, when the death he had once longed for came to him, he was almost sorry to leave it. Yet it seemed so pleasant to think of lying deep in the soft old earth he loved, and he was glad he had lived. There was not one night of sleepless agony, nor one hour of bitterness he would have missed, even if he might. It was all good, looked at from the end. Life lay very beautiful behind, and death was not terrible, only very strange.

'He died young and they buried him in the earth he loved; but there was not a tear shed over him. For why? What had he done all his life? Sold a few yards of print and ribbon, cast up a few accounts, suffered a little agony, prayed a little, doubted a little, comforted a few people who were sad; and for the rest lived much as the birds live, singing and loving and revelling in the sunshine.

'"I have that to give," said Life.

'And the mother said: "Take my child. Your best is bitter sweet, but it is sweet."

'So Death took the mother and Life the child.'

When Undine had finished her story they sat quiet for a little time. Then the girl said, 'It's because such beautiful stories come to you that you are never miserable and are always smiling. I like this story.'

'I like them too,' said Undine, 'when they come to me as I am at my work. They seem so beautiful, they make the blood run all through my body with little throbs; but when I try to write or tell them I wonder what I liked in them. But I must be going now, Diogenes, or Mr William Brown will be without a shirt and dying of the cold.' And Undine got up and put her tray upon her arm.

'Diogenes – what does that mean?'

'Why, Diogenes was a man who lived in a tub, as you are doing today; and I call you Diogenes because I like to call my friends by names that no one else has for them.'

'Am I your friend?' A strangely bright look came into the little freckled face that looked up at her out of the tub.

Undine answered, 'Yes, my only little friend.'

She was turning to go when Diogenes stopped her: 'Do you really think people do nothing but dream after they are dead? You said Death's eyes were full of dreams.'

'No, I don't think so,' said Undine, trying to balance the tray on her head and finally returning it to her arms. 'The stories come to me just as they like. I never think about them.'

'I'm sorry,' said Diogenes, still resting her folded arms on the ground and looking up. 'Last night I dreamt my rose bush had a great white rose and you had it in your hair, and you and I were walking over little sandhills. The air was so cool and it was dark as though there was going to be a great storm; I was looking up into your face, and you were looking straight out before you, and your eyes were so strange. And at last we came to the sea, and you said you were going over it. It was a sad dream, but I liked it, and when I woke up father was drunk and they were all quarrelling and I wished I had never woken up any more. It's so nice to dream.'

'Yes, dreams are nice. Goodbye.' And the little ironing woman trudged off with her shirts, leaving Diogenes with enough food for reverie, conjecture and enjoyment for the rest of the day.

The owner of the shirts, she had been told by the Kaffir who brought them, lived near the Circus; that his name was W Brown the shirts themselves told her; but to discover his whereabouts seemed a hopeless task.

Most people answered her shortly enough. One old woman, in answer to her questions, began the long story of one Bill Brown, who might be the Bill Brown she was in search of, who had lived at Graaff-Rienet, who had set out for the Fields, but who, as turned out in the sequel, had died before reaching them.

He could hardly be the owner of the shirt, nor yet the widow Brown to whose tent some well-disposed digger sent her. Undine was giving up the quest when a Kaffir woman, hearing her question, directed her to a small tent the top of which was just visible behind its larger compeers.

Making her way between the tents over broken bottles, empty tins and rubbish of all kinds, Undine soon found herself before it, and a glance through its open door convinced her that she had found the right place at last.

'Twas a tent of about the size of her own, but its interior presented an infinitely more comfortless appearance, though it was furnished with a wooden stretcher, two camp stools and a huge padlocked sea-chest.

The gravel that covered the floor was trodden into mounds and heaps of all sizes. More laths of the wooden stretcher hung down broken than were left to support the red sand-coloured bedding that lay on it. On the sea chest that stood in the middle of the tent was such a multifarious and miscellaneous collection of articles as surely never sea-chest bore before. There were tins and bottles of every description, the latter crowned with the remains of half burnt candles; there were old newspapers and shoe blacking, books and a pepper caster, pens and cigar ends, a paint box and a broken looking-glass, a microscope and combs, hair brushes, tooth brushes, boot brushes, nail brushes and a papier-mache desk on which was a silver-clasped album across which lay the broken head of a pick; these with an infinitude of other smaller and larger articles covered it. On the ground at its side lay an empty meal sack, the last of whose contents had evidently been used to compose the great leadeny-looking roaster-cake that was standing beside a tin mug of water on the sea chest; the look of the roaster-cake was not inviting, except it were to throw at the head of an enemy, yet someone had evidently tried to put it to some other use, for there were small pieces chipped off every here and there.

Close beside the sea chest, on one of the campstools leaning against the central pole, with his head hanging on his breast, sat a man. He was in digger trim, with his shirt sleeves rolled up above his elbows, perhaps to hide their frayed and worn condition, certainly not for work, for the long arms they left uncovered seemed hardly strong enough to raise themselves, still less to handle sieve or pick. His eyes were closed, but a very light tap at the doorpost caused him to raise his head and look up heavily at the white-clad figure that stood in his doorway.

If he were Mr Brown, she said, she had brought his shirts.

A slight flush came into her face.

'I don't want them; you had better take them and keep them as payment,' he said; then he drooped back into his old posture.

He was greatly changed, but, when he looked up, Undine at once recognised him as the passenger who, on that first morning on board the steamer had seemed the only glad thing in harmony with the fresh breezy water and the sweeping sea-birds.

He was in harmony with his surroundings now also, for the broken tins and bottles and the old stretcher did not look more hopelessly down-and-out and good-for-nothing than their master.

Undine looked at his wasted arms, at the empty meal sack, and the leaden roaster-cake, and listened to his hollow cough, and wondered where the long-whiskered captain and his brilliant sister might be. Perhaps they were only of the sunflower species whom only fools think to find growing in the shade.

She watched him in silence for a minute, then she stepped lightly into the tent and, putting her tray down on the floor, came and stood beside him. It was not till she had spoken twice and touched him softly on the shoulder that he seemed to hear her.

'You are very ill,' she said. 'Have you much pain?'

'No,' he answered, heavily, without raising his head or opening his eyes.

'Have you been ill long?'

'Yes – no – I don't know'; and a long hollow cough followed.

'Would you not feel a little better if you tried to lie down? It must be very hard to sit up here,' she said, gently.

'I would, but it's such a long way.'

He raised his head again and looked with his heavy eyes across the three feet that separated him from his stretcher as a man might to a land of promise across an ocean.

Undine shook out the pillows and smoothed the blanket, and putting his hand on her shoulder helped him to reach it.

He did not thank her, but dropped down on it with a weary sigh. He had bonny light curls like someone she had cared for long ago, and he had broken boots and stockings so old that the red flesh showed through. She hardly knew which drew her to him most, the curls or the boots, for there is something achingly pitiable in broken boots.

When a man who has called himself a gentleman falls to that, he can fall no lower.

CHAPTER EIGHTEEN

Little Irons and a Digger

Diogenes's little red head peeped out of her tub and she rolled herself from side to side and felt sadly disconsolate. Her rose bush was full of tender leaves, her back was not bad and the weather was glorious, but for three weeks she had had no story, and for three whole weeks her daily visitor had come only to go. She felt aggrieved and gently wronged.

'I wish he had stopped in England; it would have been a great deal nicer for *him*,' she soliloquised, her little forehead all gathered up into knots and puckers.

'England's such a nice country, they say, and there's nothing nice in this land. I wonder why he came.'

Just at that moment Undine arrived.

'Is he better?' inquired Diogenes, evidently with great interest, and her lips seemed to grow yet heavier when she had received her answer.

'I don't believe he tries to get better,' she said in an aggrieved tone.

'Don't you get tired to keep running up here all day?'

'Not tired, but I am going to look for some Kaffir men to carry his tent down next to mine; then I will be able to take care of him and iron too. How is your back this morning?'

'Well,' said Diogenes, sullenly.

'I'm glad,' said Undine. 'I'll come back again when I have got the Kaffirs. Goodbye.' And she was gone.

'I wish *he* was gone,' said Diogenes. 'It is not a bit nice any more. Heigh-ho!' And she traced with her finger on the ground Bs and Cs Undine had taught her to make.

As Undine had thought, it was a change for the better which brought the second tent into her little nest among the gravel-heaps. While one pair of hands and four irons had to skim over shirts enough in the twenty-four hours to pay for doctors, eggs, milk, medicine, and sufficient bread to keep the hands themselves going, they could ill afford to be long at rest. Now she could go on ironing all day without interruption, peeping in at his tent every time she passed to change an iron at the fire, which was built between three round stones at the back of the tent.

The doctor did not give much hope of his recovery. He was completely broken down, said the doctor, with hard work and bad living. All day he lay there as helpless as a little child, never speaking but when his mind wandered. Then he would often fancy himself talking with the mine-captain and begging him not to give up yet, to keep on a little longer, to advance a little more money. Luck must turn

159

soon. Or sometimes he was walking on the deck with the captain's pretty sister, and he would be whispering on softly for hours.

When Undine heard him she sometimes wondered whether it would not almost have been best to let him die alone, with his bit of roaster-cake in his solitary tent. He did not look much like winning the heart of any woman as he lay there moaning, with even his bonny curls cut off.

At last he grew better, and then it was hard to find time for the inevitable ironing. Let him seem ever so fast asleep, his eyes were sure to open if she rose to leave him. If she had nothing else to do for him, he liked her to sit beside him and talk.

One day she looked in at the door with a furiously red face and in one hand a hot iron that she had just been to fetch at the fire.

'Put that iron away', he said, feebly, 'till it gets cool. My eyes ache with them. They are always in your hands. I want you to answer me a question I can't answer for myself.'

'Well?' said Undine, pushing back her cap a little and leaning over to one side to balance the iron she held in the other. 'What is it? I don't think the irons have absorbed quite all my intellect yet.'

'As the spades and picks did mine. Tell me how it is that I am quite contented to lie here and be fed and nursed by you, and don't feel as though I ought even to thank you, when I would die sooner than take a broken sixpence from my own flesh and blood? How is it? I'm too weak to think.'

'You must be weak if you can't think *that* out,' she said, twisting one arm round the tent-post to keep her steady, and looking, he thought, almost beautiful in spite of her redness. 'Don't you know there are things we have to be more grateful for than being nursed and fed? You've given me something to take care of, and so, though you don't think it, you feel you have done more for me that I for you. As for getting help from our relations,' said Undine, resting her head against the pole, 'they are just the last people to go to unless one likes getting a pain in one's pride bones. One always has a lurking suspicion they are doing it from principle or necessity or something equally disagreeable; and that's why their money hurts. But my irons are getting cold,' she said, turning to go.

'Don't you ever get tired of them?' he asked. 'It's so burning hot today.'

'Oh no, I never get tired, and it's not so hot today – as it might be. I get to like it.'

She walked off, but the iron she was using must have been a very heavy one, for when she was taking it back to the fire she stumbled two or three times as though she would have fallen.

'What a very uneven little path this is,' she said to herself, thereby greatly maligning the very smooth little path over the gravel that led from the door of her tent to the fireplace. Perhaps it was by way of smoothing it that she knelt down by the water barrel and damped the crown of her head and lay there for half an hour looking very white. Anyhow, she did not say any more about the path being uneven after that.

A few days later, Undine paid her daily visit to Diogenes, who as usual lay in her tub with her rose bush before her. The discerning eyes of that small individual perceived something unusual and amiss in the face of her friend, and when Undine sat down beside the tub and leaned her hand against it, she said:

'Are you very tired today?'

'No, not at all.'

'You don't look happy. I wish I knew what was the matter; I wish you need never be tired or sad'; and Diogenes took Undine's rough little hand and rubbed it softly up and down with her chin. It was her way of showing sympathy; and it showed it more effectually than any words could have done – so effectually that it ended in making Undine cry. She pressed her face against the tub, and Diogenes fancied she heard a sob.

'Oh dear! What is it?' said Diogenes, looking up, terribly troubled at the sound. 'I did not know you could be *so* miserable. I thought you saw such beautiful things, you were always happy. I'm sure it's all that man's fault'; and Diogenes's clear grey eyes filled with wrathful but partly sympathetic tears.

'No, it is not; only I am weak and faint, and I want money.'

If her rose bush had stirred its tender leaves and said it wanted high-heeled boots and a fashionable bonnet, it would not have astonished Diogenes more.

'Thou shalt not love money; thou shalt not desire it; thou shalt despise it; it is the child of the devil, and his eldest born.' This was the little bit of ethical teaching which was sure to lift up its head in the wildest of Undine's fairy stories, and the effect on Diogenes had been so great that she often seriously debated in her own mind whether, seeing a pound lying at her feet, there would not be a certain amount of degradation in stooping to pick it up. To look up, therefore, and see her instructor's face wet with tears because she wanted money, wanted money, so puzzled Diogenes that she remained quiet for a few minutes.

Then she began to use her very practical little brains, and quickly came to certain conclusions.

'Can't you get money enough to pay the doctor?' she asked, looking up softly from under her great shock of red hair.

'No, I can get that. I want much money, almost a hundred pounds. If I can't get that I don't want any, I don't want anything.'

Diogenes drew a long breath. She felt sure that disagreeable *he* was at the bottom of it all, but she would ask no more questions. She was rubbing her chin softly up and down Undine's hand when it touched the ring upon it – Aunt Margaret's ring.

'If you were to sell this, perhaps you would get much money; diamonds are so dear and it is so beautiful.'

Undine lifted her head quickly and looked down at it. She had as little thought of it as a thing to be parted with as the hand which wore it. The one link between her and the old days. She had worn it till it seemed to have grown a part of herself. Her baby friend had touched it, pleased with its flash and gleam. It had whispered to her that truth and love were possibilities when she had sat toying with it in the great, gayly filled, empty rooms of her husband's house. It had shone on a soft hand that had so often rested tenderly on her head. It had been the sign of a great love, faithful even unto death. She moved it softly round her finger two or three times; then she drew it off.

Why sacrifice the living to the dead, the present to the past? The past is a fruitless dream, the present only is living and demands all things.

'Are you going to sell it?' asked Diogenes.

'Yes, at once,' said Undine, rising quickly, 'and I will come back soon.'

'I know she liked the ring, and now she has got to sell it,' said Diogenes to herself as soon as Undine was out of hearing. 'It's all his fault, I know it is. Perhaps she wants to send him to England. She said yesterday he was worse and would never get better if he couldn't go. I do wonder why he did not stay there,' said Diogenes, in her anger pulling so vigorously at one leaf of her rose that it came off. '*I* don't go about everywhere making everybody miserable.' Lost in the contemplation of her own virtue in abstaining from crime which by no possibility she could have committed, and finding immense satisfaction in so doing, Diogenes lay still in her tub and waited for Undine's return.

She was long gone, but when she did make her appearance, it was so radiantly, joyfully, that Diogenes felt ashamed of her tears. If she had not liked parting with her ring, there was no sign of it in her face. She had got as much as she wanted, almost more; now he would know that he could go to England, and the hope would make him well.

'I knew it was for him,' muttered Diogenes under her breath; but Undine was too glad to hear it, too glad to sit down, and soon fluttered off. She hardly felt the sandy road she plodded in, but only the little roll of notes tight-clasped in her hand, the little roll that meant hope and strength and life for him and, it might be, more than life – gladness in place of long years of weary loneliness. Even if he got well and, staying at New Rush till he had money, at last went home to find the woman who had charmed away his soul given to another, would he not curse the hand that had kept him from a quiet sleep in the New Rush graveyard?

It might be that, going home even now, he might find the bright eyes had fooled him; but Undine put the thought from her and enjoyed the sunshine of the moment.

He should never know from whom it came; it should be burdened with no debt of gratitude. Generally the work is heart-sickening, that of trying to bring joy and good to our heart's own, work in which failures are in number as gravel bort,[1] and

---

[1] Diamond dust; ie the 'dust' outnumbering the 'diamonds'.

the successes as diamonds. But for once Undine found success. The mysterious little parcel which the post brought him seemed to work in him all the wonders of the old life waters.

There were no more refusals to eat; no more weary days of stupor and relapse coming when he had wearied himself out with calculation as to the length of time it would take him to get strong and then to earn money enough for the long journey.

When the days grew warmer, he was strong enough to sit outside, among rugs and cushions on the shady side of the tent; sometimes to use his pencils; sometimes to watch Undine through the tent door as she stood smoothing away at her packing case.

Pleasant days they were, flying all too quickly, for one at least, who worked and enjoyed the present and put the future from her.

At last the time came when they were only hours that could be counted before his departure. He was still so weak that it took him a long time to get from one tent to the other, but he was to leave by the next morning's coach. The last evening came. He lay on his stretcher, and Undine sat at its foot on the skirting in the doorway, trying to make the most of the daylight. She was darning the best of his old stockings, and he all the while chatted on eagerly of the future, in spirits unnaturally high, springing quickly from one subject to another.

'You are such a genius, Little Irons, in spite of your big *kappie* and your shirts. The world shall know of you someday, and I shall be so proud of the Little Irons who came to help me when all the world would have left me to drop out of life like a dog.' Then he speculated as to where the money could have come from, then on his own course for the future; then talked of those first dreadful days of labour and failure, of the time it would take him to reach The Bay, and at last talked himself to sleep. Then she stood up and put the stockings she had mended into his bag, and moved softly about the tent collecting pencils and various trifles that still lay about.

She had just packed the last of them when a coolie, late out, passed the tent with his tray of wares upon his head. There were till two oranges left on it, so she told him to wait, and went into her tent to the broken ink pot where she kept her money. There was only one shilling in it, so one of the oranges had to go; the other she put in the pocket of the coat he was to wear tomorrow, which lay on the box at his side. There was no money left in the ink pot, but what did it matter? There would be nobody to care for after tomorrow. What did anything matter? She went to her own tent and sat down in the doorway and tried to eat her supper; but eating did not answer; so presently she sat still with her head leaning against the doorpost.

Across the road were the children of the Dutchwoman, shouting and tumbling over one another in their play. They had done so every night for the last six months, but did that night seem just like every other night to them?

He did not wake to eat his supper, and slept on straight till morning. Just at daybreak she stepped softly into his tent to wake him. The cart they had ordered to take him to the hotel would be there soon. He was scarcely ready, and Undine was still busy cutting up his tobacco when she caught the sound of the approaching wheels. He did not hear them till they were just before the tent; then he rose quickly and pressed the cut tobacco into his pouch while the driver carried out his luggage. Then he turned to wish her goodbye. The grey light was just turning into white, and gusts of cold early wind blew in though the rolled-up door.

'Goodbye, my friend, my dear Little Irons,' he said, warmly yet very gladly, and he stooped down to kiss her; but it was such a cold, trembling little face he touched that something smote his heart.

'I've been a great bother to you, dear Little Irons,' he said, resting his right hand tenderly on her shoulder. 'You will have rest when I am gone and go back to your happy, quiet old life; and I shall never forget you, never. How could I?'

She stood on tiptoe and wound a scarf round his neck.

'Don't take it off till the sun gets warm,' she said.

'Oh, I'll take good care of myself,' he answered as he passed out of the door. Then he turned round to say goodbye once more. 'Goodbye, but not for very long; I feel sure we shall soon meet again,' he said, as he took her hand in his.

He climbed up at the back of the cart, and a moment after only the faint rumbling of the wheels broke the stillness. Undine stood in the tent door.

'Meet again! Meet again!' Poor human hearts that must still their aching with such vain words. Meet again! Who ever met again? The child we love goes from us and comes back to us a man, and all others praise the change; but we, even while we run our fingers through his curls, we hunger for the little child that sat upon our knee.

We part with the friend of our childhood, and we say, 'We part only for today; through life we shall often meet again,' and it may be we clasp hands often in the years that come and talk of the old days; but we know, though we never say it, that the two who parted have never met again, that the sea of time has run up between us, and we cannot touch. Who can part, forever; only when we come so close that nothing separates us can we meet again, only when what binds us is not my need of you or your need of me nor any chance circumstance, but a deep ingrained likeness of nature that cannot pass away.

'We shall meet again someday,' said Undine as she stood in the tent door, comforting herself with this great lie.

A little after the sun had risen, she hurried along the path in the direction of the Toit's Pan Road, and stopped when she came to the last of the enclosures that lined it on either side. The coach would have to pass there, and she must see it; so she stood there waiting while the quickly moving passenger carts from Toit's Pan passed and repassed her, breaking the stillness of the quiet morning.

At last, after long waiting, it came with its great red tent, with its blowing bugle, with its eight prancing horses, with its crowded roof; and inside, just as it tore past her, she saw him. It was only a glimpse, but that was enough, for he looked bright and glad. He was speaking to the passenger who sat next him and laughing and peeling the orange he had found in his pocket. A piece of peel he threw out fell at the roadside, and she picked it up after the coach had passed.

'It is all right. He is happy, very happy,' she said, and turned to go back to her tent. 'He is happy, very happy,' she kept on repeating to herself when she got back to the tent. Remnants of the tobacco she had been cutting still lay on the old sea-chest, the boots he had worn yesterday still lay beside it, and the half drunk cup of chocolate was hardly cold. She looked in at the door for a minute, and then went to her own tent.

Her own little tent, which she had said was so full and rich to her, which was so empty and silent now. She walked up and down, not daring to sit down and rest. Well had she said to that hungry dog on that day long ago: 'Go away, and do not follow me. If you follow me I shall love you and I, I have had pain enough.'

At last she sat down by the old packing case and drew out the old papers, and the pens that had been unused so long. She took up the newspaper and scribbled all over the edges one of those stories in which the heart of Diogenes delighted. Its keynote was the very safe and comforting reflection that all love dies sooner or later; only that which has no existence, which the young dream of, lasts forever. It comforted her greatly that morning. After a few months she would be happy without him and almost forget this boy whom she had loved with a more yearning tenderness than her own little child.

'I will forget, I will forget everthing, and live only in the present; then, soon, there will be no reason to forget, for this little love will fade away like the yearning for my monkey and the madness that looks so grotesque and unreal now, and which nothing could ever again bring back – nothing.'

The margins of the newspaper were full to overflowing and she was already crossing it over in every direction, when a shadow fell across the sunlight that streamed in through the tent door.

Some coolie bringing milk he was accustomed to sell there, she thought, as she looked up to see the figure of a man with his back turned to the entrance. The opening was so low that his head was not visible, but an elegant little black cane moved slowly backwards and forwards, and there was that in the cut of the black cloth coat and the hang of the trousers that carried her back from New Rush to that first meeting before the picture in Blair House. Soon the figure turned and Undine hardly knew what she expected to see, but it was only the very ugly face of a very black nigger that stuck itself in at the doorway.

'Have you done the shirts a girl brought here yesterday?' he asked in very good English and in a very leisurely and self-possessed manner. Evidently he had taken some Englishman, probably his master, as the model upon which to form himself. Undine brought him the shirts, which the swell nigger took with the extreme tips of

165

his fingers, as though it were greatly derogatory to his dignity and he only submitted to a most painful necessity. Touching gracefully his woolless upper lip with the hand in which he held the cane, he said:

'If you want more work, I dare say you could get it if you come to our place – Mr Albert Blair's.'

The nigger rolled out the name very full and with evident satisfaction, at the same time holding out a five-shilling piece to Undine with an air that clearly evinced how greatly he scorned the performing of so trivial an action. He thought the ironing-woman was certainly half daft, or it might be drunk, for she stood in the tent door staring at him and never holding out her hand to receive the money. He was on the point of informing her of his opinion in very plain language when she said, 'You can keep the money for yourself.'

There was no doubt now as to the ironing-woman's daftness or drunkenness, for who gives five shillings for nothing? But the nigger no longer felt himself under the painful necessity of informing her of the fact, and, great as his scorn for the five-shilling piece had appeared to be, it quickly found its way into his waitscoat pocket. In reply to a question from Undine he proceeded to inform her where his master's house might be found, and wrapping up the shirts in a newspaper he had brought for the purpose, and tucking them under his arm, he walked off switching his black cane.

Near evening Undine too went out, but in an opposite direction, and forgetting today even to button down her tent door. There was not a shilling in the bottle nor a whole slice of bread in the box, yet she was not going to look for work now. She was going to Diogenes, but the walk seemed a weary long one; it had never seemed so long before. Her legs ached, her head ached, and sometimes she grew dizzy.

Diogenes was not in her tub today. She was greatly excited and the tub seemed to confine her. She was leaning against it and almost started to her feet when Undine appeared round the tent's corner.

'I've been so tired of waiting for you all these two days. I thought you would never come. Stoop down before the tub and shut your eyes tight and then look in and see what I've got for you,' cried Diogenes, giving two gentle claps with her hands, for once a perfect child in her delight. Undine did as she was told and looked in, to see the tiny rose bush adorned with one deep-bosomed red rosebud.

'Isn't it beautiful? Isn't it beautiful?' said Diogenes, enthusiastically clasping her hands. 'Pick it; it's for you. No – you must not pick it. I will – and fasten it in your hair just like it was in my dream. Oh, how beautiful!'

Undine put the iron pot down in Diogenes's lap, but Diogenes's fingers were so tremulous with gladness that she almost uprooted the rose bush before the flower was severed from the stem. 'Now,' she said, putting the old pot down at one side, 'lay down your head and I will put it in.'

Undine sat down beside her and put her head in Diogenes's lap, and the child did and undid the hair half a score of times before the flower was fixed to her satisfaction.

'Now turn round and look at me,' she said, when all was done. But it was such a weary face that looked up at hers that Diogenes's face fell also.

'I had quite forgotten he went away this morning, and you must be sorry, you've taken care of him so long,' said Diogenes, who, in truth, for the last forty-eight hours had been gloriously oblivious of every existence save that of her wonderful rosebud.

Diogenes did not know what to say; so she resorted to dumb sympathy, which she did understand, and drew Undine's face very close to her and smoothed it with the palms of her little hands.

After a long quiet she said, 'I love you better than anything, better even than my rose bush.' It was only a child's way of comforting, those few words of love and that smoothing her cheek with her little hands. A child's way, yet by it she paid back more than all the good that had been brought to her.

'It is nice to lie here and rest, but I must go,' said Undine, when the last rays of the sun were shining on the little green leaves of the rose bush, which stood just beyond the end of the tent where it could catch them.

'You are sick, too,' said Diogenes, noticing how she leaned her hand against the tub to help herself in rising.

'Not sick, only tired. I have not been so tired for many years. I want to sleep for a long, long time. I shall be better then.'

She smiled as she looked down into the earnest eyes that were fixed on her.

'Come again soon, very soon,' said Diogenes, as Undine was going out of sight.

She did not answer, but turned round for a moment and looked back at her, still smiling. The rose had fallen out of her hair and she held it in her hand.

'You look just like you did in my dream,' Diogenes said; but Undine did not hear her, for she had turned to go.

It may be that in the years to come Diogenes shall grow into a great, coarse, red woman as her mother was before her – the mother of many children, the wife of many husbands whom she may drop as easily as she does every hour the words that are not choice.

It may be – but there will come hours when the one pure and tender memory of her childhood will come back to her, and her children will wonder why she speaks so softly and the men why she has no oath to throw back at them. They would wonder if they knew it was only the picture of that summer evening at New Rush and the little slight figure standing at the tent corner with the red rosebud in its hand, and its great white *kappie*, and the yellow evening sunlight streaming over it from behind.

As Undine had said, she was tired, very tired; but instead of going home she turned slowly to that part of the camp to which her little squint-eyed guide had once conducted her.

She stopped when she came to the reed fence that encircled the home of the baby-faced golden-haired lady. She was on the veranda again this evening, but she was not alone now. Over her chair was leaning a man, whose head was bent so low over hers that the black beard mingled with the golden ripples on her forehead. They spoke very soft and low, and they did not notice Undine, for their backs were to her and their talk was very interesting. But a little boy, who sat behind them playing, now lifted his blue eyes to look at the woman on the other side of the hedge and caught sight of the bright rose she held. He slipped down from the veranda and stood before her.

'Give,' he said, and held out imperiously one small hand.

Undine dropped the rose into it and turned to go back to her tent.

'You must come,' whispered the dark-whiskered gentleman as he stooped low over the golden head. 'Come if it is for only one short half hour. *You* may allow yourself to be robbed of all pleasure, but others must not be quite forgotten, you know; even if our claim to be considered is not *very* strong.'

The lady smiled very softly and smoothed out the fringe on her sleeve with her little pink finger.

'Surely you have done enough in coming to such a place as this. You need not renounce the world *altogether*; you are too young to do penance yet'; and the gentleman's breath was warm on her cheek. Then she lifted her baby face up to his, and her eyes were just as they had been when she looked down at Undine, placid, smiling; there was no harm in them.

'I've been out two nights this week,' she said, 'and people might think it strange, you know. The doctor said he was much worse today, and he would be so angry if they told him.'

It might have ended in her not going to the ball that night, but at that moment the child passed them with the bright flower in its hand.

'What a lovely flower!' said the mother, and she held out her hand for it; but the child clasped it tighter in his fist and held it close against his little breast.

It was only a moment's work for the gentleman to unclasp the little fingers and put the flower into the mother's hand. The child did not cry; he only pressed his little thin arched lips together and drooped the lids over the blue eyes with which he looked at them. He was only a baby: there was no sin in taking it. 'You see the very gods have condescended to interfere in my behalf,' whispered the gentleman. 'This rose means that you are to go and wear it here tonight.'

He lay it very softly on her breast and whispered words, so softly that only the ear in which they were spoken could catch them; and when the mother rose to go into the house she said, 'Well just for one hour, just for one, you know.'

And so she went to the ball that night and danced, the loveliest of all the women there, with that bright flower at her heart; and all praised her and looked at her.

And that night, alone, when the nigger who had been left to watch him had gone out to spend the five shillings, Albert Blair died.

CHAPTER NINETEEN

Albert Blair

*'Vat jou goed en trek, Ferreira,
Vat jou goed en trek;
Swaar dra, swaar dra ...'*[1]

whistled the swell nigger next morning as he walked, switching his cane, in the direction of Undine's tent.

Generally she rose early, but this morning she was sleeping late and so heavily that he had to knock two or three times at the tent pole before she came to unbutton the sail.

'Do you want any needlework?' asked the nigger, touching his hat quite respectfully, for, even with a salary of six pounds a month, five shillings are not be despised.

Undine said she wanted no work.

The nigger looked disappointed. He had hoped she would take the work, and show as great an objection to accepting payment for black skirts as for ironing shirts.

'You see, my master died last night, and Mrs Blair wants her mourning quickly. Don't you think, if I was to bring some stuff now, you would be able to do it for her?'

There was no doubt today about the ironing-woman's daftness. She took no notice of his question, but said, after a pause, 'What did your master die of?'

'Well you see,' replied the nigger, resting his hand on the head of his cane and leaning elegantly forward, 'I don't rightly know. He came here just to have a look at everything, and he took ill, something wrong inside, and the doctors they won't let him travel; and this six months he's been lying here, and they've been saying he was going to die, but he never did till last night.'

Having got so far, the nigger turned round and looked across the road to see what it might be the ironing-woman saw that made her eyes look so strange. He could see nothing but just a blade or two of grass which had not yet been trodden down and which were heavy with the morning dew; so he looked at her again.

'When are they going to bury him?'

---

1   'Take your things and go, Ferreira,
    Take your things and go;
    Heavy to carry, heavy to carry ...'
These words are from the Afrikaans folksong (*lied*) *'Jannie met die hoepelbeen, Ferreira'* (Johnny with the bandy leg, Ferreira).

'Tomorrow morning. They've put him in a house in the yard; for Mrs Blair, she's frightened of ghosts.'

There was nothing to be gained by wasting more words over her just now, so the nigger resumed his *Swaar dra, swaar dra*, and, without touching his hat, turned away and walked jauntily whistling down the road.

Undine stood in the doorway and looked after him. There were sparrows hopping about at the tent-side, picking up crumbs and insects; and diggers passed with their sleeves rolled up above their elbows, walking briskly, whistling, some of them, for the morning air was fresh and made them feel that life, though it might mean small finds and hard work, was a pleasant thing and worth the having. Some of her children die every day, and Nature might go about forever in deep weeds and mourning if she took the trouble to lament for them; so she goes on smiling, though the best loved and the dearest have just gone – smiling, smiling, when our hearts are breaking. Why should the sky be clouded and the birds fly home hungry, because in one small tent a man lay stiff and white? Men whom women's hearts had yearned over died just so every week, and the world rocked on the same.

Undine slept heavily all day, a heavy sleep but troubled by many dreams; and when she woke the sun had long set. She went out to the barrel that stood at the back of the tent, and drained the last drop of water into the mug. She was thirsty, parched with thirst, but she felt no hunger. The slice of bread, very dry now, still lay upon the box unfinished.

She sat down on the side of her bed and held her head between her hands and tried to think, but her brain seemed very numb. After about an hour she stood up and went out, taking the road by which she had come yesterday evening. It was very dark, but she knew her way well.

The Compound was very quiet tonight. There was no one on the veranda, no light in the house. Only in the little tent at the back there was a light visible, and presently two men came out. The night was still and, though they spoke low, she could hear every word that passed:

'Put the candle and matches down, Jack, just there inside the door and button it down tight,' said the first man. 'I wonder they like leaving it alone like this without a soul in the place. Dogs might get in.'

'No fear of that while this dog lies here,' said the second. 'If I was not with you, I expect you'd rather be pretty near anywhere than here; he'd think no more of tearing you than of growling, if you tried to go in there alone; he don't half like it as it is, for all that I've had the feeding of the beggar for the last six months. Down, Prince, down!'

The men passed close to where Undine stood.

'I tell you what, Jack,' said the first, 'that coffin was damned heavy. My shoulders ache.'

'Charge it all in the bill,' said the second with a laugh:

'Ten little nigger boys
Fiddling over wine;
One got so jolly drunk,
And then there were nine, nine, nine.'

Then they went out at the gate, and the Compound was silent once more.

By and by Undine went round and opened the gate and walked in.

'Prince, Prince, old boy,' she called softly; for Prince had risen to his feet and uttered a low growl at the sound of approaching footsteps. 'Prince, have you quite forgotten me?'

The dog did not leave his post, but when she came close to him he laid his head against her knee.

'Prince, Prince! Oh, Prince!'

He seemed to understand her, for he uttered a long low growl, and they crouched down together at the entrance. Is *he* listening for the sound of his master's breathing in the quiet tent? Or is it only *one* who remembers how they two waited and listened, long ago?

Only the heavy breathing of the dog and the quick low breath of the woman break the stillness and are heard loud and clear in the quiet night; but in the tent, in the tent, there is deadly stillness.

It was near midnight now, and in the street passenger carts rumbled past, bearing home Toit's Pan visitors from the fast-closing houses of amusement.

Now she stood up and loosened the lower buttons that fastened down the canvas door. Stooping low, she went in, and the dog followed her, lying down close to the doorway and uttering a low short howl. Then it was quite silent in the tent, and very dark. Feeling her way along its side, her fingers touched at last the cold back of a chair, but that was not what she looked for; then the edge of a small table; then something lower than the table, long and narrow but with nothing inside. She felt that it was empty, so she moved on softly. Her hand was on the iron bedpost, then on the smooth sheet, and then on something cold – O, God – how cold!

She took the sheet down off his face, and the cheek of the living woman was pressed close to the cold face of the dead man. In his ear she whispered the wild words of love that to the living she would never utter – wild passionate words, the outpourings of a life's crushed-out love, the breaking forth of a fiercely suppressed passion. And the dead man lies so still; he does not send her from him; he does not silence her; he understands her now; he loves her now. She will see his face once more before it goes, and then she will creep close to him, and lie there, and never leave him.

In its place near the door she found the glass candlestick and matches, and when she had struck a light she came and stood with it in her hand at the bed's foot till her eyes had grown accustomed to it; then she looked up.

It was a calm white face that lay there above the sternly folded arms – a calm white face with the old smile, half scornful, half defiant, on the delicate arched lips.

The old face! What use to cry aloud to it! Mad, mad, and fool! Was there room in those sternly folded arms for her! He had lived alone and self-sufficient; he had died alone. There was no room for her now.

With a cry, as of one whose last hope has passed away, she let the light fall upon the floor, and the glass broke into a thousand fragments. But she stayed at the bed's foot till the grey light glimmered through the canvas. Then she crept out and left him.

A few hours afterwards, when all New Rush was astir again, the young wife came in to see her husband for the last time. She had never looked so lovely as that day in her flowing crape, with the great tears of fear in her baby eyes when they told her to stoop down and kiss him.

'I cannot, I cannot,' she cried; 'I am so afraid.' And as she turned to go out, the trailing crape rolled the broken glass upon the floor.

That was all that told of last night's watch.

CHAPTER TWENTY

Alone with the Stars

Water! Water!
She had slept again all day, and now that she awoke it was dark, and she was parched with thirst and there was no water – none in the barrel, none in the jug; her tongue clave to the roof of her mouth and her veins seemed scorched by liquid fire. She shook the barrel fiercely in her anger and tried to draw the tap out with her teeth. There must be some water in it, if only one could get it; it seemed to her some cruel living thing withholding life from her; and when she found she could do nothing she ran round and round the tent in the vain hope of growing cool. In her delirium it seemed that behind her a whole host of small hideous beings followed, howling – old women with long canine teeth that touched their breasts, old men with hunchbacks and little twinkling eyes which they closed tight and then opened suddenly: before, behind, they followed her; at every side they pressed her; and her thirst grew greater, till her tongue refused to move and keep them off by words.

'Water, water, water!' was all she could murmur.

And at last, as if in answer to her cry, water came. The great clouds that had made the night so dark burst, and the great torrent poured down on the earth. In an instant the heavy canvas sails were drenched, and she knelt down eagerly, holding them in both hands and sucking them. Then she lay down and let the rain fall on her till the fever left her and a great shivering seized her.

She went into her tent and climbed into the box, and her hands seemed powerless to undo her wet clothes, so she drew the blanket over her and lay there till morning.

'Mother,' said the children of the Dutchwoman opposite – 'mother, perhaps some wicked man has been to kill the Englishwoman in the little tent. Three days the sail is hanging loose, but we never see her coming out or doing ironing. We think she must be dead.'

'Nonsense!' said the mother. 'Don't you have anything to do with her; she's a bad woman.'

'How do you know that?' asked her husband, who sat at the door, smoking his pipe.

'Because I asked her the other day if the man who lived with her was her husband, and she said no. And I asked her if he was any relation of hers, and she said no. So she must be bad,' said the wife.

Nevertheless, when her work was done, curiosity led the dame over to the Englishwoman's tent. She looked in at the door and at first thought there was nothing but the three packing cases in the tent; then, in the farthest of these, which lay bottom downwards, she noticed the purple blanket move, and went up to it.

'You are very sick,' said the Dutchwoman in English, better than Boers generally speak.

Undine opened her eyes, but did not answer.

'You are very sick,' repeated the Dutchwoman.

'What is your name?'

'Undine, Undine Bock,' said Undine, slowly, as though puzzled to remember what it really was, and going back to the old name of her childhood.

'Great heavens!' said the Dutchwoman. 'Do you remember me – Sannie Muller?'

'Yes,' said Undine; but her eyes had closed again.

'Can I do anything for you?' Sannie asked with some real kindness in her voice, as the memory came to her of the little schoolmate who, in company with her monkey, had been first and foremost in all evil and forever in disgrace.

'No, thank you,' said Undine.

But the woman remained sitting by her till it grew dark; then she lit a candle and stood at her side, saying as she did so: 'I will come again during the night and see you.'

'Mother,' asked the little child who had been waiting for her in the road, as she trotted along at her side, 'is the Englishwoman very sick?'

'Yes,' said the mother. 'She will be dead in the morning.'

The Dutchwoman had worked hard all day, and when once she fell asleep she did not awake.

But the little tent had another visitor that night. Not long after the Dutchwoman left, a great, rough curly head pushed itself in at the door, sniffed for a moment, and then four black paws carried it up to the side of the box. Undine was roused by a soft warm touch on the hand and when she opened her eyes the rough old face was close above hers, looking down at her. Her mind was too confused and dull for his presence there to cause her even the vaguest wonder. She only moved her fingers feebly and called his name, 'Prince, Prince.'

He stepped over the low side of the packing case and lay down across her feet, with his head turned to one side so that he could watch her as he lay there.

A very quiet sleep followed, and Undine did not know when the candle dropped into the bottle, or when Prince moved higher up so that his head rested on her breast. She knew nothing till she woke at one o'clock. Then she raised herself a little on her elbow, looked round and fell back heavily again on her pillow.

The racking pain, the fever, the dull confusion of brain, all had vanished. Free from pain, calm and clear as she had never felt before, she lay there, yet cold, strangely cold. What did it mean, this strange feeling? She lay wondering, thinking, with her hands folded on the dog's black head. Then the truth came to her suddenly.

Death – only that, nothing more. What she had longed and prayed for; what she had looked for in the muddy pool; what she had sighed for in days of emptiness – it had come at last.

Again she raised herself and again fell back heavily upon the pillow. 'Not death, not death!' she said, 'not death! – anything else – death is too horrible and I, I am so young, so young to die!'

What was the use of crying out! She only grew stiffer and colder and her breath came slow and heavy in the closed tent. She would leave it and go out into the starlight, she would be braver there. The great horror that was upon her gave her strength, and she pushed the dog from her and crept slowly over the side of the low box. There she lay long, and then again, inch by inch, crawling on hands and knees, she reached the doorway. The skirting that crossed it, three inches high, was hard to pass, and again she lay still; but when she turned her head and caught sight of clear starlight outside, she crept on once more. Still on her hands and knees, and falling sometimes with her face into the dust, she gained at last one of the low gravel-heaps and lay down on its side.

She looked up at the old stars that she had looked up to and loved from her childhood as other men love their friends of flesh and blood – the dear old stars that had shed their light on the thatched roofs and stone walls of the old farm on the Karoo; that had looked in at the window of the little whitewashed room and on the leaves of the small brown Testament and the little child who cried and prayed there; the same and yet, tonight, looking so strange and new to her. Over the tumult and agony that reigned within, they spoke a great peace, and she lay still and watched them.

'Twas one of the gorgeous nights when the sky, shooting light from a million points, overwhelms and silences us; and the little circle of our life, that has seemed to fill all creation, sinks to its proper size – a shadow, a breath of wind that, being or not being, matters not.

High over her head was one great blue star that gave a steady and unflickering light. At this she looked with dark wide-open eyes till it seemed to speak to her as clearly as the priest speaks who stands at the bedside of the dying with bread and wine, reproof and blessing, whereby he hopes to help the soul in its last struggles among the waters.

'Is death so horrible and ghastly to you?' said the star, 'so ghastly that even the pain and suffering and despair that are in life grow beautiful in your eyes? I am only your brother,' said the star, 'a few million years older than you, and I know nothing; but I have seen some things – a few. I have seen the sun pour forth his light and heat as a great heart pours its life-blood for others. I have seen it fall on a world dead and silent, and awake it; till in place of death there was life, and for silence sound and ceaseless change. I have seen a world find birth through that light, even those strange and tiny creatures who deep at the floor of the sea have formed their graves and a new land; the waves have rolled back from it and the land that is built from their skeletons has become tree and grass and a million forms of life; on these other creatures have lived; and these again have died that others might have life; and at last man has come, to bring one of whom from the shapeless germ in which he lies plants innumerable die, and his very next of kin are sacrificed that he may grow and be. I have looked long and carefully,' said the star, 'and I have seen that the thing which you call death is the father of all life and beauty. Till life goes, till blood flows, no higher life can come. There is nothing added to Nature, nothing taken from her. She has only so much in her hand, and with that she must do all things. Would she build better, she must pull down first; would she raise a new world, an old must sink; would she double a flower, the seed of the single must go; and to make a man a million million forms have been and are not.

'Without death there is no change, without change no life; without the shedding of blood no good thing.

'If what you fear in the death that is upon you is not change but a fearful endless silence and annihilation, then take comfort,' said the star; 'I have been young and now am old; I have seen great ebbs and great flows, and myriad never-ending changes; but such death as you dream of I have nowhere seen. Nature is too poor to lose, too poor to let rest; her work is not yet done; she has other things to make.

'Mark you well, I know nothing,' said the star; 'and what you are, or I am, or the gravel is on which you lie, I cannot tell, and what we mean I cannot tell; only that which I have seen I speak of.

'The stump now burning at your side, it was a great brown lifeless stump an hour or two ago, now a lurid glowing mass shooting out flames and heat, cracking and changing every moment. It will be a small heap of ashes soon, but the light and heat were in it before the match touched it, and I know they are not lost, only doing other work in other forms.

'I have been young and now am old,' said the star; 'yet if I should say I have seen death as you fear it, I should lie. Change I have seen and desolation, but no death. Take comfort.'

And she was comforted and looked upwards with her arms folded and almost a smile on her lips.

For, as in our hours of sin and weakness, we weep because the great ever-changing, many-waved current on which we find ourselves will flow on just the same when our small wave has spent itself, so, in our moments of sight and strength, a joy, calm and mighty, comes to us when we see that the great current will flow on uninjured, unchanged by our loss, in its deathless progress.

She lay still and was comforted. And what if the star never spoke, and only her own thoughts were thrown back to her! If it be to a bedside with priest, wafer, and book, or to a gravel-heap under the stars, that peace and strength come, are they not the children of the soul, and no outcome of wafer, priest, or star? Though blessed be all three if they can call them forth in the hour of our battle the last and strongest.

She rested till it seemed as though a mist were creeping over the brilliant night sky, and then as though the smoke from the fire passed before her eyes. She raised her hands slowly as though to wave it from her; but it grew darker, and one by one the stars vanished. Then she knew that it was the shadow of death that lay between her and them.

Slowly she turned away her head, and even in that darkness could see lying between the two great stones the stump, now coal from end to end with blood-red cracks upon its surface.

The cold was growing greater, so she crept a little nearer the coal and lay with her face to it.

Was it because the glowing light, seen through the mist, brought back a night of long ago, that she heard in the dim delicious confusion the voice that had called her so tenderly under the red lamplight in the little hall?

'My little girl, my own little girl – Undine,' it said over and over, and the soft tears of gladness filled her eyes, and in delicious dreamy darkness it seemed as though his arms were close around her.

Presently the moon rose and looked over the ridge of the tent into the little yard among the gravel-heaps. The glowing stump had burnt out and gone to ashes between the great round stones.

Before them, in her little purple print, with her feet crossed and her head resting on one arm, lay Undine.

Her white *kappie* lay near her and cast a grotesque shadow, like a man's face with long nose and chin; and the light glistened on her soft brown hair.

There was nothing else to be seen in the little yard.

THE END

The Story of an African Farm

by
Olive Schreiner

Author's Preface

I have to thank cordially the public and my critics for the reception they have given this little book.

Dealing with a subject that is far removed from the round of English daily life, it of necessity lacks the charm that hangs about the ideal representation of familiar things, and its reception has therefore been the more kindly.

A word of explanation is necessary. Two strangers appear on the scene, and some have fancied that in the second they have again the first, who returns in a new guise. Why this should be we cannot tell; unless there is a feeling that a man should not appear upon the scene, and then disappear, leaving behind him no more substantial trace than a mere book; that he should return later on as husband or lover, to fill some more important part than that of the mere stimulator of thought.

Human life may be painted according to two methods. There is the stage method. According to that each character is duly marshalled at first, and ticketed; we know with an immutable certainty that at the right crises each one will reappear and act his part, and, when the curtain falls, all will stand before it bowing. There is a sense of satisfaction in this, and of completeness. But there is another method – the method of the life we all lead. Here nothing can be prophesied. There is a strange coming and going of feet. Men appear, act and re-act upon each other, and pass away. When the crisis comes the man who would fit it does not return. When the curtain falls no one is ready. When the footlights are brightest they are blown out; and what the name of the play is no one knows. If there sits a spectator who knows, he sits so high that the players in the gaslight cannot hear his breathing. Life may be painted according to either method; but the methods are different. The canons of criticism that bear upon the one cut cruelly upon the other.

It has been suggested by a kind of critic that he would better have liked the little book if it had been a history of wild adventure; of cattle driven into inaccessible *kranzes* by Bushmen; 'of encounters with ravening lions, and hair-breadth escapes'. This could not be. Such works are best written in Picdadilly or in the Strand: there the gifts of the creative imagination, untrammelled by contact with any fact, may spread their wings.

But, should one sit down to paint the scenes among which he has grown, he will find that the facts creep in upon him. Those brilliant phases and shapes which the imagination sees in far-off lands are not for him to portray. Sadly he must squeeze the colour from his brush, and dip it into the grey pigments around him. He must paint what lies before him.

Ralph Iron
(Olive Schreiner)

'We must see the first images which the external world casts upon the dark mirror of his mind; or, must hear the first words which awaken the sleeping powers of thought, and stand by his earliest efforts, if we would understand the prejudices, the habits, and the passions that will rule his life. The entire man is, so to speak, to be found in the cradle of the child.'

Alexis De Tocqueville

Contents

Author's Preface *181*
Introduction by S C Cronwright-Schreiner *185*

Part One

1. Shadows from Child-life *191*
2. Plans and Bushman Paintings *198*
3. I was a Stranger, and Ye Took Me In *204*
4. Blessed in He that Believeth *209*
5. Sunday Services *216*
6. Bonaparte Blenkins Makes His Nest *223*
7. He Sets His Trap *228*
8. He Catches the Old Bird *232*
9. He Sees a Ghost *240*
10. He Shows His Teeth *246*
11. He Snaps *249*
12. He Bites *255*
13. He Makes Love *264*

Part Two

1. Times and Seasons *271*
2. Waldo's Stranger *285*
3. Gregory Rose Finds His Affinity *300*
4. Lyndall *308*
5. *Tant* Sannie Holds an Upsitting, and Gregory Writes a Letter *321*
6. A Boer Wedding *327*
7. Waldo Goes Out to Taste Life, and Em Stays at Home and Tastes It *336*
8. The *Kopje* *339*
9. Lyndall's Stranger *346*
10. Gregory Rose has an Idea *353*
11. An Unfinished Letter *357*
12. Gregory's Womanhood *368*
13. Dreams *384*
14. Waldo Goes Out to Sit in the Sunshine *389*

Introduction

In March 1875, Olive Schreiner, aged twenty, went, at a salary of £30 a year, as governess in the family of Mr Stoffel Fouché, an Afrikaner farmer (a Boer), on the farm Klein Gannahoek in the mountain veld of the Karoo of the Cape Colony. This farm lies west of the railway, about twenty-five miles almost south of the village of Cradock. There was then no railway within 200 miles of the farm and the journey to Cradock took four hours by cart. The house was isolated, many things were primitive, and on the wild veld game was plentiful. Olive's only room was her bedroom, with a simple bedstead, a box to hold her clothes and nothing else except the books she was reading. This room was part of a flat-roofed lean-to set up against the northern wall of the house next to the kitchen and under the same roof; it was mud-floored and the roof leaked, so that when heavy rain fell she used to cover herself with an umbrella and lead the water away by a little furrow in the floor. Until she secured a basin she used to wash in the little stream in the *kloof* or ravine which ran up the mountains almost from her door. Such was the room in which she wrote at least a considerable part of what was to be *The Story of an African Farm*. She left this situation at the end of April 1876 after the eldest daughter, a powerful girl, had struck her because she had been awarded less marks than a younger pupil.

Her next situation, again as governess and at the same salary, was at Ratelhoek, a farm between Cradock and Tarkastad, belonging to Mr Martin, another Afrikaner. At Klein Gannahoek the household language was solely Afrikaans (the *taal*), and probably it was there that Olive first had to speak the 'Dutch' language; but the Martins were bilingual. The owner of Ratelhoek was in affluent circumstances and had a large, well-furnished house; Olive had excellent rooms, was kindly treated and was happy. But she was a bad asthmatic and the situation of the house was so unsuited to her chest that she eventually had to leave. At Ratelhoek, in addition to doing an incredible amount of other writing and reading, she continued working at a novel then called *Thorn Kloof*, but which was eventually to be known as *The Story of an African Farm*. She always said she had written this novel at Klein Gannahoek, and, although there is no mention of it in her 1875-1876 journal, she must have written a considerable amount of it there, as is proved by several entries in her Ratelhoek journal. For instance (in addition to the fact that it is certain she wrote the first draft of 'The Watch' in 1873), only three months after she left Klein Gannahoek, she writes that she has decided to finish *Thorn Kloof* before revising an earlier novel (*Undine*) which she had finished while at the Fouchés; in March 1877 there are references to 'A Boer Wedding', and in the beginning of December 1878 she was writing 'Waldo's Letter'. It is thus clear that, by the end of 1878, she had practically finished the novel. Later events seem to indicate she may even then have been revising it.

In March 1879 she left Ratelhoek and, at the beginning of August, was re-installed as governess with the Fouchés, at a higher salary, at Leliekloof, a farm high up in the mountain range about five hours by cart south-east of Cradock. Here she was free from asthma and was strong and well and so remained until she left; and it was here that she finished *Thorn Kloof* late in 1879 or early in 1880, for in the latter year she sent the manuscript to Mrs John Brown at Burnley, England, asking her to find a publisher.

Mrs Brown (who still lives) does not remember whether the novel had a name, but says: 'the description of Lyndall was a word-picture of Olive herself, of her own form and face,' as she knew her in 1873. At the request of Dr and Mrs Brown, a friend and relative in Edinburgh consulted a publisher of standing, who, while eulogising the novel, thought it needed some cutting down. Mrs Brown returned the manuscript to Olive at Leliekloof with this opinion and recommendation, and Olive did what, in her discretion, she thought might be necessary. As far as my knowledge goes, she received no other advice, nor do I know what she cut out or condensed except that (as she told me) the most important and longest condensation was a dream of *Tant* Sannie's, given originally in full, now represented by the paragraph that occurs early in the first chapter, beginning: 'She had gone to bed, as she always did, in her clothes.' There is an interesting entry in her Leliekloof journal in which she refers to the novel, previously referred to as *Thorn Kloof* or 'the new work', by another name: 'I have begun to revise *Lyndall*. Must leave out much, feel a little sore.' Lyndall was her mother's maiden name. I do not know when Olive decided to abandon the name *Lyndall* and to adopt the title of *The Story of an African Farm*. She told Havelock Ellis that at one time she thought of calling the book *Mirage*, with the sub-title *A Series of Abortions*, but decided against it because she found a book had already been been published under that name and because she feared also it might be open to misconstruction.

Olive left Leliekloof in February 1881, taking the novel with her, and arrived in England (which she had never seen before) at the end of March. As soon as she was settled down, she began her attempts to get *The Story of an African Farm* published, but it was rejected by one publisher after another. She was almost in despair when Chapman & Hall accepted it, acting on the advice of their 'reader', George Meredith. The story that Meredith, who was a stranger to her, assisted her in any way whatever, is wholly untrue. The first edition, a small one in two volumes, was published late in January 1883, and was soon sold out. The author's name was given simply as 'Ralph Iron', and there was no dedication or preface. This edition brought Olive £18 2s 11d. In July 1883, a second edition was published. This was in one volume and contained a short preface as well as the dedication to Mrs John Brown. The author's name, in brackets beneath the original pen-name 'Ralph Iron', appeared in the 1887 edition. Olive used to tell with amusement how surprised Mr Chapman was when, having asked 'Ralph Iron Esq' to call, a small, shy, girlish-looking young woman was ushered in, instead of the big, powerful man expected. Many subsequent editions have of course been issued. By far the largest sales have been in America, where unfortunately the book was not copyrighted.

Much of the book is clearly autobiographical, in its subjective states especially; for instance, there can be no doubt that the incidents of 'The Watch' and 'The Sacrifice' in the first chapter are actually her own childish experiences; 'Times and Seasons' (as she stated in a letter to me, given in the *Life*) are in part at least a relation of the actual workings of her own mind as a child at Healdtown (from the age of six to the age of eleven). Readers interested in the chapter 'Waldo's Stranger' may like to know who 'The Stranger' was, and how and when and where Olive met him. In June 1871, Olive, aged sixteen, was on a visit to her aunt, Mrs Rolland, at Hermon, a Native Mission Station in Basutoland, to which the Rev Mr Rolland had been appointed, and their daughter was there also. These three women were alone in the Mission House, which, Olive said, was about fifty miles from the nearest white residence. One wet, cold, dark night there was a knock. The lonely women were alarmed, but Olive opened the door and a white man entered, a member of the Cape Civil Service, who, on behalf of the Native Affairs Department, was making a tour of inspection of the Native Territories. This was 'Waldo's Stranger'. His name was Bertram, and he was about thirty years old. Like Waldo's Stranger he was on horseback and actually carried in his saddlebag Herbert Spencer's *First Principles* (which is the book the 'Stranger' is supposed to give Waldo). Bertram lent Olive *First Principles* and, before he rode away next morning, had a talk with her on Art. She says he was 'exactly like' Waldo's Stranger, and indeed, the resemblance, mentally and physically, is close. The allegory is, of course, her own, nor can it be open to doubt that, whatever Bertram said to her on Art, has been elaborated and transmuted. Bertram was to return in three days, which was thus the length of time this sixteen-year-old country girl had in which to read Herbert Spencer's great book. She had never had schooling worth anything to her: all that she knew was from intercourse with her cultured mother and from her insatiable thirst for knowledge and reading, worked upon by her precocious and penetrating intellect.

Of the characters in the novel, Lyndall and Waldo are in large part two sides of Olive herself and are so meant to be, though there were many more than two sides to her complex personality; Waldo, however ('as far as he is not myself,' Olive used to say), had an original, a man I knew; and it is remarkable how accurately Olive (who was only seventeen when she met him), has shewn a comprehension of the deeps of his nature, discernable to but few others. Lyndall is a more evident side of Olive than Waldo is; the likeness is both mental and physical. Old Otto, the German overseer, is Olive's own father, acknowledged by the family to be a true and beautiful delineation of the old man. Some of *Tant* Sannie's characteristics are founded upon a not uncommon South African type, of which the good housewife at Klein Gannahoek was, in some respects, an example; the study is, however, objective and humorous, and is not meant wholly to portray Mrs Fouché, for whom Olive had an affectionate and humorous admiration, and who was much offended and wrote Olive a violent letter when some mischievous person told her she was *Tant* Sannie. Gregory Rose is founded on an original, too (whom I knew), an admirable man whom Olive thought highly of and whose gentle side she drew lovingly and sympathetically. Strange to relate Bonaparte Blenkins (whose son I knew) also had an original, an irresponsible Irishman, though of course Bonaparte is drawn objectively and is a caricature. 'Lyndall's Stranger' (who was not Waldo's Stranger) and Em represent no one in particular, and the main incidents of the story are imaginary.

I conclude with a few opinions on *The Story of an African Farm* by some eminent persons. Lecky, the historian, held it to be among the best novels in the English language. Sir Charles Dilke, a man of unusual intellect and literary taste and of wide culture, said it was the greatest novel in the English language, greater than *The Pilgrim's Progress*. Gladstone was 'deeply impressed' by it, and 'much struck with its power and force, more than he had been with any book for a long time'; meeting her in 1889, in consequence of his admiration for the book, he got into 'deep talk' with her and 'would not let her go'. Cecil Rhodes said it 'enraptured him'; he was 'unable to account for its splendour'; again and again he referred to the concluding chapters as 'masterpieces', and to the book itself as a work of 'profound genius', pointing out that it had been written 'amid desert surroundings, with which alone, practically speaking, she had been acquainted'. Edward Carpenter, Havelock Ellis, Arthur Symons and many others have borne testimony from personal knowledge to their conviction that the book was the intimate revelation of the writer's emotional and intellectual life.

S C Cronwright-Schreiner

Rome
January 1924

PART ONE

CHAPTER ONE

Shadows From Child-Life

The Watch

The full African moon poured down its light from the blue sky into the wide, lonely plain. The dry, sandy earth, with its coating of stunted Karoo bushes a few inches high, the low hills that skirted the plain, the milk-bushes with their long, finger-like leaves, all were touched by a weird and an almost oppressive beauty as they lay in the white light.

In one spot only was the solemn monotony of the plain broken. Near the centre a small, solitary *kopje* rose. Alone it lay there, a heap of round iron-stones piled one upon another, as over some giant's grave. Here and there a few tufts of grass or small succulent plants had sprung up among its stones, and on the very summit a clump of prickly-pears lifted their thorny arms, and reflected, as from mirrors, the moonlight on their broad, fleshy leaves. At the foot of the *kopje* lay the homestead. First, the stone-walled sheep *kraals* and Kaffir huts; beyond them the dwelling house – a square red-brick building with thatched roof. Even on its bare red walls, and the wooden ladder that led up to the loft, the moonlight cast a kind of dreamy beauty, and quite etherealised the low brick wall that ran before the house, and which enclosed a bare patch of sand and two straggling sunflowers. On the zinc roof of the great open wagon-house, on the roofs of the outbuildings that jutted from its side, the moonlight glinted with a quite peculiar brightness, till it seemed that every rib in the metal was of burnished silver.

Sleep ruled everywhere, and the homestead was not less quiet than the solitary plain.

In the farmhouse, on her great wooden bedstead, *Tant* Sannie, the Boer woman, rolled heavily in her sleep.

She had gone to bed, as she always did, in her clothes; and the night was warm and the room close, and she dreamed bad dreams. Not of the ghosts and devils that so haunted her waking thoughts; nor of her second husband, the consumptive Englishman, whose grave lay away beyond the ostrich camps; nor of her first, the young Boer; but only of the sheep's trotters she had eaten for supper that night. She dreamed that one stuck fast in her throat, and she rolled her huge form from side to side, and snorted horribly.

In the next room, where the maid had forgotten to close the shutter, the white moonlight fell in a flood, and made it light as day. There were two small beds against the wall. In one lay a yellow-haired child, with a low forehead and a face of freckles;

but the loving moonlight hid defects here as elsewhere, and showed only the innocent face of a child in its first sweet sleep.

The figure in the companion bed belonged of right to the moonlight, for it was of quite elfin-like beauty. The child had dropped her cover on the floor, and the moonlight looked in at the naked little limbs. Presently she opened her eyes and looked at the moonlight that was bathing her.

'Em!' she called to the sleeper in the other bed; but received no answer. Then she drew the cover from the floor, turned her pillow, and pulling the sheet over her head, went to sleep again.

Only in one of the outbuildings that jutted from the wagon-house there was someone who was not asleep. The room was dark; door and shutter were closed; not a ray of light entered anywhere. The German overseer, to whom the room belonged, lay sleeping soundly on his bed in the corner, his great arms folded, and his bushy grey-and-black beard rising and falling on his breast. But one in the room was not asleep. Two large eyes looked about in the darkness, and two small hands were smoothing the patchwork quilt. The boy, who slept on a box under the window, had just awakened from his first sleep. He drew the quilt up to his chin, so that little peered above it but a great head of silky black curls and the two black eyes. He stared about in the darkness. Nothing was visible, not even the outline of one worm-eaten rafter, nor of the deal table, on which lay the Bible from which his father had read before they went to bed. No one could tell where the toolbox was, and where the fireplace. There was something very impressive to the child in the complete darkness.

At the head of his father's bed hung a great silver hunting watch. It ticked loudly. The boy listened to it, and began mechanically to count. Tick – tick – tick! one, two, three, four! He lost count presently, and only listened. Tick – tick – tick – tick!

It never waited; it went on inexorably; and every time it ticked *a man died*! He raised himself a little on his elbow and listened. He wished it would leave off.

How many times had it ticked since he came to lie down? A thousand times, a million times, perhaps.

He tried to count again, and sat up to listen better.

'Dying, dying, dying!' said the watch; 'dying, dying, dying!'

He heard it distinctly. Where were they going to, all those people?

He lay down quickly, and pulled the cover up over his head; but presently the silky curls reappeared.

'Dying, dying, dying!' said the watch; 'dying, dying, dying!'

He thought of the words his father had read that evening – '*For wide is the gate, and broad is the way, that leadeth to destruction, and many there be which go in thereat.*'

'Many, many, many!' said the watch.

'*Because strait is the gate, and narrow is the way, that leadeth unto life, and few there be that find it.*'

'Few, few, few!' said the watch.

The boy lay with his eyes wide open. He saw before him a long stream of people, a great dark multitude, that moved in one direction; then they came to the dark edge of the world, and went over. He saw them passing on before him, and there was nothing that could stop them. He thought of how that stream had rolled on through all the long ages of the past – how the old Greeks and Romans had gone over; the countless millions of China and India, they were going over now. Since he had come to bed, how many had gone?

And the watch said, 'Eternity, eternity, eternity!'

'Stop them! stop them!' cried the child.

And all the while the watch kept ticking on; just like God's will, that never changes or alters, you may do what you please.

Great beads of perspiration stood on the boy's forehead. He climbed out of bed and lay with his face turned to the mud floor.

'Oh, God, God! save them!' he cried in agony. 'Only some; only a few! Only for each moment I am praying here one!' He folded his little hands upon his head. 'God! God! save them!'

He grovelled on the floor.

Oh, the long, long ages of the past, in which they had gone over! Oh, the long, long future, in which they would pass away! Oh, God! the long, long, long eternity, which has no end!

The child wept, and crept closer to the ground.

The Sacrifice

The farm by daylight was not as the farm by moonlight. The plain was a weary flat of loose red sand sparsely covered by dry Karoo bushes that cracked beneath the tread like tinder, and showed the red earth everywhere. Here and there a milk-bush lifted its pale-coloured rods, and in every direction the ants and beetles ran about in the blazing sand. The red walls of the farmhouse, the zinc roofs of the outbuildings, the stone walls of the *kraals*, all reflected the fierce sunlight, till the eye ached and blenched. No tree or shrub was to be seen far or near. The two sunflowers that stood before the door, out-stared by the sun, drooped their brazen faces to the sand; and the little cicada-like insects cried aloud among the stones of the *kopje*.

The Boer woman, seen by daylight, was even less lovely than when, in bed, she rolled and dreamed. She sat on a chair in the great front room, with her feet on a wooden stove, and wiped her flat face with the corner of her apron, and drank coffee, and in Cape Dutch swore that the beloved weather was damned. Less lovely, too, by daylight was the dead Englishman's child, her little step-daughter, upon whose freckles and low, wrinkled forehead the sunlight had no mercy.

'Lyndall,' the child said to her little orphan cousin, who sat with her on the floor threading beads, 'how is it your beads never fall off your needle?'

' I try,' said the little one gravely, moistening her tiny finger. 'That is why.'

The overseer, seen by daylight, was a huge German, wearing a shabby suit, and with a childish habit of rubbing his hands and nodding his head prodigiously when pleased at anything. He stood out at the *kraals* in the blazing sun, explaining to two Kaffir boys the approaching end of the world. The boys, as they cut the cakes of dung, winked at each other, and worked as slowly as they possibly could; but the German never saw it.

Away, beyond the *kopje*, Waldo his son herded the ewes and lambs – a small and dusty herd – powdered all over from head to foot with red sand, wearing a ragged coat, and shoes of undressed leather, through whose holes the toes looked out. His hat was too large, and had sunk down to his eyes, concealing completely the silky black curls. It was a curious, small figure. His flock gave him little trouble. It was too hot for them to move far; they gathered round every little milk-bush as though they hoped to find shade, and stood there motionless in clumps. He himself crept under a shelving rock that lay at the foot of the *kopje*, stretched himself on his stomach, and waved his dilapidated little shoes in the air.

Soon, from the blue bag where he kept his dinner, he produced a fragment of slate, an arithmetic, and a pencil. Proceeding to put down a sum with solemn and earnest demeanour, he began to add it up aloud: 'Six and two is eight – and four is twelve – and two is fourteen – and four is eighteen.' Here he paused. 'And four is eighteen – and – four – is eighteen.' The last was very much drawled. Slowly the pencil slipped from his fingers and the slate followed it into the sand. For a while he lay motionless, then began muttering to himself, folded his little arms, laid his head down upon them, and might have been asleep but for a muttering sound that from time to time proceeded from him. A curious old ewe came to sniff at him; but it was long before he raised his head. When he did, he looked at the far-off hills with his heavy eyes.

'Ye shall receive – ye shall receive – *shall, shall, shall,*' he muttered.

He sat up then. Slowly the dullness and heaviness melted from his face; it became radiant. Midday had come now, and the sun's rays were poured down vertically; the earth throbbed before the eye.

The boy stood up quickly, and cleared a small space from the bushes which covered it. Looking carefully, he found twelve small stones of somewhat the same size; kneeling down, he arranged them carefully on the cleared space in a square pile in shape like an altar. Then he walked to the bag where his dinner was kept; in it was a mutton chop and a large slice of brown bread. The boy took them out and turned the bread over in his hand, deeply considering it. Finally he threw it away and walked to the altar with the meat, and laid it down on the stones. Close by in the red sand he knelt down. Sure, never since the beginning of the world was there so ragged and so small a priest. He took off his great hat and placed it solemnly on the ground, then closed his eyes and folded his hands. He prayed aloud.

'Oh, God, my Father, I have made Thee a sacrifice. I have only two pence, so I cannot buy a lamb. If the lambs were mine I would give Thee one; but now I have only this meat; it is my dinner-meat. Please, my Father, send fire down from heaven to burn it. Thou hast said, "Whosoever shall say unto this mountain, be thou cast into the sea, nothing doubting, it shall be done." I ask for the sake of Jesus Christ. Amen.'

He knelt down with his face upon the ground, and he folded his hands upon his curls. The fierce sun poured down its heat upon his head and upon his altar. When he looked up he knew what he should see – the glory of God! For fear his very heart stood still, his breath came heavily; he was half suffocated. He dared not look up. Then at last he raised himself. Above him was the quiet, blue sky, about him the red earth; there were the clumps of silent ewes and his altar – that was all.

He looked up – nothing broke the intense stillness of the blue overhead. He looked round in astonishment, then he bowed again, and this time longer than before.

When he raised himself the second time all was unaltered. Only the sun had melted the fat of the little mutton chop, and it ran down upon the stones.

Then, the third time he bowed himself. When at last he looked up, some ants had come to the meat on the altar. He stood up and drove them away. Then he put his hat on his hot curls, and sat in the shade. He clasped his hands about his knees. He sat to watch what would come to pass. The glory of the Lord God Almighty! He knew he should see it.

'My dear God is trying me,' he said; and he sat there through the fierce heat of the afternoon. Still he watched and waited when the sun began to slope; and when it neared the horizon and the sheep began to cast long shadows across the Karoo, he still sat there. He hoped when the first rays touched the hills till the sun dipped behind them and was gone. Then he called his ewes together, and broke down the altar, and threw the meat far, far away into the field.

He walked home behind his flock. His heart was heavy. He reasoned so: 'God cannot lie. I had faith. No fire came. I am like Cain – I am not His. He will not hear my prayer. God hates me.'

The boy's heart was heavy. When he reached the *kraal* gate the two girls met him.

'Come,' said the yellow-haired Em, 'let us play "coop". There is still time before it gets quite dark. You, Waldo, go and hide on the *kopje*; Lyndall and I will shut eyes here, and we will not look.'

The girls hid their faces in the stone wall of the sheep-*kraal*, and the boy clambered half-way up the *kopje*. He crouched down between two stones and gave the call. Just then the milk-herd came walking out of the cow-*kraal* with two pails. He was an ill-looking Kaffir.

'Ah!' thought the boy, 'perhaps he will die tonight, and go to hell! I must pray for him, I must pray!'

195

Then he thought – 'Where am I going to?' and he prayed desperately.

'Ah! this is not right at all,' little Em said, peeping between the stones, and finding him in a very curious posture. 'What *are* you doing, Waldo? It is not the play, you know. You should run out when we come to the white stone. Ah, you do not play nicely.'

'I – I will play nicely now,' said the boy, coming out and standing sheepishly before them; 'I – I only forgot; I will play now.'

'He has been to sleep,' said freckled Em.

' No,' said beautiful little Lyndall, looking curiously at him; 'he has been crying.' She never made a mistake.

The Confession

One night, two years after, the boy sat alone on the *kopje*. He had crept softly from his father's room and come there. He often did, because, when he prayed or cried aloud, his father might awake and hear him; and none knew his great sorrow, and none knew his grief, but he himself, and he buried them deep in his heart.

He turned up the brim of his great hat and looked at the moon, but most at the leaves of the prickly pear that grew just before him. They glinted, and glinted, and glinted, just like his own heart – cold, so hard, and very wicked. His physical heart had pain also; it seemed full of little bits of glass, that hurt. He had sat there for half an hour, and he dared not go back to the close house.

He felt horribly lonely. There was not one thing so wicked as he in all the world, and he knew it. He folded his arms and began to cry – not aloud; he sobbed without making any sound, and his tears left scorched marks where they fell. He could not pray; he had prayed night and day for so many months; and tonight he could not pray. When he left off crying, he held his aching head with his brown hands. If one might have gone up to him and touched him kindly; poor, ugly little thing! Perhaps his heart was almost broken.

With his swollen eyes he sat there on a flat stone at the very top of the *kopje*; and the tree, with every one of its wicked leaves, blinked, and blinked, and blinked at him. Presently he began to cry again and then stopped his crying to look at it. He was quiet for a long while, then he knelt up slowly and bent forward. There was a secret he had carried in his heart for a year. He had not dared to look at it; he had not whispered it to himself; but for a year he had carried it. 'I hate God!' he said. The wind took the words and ran away with them, among the stones, and through the leaves of the prickly pear. He thought it died away half down the *kopje*. He had told it now!

'I love Jesus Christ, but I hate God.'

The wind carried away that sound as it had done the first. Then he got up and buttoned his old coat about him. He knew he was certainly lost now; he did not care. If half the world were to be lost, why not he too? He would not pray for mercy any more. Better so – better to know certainly. It was ended now. Better so.

He began scrambling down the sides of the *kopje* to go home.

Better so! – But oh, the loneliness, the agonised pain! for that night, and for nights on nights to come! The anguish that sleeps all day on the heart like a heavy worm, and wakes up at night to feed!

There are some of us who in after years say to Fate, 'Now deal us your hardest blow, give us what you will; but let us never again suffer as we suffered when we were children.'

The barb in the arrow of childhood's suffering is this – its intense loneliness, its intense ignorance.

CHAPTER TWO

Plans and Bushman Paintings

At last came the year of the great drought, the year of 1862. From end to end of the land the earth cried for water. Man and beast turned their eyes to the pitiless sky, that like the roof of some brazen oven arched overhead. On the farm, day after day, month after month, the water in the dams fell lower and lower; the sheep died in the fields; the cattle, scarcely able to crawl, tottered as they moved from spot to spot in search of food. Week after week, month after month, the sun looked down from the cloudless sky, till the Karoo bushes were leafless sticks, broken into the earth, and the earth itself was naked and bare; and only the milk-bushes, like old hags, pointed their shrivelled fingers heavenwards, praying for the rain that never came.

It was on an afternoon of a long day in that thirsty summer that on the side of the *kopje* furthest from the homestead the two girls sat. They were somewhat grown since the days when they played hide-and-seek there, but they were mere children still.

Their dress was of dark, coarse stuff; their common blue pinafores reached to their ankles, and on their feet they wore homemade *velskoen*.

They sat under a shelving rock, on the surface of which were still visible some old Bushman paintings, their red and black pigments having been preserved through long years from wind and rain by the overhanging ledge; grotesque oxen, elephants, rhinoceroses, and a one-horned beast, such as no man ever has seen or ever shall.

The girls sat with their backs to the paintings. In their laps were a few fern and ice-plant leaves, which by dint of much searching they had gathered under the rocks.

Em took off her big brown *kappie* and began vigorously to fan her red face with it; but her companion bent low over the leaves in her lap, and at last took up the ice-plant leaf and fastened it onto the front of her blue pinafore with a pin.

'Diamonds must look as these drops do,' she said, carefully bending over the leaf, and crushing one crystal drop with her delicate little nail. 'When I,' she said, 'am grown up, I shall wear real diamonds, exactly like these, in my hair.'

Her companion opened her eyes and wrinkled her low forehead.

'Where will you find them, Lyndall? The stones are only crystals that we picked up yesterday. Old Otto says so.'

'And you think that I am going to stay *here* always?'

The lip trembled scornfully.

'Ah, no,' said her companion. 'I suppose someday we shall go somewhere; but now we are only twelve, and we cannot marry till we are seventeen. Four years, five – that is a long time to wait. And we might not have diamonds if we did marry.'

'And you think that I am going to stay here till then?'

'Well, where *are* you going?' asked her companion.

The girl crushed an ice-plant leaf between her fingers.

'*Tant* Sannie is a miserable old woman,' she said. 'Your father married her when he was dying, because he thought she would take better care of the farm, and of us, than an Englishwoman. He said we should be taught and sent to school. Now she saves every farthing for herself, buys us not even one old book. She does not ill-use us – why? Because she is afraid of your father's ghost. Only this morning she told her Hottentot that she would have beaten you for breaking the plate, but that three nights ago she heard a rustling and a grunting behind the pantry door, and knew it was your father coming to *spook* her. She is a miserable old woman,' said the girl, throwing the leaf from her; but I intend to go to school.'

'And if she won't let you?'

'I shall make her.'

'How?'

The child took not the slightest notice of the last question, and folded her small arms across her knees.

'But why do you want to go, Lyndall?'

'There is nothing helps in this world,' said the child slowly, 'but to be very wise, and to know everything – to be clever.'

'But I should not like to go to school!' persisted the small, freckled face.

'And you do not need to. When you are seventeen this Boer woman will go; you will have this farm and everything that is upon it for your own; but I,' said Lyndall, 'will have nothing. I must learn.'

'Oh, Lyndall! *I* will give you some of my sheep,' said Em, with a sudden burst of pitying generosity.

'I do not want your sheep,' said the girl slowly; 'I want things of my own. When I am grown up,' she added, the flush on her delicate features deepening at every word, 'there will be nothing that I do not know. I shall be rich, very rich; and I shall wear not only for best, but every day, a pure white silk, and little rosebuds, like the lady in *Tant* Sannie's bedroom, and my petticoats will be embroidered, not only at the bottom, but all through.'

The lady in *Tant* Sannie's bedroom was a gorgeous creature from a fashion-sheet, which the Boer woman, somewhere obtaining, had pasted up at the foot of her bed, to be profoundly admired by the children.

'It would be very nice,' said Em; but it seemed a dream of quite too transcendent a glory ever to be realised.

At this instant there appeared at the foot of the *kopje* two figures – the one, a dog, white and sleek, one yellow ear hanging down over his left eye; the other, his master, a lad of fourteen, and no other than the boy Waldo, grown into a heavy, slouching youth of fourteen. The dog mounted the *kopje* quickly, his master followed slowly. He wore an aged jacket much too large for him, and rolled up at the wrists, and, as of old, a pair of dilapidated *velskoens* and a felt hat. He stood before the two girls at last.

'What have you been doing today?' asked Lyndall, lifting her eyes to his face.

'Looking after ewes and lambs below the dam. Here!' he said, holding out his hand awkwardly, 'I brought them for you.'

There were a few green blades of tender grass.

'Where did you find them?'

'On the dam wall.'

She fastened them beside the leaf on her blue pinafore.

'They look nice there,' said the boy, awkwardly rubbing his great hands and watching her.

'Yes; but the pinafore spoils it all; it is not pretty.'

He looked at it closely.

'Yes, the squares are ugly; but it looks nice upon you – beautiful.'

He now stood silent before them, his great hands hanging loosely at either side.

'Someone has come today,' he mumbled out suddenly, when the idea struck him.

'Who?' asked both girls.

'An Englishman on foot.'

'What does he look like?' asked Em.

'I did not notice; but he has a very large nose,' said the boy slowly. 'He asked the way to the house.'

'Didn't he tell you his name?'

'Yes – Bonaparte Blenkins.'

'Bonaparte!' said Em, 'why that is like the reel Hottentot Hans plays on the violin –

Bonaparte, Bonaparte, my wife is sick;
In the middle of the week, but Sundays not,
I give her rice and beans for soup.

It is a funny name.'

'There was a living man called Bonaparte once,' said she of the great eyes.

'Ah, yes, I know,' said Em – 'the poor prophet whom the lions ate. I am always so sorry for him.'

Her companion cast a quiet glance upon her.

'He was the greatest man who ever lived,' she said, 'the man I like best.'

'And what did he do?' asked Em, conscious that she had made a mistake, and that her prophet was not the man.

'He was one man, only one,' said her little companion slowly, 'yet all the people in the world feared him. He was not born great, he was common as we are; yet he was master of the world at last. Once he was only a little child, then he was a lieutenant, then he was a general, then he was an emperor. When he said a thing to himself he never forgot it. He waited, and waited, and waited, and it came at last.'

'He must have been very happy,' said Em.

'I do not know,' said Lyndall; 'but he had what he said he would have, and that is better than being happy. He was their master, and all the people were white with fear of him. They joined together to fight him. He was one and they were many, and they got him down at last. They were like the wild cats when their teeth are fast in a great dog, like cowardly wild cats,' said the child, 'they would not let him go. They were many; he was only *one*. They sent him to an island in the sea, a lonely island, and kept him there fast. He was one man, and they were many, and they were terrified at him. It was glorious!' said the child.

'And what then?' said Em.

'Then he was alone there in that island with men to watch him always,' said her companion, slowly and quietly, 'and in the long, lonely nights he used to lie awake and think of the things he had done in the old days, and the things he would do if they let him go again. In the day when he walked near the shore it seemed to him that the sea all around him was a cold chain about his body, pressing him to death.'

'And then?' said Em, much interested.

'He died there in that island; he never got away.'

'It is rather a nice story,' said Em; 'but the end is sad.'

'It is a terrible, hateful ending,' said the little teller of the story, leaning forward on her folded arms; 'and the worst is, it is true. I have noticed,' added the child very deliberately, 'that it is only the made-up stories that end nicely; the true ones all end so.'

As she spoke the boy's dark, heavy eyes rested on her face.

'You have read it, have you not?'

He nodded. 'Yes; but the brown history tells only what he did, not what he thought.'

'It was in the brown history that I read of him,' said the girl; 'but I *know* what he thought. Books do not tell everything.'

'No,' said the boy, slowly drawing nearer to her and sitting down at her feet. 'What you want to know they never tell.'

Then the children fell into silence, till Doss, the dog, growing uneasy at its long continuance, sniffed at one and the other, and his master broke forth suddenly:

'If *they* could talk, if they could tell us now!' he said, moving his hand out over the surrounding objects – 'then we would know something. This *kopje*, if it could tell us how it came here! The *Physical Geography* says,' he went on most rapidly and confusedly, 'that what are dry lands now were once lakes; and what I think is this – these low hills were once the shores of a lake; this *kopje* is some of the stones that were at the bottom, rolled together by the water. But there is this – how did the water come to make one heap here alone, in the centre of the plain?' It was a ponderous question; no one volunteered an answer. 'When I was little,' said the boy, 'I always looked at it and wondered, and I thought a great giant was buried under it. Now I know the water must have done it; but how? It is very wonderful. Did one little stone come first, and stopped the others as they rolled?' said the boy, with earnestness, in a low voice, more as speaking to himself than to them.

'Oh, Waldo, God put the little *kopje* here,' said Em with solemnity.

'But how did He put it here?'

'By wanting.'

'But how did the wanting bring it here?'

'Because it did.'

The last words were uttered with the air of one who produces a clinching argument. What effect it had on the questioner was not evident, for he made no reply, and turned away from her.

Drawing closer to Lyndall's feet, he said, after a while, in a low voice:

'Lyndall, has it never seemed to you that the stones *were* talking with you? Sometimes,' he added, in a yet lower tone, 'I lie under there with my sheep, and it seems that the stones are really speaking – speaking of the old things, of the time when the strange fishes and animals lived that are turned into stone now, and the lakes were here; and then of the time when the little Bushmen lived here, so small and so ugly, and used to sleep in the wild dog holes, and in the *sloots*, and eat snakes, and shot the bucks with their poisoned arrows. It was one of them, one of these old wild Bushmen, that painted those,' said the boy, nodding towards the pictures – 'one who was different from the rest. He did not know why, but he wanted to make something, so he made these. He worked hard, very hard, to find the juice to make the paint; and then he found this place where the rocks hang over, and he painted them. To us they are only strange things, that make us laugh; but to him they were very beautiful.'

The children had turned round and looked at the pictures.

'He used to kneel here naked, painting, painting, painting; and he wondered at the things he made himself,' said the boy, rising and moving his hand in deep excitement. 'Now the Boers have shot them all, so that we never see a yellow face peeping out among the stones.' He paused, a dreamy look coming over his face. 'And the wild bucks have gone, and those days, and we are here. But we will be gone soon, and only the stones will lie on here, looking at everything like they look now. I know that it is I who am thinking,' the fellow added slowly, 'but it seems as though it were they who were talking. Has it never seemed so to you, Lyndall?'

'No, it never seems so to me,' she answered.

The sun had dipped now below the hills, and the boy suddenly remembering the ewes and lambs, started to his feet.

'Let us also go to the house and see who has come,' said Em, as the boy shuffled away to rejoin his flock while Doss ran at his heels, snapping at the ends of the torn trousers as they fluttered in the wind.

CHAPTER THREE

I Was a Stranger, and Ye Took Me In

As the two girls rounded the side of the *kopje*, an unusual scene presented itself. A large group was gathered at the back door of the homestead.

On the doorstep stood the Boer woman, a hand on each hip, her face red and angry, her head nodding fiercely. At her feet sat the yellow Hottentot maid, her satellite, and around stood the black Kaffir maids, with blankets twisted round their half-naked figures. Two, who stamped *mielies* in a wooden block, held the great stampers in their hands, and stared stupidly at the object of attraction. It certainly was not to look at the old German overseer, who stood in the centre of the group, that they had all gathered together. His salt-and-pepper suit, grizzly black beard, and grey eyes were as familiar to everyone on the farm as the red gables of the homestead itself; but beside him stood the stranger, and on him all eyes were fixed. Ever and anon the newcomer cast a glance over his pendulous red nose to the spot where the Boer woman stood, and smiled faintly.

'I'm not a child,' cried the Boer woman, in low Cape Dutch, 'and I wasn't born yesterday. No, by the Lord, no! You can't take *me* in! My mother didn't wean me on Monday. One wink of my eye and I see the whole thing. I'll have no tramps sleeping on my farm,' cried *Tant* Sannie, blowing. 'No, by the Devil, no! Not though he had sixty-times-six red noses.'

There the German overseer mildly interposed that the man was not a tramp, but a highly respectable individual, whose horse had died by an accident three days before.

'Don't tell me,' cried the Boer woman; 'the man isn't born that can take *me* in. If he'd had money, wouldn't he have bought a horse? Men who walk are thieves, liars, murderers, Rome's priests, seducers! I see the Devil in his nose!' cried *Tant* Sannie, shaking her fist at him; 'and to come walking into the house of this Boer's child, and shaking hands as though he came on horseback! Oh, no no!'

The stranger took off his hat, a tall, battered chimney-pot, and disclosed a bald head, at the back of which was a little fringe of curled white hair; and he bowed to *Tant* Sannie.

'What does she remark, my friend?' he inquired, turning his crosswise looking eyes on the old German.

'Ah – well – ah – the – Dutch – you know – do not like people who walk – in this country – ah!'

'My dear friend,' said the stranger, laying his hand on the German's arm, 'I should have bought myself another horse, but crossing, five days ago, a full river, I lost my purse – a purse with five hundred pounds in it. I spent five days on the bank of the river trying to find it – couldn't. Paid a Kaffir nine pounds to go in and look for it at the risk of his life – couldn't find it.'

The German would have translated this information, but the Boer woman gave no ear.

'No, no; he goes tonight. See how he looks at me – a poor, unprotected female! If he wrongs me, who is to do me right?' cried *Tant* Sannie.

'I think,' said the German in an undertone, 'if you didn't look at her quite so much it might be advisable. She – ah – she – might – imagine that you liked her too well, – in fact – ah –'

'Certainly, my dear friend, certainly,' said the stranger, 'I shall not look at her.'

Saying this, he turned his nose full upon a small Kaffir of two years old. That small, naked son of Ham became instantly so terrified that he fled to his mother's blanket for protection, howling horribly.

Upon this the newcomer fixed his eyes pensively on the stamp-block, folding his hands on the head of his cane. His boots were broken, but he still had the cane of a gentleman.

'You *vaggabonds se Engelsman*!' said *Tant* Sannie, looking straight at him.

This was a near approach to plain English; but the man contemplated the block abstractedly, wholly unconscious that any antagonism was being displayed towards him.

'You might not be a Scotchman or anything of that kind, might you?' suggested the German. 'It is the English that she hates.'

'My dear friend,' said the stranger, 'I am Irish every inch of me – father Irish, mother Irish. I've not a drop of English blood in my veins.'

'And you might not be married, might you?' persisted the German. 'If you had a wife and children, now? Dutch people do not like those who are not married.'

'Ah,' said the stranger, looking tenderly at the block, 'I have a dear wife and three sweet little children – two lovely girls and a noble boy.'

This information having been conveyed to the Boer woman, she, after some further conversation, appeared slightly mollified; but remained firm to her conviction that the man's designs were evil.

'For, dear Lord!' she cried; 'all Englishmen are ugly; but was there ever such a red-rag-nosed thing with broken boots and crooked eyes before? Take him to your room,' she cried to the German; 'but all the sin he does I lay at your door.'

The German having told him how matters were arranged, the stranger made a profound bow to *Tant* Sannie, and followed his host, who led the way to his own little room.

'I thought she would come to her better self soon,' the German said joyously. '*Tant* Sannie is not wholly bad, far from it, far.' Then seeing his companion cast a furtive glance at him, which he mistook for one of surprise, he added quickly, 'Ah, yes, yes; we are all a primitive people here – not very lofty. We deal not in titles. Everyone is *Tanta* and *Oom* – aunt and uncle. This may be my room,' he said, opening the door. 'It is rough, the room is rough; not a palace – not quite. But it may be better than the fields, a little better!' he said, glancing round at his companion. 'Come in, come in. There is something to eat – a mouthful: not the fare of emperors or kings, but we do not starve, not yet,' he said, rubbing his hands together and looking round with a pleased, half-nervous smile on his old face.

'My friend, my dear friend,' said the stranger, seizing him by the hand, 'may the Lord bless you, the Lord bless and reward you – the God of the fatherless and the stranger. But for you I would this night have slept in the fields, with the dews of heaven upon my head.'

Late that evening Lyndall came down to the cabin with the German's rations. Through the tiny square window the light streamed forth, and without knocking she raised the latch and entered. There was a fire burning on the hearth, and it cast its ruddy glow over the little room, with its worm-eaten rafters and mud floor and broken whitewashed walls. A curious little place, filled with all manner of articles. Next to the fire was a great toolbox; beyond that the little bookshelf with its well-worn books; beyond that, in the corner, a heap of filled and empty grain bags. From the rafters hung down straps, *riems,* old boots, bits of harness, and a string of onions. The bed was in another corner, covered by a patchwork quilt of faded red lions, and divided from the rest of the room by a blue curtain, now drawn back. On the mantelshelf was an endless assortment of little bags and stones; and on the wall hung a map of South Germany, with a red line drawn through it to show where the German had wandered. This place was the one home the girls had known for many a year. The house where *Tant* Sannie lived and ruled was a place to sleep in, to eat in, not to be happy in. It was in vain she told them they were grown too old to go there; every morning and evening found them there. Were there not too many golden memories hanging about the old place for them to leave it?

Long winter nights, when they had sat round the fire and roasted potatoes, and asked riddles, and the old man had told of the little German village, where, fifty years before, a little German boy had played at snowballs, and had carried home the knitted stockings of a little girl who afterwards became Waldo's mother; did they not seem to see the German peasant girls walking about with their wooden shoes and yellow, braided hair, and the little children eating their suppers out of little wooden bowls when the good mothers called them in to have their milk and potatoes?

And were there not yet better times than these? Moonlight nights, when they romped about the door, with the old man, yet more a child than any of them, and laughed, till the old roof of the wagon-house rang?

Or, best of all, were there not warm, dark, starlight nights, when they sat together on the doorstep, holding each other's hands, singing German hymns, their voices rising clear in the still night air – till the German would draw away his hand suddenly to wipe quickly a tear the children must not see? Would they not sit looking up at the stars and talking of them – of the dear Southern Cross; red, fiery Mars; Orion, with his belt; and the Seven Mysterious Sisters – and fall to speculating over them? How old are they? Who dwelt in them? And the old German would say that perhaps the souls we loved lived in them; *there*, in that little twinkling point was perhaps the little girl whose stockings he had carried home; and the children would look up at it lovingly, and call it 'Uncle Otto's star'. Then they would fall to deeper speculations – of the times and seasons wherein the heavens shall be rolled together as a scroll, and the stars shall fall as a fig tree casteth her untimely figs, and there shall be time no longer; 'when the Son of man shall come in His glory, and all His holy angels with Him'. In lower and lower tones they would talk, till at last they fell into whispers; then they would wish goodnight softly, and walk home hushed and quiet.

Tonight, when Lyndall looked in, Waldo sat before the fire watching a pot which simmered there, with his slate and pencil in his hand; his father sat at the table buried in the columns of a three-weeks-old newspaper; and the stranger lay stretched on the bed in the corner, fast asleep, his mouth open, his great limbs stretched out loosely, betokening much weariness. The girl put the rations down upon the table, snuffed the candle, and stood looking at the figure on the bed.

'Uncle Otto,' she said presently, laying her hand down on the newspaper, and causing the old German to look up over his glasses, 'how long did that man say he had been walking?'

'Since this morning, poor fellow! A gentleman – not accustomed to walking – horse died – poor fellow!' said the German, pushing out his lip and glancing commiseratingly over his spectacles in the direction of the bed where the stranger lay, with his flabby double chin, and broken boots, through which the flesh shone.

'And do you believe him, Uncle Otto?'

'Believe him? why, of course I do. He himself told me the story three times distinctly.'

'If,' said the girl slowly, 'he had walked for only one day his boots would not have looked so; and if –'

'*If!*' said the German, starting up in his chair, irritated that anyone should doubt such irrefragable evidence – '*if*! Why, he told me *himself*! Look how he lies there,' added the German pathetically, 'worn out – poor fellow! We have something for him though,' pointing with his forefinger over his shoulder to the saucepan that stood on the fire. 'We are not cooks – not French cooks, not quite; but it's drinkable, drinkable, I think; better than nothing, I think,' he added, nodding his head in a jocund manner, that evinced his high estimation of the contents of the saucepan and his profound satisfaction therein. 'Bish! bish! my chicken,' he said, as Lyndall tapped her little foot up and down upon the floor. 'Bish! bish! my chicken, you will wake him.'

He moved the candle so that his own head might intervene between it and the sleeper's face; and, smoothing his newspaper, he adjusted his spectacles to read.

The child's grey-black eyes rested on the figure on the bed, then turned to the German, then rested on the figure again.

'*I* think he is a liar. Goodnight, Uncle Otto,' she said slowly, turning to the door.

Long after she had gone the German folded his paper up methodically, and put it in his pocket.

The stranger had not awakened to partake of the soup, and his son had fallen asleep on the ground. Taking two white sheepskins from the heap of sacks in the corner, the old man doubled them up, and lifting the boy's head gently from the slate on which it rested, placed the skins beneath it.

'Poor lambie, poor lambie!' he said, tenderly patting the great rough, bear-like head; 'tired, is he!'

He threw an overcoat across the boy's feet, and lifted the saucepan from the fire. There was no place where the old man could comfortably lie down himself, so he resumed his seat. Opening a much-worn Bible, he began to read, and as he read pleasant thoughts and visions thronged on him.

'I was a stranger, and ye took me in,' he read. He turned again to the bed where the sleeper lay.

'I was a stranger.'

Very tenderly the old man looked at him. He saw not the bloated body nor the evil face of the man; but, as it were, under deep disguise and fleshly concealment, the form that long years of dreaming had made very real to him. 'Jesus, lover, and is it given to us, weak and sinful, frail and erring, to serve *Thee*, to take *Thee* in!' he said softly, as he rose from his seat. Full of joy, he began to pace the little room. Now and again as he walked he sang the lines of a German hymn, or muttered broken words of prayer. The little room was full of light. It appeared to the German that Christ was very near him, and that at almost any moment the thin mist of earthly darkness that clouded his human eyes might be withdrawn, and that made manifest of which the friends at Emmaus, beholding it, said, 'It is the Lord!'

Again, and yet again, through the long hours of that night, as the old man walked, he looked up to the roof of his little room, with its blackened rafters, and yet saw them not. His rough bearded face was illuminated with a radiant gladness; and the night was not shorter to the dreaming sleepers than to him whose waking dreams brought heaven near.

So quickly the night fled, that he looked up with surprise when at four o'clock the first grey streaks of summer dawn showed themselves through the little window. Then the old man turned to rake together the few coals that lay under the ashes, and his son, turning on the sheepskins, muttered sleepily to know if it were time to rise.

'Lie still, lie still! I would only make a fire,' said the old man.

'Have you been up all night?' asked the boy.

'Yes; but it has been short, very short. Sleep again, my chicken; it is yet early.'

And he went out to fetch more fuel.

CHAPTER FOUR

Blessed is He That Believeth

Bonaparte Blenkins sat on the side of the bed. He had wonderfully revived since the day before, held his head high, talked in a full, sonorous voice, and ate greedily of all the viands offered him. At his side was a basin of soup, from which he took a deep draught now and again as he watched the fingers of the German, who sat on the mud floor before him, mending the bottom of a chair.

Presently he looked out, where, in the afternoon sunshine, a few half-grown ostriches might be seen wandering listlessly about, and then he looked in again at the little whitewashed room, and at Lyndall, who sat in the doorway looking at a book. Then he raised his chin and tried to adjust an imaginary shirt collar. Finding none, he smoothed the little grey fringe at the back of his head, and began:

'You are a student of history, I perceive, my friend, from the study of these volumes that lie scattered about this apartment; this fact has been made evident to me.'

'Well – a little – perhaps – it may be,' said the German meekly.

'Being a student of history then,' said Bonaparte, raising himself loftily, 'you will doubtless have heard of my great, of my celebrated kinsman, Napoleon Bonaparte?'

'Yes, yes,' said the German, looking up.

'I, sir,' said Bonaparte, 'was born at this hour, on an April afternoon, three-and-fifty years ago. The nurse, sir – she was the same who attended when the Duke of Sutherland was born – brought me to my mother. "There is only one name for this child," she said: "he has the nose of his great kinsman"; and so Bonaparte Blenkins became my name – Bonaparte Blenkins. Yes, sir,' said Bonaparte, 'there is a stream on *my* maternal side that connects me with a stream on *his* maternal side.'

The German made a sound of astonishment.

'The connection,' said Bonaparte, 'is one which could not be easily comprehended by one unaccustomed to the study of aristocratic pedigrees; but the connection is close.'

'Is it possible!' said the German, pausing in his work with much interest and astonishment. 'Napoleon an Irishman!'

'Yes,' said Bonaparte, 'on the mother's side, and that is how we are related. There wasn't a man to beat him,' said Bonaparte, stretching himself – 'not a man except the Duke of Wellington. And it's a strange coincidence,' added Bonaparte, bending forward, 'but *he* was a connection of mine. His nephew, the Duke of Wellington's nephew, married a cousin of mine. *She* was a woman! See her at one of the court balls – amber satin – daisies in her hair. Worth going a hundred miles to look at her! Often seen her there myself, sir!'

209

The German moved the leather thongs in and out, and thought of the strange vicissitudes of human life, which might bring the kinsman of dukes and emperors to his humble room.

Bonaparte appeared lost among old memories.

'Ah, that Duke of Wellington's nephew!' he broke forth suddenly; 'many's the joke I've had with him. Often came to visit me at Bonaparte Hall. Grand place I had then – park, conservatory, servants. He had only one fault, that Duke of Wellington's nephew,' said Bonaparte, observing that the German was deeply interested in every word: 'he was a coward – what you might call a coward. You've never been in Russia, I suppose?' said Bonaparte, fixing his crosswise looking eyes on the German's face.

'No, no,' said the old man humbly. 'France, England, Germany, a little in this country; it is all I have travelled.'

'*I*, my friend,' said Bonaparte, 'have been in every country in the world, and speak every civilised language, excepting only Dutch and German. I wrote a book of my travels – noteworthy incidents. Publisher got it – cheated me out of it. Great rascals those publishers! Upon one occasion the Duke of Wellington's nephew and I were travelling in Russia. All of a sudden one of the horses dropped down dead as a doornail. There we were – cold night – snow four feet thick – great forest – one horse – not being able to move sledge – night coming on – wolves!

'"Spree!" says the Duke of Wellington's nephew.

'"Spree, do you call it?" says I. "Look out."

'There, sticking out under a bush, was nothing less than the nose of a bear. The Duke of Wellington's nephew was up a tree like a shot; I stood quietly on the ground, as cool as I am at this moment, loaded my gun, and climbed up the tree. There was only one bough.

'"Bon," said the Duke of Wellington's nephew, "you'd better sit in front."

'"All right," said I; "but keep your gun ready. There are more coming." He'd got his face buried in my back.

'"How many are there?" said he.

'"Four," said I.

'"How many are there now?" said he.

'"Eight," said I.

'"How many are there now?" said he.

'"Ten," said I.

'"Ten! ten!" said he; and down goes his gun.

'"Wallie," I said, "what have you done? We're dead men now."

'"Bon, my old fellow," said he, "I couldn't help it; my hands trembled so!"

'"Wal," I said, turning round and seizing his hands. "Wallie, my dear lad, goodbye. I'm not afraid to die. My legs are long – they hang down – the first bear that comes and I don't hit him, off goes my foot. When he takes it I shall give you my gun and go. You may yet be saved; but tell, oh, tell Mary Ann that I thought of her, that I prayed for her!"

"'Goodbye, old fellow!' said he.

"'God bless you!' said I.

'By this time the bears were sitting in a circle all round the tree. Yes,' said Bonaparte impressively, fixing his eyes on the German, 'a regular, exact circle. The marks of their tails were left in the snow, and I measured it afterwards; a drawing-master couldn't have done it better. It was that saved me. If they'd rushed on me at once, poor old Bon would never have been here to tell this story. But they came on, sir, *systematically*, one by one. All the rest sat on their tails and waited. The first fellow came up and I shot him; the second fellow – I shot him; the third – I shot him. At last the tenth came; he was the biggest of all – the leader, you may say.

"'Wal,' I said, "give me your hand. My fingers are stiff with the cold; there is only one bullet left. I shall miss him. While he is eating me you get down and take your gun; and live, dear friend, live to remember the man who gave his life for you!" By that time the bear was at me. I felt his paw on my trousers.

"'Oh, Bonnie! Bonnie!' said the Duke of Wellington's nephew. But I just took my gun, and put the muzzle to the bear's ear – over he fell – dead?'

Bonaparte Blenkins waited to observe what effect his story had made. Then he took out a dirty white handkerchief, and stroked his forehead, and more especially his eyes.

'It always affects me to relate that adventure,' he remarked, returning the handkerchief to his pocket. 'Ingratitude – base, vile ingratitude – is recalled by it! That man, that man, who but for me would have perished in the pathless wilds of Russia, that man in the hour of my adversity forsook me.' The German looked up. 'Yes,' said Bonaparte, 'I had money. I had lands, I said to my wife, "There is Africa, a struggling country; they want capital; they want men of talent; they want men of ability to open up that land. Let us go."

'I bought eight thousand pounds worth of machinery – winnowing, ploughing, reaping machines; I loaded a ship with them. Next steamer I came out – wife, children all. Got to the Cape. Where is the ship with the things? Lost – gone to the bottom! And the box with the money? Lost – nothing saved!

'My wife wrote to the Duke of Wellington's nephew; I didn't wish her to; she did it without my knowledge.

'What did the man whose life I saved do? Did he send me thirty thousand pounds? Say "Bonaparte, my brother, here is a crumb?" No; he sent me nothing.

'My wife said, "Write." I said, "Mary Ann, no. While these hands have power to work, no. While this frame has power to endure, no. Never shall it be said that Bonaparte Blenkins asked of any man."'

The man's noble independence touched the German.

'Your case is hard; yes, that *is* hard,' said the German, shaking his head.

Bonaparte took another draught of the soup, leaned back against the pillows, and sighed deeply.

'I think,' he said after a while, rousing himself, 'I shall now wander in the benign air, and taste the gentle cool of evening. The stiffness hovers over me yet; exercise is beneficial.'

So saying, he adjusted his hat carefully on the bald crown of his head, and moved to the door. After he had gone the German sighed again over his work:

'Ah, Lord! So it is! Ah!'

He thought of the ingratitude of the world.

'Uncle Otto,' said the child in the doorway, 'did you ever hear of ten bears sitting on their tails in a circle?'

'Well, not of ten, exactly; but bears do attack travellers every day. It is nothing unheard of,' said the German. 'A man of such courage, too! Terrible experience that!'

'And how do we know that the story is true, Uncle Otto?'

The German's ire was roused. 'That is what I do hate!' he cried. 'Know that is true! How do you know that anything is true? Because you are told so. If we begin to question everything – proof, proof, proof, what will we have to believe left? How do you know the angel opened the prison door for Peter, except that Peter said so? How do you know that God talked to Moses, except that Moses wrote it? That is what I hate!'

The girl knit her brows. Perhaps her thoughts made a longer journey than the German dreamed of; for, mark you, the old dream little how their words and lives are texts and studies to the generation that shall succeed them. Not what we are taught, but what we see, makes us, and the child gathers the food on which the adult feeds to the end.

When the German looked up next there was a look of supreme satisfaction in the little mouth and the beautiful eyes.

'What dost see, chicken?' he asked.

The child said nothing, and an agonising shriek was borne on the afternoon breeze.

'Oh, God! my God! I am killed!' cried the voice of Bonaparte, as he, with wide open mouth and shaking flesh, fell into the room, followed by a half-grown ostrich, who put its head in at the door, opened its beak at him, and went away.

'Shut the door! Shut the door! As you value my life, shut the door!' cried Bonaparte, sinking into a chair, his face blue and white, with a greenishness about the mouth. 'Ah, my friend,' he said tremulously, 'eternity has looked me in the face! My life's thread hung upon a cord! The valley of the shadow of death!' said Bonaparte, seizing the German's arm.

'Dear, dear, dear!' said the German, who had closed the lower half of the door, and stood much concerned beside the stranger, 'you have had a fright. I never knew so young a bird to chase before; but they will take dislikes to certain people. I sent a boy away once because a bird would chase him. Ah, dear, dear!'

'When I looked round,' said Bonaparte, 'the red and yawning cavity was above me, and the reprehensible paw raised to strike me. My nerves,' said Bonaparte, suddenly growing faint, 'always delicate – highly strung – are broken – broken! You could not give a little wine, a little brandy, my friend?'

The old German hurried away to the bookshelf, and took from behind the books a small bottle, half of whose contents he poured into a cup. Bonaparte drained it eagerly.

'How do you feel now?' asked the German, looking at him with much sympathy.

'A little, *slightly* better.'

The German went out to pick up the battered chimney-pot which had fallen before the door.

'I am sorry you got the fright. The birds are bad things till you know them,' he said sympathetically, as he put the hat down.

'My friend,' said Bonaparte, holding out his hand, 'I forgive you; do not be disturbed. Whatever the consequences, I forgive you. I know, I believe, it was with no ill-intent that you allowed me to go out. Give me your hand. I have no ill-feeling; none!'

'You are very kind,' said the German, taking the extended hand, and feeling suddenly convinced that he was receiving magnanimous forgiveness for some great injury, 'you are very kind.'

'Don't mention it,' said Bonaparte.

He knocked out the crown of his caved-in old hat, placed it on the table before him, leaned his elbows on the table and his face in his hands, and contemplated it.

'Ah, my old friend,' he thus apostophised the hat, 'you have served me long, you have served me faithfully, but the last day has come. Never more shall you be borne upon the head of your master. Never more shall you protect his brow from the burning rays of summer or the cutting winds of winter. Henceforth bare-headed must your master go. Goodbye, goodbye, old hat!'

At the end of this affecting appeal the German rose. He went to the box at the foot of his bed; out of it he took a black hat, which had evidently been seldom worn and carefully preserved.

'It's not exactly what you may have been accustomed to,' he said nervously, putting it down beside the battered chimney-pot, 'but it might be of some use – a protection to the head, you know.'

'My friend,' said Bonaparte, 'you are not following my advice; you are allowing yourself to be reproached on my account. Do not make yourself unhappy. No; I shall go bare-headed.'

'No, no, no!' cried the German energetically. 'I have no use for the hat, none at all. It is shut up in the box.'

Then I will take it, my friend. It is a comfort to one's own mind when you have unintentionally injured anyone to make reparation. I know the feeling. The hat may not be of that refined cut of which the old one was, but it will serve, yes, it will serve. Thank you,' said Bonaparte, adjusting it on his head, and then replacing it on the table. 'I shall lie down now and take a little repose,' he added; I much fear my appetite for supper will be lost.'

'I hope not, I hope not,' said the German, reseating himself at his work, and looking much concerned as Bonaparte stretched himself on the bed and turned the end of the patchwork quilt over his feet.

'You must not think to make your departure, not for many days,' said the German presently, '*Tant* Sannie gives her consent, and –'

'My friend,' said Bonaparte, closing his eyes sadly, 'you are kind; but were it not that tomorrow is the Sabbath, weak and trembling as I lie here, I would proceed on my way. I must seek work; idleness but for a day is painful. *Work, labour* – that is the secret of all true happiness!'

He doubled the pillow under his head, and watched how the German drew the leather thongs in and out.

After a while Lyndall silently put her book on the shelf and went home, and the German stood up and began to mix some water and meal for roaster-cakes. As he stirred them with his hands he said:

'I make always a double supply on Saturday night; the hands are then free as the thoughts for Sunday.'

'The blessed Sabbath!' said Bonaparte.

There was a pause. Bonaparte twisted his eyes without moving his head, to see if supper were already on the fire.

'You must sorely miss the administration of the Lord's word in this desolate spot,' added Bonaparte. 'Oh, how love I Thine house, and the place where Thine honour dwelleth!'

'Well, we do; yes,' said the German; 'but we do our best. We meet together, and I – well, I say a few words, and perhaps they are not wholly lost, not quite.'

'Strange coincidence,' said Bonaparte; 'my plan always was the same. Was in the Free State once – solitary farm – one neighbour. Every Sunday I called together friend and neighbour, child and servant, and said, "Rejoice with me, that we may serve the Lord," and then I addressed them. Ah, those were blessed times,' said Bonaparte; 'would they might return.'

The German stirred at the cakes, and stirred, and stirred, and stirred. He could give the stranger his bed, and he could give the stranger his hat, and he could give the stranger his brandy; but his Sunday service!

After a good while he said:

'I might speak to *Tant* Sannie; I might arrange; you might take the service in my place, if it –'

'My friend,' said Bonaparte, 'it would give me the profoundest felicity, the most unbounded satisfaction; but in these worn-out habiliments, in these deteriorated garments, it would not be possible, it would not be fitting that I should officiate in service of One, whom, for respect, we shall not name. No, my friend, I will remain here; and, while you are assembling yourselves together in the presence of the Lord, I, in my solitude, will think of and pray for you. No; I will remain here!'

It was a touching picture – the solitary man there praying for them. The German cleared his hands from the meal, and went to the chest from which he had taken the black hat. After a little careful feeling about, he produced a black cloth coat, trousers, and waistcoat, which he laid on the table, smiling knowingly. They were of new shining cloth, worn twice a year, when he went to the town to *nagmaal*. He looked with great pride at the coat as he unfolded it and held it up.

'It's not the latest fashion, perhaps, not a West End cut, not exactly; but it might do; it might serve at a push. Try it on, try it on!' he said, his old grey eyes twinkling with pride.

Bonaparte stood up and tried on the coat. It fitted admirably; the waistcoat could be made to button by ripping up the back, and the trousers were perfect; but below were the ragged boots. The German was not disconcerted. Going to the beam where a pair of top-boots hung, he took them off, dusted them carefully, and put them down before Bonaparte. The old eyes now fairly brimmed over with sparkling enjoyment.

'I have only worn them once. They might serve; they might be endured.'

Bonaparte drew them on and stood upright, his head almost touching the beams. The German looked at him with profound admiration. It was wonderful what a difference feathers made in the bird.

CHAPTER FIVE

Sunday Services

Service No 1

The boy Waldo kissed the pages of his book and looked up. Far over the flat lay the *kopje*, a mere speck; the sheep wandered quietly from bush to bush; the stillness of the early Sunday rested everywhere, and the air was fresh.

He looked down at his book. On its page a black insect crept. He lifted it off with his finger. Then he leaned on his elbow, watching its quivering antennae and strange movements, smiling.

'Even you,' he whispered, 'shall not die. Even you He loves. Even you He will fold in His arms when He takes everything and makes it perfect and happy.'

When the thing had gone he smoothed the leaves of his Bible somewhat caressingly. The leaves of that book had dropped blood for him once; they had taken the brightness out of his childhood; from between them had sprung the visions that had clung about him and made night horrible. Adder-like thoughts had lifted their heads, had shot out forked tongues at him, asking mockingly strange, trivial questions that he could not answer, miserable child:

> Why did the women in Mark see only one angel and the women in Luke two? Could a story be told in opposite ways and both ways be true? Could it? Could it? Then again: – Is there nothing always right and nothing always wrong? Could Jael the wife of Heber the Kenite 'put her hand to the nail, and her right hand to the workman's hammer'? and could the Spirit of the Lord chant paeans over her, loud paeans, high paeans, set in the book of the Lord, and no voice cry out it was a mean and dastardly sin to lie, and kill the trusting in their sleep? Could the friend of God marry his own sister, and be beloved, and the man who does it today goes to hell, to hell? Was there nothing always right or always wrong?

Those leaves had dropped blood for him once: they had made his heart heavy and cold; they had robbed his childhood of its gladness; now his fingers moved over them caressingly.

'My Father God knows, my Father knows,' he said; 'we cannot understand; He knows.' After a while he whispered smiling – 'I heard your voice this morning when my eyes were not yet open, I felt you near me, my Father. Why do you love me so?' His face was illuminated. 'In the last four months the old question has gone from me. I know you are good; I know you love everything; I know, I know, I know! I could not have borne it any more, not any more.' He laughed softly. 'And all the while I was so miserable you were looking at me and loving me, and I never knew it. But I know it now, I feel it,' said the boy, and he laughed low; 'I feel it!' he laughed.

After a while he began partly to sing, partly to chant the disconnected verses of hymns, those which spoke his gladness, many times over. The sheep with their senseless eyes turned to look at him as he sang.

At last he lapsed into quiet. Then as the boy lay there staring at bush and sand, he saw a vision.

He had crossed the river of Death, and walked on the other bank in the Lord's land of Beulah. His feet sank into the dark grass, and he walked alone. Then, far over the fields, he saw a figure coming across the dark green grass. At first he thought it must be one of the angels; but as it came nearer he began to feel what it was. And it came closer, closer to him, and then the voice said, 'Come,' and he knew surely Who it was. He ran to the dear feet and touched them with his hands; yes, he held them fast! He lay down beside them. When he looked up the face was over him, and the glorious eyes were loving him; and they two were there alone together.

He laughed a deep laugh; then started up like one suddenly awakened from sleep.

'Oh, God!' he cried, 'I cannot wait! I cannot wait! I want to die; I want to see Him; I want to touch Him. Let me die!' He folded his hands, trembling. 'How can I wait so long – for long, long years perhaps? I want to die – to see Him. I will die any death. Oh, let me come!'

Weeping he bowed himself, and quivered from head to foot. After a long while he lifted his head.

'Yes; I will wait, I will wait. But not long, do not let it be very long, Jesus King. I want you; oh, I want you, – soon, soon!' He sat still, staring across the plain with his tearful eyes.

Service No 2

In the front room of the farmhouse sat *Tant* Sannie in her elbow-chair. In her hand was her great brass-clasped hymnbook, round her neck was a clean white handkerchief, under her feet was a wooden stove. There, too, sat Em and Lyndall, in clean pinafores and new shoes. There, too, was the spruce Hottentot in a starched white *kappie*, and her husband on the other side of the door, with his wool oiled and very much combed out, and staring at his new leather boots. The Kaffir servants were not there, because *Tant* Sannie held they were descended from apes, and needed no salvation. But the rest were gathered for the Sunday service, and waited the officiator.

Meanwhile Bonaparte and the German approached arm-in-arm – Bonaparte resplendent in the black-cloth clothes, a spotless shirt, and a spotless collar; the German in the old salt-and-pepper, casting shy glances of admiration at his companion.

At the front door Bonaparte removed his hat with much dignity, raised his shirt-collar, and entered. To the centre table he walked, put his hat solemnly down by the big Bible, and bowed his head over it in silent prayer.

The Boer woman looked at the Hottentot, and the Hottentot looked at the Boer woman.

There was one thing on earth for which *Tant* Sannie had a profound reverence, which exercised a subduing influence over her, which made her for the time a better woman – that thing was new, shining black cloth. It made her think of the *predikant*; it made her think of the elders, who sat in the top pew of the church on Sundays, with the hair so nicely oiled, so holy and respectable, with their little swallow-tailed coats; it made her think of heaven, where everything was so holy and respectable, and nobody wore tan-cord, and the littlest angel had a black tail-coat. She wished she hadn't called him a thief and a Roman Catholic. She hoped the German hadn't told him. She wondered where those clothes were when he came in rags to her door. There was no doubt, he was a very respectable man, a gentleman.

The German began to read a hymn. At the end of each line Bonaparte groaned, and twice at the end of every verse.

The Boer woman had often heard of persons groaning during prayers, to add a certain poignancy and finish to them; old Jan Vanderlinde, her mother's brother, always did it after he was converted; and she would have looked upon it as no especial sign of grace in anyone; but to groan at hymn-time! She was startled. She wondered if he remembered that she shook her fist in his face. This was a man of God. They knelt down to pray. The Boer woman weighed two hundred and fifty pounds, and could not kneel. She sat in her chair, and peeped between her crossed fingers at the stranger's back. She could not understand what he said; but he was in earnest. He shook the chair by the back rail till it made quite a little dust on the mud floor.

When they rose from their knees Bonaparte solemnly seated himself in the chair and opened the Bible. He blew his nose, pulled up his shirt-collar, smoothed the leaves, stroked down his capacious waistcoat, blew his nose again, looked solemnly round the room, then began:

'All liars shall have their part in the lake which burneth with fire and brimstone, which is the second death.'

Having read this portion of Scripture, Bonaparte paused impressively, and looked all around the room.

'I shall not, my dear friends,' he said, 'long detain you. Much of our precious time has already fled blissfully from us in the voice of thanksgiving and the tongue of praise. A few, a very few words are all I shall address to you, and may they be as a rod of iron dividing the bones from the marrow, and the marrow from the bones.

'In the first place: What is a liar?'

The question was put so pointedly and followed by a pause so profound, that even the Hottentot man left off looking at his boots and opened his eyes, though he understood not a word.

'I repeat,' said Bonaparte, 'what is a liar?'

The sensation was intense; the attention of the audience was riveted.

'Have you, any of you, ever seen a liar, my dear friends?' There was a still longer pause. 'I hope not; I truly hope not. But I will tell you what a liar is. I knew a liar once – a little boy who lived in Cape Town, in Short Market Street. His mother and I sat together one day, discoursing about our souls.

'"Here, Sampson," said his mother, "go and buy sixpence of *meiboss* from the Malay round the corner."

'When he came back she said, "How much have you got?"

'"Five," he said.

'He was afraid if he said six and a half she'd ask for some. And, my friends, that was a *lie*. The half of a *meiboss* stuck in his throat, and he died, and was buried. And where did the soul of that little liar go to, my friends? It went to the lake of fire and brimstone. This brings me to the second point of my discourse.

'What is a lake of fire and brimstone? I will tell you, my friends,' said Bonaparte, condescendingly. 'The imagination unaided cannot conceive it: but by the help of the Lord I will put it before your mind's eye.

'I was travelling in Italy once on a time; I came to a city called Rome, a vast city, and near it is a mountain which spits forth fire. Its name is Etna. Now, there was a man in that city of Rome who had not the fear of God before his eyes, and he loved a woman. The woman died, and he walked up that mountain spitting fire, and when he got to the top he threw himself in at the hole that is there. The next day I went up. I was not afraid; the Lord preserves His servants. And in their hands shall they bear thee up, lest at any time thou fall into a volcano. It was a dark night when I got there, but in the fear of the Lord I walked to the edge of the yawning abyss, and looked in. That sight – that sight, my friends, is impressed upon my most indelible memory. I looked down into the lurid depths upon an incandescent lake, a melted fire, a seething sea; the billows rolled from side to side, and on their fiery crests tossed the white skeleton of the suicide. The heat had burnt the flesh from off the bones; they lay as a light cork upon the melted fiery waves. One skeleton hand was raised upwards, the finger pointing to heaven; the other, with outstretched finger pointing downwards, as though it would say, "I go below, but you, Bonaparte, may soar above." I gazed; I stood entranced. At that instant there was a crack in the lurid lake; it swelled, expanded, and the skeleton of the suicide disappeared, to be seen no more by mortal eye.'

Here again Bonaparte rested, and then continued:

'The lake of melted stone rose in the crater, it swelled higher and higher at the side, it streamed forth at the top. I had presence of mind; near me was a rock; I stood upon it. The fiery torrent was vomited out, and streamed on either side of me. And through that long and terrible night I stood there alone upon that rock, the glowing fiery lava on every hand – a monument of the long-suffering and tender providence of the Lord, who spared me that I might this day testify in your ears of Him.

'Now, my dear friends, let us deduce the lessons that are to be learnt from this narrative.

'Firstly: let us never commit suicide. That man is a fool, my friends; that man is insane, my friends, who would leave this earth, my friends. Here are joys innumerable, such as it hath not entered into the heart of man to understand, my friends. Here are clothes, my friends; here are beds, my friends; here is delicious food, my friends. Our precious bodies were given us to love, to cherish. Oh, let us do so! Oh, let us never hurt them; but care for and love them, my friends!'

Everyone was impressed, and Bonaparte proceeded.

'Secondly, let us not love too much. If that young man had not loved that young woman, he would not have jumped into Mount Etna. The good men of old never did so. Was Jeremiah ever in love, or Ezekiel, or Hosea, or even any of the minor prophets? No. Then why should we be? Thousands are rolling in that lake at this moment who would say, "It was love that brought us here." Oh, let us think always of our own souls first.

> *A charge to keep I have,*
> *A God to glorify;*
> *A never-dying soul to save,*
> *And fit it for the sky.*

'Oh, beloved friends, remember the little boy and the *meiboss*; remember the young girl and the young man; remember the lake, the fire, and the brimstone; remember the suicide's skeleton on the pitchy billows of Mount Etna; remember the voice of warning that has this day sounded in your ears; and what I say to you I say to all – watch! May the Lord add His blessing!'

Here the Bible closed with a tremendous thud. *Tant* Sannie loosened the white handkerchief about her neck and wiped her eyes, and the Coloured girl, seeing her do so, sniffled. They did not understand the discourse, which made it the more affecting. There hung over it that inscrutable charm which hovers forever for the human intellect over the incomprehensible and shadowy. When the last hymn was sung the German conducted the officiator to *Tant* Sannie, who graciously extended her hand, and offered coffee and a seat on the sofa. Leaving him there, the German hurried away to see how the little plum-pudding he had left at home was advancing; and *Tant* Sannie remarked that it was a hot day. Bonaparte gathered her meaning as she fanned herself with the end of her apron. He bowed low in acquiescence. A long silence followed. *Tant* Sannie spoke again. Bonaparte gave her no ear; his eye was fixed on a small miniature on the opposite wall, which represented *Tant* Sannie as she had appeared on the day before her confirmation, fifteen years before, attired in green muslin. Suddenly he started to his feet, walked up to the picture, and took his stand before it. Long and wistfully he gazed into its features; it was easy to see that he was deeply moved. With a sudden movement as though no longer able to restrain himself, he seized the picture, loosened it from its nail, and held it close to his eyes. At length, turning to the Boer woman, he said, in a voice of deep emotion:

'You will, I trust, dear madam, excuse this exhibition of my feelings; but this – this little picture recalls to me my first and best beloved, my dear, departed wife, who is now a saint in heaven.'

Tant Sannie could not understand; but the Hottentot maid, who had taken her seat on the floor beside her mistress, translated the English into Dutch as far as she was able.

'Ah, my first, my beloved!' he added, looking tenderly down at the picture. 'Oh, the beloved, the beautiful lineaments! My angel wife! This is surely a sister of yours, madame?' he added, fixing his eyes on *Tant* Sannie.

The Dutch woman blushed, shook her head, and pointed to herself.

Carefully, intently, Bonaparte looked from the picture in his hand to *Tant* Sannie's features, and from the features back to the picture. Then slowly a light broke over his countenance; he looked up, it became a smile; he looked back at the miniature, his whole countenance was effulgent.

'Ah, yes; I see it now,' he cried, turning his delighted gaze onto the Boer woman; 'eyes, mouth, nose, chin, the very expression!' he cried. 'How is it possible I did not notice it before?'

'Take another cup of coffee,' said *Tant* Sannie. 'Put some sugar in.'

Bonaparte hung the picture tenderly up, and was turning to take the cup from her hand, when the German appeared, to say that the pudding was ready and the meat on the table.

'He's a God-fearing man, and one who knows how to behave himself,' said the Boer woman as he went out at the door. 'If he is ugly, did not the Lord make him? And are we to laugh at the Lord's handiwork? It is better to be ugly and good than pretty and bad; though of course it's nice when one is both,' said *Tant* Sannie, looking complacently at the picture on the wall.

In the afternoon the German and Bonaparte sat before the door of the cabin. Both smoked in complete silence – Bonaparte with a book in his hands and his eyes half closed; the German puffing vigorously, and glancing up now and again at the serene blue sky overhead.

'Supposing – you – you, in fact, made the remark to me,' burst forth the German suddenly, 'that you were looking for a situation.'

Bonaparte opened his mouth wide, and sent a stream of smoke through his lips.

'Now supposing,' said the German, – 'merely supposing, of course, – that someone, someone in fact, should make an offer to you, say, to become schoolmaster on their farm and teach two children, two little girls, perhaps, and would give you forty pounds a year, would you accept it? Just supposing, of course.'

'Well, my dear friend,' said Bonaparte, 'that would depend on circumstances. Money is no consideration with me. For my wife I have made provision for the next year. My health is broken. Could I meet a place where a gentleman would be treated as a gentleman I would accept it, however small the remuneration. With me,' said Bonaparte, 'money is no consideration.'

'Well,' said the German, when he had taken a whiff or two more from his pipe, 'I think I shall go up and see *Tant* Sannie a little. I go up often on Sunday afternoon to have a general conversation, to see her, you know. Nothing – nothing particular, you know.'

The old man put his book into his pocket, and walked up to the farmhouse with a peculiarly knowing and delighted expression of countenance.

'He doesn't suspect what I'm going to do,' soliloquised the German; 'hasn't the least idea. A nice surprise for him.'

The man whom he had left at his doorway winked at the retreating figure with a wink that was not to be described.

CHAPTER SIX

Bonaparte Blenkins Makes His Nest

'Ah, what is the matter?' asked Waldo, stopping at the foot of the ladder with a load of skins on his back that he was carrying up to the loft. Through the open door in the gable little Em was visible, her feet dangling from the high bench on which she sat. The room, once a storeroom, had been divided by a row of *mielie* bags into two parts – the back being Bonaparte's bedroom, the front his schoolroom.

'Lyndall made him angry,' said the girl tearfully; 'and he has given me the fourteenth of John to learn. He says he will teach me to behave myself, when Lyndall troubles him.'

'What did she do?' asked the boy.

'You see,' said Em, hopelessly turning the leaves, 'whenever he talks she looks out at the door, as though she did not hear him. Today she asked him what the signs of the Zodiac were, and he said he was surprised that she should ask him; it was not a fit and proper thing for little girls to talk about. Then she asked him who Copernicus was; and he said he was one of the Emperors of Rome, who burned the Christians in a golden pig, and the worms ate him up while he was still alive. I don't know why,' said Em plaintively, 'but she just put her books under her arm and walked out; and she will never come to his school again, she says, and she *always* does what she says. And now I must sit here every day alone,' said Em, the great tears dropping softly.

'Perhaps *Tant* Sannie will send him away,' said the boy, in his mumbling way, trying to comfort her.

'No,' said Em, shaking her head; 'no. Last night when the little Hottentot maid was washing her feet, he told her he liked such feet, and that fat women were so nice to him; and she said I must always put him pure cream in his coffee now. No; he'll never go away,' said Em dolorously.

The boy put down his skins and fumbled in his pocket, and produced a small piece of paper containing something. He stuck it out towards her.

'There, take it for you,' he said. This was by way of comfort.

Em opened it and found a small bit of gum, a commodity prized by the children; but the great tears dropped down slowly onto it.

Waldo was distressed. He had cried so much in his morsel of life that tears in another seemed to burn him.

'If,' he said, stepping in awkwardly and standing by the table, 'if you will not cry I will tell you something – a secret.'

'What is that?' asked Em, instantly becoming decidedly better.

223

'You will tell it to no human being?'

'No.'

He bent nearer to her, and with deep solemnity said, '*I have made a machine!*'

Em opened her eyes.

'Yes; a machine for shearing sheep. It is almost done,' said the boy. 'There is only one thing that is not right yet; but it will be soon. When you think, and think, and think, all night, and all day, it comes at last,' he added mysteriously.

'Where is it?'

'Here! I always carry it here,' said the boy, putting his hand to his breast, where a bulging-out was visible. 'This is a model. When it is done they will have to make a large one.'

'Show it me.'

The boy shook his head. 'No, not till it is done. I cannot let any human being see it till then.'

'It is a beautiful secret,' said Em; and the boy shuffled out to pick up his skins.

That evening father and son sat in the cabin eating their supper. The father sighed deeply sometimes. Perhaps he thought how long a time it was since Bonaparte had visited the cabin; but his son was in that land in which sighs have no part. It is a question whether it were not better to be the shabbiest of fools, and know the way up the little stair of imagination to the land of dreams, than the wisest of men, who see nothing that the eyes do not show, and feel nothing that the hands do not touch. The boy chewed his brown bread and drank his coffee; but in truth he saw only his machine finished – that last something found out and added. He saw it as it worked with beautiful smoothness, and over and above, as he chewed his bread and drank his coffee, there was that delightful consciousness of something bending over him and loving him. It would not have been better in one of the courts of heaven, where the walls are set with rows of the King of Glory's amethysts and milk-white pearls, than there, eating his supper in that little room.

As they sat in silence there was a knock at the door. When it was opened the small woolly head of a little nigger showed itself. She was a messenger from *Tant* Sannie; the German was wanted at once at the homestead. Putting on his hat with both hands, he hurried off. The kitchen was in darkness, but in the pantry beyond, *Tant* Sannie and her maids were assembled.

A Kaffir girl, who had been grinding pepper between two stones, knelt on the floor, the lean Hottentot stood with a brass candlestick in her hand, and *Tant* Sannie, near the shelf, with a hand on each hip, was evidently listening intently, as were her companions.

'What may it be?' cried the old German in astonishment.

The room beyond the pantry was the storeroom. Through the thin wooden partition there arose at that instant, evidently from some creature ensconced there, a prolonged and prodigious howl, followed by a succession of violent blows against the partition wall.

The German seized the churn-stick, and was about to rush round the house, when the Boer woman impressively laid her hand upon his arm.

'That is his head,' said *Tant* Sannie, 'that is his head.'

'But what might it be?' asked the German, looking from one to the other, churn-stick in hand.

A low, hollow bellow prevented reply, and the voice of Bonaparte lifted itself on high.

'Mary Ann! my angel! my wife!'

'Isn't it dreadful?' said *Tant* Sannie, as the blows were repeated fiercely. 'He has got a letter; his wife is dead. You must go and comfort him,' said *Tant* Sannie at last, 'and I will go with you. It would not be the thing for me to go alone – me, who am only thirty-three, and he an unmarried man now,' said *Tant* Sannie, blushing and smoothing out her apron.

Upon this they all trudged round the house in company – the Hottentot maid carrying the light, *Tant* Sannie and the German following, and the Kaffir girl bringing up the rear.

'Oh,' said *Tant* Sannie, 'I see now it wasn't wickedness made him do without his wife so long – only necessity.'

At the door she motioned to the German to enter, and followed him closely. On the stretcher behind the sacks Bonaparte lay on his face, his head pressed into a pillow, his legs kicking gently. The Boer woman sat down on a box at the foot of the bed. The German stood with folded hands looking on.

'We must all die,' said *Tant* Sannie at last; 'it is the dear Lord's will.'

Hearing her voice, Bonaparte turned himself onto his back.

'It's very hard,' said *Tant* Sannie, 'I know, for I've lost two husbands.'

Bonaparte looked up into the German's face. 'Oh, what does she say? Speak to me words of comfort.'

The German repeated *Tant* Sannie's remark. 'Ah, I – I also! Two dear, dear wives, whom I shall never see any more!' cried Bonaparte, flinging himself back upon the bed.

He howled, till the tarantulas, who lived between the rafters and the zinc roof, felt the unusual vibration, and looked out with their wicked bright eyes, to see what was going on.

Tant Sannie sighed, the Hottentot maid sighed, the Kaffir girl who looked in at the door put her hand over her mouth and said, 'Mow – wah!'

'You must trust in the Lord,' said *Tant* Sannie. 'He can give you more than you have lost.'

'I do, I do!' he cried; 'but oh, I have no wife! I have no wife!'

Tant Sannie was much affected, and came and stood near the bed.

'Ask him if he won't have a little *pap* – nice, fine, flour *pap*. There is some boiling on the kitchen fire.'

The German made the proposal, but the widower waved his hand.

'No, nothing shall pass my lips. I should be suffocated. No, no! Speak not of food to me!'

'*Pap*, and a little brandy in,' said *Tant* Sannie coaxingly.

Bonaparte caught the word.

'Perhaps, perhaps – if I struggled with myself – for the sake of my duties I might imbibe a few drops,' he said, looking with quivering lip up into the German's face. 'I must do my duty, must I not?'

Tant Sannie gave the order, and the girl went for the *pap*.

'I know how it was when my first husband died. They could do nothing with me,' the Boer woman said, 'till I had eaten a sheep's trotter, and honey, and a little roaster-cake. *I know*.'

Bonaparte sat up on the bed with his legs stretched out in front of him, and a hand on each knee, blubbering softly.

'Oh, she was a woman! You are very kind to try and comfort me, but she was my wife. For a woman that is my wife I could live; for the woman that is my wife I could die! For a woman that is my wife I could – Ah! that sweet word *wife*; when will it rest upon my lips again?'

When his feelings had subsided a little he raised the corners of his turned-down mouth, and spoke to the German with flabby lips.

'Do you think she understands me? Oh, tell her every word, that she may know I thank her.'

At that instant the girl reappeared with a basin of steaming gruel and a black bottle.

Tant Sannie poured some of its contents into the basin, stirred it well, and came to the bed.

'Oh, I can't, I can't! I shall die! I shall die!' said Bonaparte, putting his hands to his side.

'Come, just a little,' said *Tant* Sannie coaxingly; 'just a drop.'

'It's too thick, it's too thick. I should choke.'

Tant Sannie added from the contents of the bottle and held out a spoonful; Bonaparte opened his mouth like a little bird waiting for a worm, and held it open, as she dipped again and again into the *pap*.

'Ah, this will do your heart good,' said *Tant* Sannie, in whose mind the relative functions of heart and stomach were exceedingly ill-defined.

When the basin was emptied the violence of his grief was much assuaged; he looked at *Tant* Sannie with gentle tears.

'Tell him,' said the Boer woman, 'that I hope he will sleep well, and that the Lord will comfort him as the Lord only can.'

'Bless you, dear friend, God bless you,' said Bonaparte.

When the door was safely shut on the German, the Hottentot, and the Dutch woman, he got off the bed and washed away the soap he had rubbed on his eyelids.

'Bon,' he said, slapping his leg, 'you're the 'cutest lad I ever came across. If you don't turn out the old Hymns-and-prayers, and pummel the Ragged coat, and get your arms round the fat one's waist and a wedding ring on her finger, then you are not Bonaparte. But you *are* Bonaparte. Bon, you're a fine boy!'

Making which pleasing reflection, he pulled off his trousers and got into bed cheerfully.

CHAPTER SEVEN

He Sets His Trap

'May I come in? I hope I do not disturb you, my dear friend,' said Bonaparte, late one evening, putting his nose in at the cabin door, where the German and his son sat finishing their supper.

It was now two months since he had been installed as schoolmaster in *Tant* Sannie's household, and he had grown mighty and more mighty day by day. He visited the cabin no more, sat close to *Tant* Sannie drinking coffee all the evening, and walked about loftily with his hands under the coat-tails of the German's black cloth, and failed to see even a nigger who wished him a deferential good morning. It was therefore with no small surprise that the German perceived Bonaparte's red nose at his door.

'Walk in, walk in,' he said, joyfully. 'Boy, boy, see if there is coffee left. Well, none. Make a fire. We have done supper, but – '

'My dear friend,' said Bonaparte, taking off his hat, 'I came not to sup, not for mere creature comforts, but for an hour of brotherly intercourse with a kindred spirit. The press of business and the weight of thought, but they alone, may sometimes prevent me from sharing the secrets of my bosom with him for whom I have so great a sympathy. You perhaps wonder when I shall return the two pounds ...'

'Oh, no, no! Make a fire, make a fire, boy. We will have a pot of hot coffee presently,' said the German, rubbing his hands and looking about, not knowing how best to show his pleasure at the unexpected visit.

For three weeks the German's diffident 'Good evening' had met with a stately bow; the chin of Bonaparte lifting itself higher daily; and his shadow had not darkened the cabin doorway since he came to borrow the two pounds. The German walked to the head of the bed and took down a blue bag that hung there. Blue bags were a speciality of the German's. He kept above fifty stowed away in different corners of his room – some filled with curious stones, some with seeds that had been in his possession fifteen years, some with rusty nails, and bits of old harness – in all, a wonderful assortment, but highly prized.

'We have something here not so bad,' said the German, smiling knowingly, as he dived his hand into the bag and took out a handful of almonds and raisins; 'I buy these for my chickens. They increase in size, but they still think the old man must have something nice for them. And the old man – well, a big boy may have a sweet tooth sometimes, may he not? Ha, ha!' said the German, chuckling at his own joke, as he heaped the plate with almonds. 'Here is a stone – two stones to crack them –

no late patent improvement – well, Adam's nutcracker; ha, ha! But I think we shall do. We will not leave them uncracked. We will consume a few without fashionable improvements.'

Here the German sat down on one side of the table, Bonaparte on the other; each one with a couple of flat stones before him, and the plate between them.

'Do not be afraid,' said the German, 'do not be afraid. I do not forget the boy at the fire; I crack for him. The bag is full. Why, this is strange,' he said suddenly, cracking open a large nut; 'three kernels! I have not observed that before. This must be retained. This is valuable.' He wrapped the nut gravely in paper, and put it carefully in his waistcoat pocket. 'Valuable, very valuable!' he said, shaking his head.

'Ah, my friend,' said Bonaparte, 'what joy it is to be once more in your society.' The German's eye glistened, and Bonaparte seized his hand and squeezed it warmly. They then proceeded to crack and eat. After a while Bonaparte said, stuffing a handful of raisins into his mouth:

'I was so deeply grieved, my dear friend, that you and *Tant* Sannie had some slight unpleasantness this evening.'

'Oh, no, no,' said the German; 'it is all right now. A few sheep missing; but I make it good myself. I give my twelve sheep, and work in the other eight.'

'It is rather hard that you should have to make good the lost sheep,' said Bonaparte; 'it is no fault of yours.'

'Well,' said the German, 'this is the case. Last evening I count the sheep at the *kraal* – twenty are missing. I ask the herd; he tells me they are with the other flock; he tells me so *distinctly*; how can I think he lies? This afternoon I count the other flock. The sheep are not there. I come back here: the herd is gone; the sheep are gone. But I cannot – no, I will not – believe he stole them,' said the German, growing suddenly excited. 'Someone else, but not he. I know that boy; I knew him three years. He is a good boy. I have seen him deeply affected on account of his soul. And she would send the police after him!' I say I would rather make the loss good myself. I will not have it; he has fled in fear. I know his heart. It was,' said the German, with a little gentle hesitation, 'under my words that he first felt his need of a Saviour.'

Bonaparte cracked some more almonds, then said, yawning, and more as though he asked for the sake of having something to converse about than from any interest he felt in the subject:

'And what has become of the herd's wife?'

The German was alight again in a moment. 'Yes; his wife. She has a child six days old, and *Tant* Sannie would turn her out into the fields this night. That,' said the German, rising, 'that is what I call cruelty – diabolical cruelty. My soul abhors that deed. The man that could do such a thing I could run him through with a knife!' said the German, his grey eyes flashing, and his bushy black beard adding to the murderous fury of his aspect. Then suddenly subsiding, he said, 'But all is now well; *Tant* Sannie gives her word that the maid shall remain for some days. I go to *Oom*

Muller's tomorrow to learn if the sheep may not be there. If they are not, then I return. They are gone; that is all. I make it good.'

'*Tant* Sannie is a singular woman,' said Bonaparte, taking the tobacco bag the German passed to him.

'Singular! Yes,' said the German; 'but her heart is on her right side. I have lived long years with her, and I may say, I have for her an affection, which she returns. I may say,' added the German with warmth, 'I may say, that there is not one soul on this farm for whom I have *not* an affection.'

'Ah, my friend,' said Bonaparte, 'when the grace of God is in our hearts, is it not so with us all? Do we not love the very worm we tread upon, and as we tread upon it? Do we know distinctions of race, or of sex, or of colour? *No!*

> *Love so amazing, so divine,*
> *It fills my soul, my life, my all.'*

After a time he sank into a less fervent mood, and remarked:

'The Coloured female who waits upon *Tant* Sannie appears to be of a virtuous disposition, an individual who – '

'Virtuous!' said the German; 'I have confidence in her. There is that in her which is pure, that which is noble. The rich and high that walk this earth with lofty eyelids might exchange with her.'

The German here got up to bring a coal for Bonaparte's pipe, and they sat together talking for a while. At length Bonaparte knocked the ashes out of his pipe.

'It is time that I took my departure, dear friend,' he said; 'but, before I do so, shall we not close this evening of sweet communion and brotherly intercourse by a few words of prayer? Oh, how good and how pleasant a thing it is for brethren to dwell together in unity! It is like the dew upon the mountains of Hermon; for there the Lord bestowed a blessing, even life for evermore.'

'Stay and drink some coffee,' said the German.

'No, thank you, my friend; I have business that must be done tonight,' said Bonaparte. 'Your dear son appears to have gone to sleep. He is going to take the wagon to the mill tomorrow! What a little *man* he is.'

'A fine boy.'

But though the boy nodded before the fire he was not asleep; and they all knelt down to pray.

When they rose from their knees Bonaparte extended his hand to Waldo, and patted him on the head.

'Goodnight, my lad,' he said. 'As you go to the mill tomorrow, we shall not see you for some days. Goodnight! Goodbye! The Lord bless and guide you; and may He bring you back to us in safety to find us all *as you have left us!*' He laid some emphasis on the last words. 'And you, my dear friend,' he added, turning with redoubled warmth to the German, 'long, long shall I look back to this evening as a time of refreshing from the presence of the Lord, as an hour of blessed intercourse with a brother in Jesus. May such often return. The Lord bless you!' he added, with yet deeper fervour, 'richly, richly.'

Then he opened the door and vanished out into the darkness.

'He, he, he!' laughed Bonaparte, as he stumbled over the stones. 'If there isn't the rarest lot of fools on this farm that ever God Almighty stuck legs to. He, he, he! When the worms come out then the blackbirds feed. Ha, ha, ha!' Then he drew himself up: even when alone he liked to pose with a certain dignity; it was second nature to him.

He looked in at the kitchen door. The Hottentot maid who acted as interpreter between *Tant* Sannie and himself was gone, and *Tant* Sannie herself was in bed.

'Never mind, Bon, my boy,' he said, as he walked round to his own room, 'tomorrow will do. He, he, he!'

CHAPTER EIGHT

He Catches the Old Bird

At four o'clock the next afternoon the German rode across the plain, returning from his search for the lost sheep. He rode slowly, for he had been in the saddle since sunrise and was somewhat weary, and the heat of the afternoon made his horse sleepy as it picked its way slowly along the sandy road. Every now and then a great red spider would start out of the Karoo on one side of the path and run across to the other, but nothing else broke the still monotony. Presently, behind one of the highest of the milk-bushes that dotted the roadside, the German caught sight of a Kaffir woman, seated there evidently for such shadow as the milk-bush might afford from the sloping rays of the sun. The German turned the horse's head out of the road. It was not his way to pass a living creature without a word of greeting. Coming nearer, he found it was none other than the wife of the absconding Kaffir herd. She had a baby tied on her back by a dirty strip of red blanket; another strip hardly larger was twisted round her waist, for the rest her black body was naked. She was a sullen, ill-looking woman, with lips hideously protruding.

The German questioned her as to how she came there. She muttered in broken Dutch that she had been turned away. Had she done evil? She shook her head sullenly. Had she had food given her? She grunted a negative, and fanned the flies from her baby. Telling the woman to remain where she was, he turned his horse's head to the road and rode off at a furious pace.

'Hard-hearted! Cruel! Oh, my God! Is this the way? Is this charity?'

'Yes, yes, yes,' ejaculated the old man as he rode on; but, presently, his anger began to evaporate, his horse's pace slackened, and by the time he had reached his own door he was nodding and smiling.

Dismounting quickly, he went to the great chest where his provisions were kept. Here he got out a little meal, a little *mielies*, a few roaster-cakes. These he tied up in three blue handkerchiefs, and putting them into a sailcloth bag, he strung them over his shoulders. Then he looked circumspectly out at the door. It was very bad to be discovered in the act of giving; it made him red up to the roots of his old grizzled hair. No one was about, however, so he rode off again. Beside the milk-bush sat the Kaffir woman still – like Hagar, he thought, thrust out by her mistress in the wilderness to die. Telling her to loosen the handkerchief from her head, he poured into it the contents of his bag. The woman tied it up in sullen silence.

'You must try and get to the next farm,' said the German.

The woman shook her head; she would sleep in the field.

The German reflected. Kaffir women were accustomed to sleep in the open air; but then, the child was small, and after so hot a day the night might be chilly. That she would creep back to the huts at the homestead when the darkness favoured her, the German's sagacity did not make evident to him. He took off the old brown salt-and-pepper coat, and held it out to her. The woman received it in silence, and laid it across her knee. 'With that they will sleep warmly; not so bad. Ha, ha!' said the German. And he rode home, nodding his head in a manner that would have made any other man dizzy.

'I wish he would not come back tonight,' said Em, her face wet with tears.
'It will be just the same if he comes back tomorrow,' said Lyndall.
The two girls sat on the step of the cabin waiting for the German's return. Lyndall shaded her eyes with her hand from the sunset light.
'There he comes,' she said, 'whistling Ach Jerusalem du schöne so loud I can hear him here.'
'Perhaps he has found the sheep.'
'Found them!' said Lyndall. 'He would whistle just so if he knew he had to die tonight.'
'You look at the sunset, eh, chickens?' the German said, as he came up at a smart canter. 'Ah yes, that *is* beautiful!' he added, as he dismounted, pausing for a moment with his hand on the saddle to look at the evening sky, where the sun shot up long flaming streaks between which and the eye thin yellow clouds floated. 'Ei! you weep?' said the German, as the girls ran up to him.
Before they had time to reply the voice of *Tant* Sannie was heard.
'You child, of the child, of the child of a Kaffir's dog, come here!' The German looked up. He thought the Dutch woman, come out to cool herself in the yard, called to some misbehaving servant. The old man looked round to see who it might be.
'You old vagabond of a praying German, are you deaf?'
Tant Sannie stood before the steps of the kitchen; upon them sat the lean Hottentot, upon the highest stood Bonaparte Blenkins, both hands folded under the tails of his coat, and his eyes fixed on the sunset sky.
The German dropped the saddle on the ground. 'Bish, bish, bish! what may *this* be?' he said, and walked towards the house. 'Very strange!'
The girls followed him: Em still weeping; Lyndall with her face rather white and her eyes wide open.
'And I have the heart of a devil, did you say? You could run me through with a knife, could you?' cried the Dutch woman. 'I could not drive the Kaffir maid away because I was afraid of *you*, was I? Oh, you miserable rag! I loved you, did I? I would have liked to marry you, would I? *Would* I? WOULD I?' cried the Boer woman; 'you cat's tail, you dog's paw! Be near my house tomorrow morning

when the sun rises,' she gasped, 'my Kaffirs will drag you through the sand. They would do it gladly, any of them, for a bit of tobacco, for all your prayings with them.'

'I am bewildered, I am bewildered,' said the German, standing before her and raising his finger to his forehead; 'I – I do not understand.'

'Ask him, ask him!' cried *Tant* Sannie, pointing to Bonaparte; 'he knows. You thought he could not make me understand, but he did, he did, you old fool. I know enough English for that. You be here,' shouted the Dutch woman, 'when the morning star rises, and I will let my Kaffirs take you out and drag you, till there is not one bone left in your old body that is not broken as fine as *bobotie* meat, you old beggar! All your rags are not worth that they should be thrown out onto the ash heap,' cried the Boer woman; 'but I will have them for my sheep. Not one rotten hoof of your old mare do you take with you; I will have her – all, all for my sheep that you have lost, you godless thing!'

The Boer woman wiped the moisture from her mouth with the palm of her hand.

The German turned to Bonaparte, who still stood on the step absorbed in the beauty of the sunset.

'Do not address me; do not approach me, lost man,' said Bonaparte, not moving his eye nor lowering his chin. 'There is a crime from which all nature revolts; there is a crime whose name is loathsome to the human ear – that crime is yours; that crime is ingratitude. This woman has been your benefactress; on her farm you have lived; after her sheep you have looked; into her house you have been allowed to enter and hold Divine service – an honour of which you were never worthy; and how have you rewarded her? – Basely, basely, basely!'

'But it is all false, lies and falsehoods. I must, I will speak,' said the German, suddenly looking round bewildered. 'Do I dream? Are you mad? What may it be?'

'Go, dog,' cried the Dutch woman; I would have been a rich woman this day if it had not been for your laziness. Praying with the Kaffirs behind the *kraal* walls. Go, you Kaffir's dog!'

'But what then is the matter? What may have happened since I left?' said the German, turning to the Hottentot woman who sat upon the step.

She was his friend; she would tell him kindly the truth. The woman answered by a loud, ringing laugh.

'Give it him, old missis! Give it him!'

It was so nice to see the white man who had been master hunted down. The Coloured woman laughed, and threw a dozen *mielie* grains into her mouth to chew.

All anger and excitement faded from the old man's face. He turned slowly away and walked down the little path to his cabin, with his shoulders bent; it was all dark before him. He stumbled over the threshold of his own well-known door.

Em, sobbing bitterly, would have followed him; but the Boer woman prevented her by a flood of speech which convulsed the Hottentot, so low were its images.

'Come, Em,' said Lyndall, lifting her small, proud head, 'let us go in. We will not stay to hear such language.'

She looked into the Boer woman's eyes. *Tant* Sannie understood the meaning of the look if not the words. She waddled after them, and caught Em by the arm. She had struck Lyndall once years before, and had never done it again; so she took Em.

'So you will defy me, too, will you, you Englishman's ugliness!' she cried, as with one hand she forced the child down, and held her head tightly against her knee; with the other she beat her first upon one cheek, and then upon the other.

For one instant Lyndall looked on, then she laid her small fingers on the Boer woman's arm. With the exertion of half its strength *Tant* Sannie might have flung the girl back upon the stones. It was not the power of the slight fingers, tightly though they clenched her broad wrist – so tightly that at bedtime the marks were still there; but the Boer woman looked into the clear eyes and at the quivering white lips, and with a half-surprised curse relaxed her hold. The girl drew Em's arm through her own.

'Move!' she said to Bonaparte, who stood in the door; and he, Bonaparte the invincible, in the hour of his triumph, moved to give her place.

The Hottentot ceased to laugh, and an uncomfortable silence fell on all the three in the doorway.

Once in their room, Em sat down on the floor and wailed bitterly. Lyndall lay on the bed with her arm drawn across her eyes, very white and still.

'Hoo, hoo!' cried Em; 'and they won't let him take the grey mare; and Waldo has gone to the mill. Hoo, hoo! And perhaps they won't let us go and say goodbye to him. Hoo, hoo, hoo!'

'I wish you would be quiet,' said Lyndall, without moving. 'Does it give you such felicity to let Bonaparte know he is hurting you? We will ask no one. It will be suppertime soon. Listen – and when you hear the chink of the knives and forks we will go out and see him.'

Em suppressed her sobs and listened intently, kneeling at the door. Suddenly someone came to the window and put the shutter up.

'Who was that?' said Lyndall, starting.

'The girl, I suppose,' said Em. 'How early she is this evening!'

But Lyndall sprang from the bed and seized the handle of the door, shaking it fiercely. The door was locked on the outside. She ground her teeth.

'What is the matter?' asked Em. The room was in perfect darkness now.

'Nothing,' said Lyndall quietly; 'only they have locked us in.'

She turned, and went back to bed again. But ere long Em heard a sound of movement. Lyndall had climbed up into the window, and with her fingers felt the woodwork that surrounded the panes. Slipping down, the girl loosened the iron knob from the foot of the bedstead, and climbing up again she broke with it every pane of glass in the window, beginning at the top and ending at the bottom.

'What are you doing?' asked Em, who heard the falling fragments.

Her companion made no reply; but leaned on every little cross-bar, which cracked and gave way beneath her. Then she pressed with all her strength against the shutter. She had thought the wooden buttons would give way, but by the clinking sound she knew that the iron bar had been put across. She was quite quiet for a time. Clambering down, she took from the table a small one-bladed penknife, with which she began to peck at the hard wood of the shutter.

'What are you doing now?' asked Em, who had ceased crying in her wonder, and had drawn near.

'Trying to make a hole,' was the short reply.

'Do you think you will be able to?'

'No, but I am trying.'

In an agony of suspense Em waited. For ten minutes Lyndall pecked. The hole was three-eighths of an inch deep – then the blade sprang into ten pieces.

'What has happened now?' asked Em, blubbering afresh.

'Nothing,' said Lyndall. 'Bring me my nightgown, a piece of paper, and the matches.'

Wondering, Em fumbled about till she found them. 'What are you going to do with them?' she whispered.

'Burn down the window.'

'But won't the whole house take fire and burn down too?'

'Yes.'

'But will it not be very wicked?'

'Yes, very. And I do not care.'

She arranged the nightgown carefully in the corner of the window, with the chips of the frame about it. There was only one match in the box. She drew it carefully along the wall. For a moment it burnt up blue, and showed the tiny face with its glistening eyes. She held it carefully to the paper. For an instant it burnt up brightly, then flickered and went out. She blew the spark, but it died also. Then she threw the paper on to the ground, trod on it, and went to her bed, and began to undress.

Em rushed to the door, knocking against it wildly. 'Oh, *Tant* Sannie! *Tant* Sannie! Oh, let us out!' she cried. 'Oh, Lyndall, what are we to do?'

Lyndall wiped a drop of blood off the lip she had bitten.

'I am going to sleep,' she said. 'If you like to sit there and howl till the morning, do. Perhaps you will find that it helps; I never heard that howling helped anyone.'

Long after, when Em herself had gone to bed and was almost asleep, Lyndall came and stood at her bedside.

'Here,' she said, slipping a little pot of powder into her hand; 'rub some on to your face. Does it not burn where she struck you?'

Then she crept to her own bed.

Long, long after, when Em was really asleep, she lay still awake, and folded her hands on her little breast, and muttered:

'When that day comes, and I am strong, I will hate everything that has power, and help everything that is weak.' And she bit her lip again.

The German looked out at the cabin door for the last time that night. Then he paced the room slowly and sighed. Then he drew out pen and paper, and sat down to write, rubbing his old grey eyes with his knuckles before he began.

'MY CHICKENS,

You did not come to say goodbye to the old man. Might you? Ah, well, there is a land where they part no more, where saints immortal reign.

I sit here alone, and I think of you. Will you forget the old man? When you wake tomorrow he will be far away. The old horse is lazy, but he has his stick to help him; that is three legs. He comes back one day with gold and diamonds. Will you welcome him? Well, we shall see. I go to meet Waldo. He comes back with the wagon; then he follows me. Poor boy! God knows. There is a land where all things are made right, but that land is not here.

My little children, serve the Saviour; give your hearts to Him while you are yet young. Life is short.

Nothing is mine, otherwise I would say, Lyndall, take my books, Em my stones. Now I say nothing. The things are mine: it is not righteous, God knows! But I am silent. Let it be. But I feel it, I must say I feel it.

Do not cry too much for the old man. He goes out to seek his fortune, and comes back with it in a bag, it may be.

I love my children. Do they think of me? I am Old Otto, who goes out to seek his fortune.

OF'

Having concluded this quaint production, he put it where the children would find it the next morning, and proceeded to prepare his bundle. He never thought of entering a protest against the loss of his goods; like a child he submitted, and wept. He had been there eleven years, and it was hard to go away. He spread open on the bed a blue handkerchief and on it put one by one the things he thought most necessary and important: a little bag of curious seeds, which he meant to plant someday; an old German hymn book, three misshapen stones that he greatly valued, a Bible, a shirt, and two handkerchiefs; then there was room for nothing more. He tied up the bundle tightly and put it on a chair by his bedside.

'That is not much; they cannot say I take much,' he said, looking at it.

He put his knotted stick beside it, his blue tobacco bag and his short pipe, and then inspected his coats. He had two left – a moth-eaten overcoat and a black alpaca out at the elbows. He decided for the overcoat: it was warm certainly, but then he could carry it over his arm, and only put it on when he met someone along the road. It was more respectable than the black alpaca. He hung the greatcoat over the back of the chair, and stuffed a hard bit of roaster-cake under the knot of the bundle, and then his preparations were completed. The German stood contemplating them with much satisfaction. He had almost forgotten his sorrow at leaving, in his pleasure at preparing. Suddenly he started; an expression of intense pain passed over his face. He drew back his left arm quickly, and then pressed his right hand upon his breast.

'Ah, the sudden pang again,' he said.

His face was white, but it quickly regained its colour. Then the old man busied himself in putting everything right.

'I will leave it neat. They shall not say I did not leave it neat,' he said. Even the little bags of seeds on the mantelpiece he put in rows and dusted. Then he undressed and got into bed. Under his pillow was a little storybook. He drew it forth. To the old German a story was no story. Its events were as real and as important to himself as the matters of his own life. He could not go away without knowing whether that wicked Earl relented, and whether the Baron married Emilina. So he adjusted his spectacles and began to read. Occasionally, as his feelings became too strongly moved, he ejaculated, 'Ah, I thought so! – That was a rogue! – I saw it before! – I knew it from the beginning!' More than half an hour had passed when he looked up to the silver watch at the top of his bed.

'The march is long tomorrow; this will not do,' he said, taking off his spectacles and putting them carefully into the book to mark the place. 'This will be good reading as I walk along tomorrow,' he added, as he stuffed the book into the pocket of the greatcoat; 'very good reading.' He nodded his head and lay down. He thought a little of his own troubles, a good deal of the two little girls he was leaving, of the Earl, of Emilina, of the Baron; but he was soon asleep – sleeping as peacefully as a little child upon whose innocent soul sorrow and care cannot rest.

It was very quiet in the room. The coals in the fireplace threw a dull red light across the floor upon the red lions on the quilt. Eleven o'clock came, and the room was very still. One o'clock came. The glimmer had died out, though the ashes were still warm, and the room was very dark. The grey mouse, who had its hole under the toolbox, came out and sat on the sacks in the corner; then, growing bolder, the room was so dark, it climbed the chair at the bedside, nibbled at the roaster-cake, took one bite quickly at the candle, and then sat on its haunches listening. It heard the even breathing of the old man, and the steps of the hungry Kaffir dog going his last round in search of a bone or a skin that had been forgotten; and it heard the white hen call out as the wild cat ran away with one of her brood, and it heard the chicken cry. Then the grey mouse went back to its hole under the toolbox, and the room was quiet. And two o'clock came. By that time the night was grown dull and cloudy. The wild cat had gone to its home on the *kopje*: the Kaffir dog had found a bone, and lay gnawing it.

An intense quiet reigned everywhere. Only in her room the Boer woman tossed her great arms in her sleep; for she dreamed that a dark shadow with outstretched wings fled slowly over her house, and she moaned and shivered. And the night was very still.

But, quiet as all places were, there was a quite peculiar quiet in the German's room. Though you strained your ear most carefully you caught no sound of breathing.

He was not gone, for the old coat still hung on the chair – the coat that was to be put on when he met anyone; and the bundle and stick were ready for tomorrow's long march. The old German himself lay there, his wavy black hair just touched with grey thrown back upon the pillow. The old face was lying there alone in the dark, smiling like a little child's – oh, so peacefully. There is a stranger whose coming, they say, is worse than all the ills of life, from whose presence we flee away trembling; but he comes very tenderly sometimes. And it seemed almost as though Death had known and loved the old man, so gently it touched him. And how could it deal hardly with him – the loving, simple, childlike old man?

So it smoothed out the wrinkles that were in the old forehead, and fixed the passing smile, and sealed the eyes that they might not weep again; and then the short sleep of time was melted into the long, long sleep of eternity.

'How has he grown so young in this one night?' they said when they found him in the morning.

Yes, dear old man; to such as you time brings no age. You die with the purity and innocence of your childhood upon you, though you die in your grey hairs.

CHAPTER NINE

He Sees a Ghost

Bonaparte stood on the ash heap. He espied across the plain a moving speck, and he chucked his coat tails up and down in expectancy of a scene.

The wagon came on slowly. Waldo lay curled among the sacks at the back of the wagon, the hand in his breast resting on the sheep-shearing machine. It was finished now. The right thought had struck him the day before, as he sat, half asleep, watching the water go over the mill wheel. He muttered to himself with half-closed eyes: 'Tomorrow smooth the cogs – tighten the screws a little – show it to them.' Then after a pause – 'Over the whole world – the whole world – mine, that I have made!' He pressed the little wheels and pulleys in his pocket till they cracked. Presently his muttering became louder – 'And fifty pounds – a black hat for my dadda – for Lyndall a blue silk, very light; and one purple like the earth-bells, and white shoes.' He muttered on – 'A box full, full of books. They shall tell me all, all, all,' he added, moving his fingers desiringly; 'why the crystals grow in such beautiful shapes; why lightning runs to the iron; why black people are black; why the sunlight makes things warm. I shall read, read, read,' he muttered slowly. Then came over him suddenly what he called 'The presence of God'; a sense of a good, strong something folding him round. He smiled through his half-shut eyes. 'Ah, Father, my own Father, it is so sweet to feel you, like the warm sunshine. The Bibles and books cannot tell of you and all I feel you. They are mixed with men's words; but you ...'

His muttering sank into inaudible confusion, till opening his eyes wide, it struck him that the brown plain he looked at was the old home farm. For half an hour they had been riding in it, and he had not known it. He roused the leader, who sat nodding on the front of the wagon in the early morning sunlight. They were within half a mile of the homestead. It seemed to him that he had been gone from them all a year. He fancied he could see Lyndall standing on the brick wall to watch for him; his father, passing from one house to the other, stopping to look.

He called aloud to the oxen. For each one at home he had brought something. For his father a piece of tobacco, bought at the shop by the mill; for Em a thimble; for Lyndall a beautiful flower dug out by the roots, at a place where they had *outspanned*; for *Tant* Sannie a handkerchief. When they drew near the house he threw the whip to the Kaffir leader, and sprang from the side of the wagon to run on. Bonaparte stopped him as he ran past the ash heap.

'Good morning, my dear boy. Where are you running to so fast with your rosy cheeks?'

The boy looked up at him, glad even to see Bonaparte.

'I am going to the cabin,' he said, out of breath.

'You won't find them in just now – not your good old father,' said Bonaparte.

'Where is he?' asked the lad.

'There beyond the camps,' said Bonaparte, waving his hand oratorically towards the stone-walled ostrich camps.

'What is he doing there?' asked the boy.

Bonaparte patted him on the cheek kindly.

'We could not keep him any more, it was too hot. We've buried him, my boy,' said Bonaparte, touching with his finger the boy's cheek. 'We couldn't keep him any more. He, he, he!' laughed Bonaparte, as the boy fled away along the low stone wall, almost furtively, as one in fear.

At five o'clock Bonaparte knelt before a box in the German's room. He was busily unpacking it.

It had been agreed upon between *Tant* Sannie and himself, that now the German was gone he, Bonaparte, was to be no longer schoolmaster, but overseer of the farm. In return for his past scholastic labours he had expressed himself willing to take possession of the dead man's goods and room. *Tant* Sannie hardly liked the arrangement. She had a great deal more respect for the German dead than the German living, and would rather his goods had been allowed to descend peacefully to his son. For she was a firm believer in the chinks in the world above, where not only ears, but eyes might be applied to see how things went on in this world below. She never felt sure how far the spirit world might overlap this world of sense, and, as a rule, prudently abstained from doing anything which might offend unseen auditors. For this reason she abstained from ill-using the dead Englishman's daughter and niece, and for this reason she would rather the boy had had his father's goods. But it was hard to refuse Bonaparte anything when she and he sat so happily together in the evening drinking coffee, Bonaparte telling her in the broken Dutch he was fast learning how he adored fat women, and what a splendid farmer he was.

So at five o'clock on this afternoon Bonaparte knelt in the German's room.

'Somewhere here, it is,' he said, as he packed the old clothes carefully out of the box, and, finding nothing, packed them in again. 'Somewhere in this room it is; and if it's here Bonaparte finds it,' he repeated. 'You didn't stay here all these years without making a little pile somewhere, my lamb. You weren't such a fool as you looked. Oh, no!' said Bonaparte.

He now walked about the room, diving his fingers in everywhere: sticking them into the great crevices in the wall and frightening out the spiders; rapping them against the old plaster till it cracked and fell in pieces; peering up the chimney, till the soot dropped on his bald head and blackened it. He felt in little blue bags; he tried to raise the hearthstone; he shook each book till the old leaves fell down in showers on the floor.

It was getting dark, and Bonaparte stood with his finger on his nose reflecting. Finally he walked to the door, behind which hung the trousers and waistcoat the dead man had last worn. He had felt in them, but hurriedly, just after the funeral the day before; he would examine them again. Sticking his fingers into the waistcoat pockets, he found in one corner a hole. Pressing his hand through it, between the lining and the cloth, he presently came into contact with something. Bonaparte drew it forth – a small, square parcel, sewed up in sailcloth. He gazed at it, squeezed it; it cracked, as though full of bank notes. He put it quickly into his own waistcoat pocket, and peeped over the half-door, to see if there was anyone coming. There was nothing to be seen but the last rays of yellow sunset light, painting the Karoo bushes in the plain, and shining on the ash heap, where the fowls were pecking. He turned and sat down on the nearest chair, and, taking out his penknife, ripped the parcel open. The first thing that fell was a shower of yellow faded papers. Bonaparte opened them carefully one by one, and smoothed them out on his knee. There was something very valuable to be hidden so carefully, though the German characters he could not decipher. When he came to the last one he felt there was something hard in it.

'You've got it, Bon, my boy! you've got it!' he cried, slapping his leg hard. Edging nearer to the door, for the light was fading, he opened the paper carefully. There was nothing inside but a plain gold wedding-ring.

'Better than nothing!' said Bonaparte, trying to put it on his little finger, which, however, proved too fat.

He took it off and set it down on the table before him, and looked at it with his crosswise eyes.

'When that auspicious hour, Sannie,' he said, 'shall have arrived, when, panting, I shall lead thee, lighted by Hymen's torch, to the connubial altar, upon thy fair amaranthine finger, my joyous bride, shall this ring repose.

Thy fair body, oh, my girl,
Shall Bonaparte possess;
His fingers in thy moneybags,
He therein, too, shall mess.'

Having given utterance to this flood of poesy, he sat lost in joyous reflection.

'He therein, too, *shall* mess,' he repeated, meditatively.

At this instant, as Bonaparte swore, and swore truly to the end of his life, a slow and distinct rap was given on the crown of his bald head.

Bonaparte started and looked up. No *riem*, or strap, hung down from the rafters above, and not a human creature was near the door. It was growing dark; he did not like it. He began to fold up the papers expeditiously. He stretched out his hand for the ring. The ring was gone! Gone, although no human creature had entered the room; gone, although no form had crossed the doorway. Gone!

He would not sleep there, that was certain.

He stuffed the papers into his pocket. As he did so, three slow and distinct taps were given on the crown of his head. Bonaparte's jaw fell; each separate joint lost its power; he could not move; he dared not rise; his tongue lay loose in his mouth.

'Take all, take all!' he gurgled in his throat. 'I – I do not want them. Take –'

Here a resolute tug at the grey curls at the back of his head caused him to leap up, yelling wildly. Was he to sit still paralysed, to be dragged away *bodily* to the devil? With terrific shrieks he fled, casting no glance behind.

When the dew was falling, and the evening was dark, a small figure moved towards the gate of the farthest ostrich-camp, driving a bird before it. When the gate was opened and the bird driven in and the gate fastened, it turned away, but then suddenly paused near the stone wall.

'Is that you, Waldo?' said Lyndall, hearing a sound.

The boy was sitting on the dam ground with his back to the wall. He gave her no answer.

'Come,' she said, bending over him. 'I have been looking for you all day.'

He mumbled something.

'You have had nothing to eat. I have put some supper in your room. You must come home with me, Waldo.'

She took his hand, and the boy rose slowly.

She made him take her arm, and twisted her small fingers among his.

'You must forget,' she whispered. 'Since it happened, I walk, I talk, I never sit still. If we remember we cannot bring back the dead.' She knit her little fingers closer among his. 'Forgetting is the best thing. He did not watch it coming,' she whispered presently. 'That is the dreadful thing, to *see* it coming!' She shuddered. 'I want it to come so to me, too. Why do you think I was driving that bird?' she added quickly. 'That was Hans, the bird that hates Bonaparte. I let him out this afternoon; I thought he would chase him and perhaps kill him.'

The boy showed no sign of interest.

'He did not catch him; but he put his head over the half-door of your cabin and frightened him horribly. He was there, busy stealing your things. Perhaps he will leave them alone now; but I wish the bird had trodden on him.'

They said no more till they reached the door of the cabin.

'There is a candle and supper on the table. You must eat,' she said authoritatively. 'I cannot stay with you now, lest they find out about the bird.'

He grasped her arm and brought his mouth close to her ear:
'There is no God!' he almost hissed; 'no God; not anywhere!'
She started.
'*Not anywhere!*'
He ground it out between his teeth, and she felt his hot breath on her cheek.
'Waldo, you are mad,' she said, drawing herself from him instinctively.
He loosened his grasp and turned away from her also.
In truth, is it not life's way? We fight our little battles alone; you yours, I mine. We must not help or find help.

When your life is most real, to me you are mad; when your agony is blackest, I look at you and wonder. Friendship is good, a strong stick; but when the hour comes to lean hard, it gives. In the day of their bitterest need all souls are alone.

Lyndall stood by him in the dark, pityingly, wonderingly. As he walked to the door she came after him.

'Eat your supper; it will do you good,' she said.

She rubbed her cheek against his shoulder and then ran away.

In the front room the little woolly Kaffir girl was washing *Tant* Sannie's feet in a small tub, and Bonaparte, who sat on the wooden sofa, was pulling off his shoes and stockings that his own feet might be washed also. There were three candles burning in the room, and he and *Tant* Sannie sat close together, with the lean Hottentot not far off; for when ghosts are about much light is needed, there is great strength in numbers. Bonaparte had completely recovered from the effects of his fright in the afternoon, and the numerous doses of brandy that it had been necessary to administer to him to effect his restoration had put him into a singularly pleasant and amiable mood.

'That boy, Waldo,' said Bonaparte, rubbing his toes, 'took himself off coolly this morning as soon as the wagon came, and has not done a stiver of work all day. *I'll not have that kind of thing now I'm master of this farm.*'

The Hottentot maid translated.

'Ah, I expect he's sorry that his father's dead,' said *Tant* Sannie. 'It's nature, you know. I cried the whole morning when my father died. One can always get another husband, but one can't get another father,' said *Tant* Sannie, casting a sidelong glance at Bonaparte.

Bonaparte expressed a wish to give Waldo his orders for the next day's work, and accordingly the little woolly-headed Kaffir was sent to call him. After a considerable time the boy appeared, and stood in the doorway.

If they had dressed him in one of the swallow-tailed coats, and oiled his hair till the drops fell from it, and it lay as smooth as an elder's on sacrament Sunday, there would still have been something unannointed in the aspect of the fellow. As it was, standing there in his strange old costume, his head presenting much the appearance of having been deeply rolled in sand, his eyelids swollen, the hair hanging over his forehead, and a dogged sullenness on his features, he presented most the appearance of an ill-conditioned young buffalo.

'Beloved Lord,' cried *Tant* Sannie, 'how he looks! Come in, boy. Couldn't you come and say good day to me? Don't you want some supper?'

He said he wanted nothing, and turned his heavy eyes away from her.

'There's a ghost been seen in your father's room,' said *Tant* Sannie. 'If you're afraid you can sleep in the kitchen.'

'I will sleep in our room,' said the boy slowly.

'Well, you can go now,' she said; 'but be up early to take the sheep. The herd ...'

'Yes, be up early, my boy,' interrupted Bonaparte, smiling. 'I am to be master of this farm now; and we shall be good friends, I trust, very good friends, if you try to do your duty, my dear boy.'

Waldo turned to go, and Bonaparte, looking benignly at the candle, stretched out one unstockinged foot, over which Waldo, looking at nothing in particular, fell with a heavy thud upon the floor.

'Dear me! I hope you are not hurt, my boy,' said Bonaparte. 'You'll have many a harder thing than that though, before you've gone through life,' he added consolingly, as Waldo picked himself up.

The lean Hottentot laughed till the room rang again; and *Tant* Sannie tittered till her sides ached.

When he had gone the little maid began to wash Bonaparte's feet.

'Oh, Lord, beloved Lord, how he did fall! I can't think of it,' cried *Tant* Sannie, and she laughed again. 'I always did know he was not right; but this evening anyone could see it,' she added, wiping the tears of mirth from her face. 'His eyes are as wild as if the devil was in them. He never *was* like other children. The dear Lord knows, if he doesn't walk alone for hours talking to himself. If you sit in the room with him you can see his lips moving the whole time; and if you talk to him twenty times he doesn't hear you. Daft-eyes; he's as mad as mad can be.'

The repetition of the word mad conveyed meaning to Bonaparte's mind. He left off paddling his toes in the water.

'Mad, mad? *I* know that kind of mad,' said Bonaparte, and I know the thing to give for it. The front end of a little horsewhip, the tip! Nice thing; takes it out,' said Bonaparte.

The Hottentot laughed, and translated.

'No more walking about and talking to themselves on this farm now,' said Bonaparte; no more minding of sheep and reading of books at the same time. The point of a horsewhip is a little thing, but I think he'll have a taste of it before long.' Bonaparte rubbed his hands and looked pleasantly across his nose; and then the three laughed together grimly.

And Waldo in his cabin crouched in the dark in a corner, with his knees drawn up to his chin.

CHAPTER TEN

He Shows His Teeth

Doss sat among the Karoo bushes, one yellow ear drawn over his wicked little eye, ready to flap away any adventurous fly that might settle on his nose. Around him in the morning sunlight fed the sheep; behind him lay his master polishing his machine. He found much comfort in handling it that morning. A dozen philosophical essays, or angelically attuned songs for the consolation of the bereaved, could never have been to him what that little sheep-shearing machine was that day.

After struggling to see the unseeable, growing drunk with the endeavour to span the infinite, and writhing before the inscrutable mystery, it is a renovating relief to turn to some simple, feelable, weighable substance; to something which has a smell and a colour, which may be handled and turned over this way and that. Whether there be or be not a hereafter, whether there be any use in calling aloud to the Unseen power, whether there be an Unseen power to call to, whatever be the true nature of the *I* who call and of the objects around me, whatever be our meaning, our internal essence, our cause (and in a certain order of minds death and the agony of loss inevitably awaken the wild desire, at other times smothered, to look into these things), whatever be the nature of that which the limits of the human intellect build up on every hand, this thing is certain – a knife will cut wood, and one cogged wheel will turn another. This is sure.

Waldo found an immeasurable satisfaction in the handling of his machine; but Doss winked and blinked, and thought it all frightfully monotonous out there on the flat, and presently dropped asleep, sitting bolt upright. Suddenly his eyes opened wide; something was coming from the direction of the homestead. Winking his eyes and looking intently, he perceived it was the grey mare. Now Doss had wondered much of late what had become of her master. Seeing she carried someone on her back, he now came to his own conclusion, and began to move his tail violently up and down. Presently he pricked up one ear and let the other hang; his tail became motionless, and the expression of his mouth was one of decided disapproval bordering on scorn. He wrinkled his lips up on each side into little lines.

The sand was soft, and the grey mare came on so noiselessly that the boy heard nothing till Bonaparte dismounted. Then Doss got up and moved back a step. He did not approve of Bonaparte's appearance. His costume, in truth, was of a unique kind. It was a combination of the town and country. The tails of his black cloth coat were pinned up behind to keep them from rubbing; he had on a pair of moleskin trousers and leather gaiters, and in his hand he carried a little whip of rhinoceros hide.

Waldo started and looked up. Had there been a moment's time he would have dug a hole in the sand with his hands and buried his treasure. It was only a toy of wood, but he loved it, as one of necessity loves what has been born of him, whether of the flesh or spirit. When cold eyes have looked at it, the feathers are rubbed off our butterfly's wing forever.

'What have you here, my lad?' said Bonaparte, standing by him and pointing with the end of his whip to the medley of wheels and hinges.

The boy muttered something inaudible, and half-spread his hand over the thing.

'But this seems to be a very ingenious little machine,' said Bonaparte, seating himself on the ant-heap, and bending down over it with deep interest.

'What is it for, my lad?'

'Shearing sheep.'

'It is a very nice little machine,' said Bonaparte. 'How does it work, now? I have never seen anything so ingenious.'

There was never a parent who heard deception in the voice that praised his child – his firstborn. Here was one who liked the thing that had been created in him. He forgot everything. He showed how the shears would work with a little guidance, how the sheep would be held, and the wool fall into the trough. A flush burst over his face as he spoke.

'I tell you what, my lad,' said Bonaparte emphatically, when the explanation was finished, 'we must get you a patent. Your fortune is made. In three years' time there'll not be a farm in this Colony where it isn't working. You're a genius, that's what *you* are!' said Bonaparte, rising.

'If it were made larger,' said the boy, raising his eyes, 'it would work more smoothly. Do you think there would be anyone in this Colony would be able to make it?'

'I'm sure they could,' said Bonaparte; 'and if not, why, I'll do my best for you. I'll send it to England. It must be done somehow. How long have you worked at it?'

'Nine months,' said the boy.

'Oh, it is such a nice little machine,' said Bonaparte, 'one can't help feeling an interest in it. There is only *one* little improvement, one very little improvement, I should like to make.'

Bonaparte put his foot on the machine and crushed it into the sand. The boy looked up into his face.

'Looks better now,' said Bonaparte, 'doesn't it? If we can't have it made in England we'll send it to America. Goodbye; ta-ta,' he added. 'You're a great genius, a born genius, my dear boy, there's no doubt about it.'

He mounted the grey mare and rode off. The dog watched his retreat with cynical satisfaction; but his master lay on the ground with his head on his arms in the sand, and the little wheels and chips of wood lay on the ground around him. The dog jumped on to his back and snapped at the black curls, till, finding that no notice was taken, he walked off to play with a black beetle. The beetle was hard at work trying to roll home a great ball of dung it had been collecting all the morning; but Doss broke the ball, and ate the beetle's hind legs, and then bit off its head. And it was all play, and no one could tell what it had lived and worked for. A striving, and a striving, and an ending in nothing.

CHAPTER ELEVEN

He Snaps

'I have found something in the loft,' said Em to Waldo, who was listlessly piling cakes of fuel on the *kraal* wall, a week after. 'It is a box of books that belonged to my father. We thought *Tant* Sannie had burnt them.'

The boy put down the cake he was raising and looked at her.

'I don't think they are very nice, not stories,' she added, 'but you can go and take any you like.'

So saying, she took up the plate in which she had brought his breakfast, and walked off to the house.

After that the boy worked quickly. The pile of fuel Bonaparte had ordered him to pack was on the wall in half an hour. He then went to throw salt on the skins laid out to dry. Finding the pot empty, he went to the loft to refill it.

Bonaparte Blenkins, whose door opened at the foot of the ladder, saw the boy go up, and stood in the doorway waiting for his return. He wanted his boots blacked. Doss, finding he could not follow his master up the round bars, sat patiently at the foot of the ladder. Presently he looked up longingly, but no one appeared. Then Bonaparte looked up also, and began to call; but there was no answer. What could the boy be doing? The loft was an unknown land to Bonaparte. He had often wondered what was up there; he liked to know what was in all locked-up places and out-of-the-way corners, but he was afraid to climb the ladder. So Bonaparte looked up, and, in the name of all that was tantalising, questioned what the boy did up there. The loft was used only as a lumber-room. What could the fellow find up there to keep him so long?

Could the Boer woman have beheld Waldo at that instant, any lingering doubt which might have remained in her mind as to the boy's insanity would instantly have vanished. For, having filled the salt-pot, he proceeded to look for the box of books among the rubbish that filled the loft. Under a pile of sacks he found it – a rough packing case, nailed up, but with one loose plank. He lifted that, and saw the even backs of a row of books. He knelt down before the box, and ran his hand along its rough edges, as if to assure himself of its existence. He stuck his hand in among the books, and pulled out two. He felt them, thrust his fingers in among the leaves, and crumpled them a little, as a lover feels the hair of his mistress. The fellow gloated over his treasure. He had had a dozen books in the course of his life; now here was a mine of them opened at his feet. After a while he began to read the titles, and now and again opened a book and read a sentence; but he was too excited to catch the meanings distinctly. At last he came to a dull, brown volume. He read the name, opened it in the centre, and where he opened began to read. 'Twas a chapter on property that he fell upon – Communism, Fourierism, St Simonism – in a work on Political Economy. He read down one page and turned over to the next; he read down that without changing his posture by an inch; he read the next, and the next, kneeling up all the while with the book in his hand, and his lips parted.

All he read he did not fully understand; the thoughts were new to him; but this was the fellow's startled joy in the book – the thoughts were his, they belonged to him. He had never thought them before, but they were his.

He laughed silently and internally, with the still intensity of triumphant joy.

So, then, all thinking creatures did not send up the one cry – 'As thou, dear Lord, hast created things in the beginning, so are they now, so ought they to be, so will they be, world without end; and it doesn't concern us what they are. Amen.' There were men to whom not only *kopjes* and stones were calling out imperatively, 'What are we, and how came we here? Understand us, and know us'; but to whom even the old, old relations between man and man, and the customs of the ages called, and could not be made still and forgotten.

The boy's heavy body quivered with excitement. So he was not alone, not alone. He could not quite have told anyone why he was so glad, and this warmth had come to him. His cheeks were burning. No wonder that Bonaparte called in vain, and Doss put his paws on the ladder, and whined till three-quarters of an hour had passed. At last the boy put the book in his breast and buttoned it tightly to him. He took up the salt-pot, and went to the top of the ladder. Bonaparte, with his hands folded under his coat tails, looked up when he appeared, and accosted him.

'You've been rather a long time up there, my lad,' he said, as the boy descended with a tremulous haste, most unlike his ordinary slow movement. 'You didn't hear me calling, I suppose?'

Bonaparte whisked the tails of his coat up and down as he looked at him. He, Bonaparte Blenkins, had eyes which were very far-seeing. He looked at the pot. It was rather a small pot to have taken three-quarters of an hour in the filling. He looked at the face. It was flushed. And yet, *Tant* Sannie kept no wine – he had not been drinking; his eyes were wide open and bright – he had not been sleeping; there was no girl up there – he had not been making love. Bonaparte looked at him sagaciously. What would account for the marvellous change in the boy coming down the ladder from the boy going up the ladder? *One* thing there was. Did not *Tant* Sannie keep in the loft *biltongs* and nice smoked sausages? There must be something nice to *eat* up there! Aha! that was it!

Bonaparte was so interested in carrying out this chain of inductive reasoning that he quite forgot to have his boots blacked.

He watched the boy shuffle off with the salt-pot under his arm; then he stood in

250

his doorway, and raised his eyes to the quiet blue sky, and audibly propounded this riddle to himself.

'What is the connection between the naked back of a certain boy with a greatcoat on and a salt-pot under his arm, and the tip of a horsewhip? Answer: No connection at present, but there will be soon.'

Bonaparte was so pleased with this sally of his wit that he chuckled a little, and went to lie down on his bed.

There was bread-baking that afternoon, and there was a fire lighted in the brick oven behind the house, and *Tant* Sannie had left the great wooden-elbowed chair in which she passed her life, and waddled out to look at it. Not far off was Waldo, who, having thrown a pail of food into the pigsty, now leaned over the sod-wall looking at the pigs. Half of the sty was dry, but the lower half was a pool of mud, on the edge of which the mother sow lay with closed eyes, her ten little ones sucking; the father pig, knee-deep in the mud, stood running his snout into a rotten pumpkin and wriggling his curled tail.

Waldo wondered dreamily as he stared why they were pleasant to look at. Taken singly they were not beautiful; taken together they were. Was it not because there was a certain harmony about them? The old sow was suited to the little pigs, and the little pigs to their mother; the old boar to the rotten pumpkin, and all to the mud. They suggested the thought of nothing that should be added, of nothing that should be taken away. And, he wondered on vaguely, was not *that* the secret of all beauty, that you look on – . So he stood dreaming, and leaned further and further over the sod-wall, and looked at the pigs.

All this time Bonaparte Blenkins was sloping down from the house in an aimless sort of way; but he kept one eye fixed on the pigsty, and each gyration brought him nearer to it. Waldo stood like a thing asleep when Bonaparte came close up to him.

In old days, when a small boy, playing in an Irish street gutter, he, Bonaparte, had been familiarly known among his comrades under the title of Tripping Ben; this, from the rare ease and dexterity with which, by merely projecting his foot, he could precipitate any unfortunate companion on to the crown of his head. Years had elapsed, and Tripping Ben had become Bonaparte; but the old gift was in him still. He came close to the pigsty. All the defunct memories of his boyhood returned on him in a flood, as with an adroit movement he inserted his leg between Waldo and the wall, and sent him over into the pigsty.

The little pigs were startled at the strange intruder, and ran behind their mother, who sniffed at him. *Tant* Sannie smote her hands together and laughed; but Bonaparte was far from joining her. Lost in reverie, he gazed at the distant horizon.

The sudden reversal of head and feet had thrown out the volume that Waldo carried in his breast. Bonaparte picked it up, and began to inspect it, as the boy climbed slowly over the wall. He would have walked off sullenly, but he wanted his book, and waited till it should be given him.

'Ha!' said Bonaparte, raising his eyes from the leaves of the book which he was examining. 'I hope your coat has not been injured; it is of an elegant cut. An heirloom, I presume, from your paternal grandfather? It looks nice now.'

'Oh, Lord! Oh, Lord!' cried *Tant* Sannie, laughing and holding her sides; 'how the child looks – as though he thought the mud would never wash off. Oh, Lord, I shall die! You, Bonaparte, are the funniest man I ever saw.'

Bonaparte Blenkins was now carefully inspecting the volume he had picked up. Among the subjects on which the darkness of his understanding had been enlightened during his youth, Political Economy had not been one. He was not, therefore, very clear as to what the nature of the book might be; and as the name of the writer, J S Mill, might, for anything he knew to the contrary, have belonged to a venerable member of the British and Foreign Bible Society, it by no means threw light upon the question. He was not in any way sure that Political Economy had nothing to do with the cheapest way of procuring clothing for the army and navy, which would be, certainly, both a political and economical subject.

But Bonaparte soon came to a conclusion as to the nature of the book and its contents, by the application of a simple rule now largely acted upon, but which, becoming universal, would save much thought and valuable time. It is of marvellous simplicity, of infinite utility, of universal applicability. It may easily be committed to memory, and runs thus:

Whenever you come into contact with any book, person, or opinion of which you absolutely comprehend nothing, declare that book, person, or opinion to be immoral. Bespatter it, vituperate against it, strongly insist that any man or woman harbouring it is a fool or a knave, or both. Carefully abstain from studying it. Do all that in you lies to annihilate that book, person, or opinion.

Acting on this rule, so wide in its comprehensiveness, so beautifully simple in its working, Bonaparte approached *Tant* Sannie with the book in his hand. Waldo came a step nearer, eyeing it like a dog whose young has fallen into evil hands.

'This book,' said Bonaparte, 'is not a fit and proper study for a young and immature mind.'

Tant Sannie did not understand a word, and said: 'What?'

'This book,' said Bonaparte, bringing down his finger with energy on the cover, 'this book is *sleg, sleg, Davel, Davel!*'

Tant Sannie perceived from the gravity of his countenance that it was no laughing matter. From the words *sleg* and *Davel* she understood that the book was evil, and had some connection with the prince who pulls the wires of evil over the whole earth.

'Where did you get this book?' she asked, turning her twinkling little eyes on Waldo. 'I wish that my legs may be as thin as an Englishman's if it isn't one of your father's. He had more sins than all the Kaffirs in Kaffirland, for all that he pretended to be so good all those years, and to live without a wife because he was thinking of the one that was dead! As though ten dead wives could make up for one fat one with arms and legs!' cried *Tant* Sannie, snorting.

'It was not my father's book,' said the boy savagely. 'I got it from your loft.'

'My loft! My book! How dare you?' cried *Tant* Sannie.

'It was Em's father's. She gave it to me,' he muttered more sullenly.

'Give it here. What is the name of it? What is it about?' she asked, putting her finger upon the title.

Bonaparte understood.

'Political Economy,' he said slowly.

'Dear Lord!' said *Tant* Sannie, 'cannot one hear from the very sound what an ungodly book it is! One can hardly say the name. Haven't we got curses enough on this farm?' cried *Tant* Sannie, eloquently: 'My best imported Merino ram dying of nobody knows what, and the short-horn cow casting her two calves, and the sheep eaten up with the scab and the drought? And is *this* a time to bring ungodly things about the place, to call down the vengeance of Almighty God to punish us more? Didn't the minister tell me when I was confirmed not to read any book except my Bible and hymnbook, that the Devil was in all the rest? And I never have read any other book,' said *Tant* Sannie with virtuous energy, 'and I never will!'

Waldo saw that the fate of his book was sealed, and turned sullenly on his heel.

'So you will not stay to hear what I say!' cried *Tant* Sannie. 'There, take your Polity-gollity-gominy, your devil's book!' she cried, flinging the book at his head with much energy.

It merely touched his forehead on one side and fell to the ground.

'Go on,' she cried; 'I know you are going to talk to yourself. People who talk to themselves always talk to the Devil. Go and tell him all about it. Go, go! Run!' cried *Tant* Sannie.

But the boy neither quickened nor slackened his pace, and passed sullenly round the back of the wagon-house.

Books have been thrown at other heads before and since that summer afternoon, by hands more white and delicate than those of the Boer woman; but whether the result of the process has been in any case wholly satisfactory, may be questioned. We love that with a peculiar tenderness, we treasure it with a peculiar care, it has for us quite a fictitious value, for which we have suffered. If we may not carry it anywhere else we will carry it in our hearts, and always to the end.

Bonaparte Blenkins went to pick up the volume, now loosened from its cover, while *Tant* Sannie pushed the stumps of wood farther into the oven. Bonaparte came close to her, tapped the book knowingly, nodded, and looked at the fire. *Tant* Sannie comprehended, and, taking the volume from his hand, threw it into the back of the oven. It lay upon the heap of coals, smoked, flared, and blazed, and the

Political Economy was no more – gone out of existence, like many another poor heretic of flesh and blood.

Bonaparte grinned, and to watch the process brought his face so near the oven door that the white hair on his eyebrows got singed. He then inquired if there were any more books in the loft.

Learning that there were, he made signs indicative of taking up armfuls and flinging them into the fire. But *Tant* Sannie was dubious. The deceased Englishman had left all his personal effects specially to his child. It was all very well for Bonaparte to talk of burning the books. He had had his hair spiritually pulled, and she had no wish to repeat his experience.

She shook her head. Bonaparte was displeased. But then a happy thought occurred to him. He suggested that the key of the loft should henceforth be put in his own safe care and keeping – no one gaining possession of it without his permission. To this *Tant* Sannie readily assented, and the two walked lovingly to the house to look for it.

CHAPTER TWELVE

He Bites

Bonaparte Blenkins was riding home on the grey mare. He had ridden out that afternoon, partly for the benefit of his health, partly to maintain his character as overseer of the farm. As he rode on slowly, he thoughtfully touched the ears of the grey mare with his whip.

'No, Bon, my boy,' he addressed himself, 'don't propose! You can't marry for four years, on account of the will; then why propose? Wheedle her, tweedle her, teedle her, but *don't* let her make sure of you. When a woman,' said Bonaparte, sagely resting his finger against the side of his nose, 'when a woman is sure of you she does what she likes with you; but when she isn't, you do what you like with her. And I ...' said Bonaparte.

Here he drew the horse up suddenly and looked. He was now close to the house, and leaning over the pigsty wall, in company with Em, who was showing her the pigs, was a strange female figure. It was the first visitor that had appeared on the farm since his arrival, and he looked at her with interest. She was a tall, pudgy girl of fifteen, weighing a hundred and fifty pounds, with baggy, pendulous cheeks and upturned nose. She strikingly resembled *Tant* Sannie, in form and feature, but her sleepy good eyes lacked the twinkle that dwelt in the Boer woman's small orbs. She was attired in a bright green print, wore brass rings in her ears, and glass beads round her neck, and was sucking the tip of her large finger as she looked at the pigs.

'Who is it that has come?' asked Bonaparte, when he stood drinking his coffee in the front room.

'Why, my niece, to be sure,' said *Tant* Sannie, the Hottentot maid translating. 'She's the only daughter of my only brother Paul, and she's come to visit me. She'll be a nice mouthful to the man that can get her,' added *Tant* Sannie. 'Her father's got two thousand pounds in the green wagon box under his bed, and a farm, and five thousand sheep, and God Almighty knows how many goats and horses. They milk ten cows in mid-winter, and the young men are after her like flies about a bowl of milk. She says she means to get married in four months, but she doesn't yet know to whom. It was so with me when I was young,' said *Tant* Sannie: 'I've sat up with the young men four and five nights a week. And they will come riding, again, as soon as ever they know that the time's up that the Englishman made me agree not to marry in.'

The Boer woman smirked complacently. 'Where are you going to?' asked *Tant* Sannie presently, seeing that Bonaparte rose.

255

'Ha! I'm just going to the *kraals*; I'll be in to supper,' said Bonaparte. Nevertheless, when he reached his own door he stopped and turned in there.

Soon after he stood before the little glass, arrayed in his best white shirt with the little tucks, and shaving himself. He had on his very best trousers, and had heavily oiled the little fringe at the back of his head, which, however, refused to become darker. But what distressed him most was his nose – it was very red. He rubbed his finger and thumb on the wall, and put a little whitewash on it; but, finding it rather made matters worse, he rubbed it off again. Then he looked carefully into his own eyes. They certainly were a little pulled down at the outer corners, which gave them the appearance of looking crosswise; but then they were a nice blue. So he put on his best coat, took up his stick, and went out to supper, feeling on the whole well satisfied.

'Aunt,' said Trana to *Tant* Sannie, when that night they lay together in the great wooden bed, 'why does the Englishman sigh so when he looks at me?'

'Ha!' said *Tant* Sannie, who was half asleep, but suddenly started, wide awake. 'It's because he thinks you look like me. I tell you, Trana,' said *Tant* Sannie, 'the man is mad with love of me. I told him the other night I couldn't marry till Em was sixteen, or I'd lose all the sheep her father left me. And he talked about Jack working seven years and seven years again for his wife. And of course he meant me,' said *Tant* Sannie pompously. 'But he won't get me so easily as he thinks; he'll have to ask more than once.'

'Oh!' said Trana, who was a lumpish girl and not much given to talking; but presently she added, 'Aunt, why does the Englishman always knock against a person when he passes them?'

'That's because you are always in the way,' said *Tant* Sannie.

'But, Aunt,' said Trana presently, 'I think he is very ugly.'

'Phugh!' said *Tant* Sannie. 'It's only because we're not accustomed to such noses in this country. In his country he says all the people have such noses, and the redder your nose is the higher you are. He's of the family of the Queen Victoria, you know,' said *Tant* Sannie, wakening up with her subject: 'and he doesn't think anything of governors and church elders, and such people; they are nothing to him. When his aunt with the dropsy dies he'll have money enough to buy all the farms in this district!'

'Oh!' said Trana. That certainly made a difference.

'Yes,' said *Tant* Sannie; 'and he's only forty-one, though you'd take him to be sixty. And he told me last night the real reason of his baldness.'

Tant Sannie then proceeded to relate how, at eighteen years of age, Bonaparte had courted a fair young lady. How a deadly rival, jealous of his verdant locks, his golden flowing hair, had, with a damnable and insinuating deception, made him a present of a pot of pomatum. How, applying it in the evening, on rising in the morning he found his pillow strewn with the golden locks, and looking into the glass, beheld the shining and smooth expanse which henceforth he must bear. The few remaining hairs were turned to a silvery whiteness and the young lady married his rival.

'And,' said *Tant* Sannie solemnly, 'if it had not been for the grace of God, and reading of the psalms, he says he would have killed himself. He says he could kill himself quite easily, if he wants to marry a woman and she won't.'

'*Alle wêreld*,' said Trana: and then they went to sleep.

Everyone was lost in sleep soon; but from the window of the cabin the light streamed forth. It came from a dung fire, over which Waldo sat brooding. Hour after hour he sat there, now and again throwing a fresh lump of fuel onto the fire, which burnt up bravely, and then sank into a great bed of red coals, which reflected themselves in the boy's eyes as he sat there brooding, brooding, brooding. At last, when the fire was blazing at its brightest, he rose suddenly and walked slowly to a beam from which an ox *riem* hung. Loosening it, he ran a noose in one end and then doubled it round his arm.

'Mine, mine! I have a right,' he muttered; and then something louder, 'if I fall and am killed, so much the better!'

He opened the door and went out into the starlight.

He walked with his eyes bent upon the ground, but overhead it was one of those brilliant southern nights when every space so small that your hand might cover it shows fifty cold white points, and the Milky Way is a belt of sharp frosted silver. He passed the door where Bonaparte lay dreaming of Trana and her wealth, and he mounted the ladder steps. From those he clambered with some difficulty onto the roof of the house. It was of old rotten thatch with a ridge of white plaster, and it crumbled away under his feet at every step. He trod as heavily as he could. So much the better if he fell.

He knelt down when he got to the far gable, and began to fasten his *riem* to the crumbling bricks. Below was the little window of the loft. With one end of the *riem* tied round the gable, the other end round his waist, how easy to slide down to it, and to open it, through one of the broken panes, and to go in, and to fill his arms with books, and to clamber up again! They had burnt one book – he would have twenty. Every man's hand was against his – his should be against every man's. No one would help him – he would help himself.

He lifted the black damp hair from his knit forehead, and looked round to cool his hot face. Then he saw what a regal night it was. He knelt silently and looked up. A thousand eyes were looking down at him, bright, and so cold. There was a laughing irony in them.

'So hot, so bitter, so angry? Poor little mortal!' He was ashamed. He folded his arms, and sat on the ridge of the roof looking up at them.

'*So* hot, *so* bitter, *so* angry?'

It was as though a cold hand had been laid upon his throbbing forehead, and slowly they began to fade and grow dim. *Tant* Sannie and the burnt book, Bonaparte and the broken machine, the box in the loft, he himself sitting there – how small they all became! Even the grave over yonder. Those stars that shone on up above so quietly, they had seen a thousand such little existences, a thousand such little existences fight just as fiercely, flare up just so brightly, and go out; and they, the old, old stars shone on forever.

'So hot, so angry, poor little soul?' they said.

The *riem* slipped from his fingers; he sat with his arms folded, looking up.

'We,' said the stars, 'have seen the earth when it was young. We have seen small things creep out upon its surface – small things that prayed and loved and cried very loudly, and then crept under it again. But we,' said the stars, 'are as old as the Unknown.'

He leaned his chin against the palm of his hand and looked up at them. So long he sat there that bright stars set and new ones rose, and yet he sat on.

Then at last he stood up, and began to loosen the *riem* from the gable.

What did it matter about the books? The lust and the desire for them had died out. If they pleased to keep them from him they might. What matter? It was a very little thing. Why hate, and struggle, and fight? Let it be as it would.

He twisted the *riem* round his arm and walked back along the ridge of the house.

By this time Bonaparte Blenkins had finished his dream of Trana, and as he turned himself round for a fresh doze he heard the steps descending the ladder. His first impulse was to draw the blanket over his head and his legs under him, and to shout; but, recollecting that the door was locked and the window carefully bolted, he allowed his head slowly to crop out among the blankets, and listened intently. Whosoever it might be, there was no danger of their getting at *him*; so he clambered out of bed, and going on tiptoe to the door, applied his eye to the keyhole. There was nothing to be seen; so walking to the window, he brought his face as close to the glass as his nose would allow. There was a figure just discernible. The lad was not trying to walk softly, and the heavy shuffling of the well-known *velskoens* could be clearly heard through the closed window as they crossed the stones in the yard. Bonaparte listened till they had died away round the corner of the wagon-house; and, feeling that his bare legs were getting cold, he jumped back into bed again.

'What do you keep up in your loft?' inquired Bonaparte of the Boer woman the next evening, pointing upwards, and elucidating his meaning by the addition of such Dutch words as he knew, for the lean Hottentot was gone home.

'Dried skins,' said the Boer woman, 'and empty bottles, and boxes, and sacks, and soap.'

'You don't keep any of your provisions there – sugar, now?' said Bonaparte, pointing to the sugar basin and then up at the loft.

Tant Sannie shook her head. 'Only salt, and dried peaches.'

'Dried peaches! Eh?' said Bonaparte. 'Shut the door, my dear child, shut it tight,' he called out to Em, who stood in the dining room. Then he leaned over the elbow of the sofa and brought his face as close as possible to the Boer woman's, and made signs of eating. Then he said something she did not comprehend; then said, 'Waldo, Waldo, Waldo,' pointed up to the loft, and made signs of eating again.

Now an inkling of his meaning dawned on the Boer woman's mind. To make it clearer, he moved his legs after the manner of one going up a ladder, appeared to be opening a door, masticated vigorously, said, 'Peaches, peaches, peaches,' and appeared to be coming down the ladder.

It was now evident to *Tant* Sannie that Waldo had been in her loft and eaten her peaches.

To exemplify his own share in the proceedings, Bonaparte lay down on the sofa, and shutting his eyes tightly, said, 'Night, night, night!' Then he sat up wildly, appearing to be intently listening, mimicked with his feet the coming down a ladder, and looked at *Tant* Sannie. This clearly showed how, roused in the night, he had discovered the theft.

'He must have been a great fool to eat my peaches,' said *Tant* Sannie. 'They are full of mites as a sheepskin, and as hard as stones.'

Bonaparte, fumbling in his pocket, did not even hear her remark, and took out from his coat-tail a little horsewhip, nicely rolled up. Bonaparte winked at the little rhinoceros horsewhip, at the Boer woman, and then at the door.

'Shall we call him – Waldo, Waldo?' he said.

Tant Sannie nodded, and giggled. There was something so exceedingly humorous in the idea that he was going to beat the boy, though for her own part she did not see that the peaches were worth it. When the Kaffir maid came with the washtub she was sent to summon Waldo; and Bonaparte doubled up the little whip and put it in his pocket. Then he drew himself up, and prepared to act his important part with becoming gravity. Soon Waldo stood in the door, and took off his hat.

'Come in, come in, my lad,' said Bonaparte, 'and shut the door behind.'

The boy came in and stood before them.

'You need not be so afraid, child,' said *Tant* Sannie. 'I was a child myself once. It's no great harm if you have taken a few.'

Bonaparte perceived that her remark was not in keeping with the nature of the proceedings, and of the little drama he intended to act. Pursing out his lips, and waving his hand, he solemnly addressed the boy.

'Waldo, it grieves me beyond expression to have to summon you for so painful a purpose; but it is at the imperative call of duty, which I dare not evade. I do not state that frank and unreserved confession will obviate the necessity of chastisement, which if requisite shall be fully administered; but the nature of that chastisement may be mitigated by free and humble confession. Waldo, answer me as you would your own father, in whose place I now stand to you: have you, or have you not, did you, or did you not, eat of the peaches in the loft?'

'Say you took them, boy, say you took them, then he won't beat you much,' said the Dutch woman good-naturedly, getting a little sorry for him.

The boy raised his eyes slowly and fixed them vacantly upon her, then suddenly his face grew dark with blood.

'*So*, you haven't got anything to say to us, my lad?' said Bonaparte, momentarily forgetting his dignity, and bending forward with a little snarl. 'But what I mean is just this, my lad – when it takes a boy three-quarters of an hour to fill a salt-pot, and when at three o'clock in the morning he goes knocking about the doors of a loft, it's natural to suppose there's mischief in it. It's certain there *is* mischief in it; and where there's mischief *in* it must be taken *out*,' said Bonaparte, grinning into the boy's face. Then, feeling that he had fallen from that high gravity which was as spice to the pudding, and the flavour of the whole little tragedy, he drew himself up. 'Waldo,' he said, 'confess to me instantly, and without reserve, that you ate the peaches.'

The boy's face was white now. His eyes were on the ground, his hands doggedly clasped before him.

'What, you do not intend to answer?' The boy looked up at them once from under his bent eyebrows, and then looked down again.

'The creature looks as if all the devils in hell were in it,' cried *Tant* Sannie. 'Say you took them, boy. Young things will be young things; I was older than you when I used to eat *biltong* in my mother's loft, and get the little niggers whipped for it. Say you took them.'

But the boy said nothing. 'I think a little solitary confinement might perhaps be beneficial,' said Bonaparte. 'It will enable you, Waldo, to reflect on the enormity of the sin you have committed against our Father in heaven. And you may also think of the submission you owe to those who are older and wiser than you are, and whose duty it is to check and correct you.'

Saying this, Bonaparte stood up and took down the key of the fuel-house, which hung on a nail against the wall.

'Walk on, my boy,' said Bonaparte, pointing to the door; and as he followed him out he drew his mouth expressively on one side, and made the lash of the little horsewhip stick out of his pocket and shake up and down.

Tant Sannie felt half sorry for the lad; but she could not help laughing, it was always so funny when one was going to have a whipping, and it would do him good. Anyhow he would forget all about it when the places were healed. Had not she been beaten many times and been all the better for it?

Bonaparte took up a lighted candle that had been left burning on the kitchen table, and told the boy to walk before him. They went to the fuel-house. It was a little stone erection that jutted out from the side of the wagon-house. It was low, and without a window; and the dried dung was piled in one corner, and the coffee mill stood in another, fastened on the top of a short post about three feet high. Bonaparte took the padlock off the rough door.

'Walk in, my lad,' he said.

Waldo obeyed sullenly; one place to him was much the same as another. He had no objection to being locked up.

Bonaparte followed him in, and closed the door carefully.

He put the light down on the heap of dung in the corner, and quietly introduced his hand under his coat-tails and drew slowly from his pocket the end of a rope which he concealed behind him.

'I'm very sorry, exceedingly sorry, Waldo, my lad, that you should have acted in this manner. It grieves me,' said Bonaparte.

He moved round towards the boy's back. He hardly liked the look in the fellow's eyes, though he stood there motionless. If he should spring on him!

So he drew the rope out very carefully, and shifted round to the wooden post. There was a slipknot in one end of the rope, and a sudden movement drew the boy's hands to his back and passed it round them. It was an instant's work to drag it twice round the wooden post: then Bonaparte was safe.

For a moment the boy struggled to free himself; then he knew that he was powerless, and stood still.

'Horses that kick must have their legs tied,' said Bonaparte, as he passed the other end of the rope round the boy's knees. 'And now, my dear Waldo,' taking the whip out of his pocket, 'I am going to beat you.'

He paused for a moment. It was perfectly quiet; they could hear each other's breath.

'"Chasten thy son while there is hope",' said Bonaparte, '"and let not thy soul spare for his crying." Those are God's words. I shall act as a father to you, Waldo. I think we had better have your naked back.'

He took out his penknife, and slit the shirt down from the shoulder to the waist.

'Now,' said Bonaparte, 'I hope the Lord will bless and sanctify to you what I am going to do to you.'

The first cut ran from the shoulder across the middle of the back; the second fell exactly in the same place. A shudder passed through the boy's frame.

'Nice, eh?' said Bonaparte, peeping round into his face, speaking with a lisp, as though to a very little child. '*Nith, eh?*'

But the eyes were black and lustreless, and seemed not to see him. When he had given sixteen Bonaparte paused in his work to wipe a little drop of blood from his whip.

'Cold, eh? What makes you shiver so? Perhaps you would like to pull up your shirt? But I've not quite done yet.'

When he had finished he wiped the whip again, and put it back in his pocket. He cut the rope through with his penknife, and then took up the light.

'You don't seem to have found your tongue yet. Forgotten how to cry?' said Bonaparte, patting him on the cheek.

The boy looked up at him – not sullenly, not angrily. There was a wild, fitful terror in the eyes. Bonaparte made haste to go out and shut the door, and leave him alone in the darkness. He himself was afraid of that look.

It was almost morning. Waldo lay with his face upon the ground at the foot of the fuel-heap. There was a round hole near the top of the door, where a knot of wood had fallen out, and a stream of grey light came in through it.

Ah, it was going to end at last! Nothing lasts forever, not even the night. How was it he had never thought of that before? For in all that long, dark night he had been very strong, had never been tired, never felt pain, had run on and on, up and down, up and down; he had not dared to stand still, and he had not known it would end. He had been so strong, that when he struck his head with all his force upon the stone wall it did not stun him nor pain him – only made him laugh. That was a dreadful night. When he clasped his hands frantically and prayed: 'O God, my beautiful God, my sweet God, once, only once, let me feel you near me tonight!' he could not feel Him. He prayed aloud, very loud, and he got no answer; when he listened it was all quite quiet – like when the priests of Baal cried aloud to their God – 'Oh, Baal, hear us! Oh, Baal, hear us!' but Baal was gone a-hunting.

That was a long wild night, and wild thoughts came and went in it; but they left their marks behind them forever: for, as years cannot pass without leaving their traces behind them, neither can nights into which are forced the thoughts and sufferings of years. And now the dawn was coming, and at last he was very tired. He shivered, and tried to draw the shirt up over his shoulders. They were getting stiff. He had never known they were cut in the night. He looked up at the white light that came in through the hole at the top of the door and shuddered. Then he turned his face back to the ground and slept again.

Some hours later Bonaparte came towards the fuel-house with a lump of bread in his hand. He opened the door and peered in; then entered, and touched the fellow with his boot. Seeing that he breathed heavily, though he did not rouse, Bonaparte threw the bread down on the ground. He was alive, that was one thing. He bent over him, and carefully scratched open one of the cuts with the nail of his forefinger, examining with much interest his last night's work. He would have to count his sheep himself that day; the boy was literally cut up. He locked the door and went away again.

'Oh, Lyndall,' said Em, entering the dining room and bathed in tears, that afternoon, 'I have been begging Bonaparte to let him out, and he wont.'

'The more you beg the more he will not,' said Lyndall.

She was cutting out aprons on the table.

'Oh, but it's late, and I think they want to kill him,' said Em, weeping bitterly; and finding that no more consolation was to be gained from her cousin, she went off blubbering – 'I wonder you can cut out aprons when Waldo is shut up like that.'

For ten minutes after she was gone Lyndall worked on quietly; then she folded up her stuff, rolled it tightly together, and stood before the closed door of the sitting room with her hands closely clasped. A flush rose to her face; she opened the door quickly, and walked in, went to the nail on which the key of the fuel-room hung. Bonaparte and *Tant* Sannie sat there and saw her.

'What do you want?' they asked together.

'This key,' she said, holding it up, and looking at them.

'Do you mean her to have it?' said *Tant* Sannie in Dutch.

'Why don't you stop her?' asked Bonaparte in English.

'Why don't you take it from her?' said *Tant* Sannie.

So they looked at each other, talking, while Lyndall walked to the fuel-house with the key, her under-lip bitten in.

'Waldo,' she said, as she helped him to stand up, and twisted his arm about her waist to support him, 'we will not be children always; we shall have the power too, someday.' She kissed his naked shoulders with her soft little mouth. It was all the comfort her young soul could give him.

CHAPTER THIRTEEN

He Makes Love

'Here,' said *Tant* Sannie to her Hottentot maid, 'I have been in this house four years, and never been up in the loft. Fatter women than I go up ladders; I will go up today and see what it is like, and put it to rights up there. You bring the little ladder, and stand at the bottom.'

'There's one would be sorry if you were to fall,' said the Hottentot maid, leering at Bonaparte's pipe, that lay on the table.

'Hold your tongue, jade,' said her mistress, trying to conceal a pleased smile, 'and go and fetch the ladder.'

There was a never-used trapdoor at one end of the sitting room; this the Hottentot maid pushed open, and setting the ladder against it, the Boer woman with some danger and difficulty climbed into the loft. Then the Hottentot maid took the ladder away, as her husband was mending the wagon-house, and needed it; but the trapdoor was left open.

For a little while *Tant* Sannie poked about among the empty bottles and skins, and looked at the bag of peaches that Waldo was supposed to have liked so; then she sat down near the trapdoor beside a barrel of salt mutton. She found that the pieces of meat were much too large, and took out her clasp knife to divide them.

That was always the way when one left things to servants, she grumbled to herself; but when once she was married to her husband Bonaparte it would not matter whether a sheep spoiled or no – when once his rich aunt with the dropsy was dead. She smiled as she dived her hand into the pickle-water.

At that instant her niece entered the room below, closely followed by Bonaparte, with his head on one side, smiling mawkishly. Had *Tant* Sannie spoken at that moment the life of Bonaparte Blenkins would have run a wholly different course; as it was, she remained silent, and neither noticed the open trapdoor above their heads.

'Sit there, my love,' said Bonaparte, motioning Trana into her aunt's elbow-chair, and drawing another close up in front of it, in which he seated himself. 'There, put your feet upon the stove too. Your aunt has gone out somewhere. Long have I waited for this auspicious event!'

Trana, who understood not one word of English, sat down in the chair and wondered if this was one of the strange customs of other lands, that an old gentleman may bring his chair up to yours, and sit with his knees touching you. She had been five days in Bonaparte's company, and feared the old man, and disliked his nose.

'How long have I desired this moment!' said Bonaparte. 'But that aged relative of thine is always casting her unhallowed shadow upon us. Look into my eyes, Trana.'

Bonaparte knew that she comprehended not a syllable; but he understood that it is the eye, the tone, the action, and not at all the rational word, that touches the love-chords. He saw she changed colour.

'All night,' said Bonaparte, 'I lie awake; I see naught but thy angelic countenance. I open my arms to receive thee – where art thou, where? Thou art not there!' said Bonaparte, suiting the action to the words, and spreading out his arms and drawing them to his breast.

'Oh, please, I don't understand,' said Trana, 'I want to go away.'

'Yes, yes,' said Bonaparte, leaning back in his chair, to her great relief, and pressing her hands on his heart, 'since first thy amethystine countenance was impressed *here* – what have I not suffered, what have I not felt? Oh, the pangs unspoken, burning as an ardent coal in a fiery and uncontaminated bosom!' said Bonaparte, bending forward again.

'Dear Lord!' said Trana to herself, 'how foolish I have been! The old man has a pain in his stomach, and now, as my aunt is out, he has come to me to help him.'

She smiled kindly at Bonaparte, and pushing past him, went to the bedroom, quickly returning with a bottle of red drops in her hand.

'They are very good for *benaauwdheit*; my mother always drinks them,' she said, holding the bottle out.

The face in the trapdoor was a fiery red. Like a tiger-cat ready to spring, Tant Sannie crouched, with the shoulder of mutton in her hand. Exactly beneath her stood Bonaparte. She rose and clasped with both arms the barrel of salt meat.

'What, rose of the desert, nightingale of the Colony, that with thine amorous lay whilest the lonesome night!' cried Bonaparte, seizing the hand that held the *vonlicsense*. 'Nay, struggle not! Fly as a stricken fawn into the arms that would embrace thee, then –'

Here a stream of cold pickle-water, heavy with ribs and shoulders, descending on his head abruptly terminated his speech. Half-blinded, Bonaparte looked up through the drops that hung from his eyelids, and saw the red face that looked down at him. With one wild cry he fled. As he passed out at the front door a shoulder of mutton, well directed, struck the black coat in the small of the back.

'Bring the ladder! Bring the ladder! I will go after him!' cried the Boer woman, as Bonaparte Blenkins wildly fled into the fields.

Late in the evening of the same day Waldo knelt on the floor of his cabin. He bathed the foot of his dog which had been pierced by a thorn. The bruises on his own back had had five days to heal in, and, except a little stiffness in his movements, there was nothing remarkable about the boy.

The troubles of the young are soon over; they leave no external mark. If you wound the tree in its youth the bark will quickly cover the gash; but when the tree is very old, peeling the bark off, and looking carefully, you will see the scar there still. All that is buried is not dead.

Waldo poured the warm milk over the little swollen foot; Doss lay very quiet, with tears in his eyes. Then there was a tap at the door. In an instant Doss looked wide awake, and winked the tears out from between his little lids.

'Come in,' said Waldo, intent on his work; and slowly and cautiously the door opened.

'Good evening, Waldo, my boy,' said Bonaparte Blenkins in a mild voice, not venturing more than his nose within the door. 'How are you this evening?'

Doss growled and showed his little teeth, and tried to rise, but his paw hurt him, so he whined.

'I'm very tired, Waldo, my boy,' said Bonaparte plaintively.

Doss showed his little white teeth again. His master went on with his work without looking round. There are some people at whose hands it is best not to look. At last he said:

'Come in.'

Bonaparte stepped cautiously a little way into the room, and left the door open behind him. He looked at the boy's supper on the table.

'Waldo, I've had nothing to eat all day – I'm very hungry,' he said.

'Eat!' said Waldo after a moment, bending lower over his dog.

'You won't go and tell her that I am here, will you, Waldo?' said Bonaparte most uneasily. 'You've heard how she used me, Waldo? I've been *badly* treated; you'll know yourself what it is some day when you can't carry on a little conversation with a lady without having salt-meat and pickle-water thrown at you. Waldo, look at me; do I look as a gentleman should?'

But the boy neither looked up nor answered, and Bonaparte grew more uneasy.

'You wouldn't go and tell her that I am here, would you?' said Bonaparte whiningly. 'There's no knowing what she would do to me. I've such a trust in you, Waldo; I've always thought you such a promising lad, though you mayn't have known it, Waldo.'

'Eat,' said the boy, 'I shall say nothing.'

Bonaparte, who knew the truth when another spoke it, closed the door, carefully putting on the button. Then he looked to see that the curtain of the window was closely pulled down, and seated himself at the table. He was soon munching the cold meat and bread. Waldo knelt on the floor, bathing the foot with hands which the dog licked lovingly. Once only he glanced at the table, and turned away quickly.

'Ah, yes! I don't wonder that you can't look at me, Waldo,' said Bonaparte: 'my condition would touch any heart. You see, the water was fatty, and that has made all the sand stick to me; and my hair,' said Bonaparte, tenderly touching the little fringe at the back of his head, 'is all caked over like a little plank: you wouldn't think it was hair at all,' said Bonaparte, plaintively. 'I had to creep all along the stone walls for fear she'd see me, and with nothing on my head but a red handkerchief tied under my chin, Waldo; and to hide in a *sloot* the whole day, with not a mouthful of food, Waldo. And she gave me such a blow, just here,' said Bonaparte.

He had cleared the plate of the last morsel, when Waldo rose and walked to the door.

'Oh, Waldo, my dear boy, you are not going to call her,' said Bonaparte, rising anxiously.

'I am going to sleep in the wagon,' said the boy, opening the door.

'Oh, we can both sleep in this bed: there's plenty of room. Do stay, my boy, please.'

But Waldo stepped out.

'It was such a little whip, Waldo,' said Bonaparte, following him deprecatingly. 'I didn't think it would hurt you so much. It was such a *little* whip. I'm *sure* you didn't take the peaches. You aren't going to call her, Waldo, are you?'

But the boy walked off.

Bonaparte waited till his figure had passed round the front of the wagon-house, and then slipped out. He hid himself round the corner, but kept peeping out to see who was coming. He felt sure the boy was gone to call *Tant* Sannie. His teeth chattered with inward cold as he looked round into the darkness, and thought of the snakes that might bite him, and the dreadful things that might attack him, and the dead that might arise out of their graves if he slept out in the field all night. But more than an hour passed, and no footstep approached.

Then Bonaparte made his way back to the cabin. He buttoned the door and put the table against it, and, giving the dog a kick to silence his whining when the foot throbbed, he climbed into bed. He did not put out the light for fear of the ghost, but, worn out with the sorrows of the day, was soon asleep himself. About four o'clock Waldo, lying between the seats of the horse-wagon, was awakened by a gentle touch on his head.

Sitting up, he espied Bonaparte looking through one of the windows with a lighted candle in his hand.

'I'm about to depart, my dear boy, before my enemies arise; and I could not leave without coming to bid you farewell,' said Bonaparte.

Waldo looked at him.

'I shall always think of you with affection,' said Bonaparte. 'And there's that old hat of yours, if you could let me have it for a keepsake –'

'Take it,' said Waldo.

'I thought you would say so, so I brought it with me,' said Bonaparte, putting it on. 'The Lord bless you, my dear boy. You haven't a few shillings – just a trifle you don't need, have you?'

'Take the two shillings that are in the broken vase.'

'May the blessing of my God rest upon you, my dear child,' said Bonaparte; 'may He guide and bless you. Give me your hand.'

Waldo folded his arms closely, and lay down.

'Farewell, adieu!' said Bonaparte. 'May the blessing of my God and my father's God rest on you, now and evermore.'

With these words the head and nose withdrew themselves, and the light vanished from the window.

After a few moments the boy, lying in the wagon, heard stealthy footsteps as they passed the wagon-house and made their way down the road. He listened as they grew fainter and fainter, and at last died away altogether, and from that night the footstep of Bonaparte Blenkins was heard no more at the old farm.

PART TWO

And it was all play, and no one could tell what it had lived and worked for. A striving, and a striving, and an ending in nothing

CHAPTER ONE

Times and Seasons

Waldo lay on his stomach on the sand. Since he prayed and howled to his God in the fuel-house three years had passed.

They say that in the world to come time is not measured out by months and years. Neither is it here. The soul's life has seasons of its own; periods not found in any calendar, times that years and months will not scan, but which are as deftly and sharply cut off from one another as the smoothly arranged years which the earth's motion yields us.

To stranger eyes these divisions are not evident; but each, looking back at the little track his consciousness illuminates, sees it cut into distinct portions, whose boundaries are the termination of mental states.

As man differs from man, so differ these souls' years. The most material life is not devoid of them; the story of the most spiritual is told in them. And it may chance that some, looking back, see the past cut out after this fashion:

1

The year of infancy, where from the shadowy background of forgetfulness start out pictures of startling clearness, disconnected, but brightly coloured, and indelibly printed in the mind. Much that follows fades, but the colours of those baby-pictures are permanent.

There rises, perhaps, a warm summer's evening; we are seated on the doorstep; we have yet the taste of the bread and milk in our mouth, and the red sunset is reflected in our basin.

Then there is a dark night, where, waking with a fear that there is some great being in the room, we run from our own bed to another, creep close to some large figure, and are comforted.

Then there is remembrance of the pride when, on someone's shoulder, with our arms around their head, we ride to see the little pigs, the new little pigs with their curled tails and tiny snouts – where do they come from?

Remembrance of delight in the feel and smell of the first orange we ever see; of sorrow which makes us put up our lip, and cry hard, when one morning we run out to try and catch the dewdrops, and they melt and wet our little fingers; of almighty and despairing sorrow when we are lost behind the *kraals*, and cannot see the house anywhere.

And then one picture starts out more vividly than any.

There has been a thunderstorm; the ground, as far as the eye can reach, is covered with white hail; the clouds are gone, and overhead a deep blue sky is showing; far off a great rainbow rests on the white earth. We, standing in a window to look, feel the cool, unspeakably sweet wind blowing in on us, and a feeling of longing comes over us – unutterable longing, we cannot tell for what. We are so small, our head only reaches as high as the first three panes. We look at the white earth, and the rainbow, and the blue sky; and oh, we want it, we want – we do not know what. We cry as though our heart was broken. When one lifts our little body from the window we cannot tell what ails us. We run away to play.

So looks the first year.

2

Now the pictures become continuous and connected. Material things still rule, but the spiritual and intellectual take their places.

In the dark night, when we are afraid, we pray and shut our eyes. We press our fingers very hard upon the lids, and see dark spots moving round and round, and we know they are heads and wings of angels sent to take care of us, seen dimly in the dark as they move round our bed. It is very consoling.

In the day we learn our letters, and are troubled because we cannot see why k-n-o-w should be know, and p-s-a-l-m psalm. They tell us it is so because it *is* so. We are not satisfied; we hate to learn; we like better to build little stone houses. We can build them as we please, and know the reason for them.

Other joys too we have, incomparably greater than even the building of stone houses.

We are run through with a shudder of delight when in the red sand we come on one of those white wax flowers that lie between their two green leaves flat on the sand. We hardly dare pick them, but we feel compelled to do so; and we smell and smell till the delight becomes almost pain. Afterwards we pull the green leaves softly into pieces to see the silk threads run across.

Beyond the *kopje* grow some pale-green, hairy-leaved bushes. We are so small, they meet over our head; and we sit among them, and kiss them, and they love us back: it seems as though they were alive.

One day we sit there and look up at the blue sky, and down at our fat little knees; and suddenly it strikes us, Who are we? This *I*, what is it? We try to look in upon ourself, and ourself beats back upon ourself. Then we get up in great fear and run home as hard as we can. We can't tell anyone what frightened us. We never quite lose that feeling of *self* again.

3

And then a new time rises. We are seven years old. We can read now – read the Bible. Best of all we like the story of Elijah in his cave at Horeb, and the still, small voice.

One day, a notable one, we read on the *kopje*, and discover the fifth chapter of Matthew, and read it all through. It is a new goldmine. Then we tuck the Bible under our arm and rush home. They didn't know it was wicked to take your things again if someone took them, wicked to go to law, wicked to – ! We are quite breathless when we get to the house; we tell them we have discovered a chapter they never heard of; we tell them what it says. The old wise people tell us they knew all about it. Our discovery is a mare's-nest to them; but to us it is very real. The Ten Commandments and the old 'Thou shalt' we have heard about long enough, and don't care about it; but this new law sets us on fire. We will deny ourself. Our little wagon that we have made; we give to the little Kaffirs. We keep quiet when they throw sand at us (feeling, oh, so happy). We conscientiously put the cracked teacup for ourselves at breakfast, and take the burnt roaster-cake. We save our money, and buy threepence worth of tobacco for the Hottentot maid who calls us names. We are exotically virtuous. At night we are profoundly religious; even the ticking watch says, 'Eternity, eternity! hell, hell, hell!' and the silence talks of God, and the things that shall be.

Occasionally, also, unpleasantly shrewd questions begin to be asked by someone, we know not who, who sits somewhere behind our shoulder. We get to know him better afterwards. Now we carry the questions to the grown-up people, and they give us answers. We are more or less satisfied for the time. The grown-up people are very wise, and they say it was kind of God to make hell, and very loving of Him to send men there; and besides, He couldn't help Himself; and they are very wise, we think, so we believe them – more or less.

4

Then a new time comes, of which the leading feature is, that the shrewd questions are asked louder. We carry them to the grown-up people; they answer us, and we are *not* satisfied.

And now between us and the dear old world of the senses the spirit-world begins to peep in, and wholly clouds it over. What are the flowers to us? They are fuel waiting for the great burning. We look at the walls of the farmhouse and the matter-of-fact sheep-*kraals*, with the merry sunshine playing over all; and do not see it. But we see a great white throne, and Him that sits on it. Around Him stand a great multitude that no man can number, harpers harping with their harps, a thousand times ten thousand, and thousands of thousands. How white are their robes, washed in the blood of the Lamb! And the music rises higher, and rends the vault of heaven with its unutterable sweetness. And we, as we listen, ever and anon, as it sinks on the sweetest, lowest note, hear a groan of the damned from below. We shudder in the sunlight.

'The torment,' says Jeremy Taylor, whose sermons our father reads aloud in the evening, 'comprises as many torments as the body of man has joints, sinews, arteries, etc, being caused by that penetrating and real fire of which this temporal fire is but a painted fire. What comparison will there be between burning for a hundred years' space and to be burning without intermission as long as God is God!'

We remember the sermon there in the sunlight. One comes and asks why we sit there nodding so moodily. Ah, they do not see what we see.

'A moment's time, a narrow space,
Divides me from that heavenly place,
Or shuts me up in hell.'

So says Wesley's hymn, which we sing evening by evening. What matter sunshine and walls, men and sheep?

'The things which are seen are temporal, but the things which are not seen are eternal.' They are real.

The Bible we bear always in our breasts; its pages are our food; we learn to repeat it; we weep much, for in sunshine and in shade, in the early morning or the late evening, in the field or in the house, the Devil walks with us. He comes to us a real person, copper-coloured face, head a little on one side, forehead knit, asking questions. Believe me, it were better to be followed by three deadly diseases than by him. He is never silenced – without mercy. Though the drops of blood stand out on your heart he will put his questions. Softly he comes up (we are only a wee bit child); 'Is it good of God to make hell? Was it kind of Him to let no one be forgiven unless Jesus Christ died?'

Then he goes off, and leaves us writhing. Presently he comes back.

'Do you love Him?' – waits a little. 'Do you love Him? You will be lost if you don't.'

We say we try to.

'But do you?' Then he goes off.

It is nothing to him if we go quite mad with fear at our own wickedness. He asks on, the questioning Devil; he cares nothing what he says. We long to tell someone, that they may share our pain. We do not yet know that the cup of affliction is made with such a narrow mouth that only one lip can drink at a time, and that each man's cup is made to match his lip.

One day we try to tell someone. Then a grave head is shaken solemnly at us. We are wicked, very wicked, they say; we ought not to have such thoughts. God is good, very good. We are wicked, very wicked. That is the comfort we get. Wicked! Oh,

Lord! Do we not know it? Is it not the sense of our own exceeding wickedness that is drying up our young heart, filling it with sand, making all life a dustbin for us?

Wicked? We know it! Too vile to live, too vile to die, too vile to creep over this, God's earth, and move among His believing men. Hell is the one place for him who hates his master, and there we do not want to go. This is the comfort we get from the old.

And once again we try to seek for comfort. This time great eyes look at us wonderingly, and lovely little lips say, –

'If it makes you so unhappy to think of these things, why do you not think of something else, and forget?'

Forget! We turn away and shrink into ourself. Forget, and think of other things! Oh, God! Do they not understand that the material world is but a film, through every pore of which God's awful spirit-world is shining through on us? We keep as far from others as we can.

One night, a rare, clear moonlight night, we kneel in the window; everyone else is asleep, but we kneel reading by the moonlight. It is a chapter in the prophets, telling how the chosen people of God shall be carried on the Gentile's shoulders. Surely the Devil might leave us alone; there is not much handle for him there. But presently he comes.

'Is it right there should be a chosen people? To Him, who is Father to all, should not all be dear?'

How can we answer him? We were feeling so good till he came. We put our head down on the Bible and blister it with tears. Then we fold our hands over our head and pray, till our teeth grind together. Oh, that from that spirit-world, so real and yet so silent, that surrounds us, one word would come to guide us! We are left alone with this devil; and God does not whisper to us. Suddenly we seize the Bible, turning it round and round, and say hurriedly, –

'It will be God's voice speaking to us; His voice as though we heard it.'

We yearn for a token from the inexorably Silent One.

We turn the book, put our finger down on a page, and bend to read by the moonlight. It is God's answer. We tremble.

'Then fourteen years after I went up again to Jerusalem with Barnabas, and took Titus with me also.'

For an instant our imagination seizes it; we are twisting, twirling, trying to make an allegory. The fourteen years are fourteen months; we are Paul and the devil is Barnabas, Titus is – Then a sudden loathing comes to us: we are liars and hypocrites, we are trying to deceive ourselves. What is Paul to us – and Jerusalem? Who are Barnabas and Titus? We know not the men. Before we know we seize the book, swing it round our head, and fling it with all our might to the farther end of the room. We put down our head again and weep. Youth and ignorance; is there anything else that can weep so? It is as though the tears were drops of blood congealed beneath the eyelids; nothing else is like those tears. After a long time we are weak with crying, and lie silent, and by chance we knock against the wood that stops the broken pane. It falls. Upon our hot stiff face a sweet breath of wind blows. We raise our head, and with our swollen eyes look out at the beautiful still world, and the sweet night-wind blows in upon us, holy and gentle, like a loving breath from the lips of God. Over us a deep peace comes, a calm, still joy; the tears now flow readily and softly. Oh, the unutterable gladness! At last, at last we have found it! *'The peace with God.' 'The sense of sins forgiven.'* All doubt vanished, God's voice in the soul, the Holy Spirit filling us! We feel Him! We feel Him! Oh, Jesus Christ! Through you, through you this joy! We press our hands upon our breast and look upward with adoring gladness. Soft waves of bliss break through us. *'The peace with God.' 'The sense of sins forgiven.'* Methodists and Revivalists say the words, and the mocking world shoots out its lip, and walks by smiling – 'Hypocrites!'

There are more fools and fewer hypocrites than the wise world dreams of. The hypocrite is rare as icebergs in the tropics; the fool common as buttercups beside a water-furrow: whether you go this way or that you tread on him; you dare not look at your own reflection in the water but you see one. There is no cant phrase, rotten with age, but it was the dress of a living body; none but at heart it signifies a real bodily or mental condition which some have passed through.

After hours and nights of frenzied fear of the supernatural desire to appease the power above, a fierce quivering excitement in every inch of nerve and blood vessel, there comes a time when nature cannot endure longer, and the spring long bent recoils. We sink down emasculated. Up creeps the deadly delicious calm.

'I have blotted out as a cloud thy sins, and as a thick cloud thy trespasses, and will remember them no more forever.' We weep with soft transporting joy.

A few experience this; many imagine they experience it; one here and there lies about it. In the main, 'The peace with God; a sense of sins forgiven,' stands for a certain mental and physical reaction. Its reality those know who have felt it.

And we, on that moonlight night, put down our head on the window. 'Oh, God! we are happy, happy; thy child forever. Oh, thank you, God!' and we drop asleep.

Next morning the Bible we kiss. We are God's forever. We go out to work, and it goes happily all day, happily all night; but hardly so happily, not happily at all, the next day; and the next night the Devil asks us, 'Where is your Holy Spirit?'

We cannot tell.

So month by month, summer and winter, the old life goes on reading, praying, weeping, praying. They tell us we become utterly stupid. We know it. Even the multiplication table we learnt with so much care we forget. The physical world recedes further and further from us. Truly we love not the world, neither the things that are in it. Across the bounds of sleep our grief follows us. When we wake in the night we are sitting up in bed weeping bitterly, or find ourselves outside in the moonlight, dressed, and walking up and down, and wringing our hands, and we cannot tell how we came there. So pass two years, as men reckon them.

5

Then a new time.

Before us there were three courses possible – to go mad, to die, to sleep.

We take the latter course; or Nature takes it for us.

All things take rest in sleep; the beasts, birds, the very flowers close their eyes, and the streams are still in winter; all things take rest; then why not the human reason also? So the questioning Devil in us drops asleep; and in that sleep a beautiful dream rises for us. Though you hear all the dreams of men, you will hardly find a prettier one than ours. It ran so:

In the centre of all things is a Mighty Heart, which, having begotten all things, loves them; and, having born them into life, beats with great throbs of love towards them. No death for His dear insects, no hell for His dear men, no burning up for His dear world – His own, own world that He has made. In the end all will be beautiful. Do not ask us how we make our dream tally with facts; the glory of a dream is this – that it despises facts, and makes its own. Our dream saves us from going mad; that is enough.

Its peculiar point of sweetness lay here. When the Mighty Heart's yearning of love became too great for other expression, it shaped itself into the sweet Rose of heaven, the beloved Man-god!

Jesus! you Jesus of our dream! how we loved you; no Bible tells of you as we knew you. Your sweet hands held ours fast; your sweet voice said always, 'I am here, my loved one, not far off; put your arms about Me, and hold fast.'

We find Him in everything in those days. When the little weary lamb we drive home drags its feet, we seize on it, and carry it with its head against our face. His little lamb! We feel we have got Him.

When the drunken Kaffir lies by the road in the sun we draw his blanket over his head, and put green branches of milk-bush on it. His Kaffir; why should the sun hurt him?

In the evening, when the clouds lift themselves like gates, and the red lights shine through them, we cry; for in such glory He will come, and the hands that ache to touch Him will hold Him, and we shall see the beautiful hair and eyes of our God. 'Lift up your heads, O ye gates; and be ye lifted up, ye everlasting doors, and our King of glory shall come in!'

The purple flowers, the little purple flowers, are His eyes, looking at us. We kiss them, and kneel alone on the flat, rejoicing over them. And the wilderness and the solitary place shall be glad for Him, and the desert shall rejoice and blossom as a rose.

If ever in our tearful, joyful ecstasy the poor sleepy, half-dead Devil should raise his head, we laugh at him. It is not his hour now.

'If there should be a hell, after all!' he mutters. 'If your God should be cruel! If there should be no God! If you should find out it is all imagination! If – '

We laugh at him. When a man sits in the warm sunshine, do you ask him for proof of it? He feels – that is all. And we feel – that is all. We want no proof of our God. We feel, we feel!

We do not believe in our God because the Bible tells us of Him. We believe in the Bible because He tells us of it. We feel Him, we feel Him. We feel – that is all! And the poor half-swamped Devil mutters:

'But if the day should come when you do not feel?'

And we laugh, and cry him down.

'It will never come – never,' and the poor Devil slinks to sleep again, with his tail between his legs. Fierce assertion many times repeated is hard to stand against; only time separates the truth from the lie. So we dream on.

One day we go with our father to town, to church. The townspeople rustle in their silks, and the men in their sleek cloth, and settle themselves in their pews, and the light shines in through the windows on the artificial flowers in the women's bonnets. We have the same miserable feeling that we have in a shop where all the clerks are very smart. We wish our father hadn't brought us to town, and we were out on the Karoo. Then the man in the pulpit begins to preach. His text is 'He that believeth not shall be damned.'

The day before, the magistrate's clerk, who was an atheist, has died in the street, struck by lightning.

The man in the pulpit mentions no name; but he talks of 'The hand of God made visible among us.' He tells us how, when the white stroke fell, quivering and naked, the soul fled, robbed of his earthly filament, and lay at the footstool of God; how over its head has been poured out the wrath of the Mighty One, whose existence it has denied; and, quivering and terrified, it has fled to the everlasting shade.

We, as we listen, half start up; every drop of blood in our body has rushed to our head. He lies! He lies! He lies! That man in the pulpit lies! Will no one stop him? Have none of them heard – do none of them know, that when the poor dark soul shut its eyes on earth it opened them in the still light of heaven? That there is no wrath where God's face is? That if one could once creep to the footstool of God, there is everlasting peace there? Like the fresh stillness of the early morning. While the atheist lay wondering and afraid, God bent down and said, 'My child, *here* I am – I, whom you have not known; I, whom you have not believed in; I am here. I sent My messenger, the white sheet lightning, to call you home. I am here.'

Then the poor soul turned to the light, – its weakness and pain were gone forever.

Have they not known, have they not heard, who it is rules?

'For a little moment have I hidden my face from thee; but with everlasting kindness will I have mercy upon thee, saith the Lord thy Redeemer.'

We mutter on to ourselves, till someone pulls us violently by the arm to remind us we are in church. We see nothing but our own ideas.

Presently everyone turns to pray. There are six hundred souls lifting themselves to the Everlasting light.

Behind us sit two pretty ladies; one hands her scent-bottle softly to the other, and a mother pulls down her little girl's frock. One lady drops her handkerchief; a gentleman picks it up; she blushes. The women in the choir turn softly the leaves of their tune-books, to be ready when the praying is done. It is as though they thought more of the singing than the Everlasting Father. Oh, would it not be more worship of Him to sit alone in the Karoo and kiss one little purple flower that He had made? Is it not mockery? Then the thought comes, '*What doest thou here, Elijah?*' We who judge, what are we better than they? – rather worse. Is it any excuse to say, 'I am but a child, and must come?' Does God allow any soul to step in between the spirit He made and Himself? What do we there in that place, where all the words are lies against the All Father? Filled with horror, we turn and flee out of the place. On the pavement we smite our foot, and swear in our child's soul never again to enter those places where men come to sing and pray. We are questioned afterwards. Why was it we went out of the church?

How can we explain? – we stand silent. Then we are pressed further, and we try to tell. Then a head is shaken solemnly at us. No one *can* think it wrong to go to the house of the Lord; it is the idle excuse of a wicked boy. When will we think seriously of our souls, and love going to church? We are wicked, very wicked. And we – we slink away and go alone to cry. Will it be always so? Whether we hate and doubt, or whether we believe and love, to our dearest, are we to seem always wicked?

We do not yet know that in the soul's search for truth the bitterness lies here, the striving cannot always hide itself among the thoughts; sooner or later it will clothe itself in outward action; then it steps in and divides between the soul and what it loves. All things on earth have their price; and for truth we pay the dearest. We barter it for love and sympathy. The road to honour is paved with thorns; but on the path to truth, at every step you set your foot down on your own heart.

6

Then at last a new time – the time of waking: short, sharp, and not pleasant, as wakings often are.

Sleep and dreams exist on this condition – that no one wake the dreamer.

And now life takes us up between her finger and thumb, shakes us furiously, till our poor nodding head is well-nigh rolled from our shoulders, and she sets us down a little hardly on the bare earth, bruised and sore, but preternaturally wide awake.

We have said in our days of dreaming, 'Injustice and wrong are a seeming; pain is a shadow. Our God, He is real; He who made all things, and He only, is Love.'

Now life takes us by the neck and shows us a few other things, – new-made graves with the red sand flying about them; eyes that we love with the worms eating them; evil men walking sleek and fat, the whole terrible hurly-burly of the thing called life, – and she says, 'What do you think of these?' We dare not say, 'Nothing'. We feel them; they are very real. But we try to lay our hands about and feel that other thing we felt before. In the dark night in the fuel-room we cry to our Beautiful dream-god – 'Oh, let us come near you, and lay our head against your feet. Now in our hour of need be near us.' But He is not there; He is gone away. The old questioning Devil is there.

We must have been awakened sooner or later. The imagination cannot always triumph over reality, the desire over truth. We must have been awakened. If it was done a little sharply, what matter? It was done thoroughly, and it had to be done.

7

And a new life begins for us – a new time, a life as cold as that of a man who sits on the pinnacle of an iceberg and sees the glittering crystals all about him. The old looks indeed like a long hot delirium, peopled with fantasies. The new is cold enough.

Now we have no God. We have had two: the old God that our fathers handed down to us, that we hated, and never liked; the new one that we made for ourselves, that we loved; but now he has flitted away from us, and we see what he was made of – the shadow of our highest ideal, crowned and throned. Now we have no God.

'The fool hath said in his heart, There is no God.' It may be so. Most things said or written have been the work of fools.

This thing is certain – he is a fool who says, 'No man hath said in his heart, There is no God.'

It has been said many thousand times in hearts with profound bitterness of earnest faith.

We do not cry and weep; we sit down with cold eyes and look at the world. We are not miserable. Why should we be? We eat and drink, and sleep all night; but the dead are not colder.

And, we say it slowly, but without sighing, 'Yes, we see it now: there is no God.'

And, we add, growing a little colder yet, 'There is no justice. The ox dies in the yoke, beneath its master's whip; it turns its anguish-filled eyes on the sunlight, but there is no sign of recompense to be made it. The black man is shot like a dog, and it goes well with the shooter. The innocent are accused and the accuser triumphs. If you will take the trouble to scratch the surface anywhere, you will see under the skin a sentient being writhing in impotent anguish.'

And, we say further, and our heart is as the heart of the dead for coldness, 'There is no order: all things are driven about by a blind chance.'

What a soul drinks in with its mother's milk will not leave it in a day. From our earliest hour we have been taught that the thought of the heart, the shaping of the rain-cloud, the amount of wool that grows on a sheep's back, the length of a drought, and the growing of the corn, depend on nothing that moves immutable, at the heart of all things; but on the changeable will of a changeable being, whom our prayers can alter. To us, from the beginning, Nature has been but a poor plastic thing, to be toyed with this way or that, as man happens to please his deity or not; to go to church or not; to say his prayers right or not; to travel on a Sunday or not. Was it possible for us in an instant to see Nature as she is – the flowing vestment of an unchanging reality? When a soul breaks free from the arms of a superstition, bits of the claws and talons break themselves off in him. It is not the work of a day to squeeze them out.

And so, for us, the human-like driver and guide being gone, all existence, as we look out at it with our chilled, wondering eyes, is an aimless rise and swell of shifting waters. In all that weltering chaos we can see no spot so large as a man's hand on which we may plant our foot.

Whether a man believes in a human-like God or no is a small thing. Whether he looks into the mental and physical world and sees no relation between cause and effect, no order, but a blind chance sporting, this is the mightiest fact that can be recorded in any spiritual existence. It were almost a mercy to cut his throat, if indeed he does not do it for himself.

We, however, do not cut our throats. To do so would imply some desire and feeling, and we have no desire and no feeling; we are only cold. We do not wish to live, and we do not wish to die. One day a snake curls itself round the waist of a Kaffir woman. We take it in our hand, swing it round and round, and fling it on the ground – dead. Everyone looks at us with eyes of admiration. We almost laugh. Is it wonderful to risk that for which we care nothing?

In truth, nothing matters. This dirty little world full of confusion, and the blue rag, stretched overhead for a sky, is so low we could touch it with our hand.

Existence is a great pot, and the old Fate who stirs it round cares nothing what rises to the top, and what goes down, and laughs when the bubbles burst. And we do not care. Let it boil about. Why should we trouble ourselves? Nevertheless the physical sensations are real. Hunger hurts, and thirst, therefore we eat and drink: inaction pains us, therefore we work like galley slaves. No one demands it, but we set ourselves to build a great dam in red sand beyond the graves. In the grey dawn, before the sheep are let out, we work at it. All day, while the young ostriches we tend feed about us, we work on through the fiercest heat. The people wonder what new spirit has seized us now. They do not know we are working for life. We bear the greatest stones, and feel a satisfaction when we stagger under them, and are hurt by a pang that shoots through our chest. While we eat our dinner we carry on baskets full of earth, as though the Devil drove us. The Kaffir servants have a story that at night a witch and two white oxen come to us. No wall, they say, could grow so quickly under one man's hands.

At night, alone in our cabin, we sit no more brooding over the fire. What should we think of now? All is emptiness. So we take the old arithmetic; and the multiplication table, which with so much pains we learnt long ago and forgot directly, we learn now in a few hours and never forget again. We take a strange satisfaction in working arithmetical problems. We pause in our building to cover the stones with figures and calculations. We save money for a Latin Grammar and an Algebra, and carry them about in our pockets, poring over them as over our Bible of old. We have thought we were utterly stupid, incapable of remembering anything, of learning anything. Now we find that all is easy. Has a new soul crept into this old body, that even our intellectual faculties are changed? We marvel; not perceiving that what a man expends in prayer and ecstasy he cannot have over for acquiring knowledge. You never shed a tear or create a beautiful image, or quiver with emotion, but you pay for it at the practical, calculating end of your nature. You have just so much force: when the one channel runs over the other runs dry.

And now we turn to Nature. All these years we have lived beside her, and we have never seen her; now we open our eyes and look at her.

The rocks have been to us a blur of brown; we bend over them, and the disorganised masses dissolves into a many-coloured, many-shaped, carefully arranged form of existence. Here masses of rainbow-tinted crystals, half-fused together; these bands of smooth grey and red, methodically overlying each other. This rock here is covered with a delicate silver tracery, in some mineral, resembling leaves and branches; there on the flat stone, on which we so often have sat to weep and pray, we look down, and see it covered with the fossil footprints of great birds, and the beautiful skeleton of a fish. We have often tried to picture in our mind what the fossiled remains of creatures must be like, and all the while we sat on them. We have been so blinded by thinking and feeling that we have never seen the world.

The flat plain has been to us a reach of monotonous red. We look at it, and every handful of sand starts into life. That wonderful people, the ants, we learn to know; see them make war and peace, play and work, and build their huge palaces. And that smaller people we make acquaintance with, who live in the flowers. The bitto flower has been for us a mere blur of yellow; we find its heart composed of a hundred perfect flowers, the homes of the tiny black people with red stripes, who move in and out in that little yellow city. Every bluebell has its inhabitant. Every day, the Karoo shows us a new wonder sleeping in its teeming bosom. On our way to work we pause and stand to see the ground-spider make its trap, bury itself in the sand, and then wait for the falling in of its enemy. Farther on walks a horned beetle, and near him starts open the door of a spider, who peeps out carefully, and quickly pulls it down again. On a Karoo-bush a green fly is laying her silver eggs. We carry them home, and see the shells pierced, the spotted grub come out, turn to a green fly, and flit away. We are not satisfied with what Nature shows us, and will see something for ourselves. Under the white hen we put a dozen eggs, and break one daily, to see the white spot wax into the chicken. We are not excited or enthusiastic about it; but a man is not to lay his throat open, he must think of something. So we plant seeds in rows on our dam-wall, and pull one up daily to see how it goes with them. Alladeen buried her wonderful stone, and a golden palace sprang up at her feet. We do far more. We put a brown seed in the earth, and a living thing starts out – starts upwards – why, no more than Alladeen can we say – starts upwards, and does not desist till it is higher than our heads, sparkling with dew in the early morning, glittering with yellow blossoms, shaking brown seeds with little embryo souls onto the ground. We look at it solemnly, from the time it consists of two leaves peeping above the ground and a soft white root, till we have to raise our faces to look at it; but we find no reason for that upward starting.

We look into dead ducks and lambs. In the evening we carry them home, spread newspapers on the floor, and lie working with them till midnight. With a startled feeling near akin to ecstasy we open the lump of flesh called a heart, and find little doors and strings inside. We feel them, and put the heart away; but every now and then return to look, and to feel them again. Why we like them so we can hardly tell.

A gander drowns itself in our dam. We take it out, and open it on the bank, and kneel, looking at it. Above are the organs divided by delicate tissues; below are the intestines artistically curved in a spiral form, and each tier covered by a delicate network of blood-vessels standing out red against the faint blue background. Each branch of the blood vessels is comprised of a trunk, bifurcating and rebifurcating into the most delicate, hair-like threads, symmetrically arranged. We are struck with its singular beauty. And, moreover – and here we drop from our kneeling into a sitting posture – this also we remark: of that same exact shape and outline is our thorn-tree seen against the sky in mid-winter: of that shape also is delicate metallic tracery between our rocks; in that exact path does our water flow when without a furrow we lead it from the dam; so shaped are the antlers of the horned beetle. How are these things related that such deep union should exist between them all? Is it chance? Or, are they not all the fine branches of one trunk, whose sap flows through us all? That would explain it. We nod over the gander's inside.

This thing we call existence; is it not a something which has its roots far down below in the dark, and its branches stretching out into the immensity above, which we among the branches cannot see? Not a chance jumble; a living thing, a *One*. The thought gives us intense satisfaction, we cannot tell why.

We nod over the gander; then start up suddenly, look into the blue sky, throw the dead gander and the refuse into the dam, and go to work again.

And so, it comes to pass in time, that the earth ceases for us to be a weltering chaos. We walk in the great hall of life, looking up and round reverentially. Nothing is despicable – all is meaningful; nothing is small – all is part of a whole, whose beginning and end we know not. The life that throbs in us is a pulsation from it; too mighty for our comprehension, not too small.

And so, it comes to pass at last, that whereas the sky was at first a small blue rag stretched out over us, and so low that our hands might touch it, pressing down on us, it raises itself into an immeasurable blue arch over our heads, and we begin to live again.

CHAPTER TWO

Waldo's Stranger

Waldo lay on his stomach on the sand. The small ostriches he herded wandered about him, pecking at the food he had cut, or at pebbles and dry sticks. On his right lay the graves; to his left the dam; in his hand was a large wooden post covered with carvings, at which he worked. Doss lay before him basking in the winter sunshine, and now and again casting an expectant glance at the corner of the nearest ostrich-camp. The scrubby thorn-trees under which they lay yielded no shade, but none was needed in that glorious June weather, when in the hottest part of the afternoon the sun was but pleasantly warm; and the boy carved on, not looking up, yet conscious of the brown serene earth about him and the intensely blue sky above.

Presently, at the corner of the camp, Em appeared, bearing a covered saucer in one hand, and in the other a jug with a cup in the top. She was grown into a premature little old woman of sixteen, ridiculously fat. The jug and saucer she put down on the ground before the dog and his master, and dropped down beside them herself, panting and out of breath.

'Waldo, as I came up the camps I met someone on horseback; and I do believe it must be the new man that is coming.'

The new man was an Englishman to whom the Boer woman had hired half the farm.

'Hum!' said Waldo.

'He is quite young,' said Em, holding her side, 'and he has brown hair, and beard curling close to his face, and such dark blue eyes. And, Waldo, I was so ashamed! I was just looking back to see, you know, and he happened just to be looking back too, and we looked right into each other's faces; and he got red, and I got so red. I believe he is the new man.'

'Yes,' said Waldo.

'I must go now. Perhaps he has brought us letters from the post from Lyndall. You know she can't stay at school much longer, she must come back soon. And the new man will have to stay with us till his house is built. I must get his room ready. Goodbye!'

She tripped off again, and Waldo carved on at his post. Doss lay with his nose close to the covered saucer, and smelt that someone had made nice little fat cakes that afternoon. Both were so intent on their occupation that not till a horse's hoofs beat beside them in the sand did they look up to see a rider drawing in his steed. He was certainly not the stranger whom Em had described. A dark, somewhat French-looking little man of eight-and-twenty, rather stout, with heavy, cloudy eyes and pointed moustaches. His horse was a fiery creature, well caparisoned; a highly-finished saddlebag hung from the saddle; the man's hands were gloved, and he presented the appearance – an appearance rare on that farm – of a well-dressed gentleman.

In an uncommonly melodious voice he inquired whether he might be allowed to remain there for an hour. Waldo directed him to the farmhouse, but the stranger declined. He would merely rest under the trees, and give his horse water. He removed the saddle, and Waldo led the animal away to the dam. When he returned, the stranger had settled himself under the trees, with his back against the saddle. The boy offered him of the cakes. He declined, but took a draught from the jug; and Waldo lay down not far off, and fell to work again. It mattered nothing if cold eyes saw it. It was not his sheep-shearing machine. With material loves, as with human, we go mad once, love out, and have done. We never get up the true enthusiasm a second time. This was but a thing he had made, laboured over, loved and liked – nothing more – not his machine.

The stranger forced himself lower down in the saddle and yawned. It was a drowsy afternoon, and he objected to travel in these out-of-the-world parts. He liked better civilised life, where at every hour of the day a man may look for his glass of wine, and his easy chair, and paper; where at night he may lock himself into his room with his books and a bottle of brandy, and taste joys mental and physical. The world said of him – the all-knowing, omnipotent world, whom no locks can bar, who has the cat-like propensity of seeing best in the dark – the world said, that better than the books he loved the brandy, and better than books or brandy that which it had been better had he loved less. But for the world he cared nothing; he smiled blandly in its teeth. All life is a dream; if wine and philosophy and women keep the dream from becoming a nightmare, so much the better. It is all they are fit for, all they can be used for. There was another side to his life and thought; but of that the world knew nothing, and said nothing, as the way of the wise world is.

The stranger looked from beneath his sleepy eyelids at the brown earth that stretched away, beautiful in spite of itself in that June sunshine; looked at the graves, the gables of the farmhouse showing over the stone walls of the camps, at the clownish fellow at his feet, and yawned. But he had drunk of the hind's tea, and must say something.

'Your father's place, I presume?' he inquired sleepily.

'No; I am only a servant.'

'Dutch people?'

'Yes.'

'And you like the life?'

The boy hesitated.

'On days like these.'
'And why on these?'
The boy waited.
'They are very beautiful.'
The stranger looked at him. It seemed that as the fellow's dark eyes looked across the brown earth they kindled with an intense satisfaction then they looked back at the carving.

What had that creature, so coarse-clad and clownish, to do with the subtle joys of the weather? Himself, white-handed and delicate, *he* might hear the music which shimmering sunshine and solitude play on the finely-strung chords of nature; but that fellow! Was not the ear in that great body too gross for such delicate mutterings?

Presently he said:
'May I see what you work at?'
The fellow handed his wooden post. It was by no means lovely. The men and birds were almost grotesque in their laboured resemblance to nature, and bore signs of patient thought. The stranger turned the thing over on his knee.
'Where did you learn this work?'
'I taught myself.'
'And these zigzag lines represent – '
'A mountain.'
The stranger looked.
'It has some meaning, has it not?'
The boy muttered confusedly:
'Only things.'
The questioner looked down at him – the huge, unwieldy figure, in size a man's, in right of its childlike features and curling hair a child's; and it hurt him – it attracted him and it hurt him. It was something between pity and sympathy.
'How long have you worked at this?'
'Nine months.'
From his pocket the stranger drew his pocket book, and took something from it. He could fasten the post to his horse in some way, and throw it away in the sand when at a safe distance.
'Will you take this for your carving?'
The boy glanced at the five-pound note and shook his head.
'No; I cannot.'
'You think it is worth more?' asked the stranger with a little sneer.
He pointed with his thumb to a grave, 'No; it is for him.'
'And who is there?' asked the stranger.
'My father.'
The man silently returned the note to his pocket book, and gave the carving to the boy; and, drawing his hat over his eyes, composed himself to sleep. Not being

able to do so, after a while he glanced over the fellow's shoulder to watch him work. The boy carved letters into the back.

'If,' said the stranger, with his melodious voice, rich with a sweetness that never showed itself in the clouded eyes – for sweetness will linger on in the voice long after it has died out in the eyes – 'if for such a purpose, why write that upon it?'

The boy glanced round at him, but made no answer. He had almost forgotten his presence.

'You surely believe,' said the stranger, 'that some day, sooner or later, these graves will open, and those Boer uncles with their wives walk about here in the red sand, with the very fleshly legs with which they went to sleep? Then why say "He sleeps forever"? You believe he will stand up again?'

'Do you?' asked the boy, lifting for an instant his heavy eyes to the stranger's face.

Half taken aback, the stranger laughed. It was as though a curious little tadpole which he held under his glass should suddenly lift its tail and begin to question him.

'I? – No.' He laughed his short thick laugh. 'I am a man who believes nothing, hopes nothing, fears nothing, feels nothing. I am beyond the pale of humanity; no criterion of what you should be who lives here among your ostriches and bushes.'

The next moment the stranger was surprised by a sudden movement on the part of the fellow, which brought him close to the stranger's feet. Soon after, he raised his carving and laid it across the man's knee.

'Yes, I will tell you,' he muttered; 'I will tell you all about it.'

He put his finger on the grotesque little mannikin at the bottom (Ah! that man who believed nothing, hoped nothing, felt nothing; *how he loved him*!) and with eager finger the fellow moved upwards, explaining over fantastic figures and mountains, to the crowning bird from whose wing dropped a feather. At the end he spoke with broken breath-short words, like one who utters things of mighty import.

The stranger watched more the face than the carving; and there was now and then a show of white teeth beneath the moustaches as he listened.

'I think,' he said blandly, when the boy had done, 'that I partly understand you. It is something after this fashion, is it not?' (He smiled). 'In certain valleys there was a hunter.' (He touched the grotesque little figure at the bottom.) 'Day by day he went to hunt for wild fowl in the woods; and it chanced that once he stood on the shores of a large lake. While he stood waiting in the rushes for the coming of the birds, a great shadow fell on him, and in the water he saw a reflection. He looked up to the sky; but the thing was gone. Then a burning desire came over him to see once again that reflection in the water, and all day he watched and waited; but night came, and it had not returned. Then he went home with his empty bag, moody and silent. His comrades came questioning about him to know the reason, but he answered them nothing; he sat alone and brooded. Then his friend came to him, and to him he spoke.

'"I have seen today," he said, "that which I never saw before – a vast white bird, with silver wings outstretched, sailing in the everlasting blue. And now it is as though a great fire burnt within my breast. It was but a sheen, a shimmer, a reflection in the water; but now I desire nothing more on earth than to hold her."

'His friend laughed.

'"It was but a beam playing on the water, or the shadow of your own head. Tomorrow you will forget her," he said.

'But tomorrow, and tomorrow, and tomorrow the hunter walked alone. He sought in the forest and in the woods, by the lakes and among the rushes, but he could not find her. He shot no more wild-fowl; what were they to him?

'"What ails him?" said his comrades. "He is mad," said one.

'"No; but he is worse," said another; "he would see that which none of us have seen, and make himself a wonder."

'"Come, let us forswear his company," said all.

'So the hunter walked alone.

'One night, as he wandered in the shade, very heartsore and weeping, an old man stood before him, grander and taller than the sons of men.

'"Who are you?" asked the hunter.

'"I am Wisdom," answered the old man; "but some men called me Knowledge. All my life I have grown in these valleys; but no man sees me till he has sorrowed much. The eyes must be washed with tears that are to behold me; and, according as a man has suffered, I speak."

'And the hunter cried:

'"Oh, you who have lived here so long, tell me, what is that great wild bird I have seen sailing in the blue? They would have me believe she is a dream; the shadow of my own head."

'The old man smiled.

'"Her name is Truth. He who has once seen her never rests again. Till death he desires her."

'And the hunter cried:

'"Oh, tell me where I may find her."

'But the man said:

'"You have not suffered enough," and went.

'Then the hunter took from his breast the shuttle of Imagination, and wound on it the thread of his Wishes and all night he sat and wove a net.

'In the morning he spread the golden net open on the ground, and into it he threw a few grains of credulity, which his father had left him, and which he kept in his breast-pocket. They were like white puffballs, and when you trod on them a brown dust flew out. Then he sat by to see what would happen. The first that came into the net was a snow-white bird, with dove's eyes, and he sang a beautiful song – "A human-God! a human-God! a human-God!" it sang. The second that came was black and mystical, with dark, lovely eyes, that looked into the depths of your soul, and he sang only this – "Immortality!"

'And the hunter took them both in his arms, for he said:

'"They are surely of the beautiful family of Truth."

'Then came another, green and gold, who sang in a shrill voice, like one crying in the market place, – "Reward after Death! Reward after Death!"

'And he said:

'"You are not so fair; but you are fair too," and he took it.

'And others came, brightly coloured, singing pleasant songs, till the grains were finished. And the hunter gathered all his birds together, and built a strong iron cage called a new creed, and put all his birds in it.

'Then the people came about dancing and singing.

'"Oh, happy hunter!" they cried. "Oh, wonderful man! Oh, delightful birds! Oh, lovely songs!"

'No one asked where the birds had come from, nor how they had been caught; but they danced and sang before them. And the hunter too was glad, for he said:

'"Surely Truth is among them. In time she will moult her feathers, and I shall see her snow-white form."

'But the time passed, and the people sang and danced; but the hunter's heart grew heavy. He crept alone, as of old, to weep; the terrible desire had awakened again in his breast. One day, as he sat alone weeping, it chanced that Wisdom met him. He told the old man what he had done.

'And Wisdom smiled sadly.

'"Many men," he said, "have spread that net for Truth; but they have never found her. On the grains of credulity she will not feed; in the net of wishes her feet cannot be held; in the air of these valleys she will not breathe. The birds you have caught are of the brood of Lies. Lovely and beautiful, but still lies; Truth knows them not."

'And the hunter cried out in bitterness:

'"And must I then sit still, to be devoured of this great burning?"

'And the old man said:

'"Listen, and in that you have suffered much and wept much, I will tell you what I know. He who sets out to search for Truth must leave these valleys of superstition forever, taking with him not one shred that has belonged to them. Alone he must wander down into the Land of Absolute Negation and Denial ; he must abide there; he must resist temptation; when the light breaks he must arise and follow it into the country of dry sunshine. The mountains of stern reality will rise before him: he must climb them; *beyond* them lies Truth."

'"And he will hold her fast! He will hold her in his hands!" the hunter cried.

'Wisdom shook his head.

'"He will never see her, never hold her. The time is not yet."

'"Then there is no hope?" cried the hunter.

'"There is this," said Wisdom. "Some men have climbed on those mountains; circle above circle of bare rock they have scaled; and, wandering there, in those high regions, some have chanced to pick up on the ground, one white silver feather, dropped from the wing of Truth. And it shall come to pass," said the old man, raising himself prophetically, and pointing with his finger to the sky, it shall come to pass, that, when enough of those silver feathers shall have been gathered by the hands of men, and shall have been woven into a cord, and the cord into a net, that in *that* net Truth may be captured. *Nothing but Truth can hold Truth*."

'The hunter arose. "I will go," he said.

'But Wisdom detained him.

'"Mark you well – who leaves these valleys *never* returns to them. Though he should weep tears of blood seven days and nights upon the confines, he can never put his foot across them. Left – they are left forever. Upon the road which you would travel there is no reward offered. Who goes, goes freely – for the great love that is in him. The work is his reward."

'"I go," said the hunter; "but upon the mountains, tell me, which path shall I take?"

'"I am the child of The-Accumulated-Knowledge-of-Ages," said the man; "I can walk only where many men have trodden. On these mountains few feet have passed; each man strikes out a path for himself. He goes at his own peril: my voice he hears no more. I may follow after him, but I cannot go before him."

'Then Knowledge vanished.

'And the hunter turned. He went to his cage, and with his hands broke down the bars, and the jagged iron tore his flesh. It is sometimes easier to build than to break.'

'One by one he took his plumed birds and let them fly. But, when he came to his dark-plumed bird, he held it, and looked into its beautiful eyes, and the bird uttered its low deep cry – "Immortality".

'And he said quickly, "I cannot part with it. It is not heavy; it eats no food. I will hide it in my breast; I will take it with me." And he buried it there, and covered it over with his cloak.

'But the thing he had hidden grew heavier, heavier, heavier – till it lay on his breast like lead. He could not move with it. He could not leave those valleys with it. Then again he took it out and looked at it.

'"Oh, my beautiful, my heart's own!" he cried, "may I not keep you?"

'He opened his hands sadly.

'"Go," he said. "It may happen that in Truth's song one note is like to yours; but *I* shall never hear it."

'Sadly he opened his hand, and the bird flew from him forever.

'Then from the shuttle of imagination he took the thread of his wishes, and threw it on the ground; and the empty shuttle he put into his breast, for the thread was made in those valleys, but the shuttle came from an unknown country. He turned to go, but now the people came about him, howling.

'"Fool, hound, demented lunatic!" they cried.

"'How dared you break your cage and let the birds fly?"
'The hunter spoke; but they would not hear him.
"'Truth! who is she? Can you eat her? Can you drink her? Who has ever seen her? Your birds were real: all could hear them sing! Oh, fool, vile reptile! Atheist!" they cried, "you pollute the air."
"'Come, let us take up stones and stone him," cried some.
"'What affair is it of ours?" said others. "Let the idiot go," and went away. But the rest gathered up stones and mud and threw at him. At last, when he was bruised and cut, the hunter crept away into the woods. And it was evening about him.

At every word the stranger spoke the fellow's eyes flashed back on him – yes, and yes, and yes! The stranger smiled. It was almost worth the trouble of exerting oneself, even on a lazy afternoon, to win those passionate flashes, more thirsty and desiring than the love-glances of a woman.

'He wandered on and on,' said the stranger, 'and the shade grew deeper. He was on the borders now of the land where it is always night. Then he stepped into it, and there was no light there. With his hands he groped; but each branch as he touched it broke off, and the earth was covered with cinders. At every step his foot sank in, and a fine cloud of impalpable ashes flew up into his face; and it was dark. So he sat down upon a stone and buried his face in his hands, to wait in that Land of Negation and Denial till the light came.

'And it was night in his heart also.

'Then from the marshes to his right and left cold mists arose and closed about him. A fine, imperceptible rain fell in the dark, and great drops gathered on his hair and clothes. His heart beat slowly and a numbness crept through all his limbs. Then, looking up, two merry wisp lights came dancing. He lifted his head to look at them. Nearer, nearer they came. So warm, so bright, they danced like stars of fire. They stood before him at last. From the centre of the radiating flame in one looked out a woman's face, laughing, dimpled, with streaming yellow hair. In the centre of the other were merry laughing ripples, like the bubbles on a glass of wine. They danced before him.

"'Who are you," asked the hunter, "who alone come to me in my solitude and darkness?"

"'We are the twins Sensuality," they cried. "Our father's name is Human-Nature, and our mother's name is Excess. We are as old as the hills and rivers, as old as the first man; but we never die," they laughed.

"'Oh, let me wrap my arms about you!" cried the first: "they are soft and warm. Your heart is frozen now, but I will make it beat. Oh, come to me!"

"'I will pour my hot life into you," said the second; "your brain is numb, and your limbs are dead now; but they shall live with a fierce free life. Oh, let me pour it in!"

"'Oh, follow us," they cried, "and live with us. Nobler hearts than yours have sat here in this darkness to wait, and they have come to us and we to them; and they have never left us, never. All else is a delusion, but *we* are real, we are real. Truth is a shadow; the valleys of superstition are a farce; the earth is of ashes, the trees all rotten; but we – feel us – we live! You cannot doubt us. Feel us, how warm we are! Oh, come to us! Come with us!"

'Nearer and nearer round his head they hovered, and the cold drops melted on his forehead. The bright light shot into his eyes, dazzling him, and the frozen blood began to run. And he said:

'"Yes; why should I die here in this awful darkness? They are warm, they melt my frozen blood!" and he stretched out his hands to take them.

'Then in a moment there arose before him the image of the thing he had loved, and his hands dropped to his side.

'"Oh, come to us!" they cried.

'But he buried his face.

'"You dazzle my eyes," he cried, "you make my heart warm; but you cannot give me what I desire. I will wait here – wait till I die. Go!"

'He covered his face with his hands and would not listen; and when he looked up again they were two twinkling stars, that vanished in the distance.

'And the long, long night rolled on.

'All who leave the valley of superstition pass through that dark land; but some go through it in a few days, some linger there for months, some for years, and some die there.'

The boy had crept closer; his hot breath almost touched the stranger's hand; a mystic wonder filled his eyes.

'At last for the hunter a faint light played along the horizon and he rose to follow it; and he reached that light at last, and stepped into the broad sunshine. Then before him rose the almighty mountains of Dry-facts and Realities. The clear sunshine played on them, and the tops were lost in the clouds. At the foot many paths ran up. An exultant cry burst from the hunter. He chose the straightest and began to climb; and the rocks and ridges resounded with his song. They had exaggerated; after all, it was not so high, nor was the road so steep! A few days, a few weeks, a few months at most, and then the top! Not one feather only would he pick up: he would gather all that other men had found – weave the net – capture Truth – hold her fast – touch her with his hands – clasp her!

'He laughed in the merry sunshine, and sang loud. Victory was very near. Nevertheless, after a while the path grew steeper. He needed all his breath for climbing, and the singing died away. On the right and left rose huge rocks, devoid of lichen or moss, and in the lava-like earth chasms yawned. Here and there he saw a sheen of white bones. Now, too, the path began to grow less and less marked; then it became a mere trace, with a footmark here and there; then it ceased altogether. He sang no more, but struck forth a path for himself, until he reached a mighty wall of rock, smooth and without break, stretching as far as the eye could see. "I will rear a stair against it; and, once this wall climbed, I shall be almost there," he said bravely; and worked. With his shuttle of imagination he dug out stones; but half of them would not fit, and half a month's work would roll down because those below were ill chosen. But the hunter worked on, saying always to himself, "Once this wall climbed, I shall be almost there. This great work ended!"

'At last he came out upon the top, and he looked about him. Far below rolled the white mist over the valleys of superstition, and above him towered the mountains. They had seemed low before; they were of an immeasurable height now, from crown to foundation surrounded by walls of rock, that rose tier above tier in mighty circles. Upon them played the eternal sunshine. He uttered a wild cry. He bowed himself onto the earth, and when he rose his face was white. In absolute silence he walked on. He was very silent now. In those high regions the rarefied air is hard to breath by those born in the valleys; every breath he drew hurt him, and the blood oozed out from the tips of his fingers. Before the next wall of rock he began to work. The height of this seemed infinite, and he said nothing. The sound of his tool rang night and day upon the iron rocks into which he cut steps. Years passed over him, yet he worked on; but the wall towered up always above him to heaven. Sometimes he prayed that a little moss or lichen might spring up on those bare walls to be a companion to him; but it never came.' The stranger watched the boy's face.

'And the years rolled on: he counted them by the steps he had cut – a few for a year – only a few. He sang no more; he said no more, "I will do this or that" – he only worked. And at night, when the twilight settled down, there looked out at him from the holes and crevices in the rocks strange wild faces.

'"Stop your work, you lonely man, and speak to us," they cried.

'"My salvation is in work. If I should stop but for one moment you would creep down upon me," he replied. And they put out their long necks further.

'"Look down into the crevice at your feet," they said. "See what lie there – white bones! As brave and strong a man as you climbed to these rocks. And he looked up. He saw there was no use in striving; he would never hold Truth, never see her, never find her. So he lay down here, for he was very tired. He went to sleep forever. He put himself to sleep. Sleep is very tranquil. You are not lonely when you are asleep, neither do your hands ache, nor your heart." And the hunter laughed between his teeth.

'"Have I torn from my heart all that was dearest; have I wandered alone in the land of night; have I resisted temptation; have I dwelt where the voice of my kind is never heard, and laboured alone, to lie down and be food for you, ye harpies?"

'He laughed fiercely; and the Echoes of Despair slunk away, for the laugh of a brave, strong heart is as a deathblow to them.

'Nevertheless they crept out again and looked at him.

'"Do you know that your hair is white?" they said, "that your hands begin to tremble like a child's? Do you see that the point of your shuttle is gone? – it is cracked already. If you should ever climb this stair," they said, "it will be your last. You will never climb another."

'And he answered, "*I know it!*" and worked on.

'The old, thin hands cut the stones ill and jaggedly, for the fingers were stiff and bent. The beauty and the strength of the man was gone.

'At last, an old, wizened, shrunken face looked out above the rocks. It saw the eternal mountains rise with walls to the white clouds; but its work was done.

'The old hunter folded his tired hands and lay down by the precipice where he had worked away his life. It was the sleeping time at last. Below him over the valleys rolled the thick white mist. Once it broke; and through the gap the dying eyes looked down on the trees and fields of their childhood. From afar seemed borne to him the cry of his own wild birds, and he heard the noise of people singing as they danced. And he thought he heard among them the voices of his old comrades; and he saw far off the sunlight shine on his early home. And great tears gathered in the hunter's eyes.

'"Ah! They who die there do not die alone," he cried.

'Then the mists rolled together again; and he turned his eyes away.

'"I have sought," he said, "for long years I have laboured; but I have not found her. I have not rested, I have not repined, and I have not seen her; now my strength is gone. Where I lie down worn out other men will stand, young and fresh. By the steps that I have cut they will climb; by the stairs that I have built they will mount. They will never know the name of the man who made them. At the clumsy work they will laugh; when the stones roll they will curse me. But they will mount, and on *my* work; they will climb, and by *my* stair! They will find her, and through me! And no man liveth to himself, and no man dieth to himself."

'The tears rolled from beneath the shrivelled eyelids. If Truth had appeared above him in the clouds now he could not have seen her, the mist of death was in his eyes.

'"My soul hears their glad step coming," he said; "and they shall mount! they shall mount!" He raised his shrivelled hand to his eyes.

'Then slowly from the white sky above, through the still air, came something falling, falling, falling. Softly it fluttered down, and dropped onto the breast of the dying man. He felt it with his hands. It was a feather. He died holding it.'

The boy had shaded his eyes with his hand. On the wood of the carving great drops fell. The stranger must have laughed at him, or remained silent. He did so.

'How did you know it?' the boy whispered at last. 'It is not written there – not on that wood. How did you know it?'

'Certainly,' said the stranger, 'the whole of the story is not written here, but it is suggested. And the attribute of all true art, the highest and the lowest, is this – that it says more than it says, and takes you away from itself. It is a little door that opens into an infinite hall where you may find what you please. Men thinking to detract, say, "People read more in this or that work of genius than was ever written in it," not perceiving that they pay the highest compliment. If we pick up the finger and nail of a real man, we can decipher a whole story – could almost reconstruct the creature again, from head to foot. But half the body of a Mumbo-jumbo idol leaves us utterly in the dark as to what the rest was like. We see what we see, but nothing more. There is nothing so universally intelligible as truth. It has a thousand meanings, and suggests a thousand more.' He turned over the wooden thing. 'Though a man should carve it into matter with the least possible manipulative skill, it will yet find interpreters. It is the soul that looks out with burning eyes through the most gross fleshly filament. Whosoever should portray truly the life and death of a little flower – its birth, sucking in of nourishment, reproduction of its kind, withering and vanishing – would have shaped a symbol of all existence. All true facts of nature or the mind are related. Your little carving represents some mental facts as they really are, therefore fifty different true stories might be read from it. What your work wants is not truth, but beauty of external form, the other half of art.' He leaned almost gently towards the boy. 'Skill may come in time, but you will have to work hard. The love of beauty and the desire for it must be born in a man; the skill to reproduce it he must make. He must work hard.'

'All my life I have longed to see you,' the boy said.

The stranger broke off the end of his cigar, and lit it. The boy lifted the heavy wood from the stranger's knee and drew yet nearer him. In the dog-like manner of his drawing near there was something superbly ridiculous, unless one chanced to view it in another light. Presently the stranger said, whiffing, 'Do something for me.'

The boy started up.

'No; stay where you are. I don't want you to go anywhere; I want you to talk to me. Tell me what you have been doing all your life.'

The boy slunk down again. Would that the man had asked him to root up bushes with his hands for his horse to feed on; or to run to the far end of the plain for the fossils that lay there; or to gather the flowers that grew on the hills at the edge of the plain; he would have run and been back quickly – but now!

'I have never done anything,' he said.

'Then tell me of that nothing. I like to know what other folks have been doing whose word I can believe. It is interesting. What was the first thing you ever wanted very much?'

The boy waited to remember, then began hesitatingly; but soon the words flowed. In the smallest past we find an inexhaustible mine when once we begin to dig at it.

A confused, disordered story – the little made large and the large small, and nothing showing its inward meaning. It is not till the past has receded many steps that before the clearest eyes it falls into co-ordinate pictures. It is not till the 'I' we tell of has ceased to exist that it takes its place among other objective realities, and finds its true niche in the picture. The present and the near past is a confusion, whose meaning flashes on us as it slinks away into the distance.

The stranger lit one cigar from the end of another, and puffed and listened with half-closed eyes.

'I will remember more to tell you if you like,' said the fellow.

He spoke with that extreme gravity common to all very young things who feel deeply. It is not till twenty that we learn to be in deadly earnest and to laugh. The stranger nodded, while the fellow sought for something more to relate. He would tell all to this man of his – all that he knew, all that he had felt, his most inmost sorest thought. Suddenly the stranger turned upon him.

'Boy,' he said, 'you are happy to be here.'

Waldo looked at him. Was his delightful one ridiculing him? Here, with this brown earth and these low hills, while the rare wonderful world lay all beyond. Fortunate to be here!

The stranger read his glance.

'Yes,' he said; 'here with the Karoo-bushes and red sand. Do you wonder what I mean? To all who have been born in the old faith there comes a time of danger, when the old slips from us, and we have not yet planted our feet on the new. We hear the voice from Sinai thundering no more, and the still small voice of reason is not yet heard. We have proved the religion our mothers fed us on to be a delusion; in our bewilderment we see no rule by which to guide our steps day by day; and yet every day we must step somewhere.' The stranger leaned forward and spoke more quickly. 'We have never once been taught by word or act to distinguish between religion and the moral laws on which it has artfully fastened itself, and from which it has sucked its vitality. When we have dragged down the weeds and creepers that covered the solid wall and have found them to be rotten wood, we imagine the wall itself to be rotten wood too. We find it is solid and standing only when we fall headlong against it. We have been taught that all right and wrong originate in the will of an irresponsible being. It is some time before we see how the inexorable "Thou shalt and shalt not," are carved into the nature of things. This is the time of danger.'

His dark, misty eyes looked into the boy's.

'In the end experience will inevitably teach us that the laws for a wise and noble life have a foundation infinitely deeper than the *fiat* of any being, God or man, even in the ground work of human nature. She will teach us that whoso sheddeth man's blood, though by man his blood be not shed, though no man avenge and no hell await, yet every drop shall blister on his soul and eat in the name of the dead. She will teach that whoso takes a love not lawfully his own, gathers a flower with a poison on its petals; that whoso revenges, strikes with a sword that has two edges – one for his adversary, one for himself; that who lives to himself is dead, though the ground is not yet on him; that who wrongs another clouds his own sun; and that who sins in secret stands accused and condemned before the one Judge who deals eternal justice – his own all-knowing self.

'Experience *will* teach us this, and reason will show us why it *must* be so; but at first the world swings before our eyes and no voice cries out, "This is the way, walk ye in it!" You are happy to be here, boy! When the suspense fills you with pain you build stone walls and dig earth for relief. Others have stood where you stand today, and have felt as you feel; and another relief has been offered them, and they have taken it.

'When the day has come when they have seen the path in which they might walk, they have not the strength to follow it. Habits have fastened on them from which nothing but death can free them; which cling closer than his sacerdotal sanctimony to a priest; which feed on the intellect like a worm sapping energy, hope, creative power, all that makes a man higher than a beast – leaving only the power to yearn, to regret, and to sink lower in the abyss.

'Boy,' he said, and the listener was not more unsmiling now than the speaker, 'you are happy to be here! Stay where you are. If you ever pray, let it be only the one old prayer – "Lead us not into temptation." Live on here quietly. The time may yet come when you will be that which other men have hoped to be and never will be now.'

The stranger rose, shook the dust from his sleeve, and, ashamed of his own earnestness, looked across the bushes for his horse.

'We should have been on our way already,' he said. 'We shall have a long ride in the dark tonight.'

Waldo hastened to fetch the animal; but he returned leading it slowly. The sooner it came the sooner would its rider be gone.

The stranger was opening his saddlebag, in which were a bright French novel and an old brown volume. He took the last and held it out to the boy.

'It may be of some help to you,' he said carelessly. 'It was a gospel to me when I first fell on it. You must not expect too much; but it may give you a centre round which to hang your ideas, instead of letting them lie about in a confusion that makes the head ache. We of this generation are not destined to eat and be satisfied as our fathers were; we must be content to go hungry.'

He smiled his automaton smile, and re-buttoned the bag. Waldo thrust the book into his breast, and while he saddled the horse the stranger made inquiries as to the nature of the road and the distance to the next farm.

When the bags were fixed Waldo took up his wooden post and began to fasten it onto the saddle, tying it with the little blue cotton handkerchief from his neck. The stranger looked on in silence. When it was done the boy held the stirrup for him to mount.

'What is your name?' he inquired, ungloving his right hand when he was in the saddle.

The boy replied.

'Well, I trust we shall meet again some day, sooner or later.'

He shook hands with the ungloved hand; then drew on the glove, and touched his horse, and rode slowly away. The boy stood to watch him.

Once when the stranger had gone half across the plain he looked back.

'Poor devil,' he said, smiling and stroking his moustache. Then he looked to see if the little blue handkerchief were still safely knotted. 'Poor devil!'

He smiled, and then he sighed wearily, very wearily.

And Waldo waited till the moving speck had disappeared on the horizon; then he stooped and kissed passionately a hoof-mark in the sand. Then he called his young birds together, and put his book under his arm, and walked home along the stone wall. There was a rare beauty to him in the sunshine that evening.

CHAPTER THREE

Gregory Rose Finds His Affinity

The new man, Gregory Rose, sat at the door of his dwelling, his arms folded, his legs crossed, and a profound melancholy seeming to rest over his soul. His house was a little square daub-and-wattle building far out in the Karoo, two miles from the homestead. It was covered outside with a sombre coating of brown mud, two little panes being let into the walls for windows. Behind it were the sheep-*kraals*, and to the right a large dam, now principally containing baked mud. Far off, the little *kopje* concealed the homestead, and was not itself an object conspicuous enough to relieve the dreary monotony of the landscape.

Before the door sat Gregory Rose in his shirtsleeves, on a campstool, and ever and anon he sighed deeply. There was that in his countenance for which even his depressing circumstances failed to account. Again and again he looked at the little *kopje*, at the milk pail at his side, and at the brown pony, who a short way off cropped the dry bushes – and sighed.

Presently he rose and went into his house. It was one tiny room, the whitewashed walls profusely covered with prints cut from the *Illustrated London News*, and in which there was a noticeable preponderance of female faces and figures. A stretcher filled one end of the hut, and a rack for a gun and a little hanging looking glass diversified the gable opposite, while in the centre stood a chair and table. All was scrupulously neat and clean, for Gregory kept a little duster folded in the corner of his table drawer, just as he had seen his mother do, and every morning before he went out he said his prayers, and made his bed, and dusted the table and the legs of the chairs, and even the pictures on the wall and the gun-rack.

On this hot afternoon he took from beneath his pillow a watch-bag made by his sister Jemima, and took out the watch. Only half-past four! With a suppressed groan he dropped it back and sat down beside the table. Half-past four! Presently he roused himself. He would write to his sister Jemima. He always wrote to her when he was miserable. She was his safety valve. He forgot her when he was happy; but he used her when he was wretched.

He took out ink and paper. There was a family crest and motto on the latter, for the Roses since coming to the Colony had discovered that they were of distinguished lineage. Old Rose himself, an honest English farmer, knew nothing of his noble descent; but his wife and daughter knew – especially his daughter. There were Roses in England who kept a park and dated from the Conquest. So the colonial *Rose Farm* became *Rose Manor*, in remembrance of the ancestral

300

domain, and the claim of the Roses to noble blood was established – in their own minds, at least.

Gregory took up one of the white, crested sheets; but on deeper reflection he determined to take a pink one as more suitable to the state of his feelings. He began:

Kopje Alone
Monday Afternoon

My Dear Jemima, –

Then he looked up into the little glass opposite. It was a youthful face reflected there, with curling brown beard and hair; but in the dark blue eyes there was a look of languid longing that touched him. He re-dipped his pen and wrote:

When I look up into the little glass that hangs opposite me, I wonder if that changed and sad face ...

Here he sat still and reflected. It sounded almost as if he might be conceited or unmanly to be looking at his own face in the glass. No, that would not do. So he looked for another pink sheet and began again.

Kopje Alone
Monday Afternoon

Dear Sister,

It is hardly six months since I left you to come to this spot, yet could you now see me I know what you would say, I know what mother would say – 'Can that be our Greg – that thing with the strange look in his eyes?'

Yes, Jemima, it is your Greg, and the change has been coming over me ever since I came here; but it is greatest since yesterday. You know what sorrows I have passed through, Jemima; how unjustly I was always treated at school, the masters keeping me back and calling me a blockhead, though, as they themselves allowed, I had the best memory of any boy in the school, and could repeat whole books from beginning to end. You know how cruelly father always used me, calling me a noodle and a milksop, just because he couldn't understand my fine nature. You know how he has made a farmer of me instead of a minister, as I ought to have been; you know it all, Jemima; and how I have borne it all, not as a woman, who whines for every touch, but as a man should – in silence.

But there are things, there is *a* thing, which the soul longs to pour forth into a kindred ear.

Dear sister, have you ever known what it is to keep wanting and wanting and wanting to kiss someone's mouth, and you may not; to touch someone's hand, and you cannot? I am in love, Jemima.

The old Dutch-woman from whom I hire this place has a little stepdaughter, and her name begins with E.

She is English. I do not know how her father came to marry a Boer woman. It makes me feel so strange to put down that letter, that I can hardly go on writing – E. I've loved her ever since I came here. For weeks I have not been able to eat or drink; my very tobacco, when I smoke, has no taste; and I can remain for no more than five minutes in one place, and sometimes feel as though I were really going mad.

Every evening I go there to fetch my milk. Yesterday she gave me some coffee. The spoon fell on the ground. She picked it up; when she gave it me her finger touched mine. Jemima, I do not know if I fancied it – I shivered hot, and she shivered too! I thought, 'It is all right; she will be mine; she loves me!' Just then, Jemima, in came a fellow, a great, coarse fellow, a German – a ridiculous fellow, with curls right down to his shoulders; it makes one *sick* to look at him. He's only a servant of the Boer woman's, and a low, vulgar, uneducated thing, that's never been to boarding school in his life. He had been to the next farm seeking sheep. When he came in she said, 'Good evening, Waldo. Have some coffee?' *and she kissed him.*

All last night I heard nothing else but 'Have some coffee; have some coffee.' If I went to sleep for a moment I dreamed that her finger was pressing mine; but when I woke with a start I heard her say, 'Good evening, Waldo. Have some coffee?'

Is this madness?

I have not eaten a mouthful today. This evening I go and propose to her. If she refuses me I shall go and kill myself tomorrow. There is a dam of water close by. The sheep have drunk most of it up, but there is still enough if I tie a stone to my neck.

It is a choice between death and madness. I can endure no more. If this should be the last letter you ever get from me, think of me tenderly, and forgive me. Without her, life would be a howling wilderness, a long tribulation. She is my affinity; the one love of my youth, of my manhood; my sunshine, my God-given blossom.

> 'They never loved who dreamed that they loved once,
> And who saith, "I loved once"? –
> Not angels, whose deep eyes look down through realms of light!'

Your disconsolate brother, on what is, in all probability, the last and distracted night of his life.

Gregory Nazianzen Rose

PS – Tell mother to take care of my pearl studs. I left them in the washhand-stand drawer. Don't let the children get hold of them.

PPS – I shall take this letter with me to the farm. If I turn down one corner you may know I have been accepted; if not, you may know it is all up with your heartbroken brother.

GNR

Gregory having finished this letter, read it over with much approval, put it in an envelope, addressed it, and sat contemplating the ink-pot, somewhat relieved in mind.

The evening turned out chilly and very windy after the day's heat. From afar off, as Gregory neared the homestead on the brown pony, he could distinguish a little figure in a little red cloak at the door of the cow-*kraal*. Em leaned over the poles that barred the gate, and watched the frothing milk run through the black fingers of the herdsman, while the unwilling cows stood with tethered heads by the milking poles. She had thrown the red cloak over her own head, and held it under her chin with a little hand, to keep from her ears the wind, that playfully shook it, and tossed the little fringe of yellow hair into her eyes.

'Is it not too cold for you to be standing here?' said Gregory, coming softly close to her.

'Oh, no; it is so nice. I always come to watch the milking. That red cow with the short horns is bringing up the calf of the white cow that died. She loves it so – just as if it were her own. It is so nice to see her lick its little ears. Just look!'

'The clouds are black. I think it is going to rain tonight,' said Gregory.

'Yes,' answered Em, looking up as well as she could for the little yellow fringe.

'But I'm sure you must be cold,' said Gregory, and put his hand under the cloak, and found there a small fist doubled up, soft, and very warm. He held it fast in his hand.

'Oh, Em, I love you better than all the world besides! Tell me, do you love me a little?'

'Yes, I do,' said Em, hesitating, and trying softly to free her hand.

'Better than everything; better than all the world, darling?' he asked, bending down so low that the yellow hair was blown into his eyes.

'I don't know,' said Em gravely. 'I do love you very much; but I love my cousin who is at school, and Waldo, very much. You see I have known them so long!'

'Oh, Em, do not talk to me so coldly,' Gregory cried, seizing the little arm that rested on the gate and pressing it till she was half afraid. The herdsman had moved away to the other end of the *kraal* now, and the cows, busy with their calves, took no notice of the little human farce. 'Em, if you talk so to me I will go mad! You must love me, love me better than all! You must give yourself to me. I have loved you since that first moment when I saw you walking by the stone wall with the jug in your hands. You were made for me, created for me! I will love you till I die! Oh, Em, do not be so cold, so cruel to me!'

He held her arm so tightly that her fingers relaxed their hold, and the cloak fluttered down on to the ground and the wind played more roughly than ever with the little yellow head.

'I do love you very much,' she said; 'but I do not know if I want to marry you. I love you better than Waldo, but I can't tell if I love you better than Lyndall. If you would let me wait for a week, I think perhaps I could tell you.'

Gregory picked up the cloak and wrapped it round her.

'If you could but love me as I love you,' he said; 'but no woman *can* love as a man can. I will wait till next Saturday. I will not once come near you till then. Goodbye! Oh, Em,' he said, turning again, and twining his arm about her, and kissing her surprised little mouth, 'if you are not my wife I cannot live. I have never loved another woman, and I never shall! – never, never!'

'You make me afraid,' said Em. 'Come, let us go, and I will fill your pail.'

'I want no milk. – Goodbye! You will not see me again till Saturday.'

Late that night, when everyone else had gone to bed, the yellow-haired little woman stood alone in the kitchen. She had come to fill the kettle for the next morning's coffee, and now stood before the fire. The warm reflection lit the grave old-womanish little face, that was so unusually thoughtful this evening.

'Better than all the world; better than everything; he loves me better than everything!' She said the words aloud, as if they were more easy to believe if she spoke them so. She had given out so much love in her little life, and had got none of it back with interest. Now one said, 'I love you better than all the world.' One loved her better than she loved him. How suddenly rich she was. She kept clasping and unclasping her hands. So a beggar feels who falls asleep on the pavement wet and hungry, and who wakes in a palace-hall with servants and lights, and a feast before him. Of course the beggar's is only a dream, and he wakes from it; and this was real.

Gregory had said to her, 'I will love you as long as I live.' She said the words over and over to herself like a song.

'I will send for him tomorrow, and I will tell him how I love him back,' she said.

But Em needed not to send for him. Gregory discovered on reaching home that Jemima's letter was still in his pocket. And, therefore, much as he disliked the appearance of vacillation and weakness, he was obliged to be at the farmhouse before sunrise to post it.

'If I see her,' Gregory said, 'I shall only bow to her. She shall see that I am a man, one who keeps his word.'

As to Jemima's letter, he had turned down one corner of the page, and then turned it back, leaving a deep crease. That would show that he was neither accepted nor rejected, but that matters were in an intermediate condition. It was a more poetical way than putting it in plain words.

Gregory was barely in time with his letter, for Waldo was starting when he reached the homestead, and Em was on the doorstep to see him off. When he had given the letter, and Waldo had gone, Gregory bowed stiffly and prepared to remount his own pony, but somewhat slowly. It was still early; none of the servants were about. Em came up close to him and put her little hand softly on his arm as she stood by his horse.

'I do love you best of all,' she said. She was not frightened now, however much he kissed her. 'I wish I was beautiful and nice,' she added, looking up into his eyes as he held her against his breast.

'My darling, to me you are more beautiful than all the women in the world; dearer to me than everything it holds. If you were in hell I would go after you to find you there! If you were dead, though my body moved, my soul would be under the ground with you. All life as I pass it with you in my arms will be perfect to me. It will pass, pass like a ray of sunshine.'

Em thought how beautiful and grand his face was as she looked up into it. She raised her hand gently and put it on his forehead.

'You are so silent, so cold, my Em,' he cried. 'Have you nothing to say to me?'

A little shade of wonder filled her eyes.

'I will do everything you tell me,' she said.

What else could she say? Her idea of love was only service.

'Then, my own precious one, promise never to kiss that fellow again. I cannot bear that you should love anyone but me. You must not! I will not have it! If every relation I had in the world were to die tomorrow, I would be quite happy if I still only had you! My darling, my love, why are you so cold? Promise me not to love him any more. If you asked *me* to do anything for *you*, I would do it, though it cost my life.'

Em put her hand very gravely round his neck. 'I will never kiss him,' she said, 'and I will try not to love anyone else. But I do not know if I will be able.'

'Oh, my darling, I think of *you* all night, all day. I think of nothing else, love nothing else,' he said, folding his arms about her.

Em was a little conscience-stricken; even that morning she had found time to remember that in six months her cousin would come back from school, and she had thought to remind Waldo of the lozenges for his cough, even when she saw Gregory coming.

'I do not know how it is,' she said humbly, nestling to him, 'but I cannot love you so much as you love me. Perhaps it is because I am only a woman; but I *do* love you as much as I can.'

Now the Kaffir maids were coming from the huts. He kissed her again, eyes and mouth and hands, and left her.

Tant Sannie was well satisfied when told of the betrothment. She herself contemplated marriage within the year with one or other of her numerous *vrijers*, and she suggested that the weddings might take place together.

Em set to work busily to prepare her own household linen and wedding garments. Gregory was with her daily, almost hourly, and the six months which elapsed before Lyndall's return passed, as he felicitously phrased it, 'like a summer night, when you are dreaming of someone you love.'

Late one evening, Gregory sat by his little love, turning the handle of her machine as she drew her work through it, and they talked of the changes they would make when the Boer woman was gone, and the farm belonged to them alone. There should be a new room here, and a *kraal* there. So they chatted on. Suddenly Gregory dropped the handle, and impressed a fervent kiss on the fat hand that guided the linen.

'You are so beautiful, Em,' said the lover. 'It comes over me in a flood suddenly, how I love you.'

Em smiled. '*Tant* Sannie says when I am her age no one will look at me; and it is true. My hands are as short and broad as a duck's foot, and my forehead is so low, and I haven't any nose. I *can't* be pretty.'

She laughed softly. It was so nice to think he should be so blind.

'When my cousin comes tomorrow you will see a beautiful woman, Gregory,' she added presently. 'She is like a little queen: her shoulders are so upright, and her head looks as though it ought to have a little crown upon it. You must come to see her tomorrow as soon as she comes. I am sure you will love her.'

'Of course I shall come to see her, since she is your cousin; but do you think I could *ever* think any woman as lovely as I think you?'

He fixed his seething eyes upon her.

'You could not help seeing that she is prettier,' said Em, slipping her right hand into his; 'but you will never be able to like anyone so much as you like me.'

Afterwards, when she wished her lover goodnight, she stood upon the doorstep to call a greeting after him; and she waited, as she always did, till the brown pony's hoofs became inaudible behind the *kopje*.

Then she passed through the room where *Tant* Sannie lay snoring, and, through the little room that was all draped in white, waiting for her cousin's return, on to her own room. She went to the chest of drawers to put away the work she had finished, and sat down on the floor before the lowest drawer. In it were things she was preparing for her marriage. Piles of white linen, and some aprons and quilts; and in the little box in the corner a spray of orange-blossom which she had brought from a *smous*. There too was a ring Gregory had given her, and a veil his sister had sent, and there was a little roll of fine embroidered work which Trana had given her. It was too fine and good even for Gregory's wife – just right for something very small and soft. She would keep it. And she touched it gently with her forefinger, smiling;

and then she blushed and hid it far behind the other things. She knew so well all that was in that drawer, and yet she turned them all over as though she saw them for the first time, packed them all out, and packed them all in, without one fold or crumple; and then sat down and looked at them.

Tomorrow evening when Lyndall came she would bring her here, and show her it all. Lyndall would so like to see it – the little wreath, and the ring, and the white veil! It would be so nice! Then Em fell to seeing pictures. Lyndall should live with them till she herself got married some day.

Every day when Gregory came home, tired from his work, he would look about and say, 'Where is my wife? Has no one seen my wife? Wife, some coffee!' and she would give him some.

Em's little face grew very grave at last, and she knelt up and extended her hands over the drawer of linen.

'Oh, God!' she said, 'I am so glad! I do not know what I have done that I should be so glad. Thank you!'

CHAPTER FOUR

Lyndall

She was more like a princess, yes, far more like a princess, than the lady who still hung on the wall in *Tant* Sannie's bedroom. So Em thought. She leaned back in the little armchair; she wore a grey dressing gown, and her long hair was combed out and hung to the ground. Em, sitting before her, looked up with mingled respect and admiration.

Lyndall was tired after her long journey, and had come to her room early. Her eyes ran over the familiar objects. Strange to go away for four years, and come back, and find that the candle standing on the dressing-table still cast the shadow of an old crone's head in the corner beyond the clothes-horse. Strange that even a shadow should last longer than man! She looked about among the old familiar objects; all was there, but the old self was gone.

'What are you noticing?' asked Em.

'Nothing and everything. I thought the windows were higher. If I were you, when I get this place I should raise the walls. There is not room to breathe here; one suffocates.'

'Gregory is going to make many alterations,' said Em; and drawing nearer to the grey dressing gown respectfully. 'Do you like him, Lyndall? Is he not handsome?'

'He must have been a fine baby,' said Lyndall, looking at the white dimity curtain that hung over the window.

Em was puzzled.

'There are some men,' said Lyndall, 'whom you never can believe were babies at all: and others you never see without thinking how very nice they must have looked when they wore socks and pink sashes.'

Em remained silent; then she said with a little dignity, 'When you know him you will love him as I do. When I compare other people with him, they seem so weak and little. *Our* hearts are so cold, our loves are mixed up with so many other things. But he – no one is worthy of his love. I am not. It is so great and pure.'

'You need not make yourself unhappy on that point – your poor return for his love, my dear,' said Lyndall. 'A man's love is a fire of olivewood. It leaps higher every moment; it roars, it blazes, it shoots out red flames; it threatens to wrap you round and devour you – you who stand by like an icicle in the glow of its fierce warmth. You are self-reproached at your own chilliness and want of reciprocity. The next day, when you go to warm your hands a little, you find a few ashes! 'Tis a long love and cool against a short love and hot; men, at all events, have nothing to complain of.'

308

'You speak so because you do not know men,' said Em, instantly assuming the dignity of superior knowledge so universally affected by affianced and married women in discussing man's nature with their un-contracted sisters.

'You will know them too someday, and then you will think differently,' said Em, with the condescending magnanimity which superior knowledge can always afford to show to ignorance.

Lyndall's little lip quivered in a manner indicative of intense amusement. She twirled a massive ring upon her forefinger – a ring more suitable for the hand of a man and noticeable in design – a diamond cross let into gold, with the initials 'RR' below it.

'Ah, Lyndall,' Em cried, 'perhaps you are engaged yourself – that is why you smile. Yes; I am sure you are. Look at this ring!'

Lyndall drew the hand quickly from her.

'I am not in so great a hurry to put my neck beneath any man's foot; and I do not so greatly admire the crying of babies,' she said, as she closed her eyes half wearily and leaned back in the chair. 'There are other women glad of such work.'

Em felt rebuked and ashamed. How could she take Lyndall and show her the white linen, and the wreath, and the embroidery? She was quiet for a little while, and then began to talk about Trana and the old farm servants, till she saw her companion was weary; then she rose and left her for the night. But after Em was gone Lyndall sat on, watching the old crone's face in the corner, and with a weary look, as though the whole world's weight rested on these frail young shoulders.

The next morning, Waldo, starting off before breakfast with a bag of *mielies* slung over his shoulder to feed the ostriches, heard a light step behind him.

'Wait for me; I am coming with you,' said Lyndall, adding as she came up to him, 'If I had not gone to look for you yesterday you would not have come to greet me till now. Do you not like me any longer, Waldo?'

'Yes – but – you are changed.'

It was the old, clumsy, hesitating mode of speech.

'You liked the pinafores better?' she said quickly. She wore a dress of a simple cotton fabric, but very fashionably made, and on her head was a broad white hat. To Waldo she seemed superbly attired. She saw it. 'My dress has changed a little,' she said, 'and I also; but not to you. Hang the bag over your other shoulder, that I may see your face. You say so little that if one does not look at you, you are an uncomprehended cipher.' Waldo changed the bag, and they walked on side by side. 'You have improved,' she said. 'Do you know that I have sometimes wished to see you while I was away; not often, but still sometimes.'

They were at the gate of the first camp now. Waldo threw over a bag of *mielies*, and they walked on over the dewy ground.

'Have you learnt much?' he asked her simply, remembering how she had once said, 'When I come back again I shall know everything that a human being can.'

She laughed. 'Are you thinking of my old boast? Yes; I have learnt something, though hardly what I expected, and not *quite* so much. In the first place, I have learnt that one of my ancestors must have been a very great fool; for they say nothing comes out in a man but one of his forefathers possessed it before him. In the second place, I have discovered that of all cursed places under the sun, where the hungriest soul can hardly pick up a few grains of knowledge, a girls' boarding school is the worst. They are called finishing schools, and the name tells accurately what they are. They finish everything but imbecility and weakness, and that they cultivate. They are nicely adapted machines for experimenting on the question, "Into how little space a human soul can be crushed?" I have seen some souls so compressed that they would have fitted into a small thimble, and found room to move there – wide room. A woman who has been for many years at one of those places carries the mark of the beast on her till she dies, though she may expand a little afterwards, when she breathes in the free world.'

'Were you miserable?' he asked, looking at her with quick anxiety.

'I? – No. I am never miserable and never happy. I wish I were. But I should have run away from the place on the fourth day, and hired myself to the first Boer woman whose farm I came to, to make fire under her soap-pot, if I had to live as the rest of the drove did. Can you form an idea, Waldo, of what it must be to be shut up with cackling old women, who are without knowledge of life, without love of the beautiful, without strength, to have your soul cultured by them? It is suffocation only to breathe the air they breathe, but I made them give me a room. I told them I should leave, and they knew I came there on my own account; so they gave me a bedroom without the companionship of one of those things that were having their brains slowly diluted and squeezed out of them. I did not learn music, because I had no talent; and when the drove made cushions, and hideous flowers that the roses laugh at, and a footstool in six weeks that a machine would have made better in five minutes, I went to my room. With the money saved from such work I bought books and newspapers, and at night I sat up. I read, and epitomised what I read; and I found time to write some plays, and find out how hard it is to make your thoughts look anything but imbecile fools when you paint them with ink on paper. In the holidays I learnt a great deal more. I made acquaintances, saw a few places, and many people, and some different ways of living, which is more than any books can show one. On the whole, I am not dissatisfied with my four years. I have not learnt what I expected; but I have learnt something else. What have you been doing?'

'Nothing.'

'That is not possible. I shall find out by and by.'

They still stepped on side by side over the dewy bushes. Then suddenly she turned on him.

'Don't you wish you were a woman, Waldo?'

'No,' he answered readily.

She laughed. 'I thought not. Even you are too worldly-wise for that. I never met a man who did. This is a pretty ring,' she said, holding out her little hand, that the morning sun might make the diamonds sparkle. 'Worth fifty pounds at least. I will give it to the first man who tells me he would like to be a woman. There might be one on Robben Island[1] who would win it perhaps, but I doubt it even there. It is delightful to be a woman; but every man thanks the Lord devoutly that he isn't one.'

She drew her hat to one side to keep the sun out of her eyes as she walked. Waldo looked at her so intently that he stumbled over the bushes. Yes, this was his little Lyndall who had worn the check pinafores; he saw it now, and he walked closer beside her. They reached the next camp.

'Let us wait at this camp and watch the birds,' she said, as an ostrich hen came bounding towards them, with velvety wings outstretched, while far away over the bushes the head of the cock was visible as he sat brooding on the eggs.

Lyndall folded her arms on the gate bar, and Waldo threw his empty bag on the wall and leaned beside her.

'I like these birds,' she said; 'they share each other's work, and are companions. Do you take an interest in the position of women, Waldo?'

'No.'

'I thought not. No one does, unless they are in need of a subject upon which to show their wit. And as for you, from of old you can see nothing that is not separated from you by a few millions of miles, and strewed over with mystery. If women were the inhabitants of Jupiter, of whom you had happened to hear something, you would pore over us and our condition night and day; but because we are before your eyes you never look at us. You care nothing that *this* is ragged and ugly,' she said, putting her little finger on his sleeve; 'but you strive mightily to make an imaginary leaf on an old stick beautiful. I'm sorry you don't care for the position of women; I should have liked us to be friends; and it is the only thing about which I think much or feel much – if, indeed, I have any feeling about anything,' she added flippantly, readjusting her dainty little arms. 'When I was a baby, I fancy my parents left me out in the frost one night, and I got nipped internally – it feels so!'

'I have only a few old thoughts,' he said, 'and I think them over and over again; always beginning where I left off. I never get any further. I am weary of them.'

'Like an old hen that sits on its eggs month after month and they never come out?' she said quickly. 'I am so pressed in upon by new things that, lest they should trip one another up, I have to keep forcing them back. My head swings sometimes. But this one thought stands, never goes – if I might but be one of those born in the future; then, perhaps, to be born a woman will not be to be born branded.'

Waldo looked at her. It was hard to say whether she were in earnest or mocking.

---

1 Lunatics at the Cape were sent to Robben Island.

'I know it is foolish. Wisdom never kicks at the iron walls it can't bring down,' she said. 'But we are cursed, Waldo, born cursed from the time our mothers bring us into the world till the shrouds are put on us. Do not look at me as though I were talking nonsense. Everything has two sides – the outside that is ridiculous, and the inside that is solemn.'

'I am not laughing,' said the boy sedately enough; 'but what curses you?'

He thought she would not reply to him, she waited so long.

'It is not what is done to us, but what is made of us,' she said at last, 'that wrongs us. No man can be really injured but by what modifies himself. We all enter the world little plastic beings, with so much natural force, perhaps, but for the rest – blank; and the world tells us what we are to be, and shapes us by the ends it sets before us. To you it says – *Work*! and to us it says – *Seem*! To you it says – As you approximate to man's highest ideal of God, as your arm is strong and your knowledge great, and the power to labour is with you, so you shall gain all that human heart desires. To us it says – Strength shall not help you, nor knowledge, nor labour. You shall gain what men gain, but by other means. And so the world makes men and women.

'Look at this little chin of mine, Waldo, with the dimple in it. It is but a small part of my person; but though I had a knowledge of all things under the sun, and the wisdom to use it, and the deep loving heart of an angel, it would not stead me through life like this little chin. I can win money with it, I can win love. I can win power with it, I can win fame. What would knowledge help me? The less a woman has in her head the lighter she is for climbing. I once heard an old man say, that he never saw intellect help a woman so much as a pretty ankle; and it was the truth. They begin to shape us to our cursed end,' she said, with her lips drawn in to look as though they smiled, 'when we are tiny things in shoes and socks. We sit with our little feet drawn up under us in the window and look out at the boys in their happy play. We want to go. Then a loving hand is laid on us: "Little one, you cannot go," they say; "your little face will burn, and your nice white dress be spoiled." We feel it must be for our good, it is so lovingly said; but we cannot understand; and we kneel still with one little cheek wistfully pressed against the pane. Afterwards, we go and thread blue beads, and make a string for our neck; and we go and stand before the glass. We see the complexion we were not to spoil, and the white frock, and we look into our own great eyes. Then the curse begins to act on us. It finishes its work when we are grown women, who no more look out wistfully at a more healthy life; we are contented. We fit our sphere as a Chinese woman's foot fits her shoe, exactly, as though God had made both – and yet He knows nothing of either. In some of us the shaping to our end has been quite completed. The parts we are not to use have been quite atrophied, and have even dropped off; but in others, and we are not less to be pitied, they have been weakened and left. We wear the bandages, but our limbs have not grown to them; we know that we are compressed, and chafe against them.

'But what does it help? A little bitterness, a little longing when we are young, a little futile searching for work, a little passionate striving for room for the exercise of our powers, – and then we go with the drove. A woman must march with her regiment. In the end she must be trodden down or go with it; and if she is wise she goes.

'I see in your great eyes what you are thinking,' she said, glancing at him; 'I always know what the person I am talking to is thinking of. How is this woman who makes such a fuss worse off than I? I will show you by a very little example. We stand here at this gate this morning, both poor, both young, both friendless; there is not much to choose between us. Let us turn away just as we are, to make our way in life. This evening you will come to a farmer's house. The farmer, albeit you come alone and on foot, will give you a pipe of tobacco and a cup of coffee and a bed. If he has no dam to build and no child to teach, tomorrow you can go on your way with a friendly greeting of the hand. I, if I come to the same place tonight, will have strange questions asked me, strange glances cast on me. The Boer wife will shake her head and give me food to eat with the Kaffirs, and a right to sleep with the dogs. That would be the first step in our progress – a very little one, but every step to the end would repeat it. We were equals once when we lay newborn babes on our nurse's knees. We will be equals again when they tie up our jaws for the last sleep.'

Waldo looked in wonder at the little quivering face; it was a glimpse into the world of passion and feeling wholly new to him.

'Mark you,' she said, 'we have always this advantage over you – we can at any time step into ease and competence, where you must labour patiently for it. A little weeping, a little wheedling, a little self-degradation, a little careful use of our advantages, and then some man will say – "Come, be my wife!" With good looks and youth marriage is easy to attain. There are men enough; but a woman who has sold herself, even for a ring and a new name, need hold her skirt aside for no creature in the street. They both earn their bread in one way. Marriage for love is the most beautiful external symbol of the union of souls; marriage without it is the most unclean traffic that defiles the world.' She ran her little finger savagely along the topmost bar, shaking off the dozen little dewdrops that still hung there. 'And they tell us we have men's chivalrous attention!' she cried. 'When we ask to be doctors, lawyers, law-makers, anything but ill-paid drudges, they say, – No; but you have men's chivalrous attention; now think of that and be satisfied! What would you do without it?'

The bitter little silvery laugh, so seldom heard, rang out across the bushes. She bit her little teeth together.

'I was coming up in Cobb and Co's the other day. At a little wayside hotel we had to change the large coach for a small one. We were ten passengers, eight men and two women. As I sat in the house the gentlemen came and whispered to me, "There is not room for all in the new coach, take your seat quickly." We hurried out, and they gave me the best seat, and covered me with rugs, because it was drizzling. Then the last passenger came running up to the coach – an old woman with a wonderful bonnet, and a black shawl pinned with a yellow pin.

"'There is no room,' they said; "You must wait till next week's coach takes you up"; but she climbed onto the step, and held on at the window with both hands.

"'My son-in-law is ill, and I must go and see him,' she said.

"'My good woman,' said one, "I am really exceedingly sorry that your son-in-law is ill; but there is absolutely no room for you here.'

"'You had better get down,' said another, 'or the wheel will catch you.'

'I got up to give her my place.

"'Oh, no, no!' they cried, 'we will not allow that.'

"'I will rather kneel,' said one, and he crouched down at my feet; so the woman came in.

'There were nine of us in that coach, and only one showed chivalrous attention – and that was a woman to a woman.

'I shall be old and ugly too one day, and I shall look for men's chivalrous help, but I shall not find it.

'The bees are very attentive to the flowers till their honey is done, and then they fly over them. I don't know if the flowers feel grateful to the bees; they are great fools if they do.'

'But some women,' said Waldo, speaking as though the words forced themselves from him at that moment, 'some women have power.'

She lifted her beautiful eyes to his face.

'Power! Did you ever hear of men being asked whether other souls should have power or not? It is born in them. You may dam up the fountain of water, and make it a stagnant marsh, or you may let it run free and do its work; but *you* cannot say whether it shall be there; *it is there*. And it will act, if not openly for good, then covertly for evil; but it will act. If Goethe had been stolen away a child, and reared in a robber horde in the depths of a German forest, do you think the world would have had *Faust* and *Iphigenie*? But he would have been Goethe still – stronger, wiser than his fellows. At night, round their watch-fire, he would have chanted wild songs of rapine and murder, till the dark faces about him were moved, and trembled. His songs would have echoed on from father to son, and nerved the heart and arm – for evil. Do you think if Napoleon had been born a woman that he would have been contented to give small tea parties and talk small scandal? He would have risen; but the world would not have heard of him as it hears of him now – a man, great and kingly, with all his sins; he would have left one of those names that stain the leaf of every history – the names of women, who, having power, but being denied the right to exercise it openly, rule in the dark, covertly and by stealth, through the men whose passions they feed on and by whom they climb.

'Power!' she said suddenly, smiting her little hand upon the rail. 'Yes, we have power; and since we are not to expend it in tunnelling mountains, nor healing diseases, nor making laws, nor money, nor on any extraneous object, we expend it on *you*. You are our goods, our merchandise, our material for operating on; we buy you, we sell you, we make fools of you, we act the wily old Jew with you, we keep six of you crawling to our little feet, and praying only for a touch of our little hand; and they say truly, there was never an ache or a pain or a broken heart but a woman was at the bottom of it. We are not to study law, nor science, nor art; so we study you. There is never a nerve or fibre in your man's nature but we know it. We keep six of you dancing in the palm of one little hand,' she said, balancing her outstretched arm gracefully, as though tiny beings disported themselves in its palm. 'There – we throw you away, and you sink to the Devil,' she said, folding her arms composedly. 'There was never a man who said one word for woman but he said two for man, and three for the whole human race.'

She watched the bird pecking up the last yellow grains; but Waldo looked only at her.

When she spoke again it was very measuredly.

'They bring weighty arguments against us when we ask for the perfect freedom of woman,' she said; 'but, when you come to the objections, they are like pumpkin devils with candles inside; hollow, and can't bite. They say that women do not wish for the sphere and freedom we ask for them and would not use it!

'If the bird *does* like its cage, and *does* like its sugar, and will not leave it, why keep the door so very carefully shut? Why not open it, only a little? Do they know there is many a bird will not break its wings against the bars, but would fly if the doors were open.' She knit her forehead, and leaned further over the bars.

'Then they say, "If the women have the liberty you ask for, they will be found in positions for which they are not fitted!" If two men climb one ladder, did you ever see the weakest anywhere but at the foot? The surest sign of fitness is success. The weakest never wins but where there is handicapping. Nature left to herself will as beautifully apportion a man's work to his capacities as long ages ago she graduated the colours on the bird's breast. If we are not fit, you give us to no purpose the right to labour; the work will fall out of our hands into those that are wiser.'

She talked more rapidly as she went on, as one talks of that over which they have brooded long, and which lies near their hearts.

Waldo watched her intently.

'They say women have one great and noble work left them, and they do it ill. – That is true; they do it execrably. It is the work that demands the broadest culture, and they have not even the narrowest. The lawyer may see no deeper than his law books, and the chemist see no further than the windows of his laboratory, and they may do their work well. But the woman who does woman's work needs a many-sided, multiform culture; the heights and depths of human life must not be beyond the reach of her vision; she must have knowledge of men and things in many states, a wide catholicity of sympathy, the strength that springs from knowledge, and the magnanimity which springs from strength. *We* bear the world, and *we* make it. The souls of little children are marvellously delicate and tender things, and keep forever the shadow that first falls on them, and that is the mother's or at best a woman's. There was never a great man who had not a great mother – it is hardly an exaggeration. The first six years of our life make us; all that is added later is veneer; and yet some say, if a woman can cook a dinner or dress herself well she has culture enough.

'The mightiest and noblest of human work is given to us, and we do it ill. Send a navvy to work into an artist's studio, and see what you will find there! And yet, thank God, we have this work,' she added quickly: 'it is the one window through which we see into the great world of earnest labour. The meanest girl who dances and dresses becomes something higher when her children look up into her face and ask her questions. It is the only education we have and which they cannot take from us.'

She smiled slightly. 'They say that we complain of woman's being compelled to look upon marriage as a profession; but that she is free to enter upon it or leave it as she pleases.

'Yes – and a cat set afloat in a pond is free to sit in the tub till it dies there, it is under no obligation to wet its feet; and a drowning man may catch at a straw or not, just as he likes – it is a glorious liberty! Let any man think for five minutes of what old maidenhood means to a woman – and then let him be silent. Is it easy to bear through life a name that in itself signifies defeat? To dwell, as nine out of ten unmarried women must, under the finger of another woman? Is it easy to look forward to an old age without honour, without the reward of useful labour, without love? I wonder how many men there are who would give up everything that is dear in life for the sake of maintaining a high ideal purity.'

She laughed a little laugh that was clear without being pleasant. 'And then, when they have no other argument against us, they say – "Go on; but when you have made women what you wish, and her children inherit her culture, you will defeat yourself. Man will gradually become extinct from excess of intellect, the passions which replenish the race will die." Fools!' she said, curling her pretty lip. 'A Hottentot sits at the roadside and feeds on a rotten bone he has found there, and takes out his bottle of Cape-smoke and swills at it, and grunts with satisfaction; and the cultured child of the nineteenth century sits in his armchair, and sips choice wines with the lip of a connoisseur, and tastes delicate dishes with a delicate palate, and with a satisfaction of which the Hottentot knows nothing. Heavy jaw and sloping forehead – all have gone with increasing intellect; but the animal appetites are there still – refined, discriminative, but immeasurably intensified. Fools! Before men forgave or worshipped, while they still were weak on their hind legs, did they not eat, and fight for wives? When all the later additions to humanity have vanished, will not the foundation on which they are built remain?'

She was silent then for a while, and said somewhat dreamily, more as though speaking to herself than to him:

'They ask, "What will you gain, even if man does not become extinct? – You will have brought justice and equality onto the earth, and sent love from it. When men and women are equals they will love no more. Your highly cultured women will not be lovable, will not love."

'Do they see nothing, understand nothing? It is *Tant* Sannie who buries husbands one after another, and folds her hands resignedly, – "The Lord gave, and the Lord hath taken away, and blessed be the name of the Lord," – and she looks for another. It is the hard-headed, deep thinker who, when the wife who has thought and worked for him goes, can find no rest, and lingers near her till he finds sleep beside her.

'A great soul draws and is drawn with a more fierce intensity than any small one. By every inch we grow in intellectual height our love strikes down its roots deeper, and spreads out its arms wider. It is for love's sake yet more than for any other that we look for that new time.' She had leaned her head against the stones, and watched with her sad, soft eyes the retreating bird. 'Then when that time comes,' she said slowly, 'when love is no more bought or sold, when it is not a means of making bread, when each woman's life is filled with earnest, independent labour, then love will come to her, a strange sudden sweetness breaking in upon her earnest work; not sought for, but found. Then, but not now – '

Waldo waited for her to finish the sentence, but she seemed to have forgotten him.

'Lyndall,' he said, putting his hand upon her – she started – 'if you think that that new time will be so great, so good, you who speak so easily – '

She interrupted him. 'Speak! Speak!' she said; 'the difficulty is not to speak; the difficulty is to keep silence.'

'But why do you not try to bring that time?' he said with pitiful simplicity. 'When you speak I believe all you say; other people would listen to you also.'

'I am not so sure of that,' she said with a smile.

Then over the small face came the weary look it had worn last night as it watched the shadow in the corner. Ah, so weary!

'I, Waldo, I?' she said. 'I will do nothing good for myself, nothing for the world, till someone wakes me. I am asleep, swathed, shut up in self; till I have been delivered I will deliver no one.'

He looked at her wondering, but she was not looking at him.

'To see the good and the beautiful,' she said, 'and to have no strength to live it, is only to be Moses on the mountain of Nebo, with the land at your feet and no power to enter. It would be better not to see it. Come,' she said, looking up into his face, and seeing its uncomprehending expression, 'let us go, it is getting late. Doss is anxious for his breakfast also,' she added, wheeling round and calling to the dog, who was endeavouring to unearth a mole, an occupation to which he had been zealously addicted from the third month, but in which he had never on any single occasion proved successful.

Waldo shouldered his bag, and Lyndall walked on before in silence, with the dog close to her side. Perhaps she thought of the narrowness of the limits within which a human soul may speak and be understood by its nearest of mental kin, of how soon it reaches that solitary land of the individual experience, in which no fellow-footfall is ever heard. Whatever her thoughts may have been, she was soon interrupted. Waldo came close to her, and standing still, produced with awkwardness from his breast pocket a small carved box.

'I made it for you,' he said, holding it out.

'I like it,' she said, examining it carefully.

The workmanship was better than that of the grave post. The flowers that covered it were delicate, and here and there small conical protuberances were let in among them. She turned it round critically. Waldo bent over it lovingly.

'There is one strange thing about it,' he said earnestly, putting a finger on one little pyramid. 'I made it without these, and I felt something was wrong; I tried many changes, and at last I let these in, and then it was right. But why was it? They are not beautiful in themselves.'

'They relieve the monotony of the smooth leaves, I suppose.'

He shook his head as over a weighty matter. 'The sky is monotonous,' he said, 'when it is blue, and yet it is beautiful. I have thought of that often; but it is not monotony and it is not variety makes beauty. What is it? The sky, and your face, and this box – the same thing is in them all, only more in the sky and in your face. But what is it?'

She smiled.

'So you are at your old work still. Why, why, why? What is the reason? It is enough for me,' she said, 'if I find out what is beautiful and what is ugly, what is real and what is not. Why it is there, and over the final cause of things in general, I don't trouble myself; there must be one, but what is it to me? If I howl to all eternity I shall never get hold of it; and if I did I might be no better off. But you Germans are born with an aptitude for burrowing; you can't help yourselves. You must sniff after reasons, just as that dog must after a mole. He knows perfectly well he will never catch it, but he's under the imperative necessity of digging for it.'

'But he might find it.'

'*Might*! – but he never has and never will. Life is too short to run after mights; we must have certainties.'

She tucked the box under her arm and was about to walk on, when Gregory Rose, with shining spurs, an ostrich feather in his hat, and a silver-headed whip, careered past. He bowed gallantly as he went by. They waited till the dust of the horse's hoofs had laid itself.

'There,' said Lyndall, 'goes a true woman – one born for the sphere that some women have to fill without being born for it. How happy he would be sewing frills into his little girls' frocks, and how pretty he would look sitting in a parlour, with a rough man making love to him! Don't you think so?'

'I shall not stay here when he is master,' Waldo answered, not able to connect any kind of beauty with Gregory Rose.

'I should imagine not. The rule of a woman is tyranny; but the rule of a man-woman grinds fine. Where are you going?'

'Anywhere.'

'What to do?'

'See – see everything.'

'You will be disappointed.'

'And were you?'

'Yes; and you will be more so. I want some things that men and the world give, you do not. If you have a few yards of earth to stand on, and a bit of blue over you, and something that you cannot see to dream about, you have all that you need, all that you know how to use. But I like to see real men. Let them be as disagreeable as they please, they are more interesting to me than flowers, or trees, or stars, or any other thing under the sun. Sometimes,' she added, walking on, and shaking the dust daintily from her skirts, 'when I am not too busy to find a new way of doing my hair that will show my little neck to better advantage, or, over other work of that kind, sometimes it amuses me intensely to trace out the resemblance between one man and another: to see how *Tant* Sannie and I, you and Bonaparte, St Simon on his pillar, and the Emperor dining off larks' tongues, are one and the same compound, merely mixed in different proportions. What is microscopic in one is largely developed in another; what is a rudimentary in one man is an active organ in another; but all things are in all men, and one soul is the model of all. We shall find nothing new in human nature after we have once carefully dissected and analysed the one being we ever shall truly know – ourself. The Kaffir girl threw some coffee on my arm in bed this morning; I felt displeased, but said nothing. *Tant* Sannie would have thrown the saucer at her and sworn for an hour; but the feeling would be the same irritated displeasure. If a huge animated stomach like Bonaparte were put under a glass by a skilful mental microscopist, even he would be found to have an embryonic doubling somewhere indicative of a heart, and rudimentary buddings that might have become conscience and sincerity. – Let me take your arm, Waldo. How full you are of *mielie* dust. – No, never mind. It will brush off. – And sometimes what is more amusing still than tracing the likeness between man and man, is to trace the analogy there always is between the progress and development of one individual and of a whole nation; or again, between a single nation and the entire human race. It is pleasant when it dawns on you that the one is just the other written out in large letters; and very odd to find all the little follies and virtues, and developments and retrogressions, written out in the big world's book that you find in your little internal self. It is the most amusing thing I know of; but of course, being a woman, I have not often time for such amusements. Professional duties always first, you know. It takes a great deal of time and thought always to look perfectly exquisite, even for a pretty woman. Is the old buggy still in existence, Waldo?'

'Yes; but the harness is broken.'

'Well, I wish you would mend it. You must teach me to drive. I must learn something while I am here. I got the Hottentot girl to show me how to make *sosaties* this morning; and *Tant* Sannie is going to teach me to make *kappies*. I will come and sit with you this afternoon while you mend the harness.'

'Thank you.'

'No, don't thank me; I come for my own pleasure. I never find anyone I can talk to. Women bore me, and men, I talk *so* to – "Going to the ball this evening? – Nice little dog that of yours. – Pretty little ears. – So fond of pointer pups!" – and they think me fascinating, charming! Men are like the earth and we are the moon; we turn always one side to them, and they think there is no other, because they don't see it – but there is.'

They had reached the house now.

'Tell me when you set to work,' she said, and walked towards the door.

Waldo stood to look after her, and Doss stood at his side, a look of painful uncertainty depicted on his small countenance, and one little foot poised in the air. Should he stay with his master or go? He looked at the figure with the wide straw hat moving towards the house, and he looked up at his master; then he put down the little paw and went. Waldo watched them both in at the door and then walked away alone. He was satisfied that at least his dog was with her.

CHAPTER FIVE

Tant Sannie Holds an Upsitting, and Gregory Writes a Letter

It was just after sunset, and Lyndall had not yet returned from her first driving-lesson, when the lean Coloured woman standing at the corner of the house to enjoy the evening breeze, saw coming along the road a strange horseman. Very narrowly she surveyed him, as slowly he approached. He was attired in the deepest mourning, the black crape round his tall hat totally concealing the black felt, and nothing but a dazzling shirt-front relieving the funereal tone of his attire. He rode much forward in his saddle, with his chin resting on the uppermost of his shirt-studs, and there was an air of meek subjection to the will of Heaven, and to what might be in store for him, that bespoke itself even in the way in which he gently urged his steed. He was evidently in no hurry to reach his destination, for the nearer he approached to it the slacker did his bridle hang. The Coloured woman having duly inspected him, dashed into the dwelling.

'Here is another one,' she cried – 'a widower; I see it by his hat.'

'Good Lord!' said *Tant* Sannie; 'it's the seventh I've had this month; but the men know where sheep and good looks and money in the bank are to be found,' she added, winking knowingly. 'How does he look?'

'Nineteen, weak eyes, white hair, little round nose,' said the maid.

'Then it's he! Then it's he!' said *Tant* Sannie triumphantly. 'Little Piet van der Walt, whose wife died last month – two farms, twelve thousand sheep. I've not seen him, but my sister-in-law told me about him, and I dreamed about him last night.'

Here Piet's black hat appeared in the doorway, and the Boer woman drew herself up in dignified silence, extended the tips of her fingers, and motioned solemnly to a chair. The young man seated himself, sticking his feet as far under it as they would go, and said mildly:

'I am Little Piet van der Walt, and my father is Big Piet van der Walt.'

Tant Sannie said solemnly, 'Yes.'

'Aunt,' said the young man, starting up spasmodically; 'can I off-saddle?'

'Yes.'

He seized his hat, and disappeared with a rush through the door.

'I told you so! I knew it!' said *Tant* Sannie.

'The dear Lord doesn't send dreams for nothing. Didn't I tell you this morning that I dreamed of a great beast like a sheep, with red eyes, and I killed it? Wasn't the white wool his hair, and the red eyes his weak eyes, and my killing him meant marriage? Get supper ready quickly; the sheep's inside and roaster-cakes. We shall sit up tonight.'

To young Piet van der Walt that supper was a period of intense torture. There was something overawing in that assembly of English people, with their incomprehensible speech; and moreover, it was his first courtship: his first wife had courted him, and ten months of severe domestic rule had not raised his spirit nor courage. He ate little, and when he raised a morsel to his lips glanced guiltily round to see if he were not observed. He had put three rings on his little finger, with the intention of sticking it out stiffly when he raised a coffee cup; now the little finger was curled miserably among its fellows. It was small relief when the meal was over, and *Tant* Sannie and he repaired to the front room. Once seated there, he set his knees close together, stood his black hat upon them, and wretchedly turned the brim up and down. But supper had cheered *Tant* Sannie, who found it impossible longer to maintain that decorous silence, and whose heart yearned over the youth.

'I was related to your Aunt Selena who died,' said *Tant* Sannie. 'My mother's step-brother's child was married to her father's brother's step-nephew's niece.'

'Yes, Aunt,' said the young man, 'I knew we were related.'

'It was her cousin,' said *Tant* Sannie, now fairly on the flow, 'who had the cancer cut out of her breast by the other doctor, who was not the right doctor they sent for, but who did it quite as well.'

'Yes, Aunt,' said the young man.

'I've heard about it often,' said *Tant* Sannie. 'And he was the son of the old doctor that they say died on Christmas day; but I don't know if that's true. People do tell such awful lies. Why should he die on Christmas day more than any other day?'

'Yes, Aunt, why?' said the young man meekly.

'Did you ever have the toothache?' asked *Tant* Sannie.

'No, Aunt.'

'Well, they say that doctor, – not the son of the old doctor that died on Christmas day, the other that didn't come when he was sent for, – he gave such good stuff for the toothache that if you opened the bottle in the room where anyone was bad they got better directly. You could see it was good stuff,' said *Tant* Sannie; 'it tasted horrid. *That* was a real doctor! He used to give a bottle so high,' said the Boer woman, raising her hand a foot from the table, 'you could drink at it for a month and it wouldn't get done, and the same medicine was good for all sorts of sickness – croup, measles, jaundice, dropsy. Now you have to buy a new kind for each sickness. The doctors aren't so good as they used to be.'

'No, Aunt, said the young man, who was trying to gain courage to stick out his legs and clink his spurs together. He did so at last.

Tant Sannie had noticed the spurs before; but she thought it showed a nice manly spirit, and her heart warmed yet more to the youth.

'Did you ever have convulsions when you were a baby?' asked *Tant* Sannie.

'Yes,' said the young man.

'Strange!' said *Tant* Sannie; 'I had convulsions too. Wonderful that we should be so much alike!'

'Aunt,' said the young man explosively, 'can we sit up tonight?'

Tant Sannie hung her head and half closed her eyes; but finding that her little wiles were thrown away, the young man staring fixedly at his hat, she simpered, 'Yes,' and went away to fetch candles.

In the dining room Em worked at her machine, and Gregory sat close beside her, his great blue eyes turned to the window where Lyndall leaned out talking to Waldo.

Tant Sannie took two candles out of the cupboard and held them up triumphantly, winking all round the room.

'He's asked for them,' she said.

'Does he want them for his horse's rubbed back?' asked Gregory, new to up-country life.

'No,' said *Tant* Sannie indignantly; 'we're going to sit up!' and she walked off in triumph with the candles.

Nevertheless, when all the rest of the house had retired, when the long candle was lighted, when the coffee kettle was filled, when she sat in the elbow-chair, with her lover on a chair close beside her, and when the vigil of the night was fairly begun, she began to find it wearisome. The young man looked chilly, and said nothing.

'Won't you put your feet on my stove?' said *Tant* Sannie.

'No, thank you, Aunt,' said the young man, and then lapsed into silence.

At last *Tant* Sannie, afraid of going to sleep, tapped a strong cup of coffee for herself, and handed another to her lover. This visibly revived both.

'How long were you married, Cousin?'

'Ten months, Aunt.'

'How old was your baby?'

'Three days when it died.'

'It's very hard when we must give our husbands and wives to the Lord,' said *Tant* Sannie.

'Very,' said the young man; 'but it's the Lord's will.'

'Yes,' said *Tant* Sannie, and sighed.

'She was such a good wife, Aunt: I've known her break a churn-stick over a maid's head for only letting dust come on a milk-cloth.'

Tant Sannie felt a twinge of jealousy. She had never broken a churn-stick on a maid's head.

'I hope your wife made a good end,' she said.

'Oh, beautiful, Aunt: she said a psalm and two hymns and a half before she died.'

'Did she leave any messages?' asked *Tant* Sannie.

'No,' said the young man; 'but the night before she died I was lying at the foot of her bed; I felt her foot kick me.

'"Piet," she said.

'"Annie, my heart," said I.

'"My little baby that died yesterday has been here, and it stood over the wagon-box," she said.

'"What did it say?" I asked.

'"It said that if I died you must marry a fat woman."

'"I will," I said, and I went to sleep again. Presently she woke me.

'"The little baby has been here again, and it says you must marry a woman over thirty, and who's had two husbands."

'I didn't go to sleep after that for a long time, Aunt; but when I did she woke me.

'"The baby has been here again," she said, "and it says you mustn't marry a woman with a mole." I told her I wouldn't; and the next day she died.'

'That was a vision from the Redeemer,' said *Tant* Sannie.

The young man nodded his head mournfully. He thought of a younger sister of his wife's who was not fat, and who *had* a mole, and of whom his wife had always been jealous, and he wished the little baby had liked better staying in heaven than coming and standing over the wagon-chest.

'I suppose that's why you came to me,' said *Tant* Sannie.

'Yes, Aunt. And Pa said I ought to get married before shearing-time. It is bad if there's no one to see after things then; and the maids waste such a lot of fat.'

'When do you want to get married?'

'Next month, Aunt,' said the young man in a tone of hopeless resignation. 'May I kiss you, Aunt?'

'Fie! fie!' said *Tant* Sannie, and then gave him a resounding kiss.

'Come, draw your chair a little closer,' she said, and, their elbows now touching, they sat on through the night.

The next morning at dawn, as Em passed through *Tant* Sannie's bedroom, she found the Boer woman pulling off her boots preparatory to climbing into bed.

'Where is Piet van der Walt?'

'Just gone,' said *Tant* Sannie; 'and I am going to marry him this day four weeks. I am dead sleepy,' she added; 'the stupid thing doesn't know how to talk love-talk at all,' and she climbed into the four-poster, clothes and all, and drew the quilt up to her chin.

On the day preceding *Tant* Sannie's wedding, Gregory Rose sat in the blazing sun on the stone wall behind his daub-and-wattle house. It was warm, but he was intently watching a small buggy that was being recklessly driven over the bushes in the direction of the farmhouse. Gregory never stirred till it had vanished; then, finding the stones hot, he slipped down and walked into the house. He kicked the little pail that lay in the doorway, and sent it into one corner; that did him good. Then he sat down on the box, and began cutting letters out of a piece of new paper. Finding that the snippings littered the floor he picked them up and began scribbling on his blotting paper. He tried the effect of different initials before the name Rose: G Rose, E Rose, L Rose, L Rose, L L L L Rose. When he had covered the sheet he looked at it discontentedly a little while, then suddenly began to write a letter.

Beloved Sister,

It is a long while since I last wrote to you, but I have had no time. This is the first morning I have been at home since I don't know when. Em always expects me to go down to the farmhouse in the morning; but I didn't feel as though I could stand the ride today.

I have much news for you. *Tant* Sannie, Em's Boer stepmother, is to be married tomorrow. She is gone to town today, and the wedding feast is to be at her brother's farm. Em and I are going to ride over on horseback, but her cousin is going to ride in the buggy with that German. I don't think I've written to you since she came back from school. I don't think you would like her at all, Jemima; there's something so proud about her. She thinks just because she's handsome there's nobody good enough to talk to her, and just as if there had nobody else but her been to boarding-school before.

They are going to have a grand affair tomorrow; all the Boers about are coming, and they are going to dance all night; but I don't think I shall dance at all; for, as Em's cousin says, these Boer dances are low things. I am sure I only danced at the last to please Em. I don't know why she is fond of dancing. Em talked of our being married on the same day as *Tant* Sannie; but I said it would be nicer for her if she waited till the shearing was over, and I took her down to see you. I suppose she will have to live with us (Em's cousin, I mean), as she has not anything in the world but a poor fifty pounds. I don't like her *at all*, Jemima, and I don't think you would. She's got such queer ways: she's always driving about in a gig with that low German; and I don't think it's at all the thing for a woman to be going about with a man she's not engaged to. Do you? If it was me now, of course, who am a kind of connection, it would be different. The way she treats me, considering that I am so soon to be her cousin, is not at all nice. I took down my album the other day with your likenesses in it, and I told her she could look at it, and put it down close to her; but she just said, 'Thank you', and never even touched it, as much as to say – What are your relations to me?

She gets the wildest horses in that buggy, and a horrid snappish little cur belonging to the German sitting in front, and then she drives out alone. I don't think it's at all proper for a woman to drive out alone; I wouldn't allow it if she was my sister. The other morning, I don't know how it happened, I was going in the way from which she was coming, and that little beast – they call him Doss – began to bark when he saw me – he always does, the little wretch – and the horses began to spring, and kicked the splash-board all to pieces. It was a sight to see, Jemima! She has got the littlest hands I ever saw – I could hold them both in one of mine, and not know that I'd got anything except that they were so soft; but she held those horses in as though they were made of iron. When I wanted to help her she said, 'No, thank you; I can manage them myself. I've got a pair of bits that would break their jaws if I used them well,' and she laughed and drove away. It's so unwomanly.

Tell father my hire of the ground will not be out for six months, and before that Em and I will be married. My pair of birds is breeding now, but I haven't been down to see them for three days. I don't seem to care about anything any more. I don't know what it is; I'm not well. If I go into town on Saturday I will let the doctor examine me; but perhaps she'll go in herself. It's a very strange thing, Jemima, but she never will send her letters to post by me. If I ask her she has none, and the very next day she goes in and posts them herself. You mustn't say anything about it, Jemima, but *twice* I've brought her letters from the post in a gentleman's hand, and I'm sure they were both from the same person, because I noticed every little mark, even the dotting of the i's. Of course it's nothing to *me*, but for Em's sake I can't help feeling an interest in her, however much I may dislike her myself; and I hope she's up to nothing. I pity the man who marries *her*; I wouldn't be him for *anything*. If I had a wife with pride I'd make her give it up, *sharp*. I don't believe in a man who can't make a woman obey him. Now Em – I'm very fond of her, as you know – but if I tell her to put on a certain dress, that dress she puts on; and if I tell her to sit on a certain seat, on that seat she sits; and if I tell her not to speak to a certain individual, she does not speak to them. If a man lets a woman do what he doesn't like, *he's a muff.*

Give my love to mother and the children. The *veld* here is looking pretty good, and the sheep are better since we washed them. Tell father the dip he recommended is very good.

Em sends her love to you. She is making me some woollen shirts; but they don't fit me so nicely as those mother made me.

Write soon to

Your loving brother,
GREGORY.

PS – She drove past just now; I was sitting on the *kraal* wall right before her eyes, and she never even bowed.

G N R

CHAPTER SIX

A Boer Wedding

'I didn't know before you were so fond of riding hard,' said Gregory to his little betrothed.
They were cantering slowly on the road to *Oom* Muller's on the morning of the wedding.
'Do you call this riding hard?' asked Em in some astonishment.
'Of course I do! It's enough to break the horses' necks, and knock one up for the whole day besides,' he added testily; then twisted his head to look at the buggy that came on behind. 'I thought Waldo was such a mad driver; they are taking it easily enough today,' said Gregory. 'One would think the black stallions were lame.'
'I suppose they want to keep out of our dust,' said Em. 'See, they stand still as soon as we do.'
Perceiving this to be the case, Gregory rode on.
'It's all that horse of yours: she kicks up such a confounded dust, I can't stand it myself,' he said.
Meanwhile the cart came on slowly enough.
'Take the reins,' said Lyndall, 'and make them walk. I want to rest and watch their hoofs today – not to be exhilarated; I am so tired.'
She leaned back in her corner, and Waldo drove on slowly in the grey dawn light along the level road. They passed the very milk-bush behind which, so many years before, the old German had found the Kaffir woman. But their thoughts were not with him that morning: they were thoughts of the young, that run out to meet the future and labour in the present. At last he touched her arm.
'What is it?'
'I feared you had gone to sleep, and might be jolted out,' he said; 'you sat so quietly.'
'No; do not talk to me; I am not asleep'; but after a time she said suddenly, 'it must be a terrible thing to bring a human being into the world.'
Waldo looked round; she sat drawn into the corner, her blue cloud wound tightly about her, and she still watched the horses' feet. Having no comment to offer on her somewhat unexpected remark, he merely touched up his horses.
'I have no conscience, none,' she added; 'but I would not like to bring a soul into this world. When it sinned and when it suffered something like a dead hand would fall on me, – "You did it, you, for your own pleasure you created this thing! See your work!" If it lived to be eighty it would always hang like a millstone round my neck,

327

have the right to demand good from me, and curse me for its sorrow. A parent is only like to God: if his work turns out bad so much the worse for him; he *dare* not wash his hands of it. Time and years can never bring the day when you can say to your child, "Soul, what have I to do with you?"'

Waldo said dreamily: 'It is a marvellous thing that one soul should have power to cause another.'

She heard the words as she heard the beating of the horses' hoofs; her thoughts ran on in their own line.

'They say, "God sends the little babies". Of all the dastardly revolting lies men tell to suit themselves, I hate that most. I suppose my father said so when he knew he was dying of consumption, and my mother when she knew she had nothing to support me on, and they created me to feed like a dog from stranger hands. Men do not say God sends the books, or the newspaper articles, or the machines they make; and then sigh, and shrug their shoulders, and say they can't help it. Why do they say so about other things? Liars! "God sends the little babies!"' She struck her foot fretfully against the splashboard. 'The small children say so earnestly. *They* touch the little stranger reverently who has just come from God's far country, and they peep about the room to see if not one white feather has dropped from the wing of the angel that brought him. On their lips the phrase means much; on all others it is a *deliberate lie*. Noticeable too,' she said, dropping in an instant from the passionate into a low, mocking tone, 'when people are married, though they should have sixty children, they throw the whole *onus* on God. When they are not, we hear nothing about God's having sent them. When there has been no legal contract between the parents, who sends the little children then? The Devil, perhaps!' she laughed her little silvery, mocking laugh. 'Odd that some men should come from hell and some from heaven, and yet all look so much alike when they get here.'

Waldo wondered at her. He had not the key to her thoughts, and did not see the string on which they were strung. She drew her cloud tighter about her.

'It must be very nice to believe in the Devil,' she said; 'I wish I did. If it would be of any use I would pray three hours night and morning on my bare knees, "God, let me believe in Satan". He is so useful to those people who do. They may be as selfish and as sensual as they please, and, between God's will and the Devil's action, always have someone to throw their sin on. But we, wretched unbelievers, we bear our own burdens; we must say, "I myself did it, *I*. Not God, not Satan; I myself!" That is the sting that strikes deep. Waldo,' she said gently, with a sudden and complete change of manner, 'I like you so much, I love you.' She rested her cheek softly against his shoulder. 'When I am with you I never know that I am a woman and you are a man; I only know that we are both things that think. Other men when I am with them, whether I love them or not, they are mere bodies to me; but you are a spirit; I like you. Look,' she said quickly, sinking back into her corner, 'what a pretty pinkness there is on all the hilltops! The sun will rise in a moment.'

Waldo lifted his eyes to look round over the circle of golden hills; and the horses, as the first sunbeams touched them, shook their heads and champed their bright bits, till the brass settings in their harness glittered again.

It was eight o'clock when they neared the farmhouse: a red-brick building, with *kraals* to the right and a small orchard to the left. Already there were signs of unusual life and bustle: one cart, a wagon, and a couple of saddles against the wall betokened the arrival of a few early guests, whose numbers would soon be largely increased. To a Dutch country wedding guests start up in numbers astonishing to one who has merely ridden through the plains of sparsely-inhabited Karoo.

As the morning advances, riders on many shades of steeds appear from all directions, and add their saddles to the long rows against the walls, shake hands, drink coffee, and stand about outside in groups to watch the arriving carts and ox-wagons, as they are unburdened of their heavy freight of massive *Tantes* and comely daughters, followed by swarms of children of all sizes, dressed in all manner of print and moleskin, who are taken care of by Hottentot, Kaffir, and half-caste nurses, whose many-shaded complexions, ranging from light yellow up to ebony black, add variety to the animated scene. Everywhere is excitement and bustle, which gradually increases as the time for the return of the wedding party approaches. Preparations for the feast are actively advancing in the kitchen; coffee is liberally handed round, and amid a profound sensation, and the firing of guns, the horse-wagon draws up, and the wedding party alight. Bride and bridegroom, with their attendants, march solemnly to the marriage chamber, where bed and box are decked out in white, with ends of ribbon and artificial flowers, and where on a row of chairs the party solemnly seat themselves. After a time bridesmaid and best man rise, and conduct in with ceremony each individual guest, to wish success and to kiss bride and bridegroom. Then the feast is set on the table, and it is almost sunset before the dishes are cleared away, and the pleasure of the day begins. Everything is removed from the great front room, and the mud floor, well rubbed with bullock's blood, glistens like polished mahogany. The female portion of the assembly flock into the side-rooms to attire themselves for the evening; and re-issue clad in white muslin, and gay with bright ribbons and brass jewellery. The dancing begins as the first tallow candles are stuck up about the walls, the music coming from a couple of fiddlers in a corner of the room. Bride and bridegroom open the ball, and the floor is soon covered with whirling couples, and everyone's spirits rise. The bridal pair mingle freely in the throng, and here and there a musical man sings vigorously as he drags his partner through the *Blue Water* or *John Speriwig*; boys shout and applaud, and the enjoyment and confusion are intense, till eleven o'clock comes. By this time the children who swarm in the side-rooms are not to be kept quiet longer, even by hunches of bread and cake; there is a general howl and wail, that rises yet higher than the scraping of fiddles, and mothers rush from their partners to knock small heads together, and cuff little nursemaids, and force the wailers down into unoccupied corners of beds, under tables, and behind boxes. In half an hour every variety of childish snore is heard on all sides, and it has become perilous to raise or set down a foot in any of the side-rooms lest a small head or hand should be crushed. Now, too, the busy feet have broken the solid coating of the floor, and a cloud of fine dust arises, that makes a yellow halo round the candles, and sets asthmatic people coughing, and grows denser, till to recognise anyone on the opposite side of the room becomes impossible, and a partner's face is seen through a yellow mist.

At twelve o'clock the bride is led to the marriage-chamber and undressed; the lights are blown out, and the bridegroom is brought to the door by the best man, who gives him the key; then the door is shut and locked, and the revels rise higher than ever. There is no thought of sleep till morning, and no unoccupied spot where sleep may be found.

It was at this stage of the proceedings on the night of *Tant* Sannie's wedding that Lyndall sat near the doorway in one of the side-rooms, to watch the dancers as they appeared and disappeared in the yellow cloud of dust. Gregory sat moodily in a corner of the large dancing-room. His little betrothed touched his arm.

'I wish you would go and ask Lyndall to dance with you,' she said; 'she must be so tired; she has sat still the whole evening.'

'I have asked her three times,' replied her lover shortly. 'I'm not going to be *her* dog, and creep to *her* feet, just to give her the pleasure of kicking me – not for you, Em, nor for anybody else.'

'Oh, I didn't know you had asked her, Greg,' said his little betrothed humbly; and she went away to pour out coffee.

Nevertheless, some time after, Gregory found he had shifted so far round the room as to be close to the door where Lyndall sat. After standing for some time he inquired whether he might not bring her a cup of coffee. She declined: but still he stood on (why should he not stand there as well as anywhere else?), and then he stepped into the bedroom.

'May I not bring you a stove, Miss Lyndall, to put your feet on?'

'Thank you.'

He sought for one, and put it under her feet.

'There is a draught from that broken window; shall I stuff something in the pane?'

'No; we want air.'

Gregory looked round, but, nothing else suggesting itself, he sat down on a box on the opposite side of the door. Lyndall sat before him, her chin resting in her hand; her eyes, steel-grey by day but black by night, looked through the doorway into the next room. After a time he thought she had entirely forgotten his proximity, and he dared to inspect the little hands and neck as he never dared when he was in momentary dread of the eyes being turned upon him. She was dressed in black, which seemed to take her yet further from the white-clad, gewgawed women about her; and the little hands were white, and the diamond ring glittered. Where had she got that ring? He bent forward a little and tried to decipher the letters, but the candle-light was too faint. When he looked up her eyes were fixed on him. She was looking at him – not, Gregory felt, as she had ever looked at him before; not as though he were a stump or a stone that chance had thrown in her way. Tonight, whether it were critically, or kindly, or unkindly he could not tell, but she looked at him, at the man, Gregory Rose, with attention. A vague elation filled him. He clenched his fist tight to think of some good idea he might express to her; but of all those profound things he had pictured himself as saying to her, when he sat alone in the daub-and-wattle house, not one came. He said at last:

'These Boer dances are very low things'; and then, as soon as it had gone from him, he thought it was not a clever remark, and wished it back.

Before Lyndall replied, Em looked in at the door.

'Oh, come,' she said; 'they are going to have the cushion-dance. I do not want to kiss any of these fellows. Take me quickly.'

She slipped her hand into Gregory's arm.

'It is so dusty, Em; do you care to dance any more?' he asked, without rising.

'Oh, I do not mind the dust, and the dancing rests me.'

But he did not move.

'I feel tired; I do not think I shall dance again,' he said.

Em withdrew her hand, and a young farmer came to the door and bore her off.

'I have often imagined,' remarked Gregory – but Lyndall had risen.

'I am tired,' she said. 'I wonder where Waldo is; he must take me home. These people will not leave off till morning, I suppose; it is three already.'

She made her way past the fiddlers, and a bench full of tired dancers, and passed out at the front door. On the *stoep* a group of men and boys were smoking, peeping in at the windows, and cracking coarse jokes. Waldo was certainly not among them, and she made her way to the carts and wagons drawn up at some distance from the homestead.

'Waldo,' she said, peering into a large cart, 'is that you? I am so dazed with the tallow candles, I can see nothing.'

He had made himself a place between the two seats. She climbed up and sat on the sloping floor in front.

'I thought I should find you here,' she said, drawing her skirt up about her shoulders. 'You must take me home presently, but not now.'

She leaned her head on the seat near to his, and they listened in silence to the fitful twanging of the fiddles as the night-wind bore it from the farmhouse, and to the ceaseless thud of the dancers, and the peals of gross laughter. She stretched out her little hand to feel for his.

'It is so nice to lie here and hear that noise,' she said. 'I like to feel that strange life beating up against me. I like to realise forms of life utterly unlike mine.' She drew a long breath. 'When my own life feels small, and I am oppressed with it, I like to crush together, and see it in a picture, in an instant, a multitude of disconnected unlike phases of human life – a mediaeval monk with his string of beads pacing the quiet orchard, and looking up from the grass at his feet to the heavy fruit-trees; little Malay boys playing naked on a shining sea-beach; a Hindu philosopher alone under his banyan tree, thinking, thinking, thinking, so that in the thought of God he may lose himself; a troop of Bacchanalians dressed in white, with crowns of vine-leaves, dancing along the Roman streets; a martyr on the night of his death looking through the narrow window to the sky, and feeling that already he has the wings that shall bear I him up' (she moved her hand dreamily over her face); 'an epicurean discoursing at a Roman bath to a knot of his disciples on the nature of happiness; a Kaffir witch-doctor seeking for herbs by moonlight, while from the huts on the hillside come the sound of dogs barking and the voices of women and children; a mother giving bread and milk to her children in little wooden basins and singing the evening song. I like to see it all; I feel it run through me – that life belongs to me; it makes my little life larger; it breaks down the narrow walls that shut me in.'

She sighed, and drew a long breath.

'Have you made any plan?' she asked him presently.

'Yes,' he said, the words coming in jets, with pauses between; 'I will take the grey mare – I will travel first – I will see the world – then I will find work.'

'What work?'

'I do not know.'

She made a little impatient movement. 'That is no plan; travel – see the world – find work! If you go into the world aimless, without a definite object, dreaming – dreaming, you will be definitely defeated, bamboozled, knocked this way and that. In the end you will stand with your beautiful life all spent, and nothing to show. They talk of genius – it is nothing but this, that a man knows what he can do best, and does it, and nothing else. Waldo,' she said, knitting her little fingers closer among his, 'I wish I could help you; I wish I could make you see that you must decide what you will be and do. It does not matter what you choose – be a farmer, businessman, artist, what you will – but know your aim, and live for that one thing. We have only one life. The secret of success is concentration; wherever there has been a great life, or a great work, that has gone before. Taste everything a little, look at everything a little; but live for one thing. Anything is possible to a man who knows his end and moves straight for it, and for it alone. I will show you what I mean,' she said, concisely; 'words are gas till you condense them into pictures.

'Suppose a woman, young, friendless as I am, the weakest thing on God's earth. But she must make her way through life. What she would be she cannot be because she is a woman; so she looks carefully at herself and the world about her, to see where her path must be made. There is no one to help her; she must help herself. She looks. These things she has – a sweet voice, rich in subtle intonations; a fair, very fair face, with a power of concentrating in itself, and giving expression to, feelings

332

that otherwise must have been dissipated in words; a rare power of entering into other lives unlike her own, and intuitively reading them aright. These qualities she has. How shall she use them? A poet, a writer, needs only the mental; what use has he for a beautiful body that registers clearly mental emotions? And the painter wants an eye for form and colour, and the musician an ear for time and tune, and the mere drudge has no need for mental gifts. But there is one art in which all she has would be used, for which they are all necessary – the delicate expressive body, the rich voice, the power of mental transposition. The actor, who absorbs and then reflects from himself other human lives, needs them all, but needs not much more. This is her end; but how to reach it? Before her are endless difficulties: seas must be crossed, poverty must be endured, loneliness, want. She must be content to wait long before she can even get her feet upon the path. If she has made blunders in the past, if she has weighted herself with a burden which she must bear to the end, she must but bear the burden bravely, and labour on. There is no use in wailing and repentance here: the next world is the place for that; this life is too short. By our errors we see deeper into life. They help us.' She waited for a while. 'If she does all this, – if she waits patiently, if she is never cast down, never despairs, never forgets her end, moves straight towards it, bending men and things most unlikely to her purpose – she must succeed at last. Men and things are plastic; they part to the right and left when one comes among them moving in a straight line to one end. I know it by my own little experience,' she said. 'Long years ago I resolved to be sent to school. It seemed a thing utterly out of my power; but I waited, I watched, I collected clothes, I wrote, took my place at the school; when all was ready I bore with my full force on the Boer woman, and she sent me at last. It was a small thing; but life is made up of small things, as a body is built up of cells. What has been done in small things can be done in large. Shall be,' she said softly.

Waldo listened. To him the words were no confession, no glimpse into the strong, proud, restless heart of the woman. They were general words with a general application. He looked up into the sparkling sky with dull eyes.

'Yes,' he said; 'but when we lie and think, and think, we see that there is nothing worth doing. The universe is so large, and man is so small – '

She shook her head quickly.

'But we must not think so far; it is madness, it is a disease. We know that no man's work is great, and stands forever. Moses is dead, and the prophets, and the books that our grandmothers fed on the mould is eating. Your poet and painter and actor, – before the shouts that applaud them have died their names grow strange, they are milestones that the world has passed. Men have set their mark on mankind forever, as they thought; but time has washed it out as it has washed out mountains and continents.' She raised herself on her elbow. 'And what, if we *could* help mankind, and leave the traces of our work upon it to the end? Mankind is only an ephemeral blossom on the tree of time; there were others before it opened; there will be others after it has fallen. Where was man in the time of the dicynodont, and when hoary monsters wallowed in the mud? Will he be found in the aeons that are to come? We are sparks, we are shadows, we are pollen, which the next wind will carry away. We are dying already; it is all a dream.

'I know that thought. When the fever of living is on us, when the desire to become, to know, to do, is driving us mad, we can use it as an anodyne, to still the fever and cool our beating pulses. But it is a poison, not a food. If we live on it, it will turn our blood to ice; we might as well be dead. We must not, Waldo; I want your life to be beautiful, to end in something. You are nobler and stronger than I,' she said; 'and as much better as one of God's great angels is better than a sinning man. Your life must go for something.'

'Yes, we will work,' he said.

She moved closer to him and lay still, his black curls touching her smooth little head.

Doss, who had lain at his master's side, climbed over the bench, and curled himself up in her lap. She drew her skirt up over him, and the three sat motionless for a long time.

'Waldo,' she said suddenly, 'they are laughing at us.'

'Who?' he asked, starting up.

'They – the stars!' she said softly. 'Do you not see? there is a little white, mocking finger pointing down at us from each one of them! We are talking of tomorrow, and tomorrow, and our hearts are so strong; we are not thinking of something that can touch us softly in the dark, and make us still forever. They are laughing at us, Waldo.'

Both sat looking upwards.

'Do you ever pray?' he asked her in a low voice.

'No.'

'I never do; but I might when I look up there. I will tell you,' he added, in a still lower voice, 'where I could pray. If there were a wall of rock on the edge of a world, and one rock stretched out far, far into space, and I stood alone upon it, alone, with stars above me, and stars below me – I would not say anything; but the feeling would be prayer.'

There was an end to their conversation after that, and Doss fell asleep on her knee. At last the night-wind grew very chilly.

'Ah,' she said, shivering, and drawing the skirt about her shoulders, 'I am cold. *Inspan* the horses, and call me when you are ready.'

She slipped down and walked towards the house, Doss stiffly following her, not pleased at being roused. At the door she met Gregory.

'I have been looking for you everywhere; may I not drive you home?' he said.

'Waldo drives me,' she replied, passing on; and it appeared to Gregory that she looked at him in the old way, without seeing him. But before she had reached the door an idea had occurred to her, for she turned.

'If you wish to drive me you may.'

Gregory went to look for Em, whom he found pouring out coffee in the back room. He put his hand quickly on her shoulder.

'You must ride with Waldo; I am going to drive your cousin home.'

'But I can't come just now, Greg; I promised *Tant* Annie Muller to look after the things while she went to rest a little.'

'Well, you can come presently, can't you? I didn't say you were to come now. I'm sick of this thing,' said Gregory, turning sharply on his heel. 'Why must I sit up the whole night because your stepmother chooses to get married?'

'Oh, it's all right, Greg, I only meant – '

But he did not hear her, and a man had come up to have his cup filled.

An hour after Waldo came in to look for her, and found her still busy at the table.

'The horses are ready,' he said; 'but if you would like to have one dance more I will wait.'

She shook her head wearily.

'No; I am quite ready. I want to go.'

And soon they were on the sandy road the buggy had travelled an hour before. Their horses, with heads close together, nodding sleepily as they walked in the starlight, you might have counted the rise and fall of their feet in the sand; and Waldo in his saddle nodded drowsily also. Only Em was awake, and watched the starlit road with wide-open eyes. At last she spoke.

'I wonder if all people feel so old, so very old, when they get to be seventeen?'

'Not older than before,' said Waldo sleepily, pulling at his bridle.

Presently she said again:

'I wish I could have been a little child always. You are good then. You are never selfish; you like everyone to have everything; but when you are grown-up there are some things you like to have all to yourself, you don't like anyone else to have any of them.'

'Yes,' said Waldo, sleepily, and she did not speak again.

When they reached the farmhouse all was dark, for Lyndall had retired as soon as they got home.

Waldo lifted Em from her saddle, and for a moment she leaned her head on his shoulder and clung to him.

'You are very tired,' he said, as he walked with her to the door; 'let me go in and light a candle for you.'

'No, thank you; it is all right,' she said. 'Goodnight, Waldo, dear.'

But when she went in she sat long alone in the dark.

CHAPTER SEVEN

Waldo Goes Out to Taste Life, and Em Stays at Home and Tastes It

At nine o'clock in the evening, packing his bundles for the next morning's start, Waldo looked up, and was surprised to see Em's yellow head peeping in at his door. It was many a month since she had been there. She said she had made him sandwiches for his journey, and she stayed a while to help him put his goods into the saddlebags.

'You can leave the old things lying about,' she said; 'I will lock the room, and keep it waiting for you to come back someday.'

To come back someday! Would the bird ever return to its cage? But he thanked her. When she went away he stood on the doorstep holding the candle till she had almost reached the house. But Em was that evening in no hurry to enter, and, instead of going in at the back door, walked with lagging footsteps round the low brick wall that ran before the house. Opposite the open window of the parlour she stopped. The little room, kept carefully closed in *Tant* Sannie's time, was well lighted by a paraffin lamp; books and work lay strewn about it, and it wore a bright, habitable aspect. Beside the lamp at the table in the corner sat Lyndall, the open letters and papers of the day's post lying scattered before her, while she perused the columns of a newspaper. At the centre table, with his arms folded on an open paper, which there was not light enough to read, sat Gregory. He was looking at her. The light from the open window fell on Em's little face under its white *kappie* as she looked in, but no one glanced that way.

'Go and fetch me a glass of water,' Lyndall said at last.

Gregory went out to find it; when he put it down at her side she merely moved her head in recognition, and he went back to his seat and his old occupation. Then Em moved slowly away from the window, and through it came in spotted, hard-winged insects, to play round the lamp, till, one by one, they stuck to its glass, and fell at the foot dead.

Ten o'clock struck. Then Lyndall rose, gathered up her papers and letters, and wished Gregory goodnight. Some time after Em entered; she had been sitting all the while on the loft ladder, and had drawn her *kappie* down very much over her face.

Gregory was piecing together the bits of an envelope when she came in.

'I thought you were never coming,' he said, turning round quickly, and throwing the fragments onto the floor. 'You know I have been shearing all day, and it is ten o'clock already.'

'I'm sorry. I did not think you would be going so soon,' she said in a low voice.

'I can't hear what you say. What makes you mumble so? Well, goodnight, Em.' He stooped down hastily to kiss her.

'I want to talk to you, Gregory.'

'Well, make haste,' he said pettishly. 'I'm awfully tired. I've been sitting here all the evening. Why couldn't you come and talk before?'

'I will not keep you long,' she answered, very steadily now. 'I think, Gregory, it would be better if you and I were never to be married.'

'Good heavens! Em, what do you mean? I thought you were so fond of me? You always *professed* to be. What on earth have you taken into your head now?'

'I think it would be better,' she said, folding her hands over each other, very much as though she were praying.

'Better, Em! What do you mean? Even a woman can't take a freak all about nothing! You must have *some* reason for it, and I'm sure I've done nothing to offend you. I wrote only today to my sister to tell her to come up next month to our wedding, and I've been as affectionate and happy as possible. Come – what's the matter?'

He put his arm half round her shoulder, very loosely.

'I think it would be better,' she answered slowly.

'Oh, well,' he said, drawing himself up, 'if you won't enter into explanations, you won't; and I'm not the man to beg and pray – not to any woman, and you know that! If you don't want to marry me I can't oblige you to, of course.'

She stood quite still before him.

'You women never *do* know your own minds for two days together; and of course you know the state of your own feelings best; but it's very strange. Have you really made up your mind, Em?'

'Yes.'

'Well, I'm very sorry. I'm sure I've not been in anything to blame. A man can't always be billing and cooing; but, as you say, if your feeling for me has changed, it's much better you shouldn't marry me. There's nothing so foolish as to marry someone you don't love; and I only wish for your happiness, I'm sure. I daresay you'll find someone can make you much happier than *I* could; the first person we love is seldom the right one. You are very young; it's quite natural you should change.'

She said nothing.

'Things often seem hard at the time, but Providence makes them turn out for the best in the end,' said Gregory. 'You'll let me kiss you, Em, just for old friendship's sake.' He stooped down. 'You must look upon me as a dear brother, as a cousin at least; as long as I am on the farm I shall always be glad to help you, Em.'

Soon after, the brown pony was cantering along the footpath to the daub-and-wattle house, and his master as he rode whistled *John Speriwig*, and the *Thorn Kloof Schottische*.

The sun had not yet touched the outstretched arms of the prickly pear upon the *kopje*, and the early cocks and hens still strutted about stiffly after the night's roost, when Waldo stood before the wagon-house saddling the grey mare. Every now and then he glanced up at the old familiar objects: they had a new aspect that morning. Even the cocks, seen in the light of parting, had a peculiar interest, and he listened with conscious attention while one crowed clear and loud as it stood on the pigsty wall. He wished good morning softly to the Kaffir woman who was coming up from the huts to light the fire. He was leaving them all to that old life, and from his height he looked down on them pityingly. So they would keep on crowing, and coming to light fires, when for him that old colourless existence was but a dream. He went into the house to say goodbye to Em, and then he walked to the door of Lyndall's room to wake her; but she was up, and standing in the doorway.

'So you are ready,' she said.

Waldo looked at her with sudden heaviness; the exhilaration died out of his heart. Her grey dressing gown hung close about her, and below its edge the little bare feet were resting on the threshold.

'I wonder when we shall meet again, Waldo? What you will be, and what I?'

'Will you write to me?' he asked of her.

'Yes; and if I should not, you can still remember, wherever you are, that you are not alone.'

'I have left Doss for you,' he said.

'Will you not miss him?'

'No; I want you to have him. He loves you better than he loves me.'

'Thank you.'

They stood quiet.

'Goodbye!' she said, putting her little hand in his, and he turned away; but when he reached the door she called to him: 'Come back! I want to kiss you.' She drew his face down to hers, and held it with both hands, and kissed it on the forehead and mouth. 'Goodbye, dear!'

When he looked back the little figure with its beautiful eyes was standing in the doorway still.

CHAPTER EIGHT

The Kopje

'Good morning!'
Em, who was in the storeroom measuring the Kaffirs' rations, looked up and saw her former lover standing betwixt her and the sunshine. For some days after that evening on which he had ridden home whistling he had shunned her. She might wish to enter into explanations, and he, Gregory Rose, was not the man for that kind of thing. If a woman had once thrown him overboard she must take the consequences, and stand by them. When, however, she showed no inclination to revert to the past, and shunned him more than he shunned her, Gregory softened.

'You must let me call you "Em" still, and be like a brother to you till I go,' he said; and Em thanked him so humbly that he wished she hadn't. It wasn't so easy after that to think himself an injured man.

On that morning he stood some time in the doorway switching his whip, and moving rather restlessly from one leg to the other.

'I think I'll just take a walk up to the camps and see how your birds are getting on. Now Waldo's gone you've no one to see after things. Nice morning, isn't it?' Then he added suddenly, 'I'll just go round to the house and get a drink of water first;' and somewhat awkwardly walked off. He might have found water in the kitchen, but he never glanced towards the buckets. In the front room a monkey and two tumblers stood on the centre table; but he merely looked round, peeped into the parlour, looked round again, and then walked out at the front door, and found himself again at the storeroom without having satisfied his thirst. 'Awfully nice morning this,' he said, trying to pose himself in a graceful and indifferent attitude against the door. 'It isn't hot and it isn't cold. It's awfully nice.'

'Yes,' said Em.

'Your cousin, now,' said Gregory, in an aimless sort of way – 'I suppose she's shut up in her room writing letters.'

' No,' said Em.

'Gone for a drive, I expect? Nice morning for a drive.'

'No.'

'Gone to see the ostriches, I suppose?'

'No.' After a little silence Em added, 'I saw her go by the *kraals* to the *kopje*.'

Gregory crossed and uncrossed his legs.

'Well, I think I'll just go and have a look about,' he said, 'and see how things are getting on before I go to the camps. Goodbye; so long.'

339

Em left for a while the bags she was folding and went to the window, the same through which, years before, Bonaparte had watched the slouching figure cross the yard. Gregory walked to the pigsty first, and contemplated the pigs for a few seconds; then turned round and stood looking fixedly at the wall of the fuel-house as though he thought it wanted repairing; then he started off suddenly with the evident intention of going to the ostrich-camps; then paused, hesitated, and finally walked off in the direction of the *kopje*.

Then Em went back to the corner, and folded more sacks.

On the other side of the *kopje* Gregory caught sight of a white tail waving among the stones, and a succession of short, frantic barks told where Doss was engaged in howling imploringly to a lizard who had crept between two stones, and who had not the slightest intention of re-sunning himself at that particular moment.

The dog's mistress sat higher up, under the shelving rock, her face bent over a volume of plays upon her knee. As Gregory mounted the stones she started violently and looked up; then resumed her book.

'I hope I am not troubling you,' said Gregory, as he reached her side. 'If I am I will go away. I just ...'

'No; you may stay.'

'I fear I startled you.'

'Yes; your step was firmer than it generally is. I thought it was that of someone else.'

'Who could it be but me?' asked Gregory, seating himself on a stone at her feet.

'Do you suppose you are the only man who would find anything to attract him to this *kopje*?'

'Oh, no,' said Gregory.

He was not going to argue that point with her, nor any other; but no old Boer was likely to take the trouble of climbing the *kopje*, and who else was there?

She continued the study of her book.

'Miss Lyndall,' he said at last, 'I don't know why it is you never talk to me.'

'We had a long conversation yesterday,' she said without looking up.

'Yes; but you ask me questions about sheep and oxen. I don't call that talking. You used to talk to Waldo, now,' he said, in an aggrieved tone of voice. 'I've heard you when I came in, and then you've just left off. You treated me like that from the first day; and you couldn't tell from just looking at me that I couldn't talk about the things you like. I'm sure I know as much about such things as Waldo does,' said Gregory, in exceeding bitterness of spirit.

'I do not know which things you refer to. If you will enlighten me I am quite prepared to speak of them,' she said, reading as she spoke.

'Oh, you never used to ask Waldo like that,' said Gregory, in a more sorely aggrieved tone than ever. 'You used just to begin.'

'Well, let me see,' she said, closing her book and folding her hands on it. 'There at the foot of the *kopje* goes a Kaffir; he has nothing on but a blanket; he is a splendid fellow – six feet high, with a magnificent pair of legs. In his leather bag he is going to fetch his rations, and I suppose to kick his wife with his beautiful legs when he gets home. He has a right to; he bought her for two oxen. There is a lean dog going after him, to whom I suppose he never gives more than a bone from which he has sucked the marrow; but his dog loves him, as his wife does. There is something of the master about him in spite of his blackness and wool. See how he brandishes his stick and holds up his head!'

'Oh, but aren't you making fun?' said Gregory, looking doubtfully from her to the Kaffir herd, who rounded the *kopje*.

'No; I am very serious. He is the most interesting and intelligent thing I can see just now, except, perhaps, Doss. He is profoundly suggestive. Will his race melt away in the heat of a collision with a higher? Are the men of the future to see his bones only in museums – a vestige of one link that spanned between the dog and the white man? He wakes thoughts that run far out into the future and back into the past.'

Gregory was not quite sure how to take these remarks. Being about a Kaffir, they appeared to be of the nature of a joke; but, being seriously spoken, they appeared earnest: so he half laughed and half not, to be on the safe side.

'I've often thought so myself. It's funny we should both think the same; I knew we should if once we talked. But there are other things – love, now,' he added. 'I wonder if we would think alike about that. I wrote an essay on love once; the master said it was the best I ever wrote, and I can remember the first sentence still – "Love is something that you feel in your heart."'

'That was a trenchant remark. Can't you remember any more?'

'No,' said Gregory, regretfully; 'I've forgotten the rest. But tell me what do you think about love?'

A look, half of abstraction, half amusement, played on her lips.

'I don't know much about love,' she said, 'and I do not like to talk of things I do not understand; but I have heard two opinions. Some say the Devil carried the seed from hell, and planted it on the earth to plague men and make them sin; and some say, that when all the plants in the garden of Eden were pulled up by the roots, one bush that the angels had planted was left growing, and it spread its seed over the whole earth, and its name is love. I do not know which is right – perhaps both. There are different species that go under the same name. There is a love, that begins in the head, and goes down to the heart, and grows slowly; but it lasts till death, and asks less than it gives. There is another love, that blots out wisdom, that is sweet with the sweetness of life and bitter with the bitterness of death, lasting for an hour; but it is worth having lived a whole life for that hour. I cannot tell: perhaps the old monks were right when they tried to root love out; perhaps the poets are right when they try to water it. It is a blood-red flower, with the colour of sin; but there is always the scent of a god about it.'

Gregory would have made a remark; but she said, without noticing:

'There are as many kinds of loves as there are flowers; everlastings that never wither; speedwells that wait for the wind to fan them out of life; blood-red mountain-lilies that pour their voluptuous sweetness out for one day, and lie in the dust at night. There is no flower has the charm of all – the speedwell's purity, the everlasting's strength, the mountain-lily's warmth; but who knows whether there is no love that holds all – friendship, passion, worship?

'Such a love,' she said, in her sweetest voice, 'will fall on the surface of strong, cold, selfish life as the sunlight falls on a torpid winter world; there, where the trees are bare, and the ground frozen, till it rings to the step like iron, and the water is solid, and the air is sharp as a two-edged knife, that cuts the unwary. But, when its sun shines on it, through its whole dead crust a throbbing yearning wakes: the trees feel him, and every knot and bud swell, aching to open to him. The brown seeds, who have slept deep under the ground, feel him, and he gives them strength, till they break through the frozen earth, and lift two tiny, trembling green hands in love to him. And he touches the water, till down to its depths it feels him and melts, and it flows, and the things, strange sweet things that were locked up in it; it sings as it runs, for love of him. Each plant tries to bear at least one fragrant little flower for him; and the world that was dead lives, and the heart that was dead and self-centred throbs, with an upward, outward yearning, and it has become that which it seemed impossible ever to become. There, does that satisfy you?' she asked, looking down at Gregory. 'Is that how you like me to talk?'

'Oh, yes,' said Gregory, 'that is what I have already thought. We have the same thoughts about everything. How strange!'

'Very,' said Lyndall, working with her little toe at a stone in the ground before her.

Gregory felt he must sustain the conversation. The only thing he could think of was to recite a piece of poetry. He knew he had learnt many about love; but the only thing that would come into his mind now was the *Battle of Hohenlinden* and *Not a drum was heard*, neither of which seemed to bear directly on the subject on hand.

But unexpected relief came to him from Doss, who, too deeply lost in contemplation of his crevice, was surprised by the sudden descent of the stone Lyndall's foot had loosened, which, rolling against his little front paw, carried away a piece of white skin. Doss stood on three legs, holding up the paw with an expression of extreme self-commiseration; he then proceeded to hop slowly upwards in search of sympathy.

'You have hurt that dog,' said Gregory.

'Have I?' she replied indifferently, and re-opened the book, as though to resume her study of the play.

'He's a nasty, snappish little cur!' said Gregory, calculating from her manner that the remark would be endorsed. 'He snapped at my horse's tail yesterday, and nearly made it throw me. I wonder his master didn't take him, instead of leaving him here to be a nuisance to all of us?'

Lyndall seemed absorbed in her play; but he ventured another remark.

'Do you think now, Miss Lyndall, that he'll ever have anything in the world, – that German, I mean, – money enough to support a wife on, and all that sort of thing? *I* don't. He's what *I* call a soft.'

She was spreading her skirt out softly with her left hand for the dog to lie down on it.

'I think I *should* be rather astonished if he ever became a respectable member of society,' she said. 'I don't expect to see him the possessor of bank-shares, the chairman of a divisional council, and the father of a large family; wearing a black hat, and going to church twice on a Sunday. He would rather astonish me if he came to such an end.'

'Yes; I don't expect *anything* of him either,' said Gregory zealously.

'Well, I don't know,' said Lyndall; 'there are some small things I rather look to him for. If he were to invent wings, or carve a statue that one might look at for half an hour without wanting to look at something else, I should not be surprised. He may do some little thing of that kind perhaps, when he has done fermenting, and the sediment has all gone to the bottom.'

Gregory felt that what she said was not wholly intended as blame.

'Well, I don't know,' he said sulkily; 'to me he looks like a fool. To walk about always in that dead-and-alive sort of way, muttering to himself like an old Kaffir witchdoctor! He works hard enough, but it's always as though he didn't know what he was doing. You don't know how he looks to a person who sees him for the first time.'

Lyndall was softly touching the little sore foot as she read, and Doss, to show he liked it, licked her hand.

'But, Miss Lyndall,' persisted Gregory, 'what do you really think of him?'

'I think,' said Lyndall, 'that he is like a thorn-tree, which grows up very quietly, without anyone's caring for it, and one day suddenly breaks out into yellow blossoms.'

'And what do you think I am like?' asked Gregory hopefully.

Lyndall looked up from her book.

'Like a little tin duck floating on a dish of water, that comes after a piece of bread stuck on a needle, and the more the needle pricks it the more it comes on.'

'Oh, you *are* making fun of me now, you really are!' said Gregory, feeling wretched. 'You *are* making fun, aren't you, now?'

'Partly. It is always diverting to make comparisons.'

'Yes; but you don't compare me to anything nice, and you do other people. What is Em like, now?'

'The accompaniment of a song. She fills up the gaps in other people's lives, and is always number two; but I think she is like many accompaniments – a great deal better than the song she is to accompany.'

'She is not half so good as you are?' said Gregory, with a burst of uncontrollable ardour.

'She is so much better than I, that her little finger has more goodness in it than my whole body. I hope you may not live to find out the truth of that fact.'

'You are like an angel,' he said, the blood rushing to his head and face.

'Yes, probably; angels are of many orders.'

'You are the one being that I love!' said Gregory, quivering; 'I thought I loved before, but I know now! Do not be angry with me. I know you could never like me; but if I might but always be near you to serve you, I would be utterly, utterly happy. I would ask nothing in return! If you could only take everything I have and use it; I want nothing but to be of use to you.'

She looked at him for a few moments. 'How do you know,' she said slowly, 'that you could not do something to serve me? You could serve me by giving me your name.'

He started, and turned his burning face to her. 'You are very cruel; you are ridiculing me,' he said.

'No, I am not, Gregory. What I am saying is plain, matter-of-fact business. If you are willing to give me your name within three weeks' time, I am willing to marry you; if not, well. I want nothing more than your name. That is a clear proposal, is it not?'

He looked up. Was it contempt, loathing, pity, that moved in the eyes above? He could not tell; but he stooped over the little foot and kissed it.

She smiled.

'Do you really mean it?' he whispered.

'Yes. You wish to serve me, and to have nothing in return! – You shall have what you wish.' She held out her fingers for Doss to lick. 'Do you see this dog?' He licks my hand because I love him; and I allow him to. Where I do not love I do not allow it. I believe you love me; I too could love so, that to lie under the foot of the thing I loved would be more heaven than to lie in the breast of another. Come! Let us go. Carry the dog,' she added; 'he will not bite you if I put him in your arms. So – do not let his foot hang down.'

They descended the *kopje*. At the bottom he whispered:

'Would you not take my arm, the path is very rough?'

She rested her fingers lightly on it.

'I may yet change my mind about marrying you before the time comes. It is very likely. Mark you!' she said, turning round on him; 'I remember your words: – *You will give everything, and expect nothing.* The knowledge that you are serving me is to be your reward; and you will have that. You will serve me, and greatly. The reasons I have for marrying you I need not inform you of now; you will probably discover some of them before long.'

'I only want to be of some use to you,' he said.

It seemed to Gregory that there were pulses in the soles of his feet, and the ground shimmered as on a summer's day. They walked round the foot of the *kopje*, and past the Kaffir huts. An old Kaffir maid knelt at the door of one grinding *mielies*. That she should see him walking so made his heart beat so fast that the hand on his arm felt its pulsation. It seemed that she must envy him.

Just then Em looked out again at the back window and saw them coming. She cried bitterly all the while she sorted the skins.

But that night when Lyndall had blown her candle out, and half turned round to sleep, the door of Em's bedroom opened.

'I want to say goodnight to you, Lyndall,' she said, coming to the bedside and kneeling down.

'I thought you were asleep,' Lyndall replied.

'Yes, I have been asleep; but I had such a vivid dream,' she said, holding the other's hands, 'and that awoke me. I never had so vivid a dream before.

'It seemed I was a little girl again, and I came somewhere into a large room. On a bed in the corner there was something lying dressed in white, and its little eyes were shut, and its little face was like wax. I thought it was a doll, and I ran forward to take it; but someone held up her finger and said, "Hush! it is a little dead baby." And I said, "Oh, I must go and call Lyndall, that she may look at it also."

'And they put their faces close down to my ear and whispered, "It is Lyndall's baby."

'And I said, "She cannot be grown up yet; she is only a little girl! Where is she?" And I went to look for you, but I could not find you.

'And when I came to some people who were dressed in black, I asked them where you were, and they looked down at their black clothes, and shook their heads, and said nothing; and I could not find you anywhere. And then I awoke.

'Lyndall,' she said, putting her face down upon the hands she held, 'it made me think about that time when we were little girls and used to play together, when I loved you better than anything else in the world. It isn't anyone's fault that they love you, they can't help it. And it isn't your fault; you don't make them love you. I know it.'

'Thank you, dear,' Lyndall said. 'It is nice to be loved, but it would be better to be good.'

Then they wished goodnight, and Em went back to her room. Long after, Lyndall lay in the dark thinking, thinking; and as she turned round wearily to sleep she muttered:

'There are some wiser in their sleeping than in their waking.'

CHAPTER NINE

Lyndall's Stranger

A fire is burning in the unused hearth of the cabin. The fuel blazes up, and lights the black rafters, and warms the faded red lions on the quilt, and fills the little room with a glow of warmth and light made brighter by contrast, for outside the night is chill and misty.

Before the open fireplace sits a stranger, his tall slight figure reposing in the broken armchair, his keen blue eyes studying the fire from beneath delicately pencilled, drooping eyelids. One white hand plays thoughtfully with a heavy flaxen moustache; yet once he starts, and for an instant the languid lids raise themselves: there is a keen, intent look upon the face as he listens for something. Then he leans back in his chair, fills his glass from the silver flask in his bag, and resumes his old posture.

Presently the door opens noiselessly. It is Lyndall, followed by Doss. Quietly as she enters, he hears her and turns.

'I thought you were not coming.'

'I waited till all had gone to bed. I could not come before.'

She removed the shawl that enveloped her, and the stranger rose to offer her his chair; but she took her seat on a low pile of sacks before the window.

'I hardly see why I should be outlawed after this fashion,' he said, re-seating himself and drawing his chair a little nearer to her; 'these are hardly the quarters one expects to find after travelling a hundred miles in answer to an invitation.'

'I said, "Come if you wish."'

'And I did wish. You give me a cold reception.'

'I could not take you to the house. Questions would be asked which I could not answer without prevarication.'

'Your conscience is growing to have a certain virgin tenderness,' he said, in a low, melodious voice.

'I have no conscience. I spoke one deliberate lie this evening. I said the man who had come looked rough, we had best not have him in the house; therefore I brought him here. It was a deliberate lie, and I hate lies. I tell them if I must, but they hurt me.'

'Well, you do not tell lies to yourself, at all events. You are candid, so far.'

She interrupted him.

'You got my short letter?'

'Yes; that is why I came. You sent a very foolish reply, you must take it back. Who is this fellow you talk of marrying?'

'A young farmer.'

'Lives here?'

'Yes; he has gone to town to get things for our wedding.'

'What kind of a fellow is he?'

'A fool.'

'And you would rather marry him than me?'

'Yes; because you are not one.'

'That is a novel reason for refusing to marry a man,' he said, leaning his elbow on the table, and watching her keenly.

'It is a wise one,' she said shortly. 'If I marry him I shall shake him off my hand when it suits me. If I remained with him for twelve months he would never have dared to kiss my hand. As far as I wish he should come, he comes, and no further. Would you ask me what you might and what you might not do?'

Her companion raised the moustache with a caressing movement from his lip and smiled. It was not a question that stood in need of any answer.

'Why do you wish to enter on this semblance of marriage?'

'Because there is only one point on which I have a conscience. I have told you so.'

'Then why not marry me?'

'Because if once you have me you would hold me fast. I shall never be free again.' She drew a long low breath.

'What have you done with the ring I gave you?' he said.

'Sometimes I wear it; then I take it off and wish to throw it into the fire; the next day I put it on again, and sometimes I kiss it.'

'So you do love me a little?'

'If you were not something more to me than any other man in the world, do you think – ' she paused. 'I love you when I see you; but when you are away from me I hate you.'

'Then I fear I must be singularly invisible at the present moment,' he said. 'Possibly if you were to look less fixedly into the fire you might perceive me.'

He moved his chair slightly so as to come between her and the firelight. She raised her eyes to his face.

'If you do love me,' he asked her, 'why will you not marry me?'

'Because, if I had been married to you for a year, I should have come to my senses, and seen that your hands and your voice are like the hands and the voice of any other man. I cannot quite see that now. But it is all madness. You call into activity one part of my nature; there is a higher part that you know nothing of, that you never touch. If I married you, afterwards it would arise and assert itself, and I should hate you always, as I do now sometimes.'

'I like you when you grow metaphysical and analytical,' he said, leaning his face upon his hand. 'Go a little further in your analysis; say, "I love you with the right ventricle of my heart, but not the left, and with the left auricle of my heart, but not the right; and, this being the case, my affection for you is not of a duly elevated, intellectual, and spiritual nature." I like you when you get philosophical.'

She looked quietly at him; he was trying to turn her own weapons against her.

'You are acting foolishly, Lyndall,' he said, suddenly changing his manner, and speaking earnestly, 'most foolishly. You are acting like a little child; I am surprised at you. It is all very well to have ideals and theories; but you know as well as anyone can that they must not be carried into the practical world. I love you. I do not pretend that it is in any high, superhuman sense; I do not say that I should like you as well if you were ugly and deformed, or that I should continue to prize you whatever your treatment of me might be, or to love you though you were a spirit without any body at all. That is sentimentality for beardless boys. Everyone not a mere child (and you are not a child, except in years) knows what love between a man and a woman means. I love you with that love. I should not have believed it possible that I could have brought myself twice to ask of any woman to be my wife, more especially one without wealth, without position, and who – '

'Yes – go on. Do not grow sorry for me. Say what you were going to – "who has put herself into my power, and who has lost the right of meeting me on equal terms." Say what you think. At least we two may speak the truth to one another.'

Then she added after a pause:

'I believe you do love me, as much as you possibly could love anything; and I believe that when you ask me to marry you, you are performing the most generous act you ever have performed in the course of your life, or ever will; but, at the same time, if I had required your generosity, it would not have been shown me. If, when I got your letter a month ago, hinting at your willingness to marry me, I had at once written, imploring you to come, you would have read the letter. "Poor little Devil!" you would have said, and torn it up. The next week you would have sailed for Europe, and have sent me a cheque for a hundred and fifty pounds (which I would have thrown in the fire), and I would have heard no more of you.' The stranger smiled. 'But because I declined your proposal, and wrote that in three weeks I should be married to another, then what you call love woke up. Your man's love is a child's love for butterflies. You follow till you have the thing, and break it. If you have broken one wing, and the thing flies still, then you love it more than ever, and follow till you break both; then you are satisfied when it lies still on the ground.'

'You are profoundly wise in the ways of the world; you have seen far into life,' he said.

He might as well have sneered at the firelight.

'I have seen enough to tell me that you love me because you cannot bear to be resisted, and want to master me. You liked me at first because I treated you and all men with indifference. You resolved to have me because I seemed unattainable. That is all your love means.'

He felt a strong inclination to stoop down and kiss the little lips that defied him; but he restrained himself. He said quietly, 'And you loved me – ?'

'Because you are strong. You are the first man I ever was afraid of. And' – a dreamy look came into her face – 'because I like to experience, I like to try. You don't understand that.'

He smiled.

'Well, since you will not marry me, may I inquire what your intentions are, the plan you wrote of. You asked me to come and hear it, and I have come.'

'I said, "Come if you wish". – If you agree to it, well; if not, I marry on Monday.'

'Well?'

She was still looking beyond him at the fire. 'I cannot marry you,' she said slowly, 'because I cannot be tied; but, if you wish, you may take me away with you, and take care of me; then when we do not love any more we can say goodbye. I will not go down country,' she added; 'I will not go to Europe. You must take me to the Transvaal. That is out of the world. People we meet there we need not see again in our future lives.'

'Oh, my darling,' he said, bending tenderly, and holding his hand out to her, 'why will you not give yourself entirely to me? One day you will desert me and go to another.'

She shook her head without looking at him.

'No, life is too long. But I will go with you.'

'When?'

'Tomorrow. I have told them that before daylight I go to the next farm. I will write from the town and tell them the facts. I do not want them to trouble me; I want to shake myself free of these old surroundings; I want them to lose sight of me. You can understand that is necessary for me.'

He seemed lost in consideration; then he said:

'It is better to have you on those conditions than not at all. If you *will* have it, let it be so.'

He sat looking at her. On her face was the weary look that rested there so often now when she sat alone. Two months had not passed since they parted; but the time had set its mark on her. He looked at her carefully, from the brown, smooth head to the little crossed feet on the floor. A worn look had grown over the little face, and it made its charm for him stronger. For pain and time, which trace deep lines and write a story on a human face, have a strangely different effect on one face and another. The face that is only fair, even very fair, they mar and flaw; but to the face whose beauty is the harmony between that which speaks from within and the form through which it speaks, power is added by all that causes the outer man to bear more deeply the impress of the inner. The pretty woman fades with the roses on her cheeks, and the girlhood that lasts an hour; the beautiful woman finds her fullness of bloom only when a past has written itself on her, and her power is then most irresistible when it seems going.

From under their half-closed lids the keen eyes looked down at her. Her shoulders were bent; for a moment the little figure had forgotten its queenly bearing, and drooped wearily; the wide dark eyes watched the fire very softly.

It certainly was not in her power to resist him, nor any strength in her that made his own at that moment grow soft as he looked at her.

He touched one little hand that rested on her knee.

'Poor little thing!' he said; 'you are only a child.'

She did not draw her hand away from his, and looked up at him.

'You are very tired?'

'Yes.'

She looked into his eyes as a little child might whom a long day's play had saddened.

He lifted her gently up and sat her on his knee.

'Poor little thing!' he said.

She turned her face to his shoulder, and buried it against his neck; he wound his strong arm about her, and held her close to him. When she had sat for a long while, he drew with his hand the face down, and held it against his arm. He kissed it, and then put it back in its old resting place.

'Don't you want to talk to me?'

'No.'

'Have you forgotten the night in the avenue?'

He could feel that she shook her head.

'Do you want to be quiet now?'

'Yes.'

They sat quite still, excepting that only sometimes he raised her fingers softly to his mouth.

Doss, who had been asleep in the corner, waking suddenly, planted himself before them, his wiry legs moving nervously, his yellow eyes filled with anxiety. He was not at all sure that she was not being retained in her present position against her will, and was not a little relieved when she sat up and held out her hand for the shawl.

'I must go,' she said.

The stranger wrapped the shawl very carefully about her.

'Keep it close around your face, Lyndall; it is very damp outside. Shall I walk with you to the house?'

'No. Lie down and rest; I will come and wake you at three o'clock.'

She lifted her face that he might kiss it, and, when he had kissed it once, she still held it that he might kiss it again. Then he let her out. He had seated himself at the fireplace, when she reopened the door.

'Have you forgotten anything?'

'No.'

She gave one long, lingering look at the old room. When she was gone, and the door shut, the stranger filled his glass, and sat at the table sipping it thoughtfully.

The night outside was misty and damp; the faint moonlight, trying to force its way through the thick air, made darkly visible the outlines of the buildings. The stones and walls were moist, and now and then a drop, slowly collecting, fell from the eaves to the ground. Doss, not liking the change from the cabin's warmth, ran quickly to the kitchen doorstep; but his mistress walked slowly past him, and took her way up the winding footpath that ran beside the stone wall of the camps. When she came to the end of the last camp, she threaded her way among the stones and bushes till she reached the German's grave. Why she had come there she hardly knew; she stood looking down. Suddenly she bent and put one hand on the face of a wet stone.

'I shall never come to you again,' she said. Then she knelt on the ground, and leaned her face upon the stones.

'Dear old man, good old man, I am so tired!' she said (for we will come to the dead to tell secrets we would never have told to the living). 'I am so tired. There is light, there is warmth,' she wailed; 'why am I alone, so hard, so cold? I am so weary of myself! It is eating my soul to its core – self, self, self! I cannot bear this life! I cannot breathe, I cannot live! Will nothing free me from myself?' She pressed her cheek against the wooden post. 'I want to love! I want something great and pure to lift me to itself! Dear old man, I cannot bear it any more! I am so cold, so hard, so hard; will no one help me?'

The water gathered slowly on her shawl, and fell onto the wet stones, but she lay there crying bitterly. For so the living soul will cry to the dead, and the creature to its God; and of all this crying there comes nothing. The lifting up of the hands brings no salvation; redemption is from within, and neither from God nor man: it is wrought out by the soul itself, with suffering and through time.

Doss, on the kitchen doorstep, shivered, and wondered where his mistress stayed so long; and once, sitting sadly there in the damp, he had dropped asleep, and dreamed that old Otto gave him a piece of bread, and patted him on the head, and when he woke his teeth chattered, and he moved to another stone to see if it was drier. At last he heard his mistress's step, and they went into the house together. She lit a candle, and walked to the Boer woman's bedroom. On a nail under the lady in pink hung the key of the wardrobe. She took it down and opened the great press. From a little drawer she took fifty pounds (all she had in the world), relocked the door, and turned to hang up the key. Then she paused, hesitated. The marks of tears were still on her face, but she smiled.

'Fifty pounds for a lover! A noble reward!' she said, and opened the wardrobe and returned the notes to the drawer, where Em might find them.

Once in her own room, she arranged the few articles she intended to take tomorrow, burnt her old letters, and then went back to the front room to look at the time. There were two hours yet before she must call him. She sat down at the dressing table to wait, and leaned her elbows on it, and buried her face in her hands. The glass reflected the little brown head with its even parting, and the tiny hands on which it rested.

'One day I will love something utterly, and then I will be better,' she said once. Presently she looked up. The large dark eyes from the glass looked back at her. She looked deep into them.

'We are all alone, you and I,' she whispered; 'no one helps us, no one understands us; but we will help ourselves.' The eyes looked back at her. There was a world of assurance in their still depths. So they had looked at her ever since she could remember, when it was but a small child's face above a blue pinafore. 'We shall never be quite alone, you and I,' she said; 'we shall always be together, as we were when we were little.'

The beautiful eyes looked into the depths of her soul.

'We are not afraid; we will help ourselves!' she said. She stretched out her hand and pressed it over them on the glass. 'Dear eyes! We will never be quite alone till they part us; – till then!'

CHAPTER TEN

Gregory Rose Has an Idea

Gregory Rose was in the loft putting it neat. Outside the rain poured; a six months' drought had broken, and the thirsty plain was drenched with water. What it could not swallow ran off in mad rivulets to the great *sloot* that now foamed like an angry river across the flat. Even the little furrow between the farmhouse and the *kraals* was now a stream, knee-deep, which almost bore away the Kaffir women who crossed it. It had rained for twenty-four hours, and still the rain poured on. The fowls had collected – a melancholy crowd – in and about the wagon-house, and the solitary gander, who alone had survived the six months' want of water, walked hither and thither, printing his webbed footmarks on the mud, to have them washed out the next instant by the pelting rain, which at eleven o'clock still beat on the walls and roof with unabated ardour.

Gregory, as he worked in the loft, took no notice of it beyond stuffing a sack into the broken pane to keep it out; and, in spite of the pelt and patter, Em's clear voice might be heard through the open trapdoor from the dining room, where she sat at work, singing the *Blue Water* –

> And take me away,
> And take me away,
> And take me away,
> To the Blue Water

– that quaint, childish song of the people, that has a world of sweetness, and sad, vague yearning when sung over and over dreamily by a woman's voice as she sits alone at her work. But Gregory heard neither that nor yet the loud laughter of the Kaffir maids, that every now and again broke through from the kitchen, where they joked and worked. Of late Gregory had grown strangely impervious to the sounds and sights about him. His lease had run out, but Em had said, 'Do not renew it; I need one to help me; just stay on.' And she had added, 'You must not remain in your own little house; live with me; you can look after my ostriches better so.'

And Gregory did not thank her. What difference did it make to him, paying rent or not, living there or not? It was all one. But yet he came. Em wished that he would still sometimes talk of the strength and master-right of man; but Gregory was as one smitten on the cheekbone. She might do what she pleased, he would find no fault, had no word to say. He had forgotten that it is man's right to rule. On that rainy morning he had lighted his pipe at the kitchen fire, and when breakfast was over stood in the front door watching the water rush down the road till the pipe died out in his mouth. Em saw she must do something for him, and found him a large calico duster. He had sometimes talked of putting the loft neat, and today she could find nothing else for him to do. So she had the ladder put to the trapdoor that he need not go out in the wet, and Gregory with the broom and duster mounted to the loft. Once at work he worked hard. He dusted down the very rafters, and cleaned the broken candle-moulds and bent forks that had stuck in the thatch for twenty years. He placed the black bottles neatly in rows on an old box in the corner, and piled the skins on one another, and sorted the rubbish in all the boxes; and at eleven o'clock his work was almost done. He seated himself on the packing case which had once held Waldo's books, and proceeded to examine the contents of another which he had not yet looked at. It was carelessly nailed down. He loosened one plank, and began to lift out various articles of female attire – old-fashioned caps, aprons, dresses with long pointed bodies such as he remembered to have seen his mother wear when he was a little child. He shook them out carefully to see there were no moths, and then sat down to fold them up again one by one. They had belonged to Em's mother, and the box, as packed at her death, had stood untouched and forgotten these long years. She must have been a tall woman, that mother of Em's, for when he stood up to shake out a dress the neck was on a level with his, and the skirt touched the ground. Gregory laid a night-cap out on his knee, and began rolling up the strings; but presently his fingers moved slower and slower, then his chin rested on his breast, and finally the imploring blue eyes were fixed on the frill abstractedly. When Em's voice called to him from the foot of the ladder he started, and threw the night-cap behind him.

She was only come to tell him that his cup of soup was ready; and, when he could hear that she was gone, he picked up the night-cap again, and a great brown sun-*kappie* – just such a *kappie* and such a dress as one of those he remembered to have seen a sister-of-mercy wear. Gregory's mind was very full of thought. He took down a fragment of an old looking-glass from behind a beam, and put the *kappie* on. His beard looked somewhat grotesque under it; he put up his hand to hide it – that was better. The blue eyes looked out with the mild gentleness that became eyes looking out from under a *kappie*. Next he took the brown dress, and, looking round furtively, slipped it over his head. He had just got his arms in the sleeves, and was trying to hook up the back, when an increase in the patter of the rain at the window made him drag it off hastily. When he perceived there was no one coming he tumbled the things back into the box, and, covering it carefully, went down the ladder.

Em was still at her work, trying to adjust a new needle in the machine. Gregory drank his soup, and then sat before her, an awful and mysterious look in his eyes.

'I am going to town tomorrow,' he said.

'I'm almost afraid you won't be able to go,' said Em, who was intent on her needle; 'I don't think it is going to leave off today.'

'I am going,' said Gregory. Em looked up.

'But the *sloots* are as full as rivers – you cannot go. We can wait for the post,' she said.

'I am not going for the post,' said Gregory impressively.

Em looked for an explanation; none came.

'When will you be back?'

'I am not coming back.'

'Are you going to your friends?'

Gregory waited, then caught her by the wrist.

'Look here, Em,' he said between his teeth, 'I can't stand it any more. I am going to her.'

Since that day, when he had come home and found Lyndall gone, he had never talked of her; but Em knew who it was who needed to be spoken of by no name.

She said, when he had released her hand: 'But you do not know where she is?'

'Yes, I do. She was in Bloemfontein when I heard last. I will go there, and I will find out where she went then, and then, and then! I will have her.'

Em turned the wheel quickly, and the ill-adjusted needle sprang into twenty fragments.

'Gregory,' she said, 'she does not want us; she told us so clearly in the letter she wrote.' A flush rose on her face as she spoke. 'It will only be pain to you, Gregory. Will she like to have you near her?'

There was an answer he might have made, but it was his secret, and he did not choose to share it. He said only:

'I am going.'

'Will you be gone long, Gregory?'

'I do not know; perhaps I shall never come back. Do what you please with my things. I cannot stay here!'

He rose from his seat.

'People say, forget, forget!' he cried, pacing the room. 'They are mad! They are fools! Do they say so to men who are dying of thirst – forget, forget? Why is it only to us they say so? It is a lie to say that time makes it easy; it is afterwards, afterwards that it eats in at your heart!

'All these months,' he cried bitterly, 'I have lived here quietly, day after day, as if I cared for what I ate, and what I drank, and what I did! I care for nothing! I cannot bear it! I will not! Forget! Forget!' ejaculated Gregory. 'You can forget all the world, but you cannot forget yourself. When one thing is more to you than yourself, how are you to forget it?

'I read,' he said – 'yes; and then I come to a word she used, and it is all back with me again! I go to count my sheep, and I see her face before me, and I stand and let the sheep run by. I look at you, and in your smile, a something at the corner of your lips, I see her. How can I forget her when, whenever I turn, she is there, and not there? I cannot, I will not, live where I do not see her.

'I know what you think,' he said, turning upon Em. 'You think I am mad; you think I am going to see whether she will not like me! I am not so foolish. I should have known at first she never could suffer me. Who am I, what am I, that she should look at me? It was right that she left me; right that she should not look at me. If anyone says it is not, it is a lie! I am not going to speak to her,' he added – 'only to see her; only to stand sometimes in a place where she has stood before.'

CHAPTER ELEVEN

An Unfinished Letter

Gregory Rose had been gone seven months. Em sat alone on a white sheepskin before the fire.

The August night wind, weird and shrill, howled round the chimneys and through the crannies, and in walls and doors, and uttered a long low cry as it forced its way among the clefts or the stones on the *kopje*. It was a wild night. The prickly pear tree, stiff and upright as it held its arms, felt the wind's might, and knocked its flat leaves heavily together, till great branches broke off. The Kaffirs, as they slept in their straw huts, whispered one to another that before morning there would not be an armful of thatch left on the roofs; and the beams of the wagon-house creaked and groaned as if it were heavy work to resist the importunity of the wind.

Em had not gone to bed. Who could sleep on a night like this? So in the dining room she had lighted a fire, and sat on the ground before it, turning the roaster-cakes that lay on the coals to bake. It would save work in the morning; and she blew out the light because the wind through the window-chinks made it flicker and run; and she sat singing to herself as she watched the cakes. They lay at one end of the wide hearth on a bed of coals, and at the other end a fire burnt up steadily, casting its amber glow over Em's light hair and black dress with the ruffle of crape about the neck, and over the white curls of the sheepskin on which she sat.

Louder and more fiercely yet howled the storm; but Em sang on, and heard nothing but the words of her song, and heard them only faintly, as something restful. It was an old childish song she had often heard her mother sing long ago:

> Where the reeds dance by the river,
> Where the willow's song is said,
> On the face of the morning water,
> Is reflected a white flower's head.

She folded her hands and sang the next verse dreamily:

> Where the reeds shake by the river,
> Where the moonlight's sheen is shed,
> On the face of the sleeping water,
> Two leaves of a white flower float dead.
> Dead, Dead, Dead!

She echoed the refrain softly till it died away, and then repeated it. It was as if, unknown to herself, it harmonised with the pictures and thoughts that sat with her there alone in the firelight. She turned the cakes over, while the wind hurled down a row of bricks from the gable, and made the walls tremble.

Presently she paused and listened; there was a sound as of something knocking at the back-doorway. But the wind had raised its level higher, and she went on with her work. At last the sound was repeated. Then she rose, lit the candle at the fire, and went to see. Only to satisfy herself, she said, that nothing could be out on such a night.

She opened the door a little way, and held the light behind her to defend it from the wind. The figure of a tall man stood there, and before she could speak he had pushed his way in, and was forcing the door to close behind him.

'Waldo!' she cried in astonishment.

He had been gone more than a year and a half.

'You did not expect to see me,' he answered, as he turned towards her; 'I should have slept in the out-house, and not troubled you tonight; but through the shutter I saw glimmerings of a light.'

'Come in to the fire,' she said; 'it is a terrific night for any creature to be out. Shall we not go and fetch your things in first?' she added.

'I have nothing but this,' he said, motioning to the little bundle in his hand.

'Your horse?'

'Is dead.'

He sat down on the bench before the fire.

'The cakes are almost ready,' she said; 'I will get you something to eat. Where have you been wandering all this while?'

'Up and down, up and down,' he answered wearily; 'and now the whim has seized me to come back here. Em,' he said, putting his hand on her arm as she passed him, 'have you heard from Lyndall lately?'

'Yes,' said Em, turning quickly from him.

'Where is she? I had one letter from her, but that is almost a year ago now – just when she left. Where is she?'

'In the Transvaal. I will go and get you some supper; we can talk afterwards.'

'Can you give me her exact address? I want to write to her.'

But Em had gone into the next room.

When food was on the table she knelt down before the fire, turning the cakes, babbling restlessly, eagerly, now of this, now of that. She was glad to see him – *Tant Sannie* was coming soon to show her her new baby – he must stay on the farm now, and help her. And Waldo himself was well content to eat his meal in silence, asking no more questions.

'Gregory is coming back next week,' she said; 'he will have been gone just a hundred and three days tomorrow. I had a letter from him yesterday.'

'Where has he been?'

But his companion stooped to lift a cake from the fire.

'How the wind blows! One can hardly hear one's own voice,' she said. 'Take this warm cake; no one's cakes are like mine. Why, you have eaten nothing!'

'I am a little weary,' he said; 'the wind was mad tonight.'

He folded his arms, and rested his head against the fireplace, whilst she removed the dishes from the table. On the mantelpiece stood an inkpot and some sheets of paper. Presently he took them down and turned up the corner of the tablecloth.

'I will write a few lines,' he said, 'till you are ready to sit down and talk.'

Em, as she shook out the tablecloth, watched him bending intently over his paper. He had changed much. His face had grown thinner; his cheeks were almost hollow, though they were covered by a dark growth of beard.

She sat down on the skin beside him, and felt the little bundle on the bench; it was painfully small and soft. Perhaps it held a shirt and a book, but nothing more. The old black hat had a piece of unhemmed muslin twisted round it, and on his elbow was a large patch so fixed on with yellow thread that her heart ached. Only his hair was not changed, and hung in silky beautiful waves almost to his shoulders. Tomorrow she would take the ragged edge off his collar, and put a new band round his hat. She did not interrupt him, but she wondered how it was that he sat to write so intently after his long weary walk. He was not tired now; his pen hurried quickly and restlessly over the paper, and his eye was bright. Presently Em raised her hand to her breast, where lay the letter yesterday had brought her. Soon she had forgotten him, as entirely as he had forgotten her; each was in his own world with his own. He was writing to Lyndall. He would tell her all he had seen, all he had done, though it were nothing worth relating. He seemed to have come back to her, and to be talking to her now he sat there in the old house.

' – and then I got to the next town, and my horse was tired, so I could go no further, and looked for work. A shopkeeper agreed to hire me as salesman. He made me sign a promise to remain six months, and he gave me a little empty room at the store to sleep in. I had still three pounds of my own, and when you have just come from the country three pounds seems a great deal.

'When I had been in the shop three days I wanted to go away again. A clerk in a shop has the lowest work to do of all people. It is much better to break stones: you have the blue sky above you, and only the stones to bend to. I asked my master to let me go, and I offered to give him my two pounds, and the bag of *mielies* I had bought with the other pound; but he would not.

'I found out afterwards he was only giving me half as much as he gave to the others – that was why. I had fear when I looked at the other clerks that I would at last become like them. All day they were bowing and smirking to the women who came in; smiling, when all they wanted was to get their money from them. They used to run and fetch the dresses and ribbons to show them, and they seemed to me like worms with oil on. There was one respectable thing in that store – it was the Kaffir storeman. His work was to load and unload, and he never needed to smile except when he liked, and he never told lies.

'The other clerks gave me the name of Old Salvation; but there was one person I liked very much. He was clerk in another store. He often went past the door. He seemed to me not like others – his face was bright and fresh like a little child's. When he came to the shop I felt I liked him. One day I saw a book in his pocket, and that made me feel near him. I asked him if he was fond of reading, and he said yes, when there was nothing else to do. The next day he came to me, and asked me if I did not feel lonely; he never saw me going out with the other fellows; he would come and see me that evening, he said.

'I was glad, and bought some meat and flour, because the grey mare and I always ate *mielies*; it is the cheapest thing; when you boil it hard you can't eat much of it. I made some cakes, and I folded my greatcoat on the box to make it soft for him; and at last he came.

'You've got a rummy place here,' he said.

'You see there was nothing in it but packing cases for furniture, and it was rather empty. While I was putting the food on the box he looked at my books; he read their names out aloud. *Elementary Physiology*, *First Principles*.

'"Golly!" he said; "I've got a lot of dry stuff like that at home I got for Sunday school prizes; but I only keep them to light my pipe with now; they come in handy for that." Then he asked me if I had ever read a book called the *Black-eyed Creole*. "That is the style for me," he said; "there where the fellow takes the nigger-girl by the arm, and the other fellow cuts off! That's what I like."

'But what he said after that I don't remember, only it made me feel as if I were having a bad dream, and I wanted to be far away.

'When he had finished eating he did not stay long: he had to go and see some girls home from a prayer-meeting; and he asked how it was he never saw me walking out with any on Sunday afternoons. He said he had lots of sweethearts, and he was going to see one the next Wednesday on a farm, and he asked me to lend my mare. I told him she was very old. But he said it didn't matter; he would come the next day to fetch her.

'After he was gone my little room got back to its old look. I loved it so; I was so glad to get into it at night, and it seemed to be reproaching me for bringing him there. The next day he took the grey mare. On Thursday he did not bring her back, and on Friday I found the saddle and bridle standing at my door.

'In the afternoon he looked into the shop, and called out, "Hope you got your saddle, Farber? Your bag-of-bones kicked out six miles from this. I'll send you a couple of shillings tomorrow, though the old hide wasn't worth it. Good morning."

'But I sprang over the counter, and got him by his throat. My father was so gentle with her; he never would ride her uphill, and now this fellow had murdered her! I asked him where he had killed her, and I shook him till he slipped out of my hand. He stood in the door grinning.

'"It didn't take much to kill *that* bag-of-bones, whose master sleeps in a packing case, and waits till his company's finished to eat on the plate. Shouldn't wonder if you fed her on sugar-bags," he said; "and, if you think I've jumped her, you'd better go and look yourself. You'll find her along the road by the *aasvoëls* that are eating her."

'I caught him by his collar, and I lifted him from the ground, and I threw him out into the street, halfway across it. I heard the bookkeeper say to the clerk that there was always the devil in those mum fellows; but they never called me Salvation after that.

'I am writing to you of very small things, but there is nothing to tell; it has been all small and you will like it. Whenever anything has happened I have always thought I would tell it to you. The back thought in my mind is always you. After that only one old man came to visit me. I had seen him in the streets often; he always wore very dirty black clothes, and a hat with crape round it, and he had one eye, so I noticed him. One day he came to my room with a subscription-list for a minister's salary. When I said I had nothing to give he looked at me with his one eye.

'"Young man," he said, "how is it I never see you in the house of the Lord?" I thought he was trying to do good, so I felt sorry for him, and I told him I never went to chapel. "Young man," he said, "it grieves me to hear such godless words from the lips of one so young – so far-gone in the paths of destruction. Young man, if you forget God, God will forget you. There is a seat on the right-hand side as you go at the bottom door that you may get. If you are given over to the enjoyment and frivolities of this world, what will become of your never-dying soul?"

'He would not go till I gave him half a crown for the minister's salary. Afterwards I heard he was the man who collected the pew-rents, and got a percentage. I didn't get to know anyone else.

'When my time in that shop was done I hired myself to drive one of a transport-rider's wagons.

'That first morning, when I sat in the front and called to my oxen, and saw nothing about me but the hills with the blue coming down to them, and the Karoo-bushes, I was drunk; I laughed; my heart was beating till it hurt me. I shut my eyes tight, that when I opened them I might see there were no shelves about me. There must be a beauty in buying and selling if there is beauty in everything; but it is very ugly to me. My life as transport-rider would have been the best life in the world if I had had only one wagon to drive. My master told me he would drive one, I the other, and he would hire another person to drive the third. But the first day I drove two to help him, and after that he let me drive all three. Whenever we came to an hotel he stopped behind to get a drink, and when he rode up to the wagons he could never stand; the Hottentot and I used to lift him up. We always travelled all night, and used to *outspan* for five or six hours in the heat of the day to rest. I planned that I would lie under the wagon and read for an hour or two every day before I went to sleep, and I did for the first two or three; but after that I only wanted to sleep like the rest, and I packed my books away. When you have three wagons to look after all night, you are sometimes so tired you can hardly stand. At first, when I walked along driving my wagons in the night, it was glorious; the stars had never looked so beautiful to me; and on the dark nights when we rode through the bush there were will-o'-the-wisps dancing on each side of the road. I found out that even the damp and dark are beautiful. But I soon changed, and saw nothing but the road, and my oxen. I only wished for a smooth piece of road, so that I might sit at the front and doze. At the places where we *outspanned* there were sometimes rare plants and flowers, the festoons hanging from the bush-trees, and nuts and insects, such as we never see here; but after a little while I never looked at them – I was too tired. I ate as much as I could, and then lay down on my face under the wagon till the boy came to wake me to *inspan*, and then we drove on again all night; so it went, so it went. I think sometimes when we walked by my oxen I called to them in my sleep, for I know I thought of nothing; I was like an animal. My body was strong and well to work, but my brain was dead. If you have not felt it, Lyndall, you cannot understand it. You may work, and work, and work, till you are only a body, not a soul. Now, when I see one of those evil-looking men that come from Europe – navvies, with the beast-like, sunken face, different from any Kaffir's – I know what brought that look into their eyes; and if I have only one inch of tobacco I give them half. It is work, grinding, mechanical work, that they or their ancestors have done, that has made them into beasts. You may work a man's body so that his soul dies. Work is good. I have worked at the old farm from the sun's rising till its setting, but I have had time to think, and time to feel. You may work a man so that all but the animal in him is gone; and that grows stronger with physical labour. You may work a man till he is a devil. I know it, because I have felt it. You will never understand the change that came over me. No one but I will ever know how great it was. But I was never miserable; when I could keep my oxen from sticking fast, and when I could find a place to lie down in, I had all I wanted. After I had driven eight months a rainy season came. For eighteen hours out of the twenty-four we worked in the wet. The mud went up to the axles sometimes, and we had to dig the wheels out, and we never went far in a day. My master swore at me more than ever, but when he had done he always offered me his brandy-flask. When I first came he had offered it me, and I had always refused; but now I drank as my oxen did when I gave them water – without thinking. At last I bought brandy for myself whenever we passed an hotel.

'One Sunday we *outspanned* on the banks of a swollen river to wait for its going down. It was drizzling still, so I lay under the wagon on the mud. There was no dry place anywhere; and all the dung was wet, so there was no fire to cook food. My little flask was filled with brandy, and I drank some and went to sleep. When I woke it was drizzling still, so I drank some more. I was stiff and cold; and my master, who lay by me, offered me his flask, because mine was empty. I drank some, and then I thought

I would go and see if the river was going down. I remember that I walked to the road, and it seemed to be going away from me. When I woke up I was lying by a little bush on the bank of the river. It was afternoon; all the clouds had gone, and the sky was deep blue. The Bushman boy was grilling ribs at the fire. He looked at me, and grinned from ear to ear. "Master was a little nice," he said, "and lay down in the road. Something might ride over master, so I carried him there." He grinned at me again. It was as though he said, "You and I are comrades. I have lain in a road too. I know all about it." When I turned my head from him I saw the earth, so pure after the rain, so green, so fresh, so blue; – and I was a drunken carrier, whom his leader had picked up in the mud, and laid at the roadside to sleep out his drink. I remembered my old life, and I remembered you. I saw how, one day, you would read in the papers – "A German carrier, named Waldo Farber, was killed through falling from his wagon, being instantly crushed under the wheel. Deceased was supposed to have been drunk at the time of the accident." There are those notices in the paper every month. I sat up, and I took the brandy-flask out of my pocket, and I flung it as far as I could into the dark water. The Hottentot boy ran down to see if he could catch it; it had sunk to the bottom. I never drank again. But, Lyndall, sin looks much more terrible to those who look at it than to those who do it. A convict, or a man who drinks, seems something so far off and horrible when we see him; but to himself he seems quite near to us, and like us. We wonder what kind of a creature he is; but he is just we, ourselves. We are only the wood, the knife that carves on us is the circumstance.

'I do not know why I kept on working so hard for that master. I think it was as the oxen come every day and stand by the yokes; they do not know why. Perhaps I would have been with him still; but one day we started with loads for the Diamond Fields. The oxen were very thin now, and they had been standing about in the yoke all day without food while the wagons were being loaded. Not far from the town was a hill. When we came to the foot the first wagon stuck fast. I tried for a little while to urge the oxen, but I soon saw the one *span* could never pull it up. I went to the other wagon to loosen that *span* to join them on in front, but the transport-rider, who was lying at the back of the wagon, jumped out.

"'They shall bring it up the hill; and if half of them die for it they shall do it alone," he said.

'He was not drunk, but in a bad temper, for he had been drunk the night before. He swore at me, and told me to take the whip and help him. We tried for a little time then I told him it was no use, they could never do it. He swore louder, and called to the leaders to come on with their whips, and together they lashed. There was one ox, a black ox, so thin that the ridge of his backbone almost cut through his flesh.

"'It is you, Devil, is it, that will not pull?" the transport-rider said. "I will show you something." He looked like a Devil.

'He told the boys to leave off flogging, and he held the ox by the horn, and took up a round stone and knocked its nose with it till the blood came. When he had done they called to the oxen and took up their whips again, and the oxen strained with their backs bent, but the wagon did not move an inch.

"'So you won't, won't you?" he said. "I'll help you."

'He took out his clasp-knife, and ran it into the leg of the trembling ox three times, up to the hilt. Then he put the knife in his pocket, and they took their whips. The oxen's flanks quivered, and they foamed at the mouth. Straining, they moved the wagon a few feet forward, then stood with bent backs to keep it from sliding back. From the black ox's nostril foam and blood were streaming onto the ground. It turned its head in its anguish and looked at me with its great starting eyes. It was praying for help in its agony and weakness, and they took their whips again. The creature bellowed out aloud. If there is a God, it was calling to its Maker for help. Then a stream of clear blood burst from both nostrils; it fell onto the ground, and the wagon slipped back. The man walked up to it.

"'You are going to lie down, Devil, are you? We'll see that you don't take it too easy."

'The thing was just dying. He opened his clasp-knife and stooped down over it. I do not know what I did then. But afterwards I know I had him on the stones, and I was kneeling on him. The boys dragged me off. I wish they had not. I left him standing in the sand in the road, shaking himself, and I walked back to the town. I took nothing from that accursed wagon, so I had only two shillings. But it did not matter. The next day I got work at a wholesale store. My work was to pack and unpack goods, and to carry boxes, and I had only to work from six in the morning till six in the evening; so I had plenty of time. I hired a little room, and subscribed to a library, so I had everything I needed; and in the week of Christmas holidays I went to see the sea. I walked all night, Lyndall, to escape the heat, and a little after sunrise I got to the top of a high hill. Before me was a long, low, blue, monotonous mountain. I walked looking at it, but I was thinking of the sea I wanted to see. At last I wondered what that curious blue thing might be; then it struck me it was the sea! I would have turned back again, only I was too tired. I wonder if all the things we long to see – the churches, the pictures, the men in Europe – will disappoint us so! You see I had dreamed of it so long. When I was a little boy, minding sheep behind the *kopje*, I used to see the waves stretching out as far as the eye could reach in the sunlight. My sea! Is the ideal always more beautiful than the real?

'I got to the beach that afternoon, and I saw the water run up and down on the sand, and I saw the white foam breakers; they were pretty, but I thought I would go back the next day. It was not my sea.

'But I began to like it when I sat by it that night in the moonlight; and the next day I liked it better; and before I left I loved it. It was not like the sky and stars, that talk of what has no beginning and no end; but it is so human. Of all the things I have ever seen, only the sea is like a human being; the sky is not, nor the earth. But the sea is always moving, always something deep in itself is stirring it. It never rests; it is always wanting, wanting, wanting. It hurries on; and then it creeps back slowly without having reached, moaning. It is always asking a question, and it never gets an answer. I can hear it in the day and in the night; the white foam breakers are saying that which I think. I walk alone with them when there is no one to see me, and I sing with them. I lie down on the sand and watch them with my eyes half shut. The sky is better, but it is so high above our heads. I love the sea. Sometimes we must look down too. After five days I went back to Grahamstown.

'I had glorious books, and in the night I could sit in my little room and read them; but I was lonely. Books are not the same things when you are living among people. I cannot tell why, but they are dead. On the farm they would have been living beings to me; but here, where there were so many people about me, I wanted someone to belong to me. I was lonely. I wanted something that was flesh and blood. Once on this farm there came a stranger; I did not ask his name, but he sat among the Karoo and talked with me. Now, wherever I have travelled I have looked for him – in hotels, in streets, in passenger wagons as they rushed in, through the open windows of houses I have looked for him, but I have not found him – never heard a voice like his. One day I went to the Botanic Gardens. It was a half-holiday, and the band was to play. I stood in the long raised avenue and looked down. There were many flowers, and ladies and children were walking about beautifully dressed. At last the music began. I had not heard such music before. At first it was slow and even, like the everyday life, when we walk through it without thought or feeling; then it grew faster, then it paused, hesitated, then it was quite still for an instant, and then it burst out. Lyndall, they made heaven right when they made it all music. It takes you up and carries you away, away till you have the things you longed for; you are up close to them. You have got out into a large, free, open place. I could not see anything while it was playing; I stood with my head against my tree; but when it was done, I saw that there were ladies sitting close to me on a wooden bench, and the stranger who had talked to me that day in the Karoo was sitting between them. The ladies were very pretty, and their dresses beautiful. I do not think they had been listening to the music, for they were talking and laughing very softly. I heard all they said, and could even smell the rose on the breast of one. I was afraid he would see me; so I went to the other side of the tree, and soon they got up and began to pace up and down in the avenue. All the time the music played they chatted, and he carried on his arm the scarf of the prettiest lady. I did not hear the music; I tried to catch the sound of his voice each time he went by. When I was listening to the music I did not know I was badly dressed; now I felt so ashamed of myself. I never knew before what a low, horrible thing I was, dressed in tancord. That day on the farm, when we sat on the ground under the thorn-trees, I thought he quite belonged to me; now, I saw he was not mine. But he was still as beautiful. His brown eyes are more beautiful than anyone's eyes, except yours.

'At last they turned to go, and I walked after them. When they got out of the gate he helped the ladies into a phaeton, and stood for a moment with his foot on the step talking to them. He had a little cane in his hand, and an Italian greyhound ran after him. Just when they drove away one of the ladies dropped her whip.

'"Pick it up, fellow," she said; and when I brought it her she threw sixpence on the ground. I might have gone back to the garden then; but I did not want music; I wanted clothes, and to be fashionable and fine. I felt that my hands were coarse, and that I was vulgar. I never tried to see him again.

'I stayed in my situation four months after that, but I was not happy. I had no rest. The people about me pressed on me and made me dissatisfied. I could not forget them. Even when I did not see them they pressed on me, and made me miserable. I did not love books; I wanted people. When I walked home under the shady trees in the street I could not be happy for when I passed the houses I heard music, and saw faces between the curtains. I did not want any of them, but I wanted someone for mine, for me. I could not help it. I wanted a finer life.

'Only one day something made me happy. A nurse came to the store with a little girl belonging to one of our clerks. While the maid went into the office to give a message to its father, the little child stood looking at me. Presently she came close to me and peeped up into my face.

'"Nice curls, pretty curls," she said; "I like curls."

'She felt my hair all over with her little hands. When I put out my arm she let me take her and sit her on my knee. She kissed me with her soft mouth. We were happy till the nurse-girl came and shook her, and asked her if she was not ashamed to sit on the knee of that strange man. But I do not think my little one minded. She laughed at me as she went out.

'If the world was all children I could like it; but men and women draw me so strangely, and then press me away, till I am in agony. I was not meant to live among people. Perhaps someday, when I am grown older, I will be able to go and live among them and look at them as I look at the rocks and bushes, without letting them disturb me, and take myself from me; but not now. So I grew miserable; a kind of fever seemed to eat me; I could not rest, or read, or think; so I came back here. I knew you were not here, but it seemed as though I should be nearer you; and it is you I want – you that the other people suggest to me, but cannot give.'

He had filled all the sheets he had taken, and now lifted down the last from the mantelpiece. Em had dropped asleep, and lay slumbering peacefully on the skin before the fire. Out of doors the storm still raged; but in a fitful manner, as though growing half weary of itself. He bent over his papers again, with eager flushed cheek, and wrote on.

'It has been a delightful journey, this journey home. I have walked on foot. The evening before last, when it was just sunset, I was a little footsore and thirsty, and went out of the road to look for water. I went down into a deep little *kloof*. Some trees ran along the bottom, and I thought I should find water there. The sun had quite set when

I got to the bottom of it. It was very still – not a leaf was stirring anywhere. In the bed of the mountain torrent I thought I might find water. I came to the bank, and leaped down into the dry bed. The floor on which I stood was of fine white sand, and the banks rose on every side like the walls of a room. Above, there was a precipice of rocks, and a tiny stream of water oozed from them and fell slowly onto the flat stone below. Each drop you could hear fall like a little silver bell. There was one among the trees on the bank that stood out against the white sky. All the other trees were silent; but this one shook and trembled against the sky. Everything else was still; but those leaves were quivering, quivering. I stood on the sand; I could not go away. When it was quite dark, and the stars had come, I crept out. Does it seem strange to you that it should have made me so happy? It is because I cannot tell you how near I felt to things that we cannot see but we always feel. Tonight has been a wild, stormy night. I have been walking across the plain for hours in the dark. I have liked the wind, because I have seemed forcing my way through to you. I knew you were not here, but I would hear of you. When I used to sit on the transport wagon half-sleeping, I used to start awake because your hands were on me. In my lodgings, many nights I have blown the light out, and sat in the dark, that I might see your face start out more distinctly. Sometimes it was the little girl's face who used to come to me behind the *kopje* when I minded sheep, and sit by me in her blue pinafore; sometimes it was older. I love both. I am very helpless, I shall never do anything; but you will work, and I will take your work for mine. Sometimes such a sudden gladness seizes me when I remember that somewhere in the world you are living and working. You are my very own; nothing else is my own so. When I have finished I am going to look at your room door – '

He wrote; and the wind, which had spent its fury, moaned round and round the house, most like a tired child weary with crying.

Em woke up, and sat before the fire, rubbing her eyes, and listening, as it sobbed about the gables, and wandered away over the long stone walls.

'How quiet it has grown now,' she said, and sighed herself, partly from weariness and partly from sympathy with the tired wind. He did not answer her; he was lost in his letter.

She rose slowly after a time, and rested her hand on his shoulder.

'You have many letters to write,' she said.

'No,' he answered; 'it is only one to Lyndall.'

She turned away, and stood long before the fire looking into it. If you have a deadly fruit to give, it will not grow sweeter by keeping.

'Waldo, dear,' she said, putting her hands on his, 'leave off writing.'

He threw back the dark hair from his forehead and looked at her.

'It is no use writing any more,' she said.

'Why not?' he asked.

She put her hand over the papers he had written.

'Waldo,' she said, 'Lyndall is dead.'

CHAPTER TWELVE

Gregory's Womanhood

Slowly over the flat came a cart. On the back seat sat Gregory, his arms folded, his hat drawn over his eyes. A Kaffir boy sat on the front seat driving, and at his feet sat Doss, who, now and again, lifted his nose and eyes above the level of the splashboard, to look at the surrounding country; and then, with an exceedingly knowing wink of his left eye, turned to his companions, thereby intimating that he clearly perceived his whereabouts. No one noticed the cart coming. Waldo, who was at work at his carpenter's table in the wagon-house, saw nothing, till, chancing to look down, he perceived Doss standing before him, the legs trembling, the little nose wrinkled, and a series of short suffocating barks giving utterance to his joy at reunion.

Em, whose eyes had ached with looking out across the plain, was now at work in a back room, and knew nothing till, looking up, she saw Gregory, with his straw hat and blue eyes, standing in the doorway. He greeted her quietly, hung his hat up in its old place behind the door, and for any change in his manner or appearance he might have been gone only the day before to fetch letters from the town. Only his beard was gone, and his face was grown thinner. He took off his leather gaiters, said the afternoon was hot and the roads dusty, and asked for some tea. They talked of wool, and the cattle, and the sheep, and Em gave him the pile of letters that had come for him during the months of absence, but of the thing that lay at their hearts neither said anything. Then he went out to look at the *kraals*, and at supper Em gave him hot cakes and coffee. They talked about the servants, and then ate their meal in quiet. She asked no questions. When it was ended Gregory went into the front room, and lay in the dark on the sofa.

'Do you not want a light?' Em asked, venturing to look in.

'No,' he answered; then presently called to her, 'Come and sit here; I want to talk to you.'

She came and sat on a footstool near him.

'Do you wish to hear anything?' he asked.

She whispered, 'Yes, if it does not hurt you.'

'What difference does it make to me?' he said. 'If I talk or am silent, is there any change?'

Yet he lay quiet for a long time. The light through the open door showed him to her, where he lay, with his arm thrown across his eyes. At last he spoke. Perhaps it was a relief to him to speak.

To Bloemfontein in the Free State, to which through an agent he had traced them, Gregory had gone. At the hotel where Lyndall and her stranger had stayed he put up; he was shown the very room in which they had slept. The Coloured boy who had driven them to the next town told him in which house they had boarded, and Gregory went on. In that town he found they had left the cart, and bought a spider and four greys, and Gregory's heart rejoiced. Now indeed it would be easy to trace their course. And he turned his steps northwards.

At the farmhouses where he stopped the *ooms* and *tantes* remembered clearly the spider with its four grey horses. At one place the Boer wife told how the tall, blue-eyed Englishman had bought milk, and asked the way to the next farm. At the next farm the Englishman had bought a bunch of flowers, and given half a crown for them to the little girl. It was quite true; the Boer mother made her get it out of the box and show it. At the next place they had slept. Here they told him that the great bulldog, who hated all strangers, had walked in the evening and laid its head on the lady's lap. So at every place he heard something, and traced them step by step.

At one desolate farm the Boer had a good deal to tell. The lady had said she liked a wagon that stood before the door. Without asking the price the Englishman had offered a hundred and fifty pounds for the old thing, and bought oxen worth ten pounds for sixteen. The Dutchman chuckled, for he had the 'Salt-*riem*'s' money in the box under his bed. Gregory laughed too, in silence; he could not lose sight of them now, so slowly they would have to move with that cumbrous ox wagon. Yet, when that evening came, and he reached a little wayside inn, no one could tell him anything of the travellers.

The master, a surly creature, half-stupid with Boer-brandy, sat on the bench before the door smoking. Gregory sat beside him, questioning, but he smoked on. He remembered nothing of such strangers. How should he know who had been there months and months before? He smoked on. Gregory, very weary, tried to awake his memory, said that the lady he was seeking for was very beautiful, had a little mouth, and tiny, very tiny, feet. The man only smoked on as sullenly as at first. What were little, very little, mouths and feet to him? But his daughter leaned out in the window above. She was dirty and lazy, and liked to loll there when travellers came, to hear the men talk, but she had a soft heart. Presently a hand came out of the window, and a pair of velvet slippers touched his shoulder, tiny slippers with black flowers. He pulled them out of her hand. Only one woman's feet had worn them, he knew that.

'Left here last summer by a lady,' said the girl; 'might be the one you are looking for. Never saw any feet so small.'

Gregory rose and questioned her.

They might have come in a wagon and spider, she could not tell. But the gentleman was very handsome, tall, lovely figure, blue eyes, wore gloves always when he went out. An English officer, perhaps; no Afrikaner, certainly.

Gregory stopped her. The lady? Well, she was pretty, rather, the girl said; very cold, dull air, silent. They stayed for, it might be, five days; slept in the wing over against the *stoep*; quarrelled sometimes, she thought – the lady. She had seen everything when she went in to wait. One day the gentleman touched her hair; she drew back from him as though his fingers poisoned her. Went to the other end of the room if he came to sit near her. Walked out alone. Cold wife for such a handsome husband, the girl thought; she evidently pitied him, he was such a beautiful man. They went away early one morning, how, or in which way, the girl could not tell.

Gregory inquired of the servants, but nothing more was to be learnt; so the next morning he saddled his horse and went on. At the farms he came to the good old *ooms* and *tantes* asked him to have coffee, and the little shoeless children peeped out at the stranger from behind ovens and gables; but no one had seen what he asked for. This way and that he rode to pick up the thread he had dropped; but the spider and the wagon, the little lady and the handsome gentleman, no one had seen. In the towns he fared yet worse.

Once indeed hope came to him. On the *stoep* of an hotel at which he stayed the night in a certain little village, there walked a gentleman, grave and kindly-looking. It was not hard to open conversation with him about the weather, and then – Had he ever seen such and such people, a gentleman and lady, a spider and wagon, arrive at that place? The kindly gentleman shook his head. What was the lady like, he inquired.

Gregory painted. Hair like silken floss, small mouth, underlip very full and pink, upper lip pink but very thin and curled; there were four white spots on the nail of her right hand forefinger, and her eyebrows were very delicately curved.

The gentleman looked thoughtful, as trying to remember.

'Yes; and a rose-bud tinge in the cheeks; hands like lilies, and perfectly seraphic smile.'

'That is she! That is she!' cried Gregory.

'Who else could it be? He asked where she had gone to. The gentleman most thoughtfully stroked his beard. He would try to remember. Were not her ears – Here such a violent fit of coughing seized him that he ran away into the house. An ill-fed clerk and a dirty barman standing in the doorway laughed aloud. Gregory wondered if they could be laughing at the gentleman's cough, and then he heard someone laughing in the room into which the gentleman had gone. He must follow him and try to learn more; but he soon found that there was nothing more to be learnt there. Poor Gregory!

Backwards and forwards, backwards and forwards, from the dirty little hotel where he had dropped the thread, to this farm and to that, rode Gregory, till his heart was sick and tired. That from that spot the wagon might have gone its own way and the spider another was an idea that did not occur to him. At last he saw it was no use lingering in that neighbourhood, and pressed on.

One day, coming to a little town, his horses knocked up, and he resolved to rest them there. The little hotel of the town was a bright and sunny place, like the jovial face of the clean little woman who kept it, and who trotted about talking always – talking to the customers in the tap-room, and to the maids in the kitchen, and to the passersby when she could hail them from the windows; talking, as good-natured women with large mouths and small noses always do, in season and out.

There was a little front parlour in the hotel, kept for strangers who wanted to be alone. Gregory sat there to eat his breakfast, and the landlady dusted the room and talked of the great finds at the Diamond Fields, and the badness of maid-servants, and the shameful conduct of the Dutch parson in that town to the English inhabitants. Gregory ate his breakfast and listened to nothing. He had asked his one question, had had his answer; now she might talk on.

Presently a door in the corner opened, and a woman came out – a Mozambiquer, with a red handkerchief twisted round her head. She carried in her hand a tray, with a slice of toast crumbled fine, and a half-filled cup of coffee, and an egg broken open, but not eaten. Her ebony face grinned complacently as she shut the door softly and said 'Good morning'.

The landlady began to talk to her.

'You are not going to leave her really, Ayah, are you?' she said. 'The maids say so; but I'm sure you wouldn't do such a thing.'

The Mozambiquer grinned.

'Husband says I must go home.'

'But she hasn't got anyone else, and won't have anyone else. Come now,' said the landlady, 'I've no time to be sitting always in a sick room, not if I was paid anything for it.'

The Mozambiquer only showed her white teeth good-naturedly for answer, and went out, and the landlady followed her.

Gregory, glad to be alone, watched the sunshine as it came over the fuchsias in the window, and ran up and down on the panelled door in the corner. The Mozambiquer had closed it loosely behind her, and presently, something touched it inside. It moved a little, then it was still, then moved again; then through the gap, a small nose appeared, and a yellow ear overlapping one eye; then the whole head obtruded, placed itself critically on one side, wrinkled its nose disapprovingly at Gregory, and withdrew. Through the half-open door came a faint scent of vinegar, and the room was dark and still.

Presently the landlady came back.

'Left the door open,' she said, bustling to shut it; 'but a darkey will be a darkey, and never carries a head on its shoulders like other folks. Not ill, I hope, sir?' she said, looking at Gregory when she had shut the bedroom door.

'No,' said Gregory, 'no.'

The landlady began putting the things together.

'Who,' asked Gregory, 'is in that room?'

Glad to have a little innocent piece of gossip to relate, and someone willing to hear it, the landlady made the most of a little story as she cleared the table. Six months before a lady had come alone to the hotel in a wagon, with only a Coloured leader and driver. Eight days after a little baby had been born. If Gregory stood and looked out at the window he would see a bluegum tree in the graveyard; close by it was a little grave. The baby was buried there. A tiny thing, only lived two hours, and the mother herself almost went with it. After a while she was better; but one day she got up out of bed, dressed herself without saying a word to anyone, and went out. It was a drizzly day; a little time after someone saw her sitting on the wet ground under the bluegum tree, with the rain dripping from her hat and shawl. They went to fetch her, but she would not come until she chose. When she did she had gone to bed, and had not risen again from it; never would, the doctor said.

She was very patient, poor thing. When you went in to ask her how she was she said always 'Better', or 'Nearly well!' and lay still in the darkened room, and never troubled anyone. The Mozambiquer took care of her, and she would not allow anyone else to touch her; would not so much as allow anyone to see her foot uncovered. She was strange in many ways, but she paid well, poor thing; and now the Mozambiquer was going, and she would have to take up with someone else.

The landlady prattled on pleasantly, and now carried away the tray with the breakfast things. When she was gone Gregory leaned his head on his hands, but he did not think long.

Before dinner he had ridden out of the town to where on a rise a number of transport-wagons were *outspanned*. The Dutchman driver of one wondered at the stranger's eagerness to free himself of his horses. Stolen perhaps; but it was worth his while to buy them at so low a price. So the horses changed masters, and Gregory walked off with his saddlebags slung across his arm. Once out of sight of the wagons he struck out of the road and walked across the *veld*, the dry, flowering grasses waving everywhere about him; half-way across the plain he came to a deep gully which the rain torrents had washed out, but which was now dry. Gregory sprang down into its red bed. It was a safe place, and quiet. When he had looked about him he sat down under the shade of an overhanging bank and fanned himself with his hat, for the afternoon was hot, and he had walked fast. At his feet the dusty ants ran about, and the high red bank before him was covered by a network of roots and fibres washed bare by the rains. Above his head rose the clear blue African sky; at his side were the saddlebags full of woman's clothing. Gregory looked up half plaintively into the blue sky.

'Am I, am I Gregory Nazianzen Rose?' he said.

It was all so strange, he sitting there in that *sloot* in that up-country plain! – strange as the fantastic, changing shapes in a summer cloud. At last, tired out, he fell asleep, with his head against the bank. When he woke the shadow had stretched across the *sloot* and the sun was on the edge of the plain. Now he must be up and doing. He drew from his breast pocket a little sixpenny looking glass, and hung it on one of the roots that stuck out from the bank. Then he dressed himself in one of the old-fashioned gowns and a great pinked-out collar. Then he took out a razor. Tuft by tuft the soft brown beard fell down into the sand, and the little ants took it to line their nests with. Then the glass showed a face surrounded by a frilled cap, white as a woman's, with a little mouth, a very short upper lip, and a receding chin.

Presently a rather tall woman's figure was making its way across the *veld*. As it passed a hollowed-out ant-heap it knelt down, and stuffed in the saddlebags with the man's clothing, closing up the anthill with bits of ground to look as natural as possible. Like a sinner hiding his deed of sin, the hider started once and looked round, but yet there was no one near save a *meerkat*, who had lifted herself out of her hole and sat on her hind legs watching. He did not like that even she should see, and when he rose she dived away into her hole. Then he walked on leisurely, that the dusk might have reached the village streets before he walked there. The first house was the smith's, and before the open door two idle urchins lolled. As he hurried up the street in the gathering gloom he heard them laugh long and loudly behind him. He glanced round fearingly, and would almost have fled, but that the strange skirts clung about his legs. And after all it was only a spark that had alighted on the head of one, and not the strange figure they laughed at.

The door of the hotel stood wide open, and the light fell out into the street. He knocked, and the landlady came. She peered out to look for the cart that had brought the traveller; but Gregory's heart was brave now he was so near the quiet room. He told her he had come with the transport wagons that stood outside the town.

He had walked in, and wanted lodgings for the night. It was a deliberate lie, glibly told; he would have told fifty, though the recording angel had stood in the next room with his pen dipped in the ink. What was it to him? He remembered that she lay there saying always, 'I am better.'

The landlady put his supper in the little parlour where he had sat in the morning. When it was on the table she sat down in the rocking chair, as her fashion was, to knit and talk, that she might gather news for her customers in the tap-room. In the white face under the queer, deep-fringed cap she saw nothing of the morning's traveller. The newcomer was communicative. She was a nurse by profession, she said; had come to the Transvaal, hearing that good nurses were needed there. She had not yet found work. The landlady did not perhaps know whether there would be any for her in that town?

The landlady put down her knitting and smote her fat hands together.

If it wasn't the very finger of God's Providence, as though you saw it hanging out of the sky, she said. Here was a lady ill and needing a new nurse that very day, and not able to get one to her mind, and now – well, if it wasn't enough to convert all the atheists and freethinkers in the Transvaal she didn't know!

Then the landlady proceeded to detail facts.

'I'm sure you will suit her,' she added; 'you're just the kind. She has heaps of money to pay you with; has everything that money can buy. And I got a letter with a cheque in it for fifty pounds the other day from someone, who says I'm to spend it for her, and not to let her know. She is asleep now but I'll take you in to look at her.'

The landlady opened the door of the next room, and Gregory followed her. A table stood near the bed, and a lamp burning low stood on it; the bed was a great four-poster with white curtains, and the quilt was of rich crimson satin. But Gregory stood just inside the door with his head bent low, and saw no further.

'Come nearer! I'll turn the lamp up a bit, that you can have a look at her. A pretty thing, isn't it?' said the landlady.

Near the foot of the bed was a dent in the crimson quilt, and out of it Doss's small head and bright eyes looked knowingly.

'See how the lips move; she is in pain,' said the landlady.

Then Gregory looked up at what lay on the cushion. A little white, white face, transparent as an angel's, with a cloth bound round the forehead, and with soft short hair tossed about on the pillow.

'We had to cut it off,' said the woman, touching it with her forefinger. 'Soft as silk, like a wax-doll's.'

But Gregory's heart was bleeding.

'Never get up again, the doctor says,' said the landlady.

Gregory uttered one word. In an instant the beautiful eyes opened widely, looked round the room and into the dark corners.

'Who is here? Whom did I hear speak?'

Gregory had sunk back behind the curtain; the landlady drew it aside, and pulled him forward.

'Only this lady, ma'am – a nurse by profession. She is willing to stay and take care of you, if you can come to terms with her.'

Lyndall raised herself on her elbow, and cast one keen scrutinising glance over him.

'Have I never seen you before?' she asked.

'No.'

She fell back wearily.

'Perhaps you would like to arrange the terms between yourselves,' said the landlady. 'Here is a chair, I will be back presently.'

Gregory sat down, with bent head and quick breath. She did not speak, and lay with half-closed eyes, seeming to have forgotten him.

'Will you turn the lamp down a little?' she said at last; 'I cannot bear the light.'

Then his heart grew braver in the shadow, and he spoke. Nursing was to him, he said, his chosen life's work. He wanted no money: if – She stopped him.

'I take no service for which I do not pay,' she said. 'What I gave to my last nurse I will give to you; if you do not like it you may go.'

And Gregory muttered humbly, he would take it. Afterwards she tried to turn herself. He lifted her. Ah! A shrunken little body, he could feel its weakness as he touched it. His hands were to him glorified for what they had done.

'Thank you! That is so nice. Other people hurt me when they touch me,' she said. 'Thank you!' Then after a little while she repeated humbly, 'Thank you; they hurt me so.'

Gregory sat down trembling. His little ewe-lamb, could they hurt her?

The doctor said of Gregory four days after, 'She is the most experienced nurse I ever came in contact with.'

Gregory, standing in the passage, heard it, and laughed in his heart. What need had he of experience. Experience teaches us in a millennium what passion teaches us in an hour. A Kaffir studies all his life the discerning of distant sounds; but he will never hear my step, when my love hears it, coming to her window in the dark over the short grass.

At first Gregory's heart was sore when day by day the body grew lighter, and the mouth he fed took less; but afterwards he grew accustomed to it, and was happy. For passion has o*ne* cry, one only – 'Oh, to touch thee, Beloved!'

In that quiet room Lyndall lay on the bed with the dog at her feet, and Gregory sat in his dark corner watching.

She seldom slept, and through those long, long days she would lie watching the round streak of sunlight that came through the knot in the shutter, or the massive lion's paw on which the wardrobe rested. What thoughts were in those eyes? Gregory wondered; he dared not ask.

Sometimes Doss, where he lay on her feet, would dream that they two were in the cart, tearing over the *veld* with the black horses snorting, and the wind in their faces; and he would start up in his sleep and bark aloud. Then awaking, he would lick his mistress's hand almost remorsefully, and slink quietly down into his place.

Gregory thought she had no pain, she never groaned; only sometimes, when the light was near her, he thought he could see slight contractions about her lips and eyebrows.

He slept on the sofa outside her door.

One night he thought he heard a sound, and, opening it softly, he looked in. She was crying out aloud, as if she and her pain were alone in the world. The light fell on the red quilt, and on the little hands that were clasped over the head. The wide-open eyes were looking up, and the heavy drops fell slowly from them.

'I cannot bear any more, not any more,' she said in a deep voice. 'Oh, God, God! Have I not borne in silence? Have I not endured these long, long months? But now, now, oh God, I cannot!'

Gregory knelt in the doorway listening.

'I do not ask for wisdom, not human love, not work, not knowledge, not for all things I have longed for,' she cried; 'only a little freedom from pain! Only one little hour without pain! Then I will suffer again.'

She sat up, and bit the little hand Gregory loved.

He crept away to the front door, and stood looking out at the quiet starlight. When he came back she was lying in her usual posture, the quiet eyes looking at the lion's claw. He came close to the bed.

'You have much pain tonight?' he asked her.

'No, not much.'

'Can I do anything for you?'

'No, nothing.'

She still drew her lips together, and motioned with her fingers towards the dog who lay sleeping at her feet. Gregory lifted him and laid him at her side. She made Gregory turn open the bosom of her nightdress – that the dog might put his black muzzle between her breasts. She crossed her arms over him. Gregory left them lying there together.

The next day, when they asked her how she was, she answered 'Better'.

'Someone ought to tell her,' said the landlady; 'we can't let her soul go into eternity not knowing, especially when I don't think it was all right about the child. You ought to go and tell her, doctor.'

So the little doctor, edged on and on, went in at last. When he came out of the room he shook his fist in the landlady's face.

'Next time you have any Devil's work to do, do it yourself,' he said, and shook his fist in her face again, and went away swearing.

When Gregory went into the bedroom he only found her moved, her body curled up, and drawn close to the wall. He dared not disturb her. At last, after a long time, she turned.

'Bring me food,' she said, 'I want to eat. Two eggs, and toast, and meat – two large slices of toast, please.'

Wondering, Gregory brought a tray with all that she had asked for.

'Sit me up, and put it close to me,' she said; 'I am going to eat it all.' She tried to draw the things near her with her fingers, and re-arranged the plates. She cut the toast into long strips, broke open both eggs, put a tiny morsel of bread into her own mouth, and fed the dog with pieces of meat put into his jaws with her fingers.

'Is it twelve o'clock yet?' she said; 'I think I do not generally eat so early. Put it away, please, *carefully* – no, do not take it away – only on the table. When the clock strikes twelve I will eat it.'

She lay down trembling. After a little while she said:

'Give me my clothes.'

He looked at her.

376

'Yes; I'm going to dress tomorrow. I should get up now but it is rather late. Put them on that chair. My collars are in the little box, my boots behind the door.'

Her eyes followed him intently as he collected the articles one by one, and placed them on the chair as she directed.

'Put it nearer,' she said; 'I cannot see it'; and she lay watching the clothes, with her hand under her cheek.

'Now open the shutter wide,' she said; 'I am going to read.'

The old, old tone was again in the sweet voice. He obeyed her; and opened the shutter and raised her up among the pillows.

'Now bring my books to me,' she said, motioning eagerly with her fingers, 'the large book, and the reviews, and the plays; I want them all.'

He piled them round her on the bed; she drew them greedily closer, her eyes very bright, but her face as white as a mountain lily.

'Now the big one off the drawers. No, you need not help me to hold my book,' she said; 'I can hold it for myself.'

Gregory went back to his corner, and for a little time the restless turning over of leaves was to be heard.

'Will you open the window,' she said, almost querulously, 'and throw this book out? It is so utterly foolish. I thought it was a valuable book, but the words are merely strung together, they make no sense. Yes – so!' she said with approval, seeing him fling it out into the street. 'I must have been very foolish when I thought that book good.'

Then she turned to read, and leaned her little elbows resolutely on the great volume, and knit her brows. This was Shakespeare – it must mean something.

'I wish you would take a handkerchief and tie it tight round my head, it aches so.'

He had not been long in his seat when he saw drops fall from beneath the hands that shaded the eyes, onto the page.

'I am not accustomed to so much light, it makes my head swim a little,' she said. 'Go out and close the shutter.'

When he came back, she lay shrivelled up among the pillows.

He heard no sound of weeping; but the shoulders shook. He darkened the room completely.

When Gregory went to his sofa that night, she told him to wake her early; she would be dressed before breakfast. Nevertheless, when morning came, she said it was a little cold, and lay all day watching her clothes upon the chair. Still she sent for her oxen in the country; they would start on Monday and go down to the Colony.

In the afternoon she told him to open the window wide, and draw the bed near it.

It was a leaden afternoon, the dull rain-clouds rested close to the roofs of the houses, and the little street was silent and deserted. Now and then a gust of wind eddying round caught up the dried leaves, whirled them hither and thither under the trees, and dropped them again into the gutter: then all was quiet. She lay looking out. Presently the bell of the church began to toll, and up the village street came a long procession. They were carrying an old man to his last resting place. She followed them with her eyes till they turned in among the trees at the gate.

'Who was that?' she asked.

'An old man,' he answered, 'a very old man; they say he was ninety-four; but his name I do not know.'

She mused a while, looking out with fixed eyes. 'That is why the bell rang so cheerfully,' she said. 'When the old die it is well; they have had their time. It is when the young die that the bells weep drops of blood.'

'But the old love life?' he said; for it was sweet to hear her speak.

She raised herself on her elbow. 'They love life, they do not want to die,' she answered; 'but what of that? They have had their time. They knew that a man's life is three score years and ten; they should have made their plans accordingly! But the young,' she said, 'the young cut down, cruelly, when they have not seen, when they have not known – when they have not found – it is for them that the bells weep blood. I heard in the ringing it was an old man. When the old die – Listen to the bell! it is laughing – "It is right, it is right: he has had his time." They cannot ring so for the young.'

She fell back exhausted; the hot light died from her eyes, and she lay looking out into the street. By and by stragglers from the funeral began to come back and disappear here and there among the houses; then all was quiet, and the night began to settle down upon the village street. Afterwards, when the room was almost dark, so that they could not see each other's faces, she said, 'It will rain tonight'; and moved restlessly on the pillows. 'How terrible when the rain falls down on you.'

He wondered what she meant, and they sat on in the still darkening room. She moved again.

'Will you presently take my cloak – the new grey cloak from behind the door – and go out with it. You will find a little grave at the foot of the tall bluegum tree; the water drips off the long, pointed leaves; you must cover it up with that.'

She moved restlessly as though in pain. Gregory assented, and there was silence again. It was the first time she had ever spoken of her child.

'It was so small,' she said; 'it lived such a little while – only three hours. They laid it close by me, but I never saw it; I could feel it by me.' She waited; 'It's feet were so cold; I took them in my hand to make them warm, and my hand closed right over them they were so little.' There was an uneven trembling in the voice. 'It crept close to me; it wanted to drink, it wanted to be warm.' She hardened herself – 'I did not love it; its father was not my prince; I did not care for it; but it was so little.' She moved her hand. 'They might have kissed it, one of them, before they put it in. It never did anyone any harm in all its little life. They might have kissed it, one of them.'

Gregory felt that someone was sobbing in the room. Later on in the evening, when the shutter was closed and the lamp lighted, and the raindrops beat on the roof, he took the cloak from behind the door and went away with it. On his way back he called at the village post office and brought back a letter. In the hall he stood reading the address. How could he fail to know whose hand had written it? Had he not long ago studied those characters on the torn fragments of paper in the old parlour? A burning pain was at Gregory's heart. If now, now at the last, one should come, should step in between! He carried the letter into the bedroom and gave it her. 'Bring the lamp nearer,' she said. When she had read it she asked for her desk.

Then Gregory sat down in the lamplight on the other side of the curtain, and heard the pencil move on the paper. When he looked round the curtain she was lying on the pillow musing. The open letter lay at her side; she glanced at it with soft eyes. The man with the languid eyelids must have been strangely moved before his hand set down those words: 'Let me come back to you! My darling, let me put my hand round you, and guard you from the world. As my wife they shall never touch you. I have learnt to love you more wisely, more tenderly, than of old; you shall have perfect freedom. Lyndall, grand little woman, for your own sake be my wife!

'Why did you send that money back to me? You are cruel to me; it is not rightly done.'

She rolled the little red pencil softly between her fingers, and her face grew very soft. Yet –

'It cannot be,' she wrote; 'I thank you much for the love you have shown me; but I cannot listen. You will call me mad, foolish – the world would do so; but I know what I need and the kind of path I must walk in. I cannot marry you. I will always love you for the sake of what lay by me those three hours; but there it ends. I must know and see; I cannot be bound to one whom I love as I love you. I am not afraid of the world – I will fight the world. One day – perhaps it may be far off – I shall find what I have wanted all my life; something nobler, stronger than I, before which I can kneel down. You lose nothing by not having me now; I am a weak, selfish, erring woman. One day I shall find something to worship, and then I shall be – '

'Nurse,' she said; 'take my desk away; I am suddenly so sleepy; I will write more tomorrow.' She turned her face to the pillow; it was the sudden drowsiness of great weakness. She had dropped asleep in a moment, and Gregory moved the desk softly, and then sat in the chair watching. Hour after hour passed, but he had no wish for rest, and sat on, hearing the rain cease, and the still night settle down everywhere. At a quarter past twelve he rose, and took a last look at the bed where she lay sleeping so peacefully; then he turned to go to his couch. Before he had reached the door she had started up and was calling him back.

'You are sure you have put it up?' she said, with look of blank terror at the window. 'It will not fall open in the night, the shutter – you are sure?'

He comforted her. Yes, it was tightly fastened.

'Even if it is shut,' she said in a whisper, 'you cannot keep it out! You feel it coming in at four clock, creeping, creeping, up, up; deadly cold!' She shuddered.

He thought she was wandering, and laid her little trembling body down among the blankets.

'I dreamed just now that it was not put up,' she said, looking into his eyes; 'and it crept right in and I was alone with it.'

'What do you fear?' he asked tenderly.

'The Grey Dawn,' she said, glancing round at the window. 'I was never afraid of anything, never when I was a little child, but I have always been afraid of that. You will not let it come in to me?'

'No, no; I will stay with you,' he continued.

But she was growing calmer. 'No; you must go to bed. I only awoke with a start; you must be tired. I am childish, that is all,' but she shivered again.

He sat down beside her. After some time she said, 'Will you not rub my feet?'

He knelt down at the foot of the bed and took the tiny foot in his hand; it was swollen and unsightly now, but as he touched it he bent down and covered it with kisses.

'It makes it better when you kiss it; thank you. What makes you all love me so?' Then dreamily she muttered to herself: 'Not utterly bad, not quite bad – what makes them all love me so?'

Kneeling there, rubbing softly, with his cheek pressed against the little foot, Gregory dropped to sleep at last. How long he knelt there he could not tell; but when he started up awake she was not looking at him. The eyes were fixed on the far corner, gazing wide and intent, with an unearthly light.

He looked round fearfully. What did she see there? God's angels come to call her? Something fearful? *He* saw only the purple curtain with the shadows that fell from it. Softly he whispered, asking what she saw there.

And she said, in a voice strangely unlike her own, 'I see the vision of a poor weak soul striving after good. It was not cut short; and, in the end, it learnt, through tears and such pain, that holiness is an infinite compassion for others; that greatness is to take the common things of life and walk truly among them; that' – she moved her white hand and laid it on her forehead – 'happiness is a great love and much serving. It was not cut short; and it loved what it had learnt – it loved – and – '

Was that all she saw in the corner?

Gregory told the landlady the next morning that she had been wandering all night. Yet, when he came in to give her her breakfast, she was sitting up against the pillows, looking as he had not seen her look before.

'Put it close to me,' she said, 'and when I have had breakfast I am going to dress.' She finished all he had brought her eagerly.

'I am sitting up quite by myself,' she said. 'Give me his meat,' and she fed the dog herself, cutting his food small for him. She moved to the side of the bed.

'Now bring the chair near and dress me. It is being in this room so long, and looking at that miserable little bit of sunshine that comes in through the shutter, that is making me so ill. Always that lion's paw!' she said, with a look of disgust at it. 'Come and dress me.' Gregory knelt on the floor before her, and tried to draw on one stocking, but the little swollen foot refused to be covered.

'It is very funny that I should have grown so fat since I have been so ill,' she said, peering down curiously. 'Perhaps it is want of exercise?' She looked troubled and again, 'Perhaps it is want of exercise.' She wanted Gregory to say so too. But he only found a larger pair; and then tried to force the shoes, oh so tenderly! onto her little feet.

'There,' she said, looking down at them when they were on, with the delight of a small child over its first shoes, 'I could walk far now. How nice it looks!'

'No,' she said, seeing the soft gown he had prepared for her, 'I will not put that on. Get one of my white dresses – the one with the pink bows. I do not even want to think I have been ill. It is thinking and thinking of things that makes them real,' she said. 'When you draw your mind together, and resolve that a thing shall not be, it gives way before you; it is not. Everything is possible if one is resolved,' she said. She drew in her little lips together, and Gregory obeyed her; she was so small and slight now it was like dressing a small doll. He would have lifted her down from the bed when he had finished, but she pushed him from her, laughing very softly. It was the first time she had laughed in those long dreary months.

'No, no; I can get down myself,' she said, slipping cautiously onto the floor. 'You see!' She cast a defiant glance of triumph when she stood there. 'Hold the curtain up high, I want to look at myself.'

He raised it, and stood holding it. She looked into the glass on the opposite wall. Such a queenly little figure in its pink and white. Such a transparent little face, refined by suffering into an almost angel-like beauty. The face looked at her; she looked back, laughing softly. Doss, quivering with excitement, ran round her barking. She took one step towards the door, balancing herself with outstretched hands.

'I am nearly there,' she said.

Then she groped blindly.

'Oh, I cannot see! I cannot see! Where am I?' she cried.

When Gregory reached her she had fallen with her face against the sharp foot of the wardrobe and cut her forehead. Very tenderly he raised the little crushed, heap of muslin and ribbons, and laid it on the bed. Doss climbed up, and sat looking down at it. Very softly Gregory's hands disrobed her.

'You will be stronger tomorrow, and then we shall try again,' he said, but she neither looked at him nor stirred.

When he had undressed her, and laid her in bed, Doss stretched himself across her feet and lay whining softly.

So she lay all that morning, and all that afternoon. Again and again Gregory crept close to the bedside and looked at her; but she did not speak to him. Was it stupor or was it sleep that shone under those half-closed eyelids? Gregory could not tell.

At last in the evening he bent over her.

'The oxen have come,' he said; 'we can start tomorrow if you like. Shall I get the wagon ready tonight?'

Twice he repeated his question. Then she looked up at him, and Gregory saw that all hope had died out of the beautiful eyes. It was not stupor that shone there, it was despair.

'Yes, let us go,' she said.

'It makes no difference,' said the doctor; 'staying or going; it is close now.'

So the next day Gregory carried her out in his arms to the wagon which stood *inspanned* before the door. As he laid her down on the *kartel* she looked far out across the plain. For the first time she spoke that day.

'That blue mountain, far away; let us stop when we get to it, not before.' She closed her eyes again. He drew the sails down before and behind, and the wagon rolled away slowly. The landlady and the niggers stood to watch it from the *stoep*.

Very silently the great wagon rolled along the grass-covered plain. The driver on the front box did not clap his whip or call to his oxen, and Gregory sat beside him with folded arms. Behind them, in the closed wagon, she lay with the dog at her feet, very quiet, with folded hands. He, Gregory, dared not be in there. Like Hagar, when she laid her treasure down in the wilderness, he sat afar off: – 'For Hagar said, "Let me not see the death of the child."'

Evening came, and yet the blue mountain was not reached, and all the next day they rode on slowly, but still it was far off. Only at evening they reached it; not blue now, but low and brown, covered with long waving grasses and rough stones. They drew the wagon up close to its foot for the night. It was a sheltered, warm spot.

When the dark night had come, when the tired oxen were tied to the wheels, and the driver and leader had rolled themselves in their blankets before the fire, and gone to sleep, then Gregory fastened down the sails of the wagon securely. He fixed a long candle near the head of the bed, and lay down himself on the floor of the wagon near the back. He leaned his head against the *kartel*, and listened to the chewing of the tired oxen and to the crackling of the fire, till, overpowered by weariness, he fell into a heavy sleep. Then all was very still in the wagon. The dog slept on his mistress's feet, and only two mosquitoes, creeping in through a gap in the front sail, buzzed drearily round.

The night was grown very old when from a long, peaceful sleep Lyndall awoke. The candle burnt at her head, the dog lay on her feet; but he shivered; it seemed as though a coldness struck up to him from his resting place. She lay with folded hands, looking upwards; and she heard the oxen chewing, and she saw the two mosquitoes buzzing drearily round and round, and her thoughts, – her thoughts ran far back into the past.

Through these months of anguish a mist had rested on her mind; it was rolled together now, and the old clear intellect awoke from its long torpor. It looked back into the past; it saw the present; there was no future now. The old strong soul gathered itself together for the last time; it knew where it stood.

Slowly raising herself on her elbow, she took from the sail a glass that hung pinned there. Her fingers were stiff and cold. She put the pillow on her breast, and stood the glass against it. Then the white face on the pillow looked into the white face in the glass. They had looked at each other often so before. It had been a child's face once, looking out above its blue pinafore; it had been a woman's face, with a dim shadow in the eyes, and a something which had said, 'We are not afraid, you and I; we are together; we will fight, you and I.' Now tonight it had come to this. The dying eyes on the pillow looked into the dying eyes in the glass; they knew that their hour had come. She raised one hand and pressed the stiff fingers against the glass. They were growing very stiff. She tried to speak to it, but she would never speak again. Only, the wonderful yearning light was in the eyes still. The body was dead now, but the soul, clear and unclouded, looked forth.

Then slowly, without a sound, the beautiful eyes closed. The dead face that the glass reflected was a thing of marvellous beauty and tranquillity. The Grey Dawn crept in over it, and saw it lying there.

Had she found what she sought for – something to worship? Had she ceased from being? Who shall tell us? There is a veil of terrible mist over the face of the Hereafter.

CHAPTER THIRTEEN

Dreams

'Tell me what a soul desires, and I will tell you what it is.' So runs the phrase. 'Tell me what a man dreams, and I will tell you I what he loves.' That also has its truth.

For, ever from the earliest childhood to the latest age, day by day, and step by step, the busy waking life is followed and reflected by the life of dreams – waking dreams, sleeping dreams. Weird, misty, and distorted as the inverted image of a mirage, or a figure seen through the mountain mist, they are still the reflections of a reality.

On the night when Gregory told his story, Waldo sat alone before the fire, his untasted supper before him. He was weary after his day's work – too weary to eat. He put the plate down on the floor for Doss, who licked it clean, and then went back to his corner. After a time the master threw himself across the foot of the bed without undressing and fell asleep there. He slept so long that the candle burnt itself out, and the room was in darkness. But he dreamed a lovely dream as he lay there.

In his dream, to his right rose high mountains, their tops crowned with snow, their sides clothed with bush and bathed in the sunshine. At their feet was the sea, blue and breezy, bluer than any earthly sea, like the sea he had dreamed of in his boyhood. In the narrow forest that ran between the mountains and the sea the air was rich with the scent of the honey-creeper that hung from dark green bushes, and through the velvety grass little streams ran purling down into the sea. He sat on a high square rock among the bushes, and Lyndall sat by him and sang to him. She was only a small child, with a blue pinafore, and a grave, grave, little face. He was looking up at the mountains, then suddenly when he looked round she was gone. He slipped down from his rock, and went to look for her, but he found only her little footmarks: he found them on the bright green grass, and in the moist sand, and there where the little streams ran purling down into the sea. In and out, in and out, and among the bushes where the honey-creeper hung, he went looking for her. At last, far off, in the sunshine, he saw her gathering shells upon the sand. She was not a child now, but a woman, and the sun shone on her soft brown hair, and in her white dress she put the shells she gathered. She was stooping, but when she heard his step she stood up, holding her skirt close about her, and waited for his coming. One hand she put in his, and together they walked on over the glittering sand and pink sea-shells; and they heard the leaves talking, and they heard the waters babbling on their way to the sea, and they heard the sea singing to itself, singing, singing.

At last they came to a place where was a long reach of pure white sand: there she stood still, and dropped onto the sand one by one the shells that she had gathered. Then she looked up into his face with her beautiful eyes. She said nothing; but she lifted one hand and laid it softly on his forehead; the other she laid on his heart.

With a cry of suppressed agony Waldo sprang from the bed, flung open the upper half of the door, and leaned out, breathing heavily.

Great God! It might be only a dream, but the pain was very real, as though a knife ran through his heart, as though some treacherous murderer crept on him in the dark! The strong man drew his breath like a frightened woman.

'Only a dream, but the pain was very real,' he muttered, as he pressed his right hand upon his breast. Then he folded his arms on the door, and stood looking out into the starlight.

The dream was with him still; the woman who was his friend was not separated from him by years – only that very night he had seen her. He looked up into the night sky that all his life long had mingled itself with his existence. There were a thousand faces that he loved looking down at him, a thousand stars in their glory, in crowns, and circles, and solitary grandeur. To the man they were not less dear than to the boy they had been, not less mysterious; yet he looked up at them and shuddered; at last turned away from them with horror. Such countless multitudes, stretching out far into space, and yet not in one of them all was she! Though he searched through them all, to the farthest, faintest point of light, nowhere should he ever say, 'She is here!' Tomorrow's sun would rise and gild the world's mountains, and shine into its thousand valleys; it would set and the stars creep out again. Year after year, century after century, the old changes of nature would go on, day and night, summer and winter, seedtime and harvest; but in none of them all would she have part!

He shut the door to keep out their hideous shining, and because the dark was intolerable lit a candle, and paced the little room, faster and faster yet. He saw before him the long ages of eternity that would roll on, on, on, and never bring her. She would exist no more. A dark mist filled the little room.

'Oh, little hand! oh, little voice! oh, little form!' he cried; 'oh, little soul that walked with mine; oh little soul, that looked so fearlessly down into the depths, do you exist no more forever – for all time?' He cried more bitterly: 'It is for this hour – this – that men blind reason, and crush out thought! For this hour – this, this – they barter truth and knowledge, take any lie, any creed, so it does not whisper to them of the dead that they are dead! Oh, God! God! For a Hereafter!'

Pain made his soul weak; it cried for the old faith. They are the tears that fall into the new-made grave that cement the power of the priest. For the cry of the soul that loves and loses is this – 'Bridge over Death; blend the Here with the Hereafter; cause the mortal to robe himself in immortality; let me not say of my Dead that it is dead! I will believe all else, bear all else, endure all else!'

Muttering to himself, Waldo walked with bent head, the mist in his eyes.

To the soul's wild cry for its own there are many answers. He began to think of them. Was not there one of them all from which he might suck one drop of comfort? 'You shall see her again,' says the Christian, the true Bible Christian. 'Yes; you shall see her again. "*And I saw the dead, small and great, stand before God. And the books were opened, and the dead were judged from those things which were written in the books. And whosoever was not found written in the book of life was cast into the lake of fire, which is the second death.*" Yes; you shall see her again. She died so – with her knee unbent, with her hand unraised, with a prayer unuttered, in the pride of her intellect and the strength of her youth. She loved and she was loved; but she said no prayer to God; she cried for no mercy; she repented of no sin! Yes; you *shall* see her again.'

In his bitterness Waldo laughed low.

Ah, he had long ceased to hearken to the hellish voice. But yet another speaks.

'You shall see her again,' says the nineteenth century Christian, deep into whose soul modern unbelief and thought have crept, though he knows it not. He it is who uses his Bible as the pearl-fishers use their shells, sorting out gems from refuse; he sets his pearls after his own fashion, and he sets them well. 'Do not fear,' he says; 'hell and judgment are not. God is love. I know that beyond this blue sky above us is a love as widespreading over all. The All-Father will show her to you again; not spirit only – the little hands, the little feet you loved, you shall lie down and kiss them if you will. Christ arose, and did eat and drink, so shall she arise. The dead, all the dead, raised incorruptible! God is love. You shall see her again.'

It is a heavenly song, this of the nineteenth century Christian. A man might dry his tears to listen to it, but for this one thing, – Waldo muttered to himself confusedly:

'The thing I loved was a woman proud and young; it had a mother once, who, dying, kissed her little baby, and prayed God that she might see it again. If it had lived the loved thing would itself have had a son, who, when he closed the weary eyes and smoothed the wrinkled forehead of his mother, would have prayed God to see that old face smile again in the Hereafter. To the son heaven will be no heaven if the sweet worn face is not in one of the choirs; he will look for it through the phalanx of God's glorified angels; and the youth will look for the maid, and the mother for the baby. "And whose then shall she be at the resurrection of the dead?"'

'Ah God! Ah God! A beautiful dream,' he cried; 'but can anyone dream it not sleeping?'

Waldo paced on, moaning in agony and longing. He heard the Transcendentalist's high answer.

'What have you to do with flesh, the gross and miserable garment in which spirit hides itself? You shall see her again. But the hand, the foot, the forehead you loved, you shall see no more. The loves, the fears, the frailties that are born with the flesh, with the flesh they shall die. Let them die! There is that in man that cannot die – a seed, a germ, an embryo, a spiritual essence. Higher than she was on earth, as the tree is higher than the seed, the man than the embryo, so shall you behold her; changed, glorified!'

High words, ringing well; they are the offering of jewels to the hungry, of gold to the man who dies for bread. Bread is corruptible, gold is incorruptible; bread is light, gold is heavy; bread is common, gold is rare; but the hungry man will barter all your mines for one morsel of bread. Around God's throne there may be choirs and companies of angels, cherubim and seraphim, rising tier above tier, but not for one of them all does the soul cry aloud. Only perhaps for a little human woman full of sin, that it once loved.

'Change is death, change is death,' he cried. 'I want no angel, only she; no holier and no better, with all her sins upon her, so give her me or give me nothing!'

And, truly, does not the heart love its own with the strongest passion for their very frailties? Heaven might keep its angels if men were but left to men.

'Change is death,' he cried, 'change is death! Who dares to say the body never dies, because it turns again to grass and flowers? And yet they dare to say the spirit never dies, because in space some strange unearthly being may have sprung up upon its ruins. Leave me! Leave me!' he cried in frantic bitterness. 'Give me back what I have lost, or give me nothing.'

For the soul's fierce cry for immortality is this – only this: – Return to me after death the thing as it was before. Leave me in the Hereafter the being that I am today. Rob me of the thoughts, the feelings, the desires that are my life, and you have left nothing to take. Your immortality is annihilation, your Hereafter is a lie.

Waldo flung open the door, and walked out into the starlight, his pain-stricken thoughts ever driving him on as he paced there.

'There must be a Hereafter because a man longs for it?' he whispered. 'Is not all life from the cradle to the grave one long yearning for that which we never touch? There must be a Hereafter because we cannot think of any end to life. Can we think of a beginning? Is it easier to say "I was not" than to say "I shall not be"? And yet, where were we ninety years ago? Dreams, dreams! Ah, all dreams and lies! No ground anywhere.'

He went back into the cabin and walked there. Hour after hour passed, and he was dreaming.

For, mark you, men *will* dream; the most that can be asked of them is but that the dream be not in too glaring discord with the thing they know. He walked with bent head.

All dies, all dies! The roses are red with the matter that once reddened the cheek of the child; the flowers bloom the fairest on the last year's battleground; the work of death's finger cunningly wreathed over is at the heart of all things, even of the living. Death's finger is everywhere. The rocks are built up of a life that was. Bodies, thoughts, and loves die: from where springs that whisper to the tiny soul of man, "You shall not die"? Ah, is there no truth of which this dream is shadow?

He fell into perfect silence. And, at last, as he walked there with his bent head, his soul passed down the steps of contemplation into that vast land where there is always peace; that land where the soul, gazing long, loses all consciousness of its little self, and almost feels its hand on the old mystery of Universal Unity that surrounds it. 'No death, no death,' he muttered; 'there is that which never dies – which abides. It is but the individual that perishes, the whole remains. It is the organism that vanishes, the atoms are there. It is but the man that dies, the Universal Whole of which he is part reworks him into its inmost self. Ah, what matter that man's day be short! – that the sunrise sees him, and the sunset sees his grave; that of which he is but the breath has breathed him forth and drawn him back again. That abides – we abide.'

For the little soul that cries aloud for continued personal existence for itself and its beloved, there is no help. For the soul which knows itself no more as a unit, but as a part of the Universal Unity of which the Beloved also is a part; which feels within itself the throb of the Universal Life; for that soul there is no death.

'Let us die, beloved, you and I, that we may pass on forever through the Universal Life!' In that deep world of contemplation all fierce desires die out, and peace comes down. He, Waldo, as he walked there, saw no more the world that was about him; cried out no more for the thing that he had lost. His soul rested. Was it only John, think you, who saw the heavens open? The dreamers see it every day.

Long years before the father had walked in the little cabin, and seen choirs of angels, and a prince like unto men, but clothed in immortality. The son's knowledge was not as the father's, therefore the dream was new-tinted, but the sweetness was all there, the infinite peace, that men find not in the little cankered kingdom of the tangible. The bars of the real are set close about us; we cannot open our wings but they are struck against them, and drop bleeding. But, when we glide between the bars into the great unknown beyond, we may sail forever in the glorious blue, seeing nothing but our own shadows.

So age succeeds age, and dream succeeds dream, and of the joy of the dreamer no man knoweth but he who dreameth.

Our fathers had their dreams; we have ours; the generation that follows will have its own. Without dreams and phantoms man cannot exist.

CHAPTER FOURTEEN

Waldo Goes Out to Sit in the Sunshine

It had been a princely day. The long morning had melted slowly into a rich afternoon. Rains had covered the Karoo with a heavy coat of green that hid the red earth everywhere. In the very chinks of the stone walls dark green leaves hung out, and beauty and growth had crept even into the beds of the sandy furrows and lined them with weeds. On the broken sod-walls of the old pigsty chickweeds flourished, and ice plants lifted their transparent leaves. Waldo was at work in the wagon-house again. He was making a kitchen table for Em. As the long curls gathered in heaps before his plane, he paused for an instant now and again to throw one down to a small naked nigger, who had crept from its mother, who stood churning in the sunshine, and had crawled into the wagon-house. From time to time the little animal lifted its fat hand as it expected a fresh shower of curls; till Doss, jealous of his master's noticing any other small creature but himself, would catch the curl in his mouth and roll the little Kaffir over in the sawdust, much to that small animal's contentment. It was too lazy an afternoon to be really ill natured, so Doss satisfied himself with snapping at the little nigger's fingers, and sitting on him till he laughed. Waldo, as he worked, glanced down at them now and then, and smiled; but he never looked out across the plain. He was conscious without looking of that broad green earth; it made his work pleasant to him. Near the shadow at the gable the mother of the little nigger stood churning. Slowly she raised and let fall the stick in her hands, murmuring to herself a sleepy chant such as her people love; it sounded like the humming of far-off bees.

A different life showed itself in the front of the house, where *Tant* Sannie's cart stood ready *inspanned*, and the Boer woman herself sat in the front room drinking coffee. She had come to visit her stepdaughter, probably for the last time, as she now weighed two hundred and sixty pounds, and was not easily able to move. On a chair sat her mild young husband nursing the baby – a pudding-faced, weak-eyed child.

'You take it and get into the cart with it,' said *Tant* Sannie. 'What do you want here, listening to our woman's talk?'

The young man arose, and meekly went out with the baby.

'I'm very glad you are going to be married, my child,' said *Tant* Sannie, as she drained the last drop from her coffee cup. 'I wouldn't say so while that boy was here, it would make him too conceited; but marriage is the finest thing in the world. I've been at it three times, and if it pleased God to take this husband from me I should have another. There's nothing like it, my child; nothing.'

389

'Perhaps it might not suit all people, at all times, as well as it suits you, *Tant* Sannie,' said Em. There was a little shade of weariness in the voice.

'Not suit everyone!' said *Tant* Sannie. 'If the beloved Redeemer didn't mean men to have wives what did He make women for? That's what I say. If a woman is old enough to marry, and doesn't, she's sinning against the Lord – it's a wanting to know better than Him. What, does she think the Lord took all that trouble in making her for nothing? It's evident He wants babies, otherwise why does He send them? Not that I've done much in that way myself,' said *Tant* Sannie sorrowfully, 'but I've.done my best.'

She rose with some difficulty from her chair, and began moving slowly towards the door.

'It's a strange thing,' she said, 'but you can't love a man till you've had a baby by him. Now there's that boy there – when we were first married if he only sneezed in the night I boxed his ears; now if he lets his pipe-ash come on my milk-cloths I don't think of laying a finger on him. There's nothing like being married,' said *Tant* Sannie, as she puffed toward the door. 'If a woman's got a baby and a husband she's got the best things the Lord can give her; if only the baby doesn't have convulsions. As for a husband, it's very much the same who one has. Some men are fat, and some men are thin; some men drink brandy, and some men drink gin; but it all comes to the same thing in the end; it's all one. A man's a man, you know.'

Here they came upon Gregory, who was sitting in the shade before the house. *Tant* Sannie shook hands with him.

'I'm glad you're going to get married,' she said. 'I hope you'll have as many children in five years as a cow has calves, and more too. I think I'll just go and have a look at your soap-pot before I start,' she said, turning to Em. 'Not that I believe in this new plan of putting soda in the pot. If the dear Father had meant soda to be put into soap what would He have made milk-bushes for, and stuck them all over the *veld* as thick as lambs in the lambing season?'

She waddled off after Em in the direction of the built-in soap-pot, leaving Gregory as they found him, with his dead pipe lying on the bench beside him, and his blue eyes gazing out far across the flat, like one who sits on the seashore watching that which is fading, fading from him. Against his breast was a letter found in a desk, addressed to himself but never posted. It held only four words: 'You must marry Em.' He wore it in a black bag round his neck. It was the only letter she had ever written to him.

'You see if the sheep don't have the scab this year!' said *Tant* Sannie, as she waddled after Em. 'It's with all these new inventions that the wrath of God *must* fall on us. What were the children of Israel punished for, if it wasn't for making a golden calf? I may have my sins, but I do remember the tenth commandment: "Honour thy father and thy mother that it may be well with thee, and that thou mayst live long in the land which the Lord thy God giveth thee!" It's all very well to say we honour them, and then to be finding out things that they never knew, and doing things in a way that they never did them! My mother boiled soap with bushes, and I will boil soap with bushes. If the wrath of God is to fall upon this land,' said *Tant* Sannie, with the serenity of conscious virtue, 'it shall not be through me. Let them make their steam-wagons and their fire-carriages; let them go on as though the dear Lord didn't know what he was about when He gave horses and oxen legs – the destruction of the Lord will follow them. I don't know how such people read their Bibles. When do we hear of Moses or Noah riding in a railway? The Lord sent fire-carriages out of heaven in those days: there's no chance of His sending them for us if we go on in this way,' said *Tant* Sannie sorrowfully, thinking of the splendid chance which this generation had lost.

Arrived at the soap-pot she looked over into it thoughtfully.

'Depend upon it you'll get the itch, or some other disease; the blessing of the Lord'll never rest upon it,' said the Boer woman. Then suddenly she broke forth, 'And she eighty-two, and goats, and rams, and eight thousand morgen, and the rams real angora, and two thousand sheep, and a shorthorn bull,' said *Tant* Sannie, standing upright and planting a hand on each hip.

Em looked at her in silent wonder. Had connubial bliss and the joys of motherhood really turned the old Boer woman's head?

'Yes,' said *Tant* Sannie; 'I had almost forgotten to tell you. By the Lord if I had him here! We were walking to church last Sacrament Sunday, Piet and I. Close in front of us was old *Tant* Trana, with dropsy and cancer, and can't live eight months. Walking by her was something with its hands under its coat-tails, flap, flap, flap; and its chin in the air, and a stick-up collar, and the black hat on the very back of the head. I knew him! "Who's that?" I asked. "The rich Englishman that *Tant* Trana married last week." "Rich Englishman! I'll rich Englishman him," I said; "I'll tell *Tant* Trana a thing or two." My fingers were just in his little white curls. If it hadn't been the blessed Sacrament, he wouldn't have walked so *sourka, sourka, courka,* any more. But I thought, Wait till I've had it, and then – But he, sly fox, son of Satan, seed of the Amalekite, he saw me looking at him in the church. The blessed Sacrament wasn't half over when he takes *Tant* Trana by the arm, and out they go. I clap my baby down to its father, and I go after them. But,' said *Tant* Sannie regretfully, 'I couldn't get up to them; I am too fat. When I got to the corner he was pulling *Tant* Trana up into the cart. "*Tant* Trana," I said, "you've married a Kaffir's dog, a Hottentot's *brakkie*." I hadn't any more breath. He winked at me; he winked at *me*,' said *Tant* Sannie, her sides shaking with indignation, first with one eye, and then with the other, and then drove away. Child of the Amalekite!' said *Tant* Sannie, 'if it hadn't been the blessed Sacrament. Lord, Lord, Lord!'

Here the little Bush-girl came running to say that the horses would stand no longer, and still breathing out vengeance against her old adversary she laboured towards the cart. Shaking hands and affectionately kissing Em, she was with some difficulty drawn up. Then slowly the cart rolled away, the good Boer woman putting her head out between the sails to smile and nod. Em stood watching it for a time, then as the sun dazzled her eyes she turned away. There was no use in going to sit with Gregory: he liked best sitting there alone, staring across the green Karoo; and till the maid had done churning there was nothing to do; so Em walked away to the wagon-house, and climbed on to the end of Waldo's table, and sat there, swinging one little foot slowly to and fro, while the wooden curls from the plane heaped themselves up against her black print dress.

'Waldo,' she said at last, 'Gregory has given me the money he got for the wagon and oxen, and I have fifty pounds besides that once belonged to someone. I know what they would have liked to have done with it. You must take it and go to some place and study for a year or two.'

'No, little one, I will not take it,' he said, as he planed slowly away; 'the time was when I would have been very grateful to any one who would have given me a little money, a little help, a little power of gaining knowledge. But now, I have gone so far alone I may go on to the end. I don't want it, little one.'

She did not seem pained at his refusal; but swung her foot to and fro, the little old wrinkled forehead more wrinkled up than ever.

'Why is it always so, Waldo, always so?' she said; 'we long for things, and long for them, and pray for them; we would give all we have to come near to them, but we never reach them. Then at last, too late, just when we don't want them any more, when all the sweetness is taken out of them, then they come. We don't want them then,' she said, folding her hands resignedly on her little apron. After a while she added: 'I remember once, very long ago, when I was a very little girl, my mother had a workbox full of coloured reels. I always wanted to play with them, but she would never let me. At last one day she said I might take the box. I was so glad I hardly knew what to do. I ran round the house, and sat down with it on the back steps. But when I opened the box all the cottons were taken out.'

She sat for a while longer, till the Kaffir maid had finished churning, and was carrying the butter towards the house. Then Em prepared to slip off the table, but first she laid her little hand on Waldo's. He stopped his planing and looked up.

'Gregory is going to the town tomorrow. He is going to give in our banns to the minister; we are going to be married in three weeks.'

Waldo lifted her very gently from the table. He did not congratulate her; perhaps he thought of the empty box, but he kissed her forehead gravely.

She walked away towards the house, but stopped when she had got halfway. 'I will bring you a glass of buttermilk when it is cool,' she called out; and soon her clear voice came ringing out through the back windows as she sang the *Blue Water* to herself, and washed the butter.

Waldo did not wait till she returned. Perhaps he had at last really grown weary of work; perhaps he felt the wagon-house chilly (for he had shuddered two or three times), though that was hardly likely in that warm summer weather; or, perhaps, and most probably, one of his old dreaming fits had come upon him suddenly. He put his tools carefully together, ready for tomorrow, and walked slowly out. At the side of the wagon-house there was a world of bright sunshine, and a hen with her chickens was scratching among the gravel. Waldo seated himself near them with his back against the red-brick wall. The long afternoon was half spent, and the *kopje* was just beginning to cast its shadow over the round-headed yellow flowers that grew between it and the farmhouse. Among the flowers the white butterflies hovered, and on the old *kraal* mounds three white kids gambolled, and at the door of one of the huts an old grey-headed Kaffir woman sat on the ground mending her mats. A balmy, restful, peacefulness seemed to reign everywhere. Even the old hen seemed well satisfied. She scratched among the stones and called to her chickens when she found a treasure; and all the while tucked to herself with intense inward satisfaction. Waldo, as he sat with his knees drawn up to his chin and his arms folded on them, looked at it all and smiled. An evil world, a deceitful, treacherous, mirage-like world, it might be; but a lovely world for all that, and to sit there gloating in the sunlight was perfect. It was worth having been a little child, and having cried and prayed, so one might sit there. He moved his hands as though he were washing them in the sunshine. There will always be something worth living for while there are shimmery afternoons. Waldo chuckled with intense inward satisfaction as the old hen had done; she, over the insects and the warmth; he, over the old brick walls, and the haze, and the little bushes. Beauty is God's wine, with which he recompenses the souls that love him; he makes them drunk.

The fellow looked, and at last stretched out one hand to a little ice plant that grew on the sod-wall of the sty; not as though he would have picked it, but as it were in a friendly greeting. He loved it. One little leaf of the ice plant stood upright, and the sun shone through it. He could see every little crystal cell like a drop of ice in the transparent green, and it thrilled him.

There are only rare times when a man's soul can see Nature. So long as any passion holds its revel there, the eyes are holden that they should not see her.

Go out if you will, and walk alone on the hillside in the evening, but if your favourite child lies ill at home, or your lover comes tomorrow, or at your heart there lies a scheme for the holding of wealth, then you will return as you went out; you will have seen nothing. For Nature, ever, like the old Hebrew God, cries out, 'Thou shalt have no other gods before me.' Only then, when there comes a pause, a blank in your life, when the old idol is broken, when the old hope is dead, when the old desire is crushed, then the Divine compensation of Nature is made manifest. She shows herself to you. So near she draws you, that the blood seems to flow from her to you, through a still uncut cord: you feel the throb of her life.

When that day comes, that you sit down broken, without one human creature to whom you cling, with your loves the dead and the living-dead; when the very thirst for knowledge through long-continued thwarting has grown dull; when in the present there no craving, and in the future no hope, then, oh, with a beneficent tenderness, Nature enfolds you.

Then the large white snowflakes as they flutter down, softly, one by one, whisper soothingly, 'Rest, poor heart, rest.' It is as though our mother smoothed our hair, and we are comforted.

And yellow-legged bees as they hum make a dreamy lyric; and the light on the brown stone wall is a great work of art; and the glitter through the leaves makes the pulses beat.

Well to die then; for, if you live, so surely as the years come, so surely as the spring succeeds the winter, so surely will passions arise. They will creep back, one by one, into the bosom that has cast them forth, and fasten there again, and peace will go. Desire, ambition, and the fierce agonising flood of love for the living – they will spring again. Then Nature will draw down her veil: with all your longing you shall not be able to raise one corner; you cannot bring back those peaceful days. Well to die then!

Sitting there with his arms folded on his knees, and his hat slouched down over his face, Waldo looked out into the yellow sunshine that tinted even the very air with the colour of ripe corn, and was happy.

He was an uncouth creature with small learning, and no prospect in the future but that of making endless tables and stone walls, yet it seemed to him as he sat there that life was a rare and very rich thing. He rubbed his hands in the sunshine. Ah, to live on so, year after year, how well! Always in the present; letting each day glide, bringing its own labour, and its own beauty; the gradual lighting up of the hills, night and the stars, firelight and the coals! To live on so, calmly, far from the paths of men; and to look at the lives of clouds and insects; to look deep into the heart of flowers, and see how lovingly the pistil and the stamens nestle there together; and to see in the thorn-pods how the little seeds suck their life through the delicate curled-up string, and how the little embryo sleeps inside! Well, how well, to sit so on one side, taking no part in the world's life; but when great men blossom into books looking into those flowers also, to see how the world of men too opens beautifully, leaf after leaf. Ah! life is delicious; well to live long, and see the darkness breaking, and the day coming! The day when soul shall not thrust back soul that would come to it; when men shall not be driven to seek solitude, because of the crying-out of their hearts for love and sympathy. Well to live long and see the new time breaking. Well to live long; life is sweet, sweet, sweet! In his breast pocket, where of old the broken slate used to be, there was now a little dancing-shoe of his friend who was sleeping. He could feel it when he folded his arm tight against his breast; and that was well also. He drew his hat lower over his eyes, and sat so motionless that the chickens thought he was asleep, and gathered closer around him. One even ventured to peck at his boot but he ran away quickly. Tiny yellow fellow that he was, he knew that men were dangerous; even sleeping they might awake. But Waldo did not sleep, and coming back from his sunshiny dream, stretched out his hand for the tiny thing to mount. But the chicken eyed the hand askance, and then ran off to hide under its mother's wing, and from beneath it it sometimes put out its round head to peep at the great figure sitting there. Presently its brothers ran off after a little white moth, and it ran out to join them; and when the moth fluttered away over their heads they stood looking up disappointed, and then ran back to their mother.

Waldo through his half-closed eyes looked at them. Thinking, fearing, craving, those tiny sparks of brother life, what were they, so real there in that old yard on that sunshiny afternoon? A few years – where would they be? Strange little brother spirits! He stretched his hand towards them, for his heart went out to them; but not one of the little creatures came nearer him, and he watched them gravely for a time; then he smiled, and began muttering to himself after his old fashion. Afterwards he folded his arms upon his knees, and rested his forehead on them. And so he sat there in the yellow sunshine, muttering, muttering, muttering, to himself.

It was not very long after when Em came out at the back-door with a towel thrown across her head, and in her hand a cup of milk.

'Ah,' she said, coming close to him, 'he is sleeping now. He will find it when he wakes, and be glad of it.'

She put it down upon the ground beside him. The mother hen was at work still among the stones, but the chickens had climbed about him, and were perching on him. One stood upon his shoulder, and rubbed its little head softly against his black curls; another tried to balance itself on the very edge of the old felt hat. One tiny fellow stood upon his hand, and tried to crow; another had nestled itself down comfortably on the old coat-sleeve, and gone to sleep there.

Em did not drive them away; but she covered the glass softly at his side. 'He will wake soon,' she said, 'and be glad of it.'

But the chickens were wiser.

THE END

From Man to Man
(or *Perhaps Only*)

by
Olive Schreiner

*'Perhaps only God knew what
the lights and shadows were.'*

– The Child's Day

Dedicated to

My Little Sister Ellie

*Who died, aged eighteen months,
when I was nine years old*

Also to

My Only Daughter

*Born on 30 April and died on 1 May
She never lived to know she was a woman*

Contents

The Prelude

The Child's Day *405*

The Book

The Woman's Day *433*

1 Showing What Baby-Bertie Thought of Her New Tutor; and How Rebekah Got Married *435*
2 A Wild-Flower Garden in the Bush *446*
3 The Dam Wall *453*
4 Showing How Baby-Bertie Heard the Cicadas Cry *468*
5 John-Ferdinand Shows Veronica His New House *480*
6 How Baby-Bertie Went A-Dancing *483*
7 Raindrops in the Avenue *496*
8 You Cannot Capture the Ideal by a Coup d'Etat *545*
9 Cart Tracks in the Sand *594*
10 How Griet Sat on the Stone Wall and Watched the Gnats *612*
11 How the Rain Rains in London *617*
12 Fireflies in the Dark *658*
13 The Veranda *687*

The Prelude

The Child's Day

The Child's Day

The little mother lay in the agony of childbirth. Outside all was still but the buzzing of the bees, some of which now and then found their way into the half-darkened room. The scent of the orange trees and of the flowers from the garden beyond came in through the partly opened window, with the rich dry odour of a warm, African summer morning. The little mother groaned in her anguish.

Old Ayah, the Hottentot woman, stood at the bedside with her hands folded and her long fingers crooked, the veins on the back standing out like cords. She said, '*O ja, God! Wat zal ons nou zeg?*'[1] and readjusted the little black shawl upon her shoulders. The window was open three inches, and the blind was drawn below it to keep out the heat. The mother groaned.

At the end of the passage in the dining room the father sat with his elbows on the deal table and his head in his hands, reading Swedenborg; but the words had no clear meaning for him. Every now and then he looked up at the clock over the fireplace. It was a quarter before ten, and the house was very quiet.

At the back of the house, on the kitchen doorstep, stood Rebekah, the little five-year-old daughter. She looked up into the intensely blue sky, and then down to the ducks who were waddling before the lowest step, picking up the crusts she had thrown to them. She wore a short pink-cotton dress with little white knickerbockers buttoned below the knees and a white *kappie* with a large curtain that came almost to her waist. She took the *kappie* off and looked up again into the sky. There was something almost oppressive in the quiet. The Kaffir maids had been sent home to their huts, except one who was heating water in the kitchen, and the little Kaffirs were playing away beyond the *kraals* on the old *kraal* heap. It was like Sunday. She drew a slight sigh, and looked up again into the sapphire-blue sky: it was going to be very hot. The farmhouse stood on the spur of a mountain, and the thorn trees in the flat below were already shimmering in the sunlight. After a while she put on her *kappie* and walked slowly down the steps and across the bare space which served for a farmyard. Beyond it she passed into the low bushes. She soon came to a spot just behind the *kraal* where the ground was flat and bare; the surface soil had been washed off, and a circular floor of smooth and unbroken stone was exposed, like the smooth floor of a great round room. The bushes about were just high enough to hide her from the farmhouse, though it was only fifty yards off. She stepped onto the stone slowly, on tiptoe. She was building a house here. It stood in the centre of the stone floor; it was a foot and a half high and about a foot across, and was built

---

1 'Oh yes, God! What shall we now say?'

of little flat stones placed very carefully on one another, and it was round like a tower. The lower story opened onto the ground by a little doorway two inches high; in the upper story there was a small door in the wall; and a ladder made of sticks, with smaller sticks fastened across, led up to it. She stepped up to the house very softly. She was building it for mice. Once a Kaffir boy told her he had built a house of stones, and as he passed the next day a mouse ran out at the front door. She had thought a great deal of it; always she seemed to see the mouse living in the house and going in and out at the front door; and at last she built this one. She had built it in two stories, so that the family could live on the lower floor and keep their grain on the top. She had put a great flat stone to roof the lower story, and another flat stone for the roof on the very top, and she had put a moss carpet in the lower floor for them to sleep on, and corn, ready for them to use above. She stepped very softly up to the house and peeped in at the little door; there was nothing there but the brown moss. She sat down flat on the stone before it and peered in. Half, she expected the mice to come; and half, she knew they never would!

Presently she took a few little polished flat stones out of her pocket and began to place them carefully round the top to form a turret; then she straightened the ladder a little. Then she sat, watching the house. It was too hot to go and look for more stones. After a while she stretched out her right hand and drew its sides together and made the fingers look as if it were a little mouse and moved it softly along the stone, creeping, creeping up to the door; she let it go in. Then after a minute she drew it slowly back and sat up. It was becoming intensely hot now; the sun beating down on the stone drew little beads of perspiration on her forehead.

How still it was! She listened to hear whether anyone from the house would call her. It was long past ten o'clock and she was never allowed to be out in the sun so late. She sat listening: then she got a curious feeling that something was happening at the house and stood up quickly and walked away towards it.

As she passed the dining room window, whose lower edge was on a level with her chin, she looked in. Her father was gone; but his glasses and his open book still lay on the table. Rebekah walked round to the kitchen door. Even the ducks were gone; no one was in the kitchen; only the flames were leaping up and crackling in the open fireplace, and the water was spluttering out of the mouth of the big black kettle. She stood for a moment to watch it. Then a sound struck her ear. She walked with quick, sharp steps into the dining room and threw her *kappie* on the table and stood listening. Again the sound came, faint and strange. She walked out into the long passage into which all the bedrooms opened. Suddenly the sound became loud and clear from her mother's bedroom. Rebekah walked quickly up the coconut-matted passage and knocked at her mother's door, three short, sharp knocks with her knuckle. There was a noise of moving and talking inside; then the door opened a little.

'I want to come in! Please, what is the matter?'

Some one said, 'Shall she come in?' and then a faint voice answered, 'Yes, let her come.'

Rebekah walked in; there was but a little light coming in under the blind through the slightly opened window. Her mother was lying in the large bed and her father standing at the bedside. A strange woman from the next farm, whom she had never seen before, sat in the elbow chair in the corner beyond the bed, with something on her lap; old Ayah stood near the drawers, folding some linen cloths.

Rebekah stood for a moment motionless and hesitating on the ox skin in the middle of the floor; then she walked straight up to the strange woman in the corner.

'Ask her to show you what she has got, Rebekah,' said her father.

The woman unfolded a large brown shawl, inside of which there was a white one. Even in the dim light in the corner you could see a little red face, with two hands doubled up on the chest, peeping out from it.

Rebekah looked. 'Was it *this* that made that noise?' she asked.

The woman smiled and nodded.

Her father came up. 'Kiss it, Rebekah; it is your little sister.' Rebekah looked quietly at it.

'No – I won't. I don't like it,' she said slowly. But her father had already moved across the room to speak to old Ayah.

Rebekah turned sharply on her heel and walked to the large bed. Her mother lay on it with her eyes shut. Rebekah stood at the foot, her eyes on a level with the white coverlet, looking at her mother.

As she stood there she heard old Ayah whisper to the father, and they both went out, to the spare bedroom opposite. The strange woman came and bent over the mother and said something to her; she nodded her head without opening her eyes. The woman made a space at her side and laid the white bundle down in it; she put the baby's head on the mother's arm. The mother opened her eyes then and looked down at it with a half smile, and drew the quilt up a little higher to shield it. Rebekah watched them; then she walked softly to the door.

'Please open it for me,' she said. The handle was too high for her.

For a moment she stood outside the closed door, looking at it, her tiny features curiously set almost with the firmness of a woman's; then she turned and walked down the passage. She saw her father and old Ayah come out of the spare room. Old Ayah locked the door and put the key into her pocket, and they went back to her mother's bedroom.

Rebekah picked up her *kappie* from the dining room table, put it on, and went out again on to the steps at the kitchen door. The sun was blazing in the yard now; the very stones seemed to throw up a red reflection. Standing on the top step in fine shade, Rebekah shivered with heat.

Then she wandered slowly down the steps and across the yard. She could feel the ground burn under her feet, through the soles of her little shoes. She walked to her flat stone. The mouse house stood baking in the sun with all the little crystals in the rock glittering. She sat down before the house, drawing her skirts carefully under her, the rock burnt so. She drew her knees up to her chin, and folded her arms about them, and sat looking at the mouse house. She knew she ought not to be there in the hot sun; she knew it was wicked; but she liked the heat to burn her that morning.

After a while the little drops of perspiration began to gather under her eyes and on her upper lip; she would not wipe them off. Her face began to get very red, and her temples to throb; the heat was fierce. She looked out at the mouse house from under her white *kappie* with blinking red eyes. She could feel the heat scorching her arms through her little cotton dress, and she liked it.

By half past eleven the heat was so intense she could not bear it, and there began to be a sound like a little cicada singing in her ears, so she got up and walked slowly towards the house, but did not go in at the kitchen door.

She went to the back, where the wall of the house made a deep shadow, and went to the window of the spare room. It was her favourite place, to which she went whenever she wanted to be quite safe and alone. No one ever went there. The beds were generally left unmade till visitors came, with only the mattresses and pillows on them, and under one bed she kept her box of specially prized playthings. She unclosed the outer shutters. The window was so low that she could easily raise the sash and climb in from the ground. She pushed it up and stepped into the room. It was beautifully cool there and almost dark: she drew up the blind a very little to let in some light. She was walking towards the bed under which her box was, when something struck her eye. On the large table in the middle of the room there was a something with a white sheet spread over it. Rebekah walked up to it; this was something quite new.

She drew a chair to the side of the table and climbed up. She lifted the top of the sheet. Under it there was another sheet and a pillow, and, with its head on the pillow, dressed in pure white, was a little baby. Rebekah stood upright on the chair, holding the sheet in her hand.

After a while she let it down carefully, but so turning it back that the baby's face and hand were exposed. How fast it was sleeping!

She bent down and peered into its face. There was a curious resemblance between her own small, sharply marked features and those of the baby. She put out her forefinger gently and touched one of its hands. They were very cool. She watched it for some time; then she climbed down and went to the wardrobe where the best going-to-town clothes were kept hanging. With some difficulty she unhooked a little fur-trimmed red cape of her own; with this she climbed back on to the chair and laid it across the baby's feet. It was evidently not warm enough, though the day was hot.

She bent down over it again. On the top of its head was a little mass of soft, down-like curly black hair; she put her face down softly and touched the hair with her cheek and kissed it. She dared not kiss its face for fear of waking it. She sat down beside it, motionless, for a long time, on the edge of the table. Seeing it did not stir, after a time she climbed down, and taking off her shoes and leaving them at the foot of the table, went on tip-toe to the bed and drew from under it her box.

It was a large soapbox with an odd collection of things in it. On the top was a dried monkey's skin and a large alphabet book with coloured pictures; below were different little boxes and bags; some held stones; one was full of brightly coloured beetles and grasshoppers she had picked up dead; in one, all by itself, was a very large bright crystal, carefully wrapped in cottonwool and tied with a string. Below was an oblong-shaped, common brown stone about eighteen inches in length; it was dressed in doll's clothes and it had a shawl wrapped round it. Beside it was a small shop-doll with pink cheeks and flaxen hair, which she had got on her last birthday; but it had no shawl and its face was turned to the wood. The stone she had had two years, and she loved it; the shop-doll was only interesting. Besides these there was a round Bushman stone with a hole in the middle, which she had picked up behind the *kraal*, and a flat slate-coloured stone with the impression of a fossilised leaf, which she found on the path going up to the mountain; and, at the very bottom in the corner was a workbox, with a silver thimble and needles and cottons inside, which she thought very grand; and two little brightly coloured boxes with chocolates and peppermints with holes through them like whistles, which she had got on Christmas Day, but thought too pretty to eat; and there was also a head of Queen Victoria, cut out of the tinsel label of a sardine tin, and which she kept wrapped up in white paper.

She took all the things out of the box and handled them carefully, deliberating for a while. At last she selected the alphabet book, the Bushman stone, the silver thimble and a paper of needles, Queen Victoria's head, and a stick of chocolate. When she had packed the other things back, she went with them to the table. She climbed up on the chair. She laid the thimble and paper of needles on the cushion on the left of the baby's head, and the Bushman stone and the tinsel Queen Victoria head on the right. Very gently and slowly she slipped the alphabet book under the baby's doubled-up arm; and then, turning back the silver paper at one end of the chocolate stick, she forced the other end very gently into its closed fist, leaving the uncovered end near to its mouth. Then she stood upright on the chair with her hands folded before her, looking down at them all, with a curious contentment about her mouth.

After a little time she got down and went to her box at the foot of the bed, and sat down upon it; to wait till the baby woke.

Her face was seamed under the eyes with lines hot perspiration and dust had left, and she was very tired. She leaned her arm on the bed and rested her head on it.

At half past one it was dinnertime, and old Ayah could not find her. She often crept in the heat of the day behind the piano or into the wagon-loft, and fell asleep there where no one could discover her. So old Ayah put some dinner for her in a tin plate in the oven to keep warm.

Then everyone went to lie down; the shutters of all the doors and windows were closed, and there was not a sound in all the house but the buzzing of the flies in the darkened rooms.

Only old Ayah did not sleep today and was sewing a piece of white calico into a long, narrow, white robe with a stiff frill down the front for a tiny baby. She sat working in the dining room with the shutters very slightly apart to let in enough light.

When she had done it she went down the passage to the door of the spare room and unlocked it.

The first thing she noticed was that the outer shutters she had left carefully closed were partly open, that the window had been raised, and the blind was an inch or two drawn up. She walked to the table. The baby lay with the sheet removed from its face, and the Bushman stone, and thimble, and needles, and a picture, on its pillow, and the alphabet book under its arm, and the chocolate stick in its hand. She glanced round. Rebekah was still sitting on her box at the foot of the bed with her stockinged feet crossed and her head resting on her arm on the mattress, fast asleep, her shoes standing side by side at the foot of the table.

Old Ayah walked up to her and shook her by the shoulder. Rebekah opened her eyes slowly and looked at her, dreamily, without raising her head.

'What are you doing in here? Couldn't you see, if the door was locked, that you weren't meant to get in here?' she said in the Cape Dutch she always spoke.

Rebekah sat up, still looking round vacantly; then in an instant all came back to her and she stood up.

'Aren't you a wicked, naughty child, letting all the flies and the sun come in! What have you been doing?'

'Oh, please don't talk so loud,' whispered Rebekah quickly, bending forward and stretching out her hand; 'please, you'll wake it!'

'Oh Lord!' said old Ayah, looking at her, 'what would your mother say if she knew you'd been in here playing with that blessed baby? You naughty child, how dared you touch it!'

'It's mine: *I* found it!' said Rebekah, walking softly up to the foot of the table.

Old Ayah came up, too.

'Oh, please,' said Rebekah, putting out her hand again, '*don't* touch it! Don't touch it! I *don't* want it waked!'

She looked up at old Ayah with full lustrous eyes, as a bitch when you handle her pups.

'O my God!' said old Ayah, 'the child is mad! How can it be yours? It's your mother's.'

'It is mine,' said Rebekah slowly: 'I found it. Mietje found hers in the hut, and Katje found hers behind the *kraal*. My mother found hers that cries so, in the bedroom. *This one* is mine!'

'O Lord, Lord!' cried old Ayah. 'I tell you this is your mother's baby; she had two, and this one is dead. I put it here myself.'

Rebekah looked at her. 'This one is dead: it'll never open its eyes again; it can't breathe.'

The old Hottentot woman began taking the alphabet book from under its arm and the stick from its hand, and took the things from the pillow.

Rebekah did not look at her; her gaze was fixed on the baby's face.

'Here, take these things!'

But Rebekah raised out her hand, and touched the baby's feet; a coldness went up her arm, even through the sheet. She dropped her hand.

'Child, what is it? Here! – take your shoes!'

She thrust the shoes into her hand. Rebekah held them, but let them slide between her fingers onto the floor; she was still staring at the table.

Old Ayah gathered up the child's apron and put into it the things she had taken from the baby, and forced the shoes back into her other hand.

'Here, take them, I say, and go away! And get your face washed and your hair done, and tell Mietje to put you on a clean dress and white pinafore. What would your mother say to see you looking such an ugly, dirty little fright?'

Rebekah turned away slowly, with the gathered apron in one hand and the shoes in the other, and walked to the door. When she got there she turned and looked dreamily back; then she went out into the passage.

After she had had her face washed and her hair brushed, and had got on a clean starched pink dress and a white over-all pinafore, she went to the dining room. Old Ayah had put her plate of warmed dinner on the table ready for her, and she sat down on the bench to eat it. She felt better now she was washed and had a clean starched dress on.

The heat outside was still very oppressive, and only a little light came in through the cracks in the shutter; and the blue flies were buzzing round everywhere in the dark. She did not feel very hungry, and played with her dinner, but she drank all the water in her mug. Then she pushed her plate from her, found her *kappie*, and went out into the great front room. All was quiet there also, and almost quite dark. She took a large worn picture book from the side table, and opened the double door and went out onto the front *stoep*.[2] The vine leaves on the front wall hung dry and stiff, and even the orange leaves on the great orange trees before the door hung curled and flaccid.

It was nearly three o'clock, and the heat was hardly less intense than at midday, though there was already shade on that side of the house. The hollyhocks and dahlias in the flower garden beyond the orange trees were hanging their heads, and the four-o'clocks were curled up tight, though the trees sheltered them.

She walked down through the flower garden, on into the orchard beyond.

All was very still and brown there. The little peach trees that stood in rows were shedding their half-ripe fruit, which fell into the long yellow grass beneath them, and the fig trees along the wall had curled up the edges of their leaves. Rebekah followed a little winding footpath among the grass to the middle of the orchard, where a large pear tree stood, with a gnarled and knotted stem. There was a bench under the tree, and the grass grew very long all about it. She looked around to find a spot where the tree cast a deeper shade than elsewhere. Here she walked round and round on the grass, like a dog, and then lay down on her back in the place she had made. It was like a nest, with the grass standing several inches high all round.

She drew up her legs, cocking one knee over the other, so that one foot waved in the air.

It was very nice. She lay for a while with her hands clasped across the top of her head, from which she had thrown her white *kappie*. The pear-tree leaves were so thick overhead you could hardly see any sky through them. She yawned luxuriously. Beyond the edges of the pear branches, here and there as you looked through half-closed eyes, were strips of blue sky, and some great, white masses of thundercloud were showing in them, like ships sailing in the blue. She watched them for a while with her eyes half shut; then she took up the book that lay on the grass at her side, stood it open on her chest against her knee, and gently waved the foot that was cocked up in the air.

The book opened of itself about the middle of a certain page. On it was a picture: Peter, a great boy with a red face, looking out through the top of the letter P, and at his feet was a little pig with a curled tail. Besides this there were in the picture, in the distance, fields and a stile, and a winding path leading far away over the hills; and in the foreground was a milestone with weeds growing around it; below was written, 'P stands for Peter and Pig'.

She had had the book ever since she could remember, she had kept it very clean; there was no torn place or mark in it; but the page of *Peter and his Pig* was brown and worn round the edges. It was her favourite picture. Whenever she looked at it she wanted to make up stories. She had made one long story about it: how people

---

2 Veranda.

were not kind to Peter and he had no one to love him but his pig, and how they both ran away together by that far-off road that went over the hill, and saw all the beautiful things on the other side. She liked this book better than her new books. She stood it up on her chest and looked into the picture. But today it had no meaning; it suggested nothing. Then she looked away again beyond the edges of the pear branches, where two great masses of white cloud were floating in the blue; they dazzled her eyes so she closed them.

Presently she made a story that one of those clouds was a ship and she was sailing in it (she had never seen the sea or a ship, but she was always making stories about them), and, as she sailed, she came at last to an island. The ship stopped there. And on the edge of the shore was a lady standing, dressed in beautiful clothes, all gold and silver. When she stepped on to the shore the lady came up to her and bowed to her, and said, 'I am Queen Victoria. Who are you?'

And Rebekah answered her, 'I am the little Queen Victoria of South Africa.'

And they bowed to each other. (The child under the tree moved her head very slightly, without opening her eyes.)

The Queen asked her where she came from. She said, 'From a country far away from here: not such a *very* nice country! Things are not always nice there – only sometimes they are.'

The Queen said, 'I have many islands that belong to me, but this island belongs to no one. Why don't you come and live here? No one will ever scold you here, and you can do just what you like.'

Rebekah said, 'I should like it very much; but I must first go and fetch my books out of the ship.' And when she had brought her books, she said to the Queen, 'Here is a little box of presents I have got for all the people who live on the farm where I used to live; for my father and my mother and the servants and the little Kaffirs – and even old Ayah. Would you please give it to them as you go past?' And the Queen said she would; and she said, 'Goodbye, little Queen Victoria!' And Rebekah said, 'Goodbye, big Queen Victoria!' and they bowed to each other, and the old Queen went away in the ship in which in she had come.

Then she was all alone on her island. (She had never seen an island except a lump of ground in the furrow, with some thyme and forget-me-nots growing on it; but when she grew up she found she had pictured that island just as a real island might have been!) The island had many large trees and bushes, and the grass and thyme and forget-me-nots grew down to the water's edge. She walked a little way and she came to a river with trees on each side, and on it were two swans swimming, with their long white necks bent. She had had a book with the picture of a swan swimming in a lake, and she had always thought she must die of joy if she should see a real swan swimming up and down. And here were two!

A little farther, on the bank of the river, there was a little house standing. It was as high in proportion to her as grown-up people's houses are in proportion to them.

The doors were just high enough for her to go in and out at; and all things fitted her. One room was covered with books from the floor to the ceiling, with a little empty shelf for her own books, and there was a microscope on the table like her father's which she was never allowed to touch; but this one was hers!

Outside, in the garden, there were little rakes and spades that came as high as her shoulder. (Rebekah had always had to dig with a man's spade that made her arms ache.) At the side of the house there were all the things lying one uses for building houses; and a pile of bricks; and a bit of bare ground where you could make as much mud as you liked and make more bricks. But she hadn't time to stay and make bricks then. She went on farther.

Presently she came to a place where the trees hung very low down over the water and the grass was very thick; and there, from a large white bush, hanging right over and nearly touching the water, she saw a snow-white pod nearly as long as her arm. It was like a pea pod but was covered all over with a white, frosted silver. She reached down over the edge and tried to pick it. It was very heavy; at last she broke it off and carried it away in her pinafore, and she sat on a bank with it on her lap. She pressed with her finger all up and down the joint, and slowly the pod cracked and cracked, and opened from one end to the other, like a mimosa pod does.

And there, lying inside it, like the seeds lie inside the pod of a mimosa tree – was a little baby. It was quite pink and naked. It was as long in proportion to her, as a Kaffir woman's new baby is in proportion to a Kaffir woman, when she first finds it. She tried to lift it out but it was tied to the pod like the mimosa seeds are, with a little curled-up string. She broke the string and lifted it out; then she wrapped it up in her pinafore and skirt and put its head on her arm and carried it home.

(The book, which was still standing up against her knee, here fell over softly into the breast of the child under the pear tree.)

When she got it home she fed it with milk from a tiny bottle as one feeds a hand-lamb, and she wrapped it up in a soft white shawl, and put it on her bed and lay down beside it. She held it close against her with one arm, and stroked its hair softly with the other hand.

'Go to sleep, my baby,' she said; 'you must be very tired this first day. The world is so large. Tomorrow you can see all the things, and I'll tell you about them.

'If you should wake in the night, my baby,' she said presently, 'and hear anything, don't be afraid: just call to me. I'll be close by. And if you hear the clock ticking, *don't* think it means any of those dreadful things – it doesn't! I'll stop it if it makes you sad. And if you want to see the angels, then just shut your eyes and press on them *hard* with your two fingers, like this ...' (The child under the tree moved her hand as though to raise it to her eyes, but did not). 'Those black things with the light all round which you see going round and round when you press your eyes, are the angels' heads; just like it says in the hymn:

"And through the hours of darkness keep
Their watch around my bed."

'They are good angels, though they are black in the middle. I always used to see them when I was a little girl and I pressed my eyes. I'll put a chocolate stick under your pillow, that you can find it and suck it if you feel lonely. *Don't* be sorry you are come into the world, my baby. I will take care of you!'

She was going to rise from the bed; then she remembered other things that had to be said, and lay down again.

'When you are grown older, I'll teach you the multiplication table and spelling, because you can't grow up if you don't know these things. I know how bad it is to learn them; I had to when I was little, and so at last I grew up.

'Kaffirs grow up without learning tables or spelling; that's why it would be nice to be a Kaffir. If you've something hard to learn, pray God to help you; sometimes he does and sometimes he doesn't. If he doesn't, it's because you've prayed wrong; but it's no use praying again on that same day, especially if it's hot; – wait till the next.'

Again there was a long pause. 'My baby, I shall *never* call *you* "a strange child"! You can climb trees and tear your clothes; but if you find any birds' nests, you mustn't take the eggs; you can just put your hand in and feel; and, if it's a very little nest, you must only put one finger in. Especially cock-o-veet's eggs you must *not* take! Kaffir boys take birds' eggs.'

Again there was a pause.

'My baby, shall I tell you a little story? It's one I made myself, and a rather nice little story.

'Once there was a little girl, and she went for a walk in the bush. And when she had gone a little way, a cock-o-veet[1] came flying up to her and took hold of her pinafore by the corner with its beak. And the little girl said, "Cock-o-veet dear, what is it?"

'And the cock-o-veet said, "Make your hand like a little round nest."

'So she made it so – so!' (The child as she lay under the tree with her closed eyes drew the fingers of her right hand together and made a hollow.)

'And the cock-o-veet sat down in her hand; and when it got up, there – was – a – little – real – blue – egg – lying there!

'And the little girl said, "Oh, cock-o-veet!"

'And the cock-o-veet said: "Put the egg in my nest, and I will sit on it and make a little bird come out, for you!" And the cock-o-veet showed the little girl where her nest was; and she put the egg in; and the cock-o-veet sat down on it, and said, "Goodbye; I'll call you when it comes out."

'And when she had gone farther she saw some monkeys sitting up in the high

---

1 *Kokkewiet*: The bush-shrike, a very handsome bird with resonant call notes of great beauty – a prime favourite of Olive's.

trees, little, long-tailed monkeys; and they put their hands out to her. And she looked up and said, "Oh, little monkeys, what do you want?"

'And they said, "Come up in the trees and have tea, with us."

'And she said, "What kind of tea do you have, oh, monkeys?"

'And they said, "Nam-nams and Kaffir plums."

'So she climbed up and sat with them on a branch, and they gave her of their nam-nams and Kaffir plums with their little black hands, and she gave them some cakes out of a little bag she had with her.

'And when they had finished the monkeys kissed her, and she kissed them, and she climbed down and went on.

'And presently she came to a place where some very large rocks were lying deep in the bush, and the trees were hanging over them, and it was dark under the rock. And the little girl thought it looked rather like a tiger's sleeping place!

'And when she looked under the rock, there *was* a great tiger lying! And she said, "Oh, tiger!"

'And the tiger winked with its eyes – so!

'And she said, "I'm rather frightened of you, Mr Tiger!"

'But the tiger said, "Come here!"

'So she came.

'And the tiger said, "You can just play being my cub if you like!"

'So she lay down by the tiger, and the tiger rolled her over and made believe to bite her.

'And the tiger said, "Cubbie, would you like to sleep a little? You look rather tired." And it made a place for her between its front legs, where she could lie down with her head on its side, and it was nice and soft.

'And the tiger said, "If the flies trouble you, I'll just switch them away with my tail!"

'And the little girl said, "I'll just leave my little bag of cakes open so that if you like you can help yourself while I'm asleep."

'And she went to sleep on the tiger. And when she woke the tiger licked all over her face and said, "Goodbye"; and she went on.

'And by and by, as she was going up a very steep road right up on the mountain, there was a lion standing right before her.

'And the little girl said, "Oh, Mr Lion!" And he said, "Come up to me!"

'So she came up; and he rubbed his head against her pinafore and she rubbed her head in his stiff curls.

'And the lion said, "Aren't you afraid to come walking in the bush alone?"

'And she said, "Oh, no!"

'And he yawned.

'And she said, "Don't you open your mouth so *very* wide, please! It's so *very* big!"

'And he said, "I'm only yawning a little; it's nothing."

'And the little girl gave him some of her cakes. She said, "I've made them myself."
'He licked his mouth and said they were nice cakes; and he said he would walk home with her. She said there was no need, because perhaps the people at the farmhouse mightn't quite like it; but that if ever he had a thorn in his foot he must let her know and she'd take it out. He said he hadn't a thorn just then, but he'd let her know when he had. So they rubbed their heads against each other, and she went away.'

(The mouth of the child under the tree was drawn in at the corners as if half smiling, a quiet smile.)

'Then the little girl went down the mountain and into her father's garden. And, just as she was going in at the gate under the dam wall, she heard something go puff – puff – puff! And she looked round, and, there, just by her, was a great puff-adder sitting up! And she said, "Oh, Puff-puffie!"
'And the puff-adder said, "Come with me, my dear!"
'And the little girl said, "But Puff-puffie, I'm rather afraid!"
'And the puff-adder said, "Don't be, my dear; *I* never bite little girls!" And she took the little girl to a hole in the wall, where all her little puff-adders were. And she said, "You can put your hand in and take a few out. They've all got little poison bags, but they don't use them. They only eat grass and sand; and they like a little drop of milk now and then when they can get it."
'And the little girl put her hand in and took out the little puff-adders, till her pinafore was full.
'And she said, "I shall not forget to bring them a little drop of milk when I have any!" And she put them back in the hole, and she wished good afternoon to the puff-adder, and the puff-adder wished her good afternoon and went to sleep under a stone.
'And then the little girl went down farther in the garden; and she hadn't gone very far when she saw a great cobra lying on the grass, with his bright eyes looking at her.
'And she said, "Oh, Mr Cobra!"
'And he said, "Good afternoon, my dear. Won't you take me on your lap and warm me a little? I'm so cold today!"
'So she held out her pinafore and the cobra climbed in: he made her pinafore quite full. And she walked to the sod wall with him and sat down on the top, where the sun could shine on him, and she sang to the cobra; and he went to sleep in her lap. – And that's the end of the story.'

(The child under the tree seemed to be dropping asleep also; her lips had ceased to move, and her breath came evenly, but her mind went on.)

'You know that's only a story, my baby. You can't really go into the bush and do so with all the animals. They don't understand – yet. Perhaps, if you could talk to them from a long way off – so that they knew what you meant – My father brought a tiger down from the bush once, that they had caught with a trap. I was sorry for him because he was shut up in a cage and looked so sad. So I saved my meat for him at dinner, and I took it out to him when the others were asleep; his eyes were quite nearly shut and his head was on his feet. But just when I put my hand in with the meat he jumped up; he tried to bite me. I didn't tell anyone.

'Only dogs understand. If a great dog comes at you, my baby, don't you run away. Just say "Sibby! Sibby! Sibby!" and make – so – with your fingers; say "P-o-o-r dog, *p-o-o-r,* P-O-O-R little Sibby!" Even if he's big, you can say "little"; dogs always like to be called "little". Even if he's got his mouth on a side – so – and you can see his one tooth, don't be afraid; just stand and talk to him. He'll understand. But other things don't. The best thing is to feed them.

'My baby, was it a nice little story I've told you? If I tell you a secret, you mustn't tell anyone else! I'm a person that makes stories! I write *books*! When I was little I used to scribble them in a copybook with a stick, when I didn't know how to write. But when I grew up I learned to write; I wrote real books, a whole roomful! I've written a book about birds, and about animals, and about the world; and one day I'm going to write a book something like the Bible. If you like to make up stories, I shall never let anyone laugh at *you*, when you walk up and down and talk to yourself. I know you *must*.

'There are some stories I didn't make that I like too. There's one I like best of all. Shall I tell it you?'

(The child under the tree moved her arms a little as if drawing something closer to her.)

'It's rather a hard story because it's a grown-up people's story; I heard it one Sunday afternoon; my father read it to my mother. They thought I couldn't understand, but I did. I don't know if I tell it right, because I only heard it once, but I often looked at the picture. I'll make it as easy as I can.

'You see, it's called *What Hester Durham Lived For.* Hester Durham was a woman, and she sat by the table talking; and the minister came and talked with her. And she said: "Oh, I wish I was dead! My husband isn't very kind to me, and my boy, whom I loved so much, is dead; and now I wish I was dead, too."

'And the clergyman (that is a minister) said to her, "Oh, you mustn't say that; perhaps one day you'll have something to do for some one."

'And so the lady went away to India – that's a land far away where black people live – and the black soldiers (they call them sepoys) wanted to kill them. They came all round the house, calling and yelling, with swords and sticks. They were only women and children there; and all of them were very frightened; even the old black ayah. But Hester Durham was not afraid. In the picture they are all standing round her and some of them have caught hold of her dress, and some are lying on the ground close to her; and you can see the men's faces outside, with their eyes very big, wanting to come in and kill them all, and their mouths open, screaming! Then it says in the Book: – "*Alone, like a rock in a raging sea, Hester Durham stood there.*"

They hadn't been *so* afraid, because she was there to comfort them. And at last the sepoys did come in, and killed them all; but – "*to comfort those frail women and children in their last hour of despair, that was what Hester Durham lived for*" – those are the words I heard my father read. It's rather a difficult story; but you'll know what it means when you're grown up, when you are five years old – I did – though it is difficult.

'I can teach you many things, my baby; poems; there's a nice one:

"The Assyrian came down ..."

'And another:

"Like mist on the mountains,
Like ships on the sea ..."

'But the nicest of all is about a woman. The Romans came and they took away her country and they beat her till the blood ran off her back on to the ground, and they were cruel to her daughters. The Romans were people who took other people's countries; and she got into a chariot and her two daughters and her long hair flying in the wind; and under the tree sat an old man with a long white beard; and he said ...

"Rome shall perish; write that word
In the blood that she hath spilt ..."'

(The child under the pear tree with her eyes still fast closed raised her right hand, and her lips moved making a low sound.)

"'Rome, for Empire far renown
Tramps on a thousand States:
Soon her pride shall kiss the ground:
Hark! – The Gaul is at her gates!"'

(The child under the tree lifted her hand higher and waved it dramatically with her eyes still closed.)
'And the Gauls did come; and they knocked at the gates, and they burned it down. "Hark! – The Gaul is at her gates!" – I'm glad they burned it. Aren't you?'
(The child's hand dropped.)
'It's a long poem. I'll teach it you. I could understand it all except "For-Empire" and "far-renown". – I don't know what "far-renown" is ...or "for-empire" ...'
(The child under the tree knit her forehead a little.)

419

'Grown-up people's things are nicer than children's. I didn't like *Jane Taylor's Hymns for Infant Minds*. You'll never have to learn them. The Bible is nice, especially about Elijah, and some texts; one beautiful one – "And instead of the thorn tree shall come up the fir tree; and instead of the briar shall come up the myrtle tree." It's just like water going – so ...! But Miss Plumtree's Bible stories are horrid! My mother used to read them to me.'

(The child under the tree turned her head a little to one side and bent it, as though bringing it nearer to something that lay on her arm.)

'My baby, do you know who Charles is? He's the boy who always plays with me. You won't mind if I love him more than you, because I've known him so very long. He always tells me stories, and I tell him stories, and we walk up and down together. He's a little older than me. He's not a *real* boy, you know! I made him up. He is the Prince Consort of South Africa, and I am the Queen.

'I don't like *real* boys. We had two came to visit us once: they were my cousins. Frank was the biggest. Before they came I meant to play with them and show them all my things; but afterwards I didn't: I wouldn't even show them my flat stone. Frank laughed at me and called me Goody-no-shoes. Well, I didn't mind that so much, it's not so bad as to be called a "tomboy", or "a strange child"! – but he was so unkind to the cat! He held her up by her tail. I don't like cats; they eat birds; but you can't do *that* to them! He used to come after me when I wanted to be alone, and say, "Ha, ha, miss! I've found you!" and he said I'd have to marry him when I grew up, but I said I never would.'

She paused for a long while.

'I liked him better than John-Ferdinand – that was his brother. One day John-Ferdinand saw the little Kaffir maid break the churn stick, and he went and told old Ayah; and old Ayah beat her. Frank and I saw it, too, but we didn't say anything. Frank said I ought to say to him ...

"You tell tale tit,
Your tongue shall be slit,
And every dog in the town
Shall have a little bit!"

'It wasn't such a very nice little poem; my mother said I mustn't say it up. I just tell you what Frank said. He knew many other little poems ...

"Four and twenty tailors
Went to catch a snail ..."

and

"Boobee-Boobee! Black-face!"

'They are not such very nice poems; but rather funny; and you can say them up if you like. I won't mind. He could make wagons – but I was glad when they went away. I don't like live boys: they are something like Kaffirs. Jan married Mietje, our Kaffir maid, and he used to beat her. I'm glad I'm not a Kaffir man's wife.

'My baby, I'm so glad you are a little girl. I'll make you a pair of thick trousers to climb trees in; these white ones tear so when you slide down, and then the people call you "tomboy"!

'Now put your arms tight round mother's neck, and hold mother tight.'

(The child under the tree turned yet slightly more onto her side, and moved her left arm as though she were drawing something nearer to her.)

'Mother will tell you just one little story before you go to sleep, a very easy one.

'Once there was a little blue egg in a nest, and the mother bird sat on it. And one day out came a bird; it had no feathers and its eyes were shut, and the mother bird sat on it. By and by the feathers began to come and the eyes opened. And one night, when the mother bird was fast asleep in the nest and the little bird was under her, it put out its head from under the mother's wing and looked. And what do you think it saw? It saw all the stars shining! And it sat up and looked at them!

'That's the end of the story.' She paused for a while.

(The child under the tree knit her brows a little, and her hand moved softly up and down on her bosom.)

'My baby, I'm so sorry I have to give you food out of a bottle – Kaffir women have milk for their babies – and cows and sheep, too – but I am like the birds.'

(She moved her hand over her little flat breast.)

'I'm so sorry. Now go to sleep, my baby. Put your arms round mother's neck. You must always try to be a good little girl: I always did when I was little – at least – I didn't always – but you must, please. Now go to sleep. Mother will sing you a little song.'

(The child under the tree made a queer piping little sound in her throat, and half-formed words came from her lips.)

'"London's burning!
London's burning!
Fire! Fire!
Bring some water! Bring some water!
London's burning!
London's burning!"'

(The song died away, and the child under the tree lay quite motionless; but her dream still went on.)

She thought when the baby had gone to sleep that she got softly off the bed and went out. The evening air was blowing over the island, and it was near sunset. She went to the side of the house where the building materials lay. She was going to build a playroom for the baby. She rolled up her sleeves and dug a foundation and filled it with stones.

(She had seen the workmen build the wagon house.) Then she mixed mud, and took off her shoes and socks, and danced in it. (She had seen the Kaffirs treading the mud to build the wagon house, but she had never been allowed to help.) Then she began to build. She took the bricks in one hand and the trowel in the other; she threw the bricks round in one hand and cut off the rough points with the trowel, as the workmen did. Then she placed each brick carefully on the layer of mortar, and tap-tapped them with the end of the handle of the trowel to see if they were quite straight.

When the little wall was two layers high, she looked round. The sun was setting on the island, and over the trees a strange soft evening light shone. There was a pink glow in the sky, and it reflected itself on everything. She stood perfectly still, holding the trowel in her hand, and looked at it. The swans were swimming up and down in the quiet water, far away, with their necks bent. They left a long snow-white mark in the water, like the swans in the picture.

> 'The swan swam in a silvery lake.
> Well swam the swan!'

A spasm of delight thrilled up the spine of the child under the pear tree. When a full-grown woman, long years afterwards, she could always recall that island, the little house, the bricks, the wonderful light over earth and sky, and the swans swimming on the still water.

After a time she half opened her eyes and looked up. Above her was the pear tree, with its stiff branches of dull green leaves. Slowly she raised herself into a sitting posture and looked round.

All about lay the parched yellow grass, and the little dried peach trees, with their shrivelled leaves and drooping yellow peaches. Everything was brown and dry; she stretched herself and yawned.

Then she stood up. Suddenly she saw a herd of little pigs a short way off, feeding under the peach trees. They had got in through a hole in the wall and were eating the fallen fruit among the grass. They would soon make their way up to the flower garden.

With a shout and whoop she rushed off after them, waving her *kappie* at them by one string. The little pigs squeaked and grunted and scattered in all directions. She chased them till she had got them in a herd all together, and drove out through one of the gaps in the sod wall. Then she stood on the wall and shouted frantically after them, still waving her *kappie*, though they were all running as fast as they could, with their little curled-up tails. She stood on the wall and waved till they disappeared behind the *kraals*.

The severest heat of the afternoon was now past, and there was a certain mellow haziness beginning to creep into the afternoon air. She shaded her eyes with her hand and looked away over the flat below the homestead, where the thorn trees grew. There seemed a kind of soft, yellow, transparent veil over it all; and there were little gnats in the air. Presently, as she stood dreamily gazing, she saw some figures moving far away in the flat below the house, near the great dam with the willow trees. The foremost figure carried something on its shoulders; it looked like Long Jan the Kaffir. Then came her father, and then two Kaffir boys with something over their shoulders that looked like spades. She could not see well; they were so far away and the soft yellow haze made things dreamy. They passed through the new lands and then they went out of sight, behind the great willow trees which grew round the dam.

She stood still, looking out at them very drowsily, thinking of nothing in particular and hardly noting them.

Suddenly a small shrill voice called from the back steps of the house, 'Get down from that wall, child, will you! Standing there with nothing on your head! You'll be burnt as black as a Kaffir before your mother gets up. Put your *kappie* on!'

It was old Ayah, who had come to the back door to throw water into the pigs' wash.

Rebekah climbed from the wall on the garden side, and walked away; but she did not put her *kappie* on; she tied it round her waist by its long strings and walked back to the pear tree. Everything seemed a little bald and empty; she had no wish to make more stories, and there was nothing to do. It seemed to her, all at once, that it was a very long afternoon. Then there came back to her the picture of her mother lying in the bed with the baby's head on her arm, which she had been trying to put from her all day. She saw the embroidered wrist of her mother's nightdress, and she saw her mother drawing up the cover to shield the baby's head. She tried to think of something else.

There was a strange little blind footpath among the grass under the pear tree on the left side. It was a few feet long, trodden hard and flat and led to nothing. She had made it by walking up and down there when she and Charles made stories and talked.

She began to walk up and down in it now, rather dragging her feet. By and by she and Charles began to talk; she talked in a quite audible voice, now for Charles and then for herself. They told each other no stories, but they began to discuss a little about the house of stramonium stalks they were going to build; he said what he thought was the best way of making the roof would be with stramonia branches; she said she thought peach branches would be stronger and better. But neither had much of interest to say that afternoon.

It began to get cooler now. The large white butterflies that had sat with folded wings during the great heat were beginning to hover over the brown grass; and there was a faint movement in the air, which showed that the evening cool was going to begin.

Then, as she walked, her eye caught sight of a white ball sticking on the bark of the pear tree. She walked round to the stem to look at it, and broke a bit of dry bark off to get it out. It was a soft fluffy ball. She put it on the ground and opened it carefully with two sticks, bending over it, her knees drawn up almost to her chest, and all her little white knickerbockers showing. Inside of it were little grey things that looked like tiny spiders' eggs. She examined it carefully and long, sticking her under-lip out over the upper. It was very curious. She was going to examine it more closely, when she caught sight of a row of black ants walking across her own footpath, like a file of little soldiers, one after the other; each one had a pink egg in its mandibles. A few inches farther was another line of little black ants returning across the footpath, probably to fetch more of the eggs which were in some nest hidden in the grass. She wheeled round; still on her heels, with a hand on each knee to balance herself, and watched them closely. Presently a huge ant, like those running up and down the stem of the pear tree, dashed into the path from the grass and seized one of the tiny ants that were carrying the eggs. The ant dropped the egg. The large ant held it exactly in the middle with its large nippers. In an instant she started up, drew her lips tighter, and seized a stick of straw, and tried to divide them; but the large one held so tightly she found she would crush both. She took two withered leaves and softly tried to separate them. The large one caught the leaf with its nippers and the small one got free; it ran away to look for its dropped egg. The large one was clinging angrily to the leaf and trying to bite it. She bent intently over it, watching it.

Suddenly she looked up. She had a curious feeling that someone was looking at her! She looked round and up into the pear tree, still balancing herself carefully in her half-sitting position; there was nothing there but the green dried leaves, and all about nothing but the long brown grass, in some places gently trodden down. In others still standing upright.

She looked back at the ants. Then she glanced round again inquiringly. Two feet from the round spot in the grass which she had trodden down to lie in was the head of a large yellow cobra. Most of its body was hidden in the grass; but its head was out and it was watching her. It was the colour of the grass, pale yellow with brown marks. Had it been there all the afternoon? She stood softly upright and stared at it. It looked at her with its glittering unblinking eyes. Then it began to move. Krinkle! krinkle! krinkle! It drew its long body out over the grass, with a sound like a lady walking in a stiff starched print dress. She gazed at it in fixed horror, motionless.

She was not afraid of snakes. When she was three years old she had carried one home in her pinafore, as a great treasure, and been punished for doing so. Since she understood what they were she was not afraid of them, but they had become a nightmare to her. They spoiled her world. Krinkle, krinkle, krinkle! – It moved away over the grass toward a hole in the sod wall, winding its long six feet of body after it.

She seized her book and ran up the path through the orchard. According to rule, she should have gone to the house and called people to look for it and kill it. But she ran quickly through the flower garden and up the steps onto the front *stoep*; then she stood still. Her heart was beating so she could hear it; she had a sense of an abandoned wickedness somewhere: it was almost as if *she herself* were a snake, and had gone krinkle! krinkle! krinkle! over the grass. She had a sense of all the world being abandonly wicked; and a pain in her left side. When her heart had stopped throbbing quite so loud, she opened the door slowly and went into the large front room.

No one had remembered to open the shutters that afternoon, though it was almost sunset; it was dusky in the room even with the door open. On the wall hung two great framed pictures of Queen Victoria and the Prince Consort in regal dress. She always played the Queen was herself, and the Prince, Charles; and once, when no one was about, she had put a chair on the side table and climbed up on it, and kissed her own hand, and put it high up where she could touch Charles's face with it.

But tonight she did not look at them. The chair in which her mother always sat stood empty beside the little work table, and the footstool before it was covered with dust. She opened the drawer of the table and took out a calico duster and carefully dusted the chair and stool. When she had put the duster back, she opened another drawer and took out a spelling book. She drew her own little square wooden footstool between her mother's chair and the open door and sat down on it, with her spelling book in her hand. She began to learn a short column of spelling which she should have learned in the morning. She held up the book before her so that the light from the door might fall on the page, and spelled out ...

'T-h-e-i-r – their.'

She repeated it a few score of times; then she went on to ...

'T-h-o-s-e – those.'

And then turned to her multiplication table. It was printed on the cover of the book. She was learning six-times. She repeated slowly over and over to herself ...

'Six times six is – thirty-six,
And six times six is – thirty-six.'

The soft, fading evening light was creeping over the orange trees outside the door. She drawled slower ...

'And, six times six is – thirty-six.
And, six times six is – thirty-six,
And, six times six is – thirty-six,
And, six times six – is – thirty-seven,
And, six times six – is – thirty-seven.'

She repeated it slowly about a hundred times, sometimes right, and sometimes wrong, looking out dreamily all the while over the book, through the open door, her mind almost a complete blank; then she paused. In a moment, something had flashed on her! She knew now what those figures had meant which she had seen walking down in the flat in the afternoon when she stood on the sod wall. She knew now what it was Long Jan was carrying; she knew why her father walked behind him, and the two Kaffir boys had spades over their shoulders. In an instant she knew well, and with an absolute certainty, that if she went down to the great dam behind the willow trees beyond the new lands, she would find there a little mound of earth, and that the baby from the spare room would be under it. All day she had not let herself think of that baby since old Ayah had driven her out of the room. She knew, also, something else; she knew at that moment – vaguely, but quite certainly – something of what birth and death mean, which she had not known before. She would never again look for a new little baby, or expect to find it anywhere; vaguely but quite certainly something of its genesis had flashed on her.

She stood up in the quickly darkening room, put her multiplication book back into the drawer, and walked straight to the door that opened into the dining room, and closed it behind her.

In the dining room also it was getting dark now, though it looked towards the west and the window was open, and here also it was very quiet. This was generally the noisy time of the day, when there was a stir and a bustle everywhere; her mother was generally giving out rations, and the herds and maids who had come from the huts to fetch their food stood about the storehouse door outside, laughing and talking. The Kaffir maids who worked in the house were generally chatting loudly in the kitchen; and the little Kaffirs, who might not approach at any other time, often stood about the kitchen steps, waiting for their mothers; and from the milking *kraal* you could hear the men shouting to the cows and calves, and calling to one another; and the dogs felt the excitement and barked; and above everything could always be heard old Ayah's voice, in a shrill, small key, giving orders everywhere, which no one ever obeyed. But tonight it was all quiet; you could only hear the lowing of the cows and the bleating of the sheep. The men hardly shouted. The rations had been given out early in the morning and the little Kaffirs had been told not to come about the backdoor.

Through the great square window the twilight was beginning to come in. She would not go to her mother's room, and she had nowhere else to go. She sat down on a deal bench without a back that stood against the wall. No one came to light the candles; and you could see the dim outlines of the tall clock in the corner, and the wooden chairs and tables standing out as shadows from the whitewashed walls. Presently, as it grew quite darker, a bat came in at the window and flapped about from side to side and went out again. Then the room grew pitch dark. Rebekah drew her legs up under her on the form, and leaned her head back against the whitewashed wall.

By and by the two Kaffir maids came in from the milk house, each carrying a bucket of milk. They had a lighted candle. They went through the dining room into the pantry; they were laughing and talking softly; the light from the open pantry door came back into the dining room.

Presently old Ayah came in from the mother's bedroom.

'What are you sitting here all alone in the dark for, child?' she said.

She went into the pantry, and came out with a large basin of bread and milk sop, and a little pannikin of pure milk. She set them down on the side of the table next to the bench with a tallow candle beside them in a low candlestick.

'Why didn't you eat your dinner, little white face?'

Rebekah sat upright; old Ayah pushed the table a little nearer to her, and she began to eat. She had not known before that she was hungry. Now she ate ravenously and drank at the milk out of her pannikin.

Old Ayah went back into the pantry and scolded the maids in Dutch because the wooden milk-pail was leaking. Very soon the maids and old Ayah came back to the dining room, and rested the pail on the end of the dining table to examine what was gone wrong. One of the maids held the lighted candle, while the other was chewing tallow to put in the cracks.

'What's the baby like, old Ayah?' asked the maid holding the light, as old Ayah examined the leak.

'A fine child,' said old Ayah, without looking up. 'She'd make four of *that* child when she was born. Its hands are nearly as large as hers now.'

The maid who was chewing the tallow pressed some down on the open seam.

'Where has *she* been all day?' she asked, nicking her head at Rebekah.

'Oh, God knows!' said old Ayah. 'I've hardly seen her. You might as well try to keep your eye on a *mierkat* among its holes as on *that* child.'

Rebekah kept on eating her supper, gazing straight into her basin, and taking large mouthfuls.

'Look at her now!' said the first Kaffir maid. 'How she eats! She's trying to swallow the spoon!'

'*Sy's 'n snaakse kind*!' said old Ayah. ('She's a strange child!')

Rebekah kept on eating steadily and looking into the basin. It hurt her so that they talked of her.

When they had done stopping the hand-pail, the two maids went to the kitchen and old Ayah went back to the mother's room. Immediately they were gone Rebekah pushed her basin with what was left in it from her and leaned back on the bench. She drew up one leg, leaned her elbow on the bench, and rested her head against the whitewashed wall. She was very tired. She watched the tallow candle fixedly; it was burning up red, and flickering a little, as the moths and night flies that came in through the open window fluttered round it. It seemed so long since she had got up in the morning. It was her bedtime, but no one came to tell her to go to bed.

Then she began to watch the wick of the tallow candle more fixedly as it burned larger and redder. She pressed two of her fingers on her eyes, half closing them; then she saw two candles; she took them away, and there was only one. She wondered how that was, and tried it again. When she moved one finger a little the one light went up slowly and stood over the other; she moved the other finger, and they came so close they were almost one. She took her hand away and looked at the candle, half closing her eyes; she did not see two candles now, but only four long rays of red light, the two higher ones darker and the two lower lighter. She was slowly getting very interested in it.

She held up her hand and let the light shine through her fingers; the hand made a long dark shadow on the wall to the left of the room. Why was the shadow so much longer than the hand, she wondered, and why did it fall just where it did? She moved her hand and watched the shadow move. If only one were grown up, one would know all about these things! She dropped her hand on her side. Perhaps, even grown-up people didn't know all. Perhaps only God knew what lights and shadows were!

She lay still watching the candle. The wick had burned so long it was beginning to droop and turn over a little on one side. The next morning she would get up early before anyone was up and begin learning her multiplication table and spelling; perhaps she would know it before evening. She would not play once the whole day nor make up stories. She would learn the whole day. It would all help to make you grow up quickly and know everything!

It was half past eight now. Her eyelids began to droop; she only kept them open with a strong effort; she could not bear to go to sleep; but her head bowed, nodding even though she leaned it against the wall.

Suddenly she sat bolt upright; her eyes opened widely. They seemed to grow larger and larger at each instant. She listened intently. From her mother's bedroom there came a sound, a loud, wailing cry. Rebekah got off the bench and stood rigid and upright. Her small sharp-cut face, pale before, became now a deadly white. There was silence for a moment; then another cry, then another, and another, each louder and longer than before. Her hands doubled into fists; she turned a bright pink. The crying went on. She raised her chin; her throat swelled till it looked like the full throat of a tiny woman; the veins stood out like little whipcords. She drew in the corners of her mouth. Again there was a cry, but this time fainter. A dark purple flush came up over her forehead; her eyelids drooped. She rushed out at the door, striking herself against it. She flew up the dark passage to the door of her mother's room. With hands and feet she struck the panels of the door till they rebounded.

'Let me in! Let me in! I say, let me in! I will – I – will – I say – I will come in!'

The baby inside had left off crying.

Rebekah heard nothing but the surging of the blood in her own ears.

Old Ayah opened the door.

'Let me in! Let me in! I will come in!'

Old Ayah tried to put her back with her hand.

'Leave me alone! Leave me alone!' she cried; 'You are killing it like the other one! Leave me alone, I say! Leave me alone!'

Old Ayah tried to hold her fast, but she caught the Hottentot woman's skirts and twisted them round with her arms and legs.

The little mother from the bed asked in a sleepy voice what was the matter.

'Don't ask me what is the matter!' cried old Ayah indignantly, in Cape Dutch. 'Ask the Father of all Evil! This child is mad!'

She wrenched her skirts free from Rebekah's grasp and thrust her into the room. Rebekah stood on the ox skin in the centre of the floor, vibrating from the soles of her feet to her head.

The candle was on a stand beside her mother's bed, and threw its light full on her as she lay with the baby's head on her arm and her hand with the white frill thrown across it. On the right side of the great four-poster bed they had pinned up a red cotton quilt, with great lions and palm trees printed on it, to keep off the draught from the open window; and the quilt reflected a soft red light over the mother and child. In the far right-hand corner of the room was Rebekah's own little cot, where she had slept ever since she was born.

'God only does know what possesses this child!' said old Ayah, fixing her twinkling black eyes on Rebekah and talking at her. 'If she were my child, I wouldn't let her come into the house at all, where respectable people live who like to be indoors. I'd just tie her fast with a chain to a monkey post outside, and let her go round and round there. Then she could eat Kaffir beans like a baboon, and climb, and scream as much as she liked!'

'What did you make such a noise for, Rebekah?' the little mother said gently. 'Did you think they were hurting the baby?'

Rebekah said nothing; the blood was leaving her head and running into her heart, and she felt faint.

'Twisting a person's clothes almost off their backs! Can't one even wash and dress a child without this little wild thing coming howling and dancing round one!' Old Ayah smoothed out her crumpled skirt.

'Do you want to see the baby, Rebekah?' asked her mother.

Rebekah walked unsteadily to the foot of the bed and stood beside the great wooden bedpost.

Old Ayah took up the baby's bath and walked out of the room with it, muttering that some children ought to live with the baboons.

'If you would like to come and see the baby, you can climb up,' said her mother drowsily, with half-closed eyes.

Rebekah waited a moment, then she clambered softly up on to the bed, and sat down at the foot, half kneeling, with her back against the post. Her mother, who was very tired, had closed her eyes. The baby's red face pressed against the mother's white breast. The light shone on them both.

Rebekah drew up her knees and clasped her arms round them, and sat watching.

'It's drinking, isn't it, eh, mother?' she said at last very softly.

'Yes,' said her mother, without opening her eyes.

'It's *your* little baby? Eh, mother?' she whispered again softly, after a long pause.

Her mother nodded dreamily.

Rebekah stroked her little skirts down over her knees. 'It *must* drink!' she said after a time. 'It *must* have milk, eh, mother? It's your little baby, eh, mother?' she added after a long pause.

But the little mother made no answer; she had dropped away into sleep.

Rebekah sat watching them.

By and by the baby moved its hand which struck out from the white flannel wrapper about it; it opened its fingers slowly; it stretched them out one after the other and closed them up again into a fist. Rebekah watched it intently.

Presently she leaned forward, resting one elbow on the bed, and slowly stretched out her other hand, and with one forefinger touched the hand of the baby. Her mouth quivered; she sat up quickly and watched them again. She leaned her head back against the post at the foot of the bed and sat gazing at them, her eyes never moving.

At half past nine old Ayah came in again, bringing in a hot-water bottle and an etna to warm the gruel during the night.

'My fatherland's force![1] You not in bed yet! Are you going to sit up till morning?'

The mother woke up. 'Have you been sitting here all this while, Rebekah?' she asked gently.

Old Ayah put the warm water bottle at the mother's feet.

'She'd never go to bed if she could help it!' old Ayah muttered. 'It's my belief, if you came in at three o'clock in the morning, you'd find her sitting up in her bed, talking to the spiders in the dark. She'd talk to the stars if she hadn't anything else to talk to, just not to go to sleep like other children!'

---

1 So Olive wrote it, but the expression is Afrikaans and should be *My Vaderland se vos*, probably a corruption of an old Nederlands expression, meaning: 'My fatherland's God'.

'Mother,' said Rebekah in a very slow, clear voice, stroking down her knees – 'mother, will you let me have *your* baby to sleep by me for a little while?'

She spoke each word slowly and distinctly, as one who repeats what he has carefully prepared.

'No, dear,' said the mother; 'it's too small; you can't have it to sleep with you yet.'

'Have it to sleep with you!' said old Ayah. 'I should think not! Why, you'd kill it!'

'I should take great care of it,' said Rebekah, very slowly, still stroking her knees, her eyes very wide open and fixed steadily on her mother; 'I wouldn't lie on it nor let it fall. I only want to take care of it and teach it.'

'Teach it! Teach it, indeed!' said old Ayah, tucking in the mother's feet. 'You just want to teach her to be a naughty tomboy like you. We'll take care she doesn't play with you and learn all your wild ways.'

Rebekah stroked her knees more heavily. 'I didn't mean to teach her anything wrong,' she said slowly; 'I wasn't even going to teach her to hate *you*.'

'Hate me! Rather! I should think not! What next? Why should you teach her to hate me?'

Rebekah turned her eyes on to old Ayah and gazed at her. 'Because *I* hate you so!' she said.

'Don't quarrel with her any more, Ayah,' said the mother; 'the child really doesn't know what she is talking about; she's half asleep already. Come, get off the bed, Rebekah, and go and undress. You can't have the baby.'

But Rebekah sat motionless. Slowly the tears gathered under her eyelids. She closed them, and the tears lay in large heavy drops under the lashes without falling.

She raised her face with its closed eyes to the canopy of the bed.

'Oh, I can't bear it! I can't bear it!' she said slowly. 'What shall I do? What shall I do? Oh, what shall I do?' She moved her upturned face with its closed eyes slowly from side to side. 'I meant to love it so! Oh, I meant – All my things – my Peter book – all my stones. Oh, if you will let me love it!' The bed shook, but no tears fell from the closed eyes. She stroked her knees with both hands. 'It's not any use! – you see – it's not any use! – I have tried! – I have tried! – Oh, I wish I was dead – I wish I was dead – I wish I was dead!'

Even Old Ayah looked at her in silence.

'The child is really three parts asleep,' said the mother. 'It's been a long trying day for her, running about with no one to look after her. She is but a baby, though she is so old-fashioned. Get off the bed, Rebekah, and old Ayah will undress you.'

But Rebekah felt her way to the foot of the bed and slid down.

'I can undress myself,' she heaved. She stood on the floor in the middle of the room with her eyes still closed, the lids swollen and fastened together, and unbuttoned her things one by one, letting them drop on the floor, until she stood there in her little white shift, her small naked shoulders still vibrating. Old Ayah brought her nightdress.

'*Dis 'n snaakse kind!*' she muttered. ('Tis a strange child!')

Rekebah slipped it over her own head, and then, with her hand stretched out, she felt her way to the bed in the corner. She climbed up over the side of the cot and lay down. The long vibrating movement still went on; it was almost as if a man were crying.

'I can't have that,' said the little mother. 'She'll go on with it half the night in her sleep. I know the child. I think she dreams of things. Take the baby and lay it by her just for a little while. It's been a long day and she's very tired.'

Old Ayah shook her head forebodingly; but she took up the baby, wrapped it in its shawl, and carried it across the room. She turned back the cover and made a place for it beside Rebekah. The child stretched out her arm for its head; the Hottentot woman laid it down on it and drew the cover up over both. Then she turned and went out, to fetch the gruel and the night light.

The elder sister slipped her hand under the shawl till she found the baby's hand; she clasped her fingers softly into its tiny fingers, and held them. With the other hand she tried to draw its body up close against her.

Presently there was a queer quavering little sound, as though someone were trying to sing; but nothing came of it; then all was quiet.

When old Ayah came back in fifteen minutes everyone in the room was quiet and asleep.

She put the gruel and night light down on the drawers, and came to the bedside to remove the baby. But when she turned down the cover she found the hands of the sisters so interlocked, and the arm of the elder sister so closely round the younger, that she could not remove it without awakening both.

Old Ayah shook her head and drew the cover up softly. She blew out the candle and put the night light down on the floor beyond the bed, and walked softly towards the door of the room with her naked yellow feet, her figure casting a long dark shadow on the wall. When she got to the door as she passed out she turned and looked back. Along the floor the night light shone, casting deep shadows into far corners, especially that in which the two children lay!

But they were all sleeping well.

The Book

The Woman's Day

CHAPTER ONE

Showing What Baby-Bertie Thought of Her New Tutor; and How Rebekah Got Married

Tucked away among the ribs of a mountain in the Eastern Province of the Cape of Good Hope is a quiet, tree-covered farm. The owner of this farm twenty-five years ago was an Englishman, a gentleman in the rough and unveneered fashion; a man fond of his books, of his trees, of his land; little given to speaking, much given to thinking, and seldom going farther than his own beacons. In truth, there was little to tempt anyone farther; the neighbours were unlettered, *velskoen*-wearing Dutchmen, or equally unlettered English settlers, and they did not often trouble their neighbours with a visit – a fact which no one regretted except the little mother who was of a lively and sociable turn and who rejoiced greatly over even the arrival of an old Boer *tante*. It was a quiet monotonous life; the farmer himself, the little mother, their children, with a score of Hottentot and Kaffir servants, completed the catalogue of the farm's inhabitants; the human inhabitants, for of wild animal life there was no want. In the bush that covered the mountainsides were leopards, who came down at night and carried off lambs from the *kraals*; in the tall trees in the bush were little grey, long-tailed monkeys, and wood-doves, and cock-o-veets, who cried and called all day; in the rocks that crowned the mountain troops of baboons climbed and fought; and down in the valley among the thorn[1] trees were mierkats and great tortoises, and hares who paid visits to the lands. Almost all day from the open windows of the house you might see at intervals the sheep among the long grass on the mountainside or down in the flat; or catch sight of, far off, moving specks, which were the goats moving in and out among the thorn trees. All day long the great glass doors and windows stood open; through them came the scent of orange blossoms from the orangery before the door, and from the garden beyond where the hollyhocks and dahlias and marigolds and four-o'clocks made a bed of colour. In springtime there was the sweet scent of the blossoms from the long orchard beyond the flower garden; and in the summer, at Christmas time, the flat was a sea of gold with the yellow flowers of the thorn trees, and the honey scent came up to the house; and in autumn there was a faint, acid smell from the

---

1 The mimosa, generally called thorn tree in South Africa; a tree with a delicate acacia leaf and long white thorns from an inch to three inches in length, and with a sweet-scented yellow honey blossom.

falling figs and peaches which lay on the ground in the brown trampled grass, and which the little Kaffirs and pigs came over the gaps in the wall to revel among.

Over the *nek* came the road from the town. It wound in and out, in and out, a line of white among the thorn trees. It disappeared altogether on the flat, till it came out near the *mielie* lands, and by the great dam with the willow trees. In that dam on hot summer nights the frogs loved to croak. Baby-Bertie, the farmer's younger daughter, said she loved to hear them as she lay in her bed at night; but Rebekah, her elder sister, said it was a sad sound and made one think of when one was a child long ago. But Bertie, Baby-Bertie, as they called her, was only fifteen and two months, and she had not a very long, long ago to think of. Rebekah, her sister, was twenty, and had once been on a visit to Cape Town, and knew a great deal, and had read a great deal, and that might make it seem a long time since she was a child; but to Bertie it was only yesterday, though she could already touch the oranges no other woman on the farm could reach, and her chin was higher than her father's shoulder. So, to her, the croaking of the frogs at night was as pleasant as the lowing of the cows when they came down the mountainside in the evening.

On one afternoon Baby-Bertie stood at the window of the spare room, putting dahlias and lilies into a slender green glass; Rebekah, her sister, knelt in the room behind her, pinning a white valance round the bed. Outside, all the flat was full of yellow blossoms, for the thorn trees were in flower. Once or twice Bertie put her head far out of the window, and looked across the flat, and drew it back again.

She was a velvety creature, with long eyelashes turned back till they almost touched her straight eyebrows. Her forehead was low and very broad, the hair hanging over it in brown curls, up each one of which you might have slipped a finger, but what one looked at most were the large round brown eyes and the velvety cheeks. Rebekah, her sister, was a small woman, with dark, fine hair, wavy and parted down the middle; she had a very white face, except when she flushed, and then it seemed as if the blood might burn through the skin. You could always see the veins in her temples. When she was a child she used to run behind the bed and kneel down and repeat Bonar's hymn:

> 'Calm me, my God, and keep me calm!
> Let Thine outstretched wind
> Be as the shade of Elim's palm ...'

because her heart beat so fast sometimes she thought it was going to burst. Now she seldom needed to pray that; she was always busy with her books and her microscope and collections of insects, and stones, when she was not busy working in the kitchen or milk room, or helping her father with his farming.

And now she was to be married the next day to her cousin Frank, who had come from Cape Town to fetch her. He was tall and large, and fair, and full, with blue eyes and a light mustache; he smoked cigars and wore very spotless shirts and collars, whether they were white or striped and coloured.

He had always wanted to have her for his wife since as a boy of eleven he came with his parents from England to visit their relations in South Africa. He had gone back to England, but ten years later he had come out again and settled in Cape Town to manage a branch of his father's business, and he had visited the farm once a year for four years, and had always asked Rebekah to marry him when he came, but she always said she could not. Now everyone was surprised: she had suddenly written to him that she would; and she was to be married the next day and the wedding breakfast was already laid out in the back dining room, with a white cloth pinned over it to keep the dust off. She was to be married in a lilac silk in the large front room; and her father and mother and Bertie and the servants would be there, and Queen Victoria and the Prince Consort would look down from the picture frames upon the wall.

Rebekah had wished there should be no feast and to be married in her little blue gardening dress, but her mother and Bertie said a wedding was no wedding without these things; and even the bridegroom laughed at the idea.

The magistrate was coming from the town to marry them, because Rebekah wanted no Church service. Frank was willing; he said it did not matter in the country where no one knew what you did, though he would have liked it done in the town where everyone would have noticed it.

He was the only man who had ever asked Rebekah to marry him, except his brother, John-Ferdinand, whom she had met when she went to Cape Town two years before, and who had asked her, but she had refused him.

Except for that visit to Cape Town and a visit to the seaside once with her mother when she was a child, she had never left the farm, except to drive into the next up-country village for the day's shopping. There the shop-clerks and young businessmen seemed people so far out of her world that she hardly knew who they were. Once the young bank clerk invited himself out to the farm and spent a day and night there, but she only spoke to him when she poured out the tea to know if he would have more, and spent the afternoon by herself in the *kloof*. His account of his visit did not encourage other young men to come; and only the little mother suspected what he had been there for. Rebekah had never been to a ball or a theatre or paid a formal call, and her world was a very little world except in the direction of books.

Now she and Bertie were getting the spare room ready, because Bertie's tutor was coming, who was to teach her when Rebekah was gone. Bertie herself had no greater appetite for books and learning than her hand-lamb for carrots, which it ate, as it were under compulsion, if you offered them to him, for fear of paining you, but under no other conditions whatever. But Rebekah and her father both said she ought to learn more.

This tutor was a delicate young man from England who had advertised for a situation on a farm where he might, in return for teaching three hours a day, receive his board.

No one had seen him, but he had good credentials, and Rebekah said men were generally better teachers than women; and everyone followed Rebekah's advice on the farm.

Bertie put her head out of the window again; but there was nothing to be seen except the flat, shimmering in the afternoon sunshine, and the white road over the *nek*.

'Perhaps Jan has got drunk and turned the cart over; or perhaps it has broken down,' she said, straining her head farther.

'It is not four yet,' her sister said.

Bertie drew her head in and took the glass with the dahlias and white lilies to the mantelpiece. She stood looking at them.

'Do you think he will like them, Rebekah?'

At this moment three little Kaffirs whom Bertie had set to watch on the top step of the loft ladder set up a series of frantic yells. Bertie put down the loose flowers she had just begun to collect and rushed from the room. Rebekah pinned on. She never seemed very much excited now, even when she found a new germ under her microscope, or when one of her grafts budded, or a new book came from town; and those were the things she seemed to care for most. Soon after Bertie put her face in at the door again.

'Rebekah, do come and see him! He's just come! He is so lovely and small! He's hardly a bit bigger than you! I thought I should be afraid of him, but I'm not a bit! He's smaller than I am. He keeps on smiling. He's got coal-black hair. He's got a little curl just like a drake's tail right above his ear! Do come and see him!'

Rebekah was pinning the last fold.

'Oh, come, Rebekah! He's shaking hands with father and mother and coming up the steps already!' She rushed out again.

Rebekah rose from her knees slowly, and then stooped to gather the flowers Bertie had thrown away in her haste; she looked round once to see that the room was all in readiness. Then she went into the front room. A little man was sitting at the end of the sofa, who certainly looked not more than twenty-five years old, though he had given his age as thirty-five in his credentials. He was sitting with his hands between his knees; but he smiled, and rose as she came in, with his face slightly turned down. His forehead was rounded and protruding, and had a gleam upon it as though oiled; his nose was small, and was rounded except at the point, where it seemed to have been sliced off, leaving a small square tip. Rebekah shook hands with him; but his restless, beadlike small eyes looked away at the piano. When she had gone out, he sat down again and talked to the little mother, who sat at her work table, while Bertie, too excited, or not venturing to come in, peeped through the dining room door as she passed.

That afternoon they had their tea at four o'clock in the little front workroom, because the wedding breakfast was laid out in the dining room. The room opened with a large window on to the front *stoep*. All the family collected there except Frank, Rebekah's cousin, who lay out under the orange trees before the door on his back on a reed mat, smoking, and whose tea had been carried out to him by Bertie. He looked very cool in a spotless gray suit, with a white shirt and no waistcoat. He was reading a yellow-backed book, and his pointer, whom he had brought with him in case there was any shooting, lay near his feet, with her head upon her paws.

Presently he lifted his hand as he read and drew her nearer by the ears; she winced a little, but crept up and put her nose against his arm. By and by, when he had emptied his cup, he raised his large not ungraceful body and sauntered to the house with the cup.

In the small sitting room the others had finished their tea and had all left, except Rebekah, who sat dreamily in her place near the window, cutting the orange peel on her plate. She had been up since five that morning, busy with housework and preparations for the next day, and was tired.

Presently there came the scent of a whiff from a cigar through the open window, and then her cousin Frank put his handsome face and shoulders in.

'All alone?' he said.

He stretched out his hand and set the empty cup down on the table. 'Come out and sit under the orange trees? It's splendidly cool there.'

'I can't; I've so many little things to do yet if we are to start tomorrow at eleven.'

He folded his arms on the window ledge and drew softly from his cigar.

'How nice you look in that dress,' he said slowly. She was dressed in white muslin, with a little blue sleeveless jacket cut away from the waist. 'I like that jacket; it shows your little waist – What a little ting-ting-kie[2] it is!' He put out his large, soft, well-shaped hand, and let it rest gently on her waist for a moment. Then he drew it back and refolded his arms on the window, and smoked. He blew a long whiff of smoke softly at her; he knew she liked it.

She began collecting the empty teacups on to the tray. There was a quiet contentment in his eye as he watched her.

'What do you think of the new arrival?' he said, taking his cigar from his mouth and holding it between his two first fingers.

'I dislike him.'

Frank laughed. 'He's not attractive. I'm sure he uses cocoanut oil for his hair. One

---

2 The ting-ting-kie is a slight, very lively bird, not much larger than a humming-bird, often seen moving quickly about among the grass and low bushes in South Africa. [The Cape wren-warbler.]

can forgive a man a great many sins but, not that.' He put his cigar between his lips again and drew a long whiff. 'Don't you think it's a little dangerous, too?'

'What?' Rebekah looked up at him quickly. 'Oh, settling him and Bertie down every day for three hours with nothing but the table to divide them and French verbs to unite them! It's a dangerous thing for any young man, or old either, to have a head of curls like Bertie's dancing within three feet of him!'

'I think ...' she said.

He blew a whiff of smoke softly towards her across the table, which did not reach her, and laughed. 'Oh, I know just what you are going to say – men should teach women and women should teach men. What difference does it make? But it's not the Garden of Eden yet! Bertie'll be the finest-looking woman in Africa in a few years. Have you noticed how she's developed since I was here six months ago?'

Before Rebekah could answer, Bertie thrust her head in at the door to say old Ayah wanted her to come and see if the cakes were done, and dashed away again; and Rebekah took up the tray to carry it out with her.

'Then you won't come out under the trees with me? I must go and be lazy alone! What a busy little ting-ting-kie! Well, tomorrow!' – He kissed the fingers of his left hand towards her and turned away from the window, his dog following close at his heels. As he walked along the *stoep* he hummed in a soft sweet tenor.

> 'Ten little nigger boys fuddling over wine,
> One got so jolly drunk, then there were nine!'

He went back and lay down on his mat under the orange trees, and Rebekah went to see if the cakes were burning.

At nine o'clock that evening Rebekah sat out on the *stoep*. It was a dark night; the beetles buzzed about, among the vine leaves on the wall about her head. She was sitting on the step opposite the front door with her back turned to it; a square of light fell from the open door across the *stoep* beside her and dimly lighted up the stems of the orange trees beyond. She rested her elbows on her knees and sat looking out into the dark. After a while she glanced through the open door. In the room behind her she could see the little mother sitting in the rocking chair in the far corner beside the work table, rocking herself and smiling and nodding her head, keeping time at the wrong places, and Percy Lawry, the new tutor, sitting at the piano, playing; and Bertie standing with her elbow on the top of the piano, with her eyes fixed on his face, so that, at a movement of his head, she might turn the page for him. She could see her lover lying on the sofa with his large arm thrown across his forehead, listening to the music, which was good; and in the room beyond she could catch sight of her father sitting at the bare table reading, with his grizzled beard pressed against his breast. She looked in for a moment, and then she looked away again.

What was she leaving it for, that quiet peaceful life. She folded her arms on her knees. What was she leaving it for? The light that streamed out from the door lay in a square about her, and the little night flies gathered thicker above her head. Tonight, almost too late, she took up the old balances and began to weigh again, as she had done before. What was she leaving it for, that quiet, peaceful life? – that life in which the right was pleasantest and easiest to do, and lay right ahead; in which there was no being torn asunder living between 'I would' and 'I must'; a life in which there was just as much to be done for others as might yield a grateful sense of satisfaction, yet leaving space for the individual life undisturbed; a placid, peaceful life into which the noisy, babbling, worried, worrying world crept only once a week through the post-bag of the boy who brought the letters and newspapers from the town; a life in which news from the outer world came to one with a freshness it could never bear for those living in the hurry and turmoil of the great streams of life; a studious life, in which one might grow wise exceedingly over plants, and suck whatever joy there was in insects and stones; a thoughtful life, in which one might read and creep into the hearts of books, as they can only be crept into when the wheels of the daily life are grinding soft and low; a life in which suffering was small, and pleasure, if grey-tinted, calm and constant. What was she leaving it for? She looked back again into the room, and then out into the dark. The scale looked heavy.

On the other hand, there was – well – a vague, insatiable hunger? Books, black beetles, well-performed duties – she had tried them all, and she was dying of hunger. Was it for that, that of which the far-off blue and purple mountains whisper when they say: 'Come! Come! Come! We have that to give you know not of! Come! Come! Come to us!'? Or was it a voice from that primal depth of nature which, before man was man, called beast to beast and kind to kind? Which, through all the ages, has summoned the human woman, in spite of the great Chaldean curse, 'I will greatly multiply thy sorrow and thy conception,' along one path? An ox at the roadside, when it is dying of hunger and thirst, does not lie down; it walks up and down – up and down, seeking it knows not what; – but it does not lie down.

She looked back into the sitting room, where her cousin Frank still lay, with his large rounded arm in its grey coat sleepily thrown across his forehead, his full, well-shaped lips almost smiling.

For four years, when he had placed the question before her, she had always decided she could not go with him. Why was it that, six months before, his face had become always present to her; and at night even she saw his hands, and heard his soft, sweet voice? She looked out again into the dark; and she knew as she sat there in the dark with her elbows on her knees, that, if she had been wholly free that night, and had to decide over again, she would yet have decided exactly as she had done.

She folded her arms closer on her knees and looked out at the dark stems of the orange trees, while the little night beetles fluttered thicker and almost rested on her dark head.

After a while the others went to the back dining room to drink coffee, and took the lamps with them; Rebekah still sat on alone in the dark, only a faint streak of light coming from the door of the dining room beyond the passage.

Then Bertie came out with a cup for her, feeling her way along the uneven stoep with her feet.

'I can hardly see you, the light has dazzled my eyes so.' She sat down beside her sister on the step, close to her, holding the coffee cup for her.

'I hope the little Kaffirs will come and call me very early in the morning, before it's light. Will you wake me if they don't? I want to go up in the bush and fetch more creepers and berries.' She slid her hand through her sister's arm and let it rest in her lap; she still held the saucer of the cup. 'If I tell you something, you mustn't tell anyone, Rebekah! But we've made an arch up in the bush, and just before you are married we are going to bring it down, the little niggers and I, and fasten it over the front door; and you and Frank will have to go out under it! Don't tell anyone: it'll be such a surprise! And we're going to fasten a paper bag of rice in the top, and just as you go out one of the little niggers is going to poke it with a long stick, and all the rice'll come down on you. All Frank's collar and shirt will be full, and your dress, but you won't mind, eh?'

She took the empty coffee cup from Rebekah and put it down, and then slipped her hand into hers, so that their palms lay against each other.

'Do you know that something happened this evening, Rebekah?' She bent her head closer. 'Frank gave me your wedding ring to try on. I went into the kitchen to show old Ayah, and when I was taking it off it fell under the woodpile, and we had such a trouble to find it. We had to pack all the wood out. Old Ayah was angry with me; she said it was unlucky to try on other people's wedding rings. She said if you did you never married and that the most dreadful thing in the world happened to you. She wouldn't tell me what. It's only a *geloofie*,³ isn't it, eh, Rebekah? Rebekah, what *is* the most dreadful thing that *could* happen to anyone?'

'It would depend on who the person was,' Rebekah said, still dreaming her own thoughts; but she drew her sister's head closer into hers.

'It must be so nice to get married,' Bertie said. 'But, when I get married I shan't go so far from the farm. I should like to be married to someone with a farm near here, and then you could come and visit me every year and I could come and visit you. It must be so nice to be married. But I should like to have a pure-white dress to be married in, not a mauve one like yours.' Bertie laid her head on her sister's shoulder. 'I suppose I shall be married some day; only I don't know whom I shall

---

3 Superstition.

find to marry here. Perhaps someone will come like Frank did – from far away. Rebekah, can I come and visit you some day soon?'

'Yes, dear, as soon as you've learned a little more you shall come to me for a long time – a year or six months if you like.' Bertie sat silent, with her cheek resting softly on her sister's shoulder, the crown of her head pressed against her sister's cheek.

Sometimes I think, if one should live to be ninety, and the sights and sounds of the world about become dim to one, that then, as one sits alone in the firelight dreaming, or out in the sunshine, the child sister who was young with us will come back and sit with us there. No one will see her; and we two shall sit there alone, she with her long, flowing hair; and we shall look out at life together with our young eager eyes that have known no mighty sorrow. I think it is, perhaps, that she may sit there with us, that we treasure her memory so all life through. We two shall be always young when we are together.

After Bertie had gone back into the house through the dark front room, Rebekah's lover came through it, feeling his way; he came out on to the *stoep*.

'Where is my little Goody-two-shoes? All alone in the dark, as usual?' He felt for her with his hands, and raised her up. 'What an unsociable little mortal it is! Come and walk with me.'

He put her hand through his arm and drew the little blue shawl she had across her arm about her. He lit his cigar, and they paced up and down on the long *stoep*. Her head hardly reached his shoulder. 'Chilly tonight,' he said.

By and by the little mother came into the front room and, when she had bid them both goodnight, left the lamp on the table; and they paced on together.

'I must go to bed now,' Rebekah said, after a few minutes. 'I have to be up so early tomorrow.'

'Don't make yourself too tired. We have a long day's journey before us.'

He drew her close up to him and before him. They were standing in front of the door where the lamplight fell full on them. He raised her hands in his and put them alternately softly to his lips. He put down his head and whispered something very softly. Her cheeks turned the colour of the pale carnation she had fastened to his buttonhole before supper.

'Goodnight, my little one! My queen! My love.' Suddenly, with a little curious caressing movement, she raised herself and put her face against the side of his as he bent.

'What is it? Do you want to say something?' She said nothing; but he thought he felt the soft touch of her lips against his neck; then she glided quickly from him.

He stretched out his arms towards her, for her to come back to him; but she shook her head softly and called out, 'Goodnight,' and the little figure in blue and white fluttered away through the front room.

He turned round slowly to pace up and down to finish his cigar before he took up the lamp and retired.

When Rebekah left him she went out into the long passage. She called out a second 'Goodnight' at the door of her mother's room as she passed, and both her parents answered it; then she went to her own room at the end of the passage.

She lit a candle and set it on the table, and then sat down on the side of her small bed. The window was standing open and the pitch darkness seemed to come in through it from outside; it looked out towards the *kloof* on the mountain, and the bush came down close to it. That little room had been hers for fifteen years, ever since she had given up to the new baby the cot in her mother's room.

It was bare and dismantled now. In one corner were two boxes, packed and corded, which contained her luggage ready for tomorrow's journey. Above the little table were marks on the wall where a bookshelf had been taken down. When her father first put it up for her, it was one little shelf containing a few children's books; but it had slowly mounted upward till there were shelves holding fifty or sixty volumes. A tall rough glass cabinet that had stood in the corner, in which she had kept her fossils and insects and her microscope, was packed up, too; and above her bed, at the head, was a square mark on the wall and the holes of four tacks. When she was a child of six she had found in an old copy of the *Illustrated London News* a rough print of Raphael's *Madonna della Sedia*, and she had cut it out and fastened it there. No one told her it was a great picture, but when she looked at the little John, and the baby with its hand inside its mother's breast glancing round, and the mother with her striped shawl looking down at it, a thrill of quiet joy ran through her, that no other picture made her feel. She called it '*My* picture'. Now it was taken down and folded away with her other things to go to her new home.

She sat on the side of her bed and looked out of the window. A curious weight and heaviness seemed suddenly to rest on her. The wick of candle which stood on the table began to burn long and red and bend over a little as the soft night breezes blew it. She snuffed it and then took up the light, and walked to the door at the end of her room which led to Bertie's.

Baby-Bertie lay on her bed with her arms thrown back on the pillow above her head. The sleeve of her nightdress had fallen back and showed her round arm, so small at the wrist, so large above the elbow; and one button at the neck had become unfastened and showed her small white throat; her face was flushed, though the window stood wide open and night air came in over the bed. The pillow was covered with a tangle of her brown curls.

Almost every night when, as a very small child, she had been moved into that room, Rebekah had lain by her to sing her to sleep; and when she grew older

Rebekah had still crept in to lie beside her to talk and caress her before she slept. Tonight Rebekah put the light down on the floor and knelt beside the bed. She put her head down upon Bertie's breast, under Bertie's arm, and pressed it there. It was as though, tonight, it was she who wanted to be caressed. But Bertie slept on – a deep, calm sleep. Presently Rebekah rose and partly closed the window, that the air might not blow so fully upon her. On a chair near the bed Bertie had laid out the lilac silk wedding dress Rebekah was to wear the next day, and the white tulle veil lay over it; the orange blossoms Bertie would gather early in the morning. Beside it, on another chair, hung the muslin gown Bertie herself was to wear.

Rebekah did not glance at them; she took up the light and went back to her room. Through the open window you could hear the baboons shouting and calling to one another high up on the mountainside.

She undressed slowly. When she stood ready at the bedside in her nightdress she took from under the pillow an envelope, and sat down again on the side of her bed and opened it. It was brown and worn, but you could still see the address. It held the first letter her cousin Frank had written to her, after his visit six months before, when she had written to him, telling him she had changed her mind and would marry him. She read it again: 'My one love! My own love! My only love!'

She had slept with it under her pillow ever since. In the envelope were parts of other letters. She took them out and looked at them. She did not need to read them; she knew them by heart. She kissed them one by one and then put them back in the envelope and the envelope under her pillow. When she had got into bed she put out the light, but two hours later she still lay awake. She could hear the baboons outside in the dark, shouting and fighting among the rocks on the mountainside.

The next day Rebekah got married.

CHAPTER TWO

A Wild-Flower Garden in the Bush

For a while after Rebekah went things seemed askew and out of tune at the old farm; but they soon made grooves for themselves and ran on smoothly enough.

In the bush the wood doves cooed to one another, and the cock-o-veets called; the little gray, long-tailed monkeys climbed the trees and slid down by the monkey-ropes; the hares and porcupines visited the lands at night by the great dam; and the leopard sometimes came down on very dark nights to prowl about the *kraals*; and snakes made their nests and reared their young in the garden and under the dam walls. The great flat stone still lay baking in the sun on hot days; and the trapdoor spiders made lids to their nests and lined them with white silk and opened and shut them, though no little child with passionately interested eyes sat patiently waiting to see them open or shut; and at evening, the *avondbloem*[1] in the grass on the mountain opened their drab-tinted flowers and sent their rich sweet scent far and wide; though the small personage that had moved among them for twenty years, as a child and woman, was gone.

If the father missed his wise little daughter when he went down to the lands to see how a new variety of wheat was doing, and had no one to advise with over his grafts and flutes, or to discuss with him new remedies for cattle disease, he said nothing, but buried himself deeper than ever in the pages of his *Swedenborg*. And the little mother, if she missed her eldest daughter on baking days, and in the vegetable garden, and every day when rations were given out, yet found great consolation from the fact that she had now a new subject to lament over.

Old Ayah said that everything had gone wrong since Miss Rebekah went, and that there was no one to keep order, or who knew how things ought to be done; but she cooked the food and scolded the little Kaffirs, just as of old, and shook her head continually over the tergiversations of mankind in general.

Baby-Bertie missed her. She cried herself to sleep for several nights after she went; but even for her time brought compensations. After a while there were long weekly letters from Rebekah and great excitement when the boy came with the post-bag over the *nek*. She told about her little house, and its furniture, and the garden; and now and then there were little parcels with bits of muslin or silk to be made up into *kappies* or aprons for Bertie or the little mother, and odds and ends for old Ayah and

---

1 *Aandblom*: evening flower (a species of *hesperantha*).

446

the servant; and all these brought a new element of excitement into life, and were something to look forward to.

And there was the new tutor. Everyone liked him at the farm, except perhaps the father; and he only showed dislike, if he felt it, by speaking even less than usual if he was by.

The little mother liked him. He would sit listening to her for hours while she lamented over the hardships of her life and described her home in England, which she had left as a girl twenty-five years before. It had been a simple country parsonage, but, seen through the refracting mist of twenty-five years of African life, it had slowly assumed always increasing proportions in luxury and beauty. The schoolmaster could paint beautiful illumined mottoes, with borders copied from the flowers, which Bertie bought him. He painted one to hang in the mother's bedroom, for her birthday, with a border of roses and lilies, and on it the motto, 'Blessed are the pure in heart.'

Bertie liked him. He did not trouble himself as to whether she remembered what he taught her; and he could play beautiful dreamy music, especially on Sunday afternoons, when Bertie, whom nothing else could keep long quiet, would crouch in the corner with her cat in her lap and cry softly, she did not know why.

When her three hours of school were over, he often helped her to work in the flower garden, which she had taken care of since Rebekah left, because Rebekah liked it so. Up in the bush he helped her to make a little garden for wild flowers, which he said would do better up there in their natural soil than down in the old soil of the farmhouse garden. She and he went often to see how the things were growing; and that was something new to Bertie, who had not been fond of the bush as Rebekah was, and had hardly ever gone there.

Then the autumn came. The gentians and everlasting flowers had died in the grass on the mountainside; and the thorn trees in the flat were covered with long seed pods, and their thorns became a more shiny white. Nothing important had happened at the farm since Rebekah left, except that one old batch of Kaffir servants had left and another had come; and the turkeys and goslings and chickens had bred out well and the yard was full; and the little mother had made two fine boilings of soap.

Then the winter passed and the spring came. It was ten months since Rebekah had gone. And then came the news she had a baby. The little mother cried. Old Ayah cried also, and said she felt sure the Cape Town servants would mismanage all the house while Rebekah was ill. And the father said, 'Rebekah? Rebekah? Can it be?' and walked out to the far lands. And Baby-Bertie first laughed and then cried, and then ran away to tell her tutor the news – and then things settled down again.

One afternoon, when everyone had risen from the afternoon nap, the little mother sat sewing at her work table in the corner of the front room. The door on to the *stoep* was open, and through it she could see Percy Lawrie, the tutor, sitting on a chair on the *stoep*, reading. By and by Bertie came round to the front of the house from the yard and sat down on the edge of the *stoep*, just before him.

She threw off her *kappie* and fanned herself with it; and then looked up towards the chair where her tutor sat.

'You aren't angry with me, are you, Mr Lawrie?' The tutor glanced down from his book at her, and then with one restless little black eye glanced in the direction of the open door where from his position he could see the mother sitting.

'No, Miss Bertie; oh no, of course not.'

'Because you said ...'

He made a quick movement as if to drive away one of the bees that was coming towards him: 'Miss Bertie, there it is close to your forehead!'

She shook her head. 'I don't mind.' Then stretching out one hand towards him with a deprecatory little gesture: 'I couldn't bear you to be angry with me! I don't like anyone to be angry with me – not even the servants! You *do* love me, don't you ?'

She looked up at him with the expression a puppy dog might have when looking up into the face of a master he half fears he may have offended.

'Certainly I am not angry with you, Miss Bertie. I have no reason to be. You do your lessons very well.'

'Baby-Bertie!' called the little mother from the sitting room, 'go to the yard and see if the hen is letting the goslings she brought out get to the little dam. Don't let her drive them back to the fowl house. Make haste.'

Bertie rose slowly and went round the house again to the yard.

A little later the mother went to the kitchen door herself and found Bertie sitting on the lowest step with her white apron full of goslings which she had been feeding, and she was going to carry down to the dam, as the hen refused to lead them. The black hen moved round her feet restlessly, anxious as to what was to become of her brood.

The mother stood on the top step.

'Baby-Bertie,' she said a little uncertainly, 'I want to speak to you.'

Bertie lifted her head and half turned it to her. The little mother hesitated.

'Just now, when you were round on the front *stoep*, I was sitting in the front room and heard you speaking to your tutor. I didn't quite like the way in which you spoke to him, dear.'

Bertie turned her head more fully and looked up into her mother's face. 'Well, I didn't mean to be rude to him,' she said; 'but after dinner, when you all went to lie down, he asked me to go up with him to see our plants in the *kloof*, and I didn't want to go because I wanted to sleep. He seemed cross about it, but I didn't mean to be rude to him.'

'Oh, you weren't rude to him, dear,' said the little mother nervously; 'it's not that.' The brown eyes that looked up into hers abashed her. 'You were quite polite to him; but you know, Bertie, girls and women don't ask grown-up men if they love them.

You are not a real baby, Bertie, although we call you so. But it's all right, my dear,' she added quickly, seeing the surprise on Bertie's face, 'only don't ask any man that again, dear. Take the goslings down to the dam.'

The little mother turned and hurried quickly into the house; Bertie rose slowly with the goslings in her apron and walked away towards the small dam beyond the wagon house, with the black hen anxiously following her.

It was about ten days after that the little mother fell ill. She had one of her bad sick headaches which sometimes kept her in bed for several days. All the house was kept perfectly still for her, and even the cocks were driven away from the back door because their crowing disturbed her. Bertie gave up all her lessons and waited on her, bringing in little basins of soup or of gruel she had made, and driving away the little Kaffirs if they came to play too near the farmhouse, and keeping everything in order like an old, experienced housewife. Even old Ayah allowed she was turning into a wonderful housewife since Rebekah left, though she would never allow she was as good. The little mother almost liked to lie in bed and see her trip softly in and out of her room, with her gruel and soup and fresh flowers, in her white muslin dress.

On the morning of the fourth day the little mother was better and fell early into a heavy sleep. About half past eleven o'clock she woke, and lay expecting Bertie to come in: but all the house was still; Bertie had put no new flowers in the vase beside her, nor brought in her lemon and water. For more than half an hour the little mother lay there waiting and wondering. Then the quiet grew oppressive; she rose and partly dressed herself, and went out into the passage. There was not a soul stirring in the house nor a sound to be heard but the far-off voices of the men as they called to their oxen ploughing in the *mielie* lands. She went to the kitchen and found old Ayah standing before the fire shredding *snysels*[2] into the soup-pot; she said she had not seen Bertie since just after breakfast; the father was gone to the far *mielie* lands and the Kaffir maids to wash the churns at the fountain. The little mother went back to her own room, but, feeling restless, she went out again to the room that used to be Rebekah's and was now Bertie's, and opened the door. Bertie was sitting there with her arms folded on the low dressing table before the window and her head resting on them. The little mother stepped gently up to her, thinking she was asleep. She laid her hand softly on her shoulder. Bertie raised her head slowly and looked into her mother's face. 'Are you ill, my baby?' she asked, bending down. Bertie said nothing. There was in the large eyes the look that an animal has when it is in pain; the mute fear of a creature that cannot understand its own hurt.

---

2 Cuttings; in this context dough cuttings, for soup.

She dropped her head upon her arm again.

The little mother saw nothing in it but the look of one who has a violent sick headache.

'You are ill, my baby, you are very ill! Lie down on the bed and let me cover your feet with the rug.' She took Bertie's arm and walked beside her to the bedside. Bertie moved heavily. You have done too much these last few days – you have taken too much care of me. Do not let your feet hang down so, dear. So – that is better! You take after me with these terrible headaches. I always had them when I was young.'

The little mother drew down the window blind. 'Lie still; I'll go and tell old Ayah to bring you hot water for your feet. We'll get Mr Percy Lawrie to ride over to Mrs de Wet's and bring some blue-gum leaves; they are wonderful things for these sick headaches.'

She trotted out of the room, forgetting wholly in her anxiety that she herself had been ill. At the kitchen door she met old Ayah, and told her what ailed Bertie, and discussed the blue-gum leaves. Old Ayah said they would have to send one of the Kaffir boys on foot for them, as, about half past ten that morning, Mr Percy Lawrie had come down from the bush and had said he must ride into the town for the post at once, himself, and had gone on the only horse in the stable.

When the Kaffir boy had been found and sent off, old Ayah made up the fire to get some warm water, and the little mother went back to Bertie with a glass of lemon; but she was lying with her face close to the wall, as though she were asleep, and did not stir when spoken to; and the little mother stepped softly out again.

That evening at eight o'clock the horse came back from the town; but there was a strange boy riding it whom Mr Lawrie had hired in the town. And there was a letter from him among the other post, in which he said that when he got to town he found a letter from his English relations awaiting him, which told him that his mother was dangerously ill and very anxious to see him before she died; it was therefore necessary for him to take the first post-cart and go on to the Bay[3] at once, if he wished to catch the next mail steamer for England; so he regretted he could not return to the farm to say goodbye. They need not concern themselves about any clothes, music, or books that he had left, but might give them away; neither need they trouble about his last half-quarter's salary, as he was leaving without notice. He thanked them for all their kindness. He did not send any special message to Bertie, but wished to be kindly remembered to all.

As soon as she had read the letter, the little mother hurried away to Bertie's room to tell her the news. She had refused to take any supper; but she had undressed herself and was still lying on the bed with her face to the wall. The little mother sat in the rocking chair by the bedside and rocked herself, and cried intermittently. She said it was always so, troubles never come singly; first she had been ill, then Bertie,

---

3 Port Elizabeth.

and now the dear, good schoolmaster had gone away in such trouble! But Bertie said nothing. The little mother asked her if she had pain; she said no, her head ached, and turned her face deeper into the pillow.

In the middle of the night the mother got up and came and stood at the door of Bertie's room, then opened it and went in softly. She thought she had heard someone crying bitterly; but when she got to the bedside Bertie was lying motionless and seemed to be asleep, with her face turned towards the dark, and the little mother went away, thinking it must have been the owl hooting, who came every night to see if any stray chickens were left out.

But the next morning very early, before anyone was up, Bertie got up and dressed herself, and went for a walk up into the *kloof*. When she came back she went straight to her room and lay down, and took nothing that day but a little tea.

In the evening a little Kaffir herd, who had been up in the bush to look for some goats, came back with the news that Bertie's little wild-flower garden was destroyed; that all the plants had been pulled up by the roots and the ground trampled flat; but when the little mother went to tell Bertie about it she took no notice, and lay with her eyes half shut.

The next day she got up at the usual time and said she was well, that her head did not ache; but she ate hardly anything, and was white-faced, with rings under her eyes; and old Ayah and the little mother agreed that she had been very seriously unwell.

As the days passed she went as usual about what household duties she had, but remained white and silent, seldom speaking to anyone and taking no interest in anything. As soon as her work was ended she went back to her own room, and closed the door and lay on the bed. The little mother thought she had been studying too hard; but old Ayah said it was a sickness which young girls often suffered from when they were about sixteen, and advised saffron root boiled in milk. Once or twice again at night the little mother thought she heard the sound of low crying, but when she went to Bertie's room all was silent, and she felt sure it must be owls on the roof.

Twice Bertie began a letter to Rebekah; but both times she tore the letter up, and it was never sent.

Of the little schoolmaster Bertie never spoke, though the little mother was always talking of him, speculating as to why he did not write again before he left Port Elizabeth, or as to whether his mother would be alive when he got to England. All the bits of music which he had left behind, with his name written on them, disappeared, one by one; and from the walls the mottoes he had painted with frames of everlasting flowers about them which he had helped Bertie to make, vanished. Only in the little mother's bedroom her motto with the painted border of lilies and roses still hung; otherwise there was nothing to recall him in the house.

One Sunday afternoon, two months after he went away, it had been a strangely sultry day, and since dinner Bertie had been lying down in her own room. About half past four the storm burst; the lightning flashed incessantly, the thunder crashing close over the roof, while the rain fell in torrents till you could not see the wagon house; the tiny stream that came down from the *kloof* was a roaring, foaming river, and all the little footpaths were rushing streams.

Just before sunset, when it was all over, Bertie came out of her room and went to the back of the house which faced the sunset, and sat down on the rough stone step at the floor of the milk room.

All the earth had been washed clean and fresh. The little streams in the footpath had ceased to run, but in all the hollows in the hard ground were pools of water, and you could hear the stream still rushing in the bed of the mountain torrent.

Baby-Bertie leaned her head back against the door; a rich, fragrant odour rose from the fresh earth; she drew the white shawl she had thrown over her head closer round her face, and sat watching the wet world. The sun was setting at the end of the great valley below the farmhouse; all the west was a bloody pall of crimson, all the east a faint reflection of its redness. On the water of the great dam by the willows, in the windows of the farmhouse, in the puddles in the roadway, on the wet leaves of the thorn trees, even there it was reflected; and the little flat and the lower hills on the other side of the valley and the tall mountains were all touched with its redness. A curious feeling came over her as she sat there watching it; it was as though a strong great hand were put out and took fast hold of her heart, that trembled and was so heavy, and held it fast. A curious quiet came over her. Was there not something that might make the past as if it had never been, and the 'I have done it' as meaningless as 'I have dreamed it'?

She sat gazing at that drenched world. It seemed as though the great hand stretched itself out and stroked her.

Slowly the crimson vanished and a faint glow lingered only at the far end of the valley.

Her father, as he passed her on his way back from the sheep *kraals*, laid his hand upon her shoulder. 'It grows late and cold,' he muttered; and she stood up and followed him into the house.[4]

When Bertie went to her bedroom that night and closed the door, she felt no terror of the room, as she had done lately; even though it was better to be there alone than anywhere else. After she had got into bed it seemed as though a great hand made an arch over her and she crept in under it and was safe. She drew the cover up high about her and clasped her arms about a pillow, as if it were a person, and drew it close to her. Even then the croaking of the frogs filled her with no horror; and when she fell asleep, she slept till morning without waking.

---

4 The author once drew attention to this rhythmic paragraph thus, and commented on it:
    Her father, as he passed her
    On his way back from the sheep *kraals*,
    Laid his hand upon her shoulder;
    'It grows late and cold,' he muttered.

CHAPTER THREE

The Dam Wall

Thorn Kloof was expecting visitors, and the life-blood stirred in its sluggish old veins. From the superannuated chairs and churns in the loft, to the china in the front room cupboard, everything was turned upside down and inside out and washed and scrubbed and renovated. Even the pigsty was whitewashed and had a new trough, and the *kraal* walls were built up higher with thorn branches.

For the visitors were many and important whom Thorn Kloof was expecting, and it behoved it to put on its best face. Even the little Kaffirs who danced about naked all day on the old *kraal* heaps knew that something unusual was about to happen, and came to the house to beg for cast-off clothing, paper collars, or old shoes, in which to bedeck their small naked bodies; and they danced about in the sunshine more contentedly than ever, with a collar, or a boot, or a torn waistcoat. All day the Kaffir maids were busy scrubbing and cleaning, laughing and chattering; and all day the little mother trotted about giving orders, and old Ayah clucked and scolded; and Griet, the little Bushman girl, whom Bertie had got from her drunken mother a little while before for a pair of old shoes and a bottle of wine, rushed about hither and thither, doing nothing, but flaunting her little yellow petticoats in everybody's face, and chattering at the top of her voice, and tormenting the Kaffir maids. Bertie herself got up before sunrise every morning to gather oranges and figs for preserves, and was busy all day making jams and almond cakes.

It was just four full years since Rebekah married, and now she was coming to visit them for the first time, bringing with her three small children, the eldest of whom was three years and three months old, and the youngest a new-born baby of eight weeks. She had almost died when it was born, and was coming home to rest for a while. Of late years she had often not written long letters though she wrote every week; she seemed always to be having a baby or nursing it, or to be otherwise engaged. Her husband was not coming with her, she wrote, as his business kept him in Cape Town, and later he was going for a six weeks' hunting trip into the Western Karoo. But her husband's brother, John-Ferdinand, was coming; he had come out again from England for his health, and was going to buy a farm in South Africa and settle there. He was coming to ask his uncle's advice as to the choice of a place.

A few weeks later there was also coming another visitor, a lady from England, who was delicate and recommended to their care by their English relatives; but no one knew much of her, or could tell what she would be like.

The excitement at the old farm was intense; everything was in motion.

One Saturday afternoon the wagon they had sent to the coast to fetch Rebekah came over the *nek*. The little mother began to cry as soon as they told her it was coming; and then everyone gathered at the back door to wait for it. Bertie would have liked to put on her *kappie* and run through the thorn trees to meet it, but she thought her mother would rather they all met Rebekah together.

At last the wagon drew up at the kitchen door, and Rebekah herself got out first. She looked smaller and more like a child than ever, with her little white face and her large eight-weeks baby on her arm. While the little mother was kissing her and crying, the driver handed down to the father a stout, fair boy of two, and then lifted down a shy boy of three, who looked like Rebekah and hid his face in his mother's skirt as soon as he got to the ground. They all gathered close round Rebekah. Bertie caught up the boy of two and covered him with kisses, and ran towards the house with him; the little mother took the baby from Rebekah and began to cry afresh; old Ayah caught hold of its long white skirt and began to cry also; and Griet did all she could to coax the shy boy to take his face from his mother's gown and let her carry him; but he kept his face carefully turned away as they walked towards the house.

They were so absorbed in Rebekah and her children they did not notice John-Ferdinand, her cousin, who had been walking some way behind the wagon, and who had now come up. He was a tall, slender man, with a very small, delicate head and face, and black hair, curling close to his head, and eyes of such an exceedingly dark blue they seemed black, except in certain lights. His fingers were very long and tapered, and his hands transparently white.

Only the father saw him, and went up to shake hands with him, and said he was glad to see him. When he went away to give orders about the oxen, John-Ferdinand stood alone by the great whitewashed brick oven that jutted out from the side of the kitchen.

He was dressed in dark clothes and wore a soft, black felt hat; he leaned his elbow almost gracefully on the oven and stood watching the unpacking of the wagon. The Kaffir maids had come up from the huts now, and were dragging mattresses, pillows, boxes, canisters, and bundles, out of the wagon, and throwing them down in heaps or carrying them into the house, all laughing, running, and talking. Over all Griet, with her small, yellow-brown, Bushman face, with its touch of Hottentot, was giving pretended orders to the Kaffir maids, and screaming in a shrill voice; tumbling in and out of the wagon over the heads of the others, doing nothing and glorying in the confusion.

Presently Bertie came to the back door to see how they were getting on. Then she noticed John-Ferdinand standing alone by the oven. It seemed to her he must feel lonely and neglected standing leaning there, no one speaking to him, and she ran down the steps towards him. He reminded her of the picture of Charles the First the night before his execution in her old school history, with his deep-blue eyes looking out so gravely. When she came near him she suddenly felt shy, and almost turned away; but he came slowly forward to meet her.

'You are my cousin Baby-Bertie, are you not? I think you were not born when I was here twenty-one years ago.'

He spoke gravely and held out his white hand. Bertie took it shyly.

'I have heard much of you from my brother and his wife; I think I should have known you anywhere had I met you.'

Bertie said nothing, and hesitated; then, seeing a large canister standing on the front box of the wagon ready to be carried into the house, she turned towards it and seized it. Her cousin came forward.

'That is too heavy for you.' He took it from her very gently and gravely. When their hands were near each other on the canister, she noticed how brown, and even rough, her hands were compared with his. She wrapped her right hand up quickly in her little silk apron as she walked behind him to the house. He put the canister down solemnly on the kitchen table; she thanked him quickly, and he went slowly out again.

That night, when Rebekah lay on the bed in the spare room, hushing her babies to sleep, Baby-Bertie came in. She had changed since the old days when Rebekah married and Percy Lawrie was her tutor. The exuberant brown curls were gathered into a knot at the back of her head, which showed better the beautiful outline of her small round neck and broad shoulders and the small round head. She had grown, as Frank prophesied, into a magnificent woman; but she had become quiet, the noisy gaiety of her early girlhood had passed, and she spoke and moved almost heavily. She would have been almost majestic if it had not been for the infant-like expression of the face, and something uncertain and almost wavering in her walk, rising from the fact that her feet were almost too small for her body. Her rich colouring was more perfect than ever; but in her round brown eyes there was a slight wistfulness, almost as though asking a personal question; and the corners of her small full-lipped mouth were more drawn in than they had been, as though always wearing a placid, half-smile.

She stood at the foot of Rebekah's bed, dressed in a white muslin gown with blue bows down the front. Rebekah's eldest son lay at her back, with his arms twisted round her neck, and her baby lay at her breast; but the little fat blue-eyed boy had already gone to sleep in his cot in the corner.

She crept on to the bed and laid her head softly on her sister's knee.

'It is so nice to have you here, eh, Rebekah,' she said slowly. 'It seems like long ago.' She uncovered the baby's feet and looked at them: 'Aren't they beautiful?' She held them in her hands. 'So soft and warm!' She held her cheek against them for a moment, and then laid her head back again on Rebekah's knee.

Rebekah smoothed her hair with her free hand. 'Aren't you very lonely here sometimes, Baby-Bertie?' she asked after a time.

Bertie smiled, the soft dreamy smile that was seldom wholly absent from her face. 'No,' she said. 'Sometimes I feel as if I should like to go to Cape Town and be with you and the children; and sometimes I feel as if I would like to go somewhere and see people and things and be where other people are.' She rubbed her cheek softly against Rebekah's knee. 'And then again I feel, no, it's better to be here shut in safely by the old mountains.' A slightly troubled look crept into her face; then she said: 'You know it isn't because I don't want to be with you, Rebekah; I am always wanting you; like when I was little.' They were silent for a time, as the little boy with his arms round his mother's neck was just dropping asleep. 'Rebekah,' Bertie whispered, as he seemed to have gone off, 'does cousin John-Ferdinand always look so grave?'

'Yes; he does not often smile; I never heard him laugh.'

Bertie lay still. 'Keep on stroking my hair, Rebekah; I like it so. Don't you like people to touch you – I mean, if you like them?' After a while she added, 'He's very clever, isn't he?'

'He took his degree well at the university.'

Bertie caressed the baby's feet softly with her hand. 'Don't you think he's very beautiful, Rebekah?'

At first Rebekah thought she meant the baby, then she understood.

'Yes, in a way. Most people think so. His beauty doesn't touch me.'

'I feel so afraid of him, Rebekah. He's not merry like Frank, who used always to be laughing and joking. Do you feel afraid of him, Rebekah?'

'No.'

'Oh!' said Bertie, and lay still.

Presently Griet came in to tell Bertie the milk was come and it was time to get supper ready. Soon after the little mother came in and sat in the rocking chair at the bedside and told Rebekah how much greater her troubles were than they used to be: the maids did less work than ever, and her father was more silent and said, 'Um! Um!' in answer, when you tried to talk with him. She said Bertie was a dear, good, beautiful child, but she spoiled Griet, and was like her father in not caring to talk much. She said how happy Rebekah must be with a husband always ready to chat and laugh, and how nice it must be to live in a town where you could get your bread ready baked, and all kinds of things you couldn't get on a farm; and she lamented on till Bertie came to call them to supper.

A few nights after, when the father and mother lay in bed, the father reading with his book open on his breast and the candle on the stand near his head, the little mother said, 'Rebekah *is* changed, you know.'

The father made a sound, which might mean attention or not, from under his thick iron-grey moustache.

'It's always, when you talk to her, as if she were thinking of something else; as if she didn't quite see you. She's different, she's quite different from what she used to be!'

'The cares of life,' muttered the father, still looking at his book, and growing sleepy.

'What cares has she?' said the little mother. 'She hasn't quite such an easy life as she would have had if she'd married John-Ferdinand. I've sometimes wondered why she didn't marry him, with the twelve thousand pounds of his own his aunt left him, when Frank had only his business. But, after all, I should have chosen Frank! He's so big and strong, and he's doing well, she says. Of course, she has a great many children and only one servant and an outside boy, and no nurse – but she will look after the children herself – Rebekah always did work harder than anyone else! She never complains, but it's as if she was thinking of something else. Even when she …'

But the father's book had dropped over on to his chest and he was breathing heavily; and the little mother put the light out.

During the days that followed Rebekah's arrival, the womenfolk at the house did not see much of John-Ferdinand. Sometimes he was out riding with the father, to look at the farms in the country round, to see if any suited him; and when he was at home he took his book after breakfast and roamed away with his rug into the bush and did not come back till dinner. After the afternoon sleep and tea he generally went for a walk again. At meal times he sometimes talked a little to the father and Rebekah about books. He was annotating a copy of Tennyson's *Idylls of the King*, and generally had it with his pencil in his pocket. The little mother feared he must feel lonely, and offered him the gun to go out shooting; but he said he never hunted; and she felt ashamed, as if she had offered him something wrong.

Yet, after the first ten or twelve days had gone, he began to stay more in and about the farmhouse. Sometimes, when in the morning Rebekah lay under the orange tree with her boys creeping about her, catching at the orange blossoms as they fell and stuffing them down her neck or making little heaps of them on the reed mat, and the baby lay on her arm, and Bertie was sitting at her feet shelling peas or peeling fruit, and chatting away softly about the wild cat that had stolen all her last brood of turkeys, or the man on the next farm who would quarrel about the beacons, or the sheep that had strayed in her father's veld, it would happen that Bertie would look up suddenly and see John-Ferdinand standing close behind them with his hands resting on the head of his cane, looking down at them; and she would at once become still and shell her peas or peel her fruit in silence, while John-Ferdinand said a few words to Rebekah, or walked on into the garden. He began also to sit a good deal, too, in the back dining room, reading at table, where Bertie passed and repassed as she went about her work between the pantry and kitchen.

One morning, when Rebekah had been there more than three weeks, Baby-Bertie was kneeling in the pantry, making Boer biscuits. She had the dough in a large wooden trough on a low bench, and the black pans she had to fill placed across and across on the end. She was kneeling on a footstool because she was too tall when she stood. She had finished kneading and was just going to begin making up, when she looked round and saw John-Ferdinand standing in the pantry door, watching her with his grave eyes, and his delicate head a little on one side.

'Rebekah isn't here,' she said quickly and shyly; 'she's gone down to the garden; and mother is in the ration room.'

'I am not looking for either of them, thank you.'

He stood still, and then came a step nearer.

'May I come in and watch you?'

He seated himself on the wooden churn that was turned upside down in the corner between the bench and the dresser. He leaned forward slightly and watched her. A lock of her brown hair had escaped and hung in one little ringed curl over her low, broad forehead; her sleeves were turned up far above her elbows and she had on a great snow-white coarse apron covering her dress.

She put the making-up board across the trough and broke off a lump of dough and began to make it up. She turned it this way and that, her downy cheeks growing pinker and pinker. First she tried to make snake curls, but they often broke in two as she was twisting them; then she made up double balls, and the one would hardly stick on to the other; she tried quickly three or four different patterns. She knew John-Ferdinand must think her so stupid, not even to be able to make up biscuits well. She would not have minded so much if the curl had not been hanging over her forehead, and she could not lift it off because her hands were doughy.

At last the six pans were full, and she stood up with a flushed face.

John-Ferdinand had not spoken once all the time.

He rose also.

'I am going for a walk in the bush up in the *kloof*,' he said. 'Will you come with me?'

'I – oh – I don't know. My hands are full of dough.'

'But you can wash them,' he said gravely, almost smiling.

Baby-Bertie called to the girl to take the pans away and went to her own room. She put on her best white dress and a large white *kappie* with embroidery round it. Then she came out without saying a word to anyone; John-Ferdinand and she walked round the back of the house and up towards the *kloof*.

First they went through the belt of small thorn trees, with seed pods just forming and the soft green this year's thorns turning white and hard, and with little honeycreepers hanging from here and there; and on, past the great round kunee trees, in whose depths you could hear the little birds hopping, though you could not see them; and on, into the real bush, where the tall forest trees grew straight and high over the bed of mountain torrent and made a great stillness in which the woodpeckers worked and there was always shade. Here the monkey ropes hung from the trees, and the Kaffir bean trees shed their great seeds till the ground was brown with them; and here and there out of the banks hung the great roots that the Kaffirs used to make medicine of. They crossed the bed of the mountain torrent, where the little stream of water, not thicker now in the dry weather than two fingers, was running among the great rocks, making clear pools here and there. On the other side of the torrent the path grew quickly steeper and the mountainside rose abruptly. She took the narrow upward footpath made by the Kaffir maids when they went to fetch wood; the nam-nams[1] and jasmine shrubs made a thick wall on either side, and the wild asparagus hung out long waving arms. By and by they came to a patch where olive-wood trees grew thick among fragments of fallen rocks covered with long dry moss. Just here, suddenly, they came to a small open space; two mighty rocks that must have fallen from their home in the crags on the mountain tops centuries before lay there, covered with long dry moss and red lichens. In the crack in one a tall slender young tree was growing, and the space between them was bare, covered only by a smooth carpet of moss and sorrel, with little fern leaves intermingled here and there; and the small, sweet-scented mountain geranium with its tiny pale blossom was growing close to the foot of the rocks. A bush of the tall scarlet geranium, with its brilliant blossoms, grew up against one rock. On the other side the bush rose like a solid wall, nam-nams and sweet-henries mingling with the larger trees.

The bare space between the rocks and the bush was just like a little almost square room, with a rich soft carpet.

John-Ferdinand broke away a branch of scarlet geranium, which left clear a little mound covered with fern and moss, close to the foot of one rock.

'Sit there,' he said. 'This is my little parlour. I come here often.'

She sat down upon the mound, and he stretched himself at her feet on the carpet of moss and sorrel.

'It is very nice here,' she said.

'Yes,' he answered.

She took her great muslin *kappie* off and laid it across her knee. 'It's quite cool,' she said.

'Yes,' he said.

Then they were quiet for a long time. At last he stretched out his hand, and from the branch of scarlet geranium he had broken he began plucking the brightest

---

1 A shrub with a small edible berry (also 'num-num').

blossoms and mixing them with the small fern leaves in the carpet. When he had gathered a tiny bunch he laid it upon her knee.

'They are very beautiful,' he said.

'Yes,' she answered. Then he stretched out his hand and scattered them again over the moss and sorrel.

'Oh – I liked them!'

'They do not belong to you. I should not have given them to you,' he said slowly. 'This is yours.'

He rose and from the wall of bush he plucked a small spray of the plumbago[2] that hung out everywhere.

'This is the sweetest flower of South Africa,' he said. He placed it on her knee close to her hand, and lay down again on the carpet at her feet.

'Those others are not for you,' he said, looking up at her. 'They are for women in crowded ballrooms and theatres. They can live there in the hot, stifling air. These are yours – they would fade there in a moment.'

Bertie touched softly with her finger the delicate blue leaves and the spirally curled buds.

He turned round on to his face again; the crushed leaves of the tiny mountain geraniums sent up a sweet aromatic odour as he moved.

'Would you mind my reading?' he asked.

'Oh no.'

He took out his book and laid it open before him on the turf, and leaned on his folded arms, reading at her feet.

Baby-Bertie fastened the sweet-henry spray he had given her with a pin to the front of her white dress; then she sat still. She could hear the wood doves cooing and the cock-o-veets calling in the cool morning air.

There was much wondering at the farmhouse and no little searching when dinner-time came near and Baby-Bertie was not to be found. It was an unheard of thing that she should wander farther than the *kraals* or the milk house, or at most the end of the orchard. Griet, Bertie's little Bushman maid, who had been sent to look for her and who had searched for her even in the oven at last, now sat down on the step of the loft ladder and howled, covering her face with her pinafore and knocking her heels against the lower rung, but partly peering out from the side of her pinafore now and then to see what effect her grief had on the group of little Kaffirs gathered below to watch her. She declared that the great spook with red eyes, whom she had

---

2 Plumbago, or sweet-henry, as the frontier children call it, is a delicate, pale blue flower, growing on a large, partly creeping shrub. Its skylike flowers are sensitive and curl up if roughly touched or plucked.

seen at the fountain the evening before when she went to fetch water, had certainly carried off Miss Bertie and eaten her. The little Kaffirs looked up at her with wonder and awe. They regarded her as a person highly favoured and much gifted.

Presently she saw Bertie coming down the *kloof* road in the hot sun, for the day had now grown warm, with John-Ferdinand following her; and the sweet-henry on her breast curled up, but still fastened there.

Then Griet got down quickly and stood with her face buried in the wall of the gable, sobbing bitterly. (She had seen Bertie go up the *kloof* road, and knew where she was all the time.) She thought Bertie would stop as she passed her to find out the cause of her grief, and when she did would pat her on the head and perhaps promise to give her the point of the sheep's tail, to console her.

But Bertie walked by her without seeing her.

'Daddy-long-legs! Why didn't he stay in his own country!' Griet whirled round from the gable wall, making her little skirts stand out all stiffly. 'Daddy-long-legs! Why did he ever come here! Taking our Miss Bertie away from us, to walk with him! Let him stay in his own country!' She whirled till there was a cloud of yellow petticoats, and the little naked Kaffirs looked on.

After that day everyone knew where Bertie was when she was not to be found in the milk room or the kitchen or the garden.

She and John-Ferdinand often went for walks. Sometimes they went in the early morning, when the dew was on the grass and you were afraid to set your foot down because you broke the spangles, and when the calves were putting their faces through the wet bars of their *kraals* and the cows were lowing for them, and the sheep had their backs dark with the dew, as they streamed out of their *kraals*, with the herd boy with his two sticks in his hand behind them; and when, as you walked through the mimosa trees and touched a branch, the dew rained down on you, and the long beams of the early sun made them sparkle like a shower of diamonds.

Sometimes they went in the evening up the steep bare spur of the mountainside that lay to the left of the farmhouse where the long waving grass grew; and they passed the herd boy coming down with his flock of curly Angora goats, a great Boer-goat leading them with a bell round his neck, and the Angoras running hither and thither on every side to have a last nibble at the few thorn trees among the long grass. Then they sat high up on the ridge and saw the sun set at the end of the valley, and the farmhouse on the other spur of the mountain below them looked like a white speck among the dark orange trees; and they watched the long curls of blue smoke rising in still air from the Kaffir huts, where the maids were lighting the evening fires with *mielie* cobs; and they saw the line of dust which hung over the road by which the sheep were going to the *kraal*; and in the dry grass about them the *avondbloem* (evening flowers) were coming out, and the air was full of the sweet night scent. Then they would walk down the steep stony footpath together, and say nothing; except John-Ferdinand asked her which was the best footpath to take, or she told him the name of one of some little night insects which began to buzz by them. They were very silent.

But especially in the middle of the day, when it was too hot to walk anywhere else, they went up to the little parlour in the bush. John-Ferdinand lay on the ground and read, and Baby-Bertie took out sewing she had brought with her and sat at the foot of the rock; and they stayed there long hours, often without speaking.

The little mother was glad she went out with him; it was a change for Bertie and it was bad to have a visitor one did not know how to entertain. No one thought it strange she should like to walk out with her cousin. Only Griet resented it. She turned up the little flattened ball in the centre of her face which was her nose whenever she mentioned him.

When Bertie was at home she was unusually silent, and went about her work more quietly than ever; only the placid half-smile that was always upon her face was deepened into something softer.

Rebekah was quiet, too. When she was not actively attending to her babies she was always reading. She read when she woke in the morning, in the grey dawn she drew back the curtain and lay on the side of the bed with her book stretched out that the early light might fall on it, while the baby lay drinking at her breast. She read at night, when supper was over and she could go to her own room and shut her door and lie reading without interruption, sometimes till the old cock at the wagon house began to crow; and often when she blew the light out she found the square of the window was already becoming dimly visible. She read in the afternoon, for a large part of the time when everyone else slept. Even when she was taking care of her children under the orange trees or in the orchard she had always a book in her hand; and if one came near to interrupt her, she looked up with an eager, sharp look – the look of a hungry dog eating a bone, when someone comes near him.

She seemed like a creature returning to its old habitat and resuming its old instincts and habits; but never, even when she was a child and first learned to read, had she read with such a concentration of almost fierce avidity. It was as though she hardly saw the world about her; even Bertie and her parents and the old farm she saw as through a mist, and only the world of her thought was real to her.

But one evening, when Baby-Bertie was in the milk room skimming the pans, Rebekah came with a mug to fetch fresh cream for her children. It was quite dark in the milk room already, and Bertie bent over the table, holding a lighted tallow candle in one hand, and the saucer in the other, with which she went over the pans, putting the cream into the little wooden cream vat at her side.

Rebekah stood still for a moment just inside the doorway. The light of the candle her sister held shed its yellow light full upon her, on her plain white dress and lovely down-turned face, and made her stand out from the dark shadows which filled the rest of the low room, almost illuminated. Rebekah stood looking at her for some seconds; then she came in and put her mug on the end of the long table. Bertie filled it. Still Rebekah waited, watching her work.

Suddenly Bertie said: 'Rebekah, I wish I was different and not like I am! I am so big and heavy! I am so stupid! I wish I were like you!' She looked up, and under her curled lashes the candlelight showed a tear had gathered.

'I can understand about work and such things,' she said slowly, looking back at her work, 'but I can't talk about books and all the clever things other people talk of. Sometimes, when father and you and Cousin John-Ferdinand are talking together at meal times – sometimes I wish I was dead. I want so to be different!' She bent down over her work. 'Rebekah, do you think anyone could ever love me who was very clever and not stupid like I am?'

Rebekah looked at the lovely face half-turned from her as it bent over its work. She almost laughed softly: 'You need not fear people will not love you, darling; you will be loved wherever you go; I am only afraid you will be loved too much.'

'Rebekah, I like so to be loved!'

Rebekah made a little caressing movement as though she would have put out her hand and touched the hand nearest her in which Bertie held the candle; then she heard the baby crying through the spare-room window and hurried away with her mug. Before Bertie had finished the milk the quiet dreamy smile had settled down on her face again.

The next morning, as Rebekah lay under the orange trees, with her book in her hand and her baby asleep on her arm, her boys playing beside her, John-Ferdinand came out of the house and appeared to be looking for someone and then turned to pass on to the orchard. Rebekah put down her book and told him she wished to go for a walk with him.

'I am sorry I cannot,' he said. 'I have asked Bertie to go with me as soon as her work is done.'

'That does not matter. I shall not keep you long.'

She rose and, calling Griet to watch the children, led the way round the corner of the house and past the *kraals*. She took the short cut through the mimosa trees towards the great dam in the flat. John-Ferdinand followed her with the copy of Milton he had been reading showing from his breast pocket. The path among the trees was so narrow that the thorns in the mimosa trees pecked at them as they passed.

When they got to the dam, Rebekah led the way along the narrow footpath that ran on to the broad top of the earthen wall that formed the dam. The path was almost overgrown with love-grass and chickweed and widows; and the great willow trees which grew at intervals hung over the path and dipped their branches into the water beyond. Rebekah and John-Ferdinand stood knee-deep among the weeds under the willows. They had not spoken all the way down, and they still stood silent for a few minutes.

On the other side of the dam, where the water was shallower, the lilies and water plants floated; and the goslings swam in and out among them and disappeared and reappeared among the chickweed and wild mustard that grew rank to the water's edge. Beyond them was a little mound where Bertie's twin sister, who had died when she was born, had been buried. Bertie often came down to weed about it and keep it clear; but during the last weeks she had forgotten it, and the weeds had almost overgrown it.

Rebekah took off her *kappie* and held it in her hand.

'John-Ferdinand,' she said, 'I wish to speak to you about Bertie.'

John-Ferdinand bowed his head gravely, to show he was attending, and looked down at her.

'She has led a lonely life here. A woman who grows up alone on a solitary farm in South Africa is not quite in the position of most other women. A child of ten, who has lived in a village or town and has gone to a school and grown up among other children, has more knowledge of the world in a thousand ways than she can have even at fifteen or twenty. She may know much of books, and be skilled in domestic labour or – she may even be exceptionally advanced intellectually in many ways; she is still a child in the knowledge of men and life. Bertie does not even know the world of books.'

John-Ferdinand bowed again, and looked down at her with his dark head delicately poised a little on one side.

'You have seen a great deal of her since you came here. I do not blame you; it was natural you should. She is the only interesting thing here, and she is very beautiful. But I am afraid she may possibly grow to care a little for you, John-Ferdinand, seeing no one else.'

John-Ferdinand moved as if he were about to speak, but she raised her hand and stopped him.

'She has said nothing of her feeling towards you to me; I am acting entirely on my own judgment. But she has seen no men in her life but a few shop clerks and farmers' sons who may have come here on business or have served her in a shop when she was in town; you are the first man of mental and physical attractions with whom she has been thrown into close contact. It has been almost inevitable that she should be attracted by you, and it has been almost as inevitable that you should feel attracted towards her. And yet, when you marry, you will probably require in your wife certain qualities which Baby-Bertie has not: more intellect and more calm strength of character. Now, if this is the case, John-Ferdinand' – she looked up at him – 'and you feel that, in spite of her great beauty, she is not the type of woman you can make your wife, then I think you ought to go away from the farm and not seek to meet her again. It is an absorbing love she would love you with, John-Ferdinand – a love you probably cannot understand. You might become all the world to her. Some women with complex, many-sided natures, if love fails them and one half of their nature dies, can still draw a kind of broken life through the other. The world of the impersonal is left them: they can still turn fiercely to it, and through the intellect draw in a kind of life – a poor, broken, half-asphyxiated life, not what it might have been, like the life of a man with one lung eaten out by disease, who has to live through the other alone – but still life. But Bertie and such as Bertie have only one life possible, the life of the personal relations; if that fails them, all fails. If you chop down the stem of a mimosa tree, years after you may come and find from the bottom of the old dead stem sprouts have sprung, which will even bear flowers, though there will never be the glory of the central stem; but an aloe has one flower, once; if you cut that down, nothing more comes. If the life of personal relations fails Bertie, all will have failed her; I want to save her from this. You are a man of principle, John-Ferdinand; I know you are a man who always does what he believes to be his duty. I think you will feel it your duty to go, if you know you cannot care for her.'

'Rebekah,' he said softly, still looking at her, 'I love your little sister. She is the one absolutely pure and beautiful thing life has ever yet shown me. From all the world of men and women I turn to her to find in her the one absolutely spotless, Christ-like thing I have known. I am a nobler and better man when I am in her presence. No other woman ever could be, or ever will be, to me, what she is. When as a youth I asked you to marry me I was drawn to your intellect, your strange intensity and delicate physical refinement and beauty, and your devotion to your duties. My feeling for her is wholly different. For the first time I understand now how men have made a god of woman – the eternal virgin mother! If I am all the world to her, Rebekah, she is more than all the world to me.'

Rebekah looked up at him and then away across the water. There was no mistaking the ring of sincerity in the man's voice; his dark-blue eyes were moist with unshed tears. They stood quiet for a moment. The willow trees sifted down the last of the spring's little dried catkins on Rebekah's brown hair and on John-Ferdinand's black felt hat.

'If I have not yet spoken to her of my love, Rebekah, it has been because she has seemed to me almost too pure and sacred a thing for me to approach. Can you understand? Have you never felt, on a solitary mountainside, that some delicate flower you have found growing there was too beautiful to be plucked? – that it was too pure for your finger to touch it? When your father has helped me to secure a farm in this neighborhood, so that I shall not need to take her far from her parents and her old home, I shall lay my love before her. I hope it will not be long before I take her to myself forever.'

Rebekah looked away from him to where the little goslings swam in and out among the water lilies.

'If that is so,' she said slowly, 'I have no right to say more, and perhaps I should not have said what I have.' She gathered together her little skirts and turned to lead the way along the little footpath. Then suddenly she turned. 'If I knew,' she said, 'that you would ever fail her, I, I with my own hand, would rather take her life and see her lying buried there, beside her little sister.' The crimson flush had risen suddenly over her face, darkening even her forehead; it died away in an instant and left the face paler than before. She walked on before him, the black widows shaken from bushes as they passed sticking fast to her skirts and to his black trousers. When they got off the dam wall she took the path along the thorn trees and walked so fast John-Ferdinand could hardly keep up with her. When they had climbed almost to the top of the long rise on which the house stood, she stood still for an instant and took out her penknife and cut a large many-horned gall growth from one of the mimosa branches. 'I am collecting these,' she said, half turning to him, 'to see whether the galls on the different species of mimosa are all quite alike, or whether they are different on different species of the tree.' Then she walked on quickly.

When they came out of the thorn trees at the *kraals* they saw the white tent of a cart which stood *outspanned* near the back door.

'The woman from England must have come,' she said. 'They were expecting her today.'

As they came nearer the house they saw Bertie standing on the top kitchen doorstep, and beside her a tall woman with square shoulders, dressed in a starched mauve cotton dress, with white collar and cuffs. Bertie, in her white muslin and blue ribbons, was motioning with her right hand, evidently pointing out to the stranger the interesting points in the landscape, from the wagon house and pigsty to the great dam and the road over the *nek*, which could all be seen to advantage from the top of the steps. As they approached the steps, Bertie and the newcomer came down to meet them. She had light hair of an almost drab shade touched with yellow and parted down the centre. It was brushed smoothly down on each side, showing strikingly the large, flat-topped, broad shape of the head. Her forehead was high and arched in the middle, and her large eyebrows were even more arched, so that between them and the pale-blue eyes below, over which the eyelids habitually drooped, almost the whole bulb of the eyeball showed under its eyelid. Her eyelashes were thick and almost white, and drooped over her cheeks readily as she looked down. She walked towards them with a long, even stride that contrasted with Bertie's wavering uneven little footsteps.

She held out a large, flat, cool hand to Rebekah and John-Ferdinand when Bertie introduced her.

It was not easy to say what her age was; it might have been anything between twenty-eight and thirty-eight; the perfect placidity of her face might make her appear older than she was, or, being old, might make her appear younger.

'You must have had a warm drive from the town,' John-Ferdinand said.

'No, it was very pleasant,' she said slowly; 'the view was very interesting.'

Then they all turned and went into the house.

CHAPTER FOUR

Showing How Baby-Bertie Heard the Cicadas Cry

'Wherein lies this woman's charm?'
This question Rebekah had asked herself more than once before Veronica Grey had been at the farm three weeks.

She looked at the angular high shoulders, at the rather large mouth, somewhat drawn down at the corners as in a fixed half-smile; at the thickening finger tips on the large, flat, snow-white hands; and at the white eyelashes – and found no immediate answer.

Everyone at the farm seemed to like her except Griet.

The father liked her. He seldom went to his *mielie* lands to examine the new varieties of grain he was experimenting with, or to the orchard to look at his grafts, but he took her with him. Her past life in a villa in the south of London could hardly have yielded her an extensive knowledge of African field growths, and she did not know a *mielie* land from a wheat field, or a bed of sweet potatoes from one of pumpkins; but she always said, 'Ah, yes,' when the father discussed the varying growth in his beds and their manures; and when she looked at the grafts she said, 'How *very* interesting!' or, 'How *wonderfully* they are growing!' and the father liked her company.

The little mother liked her. On days when she had a headache and went to lie down, Veronica came and sat in the rocking chair beside her bed, knitting, and saying nothing; and when the little mother was better and able to talk, she sat rocking and listening to all her complaints, and never tried to put a good complexion onto her troubles; she only said, 'How strange!' or, 'That is just what my mother often said!' and the little mother liked her.

Bertie liked her; she was something new to take care of. When the hand-lambs and all the poultry had been fed, and there were no sick Kaffirs to attend to, and Rebekah's children needed nothing, there was always still Veronica. She used to bring a glass of milk to her bed at six in the morning, when the cows were first milked, and little cups of broth or beaten-up egg and wine between breakfast and dinner; and she insisted on her sleeping in the next room to her own, which used to be Rebekah's, so that if she woke in the night and needed anything she might knock on the wall and not feel lonely – as Bertie herself still often felt, when she woke in the night and had to clasp a pillow to her and hold it tight in her arms to make herself feel as if there were someone sleeping by her and caring for her. She ironed

Veronica's white dresses herself, because the maids could not make them smooth and stiff enough.

John-Ferdinand liked her. When Bertie was busy with her housework, he used to read aloud to Veronica from the *Idylls of the King* or *Paradise Lost,* and she would sit knitting and listening. Often she would drop the work into her lap and sit with her hands across upon it and her blue eyes fixed on the cover of the book he was reading from; for half an hour she would sit motionless, listening; and sometimes she asked him to read a long passage over again; and that he liked most of all.

Old Ayah liked her; she said she gave no trouble and kept her room beautifully neat: there was never a thread or a scrap of paper on her carpet; and her large flat-soled thick English boots stood exactly side by side under the dressing table, toe to toe; and her gloves lay ready on the dressing table, in case she should be going out, finger to finger and thumb to thumb; and she gave old Ayah who did her room a shawl she had knitted.

As for Rebekah, she was so busy attending to her children and reading that she seldom spoke to anyone; and no one noticed that she never addressed a remark to Veronica, and generally left the room or the *stoep* when Veronica came there.

But Griet showed her dislike actively. One evening, when she went to the fountain to fetch water for the baths, she found a fine large toad under a stone, with great warts on his back. Carefully catching it with two sticks, she put it into the pail, which she carried home on her head and emptied into Veronica's bath. She hoped that when Veronica got up the next morning and stepped into the bath she might not notice it till she was in. About the time Veronica usually got up, Griet stood outside her bedroom door, first on one leg and then on the other, rolling her eyes and holding her breath, momentarily expecting to hear a step into the bath and then a wild cry and a flight across the floor. But instead a calm voice called to her from the bedroom, 'Griet, I think there is something moving in my bath; come in and see what it is and take it out!' And Griet, bursting with rage, had to come in and recapture her toad. 'How did that "thin-eyes" know that I was there!' she cried indignantly when rehearsing the story to herself as she emptied the bath; and her defeat increased her antipathy; but she contented herself with setting Veronica the cracked plate at teatime, and the bluntest knife at dinner; and occasionally putting a small drop of aloes into the coffee she took to her room in the morning; in which case Veronica always left it undrunk.

One Saturday night, when Veronica Grey had been just eight weeks at the farm, the father and John-Ferdinand came home to supper. They said they had signed an agreement with the owner of the next farm, the tops of the tall blue-gum trees about whose homestead were just visible over the *nek* when you climbed the mountainside, to sell his farm to John-Ferdinand for five thousand pounds, and to give him possession at once.

There was much talking about it at the supper that evening. Veronica Grey said she had often wondered what that farm was like, and John-Ferdinand said they should all go and see it the next week. Only Rebekah could not go, as her visit had come to its close, and she was leaving at daybreak on Monday morning in the ox-wagon to begin her journey to Algoa Bay,[1] from which she would go by sea to Cape Town.

After supper, the mother, who had a headache, went early to bed, and Rebekah went to her own room; the father sat with his books in the dining room; Bertie, who was finishing a dress for Griet to wear the next day, sat by the lamp at the centre table in the front room sewing, and John-Ferdinand sat beside her reading, but now and again he looked away from his book and watched her fingers as they sewed. Veronica sat in an armchair in the far corner of the room knitting; as she knitted, from time to time her eyes, from under their long white lashes, rested on the two who sat together at the table. At last she rose and gathered her work into its bag, and went to the little mother's bedroom.

'Would not you like me to come and sit by you a little?' she asked; and she seated herself on the rocking chair beside the bed. For a long time there was nothing to be heard but the tick, tick of her needles. By and by, however, her hands dropped into her lap and she sat looking at the painted motto that hung on the wall opposite the bed with its border of lilies and roses.

Then the little mother, who had been half dozing, woke up, feeling much better, and showed an inclination to talk.

Veronica said that was a very pretty motto on the wall. The mother lay on her side and told her all the story of Percy Lawrie, how he had stayed on the farm and taught Bertie, and how nicely he could paint; how he had had bad news from England and had gone away suddenly and they had never heard any news of him again. Veronica listened, and knitted, and rocked herself. Then the little mother gradually got drowsy again and went off to sleep.

When she was sleeping soundly, Veronica rose and rolled up her work and put it into the little bag upon her arm, and went out of the room, closing the door behind her. In the passage all was quiet, but you could hear Bertie at the piano singing sacred music, and John-Ferdinand's voice singing the bass, through the closed door of the front room. The long passage itself was dark; but through the half-open door of John-Ferdinand's bedroom at the far end shone a light. He had evidently not put his candle out when he went to supper. As she went towards her own room she passed John-Ferdinand's door. She looked round quickly; every other door into the passage was closed, and John-Ferdinand's and Bertie's voices could still be heard singing.

---

1 Port Elizabeth.

With a long, light, smooth step she passed into John-Ferdinand's room. The candle stood on the dressing table. She looked round the room. It was the first time she had ever stood alone in a man's bedroom. Her father had died in her early childhood and her brother was grown up and had gone to China before she could well remember, and in the quiet home in the south of London, where her widowed mother and four unmarried sisters lived, no men visitors had ever come. She stood just inside the door and looked round. On a rack against the wall behind the door hung a row of articles of man's clothing – coats, and jackets, and waistcoats, and trousers; under the dressing table was a row of boots, and a pair of man's slippers stood beside the bed. She walked up to the clothes behind the door and passed her hand softly over them; she took down a greatcoat and felt the velvet collar and the buttons; she rubbed her cheek gently against the shoulder of the coat. So a man's shoulder felt when you put your face against it. She took down a pair of trousers, stroked them, and hung them up again; she felt the buckles at the back of a waistcoat; then she walked to the washing-stand. There was nothing there but the ordinary soap, and sponge, and toothbrush, that any woman might have used, as John-Ferdinand did not shave but clipped his soft beard; but she touched the soap and toothbrush with her finger. She went to the bedside; there was a large braided bag before the pillows; she turned back the flap; there was a man's thick linen garment inside; she did not take it out, but stood listening to hear if anyone were coming. But Bertie and John-Ferdinand were still singing in the front room, and there was no other sound. She turned to the dressing table; there were his brushes and combs and a large bottle of lavender water. On each side of the glass was a small pile of books. She ran her fingers quickly over them. From under the looking-glass protruded the end of a closed, old-fashioned, portrait case. She drew it out and tried to open it; she moved the little hook that fastened it. Inside the case was an old daguerreotype portrait. It was the portrait of a little child of four with a mass of brown curls about its head; the face was smiling; there were dimples in the cheek and in the chin; the child seemed bursting with life and joy, and in its hand it held a bunch of flowers. The old tinted daguerreotype had the colour of life, the cheeks and lips were red. She held it sloping towards the candle, at such an angle that she could see it truly through the glass. There was no mistaking whom it represented. It was Bertie as a child, and the only photograph of her in existence. John-Ferdinand had begged the loan of it from the mother, that he might send it to Cape Town with Rebekah to have a life-size enlargement taken from it.

Veronica looked down closely into the face, and her eyes contracted slowly at the inner corners. Quickly she put the case down open on the table, and, placing her large flat thumb on the face, she pressed; in a moment the photograph had cracked into a hundred fine little splinters of glass radiating from the face, which was indistinguishable. With smooth quickness she closed the case and slipped it under the looking-glass, without one bit of glass falling from its place. She stood listening to hear whether anyone was coming. There was no one; and with one or two long, even steps she glided out of the room; with three or four more she had reached her own and closed the door.

The next day the morning broke peaceful and windless, but it promised to be unusually hot later. A deep Sunday stillness reigned about the farmhouse after breakfast. The Kaffir servants were gone to their huts to have their Sunday rest; old Ayah sat at the kitchen door slicing salad and keeping an eye on the pots inside with the Sunday dinner. Griet had gone off to the far lands to pick some green *mielies*, swearing vengeance upon all the world because she had been accused by old Ayah of breaking Bertie's photograph when she dusted John-Ferdinand's room, and had narrowly escaped the force of old Ayah's hand by Bertie's intervention. The father, in his Sunday best, was reading Swedenborg in the front room, with his hair very much brushed. The little mother was busy in her bedroom, and Rebekah with her boys was, as always, out under the orange trees upon the mats.

John-Ferdinand came out at the front door, looking for Bertie to go for a walk with him. Rebekah did not glance up from her book as he passed, and he walked on through the flower garden and down into the orchard beyond.

Of late, without actually shunning him, Bertie had seemed to elude him; it seemed almost as though she feared to be alone with him; yet when he spoke to her there was a wavering in her colour, and a soft brightening about her face she could not hide.

He wandered into the orchard. The long dry grass was brown under the trees, the young unripe peaches had fallen by hundreds into it, and the leaves of the peach trees were beginning to grow yellow for want of rain. At the great pear tree in the middle of the orchard, on the bench, which Rebekah had had put up around the stem when she was sixteen, he saw some one sitting. At first he thought it might be Bertie, but when he came closer he saw it was Veronica Grey.

She was dressed in one of her spotless, stiff cotton dresses with broad, stiff, white linen collar and cuffs; a great straw hat with only a simple band of ribbon tied about the crown lay on the bench beside her, and a book of Sunday sermons lay open beside it. The little sunbeams came through the pear tree branches and played on her smoothly brushed yellow and drab hair; but her eyes were fixed on the row of peach trees before her, and her long white fingers were clasped together upon her knee.

John-Ferdinand stood still at a little distance and watched her. It was a curious picture of placid calm, not a line in figure or dress moving as she sat under the soft playing shadows and lights. He stepped closer to her and asked her if she had seen Bertie. Without unclasping her hands she turned her face towards him and said slowly, 'No,' and then looked back again at the trees.

John-Ferdinand turned away; yet as he wandered up through the orchard the placid picture under the tree was with him. He walked through the flower garden and out at the gate at the north gable of the house, and took the little footpath among the mimosa trees that led up into the *kloof*.

Now he was thinking only of Bertie. He pictured the farmhouse among the blue-gum trees as it would be when he and Bertie lived there; Bertie, with her beautiful face and queenly figure lighting up the world about her, till lambs and servants and everyday work reflected that beauty that had made the old farm so lovely to him. He saw her as she had looked that morning at breakfast, when someone had told her that her old Kaffir man she was nursing was worse, and she had left her breakfast and gone out with a jug of hot milk in one hand, and the bottle of medicine in the other, to go to the huts and see if she could do anything for him; as deeply concerned as if it mattered to anyone but herself whether there was one old woolly head in the world more or less. A creature so full of loveliness and love for every living thing, was she not satisfying to the whole soul and body of a man? As he followed the little footpath among the trees, his mind ran on to the long years that were to come; he saw children with their mother's fawn-like eyes looking up at him and calling him father; and the thing he loved lying always in his bosom to comfort and complete his life; it was as though he looked up a long valley where ridge succeeds ridge in new colours, till the far end was reddened with sunset glory.

So far had his thoughts led him, that he had crossed the almost dry bed of the mountain torrent and had reached their little room and almost trodden on a little ungloved hand, before he saw that Baby-Bertie was before him, sitting at the foot of their rocks, with one hand resting on the moss beside her.

'Why did you come without me?' he said, as he lay down on the turf beside her, so close that his folded arms rested on the edge of her white dress. He had never before done so. 'I thought I should find you here.'

She was dressed in her best white Sunday dress, with bows all down the front, and a blue ribbon round her neck.

'Do you know what I was thinking of as I came up?' he said, after a while. 'I seemed to be looking into the future; and it seemed to me,' he added softly, 'that I was looking down a long, sunlit path that passed over ridge after ridge, each one more beautiful than the last, till the end, far beyond human sight, lay hidden in glory.

Bertie sat quiet; she was thinking of no beauty in the future, only of a hand very near to her, that she would have liked to bow down to and kiss humbly.

John-Ferdinand spoke in a yet lower voice: 'Nothing can ever alter, nothing can ever change, our happiness, that springs from such deep love. Death itself will be but going home to the Father's house to be made perfect there in that which made us loved and loving here.' He looked up at her. 'For those who love as we love, there is no parting, and no death, only eternal union.'

She listened, and the sound of his voice was music to her; but of the meaning she took in little.

'I do not like to think of what will come,' she said, bending her head. 'I like all things to be just as they are, now; never, never to change! I wish they would always be just so!'

He too at that moment seemed content with an unchanged present. He lay still watching the little hand that rested on the sorrel close to his; and once he looked up at the opening overhead, across which at intervals small thunder clouds were already beginning to move quickly against the hot blue sky. Why did it seem so hard to take that woman to his arms and tell her how he loved her? Why did she seem, without repulsing him, to move away from his hands when he meant to put them out and hold her?

It was already nearly midday, and a sultry stillness was beginning to settle down over the bush. Nothing broke it but the shrill cry of some cicadas hidden in the thickets and in the stems of the trees.

Then he rose from the ground, leaned his elbow against the rock, and bent down over her.

'Bertie, my darling,' he said softly, 'you must not miss me too much if I go away next week. I shall only be gone for a few days, that I may get all that will be necessary for our new home. And then I will come back to you, and you will come to me, and we will be together forever; never to part while life is left us. You are my wife now, already my darling; are you not?' He bent down and wound his left arm round her, half drawing her up to him. For a moment it seemed as though she would have leaped up and nestled close to him; then she loosened herself from his arms and sat clown again on the bank. 'You must not touch me, you must not kiss me – you must stand still, just where you are – against the rock – I want to say something to you – I want to tell you something.'

For a moment he tried to draw her to him again; then silently, wondering, he obeyed her. She sat on the mound at his feet. There was that in her voice that compelled him to listen, and the dimpled hand that had rested on the turf was on her knee now and quivering. Her face he could not see; he looked down at her waving hair that hung in little curls about her forehead.

For a moment she was quiet. He waited; but still she said nothing.

'My little Baby, what is it you want to say to me? I have not long ago told you how I love you, only because I thought you knew, as I knew, how you loved me.'

He bent over her again, with his face above her head.

'I do not know what to say – stand back as you were before – with your arm against the rock.'

He obeyed her, and waited.

'Long ago I had a schoolmaster; his name was Percy Lawrie. I – I liked him – I liked him very much. He was very kind to me. I liked him at first, then afterwards I hated him ... ' The hands she had now folded together in her lap were covered in the palms with a cold perspiration. 'I did not know – he said he would be angry with me – I did not want him to be angry with me – I didn't want to – I didn't know, you see!

Oh, what shall I do! – What shall I do!' She half started up, and then sank down on the mound again.

John-Ferdinand looked down at her, white, motionless.

'He went away that day – I never saw him any more!'

John-Ferdinand leaned heavily on his arm on the rock above her, his face an ashen white. The scent of the crushed geraniums on which he stood seemed to rise up overpoweringly strong; and the only sound was the crying out of the cicadas; they seemed glorying in the hot stillness of the bush.

John-Ferdinand took his elbow from the rock.

For a moment Bertie made a movement as though she would have moved up close to him; then she sat down motionless.

'Bertie, do you mean that you gave yourself to him?'

She nodded.

He waited in silence.

'My poor cousin!' he said slowly.

There was a cicada in the bush, just to the left, that cried louder and louder; its cry seemed to ring through her brain; she wondered when it would leave off.

'Let us go home, Bertie,' he said slowly.

She stood up from the mound. The bush had become very hot and deadly still; only the cicada's cry seemed ringing everywhere. She began to walk down the little path; John-Ferdinand followed her. The leaves of the plumbago bushes on either side hung flaccid and curled, and even the asparagus branches drooped, waiting for the storm that must come later. They crossed the bed of the mountain stream and climbed the bank on the other side where the great roots hung out, and the ground was covered with the fallen Kaffir beans; the leaves and dried sticks cracked under their feet as they walked. Just here, where the trees were tallest and met overhead and the monkey ropes hung down, and where there was deep shade and stillness, they met Veronica Grey coming up from the farmhouse into the bush, holding her stiff white skirt about her with one hand and in the other, which drooped in front of her, her half-open book, with her fingers between the leaves. She smiled tranquilly as she passed them.

'What a peaceful Sabbath stillness reigns up here!' she said; and she walked on higher into the bush, as John-Ferdinand and Bertie went down.

When they had got beyond the belt of tall trees where the small mimosa trees and scattered kunee trees grew, she turned suddenly and looked up at him.

'I hurt you so. I hurt you so!' she said. He looked down at her.

'It is not pain that matters, Bertie; it is sin,' he said slowly.

She looked up into his white drawn face, with its compressed nostrils. Then she gathered her skirts tight about her and fled down the winding footpath. An out-stretched branch of mimosa caught in her skirt and tore it from top to bottom; but she did not pause. In an instant she was out of sight. There was nothing, when

John-Ferdinand passed the next winding, but the tiny rag of white muslin with its blue bow hanging from a thorn, to show she had been there.

That night, at ten o'clock, all the boxes and bedding had already been packed into the ox-wagon, which was drawn out before the back door prepared for Rebekah's start the next morning before dawn. The yokes were laid out in order before the wagon, and the *riems*[2] hung over the side ready to *inspan* in the dark; and the oxen were sleeping in the *kraal*. The household had retired early, as they had to rise so soon; only Rebekah was still busy in her room arranging the clothes which the children would require to put on in the morning and tying up the last parcels.

When she had finished, she went to Bertie's room. Bertie had been there since before dinner, complaining of feeling unwell; and even the great thunderstorm which had burst in the afternoon had not revived her.

Rebekah opened the door very gently, fearing to awake her if she had dropped asleep. But Bertie was kneeling on the floor in the middle of the room, a large box open before her and a candle balanced on one corner; while Griet, with much alacrity, was adding the contents of the lowest drawer in the chest to the pile of clothes that lay on the floor at Bertie's side. Bertie was putting the articles one by one into the box.

Rebekah set down her candle on the dressing table and walked up to her, looking down with astonishment. Bertie did not look up, but went on mechanically fitting the articles in.

'Bertie, what is this?' Rebekah asked.

She did not look up. 'I am going with you,' she said shortly, in a voice almost low and gruff; and went on packing. Her face was turned downwards; her lips looked heavy and protruding; but there was no sign of her having wept.

Rebekah put her hand on Bertie's arm: 'How is this, Bertie? What is it?'

'I am going with you.' There was a dull, dogged persistency in the tone.

'But does mother know of this?'

'I am going with you.'

Griet, who had just added the very last article of the drawer to the heap on the floor, stood with her eyes rolling and glittering, delighted with the general confusion and the excitement of something unusual happening, though she did not understand what. Rebekah sent her out to go to her bed. When the door was closed, she knelt down beside Bertie.

'What is the matter, my dear one? You have always said you would not leave the farm or go with me, when I have asked you. Has anything happened?'

---

2 Rawhide thongs.

Bertie said nothing; her heavy face was still turned down. There flashed on Rebekah the remembrance of John-Ferdinand's white stiff face all that day.

'My darling, is there anything I can do to help you? Anything I can say?'

'Go and tell mother I am going with you,' she said slowly. 'Make her understand I am going. I *will* go.'

Rebekah stood up, but bent down again, putting one hand on her shoulder. 'There is nothing I might say to John-Ferdinand, which could be of any use to you, is there?'

In an instant Bertie had leaped to her feet and caught both Rebekah's hands in hers.

'Oh, no, no! Rebekah, promise me – you will never – never speak to him of me – never ask him about me – never ask him anything! Promise me, Rebekah! Promise me!'

For the only time in her life Rebekah saw Bertie transfixed with passion.

'I will do whatever you ask of me, dear one.'

Bertie sank back again on her knees before the box, and Rebekah went out to see the father and the little mother in their bedroom, and tell them of Bertie's resolve. The little mother, who had been half-asleep, woke up and began to whine that it was all so sudden; that she could not bear sudden things; that Bertie had no clothes; that she ought to have told them before; that it was unlike Bertie to take people so by surprise. But when Rebekah had explained that the new clothes could be better got in Cape Town; that the little mother had always wished her to go with her for a visit; that Bertie needed change and ought to see something of life after twenty years on the farm; and, when the father had expressed his full approval of her going, the little mother, still whimpering, insisted on getting up and going to see Bertie; but gave her consent. Bertie gave her as little explanation as she had given Rebekah. She only said stolidly she was going. And the little mother was at last persuaded by Rebekah to go back to her bedroom, still whimpering that she couldn't bear surprises; that she wouldn't have wondered if it had been Rebekah, but that Bertie took after her and never took anyone by surprise; that perhaps after all Bertie took after her father also; and she had no child who really resembled her! But she had no valid objection to make; when Rebekah had bid her good night and she found the father was asleep and she had no one to hear her, she got quietly into bed and was soon asleep.

When Rebekah had helped Bertie to pack all her things and they had strapped the last box, it was nearly twelve o'clock. They had spoken only of the work they were busied with. When all was done, Rebekah put her arm softly about Bertie and drew her head on to her breast.

'There is nothing you would like to tell me, Bertie?'

'No, nothing.' She almost drew herself from her sister; who, when she had helped her to undress, went to her own room for a few hours' rest, before the early start.

❖

At half past three the next morning the driver came and knocked at all doors and bedroom windows to rouse them, and everyone lit candles and got up.

It was still absolutely dark outside. The men were at the *kraal*, sorting out the oxen, and old Ayah stood before the kitchen fire, drawing her little yellow handkerchief tighter about her shoulders, and watching the flame and smoke go up about the kettle, and saying, '*O, ja, Heere!*' partly because she wanted to persuade herself she was quite wide awake, and partly because it was so chilly. Under the dining room table Griet, who had just awakened, was sitting upright on the skin on which she slept and rubbing her eyes and blubbering, partly with cold and sleepiness, and partly because old Ayah had told her that Bertie was going away for six months.

When old Ayah had made the coffee and put it on the dining room table, they began to file in one by one, and stood round the table drinking it and making believe to eat dried biscuit; the father in his great overcoat with the collar turned up; the little mother in her dressing gown with a shawl over her head; Rebekah in her travelling dress with a large white *kappie*; while Griet, on the bench in the corner, sat holding Rebekah's baby, the two boys having been already carried out fast asleep to their bed in the wagon. Then Veronica came in, fully dressed in her starched gown, with collar and cuffs, her hair smooth and the braids coiled carefully at the back, and a pale blue scarf over her shoulders pinned up neatly at one side. They stood round the table drinking the coffee and eating the biscuit, almost in silence. Only Baby-Bertie and John-Ferdinand were not yet there.

As Bertie came out of her bedroom into the long passage she saw John-Ferdinand come out of his room. It was almost dark at her end of the passage, and she stood still, thinking he would pass on to the dining room without noticing her. But he saw her and came up the passage towards her. She drew herself close to the wall, as if to let him pass, but he stopped when he reached her.

'Bertie,' he said, standing near her, and speaking in a slow, even voice, 'I fear you may think I dealt very hardly with you yesterday. If you feel that, by my expressing my love for you and showing it as I have done, I have at all committed myself to you, I am still willing to marry you, if you feel that I should do so! My poor cousin!'

'Oh no!' she said in a quick, thick voice. 'No! No! No!' Holding her skirt that it might not touch him, she ran down the passage to the dining room and John-Ferdinand passed slowly out through the dark front room and round to the back of the house where the wagon was standing.

A little later they were all gathered about the kitchen door steps to say goodbye. The light streamed in a great square from the door. Rebekah said goodbye and climbed into the wagon to take her baby. The father folded Bertie in his great arms and kissed her eyes and her mouth. The little mother cried and reminded her of some of the clothing she ought to buy for herself as soon as she got to Cape Town. Old Ayah and Griet caught hold of her at the same time, both crying; then Veronica, standing in the middle of the doorway, held both Bertie's hands fast in hers and looked full into her face. 'I hope,' she said, 'you will have a happy, a very happy, time in Cape Town. I shall do all I can to fill your place to your dear father and mother. Come back soon!'

Bertie drew her hands from her and went down the steps.

John-Ferdinand stood in the dark beside the oven. Bertie would have walked quickly by him and got into the wagon, but he stepped forward and put into her hand a hand as cold as hers. Then the father helped her to climb in, and the driver clapped his whip and called aloud to the oxen, and slowly the great wagon began to roll away in the dark. Bertie flung herself down on the bed beside the children and buried her face in a pillow; but Rebekah moved to the back of the wagon and sat leaning against the back plank. As the wagon rounded the *kraal* she could still see in the bright square of light at the kitchen doorway her father and mother, and Griet and old Ayah standing at the foot of the steps and Veronica standing full in the door, and John-Ferdinand slowly mounting the steps to go in. Then the house passed out of sight. Half an hour later, as the wagon was climbing the *nek*, Rebekah, who still sat looking out at the back, could see in the first grey breaks of dawn the farmhouse glimmering as a white speck among the peaceful orange trees. But Bertie still lay with her face buried in the pillow, as though she were sleeping heavily.[1]

---

[1] In those days there was no railway in the Eastern Province, and persons going to Cape Town were obliged to make the whole journey overland by wagon or cart, taking several weeks; or they might travel by wagon or cart as far as the Bay (Port Elizabeth) and take the steamer round the coast to Cape Town. Even by this route a journey such as Rebekah's would take twelve days or fourteen.

CHAPTER FIVE

John-Ferdinand Shows Veronica His New House

The old farm was curiously quiet after Bertie and Rebekah went. Veronica tried to fill Bertie's place; she poured out the tea and coffee at table, and got the mother to show her how to make bread, and even went to the milk room at night to skim the milk; but she was so curiously still in all her movements that the house seemed quiet and empty.

Griet resented bitterly her attempts to fill Bertie's place. Why should she sit in Miss Bertie's chair, attend to Miss Bertie's flowers, and even move into Miss Bertie's bedroom? And Griet, as far as she was able, took care it did not go well with the bread making; and the flower gardening did not prosper as in Baby-Bertie's time.

In the afternoon, when she was sent out by Veronica to water the flowers, after working for a little while she would carefully peer through the stems of the orange trees and look up and down the orchard; and if she saw no one coming, she would kneel down quickly and, producing from her little yellow print sleeve a sharp table knife, would slip it under the sod at the root of some balsam or larkspur or brilliantly coloured four-o'clock and cut the stem off two inches below the surface. The next day when Veronica came to inspect the garden she found it drooping, and a day or two after Griet was ordered to pull it up and throw it away. When Veronica asked her what she thought was the cause of the flowers withering, she always fixed her twinkling black eyes on Veronica's face and said, 'Worms, worms!' – a reply which satisfied Veronica, who in her ignorance of gardening did not note it as remarkable that only the annuals died, while the perennials, which would still be there when Bertie returned in six months, were left untouched. Also, why Veronica's bread never rose, and why it sometimes had a strong taste of garlic, and she had at last to leave it for old Ayah to make, was a mystery Veronica never fathomed.

John-Ferdinand had left the farm the day after Bertie and Rebekah went, to go to the next little up-country town to get workmen and material for enlarging and repairing the house on his farm, and also to buy some furniture for it. If he regretted purchasing it, there was now no way left of getting rid of his bargain.

At the end of ten days he returned to his farm; but to everyone's surprise, though it was only a half hour's ride on horseback from the old farm, he never came over. It was as though he had no wish to see the place. When he wanted the father's advice on any matter, he sent over a boy with a letter; or he asked him to come over and see him.

At last one afternoon, when he had been on his new farm over five weeks, John-Ferdinand drove over to ask the father's advice about using the dredger to enlarge his dam.

His aunt insisted on his staying to supper, and when it was over, as it was already late and there was no moon, he slept the night there.

The little mother, who was much concerned at his loneliness at his new farm and the fact that he had only a Kaffir cook, begged him to come over often; and after that night his visits were not infrequent. He generally drove over in the evening, when his day's work of superintendence was ended, and had supper with them. After supper the father went to his books, and then to bed; and as the little mother often could not sit out on the *stoep* on account of her neuralgic-headaches, and as the evenings were now too hot to sit indoors, John-Ferdinand and Veronica often sat on the *stoep* alone.

Sometimes they talked of England and the places they had both been to; oftener, as they sat in the half-darkness, he recited passages from Young's *Night Thoughts* or Keble's Hymns, which Veronica said she admired much; and sometimes they sat quiet and rested.

After a time it became almost a rule that he should drive over in the evenings, and sleep at the old farm, returning to his own early in the mornings; and on Sunday he always came and spent the whole day. In that way, as the little mother said, he got at least one good meal a day, and it was a break in the solitary monotony of his life. She told him to bring over all his darning and mending; and, as she was generally busy, Veronica did it for him.

One night, about three months after Bertie had gone, he asked the mother if she would drive over with him to his farm the next morning and help him hang his curtains, and give him advice about arranging the china and linen, which had just arrived from England, and which he had ordered before he bought the farm, in view of his marriage with Bertie.

The little mother said she could not go, as it was baking day, but that, if Veronica would go, she would send over two of the best of the Kaffir maids to help her in arranging the things; and the next morning Veronica drove over with John-Ferdinand.

They came back in the evening just as it was getting dark, and for three days running Veronica went to help him.

The next time the little mother wrote the weekly letter to Rebekah, she said: 'There is generally no news to give you from this dull place, but tonight there is great news, that will very much surprise you.

'Veronica Grey went over with John-Ferdinand to help him to arrange his house for several days, and, when they came back last night, after supper he told me and your father he wished to speak with us, and he told us he had asked Veronica to marry him, and that they were engaged and would be married in a few weeks. I was surprised, though your father did not seem to be; I think nothing surprises him. I am very glad about it. It was lonely for him there; and it will be very nice to have relations there. Veronica has been very good trying to help me since Bertie left, and I feel almost as if she were my daughter! Tell Bertie; I know she will be glad.

'John-Ferdinand had seemed ill and depressed during the last months. It's living alone there, and not getting proper food. It will be so good for him to have her to take care of him. Her health is much better now; her cough is almost gone; you would hardly know her, she looks so bright. She is not much of a housekeeper; her bread always turns out bad, and the flower garden hasn't done well since she looked after it; but she is well off and they will always be able to have good servants and need not trouble much about the farming. They seem made for each other.

'It will be very nice for Bertie, when she comes home, to have them so near for company. Tell her her hand-lamb of last year, which has been running with the sheep, has got two lambs. I hope the air is suiting her better than you said it did at first. I will write to her next week. I will make you the biltong as soon as it gets cooler. I feel so excited still about the engagement I can hardly write.'

Six weeks afterwards Veronica Grey and John-Ferdinand were married. Veronica said there was no need to wait for letters from England, as she knew her mother would be delighted to hear of her marriage; and if she were married at once she could help John-Ferdinand to get the house and farm quite straight. The clergyman came from the town and they were quietly married at the old farm, and Veronica promised the little mother when she said goodbye that they would come over every Sunday and spend the day with her. As the cart drove away with them to their farm, the little mother cried, she hardly knew why; but Griet shouted hurrah and tossed up her little skirts, and then turned round and round like a dervish, till you could see nothing but a whirl of yellow skirts and two little spindle legs; and the little mother left off crying and told her not to make such a spectacle of herself.

CHAPTER SIX

How Baby-Bertie Went A-Dancing

Tucked away among the great oak avenues in the suburbs of Cape Town was Rebekah's home. You might ride mile after mile on a hot summer's day and never feel the sunshine on you, for the great oak trees met over your head; and here and there to the right and left were houses buried behind hedges, with trees touching the roofs, and verandas, and flower gardens.

Everywhere was the scent of fir trees; and pine plantations stretched away up the mountainsides; and now and then there were vineyards stretching, acre on acre, with the sunlight shimmering through their leaves, and with white and purple grapes kissing the ground. Behind all rose the mountain's side, sloping away towards the Devil's Peak. On sunny days, as you looked up at it, it seemed as though that side of the mountain were a giant, tranquilly leaning backwards and watching with great godlike, placid eyes the pine woods and the dwellings of men curled about his feet.

It was very peaceful in the great avenues. Sometimes carts drove along and foot-passengers walked there; in summer the acorns fell, and in winter the leaves strewed the sidewalks, and the beautiful tracery of the bare oak branches showed against the clear blue sky, and the lovely green of the pines and of the flower gardens seemed the brighter because the oak trees were bare.

In the houses at night you always heard the trees everywhere rustling with a sound like the distant moaning of a sea. Yet, if you entered a train at one of the little stations, in half an hour or a little more you might be on the other side of the mountain and in the old seaport town itself, with its long streets, principally of single-storied houses, but also here and there of double, with small-paned windows, much as the old Dutch loved to build a hundred years ago. In the streets were Malays; and fish carts blowing their horns; and Dutchmen, and Englishmen, and men of all nations and colours and mixtures; and in the side streets were little Malay and Coloured children playing happily in the gutters before their doors, or sitting on the *stoep* steps with a bunch of grapes in the one hand and a lump of bread in the other; and everywhere the peaceful, sleepy life of the old South African town crept on slowly; with its open drains, and its old families, and its old quiet methods of business, still prevailing. And above it all towered the stupendous front of Table Mountain, its beetling crags seeming to look down always with a stern calm contempt on the little seething world of men below.

Round the Peninsula swept the Southern Sea, pale blue and deep green in fair weather, and black in storms; but always, whether in storm or in fair weather, restless and passionate as no other sea on earth is – the Cape of Storms.

Rebekah's house was divided from the avenue by a tall hedge of blue plumbago, so high you saw no one that was passing in the avenue beyond, except it might be their heads, if they were very tall. It was a small house, two great oak trees that grew in the backyard overhanging its roof; and before it was a little flower garden always brilliant with flowers in both summer and winter; and there was a small veranda between two jutting-out wing rooms. Under the windows ran a little rockery; and on the left side of the garden was a little rose hedge of monthly roses almost always in bloom, which Rebekah had planted when she first came to live there.

Across the rose hedge was a large house with a rough grass lawn and some oak trees growing around it; and in the rose hedge was a small gate which Frank had had put there a year after they were married, as people they knew lived next door, and he wanted a passage between the houses.

It was to this little house among the trees that Rebekah brought Baby-Bertie; and gave her as a bedroom the left-wing room, with a green wallpaper, which looked out into the flower garden.

But for a long time after she came Bertie seemed to take no interest in anything. She had no wish to see the people and the sights of the town; and for most part of the day she sat in the iron rocking chair on the veranda, watching the flower garden indifferently; she did not even notice the parrot swinging himself above her and calling to her from the cage over her head; and the needlework she had brought out lay often untouched in her lap all the morning.

When Frank came home at evening with his laughter and talk, it did not rouse her. Sometimes he brought men in for a game of billiards in the billiard room at the back of the house. Sometimes they had supper at eleven, and came out afterwards to sit on the veranda and smoke; but Bertie generally slipped away to bed, and seemed to feel no interest in them. She, who had always been fastidious about her clothes, and as a little child had loved bright ribbons and shoes, now often wore one white dress till it was frowsy and tumbled. Rebekah had never asked her for an explanation of her sudden desire to leave the farm and come with her, nor had she ever offered one; and the name of John-Ferdinand was never mentioned between them. In her heart Rebekah did not grieve if any misunderstanding had separated her cousin from her sister.

Rebekah, who had only one little Coloured maid to help her, was generally too busy with her household work and children to have much time to spend with her; but she brought her cups of soup and plates of fruit; and she bought her material to make new dresses, but Bertie put them away in a drawer without troubling to make them. Now and then a neighbour who had rooms in the large house across the little rose hedge came over through the little gate and brought her fancy work, and sat on the veranda with Bertie and talked to her. She was a Mrs Drummond, a little slight woman, with so long a neck and waist that when she sat, or until she stood beside another woman, she looked almost tall. She was always beautifully dressed; whatever she wore was graceful and was perfectly thought out. If she changed her scarf or waistcoat, she changed also her breast pin and earrings to match them; she was as thoughtfully dressed in the morning, in a cotton wrap with little moonstones set in dull silver in her ears, as in the afternoon when she wore Indian muslin and lace, or in the evening, when she wore delicate Chinese silks and little diamond stars for earrings. Even her little drawing room was softly draped in Indian silks or Oriental tapestries in a way other people's were not; there was not a hard outline or bare corner. The curtains at the window were tied back with gold filigree work that matched the brown and gold wallpaper; and her little real China tea cups matched her own slippers, and both harmonised with the Indian footstool on which she rested her feet. If you picked up in the avenue a bow she had dropped from her dress, you might have guessed it must be hers from its graceful limp fall. Other women tried to imitate her dresses and the draperies of her little drawing room, but they never made their things look quite as hers did.

She was not pretty, but she was too graceful to be plain. Her hair was neither dark nor light; and she had large white teeth which some people said were false, and some real, and which she always showed when she smiled, as she did continually, with a sudden short movement of her upper lip, which moved alone, while the rest of the face was at rest, as though it was mechanically drawn up and then suddenly let down again. Her face was oblong, and was long, like her neck and her body; and she generally preferred to sit instead of standing and walking, when it was possible, because her long neck and waist made her look more tall and graceful when the shortness of her legs was hidden. She often sat leaning a little forward, with her hands drooping over the edge of her lap, and with her head very slightly on one side, as that showed the outline of her chin, which she knew was the best point about her. She had come to the Cape from England with her husband two years before Rebekah was married; but he had gone to travel in the interior of Africa, while she had remained in Cape Town; he had gone on from Central Africa to India and Burma and the Far East, and had never come back during the seven years.

When Mrs Drummond first came, men had been very attentive to her, and women had imitated her dress and manners much. Now, the men who knew her began often to discuss her at their Club and in their smoking rooms; she had said she was twenty-eight years old when she came, and she was twenty-eight still; and they sometimes speculated as to when she would have another birthday, and as to whether the huge coil of hair at the back of her head were real or artificial; and they mimicked her little mannerisms; but the women still copied her dresses, though not quite so much as at first; and both men and women came to the croquet parties she gave on the lawn of the large house, part of which she had hired. She went to dances and receptions, and at dances still got partners, though not so many as at first; and young girls and older women still thought that if Mrs Drummond wore or did anything, it must be 'the right style'. Sometimes the men made jokes about her husband's long absence ribaldly, and the women now and then discussed it seriously; but on the whole it attracted little attention; it had come about so gradually. She had always said he was coming back in six months, or in eight, or next year (she said so still), and she showed handsome silks and embroideries she said he sent her from the East, and she told the women he wrote to her every week and was always longing to come back to her; so people never found the matter of great interest.

She had known Rebekah's husband before he married; she and her husband had come out in the same steamer, when he was returning from a visit to Europe; and it was she who had chosen the little house next door for him, when he had determined to marry, and helped him to furnish it. They were both musical, and sang in the same glee club, and had belonged to the same church choir; but at the time Bertie came they did not see much of each other. He had left the choir, and he laughed as other men did about the twenty-eight years and the large unchanging coil of fair hair at the back of her head; and the little gate that he had had put in the rose hedge, that he might go over more easily to practice his music with her, was now almost unused, and the grass grew in the path.

But as soon as Bertie came she called and offered to come and sit with her as she so seldom went out; and almost every afternoon she tripped over with the little silk bag over her arm; the bag varied to match each costume, and in it she carried the fancy work she was always doing for church bazaars. Sometimes she chatted to Bertie about her work, and told her about the bazaars; and sometimes she told her of her friends in England, her father a retired army officer, and their little place in the country; and sometimes she talked of the presents her husband sent her from the Far East, and what a clever man he was. She said he had a whole box full of manuscripts that he wouldn't print just because he didn't care to, or he might have made a heap of money; but generally she talked of dresses and the prices of things in the shops in Cape Town; and now and then she told some gossip about people Bertie had never seen, why some lady was never called on, or how a certain young girl was getting herself talked about. But generally she talked of more trivial matters. Rebekah never came out and sat with them while she was there, but sent them out tea and cake. And Bertie would sit still listening to her. Often Mrs Drummond stayed so late that when Frank came home in the evening she was still sitting there.

One afternoon, when she had just left, and Bertie sat with her hands crossed on her work and one little foot with its slipper half off dragging under the rocking chair, her brother-in-law opened the garden gate and came up towards the steps.

Rebekah had heard him and had come to the front door to meet him. She had always met him there in the first days of their marriage, when he had called out from the gate, 'Where is Goody-two-shoes?' and whistled for her; and now, when he did not call or whistle, she still met him there every day when she heard the click of the gate and the step on the gravel. As he gave her his bag in the doorway he said: 'Great news! What do you think! The immaculate John-Ferdinand writes he is to be married to a Miss Veronica Grey, a lady who was staying at the farm for her health. He says you know her. John married!' he laughed.

As Rebekah took his bag from him she glanced round at Bertie; she was sitting bolt upright and looking out over the flower garden. Rebekah drew him in; but Bertie heard him laughing from the dining room, 'I wonder whether he proposed to her, or she to him! – the saintly John!'

When Rebekah went on to the veranda again she found Bertie gone, and only her slipper lying under the rocking chair.

When supper-time came Bertie did not appear, having gone to her room feeling unwell, she said, and the next day was so unwell that Rebekah sent for a doctor, who said she was suffering from anemia and must take rest and a tonic; and for some weeks she lay about eating little, seldom even sitting on the veranda to be talked to by Mrs Drummond, but lying on a sofa Rebekah had placed there for her, often seeming half asleep. She even discontinued the short weekly notes she had been in the habit of writing home. Rebekah took care that John-Ferdinand's engagement was never mentioned before her, and she wished she could have prevented her receiving the little mother's letters, which were always full of news of preparations for the marriage.

Then came the news of John-Ferdinand's wedding. The little mother's letters were full of it: and Rebekah watched Bertie anxiously. But a strange change came over her. She lolled about no more. She seemed suddenly to wake up from a sleep. She was suddenly always active and restless. She laughed, and talked, and romped wildly with the children whom she had hardly noticed before. She began making the dresses, the material for which Rebekah had bought her when she first came. Sometimes she suddenly insisted on turning out a whole room and shaking the carpets and washing the windows herself; and then she would rush over to Mrs Drummond's to get advice about trimming a new hat. When she came back she would begin weeding a flowerbed, or go into the kitchen to make a cake. She seemed able to do anything except to rest quietly or be alone. When her dresses were made, Mrs Drummond insisted on her coming to her croquet parties and introduced her to people. Soon invitations came to her for dinner parties and dances, and, as Rebekah did not go out, she went under Mrs Drummond's care or with Frank; and Mrs Drummond taught her to dance. After a time the invitations became so numerous that she was always busy getting a new dress ready or repairing an old one, and seemed to live in a low fever of excitement. Frank took her to concerts and entertainments, and was proud of the attention his pretty sister-in-law awakened everywhere.

One evening, a little more than two months after the marriage, Bertie, who was going to a whist party with Mrs Drummond, knelt partly undressed on the floor before her sister with her back turned to her, that Rebekah might arrange her hair for her. All the while she talked restlessly about the dress Mrs Drummond was going to wear that night, and about the way she was going to change the old wedding dress which Rebekah had given her into a dancing skirt for herself. Suddenly in the midst of her talk she glanced round. 'Rebekah, aren't you laughing at me? You think me so foolish!' She turned herself round and clasped her large beautifully shaped white arms round Rebekah's little body. 'I talk of nothing but dressing and dancing! You must think me so foolish! – but, Rebekah, when you want to forget anything, you can read and think; you are so clever – and you have your children – I – I am so stupid – I can't help it!' She laid her head against Rebekah's breast and nestled to her like a little child. Rebekah pressed her lips on the bare white shoulder. 'Rebekah, you will not let me go back to the farm? You will keep me here?' she said quickly. 'I can never go back; I won't go back! – Never! Never! Promise me! Promise me!' Then, giving Rebekah no time to reply, she sprang up and ran away to her own room to finish dressing.

That was the first and last time at which, either then or afterwards, to any human being Bertie ever referred directly or indirectly to John-Ferdinand's relation with herself.

When three months more had passed, Bertie had had three proposals of marriage. One was from a very wealthy young man, whose estate adjoined a tiny fruit farm Rebekah had bought a few miles out in the country, and who had seen Bertie walking in the vineyard with Rebekah's children, and who had found out where she lived and got an introduction to her. Another was from an English officer whom she had met at Mrs Drummond's, who was spending two months at the Cape on his way to India, and who asked her to marry him the fourth time he saw her; and one was from a young beardless, penniless civil servant, whom she had danced with once or twice. Bertie refused them all. Frank and Mrs Drummond both thought her very foolish to refuse the English officer, who had appealed to both to further his suit, and who was a man with a large private income, of an aristocratic English family, and a first rate fellow. But the only suitor who seemed to concern Bertie at all was the young civil servant. She cried when she told Rebekah how miserable he looked when she refused him, and said she would not go to dances any more, if dancing with people made them miserable; but her restlessness and dislike of being quiet or alone soon made her go again.

At this time there came a letter from John-Ferdinand saying he and his wife were coming for a short visit to Cape Town, as they had taken no honeymoon when they were married, and asking Rebekah to take rooms for them in the large house next door, in which Mrs Drummond also had her rooms, and where John-Ferdinand had himself stayed when in Cape Town before.

Rebekah took the rooms; but when John-Ferdinand and his wife came, she and Bertie with the children had gone to her little fruit and vine farm, and only the servants were in the house, as Frank also was away up-country on a shooting trip.

This little farm Rebekah had bought two years after her marriage, partly with the money her father had given her as her wedding gift, and partly she had paid for it by placing a bond on it. Her husband had laughed loudly at first at the idea of her buying and farming it, but as they were married by antenuptial contract and he was not responsible for her debts, and as he was never much interested in any matter which did not immediately concern himself, he did not interfere.

Now he rather approved of it, as it saved the expense of taking the children to the seaside when they needed change, and supplied the household with fruit and vegetables free of charge. Rebekah kept an old German and his wife there to look after it with the help of a Coloured boy, and drove out herself when she had half a day to spare; and when her husband went away, as he often did for hunting or fishing expeditions, she took the children and stayed there till he came back. She herself had helped to mend the roof of the old cottage and to plaster and whitewash the walls, and with her own hands had planted and grafted trees and vines. She liked the labour in the open air, and she was studying books on winemaking so that if in time she were able to buy two vineyards adjoining she could make wine.

During the first days Veronica and John-Ferdinand spent much of their time sight-seeing, as she had never visited Cape Town before; but he introduced her to Mrs Drummond, and in the mornings, which he generally spent walking in the pine woods with his book, after the first days Veronica was invited by Mrs Drummond to sit in her private drawing room with her and work and drink coffee at eleven. They were unlike physically and mentally, but they had tastes which harmonised. While Veronica sat upright on a high-backed chair knitting heavy squares for a bed quilt, Mrs Drummond on a low settee, with her head a little on one side, chose carefully the shades of silk for an altar cloth which she was making. They discussed their work and the prices of things in Cape Town shops; and Mrs Drummond chirped continually the news of the place, especially the house over the way, and Veronica listened. She said that when Rebekah was married she went at first a great deal with her husband to dances and entertainments and dinners, but after about a year and a half gave it all up and never went out visiting any more. She said she never entertained now except little men's suppers which she cooked herself for the men who came sometimes to play billiards with her husband in the evenings and to which she never asked women or sat down herself. She said it was so strange, she thought, that they should have a billiard table, when they had such a small house otherwise and kept only one servant and a stable boy. She believed Rebekah had paid for the building of the billiard room herself. She had had it done while her husband had been away on a long business trip – the contractor who had built it had re-papered her bedroom and had himself told her that Rebekah had paid for the room as a surprise to her husband. Mrs Drummond supposed it was to keep him at home she built it. She said women didn't seem to care for Rebekah – she didn't think a woman had called there for over a year; she thought many of them didn't even know she existed, as she never went to church. She said she thought men cared for her as little as women; she had never seen a man call there, except when her husband was at home. It seemed so strange to her that Rebekah should have gone away to the farm with Bertie and the children just when she knew Veronica was coming, and looked inquiringly over the silks at Veronica.

Veronica said Rebekah was always strange.

Mrs Drummond said, Yes, she was; she used to dig in her garden with a big spade where people could see her quite well over the gate; she had heard some say that when she was out at her farm they had seem her climb up a ladder right on to the roof, mending a smoky chimney.

Veronica said some people were born with those manish ways. It was not Rebekah's mother's fault, as she was quite a sweet womanly woman.

Mrs Drummond also had much to tell of Bertie; of how dull she had seemed when she first came, and how she had improved. She told of her dancing and her dresses, and about the English officer (Bertie had not told her of her two other suitors), and she said she liked Bertie better than Rebekah.

Veronica said she thought she liked Rebekah the better of the two, though she was so strange, and not always very nice and womanly in her ways. She said it seemed to her that Bertie always cared too much to attract men's attention.

Mrs Drummond drew her upper lip up sharply and held her head a little more on a side. She said some people couldn't help attracting men's attention; and she looked very sideways with her eyes at Veronica's square shoulders and the flat foot showing below her plain skirt. She said one wondered how some women ever got married at all; but Veronica was looking down at her own square of bed quilt.

Mrs Drummond said she thought a woman ought to take care of her appearance; that Rebekah had worn the same old brown silk dress for three years whenever she went out shopping to town, only altering it a little every year as the fashions changed, that it might not look too striking. She said a woman who could afford to build a billiard room ought to dress better. They spent all the mornings together.

Sometimes in the afternoon they went into town shopping together also; and, when they did not, they all three had tea under the oak trees on the lawn out of Mrs Drummond's delicate little china cups, unless it was her croquet afternoon.

At last, the last day came of their visit to Cape Town. Then Veronica proposed to her husband that they should go and look at Rebekah's house and garden. She said the little mother would be so disappointed if they came back and could tell her nothing about it. John-Ferdinand felt sure his brother and sister-in-law would not object, and they walked over. They paced about Rebekah's little garden; the front door was not locked, and they went in. John-Ferdinand sat down in the drawing room at the table to look at some books, and Veronica went to inspect the house. The stable boy was away exercising the horses and the servant girl resting in her room across the yard, and Veronica passed alone from room to room. In the dining room she noted the things on the mantelpiece and the sideboard, and Rebekah's work basket and sewing machine on the table in the corner; she examined Rebekah's bedroom and the things on the dressing table and washing stand, and Frank's little dressing room that opened from it, with its large dressing table and new carpet and comfortable easy chair; she went through to the children's bedroom opening out of Rebekah's, and tried the handle of Rebekah's little study which led out of the children's room, but that was the only place in the house which was locked. She examined the kitchen and outer pantry and the things on the shelves, and passed down the passage to the billiard room which was built out at the left side. She examined the cues, which she had never seen before, and lifted the holland cover to look at the green cloth on the table; and went to the spare room which was now Bertie's bedroom and looked at all her dresses hanging in the wardrobe and the whole row of boots and shoes under the dressing table, and unlocked and examined the large new dressing case upon it with brushes and scent bottles heavily mounted in real silver, which Bertie had received through the post from some unknown admirer on her last birthday. She even went into the yard and lifted the lids of the tanks that held the water for the bathroom. When she had seen everything, she went back to the little drawing room.

John-Ferdinand was still sitting at the table with his elbows resting on it; his head was supported by his hands; he was looking down so intently that he did not notice Veronica's soft entrance, till she had stepped up behind him and put her large cool hands over both his eyes. 'Who is it?' she said with grave playfulness. He did not speak, but taking each of her hands in one of his, took them down from his eyes and resting them on his shoulders held them fast there, while he looked back up into her face.

'What are you studying so deeply?'

'Only this,' he said, glancing down. It was not a book that was open before him, but an album of photographs. On the page before him was a picture of Bertie which had just been taken at the request of her father and mother. Mrs Drummond, who had gone with Bertie to have it taken, had insisted it should be in full evening dress, that her beautiful arms and shoulders might show. The photographer also had tried to make what he believed to be an effective picture. He had turned her head a little over her shoulder and raised her chin, so that the lovely lines of the neck and upturned chin were not lost. He had put in her left hand a bunch of artificial flowers which she held against her breast, and he had required her to draw her lips in a smile. The picture resembled an imaginary type of beauty in a book of engravings rather than Bertie. The simplicity and directness of pose and manner, amounting almost to awkwardness, which was the character of her beauty, was lost.

Veronica looked down at the book over his shoulder. 'It is very finely taken, is it not?' she said. 'How well they take portraits here!'

He looked down at the face too. 'It's very handsome, and just like her!'

He loosened one of her hands, and with his right drew her to his side and made her kneel down beside him. He turned to her and took her face softly between both his hands and looked down into it ...

> '"And learn how pure,
> How sweet can be,
> My own wife's face!"'

he said softly.

A faint flush rose into Veronica's cheeks as he looked down into her face. He put one arm round her shoulders and drew her nearer to him.

'My wife,' he said, 'I want to confess something to you.'

But then he was silent. She crossed her hands upon his knees and looked up at him. 'What is it, my husband?'

His hand rested again on the side of the album; he was looking down at it.

'I told you once,' he said, 'on that day on the farm when we became engaged, that I had once been much attracted by my young cousin, but that we had had a difference, and I felt I could not marry her. But one thing I never told you – that, after she left the farm, she was always with me. Wherever I went I seemed to see her. I dared not come to the old place because it reminded me of her. At last I wrote a letter telling her I could not live without her, and asking her to come back and marry me. That evening, when I rode over to her father's farm, for the first time after she had left, I came over partly that I might give it to the boy who was going to the town the next morning to post. But you were so kind to me that evening – do you remember? – We sat out on the *stoep*, and I repeated that passage of Tennyson's to you that you liked so? It seemed to rest me to be with you, as if I got rid of her face as I saw it last look at me. And somehow, I did not post the letter that night, though it was in my pocket. – Looking back now, though I didn't realise it at the time, I am sure it was your influence upon me that kept me from sending it.'

'Yes, dear!' she said.

'But, do you know, I did not destroy that letter? For weeks still I kept it in my pocket, and at any moment it might have been sent. – Then came that day when you came over to my farm to help me put things right in my house. Even then I still always had the feeling that perhaps I was getting that house ready for her. – But, darling, you know what happened that afternoon when we stood together on the back veranda? I never can quite understand it. It seemed as though some power stronger than myself were drawing me to you – and my arms were about you, and your head was on my breast, and you were to be my wife, before I knew! That night, when I went to my bedroom, I burnt the letter. – But, Veronica, my wife, do you know, that even since that time, that face has come in between you and me?' He raised the palm of his hand from Bertie's portrait. 'At night I have dreamed of it; the scent of geraniums and the sight of plumbago flowers have brought it back to me, even the darkness of the night has brought it to me. It has been a white face with great innocent eyes – a child's face that I have always seen. – It has mingled with all our life together at the farm. When I saw the sheep come out of the *kraal* in the morning with the dew on their backs – when I saw the thorn trees, or smelt an evening flower, a kind of sudden trembling has come over me. – Even when you first proposed we should come here for our holiday, you know how I resisted you? And still more when you proposed we should stay here in this house near to them – I felt I could not see her – could not be near her – and yet deep in my heart I knew it was best; that I must see her again, or the spell would never be broken.' He looked down at the portrait, half of which his hand covered. 'Even since I have been here and I have heard from you how she has devoted herself to pleasure, even when you told me of her flirtation with that English military man for whom she yet cared nothing – it made no difference to me. But now – when I look at that – all is gone!' He raised his hand and dropped it again on the face of the picture. 'When I see *that*, I know it has all been an idle dream! She could never really have been mine – never been anything to me. Never have been what *you* are ...

"What have I done
That God should choose a wife for me?"'

He bent down over her. 'My darling wife! Look up at me!'
Veronica raised her eyes to his, and pressed her head close to his breast.
'Do you forgive me, my darling?'
She drew his head down with her hand so that his cheek rested on her hair; and then they heard the maid servant coming into the passage, and Veronica rose to her feet to explain to her how it was they were there.

Late that night, when Veronica and John-Ferdinand lay in bed in the large room in the boarding house, the wind was blowing through the pine trees and among the oak trees in the avenue, making them crack their great branches and tap the roofs of the houses. It was just a quarter to one when John-Ferdinand woke and lay listening to the wind; then on the other side of the large bed he heard Veronica move.
'Are you awake?' he asked.
'I have not yet been asleep,' she said.
He stretched out his arm and drew her a little nearer to him.
'You are not troubling about anything I told you this afternoon, beloved! You know it is all past?'
'Oh yes!' she said.

He drew her closer to him, her head resting on his shoulder, his arm passing under her neck.

'You trust me utterly?'

'Oh yes! my dear one.' They both lay looking upwards in the dark, and heard the wind tearing at the branches of the trees.

'There is *nothing* troubling you, my dear one?' He turned his face more towards her.

'No, nothing, dearest – at least,' she hesitated, 'there is perhaps one very little thing – such a very little thing, that you will think me foolish! You must tell me if I'm wrong. You always know so much better what is right and wise than I.'

'What is it, my dear one?' He put out his right hand and took her left that lay on the white coverlet.

She spoke slowly, lisping a little as a child might, talking to its mother: 'It's such a little thing – such a small thing – but you know, ever since we were married it has sometimes made me a little sad, I've felt as if you didn't *quite* trust me!'

'What is it? – There is nothing I know, or feel, or think I would not share with you!'

'Oh, it's only a little thing! – I've wondered sometimes,' she murmured softly, 'why you didn't tell me what you and Bertie quarrelled about! You told me you had a difference; but you never said what it was. You didn't even tell me today.'

He was quiet for a moment; then he said, 'I did not tell you because it was a matter more hers than mine. – She did not ask me to make any promise not to repeat it – she asked nothing – but I took it that she was speaking to me in confidence. I could never have told anyone but you – but you are not someone else. You are me, myself! When I speak to you I speak within my own soul.'

'But you must not tell me anything, dear, that you would rather not. I always know that what you wish to do is right! You know better than I.'

'But I want to tell you! There shall be nothing that divides between us.' He turned on his side and drew her nearer to him, so that from shoulder to feet their long straight figures lay side by side.

'The reason why I could not marry my cousin,' he said, 'was this' – and then he told her the story of the parlour in the bush and what Baby-Bertie told him.

Half an hour later the wind was still blowing as wildly as ever; but they lay asleep with their hands interclasped and his breath on her face.

The next day when all their trunks were strapped for starting, John-Ferdinand went to the station to call a cab. He returned sooner than he had expected, as he had met one in the avenue. As he came back into the bedroom, Veronica was sitting with her travelling cloak on, and her hat on the table beside her, bending over the dressing table, writing. She thought it was the maid come to begin carrying things down, till he stood almost at her shoulders. She started lightly, and spread her broad hand over the page on which she was writing.

'What is it?' he asked, bending over her.

A faint tint of roses rushed into her white cheeks.

'A little surprise for you. – A secret. – Something you mustn't know about.'

He stooped and pressed his cheek against her smooth head, and turned to help the maid carry down the packages.

An hour later they were driving through Cape Town on their way to the docks.

'I wish to stop at the post office,' she said. 'I have a letter to post about something I forgot to order at a shop, and which I want sent on to me.'

When they got to the post office he offered to get out and post it for her: but she said she was tired of sitting and would rather get out herself, and before he could speak, had jumped out and put it in the box. The letter was addressed to Mrs Drummond, but in a large, round hand, quite unlike her own angular small one. When she had put it in the box, they drove down to the docks, and in two hours they had sailed away to their home in the Eastern Province.

CHAPTER SEVEN

Raindrops in the Avenue

When Bertie and Rebekah came back from the fruit farm, Rebekah was busy putting her house right, and no one noticed that, on the first morning she went to see Mrs Drummond, Bertie did not stay so long as usual, nor was there anyone to note that, neither on that day nor the next, nor the day after, did Mrs Drummond come to see her.

But on the day after that, as Bertie sat sewing in the veranda, Mrs Drummond came with her workbag on her arm and sat in the low cane chair opposite her; and Bertie thought it must have been her own fancy which had made it seem that Mrs Drummond had not been so glad to see her when she returned from the farm.

Mrs Drummond said it was a fine afternoon, and made a remark about the new pattern she was tatting; and Bertie answered her; then they sat silent for a while, with the rich warm scent from Rebekah's flower garden coming up to them.

Then Mrs Drummond said, without raising her head, that her cousin, John-Ferdinand's wife, seemed a very nice woman. Bertie said yes, and asked Mrs Drummond if she thought it would not look better if she feather-stitched the sleeve of the baby's dress she was making. Mrs Drummond said she thought so: and then there was quiet again with only the sound of Bertie's needle and Mrs Drummond's shuttle and of their sleeves rustling against their sides as they worked. The parrot, who had been to sleep, woke suddenly and began throwing down grains of *mielies* on Bertie's head. Then Mrs Drummond drooped her head on the opposite side from the one on which it had been drooping before and said, 'Did you never go to school when you were a girl?'

'No,' said Bertie, without looking up, 'my sister taught me out of her old books; and my mother taught me to sew.'

Mrs Drummond drooped her head lower than before, looking at her work. 'So you never had any real teacher to teach you?' she said.

'No,' Bertie said. 'At least,' she added, hurriedly, 'once for a few months – I had a teacher.'

Mrs Drummond drooped her head yet lower.

'I suppose,' she said, half glancing up, 'it was a lady whom you had to teach you?'

Bertie said quickly, 'No – it was a man – he did not stay long. – Don't you think that the oranges I sent you yesterday were just right for marmalade?' she added quickly.

'Yes-s,' said Mrs Drummond slowly; then she looked up fully into Bertie's face.

For a little while Bertie heard only the click of the tatting shuttle, as it turned to let the thread out, and the tick of her own needle; the scent from the flower garden seemed to come up almost overpoweringly.

'Yes; the peels of the oranges were very fine and thick,' Mrs Drummond said slowly.

'I will go and fetch you some tea,' Bertie said quickly, rising. 'Rebekah will have made it by this time.'

'Oh, no, thank you,' Mrs Drummond said. 'I have some people coming to have tea with me, and must go at once or they will find me out.'

'Oh, please do not trouble!' she said, as Bertie darted to pick up her ball of tatting cotton which had dropped from her lap as she rose. Bertie caught it and handed it to her, and she put it in her bag. 'How very nice your sister's flower garden looks this afternoon – she always seems to have more flowers and sweeter smelling than anyone else! Good afternoon!'

Then the little figure in its large-figured Japanese silk dress fluttered across the garden and out through the gate in the rose hedge and across the lawn to the house beyond.

When Mrs Drummond was gone, Bertie sat in the rocking chair, sewing. There was a stain of red on each cheek deeper than the red of the damask rose in Rebekah's garden; gradually it turned to pale pink and then white.

The next afternoon Mrs Drummond had her weekly croquet party, but she did not send over to ask if Bertie was coming, and Bertie helped Rebekah to preserve the oranges they had brought, and did not go, but in the evening she went to explain why she had not been.

She found Mrs Drummond in her bedroom before the chest of drawers, putting them neat. Mrs Drummond did not pause in her work and hardly looked up; and when Bertie had stood beside her chatting for a little while she went away. Mrs Drummond seemed preoccupied. For two weeks after that she did not meet her again; then she overtook her in the avenue. Mrs Drummond talked of some purchases she had made in town and said goodbye at the gate. Then for a week she did not see her again. Twice Bertie had gone as far as the rose hedge, meaning to ask her whether she had done anything to pain her; but both times she had turned back when her hand was on the gate.

Then came a Wednesday evening when Bertie was going to an evening party at a house two avenues off. It was to be a young people's dance in honour of the fifteenth birthday of the daughter of the house, and, as most of the dancers would be under thirty, she needed no older woman to go with her; and Frank was going, who, as he grew older, preferred going to the dances and picnics where very young girls were rather than to those where there were women nearer his own age.

As the house was close at hand they were to walk, and Rebekah had brought Bertie to her own room to dress her, because of the large glass there.

497

'Don't you think it looks nice?' Rebekah asked.

Bertie was standing before the wardrobe door; she looked like a head of a large white hydrangea in the gauze dress Rebekah had helped her to make. 'Oh, I think it looks lovely!'

Rebekah, standing behind her, looked at the dress critically. Her own small, delicate face was drawn and white, as though needing rest. 'Your hair is not high enough if you are to wear the flowers under it,' she said.

She mounted a footstool and stood behind Bertie and unwound the coils of back hair to pin them higher.

Then Bertie said in her low, soft drawl, 'Rebekah haven't *you* ever wanted to go to dances? Don't you want to dance?'

'Yes,' Rebekah said, 'when I was a child I liked to dance. I used to go up into the *kloof* under the Kaffir-bean trees and dance and sing and throw up my arms till I got drunk and had to lie down on my face.'

'Oh, I don't mean that kind of dancing,' Bertie drawled slowly, 'alone in the *kloof*, by yourself! I mean with pretty dresses and other people to ask you to dance. I don't like you to stay alone here when I go,' she said in a yet softer drawl; 'you'd look so pretty if you were dressed in pretty dresses like me – you'd look like a fairy. Don't you think it would be nice to dance with other people, eh, Rebekah?'

'Perhaps,' Rebekah said, 'if you had someone you liked very much, and you two were quite alone – and you could go on dancing on and on forever with no one there, it might be better than dancing alone – perhaps better than almost anything. That will do, I think.' She got off the stool.

Bertie still stood impassively with her arms hanging on either side. 'Yes,' she said dreamily, 'it would be nice to dance with someone you liked very much; I never have. But, Rebekah, you know, I don't care very much whom I dance with now. It's the light and the noise and the going round and round I like. All the men: are so kind to me, too,' she added slowly, 'and all the girls also; they don't mind that I dance so much all the evening. Isn't it nice of them, Rebekah?'

'Very.' Rebekah was now fastening a white, half-blown rose on her breast.

'You know, I like it so when you go into a room, and they all look at you, and something so nice runs all up your body, when they all look at you and think you look nice. I like it,' she said slowly. 'Have you ever been to a real ball, Rebekah?'

'When I was first married. Frank went; and I wanted to go with him.'

She turned to a wardrobe behind the door and took from it a dress of black diaphanous silky material speckled all over with tiny silver spangles, each carefully cut out and sewn on separately. She held it up by the shoulders.

'How beautiful!' exclaimed Bertie, crossing her hands. 'I never saw such a dress. Whose is it?'

'I made it for myself,' said Rebekah. Bertie came nearer to touch it. 'Mrs Drummond had one from Paris, like this, only white. Frank said it was the most beautiful dress he had ever seen. When she did not want it any more I bought it from her as a pattern.' She looked down at the dress. 'I cut out each little spangle separately and sewed it on. It took me three weeks to make it.' She turned the dress over. 'This was the wreath to wear with it,' she said, holding up a wreath of frosted leaves.

'You must have looked beautiful,' Bertie said. 'Your teeth, your dark hair – and the spangles – just like the night! Did Frank like it?'

'He said it was not bad.'

'Do you never wear it now?'

'No, I keep it.'

As she was hanging the dress up, Bertie said suddenly, 'Rebekah, do you think, if Mrs Drummond was your friend, that she – that she – would really care for you – that she – that she wouldn't – take part with anyone against you?'

'I don't know, dear. I know very little of her. We have nothing in common. I don't understand her.'

At that moment Frank's voice sounded from the hall, calling out that Bertie must hurry or it would rain before they started; and Rebekah wrapped her sister up in the large, red silk opera cloak she had made for herself when she had first married and folded Bertie's white satin dancing shoes in silver paper, that she might carry them.

'Don't mend the stockings,' Bertie whispered as she turned to go, half bending over her; 'I'll darn them all tomorrow.'

They went into the hall where Frank was waiting, and Rebekah saw they had their umbrellas and waterproofs with them. The night was of inky blackness; it seemed it might rain at any moment, and Rebekah stood in the doorway holding the candle high to light them down the veranda steps and along the path to the gate. When the two figures had gone out at it, she closed the door and turned back into the house.

In the dining room she took from the work table a large basket with the week's mending in it, and, placing the lighted candle on the top, went through the room into the one where her children slept. She paused at each bed to see that the child in it was covered; and then, still carrying the lighted candle on the basket, she opened a door at the end of the room and went into the next.

The room was a small one, made by cutting off the end of the children's bedroom with a partition. She had had it before as study for herself where she could always hear the children call if they needed her at night. It was hardly larger than a closet, but there was a window in it and a small outer door, and both looked out on to the rockery and the plumbago hedge but on nothing else, and there was a small door close beside the window, which she had had put in that at any time she might run out and work a little in the garden. The walls were covered with a red-brown paper, and in the centre stood a large oblong desk with drawers; before it stood an old armchair with a deep dent where a head had often rested. A waste-paper basket stood beside it. In the corner stood the tall wooden cabinet which she had had when she was a girl to hold her fossils and insects, and which she had brought with her when she married; on a ledge in front her microscope stood. There was no other furniture on the floor, but on the walls hung three small bookshelves. One was behind the armchair, between the window and door; and in the corner beside it, on a little wooden bracket, was a tiny statue of Hercules a few inches high in old discoloured marble. This she had got from Mrs Drummond when she first married, in exchange for a length of green silk which she had had as a wedding present. Mrs Drummond told her her husband had bought it when he was travelling in Italy, but had left it behind with many other things he did not want when he set out on his travels in the Far East.

On another hanging bookshelf to the right of the desk were books of poetry, science, history and travel; all of them much-worn cheap editions except one handsome new copy of Darwin's *Variation of Plants and Animals under Domestication* bound in calf, which also she had got from Mrs Drummond two years before, in exchange for some pots of roses, to stand in her drawing room. It had been sent from England addressed to her husband, but as he was now in the mountains of Japan, and had said she need send nothing on to him, she was glad to let Rebekah have it.

On the wall to the left of the desk were three very small shelves, and on them were science primers and school books from which Rebekah had taught and most of which she had bought with the money her mother gave her for herself for drying peaches when she was a child. They were all now very old. What she felt for them was what no one feels for the books out of which they have been taught by another – it was what a full grown doe might feel for a little mountain stream, which it had found for itself when it was a very young fawn wandering quite alone and parched with thirst, and from which it had drunk. It might have tasted of many finer, clearer streams since then, but in none of them all would the water be to it like that in the little stream it found all for itself when it was a small thing, quite alone, and dying of thirst.

There was a *Cornwallis Grammar* with the back worn off with which she had followed her father about over the ploughed lands one day, trying to get him to explain to her what a preposition really was, and, when he answered her absently in the cut dried words of the book, she had gone away behind the hedge and lain with the book open before her, and prayed that she might really understand. There was a Smith's *Latin Principia,* the gilt letters worn off its side and black back; she bought it when she was nine years old with three-and-sixpence which her father gave her when he went into the town to sell his wool and she went with him. She had bought it at a shop where they had books in the window, and had carried it home pressed against her chest all the way in the cart. She knew they would laugh at her if they knew she meant to learn Latin; but at night she sat up in her own room, writing the exercises by the light of a tallow candle she had begged from old

Ayah, happy, thinking she would at last know all the Romans knew – what, she did not quite know.

On the shelf below were a number of cheap translations of Greek and Latin authors, which she had bought when she had found out she would never know Greek or Latin enough to read in the originals.

On the lowest shelf were five or six thin science primers in brown covers. She had seen them advertised in one of her father's newspapers, and she had sent money for them to a bookseller's in Cape Town who advertised them; when the parcel came by post she had opened it on her bed, and she had lain down by the books and felt nearly faint with gladness. The Botany she liked because it taught her how to examine the parts of flowers and helped to take away that almost painful longing she had felt when she looked at them to understand a little why they were as they were. The Geology she liked much; but it had distressed her because, like the botany book, it was written for people in England, and the plants and rocks and fossils mentioned she could not find in Africa. Her father had some shelves of old brown books: she had read nearly all of them; but, except the histories, none interested her much: they did not explain to her the world about her, what it was. He had one book called *Pre-Adamite Earth*, which she read and agonised and prayed over, trying to understand it; only after she had grown up she realised it was a book no human being could understand, least of all the man who wrote it. But he had a large old atlas which he gave her, which lay now on the top of her wooden cabinet. She used to lie on her back for hours, with the atlas open on her chest leaning against her drawn-up knees and with the Geography at her side for reference, and look at the different countries and seas, and picture them, and fancy she was there, especially China and Japan and Greenland and South America; till her heart got large with joy, the feeling that she was all over the world. On the shelf below were books of children's poetry, and the one or two story books she had as a child; but the books on the shelf above them were much more poetry to her. She felt so for them, that, if she had lived to be a woman of eighty and someone had suddenly come into the room where she was with one of those old worn books in his hand, her heart would have throbbed, and the memory of the hunger of the fierce young soul for knowledge, as it first looks out on life, would all have come back to her. Over the door leading to the children's bedroom was tacked the picture of the Madonna from the *Illustrated London News* which she had had pasted over the head of her bed when she was a child. It was the only ornament the room held except the little statue of Hercules in the corner.

Often at night, as she sat alone in that room, she had pictured to herself what great works of art must be like, or great orchestral music. She had seen or heard neither, but she dreamed of them, as she dreamed of what it must be to be one of a company of men and women in a room together, all sharing somewhat the same outlook on life and therefore thinking somewhat the same thought, and able to understand one another without explanation – a thing she knew was possible somewhere in time and space, which actually did exist though she might never know it.

On the brown carpet on the floor was a mark like a footpath where the nap had been worn off, running right round the desk. This was where she walked round and round, because the room was not large enough to allow other walking up and down, as she used to under the trees in the *kloof*.

For days often, and sometimes for weeks, she did not come into this room; but she knew it was there; and there was always a quiet spot in her mind answering to it.

Tonight she set the basket of darning down on the floor beside the desk and lit the reading lamp, and, when she had put the candle out, sat down in the armchair, leaning her head against its dented back.

It was a long time since she got up before sunrise that morning to warm the baby's milk, and she was tired. She was to have another child in seven months, and her legs and the lower part of her body ached; but it was never the same to her if she sat to rest in that room or any other. From her shelves, the bindings of her books looked down at her, each one a little brown face that seemed to love her. Behind each was hidden the mind of some human creature which at some time had touched her own; they were all the intellectual intercourse she had ever known. Not one was there because it was a rare or old copy, or had an expensive binding; each one was there because at some time she had lived close to it and it had penetrated her.

After a time she drew the basket nearer her and began to work. For nearly an hour she sewed on buttons and darned little worn places in little garments, till there was nothing left in the basket but a few pairs of socks and stockings; she took up one and began to darn it, but soon put it with the mended things in the basket with the unmended at the top, and then leaned back again on her chair, resting.

Outside, the rain had begun to fall; it was dropping on the thatched roof with a soft soo-o-shing sound. She lay in the chair and listened to it.

After a time she drew her chair closer to the desk, and from one of the top drawers took a book. It was an exercise book in a black cover. She laid it open on the desk.

In the drawer below were six or seven such books; some filled with the sharply pointed writing of a very small child who tries to write a flowing hand. In these were verses and short stories and little allegories told in rhyme – one very long allegory in blank verse, which was never quite finished – and one book held a story as long as a novel, and quite finished – and there were a few prose passages copied from books, which had struck the child as beautiful.

Some others were filled with the larger, more rounded handwriting of a young girl from twelve to twenty. They also held stories, but few had verses; and there were discussions on abstract questions. One book was a diary full of small daily entries, a book read, a visit found, seeds planted, but once or twice working out great plans for the life that was to be lived – countries to be visited – books to be written –

scientific knowledge to be gained – all written with absolute confidence. Now and then there were passionate personal entries, almost incoherent little calls for love and friendship; but they came not often, and some had been scratched out.

There were a couple of books filled after marriage; but the entries dwindled. Months passed in which nothing was written. After a child had been born and it had been necessary to lie still for weeks, there were dissertations on some abstract matter, or an allegory; but generally there were only short scraps; outlines of stories never to be filled in, and short diary notes of a very practical nature; on such a date the baby was weaned, or a new servant was hired, or she had planted a seed in her garden and set down the date to mark how long it took to come up. And sometimes (generally after a long interval in which nothing had been written) there were short notices, so written that no one into whose hand the book should fall would have understood them; in which dashes and letters took the place of words; such as 'Came into the billiard room unexpectedly. JD – Under the table. Ran out. Well, it doesn't matter, it doesn't matter. JF' or 'Again – again – again – today!'

Tonight she drew the book towards her. It was four months since she had opened it; she had had no time since she returned from the Eastern Province. When last she wrote she had been sitting up for a night, to make poultices for her boy, who had bad earache, and, between whiles as he slept, she had written.

She had been carrying on a long discussion with herself as to what was the real cause of that curious hunger for an exact knowledge of things as they are; of naked truth about all things small or great, material and also psychic, which seems to haunt so many of us, and which seems so little to have affected the thought and life of Europe through so many ages. She had advanced the view that, to find any true likeness to the modern feeling, we had to go back to the life and thought of classical days, especially to the life and thought in Greece in the fourth century before Christ.

Here she had had to go and make a poultice, and she had branched off on a sideline when she came back, to question if it were not just the resemblance on this point – this common desire for an exact knowledge of reality, of things exactly as they were, first and before all things – which gives us that strange sense of nearness to ancient classical thought and art. Was it not this deep reverence for reality, even in material things, which made us feel so curiously akin to, say, a little Greek statue, in which every muscle and organ have been carved with solemn care to follow life – sex organ and knee as devoutly as eye and forehead? Was it not this common hunger after a knowledge of reality as an end in itself which, in spite of the difference in our technical knowledge and outlook in many respects, yet makes us feel, when we read the page of a translation of some book two thousand years old, as if it might have been composed this morning by someone walking up and down in the pine woods behind the house, as well as by a peripatetic pacing the paths of a garden at Athens two thousand years ago? – Which makes us feel that if, in the sunshine on the gravelled path in our own garden today, a certain old man with flattened nose and rough cloak were found lying, we should be able to throw ourselves down beside him with our elbows on the earth and listen to his talk and share in his outlook, almost as we might have done two thousand years ago? Is it not this which, though we know thousands of things they never knew, yet, when we read them, makes us feel – 'My own! My own!'?

Is it not perhaps just the absence of this passionate desire to penetrate into the nature of all things and know them exactly as they are, which, in spite of their much nearer relation to us in order of time and by ties of blood and descent, makes us feel so infinitely more removed from the worthy Christian fathers and the sometimes gifted writers and thinkers of the Middle Ages (save a few heretics), and even from the mass of men of our own time – perhaps the very parents who bore us or begot us – persons who, living in the present, belong yet to that past which, accepting all things, found virtue in faith and not in a keen unending questioning of the facts of life; so that when we, who today share the new spirit, strive to come near them, we seem to be looking at them across an impassable mental chasm and through the haze of an almost infinite moral distance?

Here she had been interrupted again. When she came back she had gone on to seek more narrowly after the cause of the new spirit. – Was it because we were more virtuous, that for us a knowledge of all reality – whether it concerned the shading of the down on a butterfly's wing, the exact nature of a handful of earth, the antennae of a beetle, the movements of a planet, the how of sexual emotions or of social organisation – was to us a matter of primary importance, all wilful shutting of our eyes to it a crime, and all wilful misleading of our fellows with regard to it a social wrong? – while to men of the past, or men of the present holding the attitude of the past, such knowledge was only desirable and to be sought after if direct personal advantage to individuals could be seen to flow from it, while the wilful shutting of one's eyes to it, or the misleading of one's fellows with regard to it, might even be most virtuous actions if personal good seemed to flow from it?

She had held that it was not because we were more virtuous, but that the difference between the two attitudes took its rise entirely from two opposing intellectual conceptions of the nature of the Universe.

According to the old Christian conception, the Universe was a thing of shreds and patches and unconnected parts. Outside all we see and touch was the great individual Will, which had called into being wind and water, man, planet, star, stone, beast and plant, by the arbitrary action of its power, and which at any moment might return it all to nothingness, even the life that moves in animals having no permanence, and only that life in man which they called the soul having any future, though it had no past, and rose into being at an arbitrary *fiat*, like a stone and plant.

For the man intellectually holding this view to be true, the Universe could resemble only the heap of toys which a child gathers about it on the floor: doll, bugle, brick, book, having no subtle, living, connection with one another, being there together only because the will of the child has brought them there.

Solemnly to study each toy because, when you understand its structure, it might throw light on that of all the others, and closely to study their relation to one another – this doll lies at such an angle to that bugle – would be the work of a fool, when any moment a kick of the child might disturb all their relations.

For the man sincerely holding the old view, truth, the thing to be loved and sought after more than life, can be only a knowledge of the will of the arbitrary ruling individual, and the only thing of real importance in life must be the relation between that one indestructible element in man and the ruling individuality. Truth, as it regards the shading of a feather on a bird's wing, the movement of a planet, the order of social growth, the structure of a human body, can be of no value; it may even be a positive duty to misrepresent or repress the knowledge of facts, if they bear on, or seem to have a bearing injurious to, the relations of the individual man and the all-powerful individual.

For the man holding this view of the structure of the Universe, 'truth', in the sense in which it is a thing of value, cannot be simply the knowledge of all facts and all relations, as nearly as he can attain to it; it can be only the knowledge of certain facts for a definite purpose. The suppression of Galileo's discovery that the world moved – the habitual suppressing in art of certain aspects of life – the habit of continual questioning within oneself, not 'Is this thing true?' but 'What will be the effect of such knowledge or such a statement?' – is not, in the man holding this old view of the Universe, a sign of low morality and anti-social feeling; it is simply the logical outcome of his view of the Universe. For him to take any other course would not be rational, would not be virtuous, would not even be sane.

For us all this has changed.

Slowly advancing knowledge has forced on us an entirely new view of the Universe. Step by step we have been brought almost to the standpoint from which many an old Greek looked out on life.

For us once again the Universe has become one, a whole, and it lives in all its parts. Step by step advancing knowledge has shown us the internetting lines of action and reaction which bind together all that we see and are conscious of.

Between the farthest star and the planet earth we live on, between the most distant planet and the ground we tread on, between man, plant, bird, beast and clod of earth, everywhere the close internetted lines of interaction stretch; nowhere are we able to draw a sharp dividing line, nowhere find an isolated existence. The prism I hold in my hand, rightly understood, may throw light on the structure of the farthest sun; the fossil I dug out on the mountainside this morning, rightly studied, may throw light on the structure and meaning of the hand that unearths it; between the life that moved in the creature that ploughed in the mud of the lake shores three million years ago and the life which beats in my brain and moves in my eyes here in the sunshine today, I can see long unbroken lines of connection. Between spirit that beats within me and body through which it acts, between mind and matter, between man and beast, between beast and plant and plant and earth, between the life that has been and the life that is, I am able to see nowhere a sharp line of severance, but a great, pulsating, always interacting whole. So that at last it comes to be, that, when I hear my own heart beat, I actually hear in it nothing but one throb in that life which has been and is – in which we live and move and have our being and are continually sustained.

Having this view of the nature of the Universe forced on us, is it possible that our view of the nature and value of truth should not be changed?

The physiologist, when he seeks to study an organism, puts beneath his microscope an almost invisible spot of blood or shred of animal tissue, and devotes days or months to its study, not because he believes the individual shred or speck to be of any peculiar value, but because he knows that once rightly understood it may explain to him the nature of the entire organism of which it is a part. So we, who are dominated by this new conception of existence, are compelled to look upon the exact knowledge of even the smallest and most insignificant fact as sacred, never knowing when it may turn into the key which may unlock for us the meaning of part of that great universal life of which it is an integral fragment.

Holding this view of the Universe, we are compelled to walk almost awe-filled among even the small things of life; and, as the old Christian father, after much contemplation, was compelled at last to cry, 'There *is* no small sin – all violation of the will of God is great,' so we also are almost compelled to cry, 'There is no small truth – all truth is great!'

Holding the old conception of existence, it was quite possible to believe that, between God and man, mind and matter, soul and body, there were many chinks and crannies where a lie might creep in and hide itself and be quite innocuous. For us there is no faith in such possibility; we can no more nurse a false conception without it causing injury than a foreign substance can be intruded into a highly organised body without causing disorganisation and disease. Whether the truth concerns the feathers on a pigeon's wing or the constitution of a lump of earth or a psychological fact, we know that it is vital.

Here she had had to leave off the first night. When she began the next night she went on to discuss how this new intellectual conception of the Universe necessarily influenced our spiritual and moral outlook; how, for the man dominated by it, the existence of an extraneous will dealing arbitrarily with the things of existence was inconceivable, and the true revelation of the unseen and unknown beyond was to be found in the study of the seen and knowable about us; how, for us, the true act of religious worship was the search after a knowledge of all reality; how, for us, not less devout and religious than the old monk, who spent his life in copying and embroidering his missal or studying his gospel, is the man who today humbly devotes his life to the study of a spider's eye or the nature of a mineral, not knowing or seeking any direct benefit to flow to himself from the knowledge, but dominated by the profound conviction that the true comprehension of the smallest existence about us brings us nearer to the comprehension of the whole.

Then she went on to argue to herself that, for us, the true atheist was of necessity no longer the man who denies a knowledge of an unknown and unseen personality, but rather the man who believes that by juggling with facts he can outwit the Universe and make that which he knows is not as if it were; and that the greatest wrong a man can commit towards his fellow is the wilful misleading of him as to any reality; and the sin against the Holy Ghost – the sin which hath no forgiveness – is the conscious, wilful blinding of our own eyes to any form of reality.

So far she had scribbled four weeks before, when she was sitting up to make the poultices. Since then she had not thought of her discussion. But that morning, when she took the children to walk in the woods, she walked up and down under a pine tree, as they picked flowers, talking it over to herself. Tonight she opened her exercise book on the desk, climbed up in the chair and drew her feet back under her, partly because it was cold and she kept them warm so, and partly because the desk was a little high. She knelt up, bending low over the book, and began to write. She wrote quickly in a large sprawling hand, because she had much to say.

She went on to illustrate how our new attitude towards truth influenced all our personal relations in practical life. She illustrated it first by the feeling of the mother who looks down at the head of her little newborn baby sleeping at her breast. The old mother, if she were religious, looked down at it and prayed for it that it might cling to the dogmas which she would teach it, and, allowing nothing to turn its faith from them, at last attain everlasting joy. The new mother, when she looks down at the little head upon her breast, whispers in her heart: 'Oh, may you seek after truth. If anything I teach you be false, may you throw it from you, and pass on to higher and deeper knowledge than I ever had. If you are an artist, may no love of wealth or fame or admiration and no fear of blame or misunderstanding make you ever paint, with pen or brush, an ideal or a picture of external life otherwise than as you see it; if you become a politician, may no success for your party or yourself or the seeming good of even your nation ever lead you to tamper with reality and play a diplomatic part. In all the difficulties which will arise in life, fling yourself down on the truth and cling to that as a drowning man in a stormy sea flings himself onto a plank and clings to it, knowing that, whether he sink or swim with it, it is the best he has. If you become a man of thought and learning, oh, never with your left hand be afraid to pull down what your right has painfully built up through the years of thought and study, if you see it at last not to be founded on that which is; die poor, unloved, unknown, a failure – but shut your eyes to nothing that seems to them the reality.'

Then she scribbled on to show how the new attitude influenced the emotional relations between man and woman.

All women of the past and in the present find woman's heaven when their head rests on the shoulder of the man they love and his strong arm is about them; and as dear to the women of today as to the women of the remotest past is the love and tenderness of the man she is bound to. But yet the cry of our hearts is not the same. Beyond the cry for passionate tenderness there is another – 'Give us truth! Not jewels, not ease – nor even caresses, precious as they are to us – are the first thing we seek: give us truth. We are weary with seeking for truth and being baffled everywhere by subterfuge and seeming; in your eyes, beloved, let us never have to seek it, let it come out to meet us. The love which is not planted on a naked sincerity, which needs subterfuge and self-deception and the deception of another for its life, is a plucked flower stuck into the sand; what matter how soon it dies – it has no real life. Our love will more easily survive the most awful knowledge you can give us than the realisation that you have once willingly misled us. Should you lay your head upon our knees and tell us your heart had gone forever to another, it would be easier for us to bear than that you had fed us with one subterfuge to shield us from knowledge. The highest sacrament of love we thirst for between our two souls is an almighty sincerity; if there is not this, then for us love's holy of holies is defamed.'

She bent lower over her writing, scribbling quicker and quicker.

Then she painted the effect of our new feeling for reality upon the moral judgments we pass upon ourselves; and others.

When we lie awake in the dark of night thinking, what causes us to start and our cheek to burn? That which makes us shift restlessly from side to side, as if we were trying to shake off something, is often not the remembrance of what men and women of the past would have regarded as our greatest crime; it may be no infringement of any decalogue that ever yet was written; it may be just some written or spoken word or some act, perhaps seeming to us, even at the moment it was written or spoken or done, to be right and even magnanimous, but which falsified our relation with another or that other's relation with another or that other's relation to someone else. We remember it with a pain which manifest wrongdoings, recognised by the world, have not left; it is, when we remember it, as if a little knife cut into our heart, and we know till death comes it will always be sticking there.

She scribbled on to show how it altered our moral judgment of others; how, for us, the great criminal was not necessarily the murderer, the ruffian, the drunkard, the prostitute, or even the frank, direct, and open liar; but, maybe, a spirit encased in a fair and gentle body, rich in many graces of character and manner, openly breaking no social law and with no need to lie directly to others, because it lies always and so successfully to itself and within itself and acts persistently in harmony with that lie; a rotten apple with dead seeds and a worm at its core, and a shining surface. The old view was that the great sin lay in not speaking truth to your fellow when thereby you caused him practical loss; for us there is one infinitely greater – the sin of the soul that refuses to see the naked truth within itself and therefore can never show it. The man who lies to his fellow poisons an external relation – but the soul which lies in itself to itself, acting always a part before itself, becomes a poison, a deadly fungus that scatters its poisonous seeds unconsciously whenever it is touched.

The rain was now falling in torrents, running off the thatched roof and streaming down the rockery and along the garden path; but she scribbled on without hearing it.

She was trying now to show the effect of the new attitude with regard to truth on our feeling for art. For the man or woman holding the old view, the story, the picture, the statue in which certain artistically necessary aspects of life are intentionally suppressed or misrepresented for certain practical ends, the human nature falsely painted because it seemed undesirable to paint it as it is, the fig-leaf tied across the loin of the noblest statue, gives no pain and is still art; while, for those of us who have long set an intellectual value on sincerity, a mental habit has been formed which makes the perception of the wilful suppression of truth emotionally painful and so destroys our sense of perfection in the object in which it appears. The true reproduction of a sunrise, or a narrative that shows the working of a lofty spirit, may be more delightful art for us than the art which reproduces the texture of a lady's dress or paints the picture of a small soul; but the representation of the smallest or slightest aspect of life, if we are conscious of truth in it, in so far satisfies an emotional need in us and becomes for us, so far at least, an object of satisfaction; while no art can be art for us, however lofty its claims, which does not satisfy what has slowly become a master need of our natures. A work of art may have many other elements of beauty for us; but it must be a revelation of truth for us, or it means nothing. Better the true picture of a beggar in his rags than the wilfully false picture of a saint.

So she scribbled on, hearing nothing of the rain outside, bending low over her paper with her chin pressed down on her breast. But presently she began to write slower and slower, and presently raised herself and sat watching the lamp. Then she sank half-back in the chair, still on her knees and, after a time, began slowly drawing with her outstretched hand the pictures of faces down one edge of the page she had written on. They came out slowly, one below the other, some with sharp features, some with dark beards and curls, some with blunt features, some grotesque and some beautiful; she did not seem to be looking at them as she drew them. When she got to the bottom of the page she dipped the pen into the ink again and sat turning it round and round in her fingers and dipped it again. She was questioning in how far she had been right in her conclusions, and arguing the other side. Then she jumped suddenly from the chair and began to pace the room in the footpath round the desk. She clasped her hands behind her with the pen still between her fingers, and it made a large ink spot at the back of her little blue print skirt.

What, after all, did she know of art, except the art in literature? The book of photographs of great statuary, which she had bought at great expense, had so disgusted her with the modern fig leaves tied on with wire that she had never brought it into her study but had thrown it into a corner of the drawing room. What would she really feel if she could study plastic art in all its forms, not only Greek, Assyrian, Egyptian, Indian, not through books at second-hand, but actually, as though living, in climates that produced them![1] She shot out her hand greedily as if grasping them.

After she had walked for a time, she stopped suddenly at the door of the children's room, and, half opening it, stood listening to hear if they were still quiet and asleep; then she closed it softly and walked and walked on with her hands behind her. Her thoughts had wandered far now, though the new chain of thought was bound link by link to the old. From thinking of Greek art and literature, her thought wandered on to the old, old problem which had held so great a fascination for her, even when she was a child and read, in her father's old brown leather-covered *History of the Ancient World,* its stiff long-worded accounts of the Assyrian and Egyptian and Roman and other early empires, and had traced with a dry pen on the mildewed map in the front of the book the path over the mountains which the Goths and the Vandals and the Huns took when they came to overrun Italy and destroy Rome, till the map had worn quite thin there. It was the old, old problem that had always fascinated her: why, when a nation or a race or a dominant class has reached a certain point of culture and material advance, has it always seemed to fall back from it, and the nation or race or class to be swept away? Always the march of human progress has died out there, to be taken up again by some other race or class in some distant part of the globe or after the lapse of centuries – to die out there also after a time, never proceeding persistently in a straight line. Was there an immutable law, based on an organic and inherent quality in human nature, which caused this arrest? Was it futile for us to hope that human advance might ever proceed persistently and unbroken in one direction? Was that which governed its arrest an organic law, like that which ordains the length of a man's beard, which, however long the individual may live, when it has once reached a certain length will always stop growing? Is it absolutely futile to hope that humanity can ever advance as the fern palm grows, beautiful frond beyond beautiful frond opening one out of the other as it mounts up higher and higher? – or has the arrest and decay, so invariable in the past, being merely dependent on external and fortuitous conditions, having no one organic root in the human nature itself and therefore being possible to avoid?

That morning, when she had taken the children for their walk in the pine woods, she had been pacing up and down under a tree while the children picked

---

1 The original text read: 'Not through books at second hand, but to them all actually living, in climates that produced them!'

the bluebells among the grass, and had been arguing over the matter, almost as she used to argue with Charles under the pear tree. She had taken first the standpoint that it was organic and inevitable. Tonight, as she walked round the desk, she took the other view (which was really her own) and tried to defend the position that there was no sufficient evidence that this arrest and decay was really organic and therefore inevitable. One thing alone would be enough to account for it – the fact that a high advance in intellectual culture and social organisation has never yet been attained by any but a minute section of the human race as a whole, and always by merely a small section of the inhabitants of any single territory. That such a minute section of humanity has never been able to maintain its advance proves nothing except that humanity, being intimately in its nature a solidarity and a whole with all its parts reacting on one another, one minute fragment can never move very far ahead of the mass without ultimately being drawn back, either by internal disintegration, brought about through that body in the society itself which has not been included in the advance, or through external and violent contact with other parts of the race which have not shared its advance.

That all so-called advanced societies have, in the past, always disintegrated and fallen back does not prove that a hard rim-line exists which humanity can never surpass, and cannot prove this while we are in possession of a fact which adequately accounts for this retrogression without any such supposition.

She paced up and down quickly and more quickly with her hand behind her, still holding the pen, and went on in her thought to illustrate her view.

What was that high point of advance, intellectual and moral, which we speak of Greece having attained in the fourth century before Christ, and from which she receded so quickly and completely – was it indeed Greece which ever reached that point? What was that much vaunted culture, that high creative energy, that passionate thirst after intellectual insight, that demand for personal freedom, that search after physical beauty, but the possession of a few males who constituted the dominant class in a few cities of Greece! What was that much vaunted culture but a delicate iridescent film overlying the seething mass of servile agricultural and domestic slaves and of women, nominally of the dominant class, but hardly less servile and perhaps ignorant, who constituted the bulk of its inhabitants? As little could it be said to have been the property of the inhabitants of the land of Greece as the phosphorescent light on the surface of the ocean is the property of the fathoms of water stretching below it whose surface it illuminates. It would be as rational to expect that such a form of culture, brought into existence for a moment by a combination of happy conditions, could hand itself down from generation to generation, expanding and strengthening as it grew, as to expect a spray of shrub, plucked and placed in a vase of water in a hot-house, though it might bloom profusely for a few days, should permanently propagate itself and persistently grow when it was without ground and had no root.

But even had things been otherwise in Greece – had its women, they who alone have the power of transmitting the culture and outlook of one generation safely to the next, been sharers in the culture and freedom and labours of its males, not merely partially in the person of a few of its *hetairai,* but in that of the bulk of its child-bearing women – had every hand that laboured in the fields or the cities been that of a freeman, sharing to the full the civic rights of his State, possessing a stake in its material welfare and a culture that enabled him to rejoice in its art and share in its thought – had that happened, which never yet has happened in any land – had Greece been filled with a population homogeneous in their culture and freedom – had no untaught servile woman existed to suckle any Greek child – had no slave formed a rotten foundation stone in the social structure – had culture, freedom, and civic rights been the common property of every human who breathed on the soil of Greece – had the social super-structure been sound and homogeneous from foundation to coping stone; – even then, though the vantage gained, instead of passing away in a couple of generations, might have remained for a few hundred years and there might have been more persistent progress; yet, – could it have been even tolerably permanent?

For what was the whole of Greece itself but a mere spot on the earth's surface? What were its people but a drop in the ocean of humanity? Unless she could have walled herself in, shutting off all possibility of interaction with all the races beyond herself, sooner or later she must have been so interacted upon by the mass of humanity beyond, that change and disintegration, moral and intellectual, must have set in, and she must slowly have fallen back to the common level.

As she walked she had paused before the little statue of Hercules, and, taking it automatically from the bracket, stood holding it in one hand and softly stroking it down with the finger of the other as though she were feeling its outline: yet her eyes appeared not to see it. After a while she put it back on the stand and began pacing again.

All the civilisations of the past, in Egypt, in Assyria, in Persia, in India, what had they been but the blossoming of a minute, abnormality situated, abnormally nourished class, unsupported by any vital connection with the classes beneath them or the nations around? What had they resembled but the long, thin, slender, feathery, green shoots which our small rose trees sometimes send out in spring rising far into the air, but which we know long before the summer is over will have broken and fallen; not because they have grown to a height which no rose tree can ever attain, for ultimately the whole rose tree may be much higher than the shoot, but because they have shot out too far before their fellow-branches to make permanence possible; having no support, wind and weather will sooner or later do their work and snap them off or wither them. Next year a dozen rich young shoots may sprout from the snapped stem and survive; it may not have shot upwards and been broken off without helping in the growth of the whole tree – but it, itself, perishes.

If the whole of our vaunted modern advance, our science, our art, our social ideals, our material refinement, were to pass away tomorrow, swept away by the barbarians we nurse within the hearts of our societies or which exist beyond: would it for a moment prove that humanity had reached its possible limit of growth, and not rather that a sectional growth is no permanent growth? – that, where mass remain behind, the few are ultimately drawn back? (As the head of a tortoise, let it stretch it out as it will within certain limits, can never continue to advance while its hind legs are sticking in the mud; would it move, it must pull its hind legs forward.) Would it prove that our loftiest ideals of human progress were futile? – man moving ever in a little ring, advancing and forever falling backward as soon as the edge is reached – and not merely that the true cry of permanent human advance must always be 'Bring up your rears! Bring up your rears!'? Head and heart can ultimately move no farther than the feet can carry them. Permanent human advance must be united advance!

Then she thought suddenly she heard the baby stir. She threw her pen down on the table and took up the lamp, went into the next room and bent over his cot. But he had only turned in his sleep and was resting quietly. She bent down and turned him onto his side and put the nipple of his feeding bottle into his fist and close to his lips that he might find it if he woke. She had had to wean him because of the new baby that was coming. Then she tucked the cover in at the back of his neck and went back, closed the door softly behind her, and began to walk up and down.

If the advance of a nation or a race must always ultimately be stayed, partly because of the internal action of the undeveloped mass within itself which must in time disintegrate it, and partly because the interaction with humanity beyond itself must ultimately draw it down and back, how much more must it be the case that a solitary individual city can never reach its full development in a society far behind itself?

That the highest and most harmonious development of the individual which we dream of is never reached, and that the attempt to attain it seems always to lead to intense personal suffering or absolute social destruction for the individual striving, in no way proves that the ideal is ultimately beyond reach – an *ignis fatuus* which the human hand will never grasp. As the nation or the class which should first have developed so far that it turned all its energies entirely away from the creation and wielding of the arts of destruction and self-defence, and turned them entirely to the creation of the beautiful and useful arts which benefit all mankind, would, ultimately and probably very soon, be swept away, as long as anywhere on the earth's surface there were still races so retrograde that they devoted all their energies to the arts of destruction; and as the nation, which should have attained the moral standpoint at which it became no longer possible for the stronger to absorb all the good of life and in which therefore poverty and need become extinct, would inevitably be overcome by the wanting and miserable products in other societies where a lower moral standard prevailed, if any such society existed anywhere on the earth – so more surely the individual, who should arrive at a higher moral point of development and strive to realise his ideals in actual life, must inevitably suffer or be absolutely annihilated in a society which had not reached his standpoint; and this not because his ideal was inherently unattainable and might not be the ultimate goal of the race, but simply because, for its realisation harmoniously and successfully, it wanted more than the solitary unit, it wanted the interaction of the whole society.

A wolf who should suddenly be smitten by the idea that, instead of tearing his fellows to pieces, it would be better if they made a league of co-operation and fellowship, and for that purpose filed down his canines, would quickly become a prey to his fellows, not because his ideal was incompatible with successful animal life, for other forms have attained to it, but because its attainment by one was impossible.

So the individual primitive man in a cannibal tribe who had become possessed with the idea that the eating of human flesh was undesirable, and who had refused to capture and feed, would have become an object of scorn and probably of hatred to his tribe and might probably have died of hunger in some time of pressure, not because his ideal was ultimately unattainable, for practically today the whole of humanity has reached it, but because change in the idea of his fellows and the common carrying out of agricultural and pastoral labours were necessary to its successful attainment.

The man who dreams today that the seeking of material good for himself alone is an evil, who persistently shares all he has with his fellows, is not necessarily a fool dreaming of that which never has been or will be; he is simply dreaming of that which will be perfectly attainable when the dream dominates his fellows and all give and share. Working it alone, it fails, because the individual is part of an organism which cannot reach its full unfolding quite alone.

The man who should have reached a point of development at which sex in all its manifestations, whether physical or mental, has become a matter for reverence, and who should find his ideal reached only by a perfectly free and even comradeship between men and women at large in human society, and the personal ideal reached only in a relationship in which the mind fully shared with the body and in which the best in each half united into the perfect human creature called forth, who would desire that all that was most self-forgetful and heroic in his nature should be brought into play in the relation, as men desire to hang only the fairest wreaths before the shrine of the chief god in their temple – could such a man ever fully realise his ideal, or even attempt to realise it, without acute suffering and many-sided failure, in a society in which the brothel reigns and the ideals which the brothel presupposes, in which sex relationships are viewed by the mass of his fellows from the two standpoints of crude and selfish physical enjoyment or of gross material benefit? Might not his very attempts to bring men and women into freer and more equal fellowship in themselves seem to produce more evil than they remedied, simply because they were not ready for it? Would he himself not be almost certainly misunderstood and his personal relations end in irrevocable failure? What would this prove but that each man is but a cell in the human organism and that what his full development might be we shall never know till others share it with him?

The man whose ideal it is that, by the non-requital of injuries and the large expansion of sympathy even towards those who inflict suffering on himself, is human good and justice finally served – does his failure to evoke any response, and his final crushing beneath the hands he refused to strike, prove anything but the solidarity of humanity and that the foremost branch which grows too far beyond its fellows must ultimately be snapped off? That no individual ever yet realised in life the highest development which the mind has dreamed of proves not that perfect truth and fellowship are not attainable to humanity, but that the one alone cannot compass them.

Is it not a paradox covering a mighty truth that not one slave toils under the lash on an Indian plantation but the freedom of every other man on earth is limited by it? That not one laugh of lust rings but each man's sexual life is less fair for it? That the full all-rounded human life is impossible to any individual while one man lives who does not share it? 'Bring up your rears! Bring up your rears!'

She walked, whispering softly to herself. Outside, the rain had left off falling; only the drops fell from the branches of the trees over the roof as the wind moved them, and the great drops fell slowly from the thatched eaves; but she did not hear them, she was so happy talking to herself.

Now her thought shifted its standpoint. She imagined the mind she argued with to take a new view and to say, 'Granting you are right and that the full developed individual and the race must be hampered and limited by that of the less developed, is it not practically our duty and for the benefit of humanity that we should forcibly suppress, cut off, and destroy the less developed individuals and races, leaving only the highly developed to survive'? She imagined it to produce all the arguments for the destruction of inferior races and individuals, stating them as fairly as she could. Then she turned to the other side and stated the view which was really her own.

She walked more quickly now, but with her head still down, striking the palm of one hand now and then with the doubled-up fist of the other.

Firstly, where is any body of humans to be found impartial enough, and untouched by the warping of personal and racial prejudices, to be able to determine for the race at large just what qualities are desirable and should be preserved and which should render their possessors liable to destruction? Would not each individual composing it be warped, not merely by a weakness for his own personal qualities, mental and physical, but would not racial prejudice make impartial judgment for humanity at large impossible? – the Chinaman judging from the

Chinaman's standpoint; the Hindu from the Hindu's; the Englishman from the Englishman's? Could any but a race of crowned immortal gods, untouched by human self-love with its bias, form any conclave which should dare determine, not merely what were the ideal qualities after which they individually should strive and which they should impress on the race by preaching and example, but which would justify them in physically destroying those unendowed in them?

But, granting that it were possible to find such a body of humans on the globe (which it is not and cannot be), who would draw up an infallible code of all the qualities desirable and to be sought after by expanding humanity and of all those to be crushed and undesirable to the race, two difficulties that could not be surmounted would yet remain. Firstly that, given this almost divine conclave had succeeded in drawing up a list of all the qualities which are desirable in advancing humanity – the physical qualities of muscular strength, organic soundness, physical beauty (the idea of which differs so much from race to race and even from person to person that no representative body of humans ever could agree in what it consisted) – that general vitality and harmony of parts and forces which makes physical life a joy – the mental qualities of reason, imagination and keen and quick perception – the social qualities of sympathy, kindliness, rectitude, and all other qualities desired by humans in their fellows – and should exactly define what was meant by each quality and by its reverse: would they be much nearer the solution of the question what individuals and what races should be destroyed as a weight and drawback on the development of the race, and which saved and sacrificed for as the highest development? For no extended list of desirable or undesirable human qualities could be drawn up, all of which could be found wholly incarnate in any race or individual.

You say, and rightly, physical health and strength are among the prime necessities of the fully developed human creature. The Kaffir and the South Sea Islander have often these in their very highest perfection: are these, therefore, the races to be preserved and which others are to be sacrificed for? You say a powerful reason is essential to the advance of the race: you find your man with the powerful reason, but diseased, antisocial, using his powerful intellect only as a means of preying on his fellow, often the great criminal. You say, at least – let us kill out the hopelessly unfit, the invalid and the sickly and the consumptive: under this law you may ordain to destruction the bright, the lovely and most beneficent of the race. Has my view not as much to be said for it as yours that, if any on earth should be wilfully destroyed as the down-drawers of the race, it is not a Shelley or a Keats, who has enriched and beautified existence on earth beyond fifty thousand whole men; but that it is the man of perfect physical health, with far less intelligence, and organically incapable of living for anything but his own well-being, finding no joy in any kind of sacrifice for his fellows and transmitting his qualities as surely as the consumptive or the weak, who is really the disease point in humanity, the creature who prevents the noblest social institutions and personal relations from coming into existence, because his egoisms can always be calculated to make them unworkable? You say that keen perceptions and the power of dominating are characteristics of the to-be-preserved races: but what if to me the little Bushman woman, who cannot count up to five and who, sitting alone and hidden on a *kopje*, sees danger approaching and stands up, raising a wild cry to warn her fellows in the plain below that the enemy are coming, though she knows she will fall dead struck by poisonous arrows, shows a quality higher and of more importance to the race than those of any Bismarck? What if I see in that little untaught savage the root out of which ultimately the noblest blossom of the human tree shall draw its strength? Who shall contend I am not right?

You say, 'Let it be granted that social qualities are to count as high as or higher than intellectual or physical, then at least it will be justified that all avowedly criminal individuals and classes should be destroyed.' – But who are the criminals? You say the prostitute, the murderer, the robber, the gambler. But who are these? The judge who sits in his elbow chair sentencing the man who plays pitch and toss in the street and himself sits up till two o'clock over his cards – the king and the prince who, while every avenue of pleasure and good is open to them, hang round the tables of Monte Carlo – the poor man who opens his back cellar for gaming to make a wretched living – who is the gambler? Who is the prostitute – the wretched woman whom the policeman drags along the street, or the man, often of wealth and learning and power, whose selfish lust and gold alone keep alive the institution whose bitter fruit she is? When you have crushed and destroyed the woman prostitute, what have you done more than cut out the tiny rotten place on the surface of an apple, while you leave gnawing away in the dark at the core the worm that produced it? Who is the robber and murderer we have most to fear – the pirate who on the high seas grasps men and goods, the highwayman and the housebreaker, or the man who, shielding himself always carefully behind a law he sees works in his favour or knows how to evade, makes his wealth from the ill-paid labour of those in mines and factories working at the cost of life, and ornaments his wife and his daughters as much in blood-stained jewellery and garments as the robber who returning home puts on his wife's finger a ring cut from the hand of a living woman, or throws on his daughter's shoulders a garment spotted with a traveller's blood? Who is the man who robs his fellows of life and the fruit of their labour, that we may be sure he shall not slip through our fingers, leaving the wrong man there? Who is the gambler, prostitute, robber, murderer? Is he king, prince, judge, as well as beggar and tramp? How shall we make sure he gets judgment in exact proportion to his offence? And further, is there any definite action or state which, judging for the world as a whole, can be set down as marking out the criminal? Has not the buccaneer, the polygamist, the polyandrist been the hero and the virtuous man or woman of his community? Will any action more certainly bring down the judgment and social punishment of his society in some countries than refusing to bow the head to a passing wafer of flour, in others the eating of pork, or the refusal to take his dead brother's wife, or give his daughter to the chief harem? Have not robber chiefs been regarded as quite as respectable and unliable to punishment in their society as the wealthy wage robber and the prostitute king and the hangman who are with us? What definite action will you set down as marking the criminal?

You say that of course no definite concrete action can be set down as marking out the criminal, that it is one in one society and another in another, but that he is yet easily marked off: he is the man who in any society refuses to submit to the laws which its dominating power has instituted and who persists in facing the punishments and penalties it ordains; and that, if he were in all societies destroyed and prevented from perpetuating himself, his type might become absolutely extinct and the qualities he possesses die out from the human race.

Perhaps this would be so; but are you sure you know what you are doing? For on that broad road of opposition to law and authority, along which stream the millions of humanity too low to grasp even the value of laws and institutions about them, resisting them from an ignorant and blind selfishness which makes them believe they are improving their own conditions by violating them, there are found walking men of a totally different order – white robed sons of the gods with the light on their foreheads, who have left the narrow paths walled in by laws and conventions, not because they were too weak to walk in them, or because the goals towards which they led were too high, but because infinitely higher goals and straighter paths were calling to them – the new pathfinders of the race!

These men, who rise as high above the laws and conventions of their social world as the mass who violate them fall below, are yet inextricably blended with the stream of souls who walk in the path of resistance to law. From the monk Telemachus, who, springing into the Roman arena to stop the gladiatorial conflict, fell, violating the laws and conventions of his society – a criminal, but almost a god – up and down all the ages man has been on earth there have been found these social resisters and violators of the accepted order, the saviours and leaders of men on the path to higher forms of life.

It is true that if, persistently and with a rigor from which none escaped alive, you could in every land exterminate the resisters of social law, you might at last produce a race on earth in which even the wish or the power to resist social institutions will have died out; your prisons might be empty, your hangmen and judges without occupation. But what would you have done? Seeking to cut out humanity's corns, to remove its cataract, to amputate its diseased limbs, you would have put out its eyes, cut off its tongue, maimed its legs; unable to see or move or express, its heart would beat slower and slower and death would come.

There is no net which can be shaped to capture the self-seeking ignorant violator of law which shall not also capture in its meshes the hero, the prophet, the thinker, the leader – the life of the world!

As the oak tree cannot grow unless, with each new ring it adds, its old bark cracks and splits, so humanity cannot develop without the rupture of its old institutions and laws; and it has been exactly because the bulk of humanity have never of necessity been able to distinguish between this healthful disruptive process and decay, and have sought to crush and annihilate the particles causing it, that the growth of humanity has been as slow as it has. To suggest the more rigorous extermination of all non-law-submitting humans is simply to suggest a slow suicide as far as human development is concerned. In all ages the multitude has looked upon Barabbas as a less violent and dangerous disrupter of social laws than the Christ – not this man but Barabbas!

But you may say the criminal is, of course, not to be marked off in all societies merely as the breaker of any of its laws, for then, of course, the man who strives after better ideals would be included with the man who strives after lower; you say the true criminal is that man who, whether within or without the law, is willing to inflict suffering and loss on others for his own gain; and undoubtedly this is the true criminal. But how is he to be found, since it is not by the committal of any definite marked-off act, or by the violation of public enactments, but by the nature of his motive, that he becomes a criminal? It is certainly not a Lucrezia Borgia, adulteress and murderer, who of necessity, judged by the standard of motive and the amount of suffering caused to others, will always come out the great criminal. The fair gentle woman, never transgressing any enacted law, always seeking for love and sympathy and determined to gain it at all cost to others and all sacrifice of direct sincerity, may inflict in the course of her life an amount of suffering and wrong before which a few direct murders count as nothing; not merely by the love she takes from others or the friends she divides, but by the much more terrible distrust of human nature she awakens; by showing that, below so much gentleness and virtue, self-seeking and rottenness may lie, she strikes at our faith in our fellows, than which no more terrible wrong can be done. Yet under what code or before which tribunal could she be condemned to death? She is the snake in the Garden of Eden; yet who can swear she has poison as she glides noiselessly by? When we all lie silent in our last sleep with our feet turned upwards, if a god of life, knowing all things, should pass us, meting out judgment according as we had caused suffering in the search after our own good, would he of necessity pause over the worn-out drunkard and the street-treading outcast? Might it not also be over the woman of virtue and philanthropy or the man, hail-fellow well-met with all men, who paid his debts of honour and owed no man anything – saying 'There lies the great criminal!'?

But, you may say, granting that we cannot determine who the criminals are who should be destroyed for the benefit of the race, or the kind or degree of ill health which should be followed by instant destruction, yet surely such an ideal body of humans should find no difficulty in desiring the annihilation of all dark and primitive races who are manifestly a down-draught on humanity.

But are they so?

Is there really any superiority at all implied in degrees of pigmentation, and are the European races, except in their egoistic distortion of imagination, more desirable or highly developed than the Asiatic? Are we not in our vanity like the parvenu who, having wrung wealth out of the labour of others and surrounded himself by the results of all human toil and knowledge, stands in his gorgeous room filled with the works of art and use of all nations and, with his hands in his pockets and his full belly, looks round with infinite satisfaction at what he has accumulated about him, and says, 'All these are mine', believing really that their existence and creation have something to do with himself? Are we modern Europeans not the parvenus among the human race? From the ancient civilisations of Asia and Africa, ancient and complete, when we were merely savage, have we not got all the foundation and much of the superstructure of what we possess? Art, science, letters, all are their original creation, merely taken over by us; even our very religion, such as it is, we could not invent for ourselves, but had to take it over from a hook-nosed, swarthy, Semitic people. And, if the learning and art and industry of Asia and Africa, passing into the hands of that marvellous bloom of humanity, the Greek race, in its little span improved and enlarged what it took, it yet has been no work of ours, the Northern barbarians; we were running naked and staining ourselves with woad in our woods, when the looms of India and China were producing the delicate fabrics we seek now to imitate, when Asiatics ate from golden-flowered and delicate china, when temples and statues were raised that are our wonder and admiration, when philosophers taught and thought, and books were written and great legal systems enacted, while we sat round our fires on the dung and gambled with knuckle bones or danced war dances to the shouts of our fellows. It ill becomes us, who are but the tamed children of yesterday, to talk of primitive savages. Even today, when we have inherited all, is it so certain that our vaunted civilisation is so much statelier and on all sides wider and with nobler elements of truth lying at its foundation than the older civilisations of the yellow and brown races? Is it so sure we are the people and wisdom will die with us? Is it not possible, for instance, that there is something of deep wisdom in the Chinese ideal which gives so much of the beauty of life to the end, which gives even the woman when she is old, the mother and grandmother, so honoured and tender a place in society? Is it quite wise to sacrifice all to youth, so that every man and woman fears old age and would sacrifice all to avoid it? Must not the whole of life be more beautiful when men wait for good at the end, the joy of the sunset? Is not the religion which permeates Asia, and which came to life while our fathers still dreamed of heaven as a hall where man drank wine from the skulls of their enemies, more in harmony with the teaching of modern knowledge, which is reshaping us, than even that other Asiatic religion which we have adopted? Did not the deep-seeing eye of the Buddha, hundreds of years before the Jewish teacher walked in Syria, perceive clearly beneath all the complexities of form and individuality the unity in life upon the earth? He did not get at it as the modern man of reason, slowly, by measurement and calculation; by deep perception he knew that our little brothers look out at us from the eyes of animals, that the life of no beast and bird or insect is alien and unconnected with ours, that life flows on earth as one large stream with many divided branches, and under his mystical doctrine of the transmigration of souls he covered the same radical truth which 'evolution' expresses in other but perhaps more absolutely accurate terms. We Northern fair-skins have had great men; our glimpses of new truths, new masteries over matter, have added our grain to humanity's sum of riches even in the direction of creative art; but, when we look around us on what we call our civilisation, how little is really ours alone and not drawn from the great stream of human labours and creation so largely non-European? We scorn the Chinaman because his women compress their feet, not perceiving how infinitely more deadly and grotesque is the compression of our bodies; we ridicule, in certain Asiatic races, the pigtail of the Chinaman or the darkened tooth of the Japanese, blinded by egoism to the infinite degradation of the Northern races in their passionate strife to imitate ever-changing costumes and modes, alike so far removed from nature and beauty that even we, when a few years are past, perceive their grotesqueness and vulgarity, the slavish imitation of fashions which, by their unending change, feed on the vitals of the race through their ignoble demand on the brain of its womanhood, absorbing energy, reason, imagination, and setting, so long as their diseased reign lasts, a limit to the progress and expansion of woman and, with her, of the race. We accuse of immorality the Asiatics who consume the opium we forced upon them at the point of the sword; but we fair Northerns deserve today, as fully as when the Roman spoke it two thousand years ago, the judgment that as a people our chief pleasures were drinking and gambling; our race courses and card tables are as essential to our happiness as the dice and knuckle bones to our forebears. Is it not more than possible that, infinite as has been the debit of humanity to the ancient non-European peoples in the past, they have yet more to confer in the future?

You may answer (she walked quicker and quicker, looking down at the carpet) that no sane, informed mind could regard the old master races of the East, who have led in the path of civilisation, as consigned to destruction by their inferiority; that it is the dark and primitive races still leading a life of nature that it is so necessary should be removed and suppressed in the cause of humanity.

But not only does it ill become us, the latest tamed of all civilised races, to speak slightingly of any primitive barbarian; not only among ourselves is a race such as the Prussians, who were civilised many centuries later than the men of France or Spain, in no way considered by us inferior to these, but we hold, and perhaps rightly, that by the engrafting of our savage forebears on the older civilisations of Europe, though we mercilessly destroyed them for the time being and plunged all Europe into barbarous chaos for over ten centuries, that we yet vivified human life and that our savage eruption was in the end a benefit. The older civilisations were too nearly extinct, we say, by excessive civilisation; a backseat to the unclothed men of the woods and nomads of tents was necessary to vivify them. But if this were so, may not the most primitive races have the same function to fulfil towards us? Is it not possible that man, a creature of the plains and hills, naked and always in unbroken activity in the free air, cannot survive beyond a certain time when he goes about loaded with materials from all the vegetable and animal and mineral kingdoms which he has gathered from all quarters of the globe – as a mantis collects mud and shells to make a case for himself, when he buries himself deep among his little erections of mud and stone, shutting off from body and brain light and air, when he has so constructed life that half of his body social is parasitic and enervated by want of labour, and the half it feeds with crushed under the superimposed weight – is it not possible that the primitive man, individually and structurally as well as socially, may, in some future aeon, have the same restorative function to fulfil towards ourselves as we imagine ourselves to have played toward older decadent civilisations?

You say that the primitive barbarian is ugly and repulsive to us: were not our forebears so to Greeks and Romans? Were not Attila and the Huns so horrible, physically and mentally, in their eyes that they were believed to be the offspring of witches and evil spirits, nothing wholly human being possibly so repulsive? Was it not death to the Roman woman who wedded a barbarian? To have eaten or drunk or slept with him was disgrace. He was supposed even to have an unendurable smell. Was the difference not at least as great between the lovely cultured Greek and the trained imperial Roman, between Pericles and Virgil, and the naked and spear-brandishing long-haired savage, drinking blood from the skulls of his enemies, as between his modern descendant and any primitive savage on earth? Who shall say that, in destroying the child of nature with his perhaps simpler organisation and untried nerves, we are not destroying that of which humanity may yet in the aeons to come have need to keep the race upon the earth?

At the worst, which is fairer and more akin to the ideals towards which humanity seems to move? – the little Bushman in his open cave on the mountain brow, etching away into the rock with his little sharpened flint the picture of hunting or wild beast, and looking down in the glory of sunshine on the place below where the wild things graze, or a swell-chinned ragged woman staggering out of a public house in one of our centres of civilisation, while the man who made the drink dwells in high places? Which is lovelier here, now, or in any place or time – the troop of men and women on a South Sea island, naked and gladly disporting themselves in the water or wandering together in the sunshine and sharing their love in the open light of day, or the scene that night by night our great cities witness? Which fills us with a sense of the greatness of the human spirit – the Kaffirs on their flat-topped mountain refusing to surrender month after month, till the conquerors when they mount at last find only one or two hardly-moving skeletons – men, women and children having died with hunger – or the civilised soldier who has sworn to die, but when a tenth part of his numbers have fallen puts up the white flag, willing to take life but not to lose it?

He needs be a brave man who would dare ordain destruction to all primitive and barbarous people, who could feel so sure humanity will have no need of them on her march through the future.

But letting all those difficulties pass (she stretched out one hand with the palm extended): supposing it were possible for us to find an individual, a class or a race, so constituted that it presented in itself all the conceivable disadvantages and deficiencies which can afflict human nature and none of the advantages; supposing it were possible – which it never would be – to find anywhere a body of humans as diseased, as devoid of physical health and the vital enjoyment of life as a worn-out man of fashion and debauch, as stupid and ill shaped as a Bushman, as brutal as the savage, as false as the worst civilised man, as antisocial as the criminal, as hypocritical as the Pharisee, physically deformed and mentally wanting, combining in itself all the drawbacks of each form and stage of human growth and none of the advantages – you may say: 'Here at least we have found at last the creature or class whom, to perfect its own growth, it is necessary society should slay and mercilessly destroy.' But is this so? If such individual or race were found, would it even then be proved that the highest use which society could make of them would be to destroy them? Does not the essential element, which it is most important to develop, if human life on earth is ever to attain to its full blossoming, lie in just that very sensitiveness towards the right of existence of all other human units, that deep-seated and at last organic desire not to benefit ourselves at the cost of others, which this course of action would tend to blunt and kill? In attempting to remove the undesirable and, to us, retrograde portions of human society, are we not blunting and striking at the very existence of the quality in ourselves which is above all essential to full human unfolding? Might not an immensely more productive use be made of such undesirable elements of life, by using them as objects for the development of those broad and generous human feelings which are the crowning beauty of life? In seeking to exterminate the undesirable of the race when we find him, may not society be striking at the very heart of its own progress, inflicting a mortal wound upon itself which exceeds in deadliness any which the undesirable individuals could have inflicted on it? Is it not an act of moral suicide?

And (she stretched out her hand softly again) if even this point also were waived, if it be allowed that it might be possible to find a body of humans so perfect and impartial that they are fit to legislate for the race, and that it might be possible for them to discover persons and races so hopelessly undesirable that for the benefit of the race's growth they must be destroyed; yet there remains the second great difficulty – who would bell the cat? Supposing this body of enlightened impartial and thoughtful humans decided that tyrants, drunkards, gamblers, murderers, robbers, hypocrites and all inflictors of suffering on their kind, and stupid and blindly narrow persons were an evil to the race and should be destroyed – would this enlightened and philosophic body of persons be themselves able to carry out their edict of destruction and become captors and executioners? And, if they had to delegate it to others, would not the very persons to be destroyed be often the persons fit and able to carry it out? The debauched judge, the ignorant, stupid and narrow jailer, the brutal and stupid soldier, the bloodthirsty tyrant, the very individuals ordained to destruction, may be the most impossible to get at. You may condemn Nero but you cannot compel him to destroy himself, and you may not be able to find anyone capable and willing to do so. The very conditions of lofty intelligence and wide unbiased sympathy, which would alone endow any human being with the gift necessary for impartially judging for the race, are the very qualities which might render him unfit and incapable as executioner.

But you may say that all this is merely irrelevant child's play; that no sane person supposes you could find a body of humans wise enough and impartial enough to determine for the whole race which are the retrograde elements which must be destroyed for its benefit, or powerful enough to destroy them when it has so determined; that the same end is attained much more securely and quickly by simply allowing all the physically stronger elements in humanity everywhere to destroy the weaker; that, by the stronger everywhere destroying the physically weaker with a wonderful automatic action, all that is undesirable in humanity is killed out and all that is desirable remains. But is this so?

You say that, by this process through the ages of the past, all improvement and unfolding in life on the earth has taken place, and that nothing else is necessary to produce the fullest beauty, joy and strength for the race on earth.

But is this so? Has life on the globe or has mankind attained to its present position, low as that is in many ways, because the physically stronger has preyed on the physically, for the moment at least, weaker?

You say this is the great law of the survival of the fittest which leads to all beauty, strength and unfolding in sentient life; that to interfere with it in any way is to interfere with nature's one plan for attaining perfection.

You shelter yourself under the name of science. Are you not, and one-eyedly, perverting the teaching of great minds, as the priestly in all ages pervert and make falsehood of the perception of the great prophets who preceded them?

(She was whispering so loudly to herself that, in the next room, you would have thought she was speaking to someone beside her.)

You say all evolution in life has been caused simply by this destruction of the weaker by the stronger.

From every cave and den and nest, from the depths of the sea, from air and earth, from the recesses of the human breast, rises but one great 'No!' that refutes you. Neither man nor bird nor beast, nor even insect, is what it is and has survived here today, simply because the stronger has preyed on the weaker. The law of its life and its growth and survival has been far otherwise. From the time when, in a dimly living form, amoeba sought and touched amoeba, and, meeting, broke out into a larger form and divided into fresh forms, life has been governed, step by step, through the long march and advance in stages of life, by union; love and expansion of the ego to others has governed life. From the insect, following that unselfconscious reason we call instinct, who climbs to the top of the highest bough to fasten there her eggs where the tender shoots will first sprout to feed them, on to the bird who draws the soft down from her breast to warm the nest, who toils to feed and warm, and hovers about before the feet of the dangerous stranger that he may be drawn to attack her and not find her young, and who draws up the food from her own crop to feed them, till love becomes incarnate in the female mammal feeding her young from her breast – this is my blood which I give for the life of the world – through all nature, life and growth and evolution are possible only because of mother-love. Touch this, lay one cold finger on it and still it in the heart of the female, and, in fifty years, life in all its higher forms on the planet world would be extinct; man, bird and beast would have vanished and the cold dim dawn of sentient existence would alone exist on a silent empty earth. Everywhere mother-love and the tender nurturing of the weak underlies life, and the higher the creature the larger the part it plays. Man individually and as a race is possible on earth only because, not for weeks or months but for years, love and the guardianship of the strong over the weak has existed. You may almost estimate the height of development in the creature by the amount of mother-love and care he stands for.

You may say that mother-love forms an exception in the rule of nature, which, for perfecting life, demands the destruction of the weak by the strong. But what of the protective care of the male, not only of his own young and his related females, but of all the most helpless of his group? It is not only the sea lion who carries about his young in the bag on his own person; but through all sea life runs the defence of the weak by the stronger. Could the ostrich breed out its eggs in the wastes, where long journeys for food are needed, if the male did not daily take his hours of brooding on the nest to keep the eggs warm and care for and watch over the young with a tenderness even greater than their mother's while she goes afar to seek for food? Could the female bird of many kinds rear and feed her young without the continual aid of the male? Nor is it only parental sympathy, but a much wider feeling for the weak, which makes possible much of the higher animal life about us. It is not only for the defence of his own young that the old stag stands ceaselessly watching for danger and raises his shrill cry when he sees it approaching, at the greatest risk to himself. I have seen upon a cliff a baboon stand defending the one defile where dogs could mount, hurling them down with his hands and glancing back every moment anxiously to see how the troop of males and females carrying their young were escaping, clinging to his post till he fell torn to fragments by the dogs, saving his race and his species, not by his vast power of destruction, but by his willingness to be destroyed that others might live. The survival of the *mierkat*, so small and defenceless on the barren plains where so many other creatures become extinct in the presence of danger and of enemies, is accountable only when you know that each *mierkat* acts for all; not for their own young only, but for each other, and, for the younger and more helpless, all labour and sacrifice themselves. When the hawk approaches, if the older males and females be gone out far to look for food, tiny creatures, themselves hardly weaned, will seize all the tinier ones half an inch shorter than themselves and in desperate anguish strive to carry them off to the hole, forgetting all fear for themselves in their passionate attempt to save those who may have no blood relationship with themselves, while the older males and females grow gaunt and thin in the breeding-time, because almost all food they find is brought to lay at the feet of the young, while mothers go away to seek food which will supply the quite small with food. It is this passionate love for one another, this endless self-sacrifice of all, this devotion to the weaker by the stronger, which makes it possible for these little delicate furry creatures with their beautiful eyes and small powers of defence to survive in our terrible barren enemy-filled plains. The panther and the lion have vanished in the terrible presence of man, and many other forms of life grow very scarce, but these tiny creatures are still surviving, aided by their passionate devotion and self-sacrifice.

Then among men in their very struggles with one another, is it always the strongest fist and the fiercest heart which aids races or individuals to survive? Has not a great love lain behind those marvellous victories of which the world's history is full, where small and relatively weak nations and individuals have survived and driven back the large and powerful – a love for an idea, for a race, for a land, which, by blotting out personal considerations, has given weakness the power to protect itself and survive? The legend of the Swiss who gathered a score of spears into his breast, and so made room for his fellows to break the phalanx and win their nation's freedom, is only emblematic of one of the deepest-seated transforming and preserving forces in human nature. The legend of the mother, which in varying form almost every country possesses, who, to save her child from the bird of prey, climbed where the foot of the bravest and strongest could never tread, to recover it, is universal because it outlines the profound truth recognised everywhere that an almighty affection and the instinct for even self-immolation in the serving of others is not merely one of the highest but one of the strongest forces modifying human life. Almost everywhere in the record of human life on earth are the traces of rapine and slaughter and the suppression or destruction of the weak form by the strong; and they have left their marks not only in the heavy and to us hideously protruding jaw and beetling eyebrows of the male gorilla, dividing him from the more human female and young, but giving him that strength of bony structure which is necessary to enable him to rend and destroy; not only in the structure of the scorpion, all sting and tail, so loathsome from the human standpoint that, were it not that it bears its young about upon its back, it would seem so unredeemably repulsive as to be none other than a nightmare; but it may have given the springbuck her long graceful legs to flee from the jaws of her enemies, and have brightened the eye of the gazelle to see in the far distance the destroyer and to aid in its escape. It may even have rendered more intense some of the most complex emotions in the higher animal, because the species in which individuals were most inclined to defend the weak at their own cost may have survived where more purely self-centred varieties fell. It has played its part, and a vast part, in the history of life on earth. But to regard this destructive element in existence as the keynote to life on earth is a strange inversion. When we look from a hilltop on a herd of wild antelope on the plain below us and two old males come into conflict and desperately wound and perhaps kill one the other, the very fact that we are so struck by the incident and absorbed in watching shows it is not the universal, the all-pervading element, of the life before us. The care of the young by the mother, the drawing of sex to sex, the feeding together in good fellowship of hundreds of creatures – all this rouses no curious remark in us, because it is but of the universal substance of life that things should be so. To attempt to explain and sum up life by considering this element only is like the man who should attempt to represent a great musical symphony by playing its lower bass notes alone, like a man who should try to reproduce a great composer's masterpiece by striking all the discords in it without any of the harmonies into which they resolve themselves and with reference to which alone they have any meaning. From the mysterious drawing together of amoeba to amoeba, their union and increase, on through all the forms of sentient life, and in the life of the very vegetable world, the moving original power is always this stretching-out, uniting, creative force; shaping itself in the union of male and female, of begetting with their begotten; drawing together creatures of like and unlike kinds, bringing into all the forms of friendship and union and love, it lies at the root of existence; it shapes the petals of flowers, not for death but to call the insects to suck their sweetness and carry fertilisings to one another; it sings in the song of all song-birds calling to their mates; it blossoms into human speech; to kill, man might have been silent; but to communicate with and bind himself to his fellow, child to mother, mother to child, the sexes to reach each other, man, to reach man belonging to his social organism, man was obliged to blossom into speech. Everywhere this binding moving creative force moves at the very heart of things, growing more and more important and complex as the creatures mount in the scale of life, till it reaches its apotheosis in the artist, in whom the desire to create dominates all else, who, not from himself but by the necessity of some force within himself, is spent and must spend himself to produce that which gives infinite joy without ever being used up, over which there need be no struggle;

for not-seeing the statue or not-hearing the story or not-singing the song makes others poorer. Men have so recognised that this creative (and not the destructive) power was the fount and core of life that in all ages they have tended to call the highest intelligence they could conceive of, and therefore their supreme God, 'the great Creator'; and their devils have been destroyers. It is false to say that the mighty jaw and the almighty claw, and the stomach that is never filled and is always seeking to fill itself, are the fundamental moving power in life ...

> ''Tis love that makes the world go round,
> The world go round, the world go round!'

(She was speaking so animatedly now you could almost have heard what she said in the next room.)

But you may say that, granting love and self-obliteration in the cause of others plays a dominant part in the sentient life among kindred and groups, and that the mysterious instinct to create and continue to reproduce lies as the fundamental hidden power manifested in all we call life – granting all this, yet you must allow that, at least between species and species and distinct groups, a terrible conflict has always gone on, that this victory of the strongest jaw and the longest claw and the biggest belly has resulted in the survival of the fittest, and that, in the world in which this strife has gone on, we have many beautiful things – singing birds, flowers, the wonderful intelligence of man and beast – this has grown up under the struggle!

Yes, the struggle has gone on and the fittest have survived. The fittest? – to survive; not of necessity the fittest in any other sense in which we humans use the word.

The fittest has survived! Under water, half-buried in mud; only the outline of the jaw and two deep slit eyes show where the alligator lies. Age after age he has lain in the mud and slime. The gazelle has come down to the water to drink and has been drawn in by the mighty jaw; the little monkey, delicate, quick, high-witted, swinging from branch to branch and stretching its hands out to dabble in the water, has come too near, and the brown stump has moved and snapped it up; the human child has come to play upon the bank and disappeared; the young girl has come to draw water and only her broken pitcher has been left on the mud to show where she was drawn under; all have gone to fill the almighty maw and been crushed by the mighty jaw; the creature survives. In the ages which have passed since it came into being, many fair and rare forms have existed and passed out of existence. The little winged creatures with large eyes and brains, reptile in order but fitted for flitting in the air and sunshine, whose images we find impressed on the rocks, have gone; they may have had rare and beautiful colours for anything we know and may have had notes of song, but they are gone; fishes and birds and beasts that have been, have passed forever; even in our own ages lofty forms of life have passed and are passing away; but the alligator survives. Not because it was more fair, more beautiful, more complex, more brave, than the creatures upon whom it lived or whose stay on earth it outstayed, but because its long jaw set with serrated teeth, its dead, solid hide, its absorption simply in seeking food for itself, its torpid half-buried existence on mud banks and amid slime, fitted it to destroy the complex pulsating animals and to outlive the beautiful aerial forms which had not its almighty jaw and its mighty stomach. It was fittest to survive. The boa constrictor wakes in the morning, and before night bird and beast have been crushed in its mighty folds; it lies stupefied and torpid with the creatures it has consumed in its expansive inside. It has survived them, not because it was fairer or higher in the scale of being than they, but because so greasily and silently it could creep on them. The cobra strikes dead man and beast, and survives, not because she is braver or higher or even stronger, but because beneath that tooth she carries that little poison bag and strikes so silently and it may be in the dark.

If a ship full of poets and philosophers and men of science, bound for some distant place of meeting, were wrecked on the shore of Africa and a cannibal tribe met them, they would be consumed. The savage would rub down and oil his sides with the fat of the poet; the brain of the philosopher would frizzle before the fire; the cannibal's belly would be full of man of science and artist; in a time of famine the cannibal might survive and beget his kind, when a neighbouring tribe died out from hunger for want of timely poet and thinker! Would the fact that he had eaten poet and philosopher prove he was higher than the men who filled his belly and gave strength to his muscles? The fittest to survive – but the fittest for what else? Even when nation sweeps out nation, what does it mean? Is it always the loftier, more desirable form that survives? When the barbarian swept Greece till Athens was left like an empty and bleaching skull, is it certain that the savage was higher than the race which he supplanted? In nearly two thousand years in that land of blue seas and mountains, he and his descendants have produced nothing that the world prizes or desires. The fittest survived! – the fittest for what?

You say, at least it must be allowed that, along with this struggle among sentient beings and the survival of the strongest jaw and the longest claw and the biggest belly, rare and beautiful things have survived and are among us today?

Singing birds are with us, insects of beauty and colour, beasts of intelligence and heroic forms, and man, who, in spite of all, has instincts and powers latent within him of rare beauty, and strength, reason, imagination, sympathy and joy. Yes, this we have – but, oh, for the songs that will never be heard on earth now! – for the beauty we shall never see! – for the forms of light and glory which will never flit among earth's trees! – for the creatures of intelligence and complexity that will never tread earth's floor! – oh, the might have been, which is forever impossible now! Much has escaped – but, oh, for that which in the long, long ravening struggle of the ages, has not escaped from the strong jaw and the long claw and the poison bag! Oh, for the forms of life, perhaps higher than any we know or ever shall know, which in their very first incipience were cut away and made impossible forever! In this awful struggle (a struggle waged with no purpose of bringing the great and beautiful to life) what has been saved, we know; what has been lost, we shall never know. The gorilla and chimpanzee are with us; but what if, in some hidden forest, a yet more beneficent intelligent type arose, developing quite away from the predatory to a more social form, till, meeting with the stronger-armed heavier-jawed gorilla, it was exterminated, and one line of beneficent growth shut off forever? It is difficult to understand how what we call man ever came into being – the manikin thing with such small physical powers of defence and attack, whose young for years, in spite of mother-love and male protection, could so easily fall a prey to any wild beast, and who at its best is physically small and powerless – unless he first, for long periods, developed in some sheltered situations where attacks from predatory saurians or more modern carnivora were rare; but what if somewhere, it might be among inaccessible mountain peaks and valleys in the dim times when man was shaping, a branch existed in whom in time, having to expend no great force in purely predatory or physically self-defending directions, the germ of other faculties developed higher artistic and musical and reasoning powers, deeper and broader powers of originality, all that for the last many millenniums we have been slowly and with difficulty marching towards when the conditions of life lave allowed; if this variety ever were thrown into contact with a more gorilla-like form intent on destruction, it must have been swept away; that one act of destruction would have delayed the march of humanity for ages – nay, prevented it forever perhaps from attaining certain noble and to us desirable shapes.

If it were possible for us to land upon a planet in most things like our own and launched on its course with ours, it is quite possible we should find upon it a being as much higher, and from our standpoint more desirable, than our highest ideals are higher than our ourselves; our early stage of sentient growth might have been the same, and this difference, now so vast, might have arisen merely because, once or twice in the course of growth through the aeons, their highest intellectual and moral type might have escaped destruction by its lower. This is certain, that the lower and more brutal self which slumbers with each one of us today, with regard to which the chief difference between man and man is this, that one man's life is passed in submitting to it and another man's in struggling with and crushing it – this more brutal self, which the Christians have called inbred sin and all students of the human heart have under different names recognised – this body of qualities, which seems to some forever to limit human growth, so ineradicable and heavy in its weight it seems – has it not gained its strength and vitality, is it not still within us in such mighty force, because age after age not merely those races but those individuals in whom its existence was weakest have been killed off by the individuals most incarnate of the lower nature and not allowed to perpetuate themselves freely, either physically or spiritually? Lies are so easy to us because age after age the lying and subtle and insincere have conquered and crushed the individuals in whom sincerity and openness were budding. It is so difficult for us to consider others justly and impartially if they have terribly injured us, because age after age the individuals striking most mercilessly at whatever limited their pleasure, without consideration of justice or sympathy, have killed out and suppressed those in whom generosity and justice were beginning to dawn. Lust, divided from all love and inborn self-forgetfulness, is so dominant within thousands of us (making the world of sexual relations, which in our ideals are the highest, often the lowest, in life) because age after age the most brutally lustful has perpetuated himself, where the less lustful and brutal has failed to rape and force the woman or kill the opposing males. Because, age after age, the individual tendency to expend force in the direction of impersonal intellectual activity has again fallen victim to the individual more concentrated on personal aim, we today find the complex intellectual gift of the thinker and artistic creator so rare and so heavily conflicted with by the lower opponents. Because the stronger sex has so perpetually attempted to crush the physically smaller, the individuals who attempted to resist force by force being at once wiped out, sex has acquired almost as a secondary sexual characteristic a subtleness and power of finesse to which it now flies almost as instinctively as a crab to the water when it sees danger approaching, the struggles against which being the sternest that sex has to carry off within itself if it would attain moral emancipation. Because the larger male has so long and so mercilessly suppressed the weaker and exterminated those who refused to submit while the servile survived, we find perhaps that lowest of all human qualities, the material tendency to truckle before success and power, which in some humans seems instinctive and in them at least is ineradicable. For it is not alone through the physical destruction and annihilation of the weaker by the brutally stronger that we have suffered. What has humanity not lost by the suppression and subjection of the weaker sex by the muscularly stronger sex alone? We have a Shakespeare; but what of the possible Shakespeares we might have had, who passed their life from youth upward brewing currant wine and making pastries for fat country squires to eat, with no glimpse of the freedom of life and action, necessary even to poach on deer in the green forests, stifled out without one line written, simply because, being of the weaker sex, life gave no room for action and grasp on life? Here and there, where queens have been born as rulers, the vast powers for governance and the keen insight the sex possesses have been shown; but what of the millions of the race in all ages whose vast powers of intellect and insight and creation have been lost to us because they were physically the weaker sex, whose line of life was rigidly apportioned to them at the will of the stronger, which governed the structure of their societies? What statesmen, what rulers and leaders, what creative intelligences have been lost to humanity, because there has been no free trade in the powers and gifts of the muscularly smaller and weaker sex?

Therefore let no man lay the flattering unction to his soul that, by rushing out and destroying what is weaker than himself, or that, by using and bending to his own purposes all that live in the society in which he lives, he is thereby aiding nature in the great and lofty and perfect life on earth. The struggle between sentient creatures and the conquest by the most cunning, the most merciless, the most consuming, the muscularly or osseously stronger, has had powerful effects on the shapes which life takes on; it may have added to the keenness of the eagle's eye, the length of the springbuck's graceful bound; it may even have added to that intensity of anguished love which makes one baby *mierkat* try to drag a smaller away to safety when it sees the hawk approaching, because the little people have learned by a long racial experience what the claw and beak mean, and those who have loved and aided each other most have survived – the fittest to live, not the fittest to kill in that case! – it may have sharpened the wits of all creatures who had to escape, as the poison bag of the serpent teaches great caution in the country where it prevails (we always part the grass with our foot as we walk – though it might be just as well to walk without parting!); it has left many beautiful and curious forms of life, but has also destroyed many; it has nursed into being all the vices which lie deep buried in sentient life; it has age after age killed out among advancing human creatures the individuals who, to reason, love, or any of the impersonal ends of life, sacrificed the arts of destruction and self-defence; it has hanged its Christ and poisoned its Socrates; it has nurtured in everyone of us the brute which we shrink from in another when he turns it to us; it has killed out the winged reptile and a thousand noble, complex and brilliant forms of life, and has saved the crocodile and the python. The only strength which it directly preserves is predatory strength, strength of reason, strength of self-government, strength of affection, all the forms of strength most prized by the human creature as it advances, are not preserved of any necessity by it. The struggle between the forms of sentient life and action within a species, and the survival of those most fit to destroy, have no more made existence what it is than the road on a mountainside makes a mountain. It has modified, in some directions powerfully modified, the external forms of life, but no more made it what it is than a hatchet used to chop trees in an orchard makes the trees; the hatchet, wisely used or by accident so used, in lopping off certain branches may make the trees bear larger or more fruit; but used otherwise it may entirely destroy the tree, and, used recklessly and by chance, might cut down the whole garden. The process of pruning itself, however wisely carried on to produce certain ends, is an entirely subsidiary process, whose end, in increasing the size or abundance of the fruit, may generally be equally attained by manuring and feeding the tree; but it fails utterly to account really for the tree, whose essential life and essence lie in its power of growth, in the mysterious power of absorbing and adding to its substance in certain directions and along certain lines and of reproducing itself. All the pruning and cutting off in the world can never account for the fundamental mystery of one bud becoming a flower, for one grain of matter in the soil or particle of gas in the air being transformed into bark, for the kernel and reality of life. Pruning is a process which creates and produces nothing new, but which, wisely used, may tend to accelerate vitality and desirable variation; which, applied haphazard, may produce mixed desirable and undesirable results; and which, used unwisely, may mean absolute destruction. Therefore let no man lay the flattering unction to his soul that, by destroying all he can destroy, and using and consuming all he can use or consume, he is aiding nature in the only way possible in perfecting the human race on earth. Let him not imagine when he prates of the survival of the fittest that he is enshrouding himself and his desires in impenetrable armour; he is only an ass masquerading in the scientific lion's skin put on hind-side before!

You say that, with your guns shooting so many shots a minute, you can destroy any race of men armed only with spears; but how does that prove your superiority, except as the superiority of the crocodile is proved when it eats a human baby, because it has long teeth and baby has none? You say the fact that you can command the labour of so many of your fellow men and gratify your desires proves that you are higher than they; it proves that your belly is large and your power of filling it great; but what, in these matters, are even you compared to the old saurians with their vast claws and paws and rough tongues, who could have licked you off the face of the earth in a moment? The theory that humanity can be perfected on earth only by the stronger jawed, longer clawed, biggest bellied preying on the smaller is a devil's doctrine bred in the head of a fool.

But you may say: If the perfecting of humanity is not to be accomplished by this destruction of one part by the other, how then is it to be accomplished?

(She was walking very slowly now, and looking before her and saying nothing.)

Is it not possible only in two ways? Is there any hope of our in any way raising and hastening the rate of human advance if we cannot do it by the killing out and suppressing of individuals?

Surely there are ways. Has not the human only now, at last command of two vast means for the modifying of life and the conscious perfecting of humanity? In that strange and lovely power which enables us to see and picture that which we have not in all parts ever fully seen, in the ideals which are clear before the human spirit, have we not the goal to be moved towards? And in our powers of reason the means to find, step by step, the paths that lead to them, have we not now reached a plane of life, in which the struggle for existence that is to perfect human life need not in any sense be one between individual lives but between qualities within the individual – a struggle within each man to be fought mainly here (she raised her little doubled-up fist and laid it softly on her breast) – here, where alone each man rules omnipotently and where alone the kingdom of heaven on earth he dreams of can be brought to pass – here, where the ideal must be formed and realised, or nowhere? Has not the time come when the slow perfecting of humanity can find no aid from the destruction of the weak by the stronger, but by the continual bending down of the stronger to the weaker to share with them their ideals and aid them in the struggle with their qualities? Is it not by the passionate persistent determination to realise within ourselves our highest ideal, and then, by that strange power which makes every man's life unconsciously a voice calling to his fellows to follow, to be able to call on those who have not yet seen so far? Is it not so, and not in any other way, that the real blossoming time of man on earth will ever come? And no man liveth to himself and no man dieth to himself. It is not by destroying and crushing.

She was walking very slowly now, with her eyes wide open, but seeing nothing – then a picture leaped out before her mind that seemed to have no direct connection with the thoughts passing there: ...

She saw a great plain, and on it a woman standing, large and beautiful; a loose garment draped the lower part, but the great arms and shoulders were bare, and the long hair, turned back from the beautiful face, flowed over the shoulders; but the beautiful eyes were filled with tears and the forehead bent with pain. Beside it there was a great rush of wings and then another figure stood there, heroically large, half poised on one foot, as though just descended, and with wings half open as if ready for flight again.

She stood still. ... After a minute she turned to her desk and, leaning across it from the side, drew her book towards her and, opening it at the end, began to write quickly on the inside of the cover, the writing running diagonally across it: ...

'When the Spirit of the Ages, whose moments are millenniums, whose minutes are aeons, and whose hours are a human eternity, passed amongst the worlds of space seeing how it fared there, he chanced on a planet. A wide plain stretched there, no trace of plant or shrub was on it anywhere, and burning sands stretched everywhere; but far away in the distance rose mountains; on their sides one could see that streams flowed and that the earth was green and trees waved. Alone in the centre of the plain stood a woman's figure, bare and beautiful from the waist upwards, but clothed below in a coarse garment. Its eyes were fixed on the distant mountains; again and again as it looked it wrung its hands and tears streamed from the beautiful eyes. And the Spirit paused in its flight and lit on the earth beside her, and it cried, "Beautiful one, why do you stand here weeping alone in this desolate spot, where no fair thing is, and the snake has left its track in the sand at your feet and the only footprint is the mark of the wild beast's claw? On the mountains there is verdure; surely birds are singing among the trees and the grass is heavy with flowers; why linger here in this desolate spot?" But she wrung her hands and cried, "I cannot move; always and always I look out for one to come and deliver me and take me with him to the mountains, but he never comes." And he said, "Beautiful one, your forehead is high, your bosom is full, your arms are strong, your hands well knit; why cannot you move forward?" And she wept and raised the robe that was about her, and the Spirit saw that, while from the waist upwards she was fair and powerful, from the waist downward she was ill-nourished and loathsome. About, her feet were iron fetters, upon the limbs were marks of unhealed stripes, old gangrenous wounds festered there, and the flesh was shrunken from the bones and the feet deep sunken in the sand. And she cried, "My head is clear, my heart is sound, my arms are strong, but my feet, my feet, they bind me here! I wound and strike them, but they will not move; I bind them with chains in my anger. It is they, it is they, who keep me here!" And again she wept. Then the Spirit dropped his wing and drew nearer to her and whispered, "Despairing one, no deliverer will ever come. You, you yourself must save yourself. From those weak limbs strike off the fetters; with your strong hands bend down and heal the wounds your hands have made; remove the sand about the heavily sunken feet. When they are healed and free and strong, they, they and not another, will bear you to the mountains where you would be." And he asked her, "What is your name?" And she answered, "My name is Humanity." And he said, "When the years have flown I shall return again and see how it fares with you." And he smote his wings together and rose upwards: and Humanity was alone upon the plain.'

She wrote quickly across the inside of the cover; when that was full she went on the flyleaf opposite; then she paused a moment; at the head of what she had written she put as a title 'The Spirit of the Ages'. Then she drew her pen through the words as if not satisfied. Then she threw her pen down on the table. She looked round. All the room seemed strange; the old brown walls, the little bookshelves, the lamp throwing down its light on the worn leather cover of the desk, the old exercise book she had been writing in – they looked like things look when you come back from a long visit, when all about the house is strangely familiar and yet new.

She closed the exercise book and put it in the drawer. Perhaps some day the little allegory would enlarge itself and she would write it in fit words to make others see the picture. Probably she would never touch it again because it takes time to write things for other people. But the little picture she would never forget, because the pictures one sees are actual and one never forgets them. She walked to her armchair and sat down. She knew suddenly that she was very tired; she had been walking nearly three hours; but it was a delicious kind of tiredness, like one feels when one comes home from a long walk in the open air: as if something was resting by being used. She leaned back her head into the little dent. The rain was falling now in torrents. She leaned back listening to it. It was a delicious sound. It made her feel as though great strong arms were folding themselves about her, and a great strong hand were stroking her down softly. She lay still; but after some time she drew herself up and curled her legs under her, and turning sideways half buried her face in the dent in the chair's back. She tucked one hand under her cheek and after a while closed her eyes. Her thoughts ran around in a dreamy way now. How nice it would be to be a man. She fancied she was one till she felt her very body grow strong and hard and shaped like a man's. She felt the great freedom opened to her, no place shut off from her, the long chain broken, all work possible for her, no law to say this and this is for women, you are woman; she drew a long breath and smiled an expansive smile. Oh, how beautiful to be a man and be able to take care of and defend all the creatures weaker and smaller than you are. Then she dreamed away and half asleep made one of those little stories, 'self-to-self' stories, that she made as she was going to sleep, not for other people, too sweet and close, just for herself. She was a man, she thought, and she lived in a cottage about which there was bush and high forest, as at the old farm. It was night and she thought she was lying there and outside the trees were rustling as the wind moved them. It seemed she was lying on the earth, on mats in the hut, and beside her lay the woman she loved, fast asleep. She felt the little head on her shoulder, the soft hair against her cheek, and the little body within her arm; then she heard the wind blowing and the tree branches touching the roof as the wind grew strong. The little one beside her moved uneasily, and as it lay so close she felt the little body throb and knew it was the life within it that he had wakened. (She was him now, not herself any more.) And such a great tenderness came over him, and he drew her close and bound his limbs about her so that she was quite wrapped about, but the little wife upon his arms slept on, not knowing how she was loved. And then it was another day, and the little child was born so small and soft, and he held it in his arms and put his lips to its soft tiny lips (she felt the lips touch hers), and then he took it in both his hands and put it close into the little mother's arms against her breast and bent down over them, – and then it all shimmered away and she, Rebekah, was asleep.

She had slept peacefully in the chair for perhaps half an hour; the oil in the great transparent glass bowl of the lamp was burned down three-quarters of the way when suddenly she woke with a start and leaped to her feet. It seemed to her she had heard the front door close with a great bang. Perhaps it was her husband and Bertie come home; she stood to listen, but there was no sound of their voices. She was taking up the lamp to go and see, when she remembered it was the stable-boy's evening out, and that when he came back late he often came in at the front door instead of going round the back way to the yard where the servants had their rooms if he saw lights in the house. Still she took up the lamp; in the children's room they were all sleeping quietly, and when she went through her bedroom and the dining room into the passage she found no sign of anyone having been there, and went back to the study.

Her sleep had refreshed her, but left her stupid and dull. The rain had left off and there was only the sound of a few large drops falling from the trees over the house as the wind shook them. She yawned and stretched herself and sat down in the armchair again. She drew her workbasket to the side and put the lamp on the edge of the desk and went on darning the stockings that were left. She darned on mechanically, thinking of nothing much, but she remembered she must count the wash-clothes the next morning and ask the washerwoman about the three pairs of socks that were missing. And then she wondered whether she should mix on the sour dough now or leave it till the morning, and she decided to leave it. She watched the needle move in and out among the blue threads in the stocking almost without seeing them and was growing very sleepy again, when, just as she was darning the last pair, she heard a click at the gate and a step on the garden path that she knew was her husband's. She lit the fat-candle quickly and went to the hall to meet him. He was hanging up his cap but had still his greatcoat on.

'Where is Bertie?' she asked.

'That is what I wanted to ask you. Hasn't she come home?'

'No, I've not seen her.'

'I suppose she has. I went to have a round with some of the young ones in the back room; and a quarter of an hour ago, when I wanted to leave, I went to look for her and couldn't find her. The curious thing is she left her walking shoes and cloak and all behind her. But no doubt she's here all right.'

Rebekah turned down the side passage from which Bertie's room opened, and her husband, still in his greatcoat, followed her.

She opened the door and looked in. 'She's here,' she said. She walked in, shading the light with her hand. On the large old-fashioned four-poster bed which stretched right across the end of the room, so that there was just space for a person to stand at the foot, Bertie lay asleep. She was still in her ball dress, lying on her back in the centre of the bed, with no pillow under her head and with one arm thrown across her forehead. The train of the white skirt hung wet and draggled with mud against the white quilt. Rebekah stepped to the bedside, shading the light with her hand that it might not fall on Bertie's eyes. Frank stood beside her.

'What on earth made her run off like that? She was dancing hard when I left the ballroom.'

Rebekah gave him the candle to hold and stooped down to put a pillow softly under her head.

'What a magnificent creature she is,' he said. Her right arm was stretched at her side, and the great white rose, partly faded, was fastened at her breast. 'There's not another woman like her in the Peninsula, not in South Africa! And so unconscious! That's what men like. Young Smith came twice to talk about her to me this week. Did I think she'd ever change her mind and have him!'

He expanded his chest, his white shirtfront showing between the parted edges of his overcoat. Rebekah was smoothing the pillow.

'Women think,' he said importantly, 'that men don't see through them when they ogle and flirt and try to captivate every fellow they meet; but we do! That style of woman's all very well to dance and flirt with, but when he really wants a wife and means to settle down he looks for something different!'

Rebekah had gone round to the foot of the bed and was kneeling down, taking off the little drenched white satin slippers. 'What can have made her run home in these things?'

'Now I knew what I was about when I looked out a certain little woman!' he said, still holding the candle and smiling down. 'There were half a dozen damsels in the Peninsula thought they were quite sure of me, but I knew where on a certain farm in the Karoo a little woman was to be found who wouldn't always be running away to balls and croquet parties to flirt with other men and forgetting all about her husband and house – and a nice pretty little woman too.'

Rebekah had risen to put down the damp shoes and stockings she had drawn from Bertie's feet; he chucked her softly under the chin with his two forefingers as she passed him. 'Wouldn't take "No" for an answer, either! Smart fellow, eh? Knows what he wants when he sees it!'

Rebekah knelt down to cut off with the scissors from her chatelaine the wet draggled end of Bertie's train; if that were taken off she would be dry enough to sleep on till morning without harm, and the dress would never be any good again.

Frank had had three glasses of champagne and was in a good humour, exceedingly pleased with himself. He was an abstemious man; he took care never to allow himself more than was good for himself in the matter of drink or any other personal indulgence. Only twice in all their married life had Rebekah really seen him the worse for drink; once when he returned home at four in the morning and said he had been kept sitting up at his office to make up his books, and once on another occasion. He could drink several glasses without feeling them, but champagne always had an expansive effect on his nature, making him more sunny and talkative.

'I knew very well whom I was going to have,' he said, looking down appreciatingly at the bed where Bertie was lying and Rebekah was kneeling cutting off the train; 'ever since that day on Table Mountain when the rain came on and a certain little woman covered the lunch basket with her own waterproof and saved us from going home hungry, while all the other girls came running up to the rocks for us to help them up into shelter, timorous little darlings. I held a sunshade open over the head of one and gave her my hand, but all the while I was looking at a certain little woman down below tucking the covers in, with all the rain streaming off her. Oh, men aren't such fools as they seem.' He laughed. 'I'd always had a fancy for her since she was five and used to fight like a tiger-cat if I wanted to kiss her – "I don't love you! You're ugly! Go away! Don't come near me. You horrid, ugly, cruel boy!' He imitated the shrill agonised voice of a child, and laughed. 'But that day decided me.' He was holding the candle a little crooked.

Rebekah had heard that story often before; it was one of those he often told in expansive moods. She had even heard him tell it to the men in the billiard room when they were praising her milk punch.

'She looks pale,' said Rebekah, rising. 'I hope she wasn't ill.'

'Ill – you should have seen her dancing! A freak, I suppose, to come home like this in the wet. You can't account for a woman, my dear. I've found that out long ago. Haven't I been married seven years!' He would have touched her under the chin again but she had turned to the wardrobe to get a shawl to put across Bertie's feet. 'Is supper ready? They had good wine there, but really nothing fit to eat.'

'Yes, I got it ready before you left. You'll find the matches and lamp on the sideboard as you go in.'

He put the candle down on the dressing table and went out whistling one of the tunes they had danced to.

When he was gone Rebekah bent down to cover Bertie's feet. She stroked them softly with her hand. They were pink and dimpled as a baby's, such tiny feet for such a big woman. Then she covered them up carefully with the shawl, turning up the damp edge of the dress that it might not touch them. She put a candle and matches on a chair at the bedside, that Bertie might find them when she woke, and then she took up the light and went to the dining room.

Her husband had taken off his greatcoat, and sat at the head of the table, in his white shirt front and beamingly contented face above it.

'Won't you sit down and take some too? This *bobotie* is excellent. – No, you won't? You've been off your feed the last day or two. – Oh!' – he looked up and laughed – 'I'd quite forgotten what you told me this morning! I'm to be the patriarch Jacob, eh? – "Now Jacob had twelve sons and twelve daughters" – or was it Job?' He laughed again. 'Take a little soda water? That's more in your line at such times, I think. – Who'd be a woman! – You're always a bit off colour the first month or two.'

Rebekah sat down at the side of the table before the glass of soda he had poured out for her.

'This cold *bobotie* is really excellent.' He helped himself again. 'Had some at Brownlee's the other night, such stuff! This just wants the very *smallest* touch of cayenne, though! Is there any on the sideboard?' She rose to fetch it him. 'Just bring me the brandy too while you are up – no – on second thoughts I won't; I've had enough. I'll have milk with my soda. Did the boy clean my fishing boots?'

'Yes, but he hadn't time to polish the billiard room floor. He'll do that tomorrow before you come back.' She sat down again at the side of the table and leaned her elbows on it. 'I don't know what's the matter with the girl. She leaves all her work for him and me. And she was so good when she first came. I liked her better than I ever liked any servant before. She is so strange now; she knocks against me in the passage, though there's plenty of room to pass. She is so rude to me, as if she hated me. I can't understand it. If I ...'

He interrupted her quickly; 'I'll change my mind and have a little brandy if you'll bring it me; just a tiny drop. Pour it out for me, one dessertspoonful – so! Pure soda isn't good to go to sleep on, except for a little woman in a certain blissful condition.' He laughed more boisterously than there seemed need. 'Isn't that the baby crying?' he said.

She listened. 'I can't hear it!' But she rose and took the candle and went to see if it were all right.

He finished his supper in silence; then he rose and paced the room twice; then he stopped at the window that looked out into the back yard, and drew the blind a little aside, and looked out; but there was nothing to be seen except the dark. Then he turned down the lamp and went to his dressing room.

Now, what really happened to Baby-Bertie was this:

When she and Frank got to the house where the party was to be held they found it brilliantly lighted up, the garden and veranda full of Japanese lanterns, and light streaming from doors and windows, through which came the sound of music, for dancing had already begun.

A little sitting room on the right of the entrance had been turned into a dressing room, with a large mirror and dressing table, and Bertie went in to take off her wrappers. Behind the dressing room was a small bedroom, where the maid put away slippers and cloaks of the guests as she took them. Bertie could hardly wait to take hers off when she heard the music, and as there was someone using the glass she did not even look at herself before she hurried across the hall to the dancing room. Most of the dancers were youths and girls under twenty-one, with a few of older growth. Near the window to the right as she went in stood the daughter of the house whose birthday it was, with two other young girls and a young man. As Bertie walked up to them the two young girls turned away, but the daughter of the house accepted her congratulations, and the young man spoke to Bertie. Then two men, who had seen her coming in, came towards her from opposite sides of the room; the one who reached her first asked her to dance with him, and soon she forgot everything but the light and the music and the delicious whirl as she danced. As soon as one dance was over someone asked her for the next. Sometimes one of her partners suggested that they should go and sit on one of the closed-in verandas and talk and rest, but she always said she would rather dance. She had one dance with Frank, about eleven o'clock. He liked to dance with her, partly because he liked her and partly because he knew they looked well dancing together and men envied him his pretty sister-in- law.

After that, he had gone to the back veranda to have a smoke and to chat and romp with the younger girls from twelve to sixteen, who had gone there to play round games because there was no room for them in the dancing room.

And Bertie danced on.

Once in a dance, as Bertie passed a girl she knew, she smiled and nodded to her; but the girl seemed to be looking the other way and did not notice her. The rain poured, and left off, and poured again; but she heard nothing of it as she danced. By and by, as the band was playing a very fast waltz and she was whirling round and round with it, someone trod on her dress. The white gauze which covered the silk skirt tore from the waist to the bottom and the long gossamer flounce made a streamer behind her. She caught it with one hand and holding it together laughed and nodded to her partner, and ran away to the dressing room.

There was no one there now. She stood before the mirror to examine the torn skirt; then she began taking pins from the plate on the dressing table to pin it with. She began at the waist and pinned downwards. The throb of the dance was still in her feet. The rain had left off, only the sound of the great drops falling from the eaves and the branches of the trees outside interfered with the sound of the music which came loud through the two closed doors:

> 'Oh the torture and the anguish
> That cannot follow thee,'

the band was playing. She hurried to get back. She had to bend down very low at one side to pin on the flounce, so that her head was halfway to the floor; then, amid the music she heard the sound of voices talking in the little bedroom at the back where the cloaks were stored. She paid no attention to them but hurried on, her face pink with bending so low in a sideward position. Suddenly a name struck her – it was Rebekah's. Two old ladies who had brought three young daughters had gone to the little back room to be out of the way of the noise and dancing and were talking together. The noise of the drops falling from the eaves and the music and dancing prevented her hearing all that was said, but she heard part. 'It seems strange she should have been asked,' one said. 'Yes, but – the invitation three weeks ago ...'; and then the music broke in with a particular loud burst – 'to bring her here among our innocent young girls!'

Bertie kept on pinning; she heard 'she' and 'she says' and 'to her'. Then she heard Rebekah's name again; and then – 'but perhaps her sister did not know.'

Bertie was motionless with a pin in one hand, her figure still half bent down over her dress, but her head raised to listen.

She heard Mrs Drummond's name, and then – 'It was her schoolmaster.'

Quickly and noiselessly she raised herself; she dropped the pin softly on to the floor; she looked round the room with her deadly white face.

If she went out by the door that led into the hall, someone would be nearly sure to meet her. Again she looked round the room. There was a large French window at the side of the room which opened in the gable into the flower garden and shrubbery. It was low, and was hooked open two inches to let in the air. Softly she unhooked it and turned it back. It made no sound; she stepped out through it. Below was a bed of rose bushes; as she stepped into the bed of rich soft mould her feet sank almost ankle deep into it. She turned and closed the window softly, and with difficulty drew her feet out of the wet earth. She stepped into the gravel path. All the Chinese lanterns had long gone out with the rain, and the shrubbery was quite dark; she walked through the bushes, keeping away from the house and near the wall till she came to the gate. She opened it noiselessly and shut it again. She was now in the great avenue. She caught her skirt and threw it over her left arm, and began to walk quickly. The drops from the trees as the wind shook the branches fell on her naked arms and shoulders and ran down her back. She began to run; the skirt slipped from her arm and the train bellying out behind her whipped through the puddles of mud and water, drawing up the sticks and dead leaves. Faster and faster she ran. She turned into the next avenue. At last she was at Rebekah's gate. She opened it softly and crept up the little gravelled path to the steps. She could see there was still a light in Rebekah's study; it was shining through the window on the plumbago hedge at the end of the house. She stole up the steps and across the veranda and turned the handle of the front door without a sound; but, as she turned to shut it from the inside, it slipped from her wet fingers and closed with a loud noise. She stood still listening to hear if Rebekah was coming, but there was no sound, and she turned down the side passage and went into her own room and closed the door behind her.

She knew there was a candle and matches on the dressing table, but she did not light it. The large four-poster bed stood across the end of the little room with the window opening over it at the side; at the foot of the bed there was just room for a person to get in between the bed and the wall. She crept in and knelt up, pressing her face against the wallpaper. The old, old, terrible feeling had come back, the feeling she had lost for so many years; it was here again. Something following her, following her, following her! She pressed her face closer against the wall and folded her arms over her head. She felt as if everything in her were pressing down, down, down. It was so nice to press in there between the wall and the bed, it seemed to hold one up. If only one did not feel so cold. The cold seemed to break out from her heart over her whole body. She did not think of anything particular; she only felt so cold.

After a time she began feeling faint kneeling up there; she crept into the bed. She threw herself down on her back in the middle of the bed. After a time the faintness seemed to get better and she fell into a heavy sleep. It was so that Rebekah and Frank found her when they came into the room.

After Rebekah had covered her and left her, she slept on for a long while, a heavy, motionless sleep. Then, suddenly, she began to move restlessly and to moan. She was having a dream. She thought she was in a great round theatre like a circus; it was filled from floor to ceiling with seats which rose tier above tier over each other, and all were crowded with people. She was sitting halfway down on one side. In the circle in the centre of the theatre there was white sand scattered, and women in white dresses were dancing there, and all the crowd were looking down at them, and she looked down too. Then suddenly she noticed that the people were not looking at the women any more, they were all looking round the theatre as though they were seeking for someone; and she looked about too, to see what it was they were looking for. Then she noticed a man on the other side of the theatre just opposite her, with a great red fat face, who rose from his seat. She felt a kind of horror when she looked at him. He rose from his seat, and pointed with his great red fat finger, and cried, 'That is she!' And all the people from the floor to the ceiling rose to their feet; and still the man pointed with his forefinger and cried, 'That is she!' Then she looked round also to see who it was they were looking at – and then, suddenly, she knew it was herself they were looking at! Tier above tier, all round that vast place, the faces looked at her, and the man pointed with his red forefinger, and cried, 'That is she!' A cold sweat broke out on her (in truth it broke out on her as she lay on the bed); she tried to slip down between her seat and the one before it and hide, but she could not move. She seized the back of the seat before her with both hands and tried to force herself down, but she could not stir; she was as if fastened to the seat. And from floor to ceiling the faces looked down at her; she saw her father and her mother there and the old farm servants: old Ayah and a little yellow shawl over her shoulders, and Griet looking from under her arm; there were all the men she had danced with: high up near the roof she saw John-Ferdinand looking down at her and Veronica standing just behind him, and low down she saw Mrs Drummond with a lace handkerchief at her lips, looking at her. Everyone she had ever known was there. Then suddenly it seemed as if the white dress of one of the dancers in the circle below got torn; a long white trail hung down from it, and as the dancer swept round and round it grew longer and longer. It skirled as she whirled, it bellied out and out at the back and grew fuller and fuller; it frilled into soft billowy waves and passed over the heads of the dancers, filling all the circle below with a sea of misty white; it rose higher and higher, unrolling and unrolling; it came to the place where she sat; it passed her and rose to the ceiling and they were all suffocating. With a wild cry Bertie sprang up, struggling; before she knew where she was she was standing on the floor with the cold perspiration streaming down her, and the four-poster iron bedstead still rattling. At first she tried to remember how she came to be standing there in her clothes on the floor in the dark, and could not; then slowly she remembered everything.

Without lighting the candle she undressed, dropping her clothes on the floor where she stood. She felt for her nightdress and crept into bed; she drew the cover up high over her head. Yes, the old, old feeling she used to have at the farm had come back to her; something following her, following her, following her, and everything in her sinking down, down, down! She drew one of the pillows from under her head and laid it against her, and folded both her arms round it and pressed it to her as if it had been a person. It comforted her a little to hold it so close; it seemed to prevent that sinking feeling. She tucked the cover in tighter over her head. If she could only keep everything out.

When she woke the next morning it was already late; she could see by the lines of light through the venetian blind at her bedside that the sun was shining, though the room was still darkened with the drawn blind. Rebekah had evidently been in early, for a tray with biscuits and coffee, which was now cold, could dimly be seen on the chair at the bedside. Bertie lay still. It pained her to see the light coming in under the bars of the blind. If it could only always be night and one would never need to see anyone.

Then she heard the sound of steps coming up the gravelled path; she half sat up and raised slightly the corner of the blind; but it was only the butcher's boy coming for orders, whistling. She let it drop again. She could not bear people to come up the path.

After a time she got up and sat down in her nightgown on the floor at the side of the bed and began in the semi-darkness to put on the stockings Rebekah had put ready for her beside her boots. Slowly she drew one on; then, before she had gartered it, she drew up her knees and folded her arms about them and leaned her forehead on her arms. She sat so motionless she might have gone to sleep again.

Then suddenly she sat up and began to pull on the other. 'I will go to Aunt Mary-Anna,' she said. 'I will go to my Aunt Mary-Anna!' She began putting on her boots and lacing them up in the darkness. Her lips were puffed and her face a little swollen. There was a dull, obstinate resolution in it; the only form of strength her face ever wore. This Aunt Mary-Anna was a sister of her mother's and of Frank and John-Ferdinand's father. Many years before she had come out to visit her sister, and at the old farm had met a young man from the next town whom she had married. Later they had moved to a small town farther up-country, where her husband was a general agent, and where two daughters had been born to her, who were several years younger than Bertie. They had been sent to England now for some years to finish their education, and she had written many times to ask Bertie, who was her godchild, to come up and stay with her while they were away. But Bertie had never wished to leave the old farm till she had left so suddenly with Rebekah. Now it came to her suddenly that she might go to her aunt's; it was so far away from everywhere. She pictured to herself the long miles of rolling Karoo, the rocks and *kopjes* and sand and whole mountain range that lay between it and anywhere. She would go first by train and then by post-cart – on, and on, and on; she would have to go for days to get there.

'I must go! I will go!' she muttered, as she laced her boots in the half-dark, with her lips heavy set.

When she told Rebekah of her plan, Rebekah was not surprised. The little mother was always writing to ask when she was coming home, and it would seem a step on her way if she went to her aunt's, which was somewhat nearer the old farm than Cape Town. So Rebekah helped her to pack her things. She could not leave the next day as she wished, because she had to catch the post-cart which only travelled once a week; but three days after she left.

As she was so busy packing, Rebekah did not wonder she went to say goodbye to no one. There would not be room in the post-cart for all her things; so Rebekah hung her evening dress and smart gowns in the wardrobe in Bertie's room, where she would find them when she came next year to visit her again. But Bertie knew she never would.

CHAPTER EIGHT

You Cannot Capture the Ideal by a Coup d'État

It was four months now since Bertie had left. Spring had come; the oak trees had broken into their delicate spring green; the arms of the dark fir trees were sending out pale shoots at the tips, and near the old summerhouse in the pine-woods, where Rebekah loved to walk with the children, the ground between the pines was carpeted with bluebells, and under the pines themselves the smell of the needles was sweet.

In two months her child would be born, and she was busy making clothes for the other children to wear in the months when she could not do much more than look after the baby. She never went out anywhere except to the pine-woods; and if people said anything she never heard them. Bertie wrote to say she was happy at her aunt's, and her mother had written to say she might stay there till her cousins returned from their school in England.

And Rebekah was happy. It was one of those peaceful, halcyon times that come in life, when the absence of new daily recurring matter of pain makes possible that up-springing of joy which only that which morning by morning tramples it down can permanently keep out of life.

She was happy when she kneaded her bread or mixed the salads in the pantry, and when she sat at work at the children's clothes; it gave her exquisite pleasure to see the great streaks of yellow afternoon sunshine lie on the carpet, and at night it was a pleasure to lie awake and hear the branches of the trees move against the roof.

Her husband was more at home than he had been since they were first married; he stayed at home, not only when it was necessary to eat and sleep, or when men came to play billiards, but often without need he came home an hour earlier than usual from office and when she came back from the pine-woods with the children she found him in the rocking chair on the veranda with a magazine or paper in his hands, smoking and smiling contentedly. And on Sunday he would stay at home the whole morning, looking at the roses in the front garden or the fernery on the back *stoep*, or going round to the stables to look at his horses, or would sit in the shade on the back veranda, reading.

Perhaps life would always be so peaceful and beautiful now; perhaps all the struggle and anguish was passed; all things have to come to an end, and why not sorrow too? If one walked on silently, would not everything come right at last? She sometimes even wondered if she had not fancied that life was so hard as it had been in the past, and whether she could not have made things clearer. She was like a donkey who, having drawn a load to the top of a hill, when it goes down the other side for a little way thinks it must have been all a dream that there ever was a hillside. She was quite contented; she wanted nothing more. Even the Coloured servant girl was not quite so rude now, though she was dull and silent and would do little work. Rebekah had hired her for a year from her mother, a respectable woman on a mission-station, and it was as though she feared being sent home to her and forbore to press things too far. And the Black boy whom they had had since they were first married, and whose only regular work was to attend to the stables and yard and to his master's boots and fishing-tackle and guns, showed a particular kindness and would, when in the kitchen, help her lift a heavy pot, clean the kitchen window and weed her garden without being asked. Sometimes she fancied she caught him looking at her almost with a pitying, questioning look, which she fancied must be because he realised that physical work was unusually hard for her.

In the branches of the oak tree that grew in the yard and overhung the house, two small birds had made their nest. She had watched them carry on the first sticks and straws for the nest; now the little hen was beginning to sit for a great part of the day and her mate carried scraps of food he found about the yard and garden to her. In less than a month the little ones would be out. When she woke in the early morning as she lay in her bed and the sun had just risen, she could see clearly printed against the window-blind the shadow of their two little figures as they walked up and down on the top cross bar of the veranda or sat close together on it. In after years she knew how closely she had watched those little birds, because the memory of that time never came back to her without those two little shadows on the window-blind.

She had no time to write in her diaries because when her work was done she had to lie down and rest; but, lying on her back under the pine trees or at night when she could not sleep, she read a great deal. She had got a book about lichens and roses, and she had collected some from the roots of the fir trees and the thatch of the roof and from under the rose trees in the garden, and found them all beautifully different; she had examined them under her microscope, which she had not touched for years. All the little things of life were of much interest to her again; almost as they had been when she was a little child.

One Saturday evening Frank came home earlier than usual; before ten o'clock he said he would go to bed as he was starting at sunrise for a fishing expedition to a place beyond Simon's Town. Rebekah had packed his lunch basket, it stood ready in the hall beside his rods and tackle, so she said goodnight and went to her own room. She slept in the children's room now on a little bed between the eldest boy's and the baby's, because, now the new child was coming, she slept badly and moved from side to side when she was asleep and Frank said it disturbed him to have her in the same room. So she slept in the bed of her second little boy, who now slept in the bed in the corner of his father's room.

After she had lain in bed for some time reading, she put out the light and tried to go to sleep; her husband had already put out his; she could see there was no light from the crack under the door between the two rooms. At first she felt very sleepy, but the sense of weight and physical discomfort would not let her sleep; she moved from side to side. At last she piled the pillows up under her head and lay in a half-sitting position with her arms crossed over her head. She was more comfortable so. Her thoughts did not run in that clear ordered fashion in which they follow one another when one lies awake, simply because the brain is too busily secreting to rest, but in the disconnected way in which pictures and sounds succeed each other automatically when one is really very sleepy. She thought of little household things; she saw pictures of them, saw the kitchen shelf with the row of tins on it and the dust she must dust off tomorrow, saw the large bag of wash-clothes she must count; then she saw the little cups of moss she had been looking at under her microscope that day, so delicate and so minute the naked eye could not see them; then she saw a place in the *kloof* on the old farm deep up in the bush where some trees were growing which were covered with long hoary moss hanging down like rough hair; there were two kinds; she wondered if they were male and female of the same species, or distinct species growing side by side, because the conditions suited them both; she wondered why she had never examined them and thought she would if she ever went out to the old farm again. Then she saw the place nearby, in the bed of the mountain stream, where the great rocks were piled up and the Kaffir-bean trees hung over, and where Frank had lifted her down once; she seemed to feel his strong firmly-fleshed hands holding her as he lifted her down and his eyes with a beautiful intense light fixed on hers. It made her heart, the heart of the little tired pregnant woman lying there, beat when she remembered it, as the heart of the young girl had beaten. Then her thoughts went to the man in the next room lying there on his side, with his soft light hair pressed to the pillow and his strong shoulder showing above the cover. A great tenderness swept over her as when one thinks of one's little child, as if all the heart were being drawn out of her to him. The beautiful boy, the father of all her children! It rose and surged through her, the old wave that so often, through years since their marriage when he was away from home, had made her rise suddenly at night and fetch his overcoat and lie sleeping with it in her arms, with her face pressed to the collar where his neck had been, which came to her often in the night while she lay awake beside him and which, as she listened to his even breathing, made it seem to her the most precious thing in life – a wave that swelled and swelled till it filled her with a confident hope, and she knew when he woke there would be a new heaven and a new earth for them both. Tonight she only felt a great wish to be near him, to slip her arm under his and wind it softly round his waist – just to feel him and hear him breathe. She lay still for a while, then she got up softly; she could go in softly without making any noise and creep into bed and lie down behind him and put her arms around him without waking him, and, when she felt she was getting sleepy, she would creep back to her own bed. She had done it more than once already without waking him. She opened the door of the next room and closed it softly and slipped across the room with her bare feet; she had no slippers on, for fear of making a noise. The room was quite dark. It was a large room, looking out into the backyard, and in the far corner stood the large four-poster bedstead; near the window, close to the door by which she had entered, stood the little bed in which her second boy was sleeping.

She knew the room so well she felt her way without any difficulty to the side of the bed in the far corner; she put out her hand softly and touched the quilt at the foot; she felt upwards; it seemed to be thrown back; she felt higher; the bed seemed to be thrown open and no one there. She took a match from the box on the stand at the bedside and struck it; the bed was open; there was a dent in the pillow where the head had been, and when she put her hand down on the sheet it was warm. The match had burnt out, and she dropped the end on the floor. No doubt he was gone to the stables; he told her that, on several nights lately, he had to get up because he heard the new stallion fighting with the other horses in the stable; and the Coloured boy, though his room opened out of the stable, slept so soundly that he heard nothing. Rebekah hesitated; she thought she would climb up on the bed and wait till he came, but he was always angry when he had to get up at night, and it might displease him more if he had to talk to anyone. She turned to go back to her room. As she passed the bed of her little son her feet caught in his down quilt which had fallen on the floor; then she stooped to pick it up and pushed it in round his shoulders; then, as she was tucking it round his feet, she paused a moment and lifted the corner of the blind to see if she could see her husband. It was a dazzling moonlight night; all the veranda that ran along the back of the house and the half of the yard covered by the oak tree was in deep shadow, but over the rest of the yard the moonlight fell in a sheet of white light from the moon almost overhead. The stones in the gravel of the yard glittered; on the opposite side of the yard the rough-cast whitewashed walls of the servants' rooms and the side of the stables seemed to radiate light; even the green window shutter and the door of the servant-girl's room seemed almost black in the intense light. The outline of the oak leaves at the tips of the branches was printed in shadow on the gravel almost as sharply and exactly as at midday. Not a breath was stirring. Everything seemed to glint. Then she saw in the door of the kitchen, which formed a wing at the end of the veranda, her husband standing. In the shadow of the veranda she could see him in his grey dressing gown near the stand of ferns. Then, instead of walking across the left of the yard towards the little side passage into which the stables opened, he came straight along the veranda. Just as he came opposite the window at which she was standing he stooped and took off his slippers; he carried them hanging from the first two fingers of his right hand; he moved in past the window of the children's bedroom, and then at the end of the veranda turned up, keeping near the wall in the shadow of the oak tree; then he turned again and came out into the full moonlight, just beyond the oak tree's shadow, and stopped opposite her, before the little green-shuttered window of the servant-girl's room. He glanced back at the house quickly; then softly, with the tips of the two forefingers of his left hand, struck two short blows on the wood of the shutter which covered the glass of the closed window; light as the taps were, Rebekah heard them; she saw his white naked feet on the gravel and the moonlight on his fair hair. Then the door opened; and she saw him bend his broad shoulders and bow his head a little as he stepped down through the low door. Then it closed. She looked at the gravel glinting in the moonlight and the whitewashed wall, that seemed almost to throw out light at her. Whether she stood there for fifteen minutes or for twenty or for half an hour, she could not tell; a cold blast was blowing on her and froze her; then the door opened and her husband came out. The moonlight fell full on his face. He glanced at the house, then walked quickly straight across the yard to the kitchen door. Rebekah loosened her fingers from the blind, went slowly into the next room, the door closing itself behind her, and dropped on the little bed.

At half-past four all was quiet in the house; the dawn had not yet begun to make the darkness paler along the horizon.

Rebekah sat in her nightdress in her study with her head resting on the edge of her desk. In the transparent glass bowl of her lamp the oil was almost exhausted, as though it had burned all night. On the floor beside her the waste-paper basket held pages of paper, wholly or partially covered with writing and then torn up. At her elbow lay an envelope addressed to her husband. She sat as if asleep, but the slight irregularity of her breathing told it was not so.

When the first grey dawn was beginning to make a clearer line along the flats and even there among the trees to make the darkness less intense, she rose and took up the letter and the lamp and went into the children's room. Her teeth were chattering slightly with the chill of the morning. She opened the door in the left-hand corner of the room which led into her husband's dressing room. It was in a way the pleasantest room in the house; a large double bow window looked out into the front garden; before it stood a dressing table with a large mirror and her husband's shaving materials and silver-backed brushes arranged upon it; before the dressing table on a chair hung the clothes she had put out the night before for the day's excursion. At the back of the room was a door that opened into their bedroom, his and hers, where he lay sleeping. She put the lamp down on the table and stood for a moment with the letter in her hand. At first she laid it down among the shaving things upon the table; then she took it up and fastened it with a breastpin from the cushion on to the breast of the coat that hung over the chair. Then she took up the lamp and went back to the children's room. She was shivering violently now. She put on her little blue dressing gown and her red slippers and lay down on the stretcher between the two children's beds. The lamp, which was exhausted, flickered and she turned it out. She lay listening, but her teeth chattered. After it might be fifty minutes she heard the door from the bedroom into the dressing room open and shut. She hardly breathed; then she got softly up from the bed.

She walked up and down the room. Her steps were noiseless but her breathing short and quick; it might have been heard in the next room. Suddenly she stood still before the door; there was a sound of water running loud in her ears. Then she opened it and went in.

Her husband was standing before the dressing table in his trousers and shirt. He had just blown out the two candles by whose light he had been shaving. The blinds were drawn up to the very top; enough dawn light came in to make everything clear. He was running a red necktie under the soft collar of his flannel shirt. He raised his chin to run the knot of the tie up. Beside the shaving case on the table lay the letter with his address upon it.

She stood by, breathing heavily. She moved her hand towards it.

'You've seen it, haven't you?' she said almost thickly.

'That! – oh yes! – certainly,' he said slowly – 'but you don't suppose I'm going to get up at five o'clock in the morning to read letters?' He raised his chin higher and looked into the glass. 'Horrid little spot this – just in the very turn – always seems to catch the razor!' He dipped his finger into a silver-topped salve pot that stood open and put a small touch on the spot.

'I knew you wouldn't read it now,' she said hurriedly and softly. 'I wrote on the outside you must take it with you and read it today on the beach when you have time – between the fishing.'

He turned his face partly away from her, still appearing to look at the spot with an absorbed interest. 'Really, Rebekah,' he said quietly, 'I thought you'd become more sensible! What on earth should I read letters for from a person who is living in the same house with me and whom I can see every day! There are going to be a lot of people there and it would be very nice for me to be sitting there all day reading a letter from my wife!' He put on the lid of the salve pot with an exaggerated slowness.

Rebekah stepped forward suddenly, her hands knit in each other.

'Oh, please read it! Please, my husband! Please! I've sat up all night to write it. I had to write it! – Oh, please – please! I haven't meant to hurt you; I've tried to be gentle! – Oh, please, please! It's something I know! – Oh, please, please read it!'

With his face still partly turned away from her as if he were looking for something on the table, he said, 'Now really, Rebekah, this is too bad! You've been so decent and sensible the last few years, I'd thought you had given up this kind of thing. You, the mother of three children and on the point of having another, to go on in this nonsensical way!'

He sat down on the chair and began to tuck the bottom of his trousers into his boots. 'No, I'll *not* read the letter; and I shall *not* take it with me!'

'Oh, please read it! Please read it!' She looked at him with distraught eyes; then she knelt down between his knees and looked up at him.

'Oh, please, please, my husband! I sat up all night to write it! – I will go mad if you don't! – I can't bear it any more! – I can't – I can't – I can't!' She beat with her hands softly, softly, up and down on the grey trousers that covered closely his powerful legs on either side of her; they moved up and down so fast they seemed at last like butterfly wings fluttering; you could hardly see them. 'Oh, please, my dear husband, please!' Her eyes, as she looked up at him, seemed not to see him.

He looked down at her, doubtful just what line to pursue.

Then he shook himself roughly free from her and stood up. 'Really, Rebekah, you shouldn't make such a damned jackass-fool of yourself! – It's Mrs Drummond, I suppose, you are jealous about again – with her false hair and false teeth and eyebrows getting darker every day as she grows older. It's ridiculous! It's ridiculous!' He knew he had hardly spoken to Mrs Drummond for three months, and was glad to turn matters in that direction. 'I simply won't come home at all if I'm to be met in this way.' He turned and seized his Norfolk jacket from the chair. 'You've seemed so awfully sensible the last years! I thought you had got over this idiotic tom-foolery.' He spoke a little more gently.

She had risen and stood looking at him with her arms crossed above her head.

'Please read it! – Please read it!' she spoke in a low almost inaudible whisper; 'I sat up all night to write it! – I haven't slept – Oh please – please help me! – I can't – I can't – '; she beat her head softly with her two hands.

'Then why the dickens don't you sleep! If you choose to sit up all night making an ass of yourself, is that any reason you should come here howling to me? "You know, you know", – some nonsense you've trumped up. If you don't care anything for me or yourself, you might at least think of your duty towards the child. It can't be very good for you to be going on this way.'

'The child – oh, the child – my duty towards the child! – I – don't – do – my duty – towards – the – child!' She raised a long low cry, like a stricken dog. She turned away from him.

He seized her arm. 'Look here, Rebekah, be silent at once! How dare you make such a noise in this house!' His anger was not assumed now, it was real. 'Do you want to wake the children, and have them running in to see what's the matter? If you've no sense of right, or shame, or decency left in you, please remember I have. You are not fit to be allowed to have children at all if you conduct yourself in this manner!'

He took up his thick gloves and the little case with extra fishhooks and thrust them into his coat pocket.

She stood looking at him silently with her arms still folded over her head.

'I hope you'll be a little more sensible when I come back; you're acting like a mad woman now!'

He turned to the door at the back of the room, banging it to behind him so that the wall seemed to shake. She heard him shut the bedroom door in the same way; then for a little while he was in the front hall taking up his fishing rods and the luncheon basket; then she heard him going down the garden path, the footsteps she knew from all others in the world, that she had spent so many scores of hours in her life in waiting for. The gate closed. Then in the avenue, just outside the gate, on the other side of the tall plumbago hedge before the window, someone met him.

'Where are you off to so early?' The voices raised in the still damp morning air came clearly into the room.

'Going fishing. And you?'

'Off for a tramp; getting too stout. Were you at the club last night?'

'No; I came home early. Had business.'

'You didn't hear the latest, then?' The man's voice sank; then she could hear, as she stood there, only a scattered word here and there as they spoke. It was evidently some club story. Then a thick, jovial guffaw of laughter burst from her husband.

'Well, see you tomorrow.' She heard him laugh again as he walked one way and the man the other.

She stood still. The dawn light was coming full into the room now; soon the sun would rise. She looked at her letter lying on the table; she took it up and twisted it slowly with both hands till it was a stiff twisted roll. She walked into the children's room. The back veranda and the oak tree made it still almost as dark as night there. She walked to the stretcher and lay down on it on her back, the letter still clasped tightly in her hand. It was so early that not even the bread and milk carts had begun to go up and down in the avenue. There was dead silence. Presently the birds began to twitter in the oak tree outside. She lay with wide-open eyes looking up as the dark shadows of the rafters in the ceiling became slowly visible. The letter was pressed by her hand against her body.

After a while the youngest baby woke. He raised his head and called imperiously to be taken into her bed to play, as was the custom. Finding no one took any notice of him, he laid it down again, and lifting his small legs into the air began to play with his toes.

What the letter, which Rebekah held twisted in her hand, contained was this:

My Husband,

You must read this letter. I am writing it in the night. I know what has happened tonight. I know where you have been. Do not think that it is because of this that I write.

We have lived together for years now, and we have never spoken the truth to one another, nor opened our hearts; yet we are bound together; and all we do or think reacts upon the other. You know that when I have tried to speak to you of our relationship you have silenced me. And when I have written you have not read or have not answered what I wrote.

But tonight I *must* write; and you *must* read what I write.

I love you my husband. Oh! I have loved you so, you – [This sentence she had scratched out so that it was not legible, and went on.]

In the years before we were married, when you were asking me to marry you, and after we were engaged, I never doubted your love for me. My fear was always that I could not love you with a love as great and intense as yours. If there was any absence of truth and openness between us, I thought it would rise from my nature. Your frank, careless nature seemed to me of necessity more truthful and beautiful than mine, which was more reserved and perhaps complex. Those letters you wrote from England and after your return from the last voyage seemed to wrap me round with a flame of love.

Even now I wake in the night sometimes and the cry from them seems to come back to me, 'My one love, my own love, my only love – come to me!' and sometimes I seem holding your letter in my hand in the garden under the pear tree, and reading, 'My Queen, my Queen, I need you! I need nothing but you, my love!' – and, when you have wondered why I have suddenly put my arms about you in the dark and crept close to you, it has been that cry I have heard call me. It has been possible for me to go on living during these last years because I have heard it. When I have felt my self-respect dying, and a leaden humiliation of despair creeping over me, that has saved me. I want you to know that, whatever has happened in the years since we were together, or whatever may happen in the years to come, I never have doubted, and never shall doubt, the truth of your love for me then.

When we had been married two days, I knew I had been mistaken in thinking my love for you was not great enough; it rose in me as a wave that swept all, even my old self, away before it. When we had been married six months, to cook your food and listen for your step coming up the gravel path, to watch you sitting in the armchair to smoke, made the world quite beautiful to me. I had only one regret – that I had not accepted you when you first asked me, so that we might have had the years together which I wasted away from you.

'When you went to dinners or dances I wanted to go too, because it was beautiful to see you walking about and talking to the other people, and at night the happiest time of all was when I lay awake and heard you breathe close to me.

After we were married you began to express your love less to me in words and caresses; but that seemed to me so right. When you are seeking to make your love known you must speak of it even in crude language; but when union is complete then the silence of fellowship and trust expresses it. When I felt the need of laying my face against your knee if I were sitting near you, or something compelled me to stand behind your chair and touch the little curls at the back of your neck, and you were seldom impelled towards me in the same way as you were before we married, I thought it was because your deeper man's nature had not need for these small forms of expression when the central union was there.

Even afterwards, when you went for a day's fishing or to a dance or dinner and suggested it might be better for me not to go too because I had a baby coming, or afterwards had it to nurse, I never thought you did not want me; I thought you were afraid I might get tired. And even once or twice when you had decided to go to a place and I said afterwards I would go with you, I thought it was because you felt I was going for your sake.

Never, for one moment, in all that first year and a half, did it ever once come within the range of possible thought to me that you did not love me just as you had. It would have been as mentally, I might almost say as physically, impossible for me to have doubted your loyalty or dreamed that you had put another woman in my place, even in your thoughts, without telling me of it, as it would be for me now, if one of my little children climbed up in the chair behind me, to dream that it had a knife in its hand and was going to run it in under my shoulder blade and stab me to the heart.

There are things one cannot think.

If you had been surrounded by all the most beautiful, all the most talented, all the most brilliant women in the world, it would never have struck me to fear them. What could they all be to you compared to me; I was your nearest, I was your dearest – I was your wife!

As I have never suspected that my feet were trying to fling down my body, so I had never suspected any hidden thought or act of yours.

You may ask, did I not know that sometimes after men and women had married they might find they had made a mistake, that, however loyal and true was the love they had given, they might find some human creature who might have been more to them than the one they married?

And I answer, yes, I had thought of this; it had seemed to me the great attendant tragedy that waits on human marriage. It was because of this fear that, passionately as you drew me, I wanted two years before I gave myself to you. For I said always, 'Can I give him that love which is forever till death without possibility that another shadow may fall on it and darken it?' And it was only when the greatness of your love and your need of me had burned away all doubt of myself that I gave myself to you. Even if the thought of that shadow had come to me after we were married, which it never did, I should not have feared you, for I should have known that, if either of us saw such a shadow approaching, we would have gone straight to the other and laid all before them for advice and help; and I had never doubted that two souls true to each other would have found a way to the light. But after we were married no such thoughts ever came to me.

But, you may say, did I not know there were men and women to whom marriage was only a form, who freely entered on a lifelong union meaning some day to violate it, and who took the soul and body of a creature into their hand meaning to betray it?

And I answer, yes, I knew that there were such things, as I knew there were thugs and assassins and slow poisoners and professional murderers, – but that such things would ever enter into my personal life and play a part there I had never dreamed.

I have always known there were octopuses in the sea with tentacles twenty feet long which, if they caught you, would drag you down and absorb you; I have always known that there were somewhere in the world basins of boiling mud into which if a man slipped suddenly he would be swallowed up, and that sometimes there were rifts in the earth in which whole villages and cities disappeared; but I had never thought, when I was walking alone on the seashore, that a tentacle might stretch out and drag me down, or when I was walking among the Karoo bushes that a basin of boiling mud might appear before my feet and I slip into it or the earth rend open and swallow me.

These things I knew existed somewhere in time and space – but what were they to me?

I knew of them as I knew that there were women in the streets of great cities willing to sell their bodies, and men prostitutes who fell so low that they bought them (I had even shuddered walking down a street thinking I might without knowing it have passed such an one!); I knew of them as I knew there were shipwrecks in northern seas, where men and women with frozen hands clung to spars and masts till slowly the frozen fingers relaxed their grasp and they fell back with a thud into the sea; I knew of these things, but that they could ever enter my life, or had anything personally to do with me, I had never for one moment supposed. For me, personally, they had no existence.

I knew you were friendly with many men and women; and I liked to see you with them; you always looked to me like a great blare of sunshine among dull uncoloured masses; when I saw you dance or talk with other women, how happy they must think me to be part of you.

When you introduced me to Mrs Drummond I rather shrank from her because she seemed to me cold and narrow, but I knew she had come out in the same steamer with you and had been very kind in helping you to buy the furniture and get the house ready for me, and I tried to be polite to her as I was to all your friends. I was glad she could play your accompaniments and when you practised your parts in the choir; and as you both sang and went to the same church it seemed most natural and right you should walk home with her; and I was glad you had her croquet parties to go to next door, just as I was glad to economise that we might have money to build the billiard room, because both made life pleasanter for you. I knew you admired her dress; I who hardly ever notice dress admired it too, but I did not think you liked her even as well as most of the women we met, for you often said small slighting things of her that you never said of them. If anyone had said to me that you loved Mrs Drummond as well as half the tip of my little finger, I should have laughed, because you and I were one in a living circle; outside was all the world we loved and liked and helped wherever we could – but it wasn't us.

You must please forgive me for taking so long to tell you this, but we are talking now for all the rest of our lives and we must understand one another. You can't if you don't know how happy I was then.

Oh, please give up just one morning to reading this; it's for all our lives.

Do you remember that night you went out to the whist party? I was going, but you said it was damp and might rain and I must run no risks while I nursed, so I stayed at home. I sat sewing in the dining room till half past ten; then, though I knew it was early, I went and sat in the rocking chair on the veranda that I might hear your steps when you came. I had not sat there ten minutes when I thought I heard your steps coming down the avenue. No one else could have heard them, but I always did even from the corner. It seemed to me your steps stopped at the gate next door, and that I heard it open and shut; it was such a still dark night one heard everything very clearly. I thought you were taking the short cut and coming across the lawn and through the rose-hedge gate, and I went down to meet you at the gate, but as I walked I fancied I saw the figure turn up and go towards the other side of the great house. It was so dark one could only see very dimly, and there was no sound on the grass. I thought you were going to the door on the other side of the house, and no doubt were going to fetch the music you had lent Mrs Drummond to copy two days before. I was standing at the gate, when I saw against the yellow silk blind of Mrs Drummond's little drawing room the shadow of your shoulders and head. You were taking off your coat. Then I knew you must be going to practice the music with her and could not be back directly. At first I felt inclined to run over and sit there while you sang, but I never liked going to Mrs Drummond's; and it was drizzling, so I went back to my needlework in the dining room.

It was a little after half past eleven when I heard the front gate in the avenue open and your steps coming quickly up the path. I ran to the front hall. You were just going to take off your coat. You kissed me, and said you were rather late, but you had tied, so you had to stay and play a deciding rubber. Your face was flushed as if you had been walking fast. I was helping you to take your coat off, and I said, 'Wasn't it strange? I thought I saw you going up to Mrs Drummond's more than an hour ago.' You pulled your coat out of my hand and turned round on me and said, 'So, you go peeping, watching me in the dark!' And I laughed; I thought you were playing with me, as you often did then. I caught your arm to lead you in to supper, and said, 'See what I've got for you.' You threw my hand off so that I almost stumbled against the other side of the passage. I still thought you were playing, and I tried to catch you again, laughing.

Then you said, 'I suppose you fancy I am always running after other women; and you do nothing but pry, and try to find out! – I haven't seen Mrs Drummond since the day before yesterday when she came to fetch the music!' I looked up at you and saw then you weren't playing. You said, 'That's what comes of being eaten up with jealousy! You are making an idiotic fool of yourself!' and you walked towards the dining room; and then I knew you meant what you said. Frank, I walked after you, but I didn't know what I was doing. It was as if each word you said was the blow of a great iron bar falling on my head. All the words you said to me that night start out at me even now sometimes in the middle of the night when I wake suddenly; and sometimes when I am busy with my housework I suddenly hear them ringing in my ears. I ran into the dining room after you and tried to put my hands on your shoulders and ask you what it was, but you shook me off you. You said many things. You said I thought you went to service only to walk home with Mrs Drummond; you said I followed you everywhere; you said I even asked the servants about you! Oh, Frank, Frank! I couldn't say anything, I could only look at you. You said you wouldn't have any supper and you went into the bedroom and banged the door. I ran to the door to go in after you, and then I couldn't, and I ran out into the front garden and walked up and down in the drizzle. I didn't know what it was, or what I should do. Afterwards I saw you through the window come out of your bedroom and sit down to eat your supper. I wanted to run in and beg you to tell me that you had never said those words – that it was a horrible dream, but I couldn't. Afterwards you went back to the bedroom, but I still walked for a long time. Afterwards I went into the house, and then I wrote a letter to you. You see, what had stunned me was that you had thought it possible for me to doubt you. I told you I couldn't, I didn't. I told you how I had trusted your love, and I begged you to forgive me if I had ever done or said anything that made you feel I doubted it. Of course, when you said you had been kept playing, I knew I had been mistaken and that it must be another man. I told you that, wherever you went or whatever you did, I could never doubt you, that I know your nature was much nobler and simpler than mine. I begged you to forgive me for anything I had unconsciously done.

When I knew you would be fast asleep I went into the bedroom and put the letter on the stand beside you. I thought how you would open it in the morning and read it and turn and take me in your arms and lay my head upon your shoulder and tell me you would never think I doubted you again, and explain to me how it all happened. I lay awake at your back all night waiting for the morning, but just when the dawn was coming I fell asleep. When I woke it was not late, but you were gone and the letter was gone too. I got up quickly and put on my dressing gown, and went into the dining room. You were just finishing your breakfast. You got up and kissed me and said you had had something to eat as you had to catch the early train, and began to take up your things. I put my hand on your arm to say something, but you said you had to go at once, and you kissed me quickly and went. When you were gone I saw my letter, torn very, very small, in the waste paper basket by the fireplace. I couldn't understand it that you had not spoken to me of it. I thought perhaps your heart was still too sore; and yet you did not seem bitter, you looked just as always. Though you had kissed me so quickly, you had been kind to me, even more kindly than sometimes. Then I remembered I had heard older women say that no woman understands what a man is till she has been married for some years; that unmarried women never understand men. I thought that perhaps, though you had forgiven me, the pain your man's nature had felt as though I had mistrusted you was so deep you could not speak of it as a woman would have done. I thought of my father; but he was always silent and reserved, and you spoke always to everyone you met about everything. I thought of the silent agony you must have felt all those days when something I had done had made you think I doubted you, showing no sign at all, and I felt I must learn to understand you. The only thing I could think of that might have made you think I mistrusted you was that I always stood waiting at the door for your steps when it was time for you to come home. You had liked it when we were first married; you called me your little watching bird. I thought that, when we were both in bed that night, I would creep very close to you and ask you in a whisper to explain to me what I had done. That couldn't hurt you. I walked up and down a long time thinking; then I stood at the table, breaking some biscuit into a basin for the baby's breakfast before I went to dress, when the servant opened the door; she said the servant girl from next door wanted to see me. I told her to bring her in. She came and held out her hand with a little twisted bit of white paper in it; she gave it me. She said she had picked up what it held when she was sweeping the floor of her mistress's rooms just now and thought it belonged to you. I opened the paper; inside was one of the gold sleeve links I gave you on your last birthday with your initials and mine on it. The night before I had put them into your white shirt ready for you before you went out to play whist. I gave her some money, and then I mixed the baby's food and gave it to the girl to give him; and then I walked up and down with the sleeve link in my hand, and then I went to your dressing room. Over the chair was the shirt; there was a link in one sleeve and none in the other.

Perhaps you will find it hard to believe (I can hardly believe it now), but in the white daze that came to me when all the world seemed to have worn away from me, though I knew you had lied to me, the only feeling I had was that in some way I must so terribly have made you misunderstand me, that you could not pursue a simple kindly human relation without having to lie to me about it. In my darkness all I could think was that you had noticed my cold shrinking from Mrs Drummond, from the first day I met her, that you had attributed it to resentment on my part to your politeness to her, and that you had in consequence felt you could not go to see her openly but had to hide it from me. I can't understand it now, but that was how I felt. I resolved that, by great kindness and politeness to her, I would show you that I have never misunderstood your friendship for her. I remembered that, though you had often spoken slightingly of her, you had always wished me to go to see her and invite her to our house. At once I sat down and wrote to her. I told her I was going to shop in town that afternoon and asked her if she would come with her work and spend the afternoon at my house so that my baby would not be alone with the servant. It was the first favour I had ever asked of her, and I thought she would understand what it meant; and I resolved to stay away till long after your time for returning. I sent the note over with the largest bunch of roses I had ever cut from my garden, and when her answer came I spent the morning making tea cakes for her and you while I was away. It seemed to smooth my brain.

I went in the afternoon and I did not come back till long after I knew you would be home, so that you might have a long time with her. When I came home she had gone, but you had brought two men for dinner with you. You seemed in very good spirits; after dinner you sang comic songs in the drawing room, before you went to the billiard room. It was nearly twelve when they went. I thought you would say something to me; but you said you were dead tired, and you got into bed at once when you came from your dressing room, and lay on your shoulder and closed your eyes, and I could say nothing.

The next morning when I kissed you in the passage before you went out, I asked you if you had read the letter. You laughed and chucked me under the chin, and said, 'Don't be a silly little woman, don't be a little fool,' and hurried out. And I saw you did not mean to speak of it; and I could not.

I noticed that you did not go over to Mrs Drummond as you usually did; and she did not come to our house; but I sent her cakes and flowers; and I knew one day you would take me to you and say, 'I know you have always trusted me, little woman,' and then my heart would rest. But while you held me from you I could not speak.

One day I sent over some flowers to Mrs Drummond, and the servant said she had gone to Somerset Strand for a holiday and would be gone some time.

I think she'd been gone about two weeks when the post-boy brought the letters to the door. We were at breakfast, and I went to fetch them; I saw the top one was addressed in Mrs Drummond's handwriting to you at your office, and had come by mistake to the house. I passed it to you across the table. I didn't wonder she wrote to you; I knew you did all her business for her; and there were many things she might write about. You glanced at the first sheet and said she wanted you to pay some accounts for her; and you put it in your pocket. Then you took up a half-sheet that had been enclosed. You began to read it; then you said, 'Oh, this is some woman's business for you,' and you passed it on to me. It was marked PS, and began, 'Please tell your wife there is a woman here who makes very good *ingelegte vis* (pickled fish) if she wants any;' and then she went on to give the price and to say how she packed it in stone jars which had to be returned to her when they were empty; and then without any break went on, 'Tomorrow will be the 27th of January, that never-to-be-forgotten and best and dearest of all days of my life which first brought you to me. Do you remember?' – Then I read no more. I handed the sheet back to you. You took it, almost without looking at it or me, and tore it up and threw it into the waste paper basket behind you. Then you stood up and gathered the rest of your papers together. You didn't notice me. Then you went out; I didn't go with you to say goodbye at the door. I only sat. Then I heard your feet go down the path. And then an impulse came on me to stoop down and gather together the bits of paper in the basket and piece them and read them. I knew if I waited an instant I should do it. I grasped them up in my two hands and ran to the kitchen fire and dropped them in. I didn't want to know what more she had written; I wanted to forget what I had read. I held my brain stiff that I might not realise it. Only I knew that, from the moment I read the letter, there has always been a burning pain at my heart that has never quite gone and a weight that never was there before. All the day I worked and cooked to keep myself from thinking. It was only late in the afternoon that I was forced to see what the letter meant. I did not think for a moment you loved her or could have been physically unfaithful to me by so much as the pressure a hand, but I knew there was a friendship between you greater than you let be seen; that perhaps she loved you, and that it was your consciousness of this had made you fancy I mistrusted you. Further I would not look; I let down an iron door without a crack between that part of my brain which knew about it and the rest of my mind; and I worked without stopping. But I was conscious there was a deadened part of my brain lying behind that iron door all the while, waiting to come to life. I had talked so much to myself always about the duty of not shutting one's eyes to anything and facing all facts; and now I was trying to keep my eyes shut.

It was two days after that you said you had to go up to Robertson and Worcester on business and you would be gone five days.

For the first two days after you left I was busy; I turned the whole house out and had the yard and out-buildings cleaned. On the third day I got a letter dated 'Worcester' saying you would be back in three days.

The next day I was sitting sewing in the front room about ten o'clock, when a curious thing happened to me. I had had a restless feeling that I could not understand ever since I got up. But I sat sewing quietly. Suddenly a feeling came to me that I must go to Muizenberg. I had never been since just after we were married when you took me to spend a day there. I had never since thought of going there. Now, as I was glancing up from my work at the bees humming above amongst the flowers, it came, not as a desire, but as a pressing necessity, that I must go. I don't think I even questioned myself as to why I should go; it only seemed to me an imperative command: I must go. I had never taken a holiday by myself since I was married, nor ever left the house while you were away. I went to the back yard and told the boy to *inspan* the buggy and the girl to dress that she might hold the baby while I drove. I felt a kind of wild exhilaration and excitement upon me. It was only after we had started and driven some distance that it struck me how very strange it was we should be going. I thought the kind of excitement, almost fever, that was upon me must be a reaction from the many days I had been holding myself down so. Everything looked so beautiful – the green trees, the bushes with the sun shining on them. When we got to Muizenberg it was midday, there was a light southeaster blowing, the blue water was sparkling in the sun. At Farmer Peck's I told them to take the horses to the stable and feed them. They said their early dinner was over. I said I should go down to the beach for an hour and then return to have coffee and bread. But I asked them to show me a bedroom to lay the baby down in, as he had dropped asleep. They showed me into a little room, and I told the girl to sit by him till he woke and then bring him to the beach to me. Just as I was going out through the front room I saw hanging over a wooden chair near the door a cloak. It was of soft maroon colour and lined with silk and edged with fur. It struck me as familiar; then I recognised it was Mrs Drummond's. No one else in Cape Town had a cloak like that. A feeling of heaviness came over me; I did not want to see her on the beach where I had come to be glad. It seemed strange she would have come there from Somerset Strand. Then I saw, partly hidden by her cloak, on the same chair was a man's overcoat. I was going out when something struck my eye. Out of the pocket of the coat was hanging part of a blue silk muffler with white squares upon it. I stood looking at it. I gave you such a muffler at Xmas. In the corner I had worked initials in white silk. They were there. At first I seemed dulled. I couldn't touch them, I only stood looking at them. I only felt I wanted to creep away and hide. If the girl had not been there I think I should have crept into the bedroom and hidden beside the bed. It was only for a moment, and then the feeling came over me I must run out and look for something, I didn't say to myself what. I rushed out; I did not keep to the road; I almost leaped over the bushes and stones on the way to the beach, and all the time I was crying out aloud with my teeth tight, 'It's a lie! It's a lie! It's a lie! It isn't he! It isn't he!'

When I got to the sandy beach it was lying there all so calm and beautiful. Not the mark of a human foot was upon it, and only the great white seagulls were flying over the sea. I stood suddenly still as though a great hand were laid on my forehead. Had I been mad? It was all a dream!

I stood and looked at the sea and sand and the great white birds for quite a long time, and then I began to walk slowly to the part where the rocks lay. The tide was high and running softly in and out among them. I got to a little rise where the stones lay just below me. There was not a sign of a human creature anywhere.

Then quite close to me, just below, I heard voices. There was a large flat rock with the water washing round its base; on it lay a smaller rock and over the top of it I saw two heads of people who were sitting on the large rock and leaning back against the smaller. Of the head of one only a little black bonnet with an aigrette standing up could be seen, but I saw the felt hat and the row of tiny curls and the broad thick neck of the other. I could not doubt any more. She said something and then you answered her and bent your head a little and laughed, and then she laughed, that little snipped-off laugh I knew. I couldn't doubt any more. You could have heard me breathing where I stood, only the water ran in and out among the rocks, gurgling. If you had turned and seen me, perhaps all our lives would have been different, because I had lost all control of myself that day. I knew if I heard your voice again (my voice! – my voice!), I should shriek and rush down to you. So I turned and ran. I felt the one thing was I must escape. I gave the boy ten shillings to *inspan* quickly and I got the girl and baby. I saw the woman of the place standing in the door looking at me as if she thought I was mad. And then we started. We had the wind in our faces. It was the feet of the horses that saved me. They got wilder and wilder; they kicked up the mud and stones into the air. Sometimes as I looked from their heads I caught sight of their feet. I held hard; I didn't touch them, but they knew they had to go. When we had gone some way, some Coloured men working in a field ran out and tried to stop them; they thought they were trying to run away; but I shouted to them to let us go. When I got near to the suburbs a policeman came up and stopped me; he said I could not drive so fast among the houses. So I took the road down into the flats, and we drove round miles, but we got home at last. It was because they helped me that day that when last year you wanted to sell one of them who had broken his knees, I bought him from you and put him on my farm to do nothing.

It was three days more before you came home: I had had a miscarriage during

562

that time. The doctor said I was very ill, and when you came you only kissed me and went away, because the fever was high. They thought it was my body caused it, but it was my brain. I was in hell. Night and day I heard Mrs Drummond's laugh, and I heard your voice, that low voice I know, speak to her. It seemed as if I was gnawing my own soul. They said if I got out of bed and walked about I should bleed to death; and I sometimes felt I must get up and end it all. The third night after you came back I slept heavily, and when I woke in the dawn such a curious calm had come to me. You were sleeping in the spare room, and the nurse was lying in the bed in the corner. I began to think I could see things quite calmly and clearly, as though they did not concern me.

What if you loved Mrs Drummond? What if after you married me you found I was not what you thought, and she was the woman who could satisfy you? What if you had deceived me about her and your feeling for her, because your love for her was so infinite that you could not risk my knowing of your friendship?

If I had had a son and he had loved another woman not his wife, and he had come and laid his head on my breast and told me about it, would I not have sympathised with him and tried to help him to find a way that was truthful and open? And should I sympathise with you less and help you less, who were more to me than all the sons I would ever bear? I thought it all out in the dawn, and during the day I got a pencil and wrote to you. Oh, I know it was tender, because I felt to you then as I can't even now; I only wanted to help you and give myself up for you. I told you I knew you cared for Mrs Drummond, but I didn't tell you how I knew or what I had seen because I wanted *you* to tell *me* everything. I only told you that I knew you cared for her more than you allowed to me and that I did not blame you if, after you married me, I had disappointed you and you felt you needed her friendship. I told you that if you wanted to see more of her than you could as things were, I would go for a long visit to my mother with the children, and I would ask her to come and keep house for you while I was away. I should tell everyone before I went that I had asked her, so there would be no scandal; and if, when you had been with her two or three months, you wished then I would stay away forever, you could sue me to return, and, when I did not return, you could get a divorce, and no one would blame you. And then if you and she wished to marry I would write to her husband, and I would beg him to act as I had done, and make it possible for you to be happy together. I told you how much I loved you, but that the joy of helping you do what was best for you would cover my pain and heal it at last. Oh, I know I wrote tenderly, because I never felt so tender to my little baby when it lay sucking at my breast as I felt to you that day. Even to Mrs Drummond I felt no bitterness; if you loved her, why should I judge her! For three days I kept the letter in my breast, because I didn't think it fair to give it you while I was lying in bed, because you could not have spoken as you would. Even after I got up I kept it for three days. I always seemed to feel a hot place where it lay in my heart; I thought you would understand all when you read it.

I could not give it you myself, because my breath got so short when I came near you; so I gave it the servant to give you on Sunday morning while I was still in bed. After breakfast when I got up I went to the billiard room where you were practising with the balls.

I waited a little, and then I asked you if she had given you my letter. You said yes, and kept on playing the balls as though you had hardly heard me. I asked you if you had read it, and you said yes, and went on playing. And then I asked you if, when I went to visit my mother, you would like me to ask Mrs Drummond to come and keep house for you. And you burst out laughing; you said I must be very hipped to think of such a thing; that Mrs Drummond would run up enough bills in a month to run our house for a year; you said I must be completely hipped to write such nonsense. You kept looking at the balls as if all your thoughts were with them. You said I seemed to have Mrs Drummond on the brain; that the only excuse for me was that I was ill. You said that if there was only one woman in the world, and that woman Mrs Drummond, you wouldn't marry her. That any man who had the settling of her business for her, and the sending to England of cheques for her dresses, would have only one feeling about her and that was pity for her husband; and then you laughed again. You asked me why I wasted my time writing such nonsense, and you went on playing. And then it was suddenly as if something broke in me, and I lost my self-restraint. I cried out I knew you loved her, I knew everything; and I begged you to tell me the truth; and I threw myself down at your feet and I clasped them and I told you I was quite willing you should get a divorce from me, and I would go away and take care of the child and would love you all my life just the same, and I kissed your feet and cried out to you, 'please to tell me the truth,' and told you I loved you. I begged you only to speak the truth to me, nothing else. And then you pushed me from you and swore; you said I must be mad to talk such nonsense about a divorce and leaving you. You said even my illness did not make any excuse for my making such a miserable exhibition of myself, and then you went away.

You may say, why didn't I tell you exactly what I had seen and knew. Oh, didn't you see I couldn't? It was *you* who had to tell *me*! I would have taken your last chance from you! Would you have been any greater, would you have been any better, because I had forced your hand? Then I saw what you wanted was not truth between us, but just to be left alone to lead your own life.

I was ill and had to go to bed again; and you never referred to what had happened; and I never did. But you knew that, if you wished it, you could be free and that I would not keep you.

It was about two weeks after that that something else happened. I was about again, but hadn't done any work in my garden. I hadn't seemed to care what happened to it. But one morning the sun was shining and I had a feeling I wanted to put it neat. I took my mat and sat on the ground picking up the weeds and rubbish that had blown in. I was tired, and was just going back to the house, when I saw a quantity of dried leaves and bits of paper gathered among the forked roots of my large rose tree, and I sat down on my mat by it to clean it out. I was scratching the rubbish out with my fingers and the trowel when I pulled out half a sheet of notepaper yellow with the mud and rain and a little bit scorched at the bottom as if it had been thrown into the fire. I threw it down with the other leaves and rubbish before me, and then I saw my name on it. It was written in a clear round hand that I knew was Mrs Drummond's. It was a letter dated three months before, therefore before I saw you go to Mrs Drummond's that night. It began, 'My Friend' – but from what came next I saw it was to you. You and she had evidently been discussing me. She spoke of marriage generally, and then quoted with inverted commas what you had said about our relation to each other, even our physical relation. She began to comment on what you had said, then came the bottom with the last line burned off. I did not turn it over to read what was on the other side. For a little time I sat as if I was dead. Then I took my trowel and cut at it. I chopped and chopped it till it was the finest fragments; I chopped at it till it disappeared into the ground and there was not a sign of it left.

I had believed, older women had told me, that a man never talked of his wife to other women, that he might be unfaithful to her, that he might humiliate her into the dust at his own feet, but that, as long as she was his wife, he never allowed any other woman to speak of her, as long as she was a part of himself he put his hand out over her and covered her as a man covers the nakedness of his own body. I had never doubted it. I think it is because many women believe this that they stay on with men, when their hearts are breaking: they say, 'Am I not still his wife?'

Afterwards, Mrs Drummond came back and you never went to her croquet parties and seldom saw her. I knew it wasn't only when I was by you avoided her, because she often came over when she expected you would be home and seemed always restlessly looking for you. But oh, I didn't care; nothing mattered. When she looked at me there were little contractions in the inner corner or her eye that come to some women when they look at another whom they hate; but nothing mattered to me. I knew I would have given you up to her if you had really loved her.

One night I was putting the children to bed and you were smoking on the veranda with some men. I came to your dressing room to put your clothes ready for the next morning, and I could hear what was said. They were discussing Mrs Drummond. One man laughed and said she was ten years older than she professed to be. The other talked of her husband, and laughed about the way she always professed he was longing to come back to her, but he never returned. And you laughed and said you had heard she was bald at the top of her head and had two wigs, one to wear by day and the other at night, so that if she were taken ill suddenly no one might find out. And then you all laughed. Oh, don't think it comforted me to hear you laugh at her. The only thing that could have saved me would have been to believe you loved her with such a mighty passion that it swept all before it, even me! It made me see the thing I was trying to press from me with both hands that I might not see it. The less your love for her, the lower I fell, and you. Was it for this you had put me from you!

After that, when I was expecting Frank [her baby] I became very weak; the doctor said my heart was going, that I was bearing too quickly and working too much. Oh, it wasn't the childbearing or the work or the miscarriages; a woman can bear all and do all if the arms of a man are tight about her. I had loved so to bear for you and to work for you. Now nothing mattered; I couldn't read, I couldn't think! Oh, it isn't only the body of a woman that a man touches when he takes her in his hands; it's her brain, it's her intellect, it's her whole life! He puts his hand in among the finest cords of her being and rends and tears them if he will, so that they never produce anything more but discord and disharmony, or he puts his hand on them gently, and draws out all the music and makes them strong. Oh, it isn't only her body a woman gives a man – [This paragraph Rebekah had not finished and had scratched out.]

Some time after that, but just after Frank was born, you said you must go into town by the early train; you had always gone by the late one because you said you hated the crush of the business people and the children going to school; but you said you had more business. You always seemed angry and irritable if you thought breakfast would be late; I thought your work was troubling you. You seldom noticed me or the children, and seemed always absorbed. One night the girl was out, and I brought the tray with refreshments to the billiard room myself. One of the men was hanging up the rest as I came in, and his back was to the door; he was laughing, and he said something about 'that young *inamorata* of yours who is so faithful to you in the train'. He turned and saw me and took up his cue and began to play. I took no notice of what he said; I did not even know to which of the men in the room he was speaking. I took it as some man's joke; but afterwards I remembered.

One evening you decided suddenly to go the next day to Simon's Town, and you had some papers at the house you said it was necessary should be in your office the first thing in the morning. I said I would take them in for you, and you gave me them before you started in the morning in the leathern handbag you always carried with your initials on it. I thought I would make sure they were in time, and I hurried to catch the early train. I had just taken my seat in the carriage when a girl put her head in as if she were seeking for someone and went on. In a few moments she came past again, still looking in at the windows. She was just going by, and then it seemed she caught sight of something. She looked up at me and stared, and then, just as the train was moving, jumped in. She was a stout girl of about fourteen or fifteen, but wearing very short dresses and with a satchel of schoolbooks on her arm. She sat down opposite me, and as she stuck her feet out across the carriage you could see the great thickness of her legs. She had a great head of short curly black hair, very tousled and standing out at the sides, with a red jelly bag stuck on the top. She had large, round, dark eyes, and beautiful white teeth; and, though her mouth was very large, she would have been good looking if her round face had not been covered with pimples with little blackheads. As she sat opposite me she stared at the bag on my lap and then up at me; and then she tossed the end of the jelly bag from one side of her head to the other and stared again. I felt she was coarse and unpleasant, but I soon forgot about her. When the train got to Cape Town she jumped out and ran up the platform at once; when I came to the gate she was standing there watching the men from the smoking carriages as they came up. I passed her and went out of the station. When I was crossing over to the other side of the road I happened to look back and saw her standing before the station, staring after me. I hurried on to the office and forgot all about her. I gave the bag in at the office and went to Adderley Street to do some shopping. I had finished and was going slowly down the street to the station, when suddenly something struck my brain; it seemed as though a cold hand had grasped my heart, crushing the life out; in a moment I knew everything just as I know it now. I knew what the man meant in the billiard room; I knew why you went to town by the early train; I knew why the girl stared at your bag and at me. I had no ground for knowing it; one moment before I knew nothing, I was thinking of my purchases. It flashed out on me as a moving picture in a street flashes on your eye; you see all parts of it almost in a second. It was like when one makes a story; one does not think, all the characters flash out before you in a moment speaking and acting – you *see* them!

When you came back that night you were as usual, and the next morning you went to town by the early train. I tried all day to put the thing that had flashed on me away from me; I tried to say it was a fancy; but deep in my heart I *knew* it wasn't. You came back at midday for dinner because it was Saturday; at dinner you said I was looking very pale, and you said I ought to take the children and the servant and go into the pine woods for the afternoon; you said you were going to the flats to see a friend, so you would not be at home. I thought it kind of you to think of how I looked; almost gladness came to me. At three o'clock I took the children and the servant and went; you were still reading the papers on the front *stoep*; you said as soon as you had finished you were going and would lock the front doors; the stable boy was at the back and could look after the yard entrance. When we got up to the old summerhouse and had been there for some time the girl found she had forgotten the basket with the baby's feeding bottle, and I said

I would go back and fetch it. When I got there the stable boy was sitting before the back gate cleaning harness, and when I went into the house all the front doors and windows were locked, and I thought you had gone out. I had got the bottle and was just going out of the dining room into the passage that leads to the kitchen and billiard room, when I heard a noise of laughing and shouting. I went into the passage; at the far end the door of the billiard room was open and I saw two figures chasing each other round the table; the one seemed to me to be you, and the other the girl I had seen in the train. I walked straight down the passage to the door of the billiard room. You had caught her by that time; she was lying on the floor on her back; her legs were under the billiard table but her head out, and you were kneeling on the floor at her head bending over and tickling her. Your back was to the door. She was gasping with laughter and kicking with her feet against the underside of the table and crying between the gasps, 'You horrid man – I'll pull your moustache again – like I did the day before yesterday!' And you said, 'Will you! Will you! Will you!' and kept on tickling her. The soles of your feet were turned to me as you knelt, and I saw your beautiful broad shoulders and the curls above your thick neck as you bent over her. You said something in your soft thick way between your half-closed lips; only she could hear it, and she laughed louder. Then I turned and ran; I ran as I have never run in my life. I threw down the basket in the kitchen and my cloak caught the door and closed it loud behind me; I ran across the yard and up the side passage by the stable boy and up through the woods and up the mountain. I climbed and climbed; when I got to the blockhouse I dropped on my face, but as soon as I had breath I got up and I climbed till I climbed so high there were only the crags of the mountain above me where the gorge comes down to the silver trees. Then I lay on the ground. I was deaf and blind. I heard nothing to the outer world; only inside my brain I heard always – 'The father of your children! – the lord of your body! – the owner of your life!' When I called your name aloud 'Frank! – Frank!' – that was the answer that came back to me. All the time I ran up the mountain and all the time I lay there, the only thing I saw was your broad back and the curls about your neck and the girl's legs with the rim of the red flannel petticoat that showed as she kicked and laughed.

    When it was dark I felt my way down the mountain back to our house. It was half past eight when I got there, but you had not come back. I went to bathe the children. Afterwards you came in; you were very friendly and in high good spirits. You came into the bedroom and stood by the bath, and said how nice and fat the baby was growing, and squirted him with water; you didn't notice that I said nothing. But afterwards, when we were at supper, sometimes as you ate you glanced up at me from under your eyebrows; as if you had heard the door slam or the stable boy had told you I'd been home. You didn't say anything, but, just as you got up from the table, you half turned and said quickly, 'Oh, by the way, there was a girl here this afternoon, the station-master's cousin or niece or something of the kind. She had some lace her aunt had made to sell, and she wanted to see if you would buy it. I told her you were out and she must come again when you were here; it wasn't in my line!' and then you laughed your little laugh and went out of the room.

Perhaps you'll say again, why didn't I speak to you directly and tell you what I had seen? Oh, I couldn't, don't you see I couldn't! If you had sworn at me, and spoken as you spoke before, I would have died, and my baby was six weeks old.

The next day was Sunday and you stayed at home, and you played with the children. But I was in hell, wandering in the dark.

On Monday morning you went to catch the early train as usual. I was washing the baby; and suddenly the feeling swept over me that I *must* follow, that I *must* see you meet her. I hadn't a definite plan of saying or doing anything, just the feeling I must go. I laid the baby down on the bed and put on my hat and without dressing I ran down the avenue after you, till I got to the place where the second avenue turns to the station; then I stopped. An awful wave of humiliation swept over me, and I turned and came home again.

All the week you were the same as usual, only in better spirits; you sang and whistled more. Late the next Sunday afternoon you said you were going to visit a man and would go straight from his house to church and I need not expect you back till nine o'clock for supper. About an hour after you left someone came to say the old Malay cook we had when we were first married was very ill and wanted to see me. I went and stayed with her nearly an hour. When I came out it was beginning to get dark; so I didn't take the short cut through the woods; I went the long road past the station. When I got near the station it was almost dark; I saw, without noticing, a man's figure standing near a gate in a hedge in the road. It had never struck me it was you, as you had gone in the opposite direction. As I got nearer I saw in the dusk a woman standing inside the gate, leaning over it and evidently talking with the man. As I was almost opposite the gate on the other side of the side-road under the fir trees, I saw suddenly that it was you and the girl I met in the train. You were saying goodbye to her, and you had her hand; you were holding it between both yours, and you drew yours slowly and softly away till her hand fell, as you used to say goodbye to me at the farm. You turned away and walked slowly up the road in the other direction, and I took the turn towards our house. That night, when you had gone to sleep, I lay awake behind you, thinking and thinking.

It seemed to me I might have been unjust, in the bitterness of those last days. I had understood that you should love Mrs Drummond with her refined face and her graceful figure and her beautiful dresses and her many tastes in common with yours and her years almost the same. It had seemed quite possible to me you loved her with great love; I had been able to make so many justifications for you in my own mind – this had been so different. I had envied Mrs Drummond when you sat on the rocks with her and called her 'my friend'. *This* had only filled me with a creepy horror, that had passed from her to you. Now, when I remember how you stood at the gate drawing her hand through yours, the thought came to me that perhaps I had been unjust. What if it were that very sensitiveness and refinement, which Mrs Drummond and I had each in our own way, which ultimately repelled you from us when you came close to us and made you feel you could not permanently love us? What if your nature required just that animal element, without thought and without self-restraint, to draw out its depth of loyalty and love? What if the round pimpled face, and the loud laugh, and her stare which filled me with horror were the things your nature needed to draw you permanently? Was there not a whole side in your laughter-loving, sport-loving nature which was nearer her than to me or Mrs Drummond? Was there not even a likeness between your rounded face and figure and hers? Might not she much more easily be mistaken for your child or your sister than I? And must not like seek like? Had I any right to think there could be nothing beautiful and tender in your feeling for her because I could not have loved her? I even said to myself that perhaps I had been wholly unjust to you. What if after all there was nothing of sex in your feeling for her, if you simply longed for young light-hearted society and romped with her as you might with your own boys, when they were older? What if you concealed it from me simply because you thought I could not sympathise with or understand your feeling? Was not what I had thought the terrible sex-desire of a man, who had already brought a child into life, for a child less than half his age, merely a paternal joy in young life? Was it not the same desire to gambol with a young creature which made you squirt the water in the baby's face where I only wanted to kiss it and sing to it? Was it not the same feeling that made you care only for awkward gambolling young puppies, while I cared for older more matured animals? Was it not perhaps I, who had thought myself large and able to sympathise with others, who was really small and narrow, measuring you by my own little standard? I thought so long lying there behind you, that at last I had persuaded myself it was I who was wrong in not giving you a larger generous sympathy. Oh, can't you see I had to! If a woman loses her feeling of honour for the man she has given herself to, then she'd better be dead! Her love for him is like a little lamp that she carries in her breast, that she must shield with both hands from every wind that blows, because if it goes out it means death to her.

The next day I sent the servant to the station-master's wife with a letter to say I had been out when her niece called with the lace, but if she would come again that afternoon at five I would be glad to see it.

At five o'clock I had spread the table in the veranda with cakes and preserves, and soon after five the girl came. She looked hard at me as she was walking up the path; she handed me a bit of paper with a small bit of crochet lace in it. I asked her to sit down at the table and made her tea. I offered her six shillings for the lace; I knew it was only worth one, but I wanted to show her I felt friendly. I tried to talk to her about flowers and fancywork, but she hardly answered me. She sat eating cake, picking the plums out with her fingers, and looking every now and then at the gate. At last she asked what time you generally came home. I told her you would be home soon. A curious half-smile came over her mouth; it was as though she thought I knew nothing of your friendship with her and I was unconsciously playing into her hand. It was a look – a little of triumph, almost of scorn.

When she saw you come in at the gate she drew herself up and all her face changed. She looked full at you and smiled, all her white teeth showing when you said good day to her. I showed you the lace and told you what I gave for it, and went away at once to make you fresh tea. I was gone a quarter of an hour; when I came back with the tea she was sitting alone eating dates; she said you said you had to go out again at once. I picked her a large bunch of roses because she said she had none in their garden, and I asked her whenever she wanted some more to come any afternoon and fetch them.

When you came home to dinner you did not mention her, but when you were undressing in the evening you said, 'What on earth made you give six shillings for that bit of lace? It wasn't worth one; but it's your own money if you like to squander it.' You didn't say anything more about her.

Twice the next week she came, about five, to fetch roses. I always gave her tea and cake, and never mentioned your name to her. The first time when you came home you stopped and said a few words to her, and then walked on into the billiard room; the second time you hardly spoke to her, and went straight in. She waited very long, but you did not come back. Then just as she was going down the path to the gate you came to the dining room window and looked out. She was just shutting the gate. You said, 'What monstrous legs that girl has! She'll be a tower of fat and deformity before she's twenty-five.' As I was putting the tea things together you said, 'What on earth do you have that great lolloping larrikin of a girl here for? If you want to have her, I wish you'd take her into the drawing room and keep her out of my way.'

The next day you said you wanted breakfast at the old time, as there was no need for you to go in by the early train. For nearly two weeks after that the girl never came again. Then one afternoon I saw her coming up the path: she looked very heavy and sullen. I went in and got her tea. She did not keep on eating cake as she generally did; she crumbled it up in her lap and kept her eyes fixed on the ground or looked up staring at me. She said not a word, only moved her head sullenly in answer to my remarks; and I felt as if she had some purpose in coming. I cut a large bunch of roses for her; she seized them and, hardly saying goodbye, turned to go. When she got to the gate she turned and flung the roses all over the path. 'We've got flowers of our own,' she said; 'we don't want yours!' Then when she had got outside the gate and had shut it she turned and leaned her folded arms on the top. I was standing before the veranda on the path. She looked full at me with her eyes very wide open, then she burst into a loud artificial laugh with all her white teeth showing. 'You think you've got him all to yourself, do you? You think because you've taken him away from me you've got him! He doesn't care two straws for you! He'll go after another girl; I expect he's got one already!' She opened her mouth wide and laughed, and then she went away.

Then I knew you had deserted her, and there was no use my trying to do anything. I have never tried to have anything to do with a woman who was your friend.

And after that the dark closed in about me. It wasn't faith in your love I had lost – it was all faith in life. I didn't care for anything any more – not for the children, not for the house, not for books, not for nature; I only wanted to die. I did my work because I must, but the only time I felt glad was when I thought of death; it seemed that then there was a faint stirring at my heart like hope. And sometimes in the morning, just when I woke, there used come a feeling to me that somewhere, somehow, sometime, something would come to help me, some person, some man, some woman, some book. Sometimes in my dazed state I have even gone out and looked up and down the front avenue as if I thought some visible human being was coming to help me. Nothing goes on always in this world; it seemed I couldn't be left always in my despair. Life can't go on forever letting a human creature seem alive who really is dead.

And at last help did come, but not from a man, or a woman, or a book. You had gone away for three weeks to the Eastern Province by sea, and it was the day after you left. I was sitting in the rocking chair on the *stoep* with a newspaper on my lap, open, but I was not reading. As I looked mechanically at it, my eye caught certain words. It was a small wine garden to sell just beyond the suburbs. It gave the price and the agent's name. I read it once or twice mechanically. Then suddenly I grasped it and began to think. I got up and began walking up and down with the paper in my hand. I had thought that, if once I could find some man or woman to whom I could tell everything and who would hold my hand tight and let me creep close to them I should be saved. But this did it! I had the money my father gave me when I was married; it would almost pay for the ground, and I could raise a mortgage for the rest of the money to work the farm with.

I thought all the morning, and in the afternoon I went to see the agent and the farm.

He would not give me the deeds till he had seen you and you had given your consent, because I was a woman. But I paid him the money and he gave me possession at once. I put my old Malay cook and her husband and son there, and for three weeks I and the children lived there. They played in the sun on the grass, and I worked. I climbed onto the roof and pulled out the old thatch and helped the man to re-thatch the shanty. We cleaned and planted; before you came back it was almost in order. The seeds I had planted were coming up, and the vineyard was clean. I could not study, and I dared not feel; but I could still work; it was my hold on freedom and life; and it has been so to me ever since.

Frank, you must forgive me that I write to you in detail; I know it will tire you. But it is for all our lives. You must understand where I stand, and how I stand there, because now the silence between us must end.

I need not write fully about the things that have happened later; they have always kept on happening, and I think you have suspected that I suspected them. Sometimes for a little time nothing happened, and then a hope rose in me that things had changed; but they always did happen at last, and I have realised what we have to deal with is not an isolated event but a permanent condition. Such little things – but they always keep on happening.

Do you remember two Xmases ago when we were walking down Adderley Street to buy the children presents? I was walking just a little in front of you looking in at the windows when I heard a rustle of silk skirts and someone running down the pavement behind us. I glanced back and there was a woman with a red dress and black bonnet with red roses in it; she had just caught hold of your arm from behind and called out 'Hello!' You turned quickly towards her; I heard you say three words in a low voice: I could not fully catch them, though I think I know what they were, and you glanced at me. In an instant she let your arm go, and stood looking at me with her head a little on one side with that half-curious half-contemptuous smile I saw first on the station-master's niece's face, but which I have seen since so often. Then she laughed softly and drew her skirt up tight about her and crossed to the other side of the street, and you came quickly to my side. I think you must have noticed that I saw her catch your arm, for presently you said, 'I wonder who that woman can have been that came up to me just now? Seems she mistook me for someone else.'

I said, 'Have you not seen her before?'

You said, 'Oh, I may have. Rather expect she's one of the actresses that came over on the steamer with me last time I came from Port Elizabeth.' And then you began talking about the toys in the window. All these years they've kept on happening. Once you sent me a note from the office to say you had to make up the quarter's books and you wouldn't be home till very late; I mustn't sit up for you. At four o'clock you came home in a cab. Your face was swollen with tiredness and you dropped on the bed and went to sleep at once. I kept the house very quiet the next morning because I thought after your hard work you needed sleep. At nine o'clock your clerk came and said he wanted the key of the safe to get out a document. I said I didn't like to wake you because you had sat working so late making up the books.

He looked at me surprised and said, 'But we made up all the books last week!'

Another time, perhaps you remember it, I went into town to buy new oilcloth for the billiard room. I thought I would ask you to come with me to choose it. When I got to the office it was closed up. The caretaker said you had given the clerks a holiday to go to the races, and had closed at eleven o'clock. I bought the oilcloth and went home. In the evening you were an hour late for dinner. I went to the door to meet you. I was just going to say that I wished I had known you were going to the races, because I had never seen any and would have gone too, when you said you were afraid you had kept dinner waiting but there had been such a succession of people in the office all day you'd had no breathing time. You said your head ached and you did not want dinner, only a cup of coffee on the veranda. I could not understand why it was you should wish to hide from me you had gone, but the next day a woman came (it was Mrs Drummond, but Rebekah did not say so) and asked me if I had been to the races. I said I had never been to races. She said she thought I must have been, as someone had said they had seen my husband driving in a carriage with the girl who kept his books and two others, but that she had felt sure it must be me and some of my friends; and she looked at me to see how I felt it. A few days after I met a man in the avenue who stopped to say good day to me. He asked if I had been at the races the week before: I said I had not. He laughed and said, 'You should look after your husband a little; you shouldn't let him be so gay!' And he looked at me with a curious inquiring smile. One of the strangest things to me has been how not only women, but men, men who call themselves men, come close to you and prod their fingers into your wound to see how much you feel; it is like when wild animals gather round the wounded one of the herd and prod it with their horns when it falls wounded. It came to this at last, that I felt as if nothing mattered to me if people didn't come and talk to me of you and show me that they knew. There was a cow at the farm one day whose side was torn open by a barbed wire fence so that her entrails hung out; she tried always to turn that side away from the other animals, and they seemed always trying to come round to it, till we shot her.

Perhaps you will say if life has been so cruel to me, why haven't I left you and gone home to my father? Oh, you know I asked you to divorce me or send me away if you wished, and you said nothing. I have often asked myself why I didn't get up and go. Is it perhaps the spirit of those old ancestresses of mine who for millions of years have followed the man over steppes and through deserts and across mountains, with stripes and burdens, always following, following, following, – which today cries out in us, 'Follow – follow – till he sets you free!' I do not know how it is that I, who would bear binding to no other human creature, feel an iron chain about my heart binding me to you. Often I have said, 'Why do I not get up and go!' – and then something cries out in me, 'If he should need me! – If he should want me! – If I am good for him!' When I have thought of leaving you against your will, it has been as if I left my little child while it cried for me; something begins to bleed inside of me.

When I went last year to visit my mother at the farm even my brain seemed rigid. But when I saw the places where I had been when I was a little child, when I saw the long moss still hanging from the tree in the *kloof* and picked up the Kaffir beans that had fallen from the trees and saw the old great pear tree under which I used to play, I walked about alone and cried for joy, and my heart came back again to me soft, like before I married. I felt as if something went out from me and clasped itself about everything. I wanted to read and to think again; and when I had been there a month such a strange tenderness to you sprang up in my heart. It seemed all my fault that I had not wound my arms about you and made you talk about things to me, and so we should have got to understand each other. At last I had only one desire, a hunger to see your face and to hear your voice. And when you wrote a letter in which you said you missed me and the children and would never let us go so far away again, I packed up my things and came home a month sooner than I had meant. I thought when I came back the past was going to be past, that what I had wanted for so long was going to happen, because deep hidden in my heart there had always been a hope; I see it now.

And when we came back all did seem better; you spoke kindly to me almost as you spoke to other women, and never spoke roughly to me before the children and servant; but you wouldn't let me come near enough to you to speak of anything. I was glad you had Bertie to go out with, and when I knew this child was coming I was glad, almost as when the first was coming; the other two had been so terrible.

After Bertie was gone things seemed just as bright; you still cared to stay at home and seemed happy here with us. I thought I was making you happy; I didn't want anything more; it seemed I could let an iron curtain down between me and the past; I could be quite satisfied just to live peacefully and attend to you and the children and feel you near me, and nothing ever happening. Oh! I asked so little, so little!

Now tonight what has happened has made me feel we must speak the truth to one another. I have been afraid of you all these years; I have been afraid if I wrote or spoke to you and you answered me as you did years ago, something would break in me. But tonight I am not afraid.

Do not think that, because what happened in the yard tonight would give me the legal right to freedom in any court, therefore I write to you, who have been silent so long. In the eyes of the world it might seem a grosser and more brutal thing – but not in mine. When I saw you and Mrs Drummond on the rocks at

Muizenberg, and when I picked up the letter beginning 'My Friend', in which you discussed marriage and me, my youth died in me, and it will never come back; this is not so great. When I saw you in the billiard room that day you did not inflict such anguish on me as when in the last years you have often sat talking with women in the same room with me, bending perhaps over a young girl, plain it might be, with the same passionate light in your eyes begging for a return of sexual feeling, which you once turned on me, not caring that I was present to see, or the glances other women directed to me; and when, just because it meant nothing permanent and she might pass out of your life in a few days, it has inflicted deeper humiliation on you and me and the bond that bound us. It is the lightness of the attraction which could come between your manhood and my womanhood that is the measure of our degradation.

I do not know whether other women feel so, but I can understand, I can almost sympathise with, a wave of black, primitive bestial desire surging up at some moment in life in a nature otherwise pure and lofty. I can imagine it for an instant sweeping all before it, so that the creature itself cried out in the pain of a grasp it cannot comprehend, which drives it forward to action it abhors – the resurrection of that long-buried animal past, when man on earth knew not of love and loyalty; and I can understand that the creature, man or woman, should shrink with horror from the force within them while they fell before it. There are lands where, in the course of centuries or scores or decades of years, the earth rends and opens and sulphurous fumes desolate it and darkness covers it; and yet men live in it and love it and it is still a fair land, except at that rare and terrible moment when the convulsion falls on it; but a land that always trembled, that was never still, when from every smallest crack the foetid fume rose, and a fine, almost imperceptible, fall of ashes covered it: the very dogs would leave it – no man would live there!

Do not think that I am taking a mean advantage because tonight you have weakly committed yourself into my hand; it is not what you have done that makes me speak; it is because something has happened in me that never happened before. I feel that tonight the end has come, and you and I must speak openly and sincerely to one another. I am not afraid of you. I am not a woman speaking to the man who owns her, before whom she trembles; we are two free souls looking at each other. If you will not read this letter, then you shall hear me speak. But that long life of silence and repression and deception ends here. You must hear me.

It seems to me that there are just three possible courses open to us.

The first is, that you should get a divorce from me. As I told you years ago, when I thought you loved Mrs Drummond, if you wish for one I shall do all I can to make it easy for you. I will go to my parents; you can demand my return, and, when I refuse, divorce me. Then all blame will rest upon me. I have my farm and

I can work. I will support the children, but for your sake, for yourself, I think you ought to. This seems to me the best plan; then we shall both be free to lead our lives – such as they can be now.

The second is, if you do not want the disgrace of a divorce (I know you will fear it; I do not fear it; it will not touch me), that we should separate. I can go on my little wine farm; it will not attract much attention; you can come sometimes, if you will, to see the children. We can each lead our own lives; but it will not be so right as if the tie were utterly severed and openly.

Then there is a third. If, if it so happens that you still think you love me and do not wish me to go from you, then there is yet one course open for us. You must meet me, fairly and straightly, as one man meets another, and speak to me as one speaks to one's own soul. You must tell me what you feel, what you desire and wherein you think I have failed, as I have told you in this letter. There must be no subterfuge or concealment between us. Then if you still wish to possess me, I will live with you; as long as you are loyal to me I will be loyal to you; I will bear children for you. I will forget the past; never by a word or a sign shall I recall it.

Oh, Frank, Frank, I have loved you! Oh, even now I love you, as you have not known, as you never will know! Only once in all the years we have been together has it ever seemed for a moment to have gone out. We were sitting at dinner at the time you were still friendly with the station-master's niece. You were eating with your eyes fixed intently on your plate, but evidently not thinking of what you were eating. As I looked up at you, as I looked at your mouth and your jaw, a wave of horror swept over me. It was not as if you were the man who was myself, but any other man whom one might see at a restaurant for the first time. The horror and shrinking swept over me so I rose and left the table. If I had continued to feel so, then I must have left you at once. But it passed almost immediately and remained only as a terrible memory. It may have been some thought that was in your mind, written on your face for the moment, which affected me so, but, except then, never in the darkest moment has my love died. You have never been to me as another man.

Frank, I have tried to blame myself; I have sought, as a rat in a trap seeks a way of escape, to find out I was wrong and you were right. I have tried to understand you. I do even now see there may be elements in your nature forcing you almost irresistibly to certain courses of action that I cannot rightly understand, because those forces are not in me. I see that I must be unjust to you if I measure you by my standard. Can love and marriage and the relationship of human to human have the same meaning to you and to me, when in everything else we differ? Sometimes I have lain awake whole nights thinking over it.

You care for wild animals. You will spend days in the blazing sun or the cutting winds, you will creep on hands and knees over rough *kopjes* or through the mud of *vleis* to stalk a buck or a bird you have fixed on. When you get near it you shoot it; when you get to it, you pick it up and turn it over in your hand, or you kick it over with your foot. That is the end; you have got it. You sometimes care so little for a buck you have spent half the day in stalking that, rather than carry it back on your shoulder to the cart, you will give it to the man that is with you. Only if one who is shooting with you should say his gun brought it down, then it becomes of importance to you, and rather than let him have it, you would battle over it.

I have cared for wild animals too. I had a wood-dove that the Kaffir boys had caught and crushed in their stone trap; I bought it from them with the only sixpence I had, and I nursed it and cured it. It made a nest in the garden, and sometimes when I woke in the morning it was fluttering round my bed or sitting on the rail at the bottom singing and waiting for me to wake. I had a raven they shot in the land and broke its wing and leg. I tied splints to it, and, though it could never fly, it lived; and when I went out in the morning into the yard a thrill of joy used to come over me when I saw it hop out of the wagon house with its one stiff leg and its head on one side coming to peck at my skirt that I might pick it up and let it ride on my shoulder. I also had a passion for wild animals; but it has been to possess them and know they knew me and wanted me.

If you have a spare day, you go fishing, and you stand on the rocks from the morning to the evening, sometimes soaked with spray to bring a few fishes to land. I have seen your eye gleaming and your whole being intent as you have seen your float move or have reeled one to the shore. And yet, when you had them, when you had put your fingers through their gills, your interest in them was ended. You threw them into the basket with the others. Only if it were a very large one, and you wanted to take it home and weigh it and tell your friends its size, would you often care to take it home. I have known you to give a whole basketful to the Coloured boys on the beach because they were not worth carrying. I would not. I would not endure the labour you go through in catching them for anything but to save my children or someone dependent on me from absolute hunger. Yes, if I were standing in the water and a fish should creep up to me and glide between my feet and over them, not fearing me, I should stand still shivering with delight every time its beautiful body touched me. I have always dreamed of having a tame fish, one that would come to me when I called and I lie with its slow palpitating beautiful belly on my hand in the water and let me feel it.

Only once I tried to capture a thing, when I was six years old, and I saw for the first time one of those great purple butterflies with the golden eyes on their wings. It seemed so beautiful, I desired it so passionately, I think I would have committed a crime to have it. I ran after it all the way to the great dam and through the *mielie* lands, though I knew I should not go so far, and when it sat on a Karoo bush I fell down on it and caught it. When I stood up and looked it was crushed, and the fine fluff was clinging to my hand. I lay down on the ground and cried beside it. You see, what I had really wanted was not to catch it, but to have it, and I thought I could if I caught it. I don't think since then I have ever wanted to catch anything that has tried to escape from me, an animal or a human creature. I have understood that what I wanted from living things was what they could *give* me, not what I could take from them. The supreme moment to me is not when I kill or conquer a living thing, but that moment its eye and mine meet and a line of connection is formed between me and the life that is in it. It knows and understands me and we are united by something within us. Then it is mine; and I want it.

There is the same difference between us in everything. If I have a few hours to spare on an afternoon, I like to go to the blockhouse on the mountain and lie down and see the town below me and the Bay and the mountains and the bush. I lie and look at it till I feel it all belongs to me. And my little life, which sometimes seems so small when I am shut up in the house alone, grows great and beautiful. And I have my half-holiday.

And if you have a free afternoon, if you have no animal to pursue, you go to the cricket ground or play croquet; you strike or chase the balls; even if they are not alive, you have the pleasure of trying to do it better than another man; and, if you cannot play yourself, you watch others do it; you are pleased so there is winning, conquering, taking – sport!

If you have a dog, you like it because it is thoroughbred and wins prizes at shows or hunts well, and you flog it when it makes mistakes. The dog I have loved best was a terrier of no full breed. For six years it slept at the foot of my bed; and even now, when I wake in the night, something in me cries out to feel it creep softly up in the dark and lie between my arm and my side with its little head on my shoulder and its little heart beating against my side; and if there were another world where we could see again the things we have loved here, one of the first things I should ask to see would be those eyes which when I woke I used to find watching me, when it lay with its two paws on my chest waiting for me to wake.

And, sometimes, I have asked myself, if we feel so differently with regard to everything in life, is it not also inevitable we should feel differently about love? What if for you a woman is only 'sport'? What if there is something irresistible in your nature which compels you to feel that the woman who has once wholly given herself to you is a dead bird, a fish, through whose gills you have put your fingers?

Long ago you met Mrs Drummond secretly and got letters from her; you were careful I should not see and seemed to care much for her, but as soon as I said that I would go away that you might have her for six months in the house with you, and that if you wished it you could divorce me and marry her – then you cared nothing more for her; when she waited at the gate for you, you tried to avoid her; when she asked you to her parties, you never went; when she waited about for you and sent you presents and you knew you could absolutely possess her, she had no more value for you. Only two years ago, when the old Major was so attentive to her and was always coming to see her, you too went to see her and took her out till he left off coming, and then you left off going to her too, till last year, when there was gossip about the young bank clerk who came so often to see her; then you went to church with her and brought her home and went to her croquet till she left off having anything to do with him; and then you left her too. You liked to meet the station-master's niece and go to town with her while it was secretly done, but when I asked her here and you could have seen her every day in your own house, then you avoided her and you got to dislike her following you and waiting for you. Hasn't it always been so, you haven't cared for any woman for long?

I have sometimes thought that perhaps if I had been a different woman – not if I had taken more care of your house and the children, not if I had been more eager to satisfy the wants of your nature, not if your touch had been more precious to me – but if, when you came home, you were never quite sure who you would find had been taking tea with me; if, when I went for a walk in the woods, you were never quite sure that it was alone; if, instead of showing all my letters and telegrams to you, you had noticed that I tried to prevent any falling into your hands; if I had carried on a long correspondence with a married man, whose letters you never saw or mine to him, and met him when you were from home; if, at balls and assemblies, you had seen me sit with men of my own age and men much younger bending over me, and you had seen my cheeks burn and my eyes grow bright with a colour they never wore for you – then perhaps you would have been able to keep on loving me! I have thought that perhaps the only woman you could have kept on loving all your life would have been a woman of whom you were never quite sure, that there must be at least a flutter in the bird's wings, a possibility of its again taking flight, to make it of value to you!

If I am mistaken in this, tell me so. But if I am not, if you know it to be true, why should we not both face the fact plainly? If it is not possible for your nature to keep on caring for a thing that absolutely belongs to you and yields no excitement of chase, is it not as unjust to demand it of you as it would be to demand of me with my nature that I should desire to kill things simply because they were alive and I saw them move?

I sometimes think that why you were attracted to me, when I was a little girl and you first saw me, was simply because I always ran away from you to hide in the bush; if I had hung about you and wanted to play with you, you would have driven me away; but when I climbed into the top of the willow tree and you set the dogs to find me and stood at the bottom of the tree declaring you would stay the whole day if I did not come down and play, and I refused, then you liked me. I believe that afterwards it was the fact that I noticed no man, that I had accepted none of the proposals made me that drew you to me. You loved me then. When you lifted me off the rocks, when I hurried in late to breakfast and you rose and drew out the old wooden chair for me, as you looked down at me, the light upon your face seemed to me God's light shining out upon my life; when I think of it even now, I want to push everything from me and run to you and creep close to you – even now. After we were married I never saw it again on your face for me – my light; but I saw it shine on your face for others. In a ballroom I have seen you stoop to pick up a fan dropped by a young girl you did not know and who did not know you; as you have handed it her, her face has burned softly crimson and then white and she has gone away fingering the fan softly, and I know at night she has dreamed of the face with the light upon it.

I have seen it play on your face as you helped a woman much older than yourself into a carriage; I have seen it come for a girl you were saying an ordinary goodbye to at a railway station, and my heart has beaten with the feeling that when you turned to me it would shine on me also, but it has been dead when you turned and said, 'Are you ready, Rebekah?' I have seen you on a sofa beside a girl not young, not beautiful, bending over her, with the light upon your face so clearly that every person in the room has noted it and in a way quietly smiled, and the woman has thought she had won you wholly and looked up at me with the scorn of the victor; but the next week or the next month it has been just so for another woman. What is it but the old, old lure-light, the decoy-light, that through the ages has led woman on, crying to her, 'Here is light! Here is warmth!' and when she has followed it up hills and down valleys and, reaching it, stretches out her hands to warm them, she finds a few white ashes.

If the fish could see it, is it not the same light that burns with deep intensity in the eye that watches him rise slowly to take the bait? What is it but the *ignis fatuus* which leads woman on to surrender and toil and bear for man, the very memory of which, even when it has gone, binds her to him so that she cannot break the tie? Oh, now, even now, when I know what it means, something in me cries out to see it once again, my light, for me, just once before I die! [She scratched out this last sentence.]

Sometimes, in hours of great darkness, it has come to me that perhaps there is nothing strange in our fate; that perhaps in all these houses with their tender gardens and their little front gates, and between all these men and women whom one sees walking smoothly to church together and going out to dinner and sitting on the *stoep*, there lies the same ghastly reality that the strange joy which fills the heart of the man and the woman we see walking alone together as they plan their future home and life, from whom we turn away when we meet them in the pine woods lest we should trespass on the beautiful solitude – that perhaps in the end it all comes to this – that the love and fellowship which we are taught to look to as our end in life, which compensates us for all that larger world of duties and actions, which we dream of from our earliest girlhood as that which is to consecrate our lives, means in the end only this – an hour's light, and then a long darkness; the higher the flame has leaped, the colder and deader the ashes.

If I believed this always, if it came to me otherwise than as a nightmare, I would not live; because human life would be false at its core. Even the animals know what love is; the eagle mates once and never again, they say, if its mate dies; the singing birds mate with a companion whom they tend and follow; even those beasts whose union is a moment of sensuous life have no deception; the moment after, both are free; the wide world is before them; the very polygamous beasts do not win their partners by protestations of eternal love; each is free to form another union when it will. Is man the creature whose love is a falsehood by nature; who has one decoy song, crying, 'My love is eternal', which in the anguish of child-bearing and the years without freedom she is to hear no more? For in spring the bird may call to a new mate and she to whom he cried last year answers to a new call; is woman the only creature for whom there is no spring, and no fresh call when the old song is dead? Is the passion cry with which the man follows one woman for weeks or months or years, chanting that his love ends only with death, with no refrain to say that its death hour is possession and that its life is long because it passes on endlessly to others – is this always a conscious or unconscious lie?

Sometimes I have believed this – but it is only in a nightmare. When I wake from it I know that the loveliest thing that has blossomed on the earth is the binding of man and woman in one body, one fellowship, and I know that all the failures are only the broken steps which Humanity builds in stairs she is shaping for herself to climb by, which she will have to rebuild better in the future. All man's love cry is not delusion, and the dreams we have dreamed in our girlhood will have their realisation though it may never be by us.

And, when I see this, the feeling comes over me that, oh, somewhere, the woman must exist whom you could love; perhaps some young girl or some older riper woman, who, if you could meet, would draw out all the tenderness and beauty and self-devotion of your nature which I have never been able to touch, whom you would be loyal to, not for her sake but for your own, because she was yourself. And sometimes it has even come to me that perhaps, at a future day, I might be that woman, that perhaps we may yet meet each other and understand each other, and all the past ...

She had scratched out the whole of this unfinished paragraph. When she wrote next it was with another pen and more hurried and illegible.

Oh, can't we speak the truth to one another just like two men? Can't we tell each other just what we think and feel? If you can't love me, tell me so; do not be afraid of hurting me. If you feel you cannot love one woman long and that only a succession of women can make you happy, I will try to understand. I will try to be a man with you. Oh, nothing can be so terrible as this awful silence that has been between us through these long years. It is that that has crushed me, always to hold myself down with an iron hand. I do not ask you to love me, only to speak the truth to me, as you would if I were another man.

O Frank, my love, my husband, I have loved you, I have loved you! You will never know how I have loved you! If there were any woman you loved more than all the world, I would do everything in my power to bring her to you. If you had a little child that was yours and not mine, I would take it to my heart and love it as if it were my own. If you, if you don't love me, but you want me still to live with you, I will do all you ask of me; but, oh, we must speak the truth to each other, we must speak the truth. It is this life of lies and subterfuges which we have been living which is dragging down both our souls to hell.

Here she seemed to have paused a long time and paced the room, for the handwriting when she went on was suddenly quite changed and almost illegible.

O Frank, my love, my husband, please help me! I want to do what is right and I cannot see the way! I am like a little child that has lost itself in the wood and it is dark everywhere. Oh, please take my hand and help me. You are much stronger than I; you are the only human being who can help me. Take my hand in yours and let us find the path.

Here it ended suddenly.

This was the letter held twisted in a roll in her hand as she lay looking at the shadows among the rafters. The baby had grown tired of playing with his toes and had dropped asleep again, and there was no sound in the room but the even breathing of the still sleeping children.

Then Rebekah stood up and went out onto the back veranda. Dressed still in her blue dressing gown, with only the little blue slippers on her bare feet: she walked up the side passage of the yard, past the closed stable door, and out at the back gate.

There the early morning sunlight was shooting down a clear light through the young green oak leaves and playing delicately on the ground; below and beyond, where the pine trees began, single shafts of light fell through the tall branches across their stems and onto the moss and pine needles, wet with the early morning dew. Rebekah stood with her back to the outer wall of the stable gazing into the woods, but her eyes were sightless. Then she began slowly walking up and down close to the wall. Her feet made a little pathway among the weeds and the bits of dry straw that had blown there from the yard gate. Presently she leaned the crown of her head against the roughcast whitewashed walls and looked downwards. She watched the little weeds at her feet and the bits of straw against the wall. Then something rose and surged through her; from her feet it seemed to mount till it reached to her brain and swept all before it. She would go into the house and gather them all in her arms, those children born of lust and falsehood, and they and she and the unborn would pass away together! For an instant the impulse seemed to gain upon her with fearful force. Then slowly her will took command again and she annihilated it. But in years that came, when in some chance newspaper she had read of a woman in despair who had taken her children out of life with her, to her it was no impossible nightmare; she knew the steps by which a woman's soul may pass, till it stands looking down into that awful abysm.

She stood motionless, but with her head pressed to the wall, so that tiny fragments of the rough plaster clung to her soft brown hair. She tried to think; but, like a mockery, from a voice outside herself, broke in the old proverb she had read first in the little brown history, 'You – cannot – make – a silk purse – out – of – a sow's – ear!' And still she paced up and down trying to think.

A Coloured man, passing through the woods early to look for his master's cow, paused for a moment in the distance to look at the little figure in its blue dressing gown with bare slippered feet pacing up and down, with its low bent head – and then, wondering, passed on.

At last, as she walked, that quiet on-looking self, which, except in moments of rare anguish of body and soul, can always regain the mastery, woke in her. She walked along slowly. The question came, 'Why are you agonising here? Are *you* the only creature in the world who has suffered wrong? If life has no value to you, are there not others weaker than yourself to whom you can make it of value? Because in your anguish you are alone and no hand comes to help you, can you put out your hand to none? Are you the only woman in the world who has suffered?'

She raised her head; as she looked up she saw for the first time the green and golden glory of the light through the young oak leaves and the bright shafts shooting through the dark branches of the pine-wood and the soft moist earth below. She raised herself and stood looking at it; it seemed as if a soft dew were falling on her mind.

'When all hope is dead in your own life, is there yet nothing left to live for? Are there not others?' She stood looking at the morning world, like a soul come back from a long journey; then she walked in at the little gate. The door of the stable was open now and the stable boy had evidently taken the horses out to exercise. At the end of the passageway she turned into the yard. The milkman had evidently been, for the milk can stood in the stand at the kitchen door, but there was no sign of any other creature moving except two sparrows walking in the sunshine on the gravel of the yard. The green wooden shutter of the servant-girl's bedroom was thrown open; but the door was still shut. Rebekah passed across the yard to it, then she stood for a moment and glanced back at the sparrows and the sunshine; and then she knocked at the door. At first there was no answer, and she knocked again. Then a voice called out in Cape Dutch, 'Who is there?' And Rebekah said softly, 'It is I,' and opened the door. She stood for a moment before she stepped down the one step that led into the room.

Before the window on the side of her single bed the servant-girl was sitting. She was half dressed: her short black wool, with difficulty parted, was combed out to stand in two solid masses on each side of her head; her small dark face, with its puckered forehead even a little blacker than the rest, was raised as Rebekah opened the door. She had on a red-striped flannel petticoat and a pair of crimson satin corsets, embroidered with white flowers; above the corsets, from a mass of frilled white lace, showed her puny black arms and bare shoulders; on the bed beside her lay a white nightdress heavy with bows: on the other side lay the serge dress she was just going to put on. The girl placed a closed fist on each of her hips, and raising her chin in the air looked at Rebekah through her half-closed twinkling eyes.

'*Wat wil jy hê?*'¹ she said, throwing her chin yet higher.

Rebekah stood silent; all she had determined to say passed from her. The girl threw back her head farther and burst into a laugh intended to be defiant but with an undertone of fear, all her white teeth showing between her thick dark lips as she sat with her fists on her hips.

Then, as Rebekah looked at her, Rebekah knew that it was with that girl even as it was with herself that day.

Softly she turned and went out; she closed the door behind her. Almost on tiptoe, softly and quickly she ran across the yard, like one who fears something that is following them and tries to escape.

She disappeared through the back door.

It was late that night when Frank returned. He had had a successful day's fishing. The friend with whom he had driven had put him down at the gate. As he walked up the path he saw the front door open and the lamp burning on the stand, but Rebekah was not there to meet him and take his bag.

He set down his things on the hall table and went into the dining room. The lamp was lit, his supper was laid ready, his soda water was cooling in the window, but no one was there. He passed into their bedroom; it was dark; but in his dressing room

---

1 'What do you want?' The pronoun '*jy*' in the Cape Dutch language, the only language of the Coloured people of the Western Cape, was the most extreme insult when applied to a superior. It was used politely only to children or servants. Even equals would avoid its use as much as possible.

a light was burning and his change of clothes hung ready for him over the chair, but there was no sign of anyone stirring in the house though it was not yet eleven. The servants were, of course, in bed, but it was the first time in all his married life, except when Rebekah was in childbed or suffering from a miscarriage, that he had come home at such an hour and found no one to attend to him.

He washed and changed his fishing clothes for the light-grey lounging suit; then he opened the door into the children's bedroom. That room also was dark, but from the crack under the door he saw there was light in Rebekah's study. He felt no particular wish to call her just then, so he went to the dining room and sat down to his supper. He enjoyed the chicken and *bobotie* and even took three glasses of wine; but as he finished a sense of the strangeness of things came over him that he did not like. He took a cigar and lit it and went on the front veranda to smoke. After a while he sat down in the rocking chair, but he felt restless. When his cigar was half done he threw it away and lit another. Perhaps, after all, it would be better to go and see Rebekah now and have it over; it was most unlikely she would speak about anything that had happened in the morning; she never did if you gave her time – she was an awfully sensible woman if only you gave her time – gave her time! He took his new cigar between his first and second finger and lounged away to the study door in an almost exaggeratedly easy style, as though he were preparing himself for a certain attitude of mind.

He opened the door without knocking and walked in easily.

'Hello, old girl!' he said, and seated himself on the edge of her desk with one knee thrown over the corner and the hand with the lighted cigar resting on it.

'Had a good day!' he said, 'the best I've had this season. Thought everyone was dead in the house when I came home, it's so quiet.' He raised his cigar to his lips. 'Hope Wilson came and fetched those two cues to mend. Don't like giving the other fellows my favourite cues!' He looked at the smoke from his mouth rather than at her. 'Think I shall go to bed soon; I'm awfully tired!' He expanded his chest and raised his shoulders as people do who yawn, but no yawn came. He knocked some imperceptible ashes off the tip of his cigar with his little finger.

Rebekah, who had been sitting in her chair when he came, still sat there leaning back, with her head a little raised. Now she leaned forward a little and laid her hand on a large sheet of open blue foolscap paper on the desk on which there were some lines written in large clear characters.

'You must take this,' she said slowly, 'whether you wish to or not' – she was looking full up at him – 'and tomorrow I want your answer.'

He put his cigar back into his mouth and looked at her. He had an unpleasant sensation that she was looking at him as if she were looking at a tree or a wall – or any other man – not at him. The little sensitive almost imperceptible contraction about her mouth and eye, that he was always accustomed to see when she looked at him and spoke, seemed not there.

'Last night,' she continued, 'when I wrote that letter that you called a book and would not take, I said there were three lines of action on which I was willing our future relationship to each other should be based – now there are only two!'

He took the cigar from his mouth as if to speak, but something stopped him.

'They are there,' she said, moving the paper towards him.

'They are short, and will not take you more than sixty seconds to read.' She rested her fingers on the paper as she spoke. He had an unpleasant sensation as he looked at her that she was growing physically taller and larger at the moment.

'Either,' she said, looking at him, 'you must procure a legal divorce from me; in which case, both you and I will be free and may marry again, or not, as we wish. I would take the children to my farm or to my parents; if you wish it, I will support them; if, as I hope you do, you feel it is your duty, you can assist in their support. Under any conditions, we shall be free, and I think this is the best course; it is the one I prefer.' She let her fingers drop on the paper. 'If, on the other hand, you do not like these conditions, if you are afraid of what the world will say, then there is another course.' She looked at him, but, as though absorbed in her own thought, she hardly seemed to see him: 'I will, if you wish, continue to live in this house. I will look after your children and I will attend to your material wants; I will provide for my personal needs as I have already done for some years; but you will understand that, from tonight, you and I will never be anything more to each other than any man or woman who pass each other in the street for the first time. You will be free to lead your own life, to think your own thoughts, to form your own friendships; but you will understand that I also am equally free. Last night I gave you the choice of a third course; tonight there are only these two. You can let me know your decision tomorrow before twelve o'clock.' She pointed to the paper on the table.

He looked down at her. For a moment he thought of bursting into a fit of rage such as had always silenced her; he would say he was shamefully treated, swear at her, and violently close the door. But that intuitive perception, which in him took the place of reason and was almost preternaturally keen where his own interests were concerned, told him it would be useless now.

He looked down at her curiously. 'Oh, it's all too ridiculous, Rebekah. What do you mean? You are a tired little woman' – he spoke gently – 'your condition makes you take these silly little fancies into your head! You need a good night's rest. How you live, with so little sleep as you take, I don't know! I'd be a washed-out rag! – I'm jolly tired too tonight,' he said slowly, rising from the desk and drawing back his shoulders. 'I've had a long, tiring day of it. I can hardly keep my eyes open.'

She rose too. 'Take that paper,' she said quietly. 'I have put it down in writing to avoid any mistake. I have kept a copy.' She folded it up and held it out to him. He was going to speak; he looked into her face, and a sense of something that seemed almost preternatural and inverted came over him. It was as if a man called to his own dog, who had followed him for years, and it walked by with its head down, no quiver even in its tail, and turned a dead eye on him. He took the paper from her, holding it a little in one hand, while in the other he held the lighted cigar. He moved almost awkwardly from one leg to the other.

'Well, I'll take it, of course, as you want me to,' he said; 'but you know it's absolutely ridiculous! You're tired tonight, that's what it is!' He tried to smile, but it died away at the corners of his mouth in a kind of twitch. 'Of course, you must know it's all nonsense. I'm just taking it not to upset you tonight.' He put it in his pocket. 'I'm really awfully tired! I think I'll turn in. I suppose you're going to sit up a bit?'

He turned towards the door; when he had opened it and was going out, he began to recover himself; he turned and looked back at her with the door in his hand.

'Oh, this is all very well, you know,' he laughed, but with his mouth a little on one side; 'we know what'll happen before tomorrow morning! It won't be dawn, a fellow'll just be having his first sleep and he'll feel a tickling at the back of his neck; some small individual shedding tears upon it and combing out little curls with her fingers – kissing them too! – Eh?' He laughed again. 'Happened before – hasn't it?'

Rebekah was still standing by the desk, staring at him. 'It'll be all right in the morning! – Eh? – Good night!'

He shut the door behind him. When he was on the other side, the smile died out. Deep in his heart he knew it would not be all right in the morning. He had seen the look on the face of women before, and he knew what it meant. Without the shadow of a doubt he knew that the quicklime had ceased to act, that the net was broken, that the bird was out! He walked through the dark bedrooms into the dining room and took the paper from his pocket and read it under the hanging lamp. There were only twenty lines in a neat round hand, stating two alternatives. He walked up and down the room once or twice with it in his hand; then he put it in his pocket and walked to the window, lifting the corner of the blind a little. The window of the dining room looked out into the backyard as the window of the bedroom did. The white moonlight was flooding the yard; when he looked across it to the servant's room it seemed to him that both door and window stood wide open. He put his face close to the pane. The door to the servant's room was exactly opposite the dining room window, and as the moonlight fell in at the open door it seemed to him that the green box which had always stood just inside the door was not there.

He drew a soft, almost noiseless, indrawn whistle, and let the blind fall. He paced the room twice; then, glancing round to see that the door into the bedroom was closed, and listening to hear if there was any sound, he went out into the backyard. At first he walked as if to go to the stable passage; then, glancing once back at the house, he walked to the door of the servant's room and looked in.

It was empty. A great splash of whitewash lay on the earthen floor where the patch of moonlight fell in through the door; the room held nothing but a bare iron bedstead standing in the centre, and there was a strong smell of fresh whitewash. So that was it!

A flush of anger rose to his face as he turned quickly and walked to the house. Was it that devil of a stable boy? He had given him ten shillings twice, just to keep quiet in case he had noticed anything. Was it the girl herself who had talked? – you never could trust a nigger, do what you would for them! Had Rebekah noticed anything for herself? He walked into the dining room and took another cigar from the mantelshelf and bit off the end, throwing it into the waste-paper basket, but he did not light it. It had all come of being too soft hearted! He ought to have sent her away two months ago, when she first told him, instead of listening to all her nonsense. If her mother did cut up rough about it he could easily have settled it with money. It was all nonsense about her coming to talk to Rebekah about it – she would have had nothing to gain! And now Rebekah knew! He had been an absolute fool – that was what he had been!

He bit the end of his cigar again, forgetting what he had done, and began to pace the room once more with the unlighted cigar between his first and second fingers. After a while he lit the cigar and began to smoke, blowing clouds of smoke, and his brain began to work smoothly and quietly. He faced the entire position now that there was no escape. Whatever the girl might do and wherever she might go, it really did not matter, now Rebekah knew! At the worst, if she did turn up again, it would only be a matter of a few shillings a week: – A dirty, beastly little nigger! – but perhaps it would never be born? There flashed through his mind the rate of infant mortality among the Coloured population which he had seen in some paper: at the worst that could be all set right with money; there was no need to think of it.

Then he walked, smoking more slowly and looking down. After a time he went and stood still before the mantelpiece, deep in thought. Then he sat down at the little desk in the corner where Rebekah wrote her orders and kept her accounts. He took a sheet of paper and wrote:

Dearest Wife,

A certain little person was so cut-uppie tonight that I quite forgot to tell her I have to start for Caledon before five o'clock tomorrow. I have to go and see about some farms; the man will be waiting for me at the hotel with his cart. I shall be gone from a week to ten days. I won't wake you and the children, as no doubt you will be asleep when I start. I'll write if there's any chance, but it's not very likely, as it's an out-of-the-way part. Expect me when you see me. Take care of yourself and the children.

Your loving husband,

Frank

He put it in an envelope and closed it and put it in his breast pocket. Then he turned out the lamp and went to his dressing room. He put the few clothes he would need into a small portmanteau and stood it out of sight behind the door; then he undressed. He listened for a moment near the door of the children's room, but there was no sound, so no doubt she was still in her study. He took up the lamp and went to the bedroom, set it down on the stand at the bedside, and then, before he took off his dressing gown and opened the bed, he sat on the bedside with his legs stretched out and folded across each other; and for a long time he sat looking down at his bare feet. Then he took Rebekah's paper out of the pocket of his dressing gown and read it again. An angry flush rose to his face and dyed it red at the top of his forehead. 'And in that case, both you and I would be free to marry again.' (How could Rebekah write a thing like that! She, whom he had always looked upon as the type of all that was pure and womanly, to talk of giving herself to another man! He crumpled the paper in his hand. No, there would be no divorce. It was impure, it was unclean for her even to talk of such a thing. It was enough to kill all a man's faith in women! He rose as if to pace the room, then he sat down again. But of course there was no need to consider, that – the scandal – the gossip – and, what would be gained by it? He fell to considering the other preposition. After all it was not so bad! If she said she would do a thing, she would go through with it. She would be always there to look after the house and children; no one would know anything; if there was one thing you could depend on Rebekah for, it was to hold her tongue. A more placid look came over his face and all signs of anger died. Even if she carried out what she said she would, it would not be bad. When a woman has borne four children and had several miscarriages, she's not just what she was when you married her, and after seven years of marriage it would be nonsense to pretend there was very much romance: – a slight placid expansion, almost like a smile, spread over his lips and drew back the corners of his mouth; it was the look of deep, inward contentment with himself and the world that made people call him the best-tempered, jolliest man in his club. – She was not the only woman in the world! A dreamy smile played over his face, as if he were recalling past events. If only he got away for ten days, and avoided discussing matters while they were hot; that was the great thing. At the end of that time when he came back – well, if it had to be discussed – his forehead contracted a little at the thought – it would be quite a different matter from discussing it now. Give her time, give her time! Rebekah was a sensible woman if you gave her time and didn't take her on the hop while she was warm. He sat looking down at his feet. Who could tell but that, after a time, she – then he stopped, and knit his forehead; he knew that, as between him and her, things were at an end forever. He got up and threw his dressing gown over a chair. It was all a damned nuisance! But it was no use worrying about it any more. He got into bed. At the head of the bed a little silk satchel hung in which Rebekah always put the daily papers for him to read after he got into bed. He took out the evening's sheet and began to read the account of the last cricket match at Sea

Point. He ran his eyes carefully down the row of figures, noting who had done well and who had not, but his thoughts wandered, and when he had gone twice over the figures he stuck the paper back in the holder; he turned the lamp out and drew the cover up over his shoulder and turned his face on one side. – After all, the great thing was just to give her time! Things would all settle themselves somehow! In ten minutes he had gone to sleep.

When her husband had closed the door of her study, Rebekah stood silent for a moment looking at it. Then she sat down in her armchair and leaned her head back against it. She folded her hands over her head and looked up at the dark little ceiling. She drew a long breath; but it was not the ceiling of the little room she saw as she sat there staring upwards. It was as though a vast dome were reared over her, as though a dark pall, which for years had been stretched out just above her, were folded up and removed and she looked up into almost infinite space. So wide, so still, so peaceful; and she was alone there.

After half an hour she stood up; as she turned out the lamp and lit the candle to take to the room, a curious sensation came to her, as if she were a little child again. Even the candle she had lighted and held in her hand seemed like candles used to long ago. At the door of the room she turned and looked back; she seemed to have come from a long journey and to be seeing it all again – the little statue of Hercules in the corner which she had bought when she first married, her shelves with the books, the cabinet with the fossils in it that she had loved so; she saw them all as she used to see them. It seemed as if some great crease of anguish which had lain in her brain for years had smoothed itself out.

She closed the door and went to her little stretcher between the boys' beds. She had not slept for thirty-six hours. She undressed and put out her light, and in a few minutes was in a deep unbroken sleep.

When the stable boy brought the coffee to her door early the next morning, he told her that his master had called him before daylight to make coffee and to drive him to town, and he gave her a letter his master had left for her. She opened it before the window and read it. A relaxation passed over her lips as she finished it: it was not bitterness, it was not disappointment; it was a placid recognition of the inevitable which always repeated itself.

He did not return till the eighth day. A nurse met him at the front door. She said Rebekah had been confined four days before of a seven months' child. She had had a bad time, and, until the day before, her life had been despaired of. The child, she said, was very puny, but it was alive. She had driven out to her farm twice, once the day before he left and again the next day, and the jolting might have been too much for her, otherwise there was no explanation of her illness. He could not see her, the nurse said, but he might see the child. She took him into his own bedroom. Rebekah lay in the children's room, where she had been taken ill; she had refused to be removed into the large room. From the small bed in the corner the nurse took up a pillow and uncovered on it a tiny morsel of flesh, eyebrowless, hairless, with a small wizened face. He had been proud of his other children; they had all weighed ten or twelve pounds, and people had called them prize babies; he had even boasted of them to men at his club. For this sorrowful, tiny thing he had a feeling of horror, almost of loathing; he turned away from it quickly. He told the nurse as Rebekah was so ill he would go to an hotel in town, to save giving trouble in the house; but he asked her to let him know at once if she were worse or there was anything she needed, and he would himself try to come out in the evening to hear how she was.

He went to his dressing room and filled his portmanteau with the things he would need in town, then carrying it in his hand he walked through the dining room. The room looked dusty and unused. On the table in the corner stood her work basket, on the top of which lay one of his white shirts onto which she had been sewing a new wristband; the needle was stuck upright into the work with the thimble balanced on the top, as she had left it the last day when she was taken ill. As he looked at it, a sensation of what was perhaps the sharpest pain he ever felt in the course of his life over anything that did not touch him personally ran through him. He passed on quickly to the front veranda and down the garden path. All her lilies and roses were in bloom, and as the sun shone on them the mignonette and verbena sent up a strong scent; the trowel she had been weeding with lay in the soft mould near the garden gate. He hurried out quickly and shut the gate and walked down the avenue.

After all, it was not his fault if she chose to go driving out two days running in a jolting cart. She had said she was not going to the farm again till after the baby was born – and she might yet get well again! As he passed the little suburban chemist's shop at the corner, he went in and bought two bottles of scent of a kind he knew she liked when she was ill, and ordered the chemist to send it up at once to the house with a cut-glass spray. After he got into the train he resolved to go and buy three books he had heard her say she would like and a little ring they had seen in the window of a jeweller's shop in Adderley Street the last time they were out together, which she had admired. She so seldom noticed jewellery or anything of that kind; and he had never given her anything since they were married. When he got out he went to the bookseller's and ordered the books to be sent out at once; then he walked up the street to the jeweller's; just as he was going in he stopped; after all, the ring would cost seven or eight pounds, and she might not really care for it; anyhow, he could get it later. Then he walked on to his office. It was too late to settle down to work before lunch, so he soon went out. On the way to the club he met a friend who condoled with him on his wife's serious illness and they went in and had a drink together – a thing he seldom did – and they had a short game of billiards together before lunch. After lunch he felt better and went back to his office.

When the office closed he went out to the suburbs to hear how his wife was. The nurse met him at the door; she said Rebekah had been sleeping quietly the greater part of the day, that the fever had quite left her and the doctors thought the danger was passed. She had asked to see the baby – a thing she had not done yet. He said he would not come in, and walked down the avenue again. After all, she was *not* going to die; she would have had to be ill and have the baby some time; perhaps it was just as well it came when it did! It would be a week certainly before he could see her, and then probably a fortnight before they could discuss things. It would be very different from discussing everything while it was still fresh! After all, how much better it was to let things slide! Men made half their own troubles by walking up to things and grasping hold of them. Perhaps it was just as well everything was as it was!

A little lower down the avenue he met an old friend, who asked how his wife was and condoled with him and asked him to come in to dinner. All the family were very kind and sympathetic and after dinner the two elder daughters played and sang for him.

CHAPTER NINE

Cart Tracks in the Sand

Up-country, in the red Karoo, was the town where Aunt Mary-Anna lived, red Karoo to right of it, red Karoo to left. A river bed ran below the town, in winter full of dried mud banks and reaches of gravel and bare stone, but, in the summer rains, coming down red and full, the dark sand-laden water lying level with the banks and bearing on its waves trees and stumps, the carcasses of drowned animals, and even sometimes at long intervals a human corpse.

All round the plain were flat-topped mountains, some broken into jagged points, but still bearing the marks, in their flat structure, of what had been the shores of seas and lakes, the remains of whose mammoth amphibious beasts lay still within the stratified shale, turned in the course of the ages to stone themselves.

There were three churches in the town and a great square full of sand with shops and houses round it, where, in the early morning, buck wagons drawn by long teams of oxen rolled slowly in, laden with produce from the country, skins and pumpkins and firewood, bags of meal or *mielies* and sometimes butter and garden growths; and the little market master held the morning market. There the townsmen gathered to hear the latest news and send round the latest gossip, till by eight o'clock they had all gone home to their breakfasts, the wagons had rolled out and the square was left empty and silent enough all day, crossed occasionally by customers making their way to the different shops or businessmen going home to their meals, and, at eleven o'clock, by streams of men coming to the hotel at the corner where they went to have their morning drink of soda and brandy and to smoke and chat for a while on the hotel *stoep*.

Three times a week the post cart with its dusty wheels and horses came in, blowing its bugle and bringing its news from the outer world, and everyone hurried to the post office to get his letters. And twice a week came Cobb and Co's great coaches, swinging on their great leather straps; and their teams of six horses, bearing passengers to and from the Diamond Fields, drew up before the hotel door, when for two hours the town was alive and excited with the new arrivals; then the horses would be put in again and pass away in a cloud of dust and the town would be left to its silent monotony.

There were two croquet clubs in the place frequented by the members of two churches which formed the two great cliques; there was a courthouse where occasionally the members of one church gave a dance which the other church thought wicked and never went to, and once or twice a year some travelling showman would arrive and give an entertainment there. Every year the members of each church had a large Sunday School picnic to which all the members of that congregation went; and sometimes a lady would give a high tea and invite a few friends, for no one dined late there.

In the upper part of the town there were rows of little flat houses, generally kept shut up and empty, where the Dutch farmers stayed when they came in once in three months to the Lord's Supper (*Nagmaal*) and now and then to the Sunday services in the weeks between. But on Monday they all went out again, and the houses were left empty, and the town to its English inhabitants.

During nine months of the year, while the winds blew, clouds of dust whirled along the streets before thunderstorms; when the gusts came, great clouds of sand rose from the market square and met the still mightier clouds raised from the wide sandy plain; and the town was shrouded in sand.

It was a dull narrow little life enough, lived there among the flat-roofed houses, far removed from the currents of life and thought of the great world beyond.

Yet, if some summer morning you rose at half past four and went out to the *kopje* at the end of the town and climbed its round black ironstones, and stood looking down at the little town with its long rows of houses and the little brown huts of the Kaffir location sleeping at your feet in the still blue morning air, while the damp of the night yet rested on everything and nothing moved or stirred, except where here and there a Kaffir servant might be seen hurrying from the location to the town, her shawl drawn tight about her to shut out the chill morning air; till by and by, from some of the chimneys in the town, long blue curls of smoke began to rise, standing upright and almost motionless in the still air; then suddenly the bleak moist stone on which you stood turned golden at your feet; a shaft of light had shot across the plain and struck it; another came, and the little ice plant in the crevice of the rock at your feet glittered in every crystal drop; then another, and the whole plain was golden and the roofs of the little flat houses glinted – then the town was beautiful.

Bertie's aunt and uncle lived in a street leading out of the square, so close to it that from the front windows you could see half across it. It was an old dingy house, a foot lower than the street and the water furrow above, with a little strip of flower garden six feet wide and a low paling before it.

Her uncle's business place was on another plot across the square. He was a general agent; he held auction sales, conducted cases in the little Magistrate's Court, drew up wills and managed estates, and speculated on his own account. He was thin, silent, and rather hatchet-faced: he was regarded by his fellow townsmen as a clever businessman, though he was said to have lately burnt his fingers in some speculation and to have lost on a company he had fitted out and sent up to the

Diamond Fields; he was hard in business matters and said to love money; but he was a leading man in the church of which he was a member and was regarded as one of the principal men in the town. More than twenty years before he had married Bertie's aunt, whom he had met when on a visit from England to her sister, the little mother at the old farm; and had brought her to his little up-country town, where they had lived in the same house ever since, with the same furniture and the same strip of flower garden, and where their two daughters, now in England, had been born. Her aunt was not unlike the little mother in feature, but tall and thin and much less pretty, and with a cold measured manner. Her head, like Bertie's, was small compared to the size of her body, and three rows of short faded white curls hung on each side of her head. In the chapel she was the leader at prayer meetings and all religious gatherings and was one of the most esteemed women of the town.

Besides her uncle and aunt, there was no one in the house but Dorcas, the tall heavy-faced Kaffir servant, who always wore a red handkerchief bound across her head and helped in the kitchen.

Once Bertie might have found the dingy, flat little house with its three inhabitants lonely. Now she loved it.

On the first day when Bertie was unpacking her clothes her aunt admired her mantle, and Bertie had begged her aunt for her old silk shawl and out of it by the next Sunday had made a mantle exactly like her own, and had remade her aunt's bonnet and retrimmed it with lace from one of her own ball dresses; so that when Aunt Mary-Anna appeared in chapel everyone thought it was a new mantle and bonnet. Some said that if the general agent were really in business difficulties she should not purchase such expensive things, others that perhaps they were presents from a rich niece in Cape Town, but everyone admired them.

The next week Bertie got from her uncle a large roll of flower-covered chintz that had been lying in his sale room for months and with it made covers for every chair and sofa, till all the old dingy furniture blossomed out in pink roses. And the next week, when her aunt went to a farm for three days, she bought with her own money some cheap wallpaper and, with Dorcas to help her, repapered the passage and the front parlour, she standing at the top of the ladder and Dorcas at the bottom; and she took up the carpet in the parlour that had lain there for twenty-four years and cut it down the middle and resewed it so that the worn centre came to the sides, when, by placing furniture over the worn patches, it looked like a new carpet; so that when Aunt Mary-Anna returned she was filled with surprise and delight; and the house looked as if the general agent were refurnishing.

Early in the morning Bertie was up making curry and hot rolls for breakfast; for dinner and supper she made *sosatie* and *bobotie* and pumpkin fritters and puffs and grilled chops, as she had learned from old Ayah; and the hatchet face of the general agent, who for twenty-four years had suffered from bad cooking, seemed to be perceptibly filling out. When she had no cooking to do, she rummaged her aunt's old wardrobe and boxes and, from ends of lace and bits of old material, shaped little caps and aprons, and, by unpicking and cleaning and reshaping old dresses, made her aunt's wardrobe full of wearable dresses.

'I really don't know how we ever got on without you,' her aunt used to say. 'You must never leave us, or, if you do, you must promise to remain for eight months after the girls come home, so that they may learn from you.'

Even her silent uncle praised her food, and, as he passed through the kitchen where she was stooping over a pot, stirring its contents, would say, 'Our little cook must not burn her face too much, though I know it's something good she's going to turn out'; and Bertie's cheeks would flush a deeper red, more with pride and happiness than from the heat of the fire.

Even Dorcas liked her; she coaxed her so gently, and, when Bertie had given her a white silk handkerchief to tie in with her red one on Sundays and had shown her how to arrange it round her head and had made her a cotton blouse with red butterflies on it, Dorcas would do anything for her.

'I am very, very happy here,' she wrote to Rebekah; 'I should never like to go away. Everyone loves me.'

After the first Sunday when Bertie appeared in church, the ladies of the town had called to see her, and her aunt said it was necessary she should return their calls with her; but after that she refused to go out. She accepted no invitations to picnics or parties and declined to join the croquet club. At first her aunt tried to persuade her to go out; but when she found she really did not wish to go and that Bertie's staying at home gave her more time to attend prayer meetings and classes and to fulfil her duties as leading woman in the church, she gave way; and the only times when Bertie was ever seen out were when she went twice to church every Sunday and once on a week night, and when she now and then went out shopping for her aunt. The mothers of the place all praised her and held her up to their daughters as an example of devotion to hard work and duty.

When she first came the young girls of the place felt to her much as the ducks in a farmyard might to one that had wandered in from the open. They all said she was not nearly so pretty as the men said, that she looked proud and her curls were not natural. But when, after some weeks, they found she never crossed their paths, when she had lent them the patterns of her dresses and had helped two of the prettiest girls in the place to make bonnets for themselves exactly like her own, they all said she was nice and much the prettiest girl that had ever come to the town, and that her curly hair was beautiful, and that they thought her aunt unkind to keep her so much at home.

The young men had not many opportunities of seeing her except in church; two, who had always gone to the other church, began to attend there, and two who had sat in the centre moved into a wing so that they sat opposite the general agent's pew. On Sunday and week nights such as knew the general agent and his wife hurried to the church door and tried to walk home with them. But Bertie seemed always to manage to walk between her uncle and aunt; and if they spoke across to her as they walked she said 'yes' or 'no' and seemed not to see them. And if she went to a shop to buy anything, and the young shopman spoke to her of the weather or the dust or of anything but business, she answered him quickly and softly and went out.

Even the magistrate's clerk, who wore a black coat and carried a little walking stick, and said there was no one in the town he could associate with, and never took notice of any girl, called three times formally at the general agent's after Bertie came; but as she did not appear, he had to content himself with sitting opposite the general agent's pew.

Bertie was very happy all day. If ever, as she worked, a thought came to her she did not like, she put it from her quickly, saying within herself: 'They all love me here! I will never go away! They will always let me stay.'

Only at night when she had gone to bed and put out the light and was just dropping off to sleep, suddenly the old dream which she used to have on the farm when she was a little child used to come back to her – she was running down the road in the dark and on, behind her, came something with heavy breath; she knew its tongue lolled out and she heard its steps, and as she ran it came nearer and nearer! – till she woke shrieking; and Rebekah used to hear her and come from her bed and lie beside her and sing 'London's Burning! Fire! Fire!' till she went to sleep.

Now it often came back to her; she would wake with the bed trembling beneath her and would sit up wringing her hands, before she remembered where she was. Then she would lie down quickly and pull the cover close over her head and take a pillow and hold it longways against her and clasp it tight, with both arms around it, so that it seemed like something living she was clinging to.

One day at breakfast her uncle brought the post in and gave her a letter. She read it, sitting behind the coffee-urn at the head of the table.

'I hope you have no bad news, my dear,' Aunt Mary-Anna said.

'Oh no,' Bertie said, 'it's from mother.' But when breakfast was over she hurried to her own room and knelt down beside the bed and laid the letter open before her and read it through. As she read her cheeks darkened slowly to a red as deep as the darkest of Rebekah's roses in the garden at Cape Town. She buried her burning face in the letter – and knelt motionless. What the letter said was this:

My dear Baby-Bertie,

I am glad you are so happy at your aunt's, but I wish you could come home by Xmas-time. John-Ferdinand and Veronica come over and spend every Sunday with us and generally drive over once a week, so I'm not so lonely. But Veronica is going to have a baby at Xmas-time and I shall have to go and stay with her for some weeks. Of course, old Ayah can stay and look after the house and your father, but come if you can, unless your aunt very much wants you and you want to stay.

Then came much farm news that she read without noting; then came the PS:

Veronica is looking so well. ... She has a lovely colour and her face is getting quite round. ... You would hardly know her.

After a time Bertie lifted her face from the letter; it was growing slowly white; she put it in her breast and went to knead the bread in the kitchen.

After dinner, when her aunt was asleep and her uncle had gone to his business, she slipped out and went to a shop across the square. There she bought the finest muslin and lace and embroidery the town held and needles and thread even finer than those she generally used; then she slipped back to her own room and all the afternoon sat cutting out and sewing. She got up early the next morning as soon as the sun rose and went back to her work, and at night she sat sewing at her bedside till one or two o'clock. Her aunt noticed that now, as soon as her work was done, she went to her own room, but thought she was doing sewing for herself.

Slowly the scores of little tucks and the fine embroidery shaped themselves. At the end of a week there were two tiny armholes. Again and again she would stop in her work to put her fingers into them and fill them out. At the end of a fortnight the long white robe with its delicate invisible stitching was almost complete. At night, before she put it away, she would lay it out on the bed, putting a pillow at the top and filling it out so that it almost seemed there was something inside it; and she would stand across the room looking at it. One day it was finished. She packed it in white tissue-paper with a few little bits of fresh lavender put in it. She tied it with pink ribbons and packed it into a handkerchief box with red rosebuds on the lid; then she carefully folded brown paper round it and tied it with string across and across. When her aunt went to sleep after dinner, again she stole out and went to the post office and stamped it and sent it off. After it was gone she was always picturing how it travelled: it would take seven days to reach the farm; it might have to wait two days at the post office in the village if no special messenger came to fetch it; then on Sunday morning it would get to the farm; someone would open it. She never would let herself think any further; she began picturing the journey over again.

The poet, when his heart is weighted, writes a sonnet, and the painter paints a picture, and the thinker throws himself into the world of thought, and the publican and the man of business may throw themselves into the world of action; but the woman is only a woman – what has she but her needle? In that torn bit of brown leather brace worked through and through with yellow silk, in that bit of white rag with invisible stitching, lying among the fallen leaves and rubbish that the wind has

599

blown into the gutter or the street corner, lies all the passion of some woman's soul finding voiceless expression. Has the pen or the pencil dipped so deep in the blood of the human race as the needle?

After that the summer began to grow hotter, every afternoon clouds of dust wheeled along the streets and over the plains; and now and then a thunderstorm broke at four o'clock and laid the dust for that day.

The week before Xmas the post brought no letter for Bertie, but her aunt came into the kitchen where she was shelling peas and said she had had a few lines from the little mother, who could not write to Bertie because at six o'clock on the day she wrote Veronica had had a fine little boy. Mother and child were doing well. Bertie went on shelling the peas and got dinner ready; after dinner she went to bed with a sick headache and did not come to supper, but early the next morning she was up kneading the bread and said she was quite well. Some days after that came the news that Rebekah also had a little son, born prematurely, and that she was very ill; then news that she was better. Then a long time passed when nothing happened.

Slowly the summer heat began to die and the nights to become cool, sometimes almost sharp. All the housewives were busy plucking fruit and drying and preserving. Bertie had made rows and rows of bottles of peach and quince jam which lined the shelves of her aunt's pantry; and now she was making watermelon preserve. Her aunt's daughters would be out in five months, and everything was being got ready for the teas and suppers when they came.

Then a curious experience began to come to Bertie. It was as though a weight seemed always resting on her; it might be the change to the autumn's coolness, but something heavy seemed always pressing on her. She tried to shake it off; but from being a vague feeling it grew till it almost took definite shape. Sometimes if she went out to a shop or to carry a message to her uncle's office, if girls she met passed her and she wished them good day they returned her greeting, but, if she did not, they seemed to pass without seeing her. When one of her aunt's women friends called and she went to open the door, they did not smile, but asked gravely if her aunt was in. It might have been her fancy, but it seemed to her that when her uncle and aunt spoke to her they did not look at her, and they spoke more seldom. A curious silence seemed to have settled down on the house. One morning, when her aunt was having her breakfast in bed and Bertie sat, as she always did, at the table behind the tray, she looked up suddenly and saw her uncle, who sat at the other end of the table, looking at her intently over the top of the newspaper he held. The moment he saw she had noticed him he dropped his eyes and raised the paper so that only the top of his head was visible over it; and several times, when she came into a room where her uncle and aunt were, they were talking together in a low tone, but stopped at once when she came in.

On Sundays after church there were still some young men about the door, but, if the general agent did not speak to them, they did not force their company as they used to, and the three walked home alone together. One Sunday the magistrate's clerk, who had never waited near the door like other young men, walked straight up to them and forced his way in between Bertie and her uncle and walked next to her, talking to her; but there seemed something strange in the way he walked and talked, looking round at all the people they passed, as if he were challenging them to see where he walked. That afternoon, when her uncle and aunt were sleeping, Bertie sat alone in her bedroom with her hands in her lap; it seemed to her all the while that a lump kept rising in her throat and she wanted to cry, though she could not tell why.

The autumn was closing in fast now, the leaves were falling from the trees in the street and filling the furrows and covering the sidewalks in the lower part of the town. In the gardens everything but the winter crops was drying out.

One afternoon about five o'clock Bertie sat in the little parlour that looked out across the garden into the street; she sat sewing before the window on the little low chair on which she always sat, and her aunt sat opposite in a high-backed cane rocking chair, knitting. For nearly an hour they had sat there with no sound but the click of Aunt Mary-Anna's needles to break the silence. The sky was becoming slightly overcast as though it was going to rain, and the light was already beginning to grow duller in the little low room. Suddenly Bertie leaned forward and laid her hand, with the threaded needle in it, on her aunt's knee.

'Aunt Mary-Anna,' she said quickly, in a low, slightly thick voice, 'have I done anything to displease you? Are you angry with me?'

'No, Bertie, no,' she said, knitting quickly. She dropped three stitches but knitted on without noticing them.

'I was so afraid I had done something to displease you,' Bertie said, looking up at her.

'No – you have done nothing to me, Bertie.' She knitted on without looking at her. 'And yet,' she said, after a pause, 'it is perhaps quite as well you spoke, because I have been wishing to speak to you. Your uncle and I think' – she waited a little – 'it is perhaps quite as well you went home. In fact, your uncle wrote yesterday to your father, and posted the letter today, to say you would be leaving by next Thursday's post cart, and they must send to meet you at the town next week.'

Bertie sat upright in her chair, looking at her aunt with wide-open eyes.

'But I can't go home, I don't want to go,' she said, in a low thick voice. 'You said I could stay here with you. Oh, what have I done?'

For a moment Aunt Mary-Anna knitted on blunderingly, then she stopped and looked at Bertie. 'There is no need for us to discuss the matter, my dear. You have been very kind and of great use to me, and your uncle and I will always be grateful for the many ways in which you have helped us. But we both think it best you should go home now. You have been here nearly six months and your mother may be wanting you.'

'But you said I could stay! Oh, please let me stay! I don't want to go! I can't go back there!' She laid her hand again on Aunt Mary-Anna's knee and looked up at her with large wide-open eyes.

Aunt Mary-Anna hesitated. Then she drew herself up. 'Perhaps I had better tell you the truth, Bertie. It is as well you should know it. People here have been saying very strange things about you.' Bertie looked up into her face with eyes that seemed to grow wider. 'Your uncle heard something first in the town, and he told me; and afterwards the minister's wife called and told me the same thing. She said she felt it her duty to tell me what people were saying. It is the common talk of the town now. I don't believe a word of it, neither does your uncle; and I have told everyone so who has spoken to me. And after you have gone I shall deny it everywhere. But with my two girls coming home, you will understand, Bertie, that, as it is something regarding your conduct as a young girl, I could not have you staying on here with them. It may be all perfectly untrue, my dear' – there was something almost of kindliness in Aunt Mary-Anna's tone – 'but a woman's character is like gossamer, when you've once dropped it in the mud and pulled it about it can never be put right again. With a man it's different; he can live down anything. People say, 'Oh he was young, he's changed.' They never say that of a woman; the soap isn't invented that can wash a woman's character clean.'

Bertie leaned farther forward, looking at her. Her aunt moved restlessly.

'Of course I don't believe a word of it; it's just silly talk of what happened when you were a schoolgirl of fifteen. I know there's no truth in it. But that doesn't make any practical difference. You are one of the best girls I ever knew.' Bertie leaned yet more forward and laid her hand on her aunt's knee.

'But if it is true?' she whispered.

Her aunt drew herself up suddenly and looked down at her wide eyes. Bertie stretched out both her hands; it seemed as if she would have caught hold of her aunt's hands. 'I'll tell you – I'll tell you everything ...!'

Aunt Mary-Anna rose quickly. 'Really, Bertie, I am astonished at you! I will beg of you to tell me nothing. If there is any truth in what they have been saying about you, the least you can do is to keep quiet about it. I have asked you no questions, and you should at least leave me the power of denying it. You have cost me trouble enough as it is. Your mother and Rebekah did very wrong in letting you come here, knowing I had young girls.'

'Oh, they don't know! No one knows! I have only told one person about it!' Bertie rose and stood before her. A blind look was in her eyes as though she saw nothing; she moved her hands aimlessly. 'I was so young,' she wailed suddenly. 'Oh!' – she moved her hands.

'Will you lower your voice, Bertie! Do you want Dorcas, who is in the kitchen, to hear everything you say! If you want to tell anyone about it, tell your mother and your sister.'

'Oh, I can't! They must never know! They think I'm a baby still! – Oh, I can't go home! I never can never go home!'

'You must go home,' said her aunt quietly, 'and not later than by next Thursday's cart.'

At that moment there was a sound at the front door and of feet in the passage, and then the general agent flung open the door of the little parlour. Beside him shuffled a little figure. He ushered him in. Aunt Mary-Anna turned quickly to the door; but Bertie still stood motionless before the window, where the quickly fading light fell full on her. She had a little crimson rosebud fastened at the throat of her white dress, which made her face of a more deadly paleness under its cloud of brown curling hair, and the eyelashes of her drooping eyes seemed printed on her cheeks. Aunt Mary-Anna stepped forward to greet the visitor, whom she had evidently met before. She shook hands with him and asked him if he had arrived by that evening's coach from the Fields.[1]

He was a small man of about fifty, with slightly bent shoulders and thin, small limbs. His face was of a dull Oriental pallor, and his piercing dark eyes and marked nose proclaimed him at once a Jew; above a high square forehead rose a tower of stiffly curling, grey, upright hair. He spoke with a strong foreign accent. The general agent introduced him to Bertie. She gave him a cold dead hand without looking at him and then turned slowly to the window and with her back to the room stood looking out, her hands hanging lifeless at either side. The Jew took his seat on a small chair in the dark corner between the sideboard and the wall, and twisted his feet into the legs of the chair. The general agent begged him to stay to supper; he assented shortly and sat looking keenly about the room, now at Bertie's figure as she stood before the window, and then at the furniture, at the hanging lamp and the old piano and what-not and then back at Bertie. Her aunt asked her to go and get supper ready, and she left the room without looking round. Presently her aunt came into the kitchen and asked her to prepare the best supper she could, as their visitor was a man with whom her uncle had business dealings and wished to entertain as well as possible. She carried a lighted lamp into the parlour, where the general agent was inquiring from his guest the state of affairs at the Fields and the condition of the country through which he had passed, to all which inquiries the Jew answered shortly and looked keenly about him. He was a moneylender and diamond speculator whose home was in London but who had come to South Africa several times since the discovery of diamonds, and he had lent the general agent a large sum of money at a high rate of interest with which the agent had financed the diamond-digging venture that had failed. He knew it was to attend to this matter that the Jew had broken his journey from the Fields to England at the little town, and that, if the Jew pressed for immediate payment, it meant his insolvency, and he talked with unusual

---

1 The Diamond Fields.

fluency and suaveness; but the Jew did not trouble himself to make conversation, and when the general agent ceased to speak there were long pauses.

When Bertie had prepared the supper she went to her aunt's bedroom, where her aunt stood before the glass putting on her best cap and collar and arranging her curls. Bertie who stood in the doorway said that all was ready, but that her head ached and she would like to go to her room instead of going to supper. Her aunt ran her curls round her fingers and said without looking back, 'You will do nothing of the kind, my dear. The least you can do for the few days you are still here is to allow no one to see that anything unusual has happened. You will at least come to the table if you do not care to eat.' Then she added, as she patted her curls, 'You will also please note, Bertie, that you need not refer again to anything that passed between us this evening while you are here. Your uncle has taken your seat in the post cart that leaves on Thursday. He has not mentioned to your parents why you are going; he simply said that as your mother seemed to need you we could not think of keeping you here longer. One thing I should like to say to you, Bertie: never attempt such confidences as you were desirous of making to me this evening. If a woman has made a mistake there is only one course for her – silence!' Her aunt still looked into the glass and Bertie withdrew softly from the door.

At the supper table Bertie sat in her usual place behind the tray at the head, with the great coffee urn before her. Her aunt sat on the right side of the table and the Jew on the left and her uncle at the other end.

The Jew ate hurriedly and absorbedly, as people do who have lived through much of their life alone: he bent low over his plate, shovelling in the *frikkedel* and gravy with his knife and seldom looking up. Once or twice as he ate his eye passed from his plate to the end of the table where Bertie sat silent, her cheeks so pale they were almost sallow and her eyelashes almost resting on them as she looked down at the plate on which she toyed with her food.

When the supper was almost done, in answer to some remark of the general agent's as to the colour of diamonds, the Jew took from an inner breast-pocket a small parcel wrapped in oilskin and carefully tied. He removed the oilskin and took out a small brown paper parcel, from the inside of which he took a small round japanned box. He opened and poured carefully into a plate a little shower of white, yellow-tinted stones, which glittered softly in the lamplight. He put the plate between himself and the general agent and began touching the different stones with his bent forefinger, describing their various qualities and values. The general agent's wife leaned forward to see them. He passed the plate over for her to examine them more closely. When she had handed the plate back to him, the Jew looked up to the end of the table where Bertie sat. 'And ze young lady, vill she not see too?' he asked.

Bertie lifted her eyes heavily. He passed the plate up towards her; she put it down at her side, looking at them with her indifferent drooping eyes. 'They are nice,' she said slowly, and was going to return the plate, when the Jew bent forward. 'Vitch zinks she is the best now?' he said, with his head a little on one side.

Indifferently, with her finger Bertie touched a small perfect octahedron stone. 'This,' she said, and handed the plate back to the Jew.

'Ha-ha! Zat is very good! It is small, but it is ze best. Ze young lady has a good eye.'

He put the stones back into the little box and returned it to its wrappings and put it into his breast-pocket. Then they rose. The general agent invited him to return to the parlour; but he said he must leave. He shook hands with Bertie and her aunt.

In the hall, when the general agent and helped him on with his coat, he turned to him for a moment and said, 'Ze young lady, does she live viz you?'

The general agent explained that she was his wife's niece and only on a visit, and was to leave in two days. The Jew made an appointment to meet him at his office the next morning to discuss business. The general agent opened the door for him and wished him goodnight; the Jew shuffled out into the street, and the door closed behind him.

It was a glorious night. Up above, ten thousand stars were throwing down their points of light brighter than any diamonds and making dimly visible even the outlines of the houses in the dark town. The Jew began to shuffle through the thick sand in the street and the yet thicker sand of the square. But he saw neither the bright lights above him nor the dark earth about him.

Far away, across the mist of fifty years, he saw again a little garret room under the eaves in a North German city, where a small dark-eyed boy and girl played together when their parents had gone out to their work and had locked them in. He saw again the little garret window, through which they crept out onto the roof where the tall chimneys rose. Again they played at being storks, and, with tiny fragments in their mouths of the brown bread their parents had left them to eat during their absence, pretended to feed tiny imaginary storklings in an imaginary nest between the chimneys; again he heard the little girl's cry of admiration at his courage and of terror lest he should fall when the boy walked to the extreme edge of the roof to peer down into the street below; again he held fast the skirts of the little girl as she crept back through the window lest they should sweep against the box of mignonette their mother had planted there and break them. And then it was later, and a boy of seventeen and a girl of sixteen whose parents had died in Germany were living alone in London in an East End garret whose roof sloped to the floor at one side. Again it was early morning and the boy with the black curls hanging into his neck and an old black bag over his shoulders paced the streets of Bloomsbury; again he felt the nip of the fog-laden London morning air in his nostrils, and again he felt the fresh young blood coursing through his veins as the boy raised his cry, 'Old clothes! Old clothes!' and raised his eyes anxiously to the grim rows of houses to see if from door or window came an answering beck or nod. And then it was evening and the bag was full, and, up the flights of stairs in the East End lodging-house, the boy was mounting three steps at a time. Then he saw the door open and the pile of clothes on the floor and the girl in the fading light at the little sloping window bending over her work, till she raised her dark soft eyes with their curled lashes to greet him, and they prepared their evening meal of fried fish on the little stove in the corner, and to save light and keep warm sat down on a heap of clothes before the stove and ate it together from one plate; and when it was ended sat talking of the prices she had got at the shops for the clothes she had repaired, and the things he had in the bag. When she grew tired, she laid her head on his knee, and, staring at the small bed of coals, he talked of the future, of the time when their savings would have mounted and they too would possess a tall house in Bloomsbury. He talked of the jewels he would buy her and the carriage they would keep, and she talked of the food she would see he had and the things they would do for their aunt and her children in Germany who were the only relations they had. And all the while, as he saw the pictures, he saw also dimly Bertie's face at the head of the table, with the thick furling hair above the low forehead and the large eyes with the curled lashes that had waked the old pictures.

He struck his foot against the lowest step of the little hotel *stoep* and swore and shuffled up them. In the bar the men were gathered drinking and talking; he went in and sat for a while listening, now and then putting in a remark to see if no news as to the general agent's monetary position was to be gathered, and then he went upstairs. When he had undressed and put his oilcloth-wrapped parcel under his pillow, he got into bed and blew out the light. His long day's journey on the coach had tired him, but he could not sleep. First his thoughts travelled over the news he had heard of the general agent in the bar room: would it, or would it not, be best to push him? Then his thoughts travelled back to the Diamond Fields, to the man he had left at the River Diggings to buy claims for him, to New Rush[2] and his claims there. Then they led back to London, to the tall grim house in Bloomsbury, where hundreds of houses, equally yellow and dull and deadly in their exact likeness to one another from attic to basement, filled the long weary street in which he had lived alone for twenty years, with only Martha, his grimy broad-shouldered housekeeper, and later on her weak-eyed short-witted son, with a gait like his own, to keep him company. He wondered irritably if the woman was not burning too many coals and using too much food during his absence and whether Isaac always remembered to lock the area gate; and then he saw Bertie sitting at the agent's table, with her large eyes and her drooping lashes and the curly hair that had brought back the past. He tossed wearily. He lit the candle and looked at his watch; it was half past eleven; then he blew the light out and tried to sleep again. But when the clock struck twelve he was still lying staring up into the dark.

Then the Jew rose; he lit the candle and took from under his pillow the parcel of

---

2 Now Kimberley.

stones. Carefully he opened it and, examining the stones, selected the one which Bertie had touched that evening. He held it in the palm of his hand, looking at it by the candlelight. Softly he touched it with the forefinger of the other hand, caressing its soft soapy surface as a mother might the hair of a child with which she was to part. He extended his arm, holding it close to the candle, and drew back his head that he might look at it from a distance; then he put it down on a fragment of the brown paper and wrapped it carefully in it; then he cut off a piece of the oilskin and folded it in that; then he tied the tiny parcel carefully and put it in his purse. He refolded the large parcel and put it with his purse under the pillow. Then he got quickly into bed and was soon asleep.

The next morning the Jew visited the general agent's office; he discussed their business; he asked at what rate the general agent would be willing to pay if he left the money due now in a few weeks for another two years, and what securities he could give; but he gave the general agent no definite answer as to whether he would accept his terms or not, but said he should hear from him later in the day.

As he was turning to go the Jew took from his purse the small brown parcel and handed it to the general agent.

'Ze young lady, she liked zat stone. Vill you say I have ze honour to present it to her viz my compliments?' Then he went out at the door without waiting for thanks.

When the agent went home to dinner he gave Bertie the gift. She opened it with no sign of pleasure. At his request she wrote a note of three lines thanking the Jew. After dinner, when she had gone to her room to finish her packing, Aunt Mary-Anna turned to her husband. 'Why did he give it her?' she asked.

'How can I tell?' asked the general agent. She looked at him. 'Is he married?'

'For all I can tell he may have a wife and half a dozen children in Hamburg or England or wherever his headquarters may be!' But he divined her meaning as the slowest people who have lived together for twenty years will do without words.

'The idea did just flit across my mind also,' said the general agent, answering her thought, 'but it's ridiculous. No doubt he admired her; she's the kind of woman every man finds attractive. But Jews don't marry Christians, even supposing him to be unmarried. A Jew will eat sucking pig, he will be a Christian in all his manners and customs, but when it comes to legal marriage, he's a Jew. It's a ridiculous idea, and he's leaving tomorrow.'

'It's very strange he should give away a valuable stone like that to a girl he has only exchanged three words with!'

'Not at all. You never can account for what a Jew will do. I've known a Jew give thirty pounds for a Sunday School picnic for Christian children, when he would have wrung ten shillings out of a starving man who owed it him: a Jew has whims like a woman.' He went back to his office.

That evening Bertie had finished all her packing; her large box stood ready locked and tied to go by transport wagon, her small portmanteau and hat box were standing ready at the foot of her bed, to be put in the post-cart the next morning. Her aunt had gone out to a mothers' prayer meeting, and at four o'clock Bertie took a ball of cotton and a crochet needle and went to the low rocking chair before the parlour window where she sat every afternoon. For a time she crocheted, then she rested her hands on the ball in her lap and looked out of the window across the four feet of garden, with its faded geraniums and pinks and across the little green paling into the street. After a time she leaned her forehead on the window ledge. The world was so large, so large, why was there no place for her? Her thoughts went back to Rebekah's house among the oak trees at Cape Town and the old farm with the bluegums, to John-Ferdinand's homestead almost showing over the *nek*; and she felt a hand laid on her heart. She thought of the whole world, of the Far East that Rebekah taught her of when she was a little girl, of India with its swarming millions and Juggernaut cars and palm trees, of China with its pagodas and little bells: there, there, far away, if one could only get there, one would be lost among all those millions, there one would be free. Why, why was there no place for her in the world where she could go and no one ever find her! Slowly the tears gathered in her eyes and fell upon her lap. Only a few hours and she would be in the post-cart, and then a few days more and she would be at the farm, and John-Ferdinand and Veronica would come over to see her. She moved her hands passionately in her lap. Then the front gate clicked. She sat up and dried her eyes. Dorcas had answered the knock and opened the parlour door and ushered in the Jew. Bertie rose to meet him; the tear stains were still upon her cheeks, but she held out her hand passively to him. He asked if her aunt were in, as he had come to say goodbye. Bertie said she was out but would be back in a very short time: she was expecting her every moment. The Jew sat down on a small stiff-legged chair to her left, and Bertie sat down passively in her low seat. She made no effort to speak, but turned her face towards the window, so that only her profile was visible to the Jew.

For a few moments he sat quiet, then he said, 'It looks it vill rain tonight! It grows dark.'

'Yes,' said Bertie slowly. And then there was a long silence. The Jew sat watching her with his keen eyes, his feet twisted round the two forelegs of the chair.

'You are not vell?' he asked at last, bending forward.

'Yes – yes – I am quite well, thank you.' She still looked out of the window. The Jew watched her.

'You vill go away tomorrow?' he said presently.

'Yes,' she said slowly.

'I go on viz ze post-cart. You viz it too?'

'Yes,' she said, without looking at him.

Then there was a long silence and the Jew thought of something to say.

'You vill like zat you go to your home and your family again?'

Bertie turned her face slowly from the window. 'No,' she said slowly, and then turned it back again. The tear marks were clearly visible on her cheeks. The Jew felt curiously perturbed.

'Vat is it zat you cry?' he said suddenly, bending forward low; 'your uncle, your aunt, are zey not good to you?'

'Oh yes, yes, they are.'

The Jew waited a moment and looked at her motionless figure.

'Ven you shall vish to stay longer, shall I not speak viz your uncle zat he let you stay?'

'Oh no, no!' Bertie started and looked round at him. 'Don't, don't say anything to him!'

'Ven I speak to your uncle he shall let you stay. He shall hear vat I say!' A little gleam of conscious power crept into the Jew's eye.

Bertie had half started up, moving her hands quickly; the ball and crochet needle fell to the floor. 'I don't want to stay here,' she said. Then she sank back into the chair. Suddenly she bent forward to the Jew: 'I want to find work, some place where I can work. You – you have been all over the world; don't you know where I could get some work?' Her hands interclasped themselves in her lap. 'I can do nearly anything,' she said, with her eyes now wide open and fixed on him, 'that a woman does with her hands. I can cook and sew, and I can trim hats; I could take care of a baby or house. Wouldn't anyone at the Fields want me? I could do anything. I wouldn't mind working hard.' She looked full up into the Jew's face.

'Ze Fields is not ze place for you!' he said. His eyes swerved from her face and fixed themselves on the hands in her lap, rounded and dimpled and so small for her large body. 'You are for ze joy, ze life, ze beautiful clothes, ze beautiful zings: you are not for ze hard work!'

'Oh, I can work!' she said, bending closer to his knees. 'I could do anything. If your wife wanted someone to help her, I could do all she wanted. I wouldn't mind going to another land, I would like it. If I could only ...'

They saw the shadow of Aunt Mary-Anna's figure fall across the window as she passed it. The gate clicked and she opened the front door. Bertie drew back and sat upright in the shadow of the curtain. The Jew rose to his feet as she entered the parlour. He said he had done himself the honour to come and wish her goodbye and to thank her for the very good supper he had had the night before.

Aunt Mary-Anna thanked him properly for the diamond he had given Bertie and asked him to stay to supper again. But he declined, as he had business. He shook hands with Bertie without addressing her, and her aunt conducted him to the front door.

It was half past one that night. Bertie lay in the bed in the dark. She had slept for an hour after getting into bed, but since then had lain awake. Again and again she tried to draw the pillow to her and pull the cover over her head; but no sleep came. She lay now looking up into the dark. She heard the clock in the dining room strike the half-hour. Every moment brought nearer the time of her going, and then the journey, and then the arrival at the farm. Again and again she went over the steps that always ended with the arrival of John-Ferdinand and Veronica from their farm. She listened to the deadly stillness in the house and felt the inevitableness that drew her on; she must start the next morning, she must arrive at the farm, she must see them all. She turned onto her side; the curls on her forehead were damp with a chilly sweat. The clock struck two. Then she threw back the cover and stepped out of bed. In her white nightgown she walked to the door and opened it and walked softly with her bare feet across the little passage and opened the kitchen door. From the large uncurtained window a great square of dazzling moonlight fell on the stone-paved floor, making every crack visible in the stones where it lay and lighting up dimly the whole kitchen, so that even the pots on the wall and the legs of the table and chairs were visible. On the floor before the fireplace, wrapped in her brown blanket, Dorcas the Kaffir girl lay, with only a fragment of her red handkerchief showing at one end of the living brown roll. Bertie glided softly across the floor and knelt beside the roll with one knee on the floor and one raised.

'Dorcas! Dorcas!' she called softly. Dorcas did not stir.

'Dorcas, please wake!' She touched her softly. 'Oh, please wake, Dorcas!'

Dorcas gave a low guttural sound; her head protruded lightly from the blanket like a caddis worm creeping out of its case; but her eyes were fast closed.

'I'm so lonely, Dorcas! Oh, please let me hold your hand!'

Dorcas snored and turned slightly on her side. Bertie put down her hand under the blanket and took the thick coarse hand of the Kaffir woman and held it tight in her own. 'I'm so lonely, Dorcas!' But Dorcas moved heavily and then lay motionless. Bertie shivered; after a while she withdrew her hand and rose softly and glided with her naked feet back to her own room.

At half past four the post cart driver had *inspanned* his horses and had drawn up before the post office on the square and was blowing a great blast on his bugle, while the cold sleepy postmaster was dragging out the bags. Twenty minutes later he had drawn up before the general agent's door and blew another blast. Bertie, who had long been up and dressed, went to her aunt, who was still in bed, while the general agent, who had risen hastily and put on his slippers and dressing gown, carried her hat box and portmanteau to the front door. When Bertie got to the door the four grey horses were champing their bits and moving their heads in the sharp morning air; the Coloured driver was fastening her hat box and portmanteau onto the back of the cart, while before the front seat the post bags were packed higher than the splash board. On the back seat of the cart sat the little Jew wrapped in a fur-lined coat whose turned-up collar hid almost all but the sharp eyes and nose that looked out above them. The general agent stood shivering on the doorstep, with his hands in the pockets of his dressing gown, and was remarking to the Jew that it would be warmer as soon as the sun rose. All the square and the street had been drenched with a heavy night dew, and the moist trees and houses looked damp in the still morning air. The Jew moved his head in greeting to Bertie, who had a thick grey veil drawn over her face; and, when the man had fastened on her luggage at the back and had climbed into his place on the front seat with his legs hanging over the post bags and had gathered up the reins, the general agent turned to Bertie and helped her into the cart to her seat on the back bench beside the Jew. He passed her up her little handbag and asked the Jew to take care of her, as far as their path lay together, and asked her to write and tell of her arrival as soon as she got to the farm; he raised his arm to shake hands with the Jew over the side of the cart, and the Jew told him he would hear from him from the Bay in a few days' time.

The driver put the bugle to his lips and blew a loud call, then he drew the reins closer and the horses made a great turn and swept out of the street into the square. The general agent looked after them for a second and then went back into the house and closed the door. As they crossed the square and swept out at the upper end past the hotel, Bertie raised her veil a little and looked out over the back of the cart at the square with the sleeping houses and the church like a great damp white angel watching over it.

Then they passed out of sight and there was no trace of them but the deep tracks of cart wheels across the damp sand of the square.

CHAPTER TEN

How Griet Sat on the Stone Wall and Watched the Gnats

It was a rich yellow afternoon. All the valley was filled with a haze, through which you saw the outline of the hills and the trees and the flats through a sheen of gold. The air was so thick it seemed you might have cut it with a knife, and yet so clear you could see the farthest object through it, and so warm and balmy you had only one wish, to sit still in it and breathe it.

On the kitchen doorstep old Ayah sat working, hemming a yellow handkerchief that was pinned to her knee. Every now and then she would rest her hands in her lap and look away up the valley, and then sigh deeply and take a pinch of snuff and say slowly, 'Ach! – ja, God,' and then take up her sewing, till her hands fell to rest again.

A way off, on the stone wall that ran from the wagon house, which broke off suddenly and left a large gateless opening for carts and wagons to come through and then was continued to the sod wall of the garden, Griet sat. She had a piece of blue sewing in her lap, but it was tucked in between her knees; her little bare heels tapped slowly against the wall as she swung them to and fro, but her head was thrown back as far as it would go, and she was looking up into the air where dozens of gnats were wheeling their flight above her; she turned her head slowly from this side to that, following them, and sometimes pretending to snap at them. Presently she glanced round to see if old Ayah was watching her, but the afternoon was too balmy and peaceful for old Ayah even to trouble herself with other folks' concerns. So Griet went on looking up.

Suddenly she closed her mouth with a snap and threw her chin down onto her breast. Her eye roved far off across the flats, not where the road came over the *nek* from the town, but round the hill from the next farm. She bent her head a little on one side to listen, as for all the long generations of the past her foremothers had listened on the great pathless plains for the coming step of the antelope that meant food, or of the enemy that meant war – death. Then she raised her head and looked. Yes, there, coming through, moving among the mimosa trees, whose branches seemed white with thorns everywhere now their leaves had fallen, was the yet whiter tent of a cart. Griet looked round; but old Ayah had observed nothing. She took up her sewing and bent devotedly over it. The cart went out of sight at the drift and then came out near the dam, clearly visible now. Griet looked at it, wrinkling her little flat nose scornfully, and then bent down over her work, sewing on diligently, and began humming the verse of a hymn to herself.

Then the cart came out at the *kraal* just below her. On the front seat sat John-Ferdinand; his broad felt hat covered the large dark eyes that looked out gravely above his close-curling pointed beard. Behind him on the back seat was Veronica in a light print dress, her face shaded by a large mushroom-shaped straw hat bound round with white muslin. On her arm lay the baby, wrapped in a white shawl. Griet did not raise her head but bent low over her work as the cart passed her into the yard. It came so quietly that old Ayah, who was growing a little deaf, did not notice it till it drew up a few feet from the kitchen door. 'Child of sin!' she cried to Griet, 'why did you not let me know people were coming, that I might have had coffee ready? Go pick up chips to make the kettle boil quickly; there are always eyes enough in your head when there is nothing to be seen but, when there is, you are as blind as an earth-snake!'

Meanwhile John-Ferdinand had fastened the horses' heads to the horse post, showing he did not intend to stay long; and, when he had helped Veronica out with the baby, they walked into the house, Griet walking slowly to the wood pile beside the wagon house, where she carefully searched among the piles of mimosa cuttings for the very greenest and sap-oozing chips. With these drawn up in her print dress in front, she walked slowly to the house, flaunting her little short skirts superciliously with each step and wrinkling her nose slightly as she passed the cart.

In the little whitewashed dining room, when John-Ferdinand and Veronica entered it, the father was still sitting at the table in his shirt sleeves with his spectacles on his nose, his volume of Swedenborg open before him; but he seemed to have been half asleep as he took his glasses quickly off his nose and wiped them before he rose to welcome his visitors. The little mother had heard the sound of their voices and ran in from the bedroom, where she had been lying down, her little pink print dress still crumpled as she had lain in it.

'Oh, I am so glad to see you,' she said. 'Why didn't you let me know you were coming this morning when I sent the boy over for the sour dough? I should have had the cakes ready.'

'We did not know we were coming,' said Veronica. The little mother tripped away into the kitchen to see if the kettle was on.

Veronica had seated herself in the chair in the corner near the door; her face, which had been painfully long and straight, had filled out so that it was a long smooth oval; there was a warm rose colour in her cheeks, and her blue eyes, though still with deep-set orbits under the high arched brows, were fuller and had a light in their pale blueness they never wore in her maidenhood. She removed the shawl and hood from her child's head and laid it to her large white bosom, against which it pressed its little fingers and thumb, while she drew across it a small lace handkerchief, partly concealing it. John-Ferdinand stood somewhat awkwardly beside her, while the father, still rubbing his glasses, asked if he would not *outspan*.

Before he had answered, the little mother had hurried back.

'The boy came again from the town this morning. It will be three weeks next Thursday since the day they wrote she was leaving. I can't understand why your uncle doesn't write; he must have got our letter asking why she didn't come! I haven't slept all this week. Your father says if she was ill they would have written, but I ... ' She looked suddenly from John-Ferdinand to Veronica: 'You haven't any news, have you?'

John-Ferdinand looked down at his wife. 'Yes, aunt; that is why we came over; we have a letter from uncle,' said Veronica.

'Oh, she's ill! She's dead,' cried the little mother, wringing her hands and dancing before Veronica like a little child.

'No, dear aunt; no; she's quite well. They are well.' John-Ferdinand put into his wife's hand a letter and walked quickly past her into the front room and out on to the *stoep*. The father sat suddenly upright looking at her; and Veronica, with her right hand, took the letter from the envelope. The little mother stood before her motionless.

'It's from her uncle,' Veronica said, slowly unfolding the letter; 'he asked us to come over and see you about it.'

Then, partly reading and partly explaining, Veronica began to give the contents of the letter. The general agent wrote that she had left, as he said she would, by the Thursday's post cart, and he had not doubted she had arrived home safely till, on the day before he wrote, thirteen days after her leaving, he got letters from the farm saying she had not come; on the same day he had also received a letter from Bertie without any date or address saying she did not wish to return home, and that she had of her own free will and at her own request gone away with the Jew who had been her fellow-passenger in the post cart. She said she did not wish anyone to follow her, but that she would write shortly to her mother and Rebekah when she had reached her journey's end. Where that would be she did not say. 'Has she married him – married him! A Jew – a man we know nothing of!' cried the little mother. 'Oh, if Rebekah were here!'

'I don't think she has married him, dear aunt,' Veronica said, holding down the letter; 'from what her uncle writes I should say she has gone to live with him but is not married.'

The little mother stood transfixed, but the father rose and tore the letter from Veronica's hand to read it himself. With a faint helpless little cry the mother ran out of the room and to the *stoep* where John-Ferdinand stood looking into the dark green of an orange tree. She stood before him, stretching out her hands to him. 'Oh, please explain to me, please explain! I can't understand. Oh, it's so terrible! Tell me what it is!'

John-Ferdinand took her hands in his. 'My dear aunt, it is our Father's will. We cannot understand the strange and terrible dispensations that come to us in life. We can but submit.'

'But Bertie! My little Bertie!' she cried. Then she tore her hands from his and ran back into the dining room. 'Oh, where is she? Where is she?' The father stood with the letter in his hand, still reading it, unconscious of anyone's presence. 'You must go to fetch her back! John-Ferdinand must go, Rebekah must go.'

Veronica had taken her breast from the baby, who had now fallen asleep, and was drawing her dress back over it. 'My dear aunt, in the part of the letter he is reading now, Bertie's uncle says he has no idea where she and the man have gone; it may be to the Diamond Fields, to the Free State, to the Transvaal, to England, to South America, to Cape Town; and he says, very wisely, that we should make no fuss and not make public inquiries and let the thing get into the papers. He knows the man slightly, who, he says, is very wealthy and is sure to be kind to her; and there are other people to think of, his children and Rebekah's and mine. A thing like this, if it is once talked of, is never forgotten, never. For Bertie's sake, for all our sakes, it must be kept quiet.'

The father held the letter in his hand. The little mother looked, almost silenced by the whiteness of his face.

'You see,' said Veronica slowly, 'whatever has been done is done. For Bertie's own sake, for the sake of the innocent who would suffer with her, we must not act hastily. She is over twenty-one and of full age; she has a right to do as she wishes.'

'I will start tonight. I will go to her uncle and learn all he can tell me,' the father said; 'we must bring her home.' The mother flung herself upon his breast with her arms about his neck: 'Oh, she was my little baby – she was such a child! – she knows nothing!'

Twenty minutes later John-Ferdinand and Veronica, with the baby in her arms, walked through the kitchen. There was nothing they could do for the old people, and they felt it better to leave them. Old Ayah, who had just come back from the milk room with fresh cream and butter, apologised that there was no tea. Not only had the chips burned faintly under the kettle, but Griet had absently put two beakers of fresh cold water into it before she slipped off to her old seat on the wall.

John-Ferdinand helped his wife and child into the cart, loosened the horses' heads from the stake and turned the cart round; then, mounting the front seat, drove slowly away. As the cart passed through the gap in the wall, Griet on her perch seemed deeply absorbed in her sewing and did not once raise her head to glance at it, but as soon as it was once well through and passing down beside the *kraal*, she threw down her work and, extending her arms with the thumbs sticking outwards towards the back of the car and the fingers pointing inwards towards herself, raised a low snort of scorn and disapproval. Then she sat still watching it as it passed slowly down the rise among the thorn trees.

In the house a strange stillness reigned. In the little whitewashed dining room, with the afternoon sunshine playing on the wall, the father sat with his shirt-sleeved arms stretched out on the table and his head resting on them; his volume, which had fallen, was lying on the floor at his feet.

In the bedroom on the great bed on which her children had been born the little mother lay, with closed eyes, sobbing noiselessly, while old Ayah laid rags damped with vinegar and water on the forehead and wrists. As she bent she sighed deeply with sympathy; not that the little mother had yet told her what happened, but she felt that some bad news had come which had some connection with Bertie, and she had a vague feeling, for which she could give no reason, that the bearers of the news were somehow to blame for it.

Griet watched the cart till it had passed the great dam and the last glint of its white tent had been lost among the thorn trees beyond; then, seeing that no one called her and a dead stillness reigned everywhere, she fell to her old occupation and, with her head back as far as it would go, watched the gnats as they buzzed above her in the warm yellow air.

CHAPTER ELEVEN

How the Rain Rains in London

The Jew beat his feet on the pavement. It was eleven o'clock and a rainy night. Up and down the street the rain was falling; it made a wall so dense it almost shut out the light of the few gas lamps that glimmered through that long Bloomsbury street. The raindrops hung in beads round the hat of the cabman whom the lamps of his cab made dimly visible as he sat on the front seat.

The Jew went up the house steps and rang the bell loudly; then without waiting he rang again. There was a sound in the passage and then the door opened a few inches. The Jew kicked it wide. Inside, a figure could be seen holding a lighted candle.

'Vhy ze davil can you not come ven I ring? And vhy you not light ze hall lamp?'

Then he turned down the steps and opened the cab door, helping Bertie to alight. She was thickly veiled and wrapped from neck to feet in a fur cloak. The Jew led the way up the steps into the hall.

On the large, new, empty hat-stand the candle was standing, and the woman who had held it stood on a chair lighting the hall lamp. There was an overpowering smell of paint and varnish and oilcloth everywhere. In the back of the passage behind the stairs a moving figure was dimly visible.

'Isaac! Isaac! Vhy you not come and bring ze zings in?'

From the back of the hall the figure shuffled forward slowly. It was a youth of about seventeen, with a high, narrow, sloping forehead, above which rose a tower of strongly curling hair like the Jew's but of a pale sandy colour, though further, except in the shuffling gait, there was nothing to recall the Jew. He had a long straight nose slightly crooked, the tip of which was so sharply a four-sided square that it almost suggested that the point had been artificially cut off instead of being the work of nature. He had weak, bleared, blue eyes, and walked with his shoulders bent and his head stretched forward as if trying to see. He shuffled past Bertie without seeing her.

The Jew nodded at the candle. 'You take ze lady upstairs to ze room,' he said to the woman; and he followed Isaac out to the cab.

The woman who had descended from the chair took up the candle. She was a woman of about forty; her grizzled dark hair, drawn into an untidy knot at the back of her head, hung over her forehead till it almost touched her heavy eyebrows. She began without a word to mount the stairs, and Bertie followed her. She was short and broad-shouldered, and Bertie noticed, as she followed her, that the wrist of the hand in which she held the candle was almost as thick and strong as a man's and a little hairy. Her shabby black dress had a three-sided rent at the back and hung down, almost touching the stairs as she mounted. On the first landing she stopped and opened a door, and Bertie followed her into a large room. Here the smell of new paint and new furniture was even stronger than below. There was no light in the room, but the woman led the way with the candle. Bertie saw the glittering of a great cut-glass chandelier hanging from the roof in the centre of the room and of chairs and sofas and mirrors everywhere. The woman opened a small door in the folding-door which cut off the room from the one behind it, and Bertie followed her in. Here a great coal fire was burning, the warm light making visible the great bed and large drawers and wardrobes with glass doors. On the dressing table the woman put down the light. Drawn up before the fire there was a sofa covered with purple velvet. Bertie sat down on it. For a second the woman glanced at her curiously, then went out and closed the door. Bertie took off her hat and laid it on the head of the sofa and unbuttoned her fur cloak, but did not take it off. In a few moments the Jew and Isaac came bringing up the luggage, which Isaac set down within the door and went. The Jew came up to her. 'You like ze fire?' he said, looking down at her. 'I vill tell ze woman zat she bring you some supper.' He took a little bunch of keys out of his pocket. 'All ze drawers, ze wardrobes are your sings in; ven you vant zomezing you vill open zem!' He put the keys on the mantelpiece. 'I vill go down now to my office – it below – and see some letters of business, and vill come up soon.' He stood looking at her anxiously, shifting from one leg to the other. 'Ven you want anyzing you will ring? – You are tired?' He looked down at her. 'I vill tell ze woman zat she bring your supper soon,' he said; then he went out and closed the door.

When he was gone she opened her cloak yet further and threw it partly back; once she glanced round the room and then she looked back at the fire. She was very tired. For two weeks the Jew had delayed their journey at Madeira that the repairs and furnishing might be completed before they came. She had only landed that day, and the journey in the damp chill air, to which she was unaccustomed, had made her very heavy. After a little she leaned back on the purple velvet pillows and drew up her feet, and lay with one arm over her head and the other hanging at her side, looking at the fire. How soft the velvet cushions were!

In about ten minutes there was a knock at the door and, no one answering, it was pushed open. The woman looked in; she was carrying a silver tray with the supper set on it; she put it down on the dressing table. She looked at Bertie; from her slow even breathing it was evident she was fast asleep. After a moment the woman walked toward the sofa from behind and, coming to the top, bent down over it. The firelight was shimmering on the silk linings of Bertie's open fur cloak and cast a ruddy soft light on her face; she bent over Bertie a little; like her son she was near-sighted and saw nothing clearly till she came close. She bent her face low over Bertie and noticed the roundness of her snowy throat and the fullness of the little rounded chin, and looked at the long curled lashes on the pink cheeks; she put out one thick unwashed grimy finger, almost as if she were going to feel the cheek to see if its soft curves were real; then she turned and went softly out of the room with a not unpleased smile about her mouth as she closed the door.

About half an hour later the Jew came up. When he left Bertie he had gone down to a room on the ground floor; originally it had been the back dining room of the house, but the Jew had bricked up the door between it and the front room, and for nearly twenty years it had been his home. Here he lived and ate and slept when at home, while the rest of the house, which Martha attended to, had been let to lodgers. There was a stretcher on one side with a folded grimy quilt; a little iron stove was in the corner with a black kettle on it, on which the Jew made himself hot water without the trouble of calling anyone. In the other corner was a large sofa; the table was covered with papers and documents; an old cracked lamp, blackened with age, hung over it, and the paper was faded yellow, grimed with the smoke and wear of twenty years. When all the rest of the house had been renovated and refurnished, this room alone had been left untouched. Here for twenty years he had eaten, drunk, slept and sat up to work at night and the mustiness and the grime were home to him.

When he went into it that evening he took off his new black coat, hung it behind the door, put on a short black jacket, greasy and shiny, and sat down at the table to his papers. Most of them were bills for the decorating and furnishing of the home. There were long bills from silversmiths for cutlery and plate; there were yet longer bills from the Bond Street dressmakers, to whom he had sent Bertie's measurements with orders to supply her with a complete lady's outfit with which to fill the drawers and wardrobes in her room; there was a lengthy bill from his agent, who had been obliged to compensate the lodgers turned out of the house without the full month's notice. He added up the costs and sat looking down at the large total they came to, with a certain gleam of satisfaction. Yes, it had cost well.

Then, before he went on to the other papers, the Jew rose. He put off the little jacket and put on the black coat, and for a moment looked into the little cracked, eight-inch looking glass that hung on the wall, to see that his front hair stood up straight; then he went up the stairs to Bertie's room. After knocking twice and getting no answer, he opened the door and saw her still asleep on the purple sofa. Very softly he closed the door and walked on tiptoe to the foot of the couch. She was still fast asleep with the firelight playing on her. Very gently, to make no sound, he knelt down on the floor, loosened the buttons of her little shoes, drew them off and placed them on the floor. He ran his hands very softly, so softly along the curves of her feet, so tiny for the body. He looked at them for a moment, he put down his face as if he were going to press the soles against it, as women press the feet of little children. Then he rose and went to the bed and fetched a large down pillow. She was lying so low in the pillows that her feet almost hung over the end of the sofa; he slipped the cushion very carefully under them to raise and support them. Then he went to a wardrobe and discovered a large white fluffy shawl. He heaped it softly over her feet, tucking it in at the sides of the pillow. He blew out the candle, that its light might not add to the glare of the fire; then he stood looking at her for a few seconds with his hands curved before him; and then he went down to his room and his greasy coat to go on examining his letters.

When Bertie woke the next morning it was half past eight. She raised herself on the sofa. Someone had been in and built the fire, for it was burning still. She stood up and threw from her the fur cloak in which her arms had been all night. A curious dull grey light came through the two windows at the other end of the room (it seemed hardly like daylight) and a far-off roaring sound, like a million sounds breaking into one. Bertie listened to it for a minute and then walked towards the windows. Her little stockinged feet sank noiselessly into the soft pile of the carpet as into moss by the rocks in the *kloof*. She drew up both blinds and stood before a window looking out. A grey damp was everywhere. It seemed to ooze out of the walls of the buildings opposite, to ascend from the ground as much as come down from the sky. Opposite were the backs of houses in the next street, all built of the same dead yellow-grey brick, and all oozing. There were rows of windows all alike. Out of two windows on a top floor a line was stretched and a shirt was hanging out on it, but it was not drying; the water dripped from its sleeves as they hung down. Up above, in what looked like a loft, a window was open and a boy's face looked out, then the window closed. Down below, between the tall houses, tiny backyards with high walls were crushed. She pressed her face against the window to look down into them. In one were a few broken flower pots lying in the wet, and a great grey cat was stealthily walking along the top of the wall, drenching wet but seemingly accustomed to it, for it did not try to climb down. There was a pungent curious smell that seemed to burn in her nostrils, something like when they burned *harpuis*[1] bushes on the lands at home. Bertie wondered what it was; she shivered; she looked out for a moment longer, and then turned back to the room. There all was beautiful. The soft double-piled carpet had pink roses in it; on the great brass bed was a blue embroidered satin quilt. There were two great mahogany wardrobes with two mirrors in each and two chests of drawers with brass fittings; the dressing table had another large mirror and there was another over the mantelpiece that reflected the whole room; besides the velvet sofa there were two armchairs and a table with a purple velvet cover. Bertie walked about softly, touching the things with her hands: how wonderful and beautiful it was; and it was hers, all hers. She ran her finger along the edge of the brass bed, of the tables and chairs; even the white marble of the fireplace seemed beautiful to her; she had never seen it before. She thought of the little stained deal wardrobe in the best bedroom at home, and the little deal dressing table with the muslin on it; and a curious kind of pain came to her. She took the keys from the mantelpiece and began to open the drawers and wardrobes.

---

1 Resin.

In the drawers were piles of linen so delicate she hardly liked to touch it roughly; she laid out on the bed a nightgown with so much of fine lace and soft ribbons falling about it that at first it seemed to her it must be an evening dress. In the wardrobes hung gowns in silk and muslin and velvet and lace. She took them down and looked at them in turn. Then she came to one: all her life she had dreamed of having a dress made of thick black silk, with large blue daisies with white centres embroidered in raised work all over it at intervals. Her mother had had such a bit of silk in a patchwork quilt she had brought from England with her. Once on board ship the Jew had asked her what sort of a dress she would like best, and she had described it made of such stuff, quite plainly and with a long train, and a fine lace scarf to throw over the shoulders and hang down in front. In the wardrobe were the dress and the scarf. She put the dress on and hung the scarf about the low body so that the long ends hung down, and then she walked up and down in it. There were three mirrors where she could see herself in the dress; it was as beautiful as she had thought. Then there was a knock at the door and the woman stood there with a tray of breakfast; on the tray was a note from the Jew saying he had had to go to his office in the City before she woke but he would be back for lunch at one. Bertie sat in one of the purple velvet chairs with her breakfast beside her on a little table, and ate it luxuriously. She was hungry; she had not eaten since early the afternoon before. Then she leaned back and fanned herself. There was a black fan with daisies on it that was attached by a silk cord to the side of the dress, and she fanned herself, not because it was hot, but to use it. When she was tired of looking at the dresses she went into the next room. It was a large oblong room with two windows; the great cut-glass chandelier hung from the centre of the ceiling; on the mantelpiece and stands there were vases and candlesticks with cut-glass pendants that glittered; the couches and chairs were covered with crimson-coloured velvet, as rich as the purple in the bedroom; the carpet was as soft and deep; the velvet curtains at the window were lined with rich satin and had cords and ball-fringe, as heavy as the curtains in the picture of Queen Victoria that hung in the front room at the farm. Bertie touched them and rubbed her cheek against them. How wonderful and soft they were! She walked about touching all the things. She rang for Isaac to make a fire in the room and then she went and stood at the window and looked out at the houses in the street; all the houses were the same, high and yellow and dark, and the rain dropped from them. Far down at the end of the street she could see a square opening; cabs drove up it, and a postman with the rain dripping from him walked quickly up the street knocking at all the houses. She shivered and turned away and went back to sit by the fire. At one she had put on a beautiful white woollen dress made like a Greek robe, and the Jew took her down to lunch in the great dining room below stairs; it had an immense sideboard and pictures of fruits and hunting, and the great mahogany chairs were so heavy she could hardly lift them. After lunch the Jew went away again and she looked at her dresses.

At four he came and told her to get ready and he would take her for a drive. The carriage came to the door; the coachman had a livery, but had an overcoat over it; Isaac had the same livery and overcoat and sat beside him. She and the Jew got in; it was still raining, but it was close and warm inside in her furs, and she looked out through the windows at the damp people hurrying by. The Jew took her to many shops. At the milliner's she asked the price of a hat. 'Zat is nozing! Zat is nozing! Take vot you vill'; and he made her buy three hats. At other shops she bought gloves, sweetmeats, flowers, lilies, and orchids that cost sovereigns a bunch, though she thought only a few pence. At one jeweller's the Jew bought her a diamond bracelet and emerald earrings. She bought ornaments and knick-knacks, all kinds of things she had never seen before. When they got into the carriage at last, the front seat was piled so high with parcels that they kept falling down. When they got home the Jew went to his room to work till dinner, and she unpacked and rearranged her things. She rang the bell and made Isaac go and call the Jew to see how she had arranged the flowers about the drawing room, and she pinned a buttonhole into the Jew's coat. At dinner she wore a low white dress with roses wreathing on the bodice. It seemed to her at first extravagance to wear such a dress for an ordinary dinner; but there were none commoner. The dinner was laid out with much silver and cut glass, and there were many courses and three kinds of wine. She had only seen things something like that when there was a grand dinner party at Cape Town. The Jew had ordered the best cook that money could buy through his agent. Bertie would not take wine, she wanted lemonade, and Isaac had to go out and get it for her; but she ate three helpings like a child of some wonderful cake with cream and almonds in the middle. She made the Jew pull crackers with her, and when a yellow crown came out of one she made him put it on, and she put on a bishop's mitre. When they went upstairs her train was so long she nearly fell over it, and she told the Jew he would have to carry it for her. When the Jew had taken her up to the drawing room he soon went back to his little office, and she sat by the fire and looked at some of the purchases, and then listened to the roar of the city till she got tired and cold and went to bed. All the next morning she tried on her dresses and cloaks and hats. The Jew could not come back to lunch, and had ordered hers to be sent up to her; but he came at four o'clock to take her out in the carriage. She asked him to take her to a shop where they sold materials for fancywork, and she bought work of every kind, and workboxes and a worktable and a workbasket, and all the evening while he wrote in his room she sat by the fire knitting him a silk purse. When he came up at eleven o'clock she was bending over her work with a flushed face, and asked him if he liked the pattern. He could hardly get her to go to bed she was so interested in her work.

The next day it rained too heavily to go out at all; she sat all day working, finishing the purse, and began a pair of slippers. The day after she was so busy working at the slippers she said she did not want to drive. But in the evening, when the Jew came from his office at bedtime, she was sitting before the fire with her work in her lap staring into the blaze.

Suddenly she looked up at him. 'Do you think by this time they have the letter I wrote?' she asked.

'Vhy, no,' the Jew said, looking down at her. 'It takes long.'

She sat still looking into the fire. 'But don't you think I ought to write and send them my address?' she said presently. 'I told them I was well, and you were kind to me, and I was happy; but perhaps they want to know just where I am.' She waited a moment. 'Perhaps they are anxious.'

The Jew looked down at her with his bright eyes. 'Vhy you vish to tell zem vere you are? I give zem ze address of my partner in Zous America, zat zey may sink ve are zare. Do you vish zat zey come here to fetch you?' He looked keenly at her.

'Oh no, no!' Bertie said, raising herself. 'Oh no, I never want to go back to Africa! I am so happy here with you; you are so kind to me. I – only – sometimes – I am afraid they are anxious. I – I am afraid of that.'

'Ven zey sink you go on to Zous America as soon as you come here it will be nine ten months before zey come to you here; do you vish zey come soon?'

'Oh no, no, I want to stay here. You won't let anyone take me back to Africa, will you?' She raised herself.

'No, no!' he said. She took up her slipper and began working again; but soon the Jew said it was time to go to bed.

Every morning the Jew went to the City at eight and Bertie had her breakfast in bed, and in the morning she tried on her dresses and did fancy work, and at one Isaac brought her lunch up on a silver tray to the drawing room. The Jew had made her understand he did not wish her to go to the lower floor when he was not there, that her world was the first floor. After lunch she lay on the bed and tried to sleep, and then before the Jew came she dressed herself again, and if he was early enough and the weather not too bad they went for a drive in the closed carriage. When they came home she dressed again for dinner and did her hair and they went down to the dining room and had dinner, with the silver and glass and the massive furniture about them, and then the Jew went to work in his little office and she sat in the drawing room. Though it was summer, it was a wet summer, and however warm the day might be she kept large fires burning night and day in the drawing room and bedroom. The light of the fire was the only thing that gleamed.

One afternoon, when it was raining too heavily to go out, she asked the Jew what was in the floors above her, and, as she wished to see them, he took the keys and opened the door. There were three floors with the garret, but there was nothing in any of the rooms. They had been painted and papered and decorated, but they were quite empty. She said to the Jew it would be nice if they furnished them. The Jew asked what they should do with them. She looked round and said perhaps when he had visitors; but he said he never had visitors, and they locked them up and went back to the drawing room.

The next day when the Jew came home it was pouring with rain. Out in the streets as he drove up he saw an organ grinder and with him a boy of eleven standing in the rain turning their barrel organ. When he went upstairs he found the front window of the drawing room wide open and Bertie standing before it, the rain beating in on her white dress as she threw out to the man and boy little balls of crystallised fruits and sweets wrapped in paper. She had just wrapped a box of chocolates in her lace pocket handkerchief and thrown it out to them when the Jew came up. 'Catch! Catch!' she called out, flinging it. The Jew came up to her. 'Oh, look at that poor little boy! Do give me some money to give them! They've been playing so beautifully. It makes one's feet jump. I've been dancing all round the room by myself while they played. And I haven't anything to give them but sweets.'

'Look, look how vet you are!' the Jew cried, pulling down the window. He touched her dripping sleeves and bodice with his finger. 'You must not talk viz people in ze street. Bad people zat vill come and steal all ze sings!' The Jew turned quickly and went downstairs. He sent Isaac to tell them that if they ever came again he would send the police after them, and Isaac was to be always on the watch lest they or others should return. When he went upstairs again, he impressed on her that never again under any condition must she open a window and speak to anyone in the street; nor under any condition must she ever speak to anyone to whom he had not introduced her. In Africa you could do these things, but not in London. She listened to him quietly. 'You like ze music?' he asked. 'Oh yes,' she said, 'dance music I like. It makes me dance all over. I'm never tired when near dance music.'

The next day, when they returned from their drive and Bertie came back into the drawing room, there was a grand square piano, the most richly toned that money could buy, standing between the window and the door. With a little cry of joy she sprang towards it and flung her hat and gloves upon it and opened it. The Jew, who was following her closely, looked on with delight. She drew out the rich music stool and seated herself on it, still wearing her fur cloak. She opened it and began to play. 'I can't play very well, you know,' she said, half turning to the Jew, who stood beside her, 'not real grand music, but if I hear a thing I can always play it; and they always got me to play for them at dances because I kept the time so.'

She started a waltz, swaying her head gently from side to side.

'Oh how beautiful! It's a lovely piano! I never saw one like it.' Then she paused and began a reel. 'This is the *vastrap*,[2] she said, half turning her face to the Jew, who stood beside her, and nicking her head at the end of each part where the final step came. 'It's what the Hottentots dance; I learnt it from hearing them play it on the

---

2 The *vastrap* is a kind of wild Highland fling danced by Hottentot or Bushmen servants at the Cape.

concertina. When Rebekah used to set me to practice my scales, I used to try to practice them, and then suddenly I used to find I was playing this!' She was smiling and nicking her head all the while she talked: 'You should see their old *velskoens*[3] flying when they dance, all full of holes!'

She played louder and louder and with more emphasis. Then suddenly she put her arms down on the notes and rested her head on them. She was motionless. The Jew stepped closer and put his hand on her shoulder; it was quaking. 'Vat is it?' he asked. Her shoulders were slowly convulsed, and then wild suppressed sobs broke that seemed rending her shoulder.

The Jew moved from one foot to the other with his hands extended, as an old hen might shuffle whose chicken was in a convulsion she could not understand. 'Vat is it? ... Vhy ... " He bent over her. Are you not vell?'

She made no answer, the sobs growing wilder till her whole body seemed convulsed by them.

'You are tired? Ve have go to too many shops zis afternoon?' He put his hand on her, then he hurried downstairs to get her a glass of wine. When he came back she had left the piano and had thrown herself on her face on the sofa in front of the fire in her bedroom and had buried her face in the pillows. She was sobbing, but more slowly. He pressed her to take the wine; but she said she could not, her head ached and she would lie on the sofa and try to go to sleep. He covered her feet with a rug and built up the fire and stood looking at her as she lay extended, with questioning anxious eyes. She did not move again till just before dinner, when she dressed herself and came down and said her head was better.

After that she seldom played on the piano, and after a while not at all. As the summer passed it grew damper and duller, and she often declined to go out driving when the Jew came home. He never took her to the parks or places where she could see fashionable people walking about, but always offered to take her to the shops. Generally she said she needed nothing; but whenever she went out she still went to the flower shops and brought back the carriage filled with flowers, with which she decorated her drawing room and bedroom; and she went to the confectioner's after and brought back boxes of sweets, which she munched all day as she sat before the fire. She seldom did fancy work now; she had made all she could think of for the Jew, and the great sofa cover she began lay untouched day after day.

One evening the Jew came back later than usual and found the drawing room door locked and the other door on the landing which led into her bedroom locked too. She came quickly to the door and opened it. He asked her why it was locked. She had a large fire burning and the room was bright with it. 'I don't know,' she said, resting her hand on his arm. 'I nearly always lock them now when you are away. I

---

3 *Velskoens* (skin-shoes) are the home-made shoes of undressed leather generally worn by them.

don't know what it is,' – she drooped her head lower to his – 'but I feel so lonely. I'm so afraid,' she said softly.

'Afraid? Afraid of vot?' the Jew asked her looking up at her.

She still kept hold of his arm. 'I don't know,' she whispered softly, with the other hand shutting the door; 'but I always feel as if something was following me, as if something was coming upstairs after me. I can't go to sleep because I'm afraid it'll be just behind me when I wake, so I keep the doors locked – I'm so lonely,' she said, after a pause. She took her hand from the Jew's arm, and they walked to the fireplace.

'Ven you are alone,' said the Jew, 'vy do you not call Marzer zat she comes and sits viz you? I vill tell her.'

'Oh, no, no!' Bertie said hurriedly. 'I don't want her.' She stooped to the Jew and said, almost in his ear, 'It's *her* I'm afraid of! Her wrists are so large!'

'Did she ever zay zomesings to you zat you not like?' the Jew asked, his eyes flashing quickly.

'Oh no,' Bertie said, 'she's never spoken to me once; Isaac brings the things up. And when she does the bedroom I come in here. But I see her looking at me. Sometimes, when we come up from dinner, I see her looking up the stairs after me! But! – but,' Bertie hesitated, 'it isn't her fault; it isn't really her I'm afraid of; it's – I sometimes feel as if something was just behind my left shoulder, and when I look back quickly it seems I'm just going to see it – but I never do! It's always my left shoulder.' She glanced round.

The Jew looked at her with a curious questioning face. He thought for a little and then he proposed that, whenever she felt lonely, she should ring for Isaac and let him come and sit on the chair just inside the door. She said she would feel safe then; she was not afraid of Isaac. After that day Isaac had orders to come and sit with her whenever she rang. But the Jew always impressed on him he was to answer no questions she asked, nor to carry out any letters to post for her, nor to give her any money.

The first day when Isaac came up she tried to talk with him once or twice. But the convulsions he had had as an infant, while they seemed to have left his brain more or less intact (for he could do his mother's shopping, making better bargains than she could, and showed an exceeding keenness where money matters were concerned), seemed to have broken the full relation between the brain and the organs of sense; he could not tie a shoe lace except very slowly and not exactly, and, when he spoke a word, it was only slowly and after much consideration that the brain carried the order to the tongue. Bertie found he did not easily answer her and after the first day made little effort to speak to him. Every day she rang he came and sat on the chair just inside the door in his green livery with silver facings and buttons, one hand spread open on each of the knees he kept close together before him, and with his head stretched a little forward, the blunted tip of his nose always turned to the fireplace at the far end, his faint blue eyes fixed and striving to see everything where Bertie sat before the fire – as a worshipper at the far end of a cathedral looks to the altar with its lights and incense and flowers and its slowly raised chalice which announces a sacred presence. He watched, breathing slowly while she dozed in her chair. His breath became a little quicker when she rose and moved or stirred the fire; his eyes were fixed on the bedroom door when she went in to change her dress, and when she came back he noted everything she had on – the little diamond earrings, the belt, the comb in her hair – and when sometimes she drew her chair, so that as she sat before the fire he saw nothing but the little crown of brown curls on top of her head, he watched that. He watched with an intensity of interest when she put a sweetmeat between her lips and sucked or broke it. She always shared her chocolates and crystallised fruits with him; but he never ate them while he sat there; and his mother could never get him to go and do her shopping; he was always waiting in the kitchen passage for Bertie's bell to ring.

When he had been three days she proposed that he should help her move the furniture. She put the tables where the sofa had been and the sofa where the chairs had been, and they moved the piano. When the Jew came back that afternoon Bertie showed him quite excitedly the changes she had made and asked him whether he did not think it nice. During the next few days they moved everything in the room; at the end of a week all the furniture and all the pictures had been turned round and everything had been in the place of everything else; then she began to get tired of moving them, and after a few days they remained where they were.

As the summer grew older it grew damper and more oppressive. She generally refused when the Jew offered to take her out in the carriage; she liked better to rest in her armchair close to the fire, eating sweets.

One afternoon he was driving her down towards the Strand to a place where he had heard Persian sweets were kept. There was a block in the large street and they had to turn down Seven Dials. So many vehicles had come that they had almost to stand for some moments; she rubbed the damp from the windowpane and looked out. There was a low dirty shop at her left, in the window of which were boxes with rabbits and kittens and some cages with birds. Next to the shop a door stood open that led directly up a flight of stairs; in the open doorway were five children in ragged clothes with matted hair and no shoes on their feet, the eldest holding an almost naked and very dirty baby of a few months old in her arms. The rain beat in through the open door upon them as they pressed on one another and looked out into the muddy street from which the pouring rain had driven them.

'Oh, do look at them,' she cried to the Jew, 'so dirty and so ragged, and no shoes on their feet! Oh, do give me something to give them.'

The only thing the Jew had never given her was money. He gave her two half-crowns, and as the carriage moved on she opened the window and threw them in at the open door; but the carriage was already moving on, and the Jew said she must shut the window to keep the rain out.

That evening, when the Jew came up at half past nine, instead of finding her dozing in the armchair, she was sitting back in it with her eyes wide open staring interestedly into the fire, so absorbed that she did not turn, as she always did if she were awake, to nod or say some word to him when he came in. He sat down in the straight-backed chair near her; but she sat with her soft eyes unusually bright staring at the blaze.

Suddenly she asked him, but rather dreamily without looking at him, what the price of cocoanut matting was.

The Jew stared at her. 'Vhy,' he said, 'you vant some?'

'No,' she said slowly, 'I don't want any; I'm only thinking.'

He told her the price. She was dressed in a red silk dress, and about her shoulders hung a cream lace scarf; she looked very beautiful leaning back there, and the Jew thought she had almost a smiling look about her face, which she seldom had now.

'And what is the price of whitewash?' she asked slowly, presently. 'At the farm we used to pay three-and-six for lime, but up at my uncle's it used to cost four shillings.'

The Jew gazed at her. 'But vot do you vant ze lime for?'

'Oh, you see,' she said slowly, her Cape drawl becoming intensified, as was always the case when she tried to make anything but a very short speech or to explain anything, 'I was just thinking, if someone gave me thirty pounds and said I could have that house and all those children that we saw in the door today and said I must put everything right, how I would do it: I don't know if I could do it with thirty pounds, but I think I could. You see,' she said, interfolding her hands in her lap, 'I would first get a big bath and wash them all and cut their hair quite short, and I'd buy that blue stuff for three pence a yard I saw the other day and make them all blouses or frocks, and I would make them warm petticoats. The boots and socks would be dear,' – her voice got more dreamy – 'but all the other things I would make myself. I'd put alum-wash all over the floors and ceilings first, and then I'd whitewash. How many rooms are there, do you think, in a house like that? It's not high, like this.' She turned her head and looked at him. 'I should think there were four, eh? – I could do it for the thirty pounds, I'm sure, and buy new furniture, but it's the cocoanut matting I'm not sure of. For fifty I could do it! Cocoanut matting is such a help. It keeps a house clean. I could whitewash, myself,' she said, after a pause; 'the stairs one could have planed down; they are so very dirty. That second little girl would be very pretty if she was clean, and the boy too.'

She had looked away from the Jew back into the fire. He had never heard her talk so much before; he said not a word and sat staring at her, as he always did when they were together. Presently he asked if she was not sleepy, but she said it was early yet, and he went back to his office to work, and she sat looking at the fire. She had not untied the ribbon round the packet of sweets that lay in her lap and which she had brought with her after dinner to eat. The next day, when she drove out, she asked him to take her that way again; she leaned out when they came past the house, but the door was shut.

As the summer grew old it rained rather less, but the air grew heavier and more dull. Bertie now refused to drive out at all, and sat by the fire. She ate less and less but was growing very stout. At night, when the Jew woke, he somehow often felt the bed shaking, and when he looked at her she was crying. Sometimes she seemed to be crying in her sleep; but when he roused her and asked her what it was she said it was nothing, that her head ached. She began now seldom to ask Isaac to come and sit in the drawing room, and she cried nearly all the time. From the time the Jew left in the morning till he came back in the evening she sometimes cried. She shut the door so that no one could hear her, and walked about the rooms wringing her hands and crying. She did not know why she cried except that there was always a pressure on the top of her head and that everything was pain to her. She would be quite quiet and she would go and look out from the front window at the long row of yellowish drab houses opposite with their tiers of windows one above another, and she would fall at once into a passionate crying that nothing would stop for hours. If she was standing near the window and happened to stroke down the great soft velvet folds of the curtains, it would make her cry, or unfolding a dress, or opening a packet of sweets. Everything she saw or heard made her cry. When she woke in the morning and heard a voice outside say, 'Old clo'! Old clo'!' it made her draw the cover over her head. At dinner sometimes, just as she was going to eat, she used to burst out wildly crying and the Jew could do nothing to comfort her or stop the crying. She left off having Isaac to sit with her – she said she was not frightened – and passed most of her time lying on the sofa in the bedroom before the fireplace, with a white shawl over her head. The Jew bought her one day the most astonishing collection of things – jewellery, hats and knick-knacks – and sent them home all at once. When he came home in the evening she put her arm on his shoulder and thanked him, but the next morning he found them still all piled on the sofa in the drawing room, and some of the parcels were not even opened. When he asked her if she were ill, she said no, and when he asked if she wanted anything she said no. The only thing she ever complained of was a feeling of pressure on the top of her head. She wept so persistently that there were sometimes not six hours in the twenty-four when she was not weeping either waking or asleep. Sometimes the Jew lit the candle and, raising himself on his elbow, watched her weeping in her sleep till the pillow under her face was wet, the great tears bursting from under her eyelids. He had never dreamed that a living thing could weep so.

At last he sent for a doctor, an old Jew he had known for years. He examined Bertie carefully and said there was nothing organically wrong with her; she wanted change and excitement and overall exercise. He ordered she should live no more on milk and biscuits but should take a glass of wine with her meals and a glass of stout before she went to bed at night to make her sleep. He said she was right in not caring to drive in a closed carriage, that every day for at least an hour she must walk, and walk quickly. The Jew thought over it all and made plans. That evening when he came home he told her to dress in her best dress and jewels; he would take her to a theatre. She rose from the sofa and began at once to take her dresses from the wardrobe. She tried on ten before she decided on one to wear; it was a white heavy satin; with it she wore a small diamond and emerald necklace the Jew had given her, and a star in her hair above her forehead.

They had an early dinner, and she talked and laughed and drank the two glasses of champagne instead of the wine she always took with her meals. Afterwards when the carriage was waiting and he went to fetch her, he met her fully dressed on the landing outside the drawing room and was stricken dumb with her glittering beauty. Only the tiny feet, which hardly supported her large body, and gave her the slight uncertain swaying movement as she walked, took from her absolutely regal grandeur. He covered her with her cloak and took her to the carriage. She talked and laughed all the way. The Jew had taken a box. He placed her where she saw the stage well, just below her, but he drew the velvet curtain a little so that she was sheltered from the audience, and he sat between it and her and watched.

They were playing already, and for a little while she kept asking questions. In Cape Town there was no theatre, and she had only seen two domestic little plays very badly set. In the first act there was a harvest scene. Men and women in country dresses appeared tossing hay and a wagon came on the scene, and behind a hayrick a young man declared his love to one of the pretty haymakers in a sun-bonnet and asked her to marry him. Bertie was so deeply interested she leaned forward pressing before the Jew and resting her elbows on the edge of the box, looking down.

Then the curtain fell. When it rose the lights were turned down in the theatre, but on the stage it shone brilliantly; the crowd of women had returned who were haymakers in the last scene. Robbed of almost all their clothing, their lower limbs made more obtrusive with flesh-coloured tights, some wearing a few yards of spangled gilt about their waists, some only with bandages of silk drawing between their legs, the trousers cut away even from the hips, the women leaped and flung their limbs in smooth contortions. She sat gazing at them. Presently she put her head closer to the Jew's. 'Aren't they women?' she asked, 'the same that were here a little while ago?'

'Yes,' the Jew said; 'now zey dance.' Bertie's hand shaded her face away from him as she looked.

'Why do they do it?' she whispered.

'Zey get money, zey pay zem for ze dance!'

A moment after Bertie had drawn herself back in her seat into the shadow of the box. When the Jew looked round at her he thought he saw tears on her cheeks; when he went near her he found she was shaking convulsively. He asked her whether she felt ill. She only sobbed for answer; the tears were pouring down her cheeks. He asked her whether he should take her home. She nodded and sobbed, 'Yes, yes!' He wrapped her up and led her out. As she passed down the corridor she sobbed aloud, and the attendants looked curiously at her. When he got her into the carriage she sat back with her head in the corner, her white lace scarf wrapped completely over her face, sobbing heavily.

'Are you sick? Are you tired?' the Jew whispered.

'No, no!' she said, but sobbed louder, while he looked at her anxiously. His attempt at amusement seemed to have failed utterly.

When they got home she went straight upstairs and into her bedroom and, dressed as she was, flung herself face downward on the sofa before the fire. In half an hour the Jew came up with the glass of wine the doctor had said she must always have before she slept. The fire was burning low and she had not lit the lamp, but he could see her lying motionless and silent with the shawl still over her head. He touched her arm and asked her to sit up and take it. She raised herself, but, just as she was going to take it, threw herself on her face on the pillows, sobbing, 'Why don't their mothers fetch them home?'

'Vot?' said the Jew, bending over her with the glass in one hand.

'Why – don't – their – mothers – fetch – them – home?' she cried, her face half choked in the pillow; 'they are women! – they are women! – and – the – the men – they – they – they –' She sobbed incoherently.

The Jew put his hand on her softly. It was the first time she had ever tried to explain to him what she was crying about; was it always something so unintelligible?

'Vitch men? Vot men?' he asked. The ballet-dancers and the men in the front rows of the stalls had completely passed from his mind. She made no answer, but sobbed more quietly.

'Come, drink zis!' the Jew said coaxingly, as one speaks to a little child. 'It vill do you good. Ze doctor says you are very veek! Here –' He drew her with his hand. Slowly she sat up; he put the glass to her lips and she drank the contents; then she rose, a sudden dead quiet having come to her crying. She stood in the dull glowing light of the fire in her white satin dress, and she folded her arms on the mantelpiece and leaned her forehead on it.

'Do you feel better?' asked the Jew.

'Yes,' she said. Then in an instant the wild sobs convulsed her again. 'And – some of them – were – so – young! – and – no – no – no one –'

The Jew bent close to her, but could not distinguish the word in her sobbing. 'You are very tired,' he said gently, 'shall I light ze lamp and you go to bed and rest?'

'No – no – I – like the dark!'

She still kept her forehead on the mantelpiece.

'Shall I not take off your shoes?' said the Jew; but she shook her head and sobbed a stifled 'Thank you.'

As she stood there quite quiet again and there seemed nothing for him to do, the

Jew said he would go down and write for an hour and then come up again. And when he came up she was in bed and asleep.

The next morning, before he went to business, he told her that it was the doctor's order she should walk every day for an hour; that at eleven every day she must be ready and Isaac would walk out with her till twelve. He begged her to be careful never to speak to anyone; he impressed on her that London was not like South Africa, and that if one spoke or even looked at anyone terrible things might happen. He spoke long to Isaac, telling him exactly the path they were to go: down the street through the square into Oxford Street and along it, but never farther than Oxford Circus; then to come back, to walk close behind his mistress, to speak to no one, and, if anyone came to speak to her or stared much at her, to stand close behind her, and to come and tell the Jew everything as soon as they returned. 'Ven one should look at her, Isaac, ven one should walk after her, you vill tell me, Isaac,' the Jew said, his keen eyes fixed on Isaac; and though Isaac only nodded and said nothing, the Jew knew it would be done.

At eleven Bertie dressed herself very carefully in her smartest walking boots and cloth dress and walking hat. It was the first time she had walked, and she was even excited when she and Isaac started, Isaac in his best livery with gilt buttons walking behind her, carrying the water-proof galoshes and umbrella the Jew said he must always carry.

She enjoyed the walk and when the Jew came home told him of much she had seen, and asked questions about the cabs and omnibuses. She dressed herself carefully for dinner that evening, ate well, and did not cry all the night; and the Jew thought her cure had been found.

For some weeks she went every day. The early autumn was coming in drier and warmer than the rainy summer. The air was sometimes hot and oppressive, but she went every day. For some time she dressed herself very carefully when she went out, and noticed closely all she saw and looked in at the shop windows; but after a while she became careless and walked more slowly and looked more down on the pavement. There were four things she always noticed, one a large place with its windows full of books. Before Rebekah married she had once bought some second-hand books, on the outside of which a yellow card was pasted with the words 'Mudie's Select Library, New Oxford Street'. The first day she looked in at the window and saw the books it came to her with a strange thrill how Rebekah had sat under the orange trees and in her bedroom reading from a book. Always, without missing, every day she stopped at that window. She read the names of the books over and over, without thinking what they meant, and went on.

Another thing was far down the great street; there was a dark house that stood far back from the pavement, and out of huge doors upstairs men were nearly always throwing into carts or wagons below brown stuff with a smell like malt. She never passed without looking at it. She disliked the strange dank smell. She never asked what it was, but all her life it came back to her with sickening remembrance of the long walks.

The other thing she always looked at was a shop window a little lower down. It was full of filters of all kinds, and there was a little fountain there that played with three small balls. The water came up like a tiny geyser and threw the balls in the air and always as they fell the water caught them again and threw them up. Every day she looked at them. The first day she had looked with interest; afterwards it became a terrible compulsion – she must look. She knew just how long it would be before they fell and how the water would catch them up again, but she had to look. She felt a kind of sick shrinking; yet she always had to watch them always do the same thing – they were always the same, like the curtains in the drawing room and the chair before the fire and the sofa in the bedroom, always the same. They all made the dull feeling in the top of her head worse.

At first she had looked at the streams as they passed her, men and women, old and young, all pressing onward somewhere, up and down – people in omnibuses, people driving, people walking; and a strange feeling always came to her that they were not really people, but like the people from the photographs which you look at through the two glasses, who move when you pull a string and shake their heads and jaws. And sometimes the thought would come to her that they *were* people; that they were people living just as people lived in Africa, with their homes, and relations, and people they visited, who had children and felt and laughed; that each one was real and alive, just as much as the people she had known. And sometimes a strange feeling used to come to her that she must go up to someone and put her head on their arm and say, 'Talk to me, please talk to me!'

But after a while she left off noticing the people. She took no care about her dress any more, put on anything that lay nearest and walked all the while looking down at the paving stones. She got to know them all; after the very large one came the small ones and then one cracked across. When she came home, often she remembered nothing and had seen nothing but the paving stones and the window with the balls and perhaps Mudie's and the malt place. Often, if it was at all damp or chill, she would not go at all though she knew the Jew wished it.

One day, a dull brown day with no rain, but the thick sky just above the roofs of the houses and damp autumn thickness everywhere, when Isaac came at eleven to tell her he was ready, she was lying dozing on the sofa in the bedroom in the pink silk dressing gown she had worn since she rose. She did not take it off, but pinned it carelessly round her waist with two pins to shorten it, but so that it showed here and there a glimpse of her white heavy-laced petticoat. Over it she put on the great fur coat she had thrown over a chair when she returned the day before and which reached almost to the bottom of her dress. She took from a wardrobe, almost without looking at it, a steel-blue French bonnet and without looking in the glass placed it on her roughened curls and tied it under her chin; she took up a pair of gloves, but, instead of putting them on, thrust them into her coat pocket. She did not trouble to put on her walking boots, but followed Isaac out into the street still wearing her little high-heeled patent leather shoes with paste buckles; she followed him heavily and when he dropped behind her she walked, looking down, hardly seeing the shop with the filters or noticing anything as she walked. When they got to the end of the walk they turned to come back down the same side of the street. For a moment or two she stood passive, looking into the great plate-glass window of a shop where tiers of new autumn hats and dresses were displayed. She looked vaguely at them for a moment, conscious only of the heavy grey sky above. Then she looked round and saw, standing close beside her also looking in at the window, two ladies. The elder one was about forty, older than Rebekah and rather taller, with her hair, which was already partly grey, turned back from her forehead instead of being worn turned down at the side as Rebekah wore it; her eyes were blue, but there was the same full high forehead, the same delicate sharp marked nose dominating the face, a delicate strong rounded little chin and the sensitive strong mouth. She was dressed in a sealskin jacket with a little brown bonnet and skirt, just as Rebekah might have dressed. The girl beside her was about sixteen with very light hair and the exquisite pink and white skin which Northern women often have; her large blue eyes and her dreamy mouth were smiling as she looked in at the window.

Bertie looked at them, and an irresistible impulse came over her; she put out her hand and laid it softly on the sleeve of the sealskin jacket. The woman glanced down quickly, as everyone glances at being touched in London. For an instant she looked at Bertie and took it all in – the beautiful round white face with its fringed eyes, the little fifteen-guinea French bonnet tied a little askew on the natural curls, the ninety-guinea sealskin coat with the edge of pink silk showing below it, and the points of white petticoat with priceless lace that had tipped here and there in the mud; she looked at the little house-shoe with the paste buckle and the ungloved hand with the rings. All her face hardened. If she had asked her why she touched her, Bertie would have spoken; but she turned and said to her daughter, 'Dear, we must go now.' The girl who had noticed nothing smiled and turned from the window. Bertie stood looking after them with her head on one side as they disappeared into the crowd. Then she turned and walked back. She walked so slowly that it sometimes seemed to Isaac she was going to stand still. When she got home she went upstairs to the bedroom and lay on the sofa before the fire.

From that time the Jew found it impossible to make her go out for a walk. She said she was tired or was cold. Some days she lay in bed till twelve o'clock and sometimes till five. If she got up earlier, she generally half-dressed in a loose dressing gown and lay on the sofa in the bedroom or sat in the chair before the fire in the drawing room with a great shawl wrapped round her. She ate more than she had eaten, and she never cried now; she drank two or three glasses of wine for dinner and with her lunch, and the Jew brought her up something before he went to bed. But as the time passed the Jew grew anxious; he almost wished she would have the old wild fits of crying. Her face grew whiter and whiter and stouter, till under her little round chin a double chin was gathering. She never spoke unless he spoke to her, and, when he brought the carriage, only if he insisted on it would she put something on and drive out with him. She never complained of her head any more, and she never asked Isaac to come and sit with her; she said she was not afraid. Nine months before she had looked much younger. Then she was like a girl in her early teens; and now she looked ten years older than she was. Her face was still very beautiful, but it was the heavy pallid face of a woman who might be thirty or more. She never asked if there were letters from her friends or referred to the Cape.

Again the Jew called in the old doctor. He said again she ailed nothing organically; she needed change and fresh air, and advised the Jew at once to take her to the seaside. The Jew was obliged to start for Hamburg on business at the end of the week, but before he left he went to St Leonards-on-Sea and took rooms for her, and the next day he took her and Isaac down.

The rooms he had taken for her were in a house facing the sea, kept by a widow woman who was a cousin of Martha's and whose husband had owed the Jew money. He had been kind to her and started her in this house. He lad hired all the rooms from her for the time of Bertie's stay, stipulating that no other lodger should be taken; but the rooms really reserved for Bertie's use were the drawing room on the first floor and the bedroom opening from it, also a tiny closet on the first floor just outside her door where Isaac was to sleep. She had been almost excited when the Jew told her she was going to the sea; she had begun at once to pack her boxes, and had laughed several times.

They got there late in the evening when they could see nothing, and Bertie was still in bed when the Jew left the next morning. He gave many parting instructions to Isaac never to leave his mistress for a moment, and to tell him when he returned if anyone had spoken to her or come to sit by her on the beach.

When Bertie had had her breakfast and was dressed, she called Isaac and walked out on to the esplanade. As far as the eye could reach, long rows of grey houses, three or four stories high, rose on the right hand; almost as far as the eye could reach the solid stone pavement stretched, and to the left, under a grey sky, was the grey sea, breaking with a soft 'sushing' sound its dull water on the long beach of rounded boulders and grey pebbles. She stood looking at it for a little while, then she began to walk along the stone pavement with the tall grey houses to her right and the sea to her left, and Isaac followed her. Here and there were still a few bathing houses and a few people bathing in the grey water, as the air was still and warm though so dull. On the stone pavement here and there were bath-chairs with invalids in them being pushed by men, sometimes with other persons walking beside them; and there were nurses wheeling babies in perambulators, or little groups of children down on the pebbles playing. In only one spot the long endless line of pavement was broken, where in the middle of the esplanade stood a little group of shops under one roof – a fish shop, a chemist's, a greengrocer's, a flower shop. She stood for a while looking in at the windows. She wanted nothing. Then she walked on for half a mile, then they turned and walked back again. After a time they came to where a great square of houses all exactly alike opened onto the esplanade; but here there were more people, and she turned back and walked up the pavement again to the point where they first turned.

After an hour and a half they went back into the house; she took off her walking things and walked about the great empty drawing room with the windows looking out on the esplanade and the sea. She looked at a glass bowl with some goldfishes on the side table and at two little Dresden figures holding vases on the mantelpiece; and then she went into the bedroom and drew down the blind and lay covered on the bed till lunchtime.

Every day she and Isaac walked out on the broad pavement, with the sea on the one hand and the rows of houses on the other; every day she stopped at the little building in the middle of the pavement with the little shops; she noticed how the fish was crimped at the fishmonger's, and the large Persian cat at the greengrocer's; then she walked on another half-mile and they turned. She began to know the stones as she had known them in Oxford Street, the large stone with the cracks and the place fifty yards on where there was the bluish stone. Sometimes she looked up at the houses, the tall stuccoed houses stories high, and then would come to her the strange thought that they were real houses, houses where men and women lived like at the Cape. They were homes. Once she noticed specially a man with a tall silk hat run up the steps and open the door with a latch-key; he was going home to lunch just as Rebekah's husband might go home; once she saw three girls come out with tennis racquets, laughing and talking; they were going to play; and once she noticed a mother come back with some little parcels, and the children upstairs waved at her from the window till she went in and the door shut. They were real houses, with real people; it was not a nightmare; they were all real; it was she and Isaac walking up and down, up and down on the pavement, that were so strange.

One day the sky had changed from grey to a dark heavy leaden blue; it seemed to rest just on the roofs of the grey houses; and the sea was very dark when Isaac came at eleven to ask whether she would walk; he said he thought it would rain, but she walked to the front door and Isaac followed her, carrying her umbrella and cloak. They passed the shops and came to the place where she generally turned, but she walked on. They passed more and more houses, still in an unbroken row, with the stone pavement stretching on with the pebbles below and the grey muddy sea breaking softly on them. She walked on till there were no more people on the pavement and the row of houses to the right was growing smaller. The esplanade itself grew narrower. To Bertie it seemed they walked for miles; then both houses and esplanade ended. At the end of the esplanade some steps with iron handrails led down to a curved pebbly beach and the houses died away, leaving a bit of cliff-like rise with gorse bushes upon it. Away in the little bay there were stakes sticking in the water and what looked like wickerwork baskets showing in some places; there were no human creatures in sight except some men loading two carts with pebbles from the beach, and higher, near the houses, some men digging what seemed to be the foundation for a new house. She stood resting her hands on the top of the iron railing that ran along the end of the esplanade; her eyes looked far out across the dull grey waters, to where, some sixteen miles off, a small grey headland jutted out into the sea, strangely clear in the humid blue water-laden air. Presently Isaac touched her on the sleeve: 'It is going to rain,' he said. She shook her head without moving her eyes from the distance. A few more large drops fell on her, and he opened the umbrella, but she put out her hand to keep him from holding it over her and went down the steps. She sat down on the pebbles with her back to the wall of the esplanade; she drew up her knees and folded her arms round them and sat looking out across the grey water of the little bay with its stakes and baskets, away to the grey headland dimly visible in the blue moist air. Isaac came down the steps too and stood on the pebbles a few yards from her. Quickly as the rain began to gather in about them, the few large drops became a thick haze, coming partly from the sea and partly from the land, that grew damper and damper. After a while the outlines of the distant headland vanished and from all sides the rain was creeping up. Slowly it blotted out the distant landscape, and then the posts standing out in the water in the little bays nearby and the baskets vanished. The men loading the pebbles from the beach had turned up the collars of their coats and driven away. The men digging the foundations had put their tools together in the trench and were walking away. Isaac moved from one foot to the other, looking at Bertie, the rain beginning to run down him. The water was beginning to gather round the brim of Bertie's fur hat in large drops and to run slowly down her fur cloak.

After a while the gloved hands she kept clasped round her knees were soaked, and the small streams ran down from her cloak and dress and made little puddles in the pebbles and earth about her. The wall of rain closed in, so that nothing farther than a few feet away was at last visible. And the water streamed down the steps. Then she looked at Isaac and saw him shivering where he stood three feet away from her, holding her closed umbrella and waterproof as the rain ran off him.

She rose. 'Let us go home,' she said. She climbed the step and they walked home along the dripping parade on which there was now no one, seeing nothing farther than two feet before them for the blinding drizzle. When they got into the house she undressed and went to bed and had her meals brought to her room and did not get up again that day.

The next day she got up, but the rain was falling; she went to the drawing room windows after breakfast, but the grey rain was falling on a grey sea, and the great stones of the parade lay wet. She shivered and shuddered and went to her bed and drew the down quilt over her head and slept all day.

The next day and the next it rained and she did not go out. But the next morning the rain had left off. It was grey but no rain was falling. Before eleven o'clock she rang the bell and Isaac came. 'Isaac,' she said, standing before him and looking into his face, 'is there any country here? I want to go into the country.' She spoke very slowly that he might catch each word.

'Country,' he repeated.

'Yes, country. I mean a place where there are no houses and people. In my country where I come from we call it veld.'

Isaac looked at her. 'No houses, no people – country,' he said slowly. He seemed to be considering, then he said slowly, 'Yes, I can show you. Come.' And Bertie went into the bedroom and got ready, and they went out together.

He led her in the opposite direction from the one they always walked in, past many shops and hotels and busy streets and a little fishing quarter where the fishermen's nets were out drying on the beach and little children played, then up a hill where there were little houses about and the town lay at your feet, and into a hollow where there were still more houses. Then they climbed another rise; the path went up among rough grass and some gorse bushes along the cliff. Isaac walked on before, Bertie climbing after him in her dark puce-coloured silk dress, holding it high above her laced white petticoat to keep it from the mud into which their feet sank as they climbed. Then the path ran along the top of a cliff. To the right was the grey sea, with many little fishing boats out on it; overhead was the drab sky; the footpath was full of white chalky mud which clung to their boots. Then they came to a broken fence partly of brambles. Isaac helped her to get through, and they walked on a little farther. Here was another hollow leading down to the cliffs and the grey sea. There were a few bushes and small trees growing below. Nearby, a few yards from where they stood, was a great building which was closed and seemed unused; it had a red roof covered over with a fine yellow lichen that stained it everywhere. Far off there were more houses. Suddenly Isaac turned round and stood still; she also stood still.

'This – this,' said Isaac slowly, 'is country.'

She looked about her.

On the slope about them everywhere there were the marks of cows' feet, which had sunk deep into the soft soaked turf. Some of the footprints were full of clear water, in which some blue flowers had been growing which raised themselves stooping and half crushed. She looked round at the grey sky, at the damp bushes, at the barn a few hundred feet off with its red roof, damp with yellow lichens, and at the mud and grass at their feet. The high heels of her little shoes were sinking deep into the grass as the cows' hoofs had done. She drew her skirt tight about her and stood looking.

'Let us go back,' she said, and turned, Isaac following her.

She led the way through the hedge and along the path upon the edge of the cliff, Isaac patiently following her. They passed the fishermen's houses and the streets with shops and hotels and got back to their own quarters with its long hopeless row of grey tall houses and its long endless pavement and grey sea breaking on the round grey pebbles and shingles. Bertie went straight up to her bedroom, took off her little wet shoes, and curled herself under a great shawl on the bed, took only a glass of wine with a biscuit for her lunch and did not rise till late in the afternoon.

That evening the Jew came. He had only returned from Hamburg that day.

He asked her whether she would like to stay longer where she was, but she begged him to take her back with him the next morning; and the Jew chuckled much to himself as he lay in bed that night thinking her life with him could not be so unbearable if she were so glad to return to it.

When Bertie got back, for the first two or three days she ate more and was a little less pale, but then she sank back into her old life. It was duller and damper now, so she never went out. She kept the blinds nearly always drawn down, but great fires burning night and day and lamps lighted if the fog were a little dark. She wore always one dress, a crimson velvet gown, loose and long, which had cost forty guineas. She put it on in the morning and wore it till night, never changing it for dinner. When the point lace about the neck and shoulders grew soiled she did not remove it, but threw a lace scarf over it.

All day she sat deep in the armchair before the fire or lay on her sofa in the bedroom. For lunch she took nothing but a glass of ale with biscuits and at dinner she ate little, though she took some glasses of wine; yet her face and figure grew quickly heavier.

She never referred to her friends in Africa or spoke of her letters to them; a complete silence seemed to have fallen on her, and, unless it was quite necessary to answer some question the Jew put to her, she never spoke.

One evening as the Jew sat in his room writing, he looked round to see Isaac standing behind him and asked what he wanted. For a moment Isaac paused, drawing his power of speech together. Then he said slowly, bending his face near to the Jew's, 'The – lady likes – cats!'

The Jew started up. 'Cats!' He looked at Isaac.

'Yes,' said Isaac slowly. Then knitting his hands together as if for a great effort, so that the knuckles cracked, he said, 'I was – cleaning – the window – she came – she saw a black cat on the wall – she said, "Catch it for me; I – like – cats!"'

The Jew stared at him; no one had ever before heard Isaac attempt a description. The Jew had a horror of all living creatures except storks, and cats he shrank from especially. 'Cats?' he said, 'cats?'

Isaac nodded, 'She – likes – cats.'

The Jew looked at him doubtfully. 'Can you get her one?'

'Three,' said Isaac slowly, 'kittens.'

For a moment the Jew hesitated, then took from his pocket a ten-shilling bit and put it into Isaac's hand.

'You vill get zem, Isaac. Zey vill be small and not to make a noise!' Isaac nodded.

The next morning while Bertie still lay in bed, eating her milk and biscuit, someone tapped at the door. In answer to her question, the door was slowly pushed open a little and a basket thrust in; then the door was closed. A little wheezing sound from the basket made her leap out of bed and go to it. Half an hour after when the Jew, who had just finished his breakfast, went up to say goodbye to her, he was astonished to hear shouts of laughter through the closed door; not knowing Isaac had already brought the kittens, he was astonished at the door to see Bertie kneeling on all fours in her white nightdress; on the hearthrug before he fire, one kitten was lapping milk from a saucer before her, one was mounted already on her back, and one, as he knelt with her head down, was leaping up at the long loose braid of curly hair hanging over her shoulder and tying to hold it with his paws.

She looked up laughing, 'Oh, aren't they lovely! One's climbed right on my back – look how this one plays with my hair; it means to climb up by it!' She half raised herself, taking the one off her back. 'There are two black and white and one grey and white; look, its eyes are quite blue; the other two are browny!' She stood up, still holding one in her hand. 'Oh, did you get them for me? It was so kind of you ...' She rested her hand on his shoulder; standing in her white nightdress she looked like a tall white angel beside his little dark figure; the top of his head barely touched her chin. Then she stooped to pick the others up and gathered them all three in her arms, pressing her face against each. She asked the Jew whether it would be possible for him to let her have the carriage in the morning, as she wanted at once to go and buy some things for them. The Jew was very busy, but he returned at eleven o'clock and took her out.

She bought three exquisite little china bowls, decorated, one with a rose, one with holly and one with larkspur. She bought three rolls of ribbon exactly to match the flowers on each bowl and three tiny real silver bells. When she got home she tied on each its bell with a ribbon to match its bowl and gave each one the name of the flower on its bowl, Holly, Larkspur, and Rose.

When the Jew came home at night, she rushed to the door and brought him to see them all drinking milk in a row, each out of its own bowl with its own little ribbon and own little bell.

At night she put their basket close by her bed on a chair where she could put out her hand and feel them. But the next day she was not satisfied with the basket, and drove out with the Jew in the afternoon to order a cradle she had thought of. It was of white wood, in three little compartments, all joined together and on rockers, with three little hoods, one over each compartment. The next day the cradle came and she spent three days lining it; from early morning when she rose till near midnight she was lining and draping it; she made the kittens tiny down mattresses and down pillows and tiny blankets and sheets, each with the kitten's name embroidered in silk in the corner; she made three little satin quilts with the flower of each kitten embroidered on it in silks; she edged them all with real lace. When the Jew came up to bed she took him into the bedroom and showed him the three little kittens lying before the fire, each in its own division in the cradle with its head on its own little pillow and tucked in under its own little quilt. 'Isn't it lovely?' she said, peering down at them; 'just like little babies, eh?' She bent over them and smoothed their little sleeping heads softly with her hand. The Jew looked down at her with astonishment.

'Do you like babies?' he said after a time.

'Yes – of – course,' she said slowly.

'You see,' – she raised herself – 'you can put your foot on the end of the rocker – like this – and rock them all at once if they want to wake.' And she stood rocking them softly with her foot. The next day she made three little silk bags and hung them in a row by the drawing room fireplace, and in each was a tiny silk handkerchief, embroidered with a kitten's name, with which to wipe their mouths after they had drunk milk.

For two or three evenings after they came she dressed herself in white for dinner and carried all the kittens down in her arms. They walked about the table and had three little china plates set at the end into which she put tit-bits.

The Jew turned cold with horror when they walked to his end of the table and put their whiskers into his glass and even their paws on the end of his plate, though he said nothing. She fed them with tiny morsels of chicken held between her lips and gathered them all up into her breast to carry upstairs again.

For nine or ten days when the Jew came home she sat for half an hour telling him all they had been doing – one had climbed onto the piano and broken a glass vase and one had been found asleep in the folds of the window curtain. Sometimes she asked the Jew to drive her out in the carriage as she said change of air was good for them, and she held them to the closed window to let them see the fog and dark of the street; but after that the excitement began to die down. When she had had them three weeks she had dropped back into the old life; she still fed them three times a day, but generally she put the food all in one bowl; their ribbons were unchanged for three or four days; they slept in any compartment of the cradle, and she never took them down to dinner; they went if they chose. Sometimes she stroked them as they climbed about her, and she let them sleep in her lap; but she spent her day silently dozing before the fire or watching it with wide-open eyes.

One rainy evening, just before dinner, she sat dozing before the fire in her red velvet gown with the lace scarf twisted about her throat. The Jew was in his little office downstairs, working at his books; the French cook who came in every day to make the dinner was busy dishing up with Martha in the kitchen, and Isaac was in his little room in the basement, dressing to wait at table, carefully brushing his hair before the little glass upon the wall to see if it were perfectly straight – as he always did before he went into Bertie's presence. Then there was a knock at the front door. Isaac not being ready, his mother went. In the doorway stood a tall handsome man of about thirty, whom she knew well as the son of the Jew's only surviving cousin, with whom thirty years before the Jew had quarrelled hopelessly because she had insisted on marrying a wealthy Christian; but he had partly made up the difference with the son, whom he sometimes asked to his house and often gave money to. It was supposed by the few who knew the Jew's affairs that, in spite of his being a Christian, the Jew might yet make him his heir, as he had no other near kin living; and Martha had never regarded him with favour. He asked if his cousin were in, and stepped into the hall. He stared round in astonishment at the change which had passed over the place since he was there last, glanced at the double-piled carpet on the stairs and at the glass and silver on the lighted dining room table visible through the open door. The Jew, hearing sounds in the passage, came out of his den as his young cousin was taking off his overcoat and hanging it in the hall.

The young man turned and shook hands with the Jew. He apologised that he had not been able to see him for so long but for the last year he had been travelling abroad. As he spoke he glanced round and in at the dining room door; and at that moment Isaac passed them with two dishes for the dining room.

'You have made things very comfortable here, I see,' he said.

The Jew gave him no explanation and asked him into his den, but when half an hour had passed and the young man made no sign of going, he asked him whether he would not stay to dinner and went up to the drawing room to see Bertie. She was lying back in her armchair with one kitten asleep on her shoulder and two playing with a worsted ball on the hearthrug.

'It is dinner time,' he said.

'Yes, I don't know why Isaac has not rung the bell,' she said slowly.

The Jew looked down at her. 'My cousin is here; he comes to dinner too.'

'Yes,' she said, slowly stretching herself and preparing to rise.

'You vill not dress you a little?'

'No,' she said heavily, 'this will do.' She put the kitten down on the floor and ran her fingers indifferently through the brown curls above her forehead but without looking in the glass. Then she turned and walked slowly towards the door, the Jew following her. She went straight to the dining room and took her seat at the table, while the Jew went to his den to where his cousin waited.

When he brought him into the dining room, 'This is my cousin,' he said, pointing his hand towards him, but he gave Bertie no name. Bertie half rose, and a look of surprise came over her face. She merely bowed her head slightly and sat down again. (She had expected to see a man of the Jew's age and type. But the visitor was quite six feet high and nothing suggested the Jew but the brilliancy of his dark almond-shaped eyes with long lashes like her own and a slight curve in his finely shaped nose. His forehead was broad and smooth, shaded by smooth wavy black hair; his jaw and chin were powerful and well shaped, and the voluptuous fullness of the much-arched lips did not take away from their strength; they also closed firmly.)

The Jew showed him to a seat on the right side of the table opposite to Bertie, where Isaac had set a place for him. Between him and Bertie, somewhat obscuring her, was a silver stand full of flowers; but across it he was able to note the full voluptuous beauty of her figure even in the loose velvet gown, the richness of the curly hair above the flower-like white face and the perfect shaping of her arms which the wide drooping sleeves of the old dressing-gown made visible almost to her elbows.

Isaac handed round the soup. The Jew began to discuss the Stock Exchange in Paris, where his cousin had been spending some months, and Bertie, with eyes fixed on her plate, ate silently. It was not till the third course had been reached that the Jew's cousin, leaning forward a little to the side to escape the vase, said to her: 'These flowers are very beautiful. One hardly expects to see such flowers at this time of the year.'

'Yes,' Bertie said slowly, without raising her eyes from her plate. Then the Jew asked him another question, and it was only when they were finishing dessert that the visitor once again addressed her; there were oranges on the table and he was explaining the signs by which he knew these came from the South of France, and he described the orchards there.

'Perhaps you know the South of Europe?' he said, leaning forward and speaking to Bertie again.

'No,' she said slowly, hardly raising her eyelids and head.

The Jew glanced sharply from one to the other, but Bertie had not raised her head nor glanced at the visitor and was passively picking her walnut out of its shell.

The Jew's cousin at once reverted to a business topic. He saw at once Bertie had not been born in England, and it puzzled him to guess where she came from; he had thought his question might lead to an answer.

Soon Bertie rose; she bowed slightly towards them at the table without saying anything and slowly moved towards the door. Without seeming to do so the Jew's cousin noted everything – the queenly body, the small lovely round head and neck, the long trailing untidy velvet gown, the slight swaying motion in the walk, the little hand hanging at her side with three rings on it.

When she had gone out he glanced at the Jew for a second to see if he would refer to her, but the Jew passed the wine bottle to him and told him how much he had paid per dozen when he bought it. When they had emptied their glasses he took him to his den; the young man stayed three hours longer than he had ever done before, but the Jew made no offer to take him to the drawing room, nor did he in any way refer to Bertie or explain her presence.

When he had left, the Jew went upstairs. He found Bertie as always in the chair before the fire; the kittens had gone to bed and she was lying back holding a large fan to screen her face from the hot blaze. The Jew stood for nearly four minutes beside her on the hearth rug. Then he said, still looking into the blaze, 'Vell, vot zink you of my cousin?'

She laid the fan down and stared into the fire.

'He's not like you,' she said.

The Jew looked keenly at her. 'He is young,' he said. 'He is handsome?'

'Yes,' she said slowly, 'he is handsome – but,' she added yet more slowly, turning her head towards him, 'he's not so nice as you.'

The Jew waited a moment. 'Do you not like him?'

She waited; then she said, dreamily looking at the fire: 'On the farm where I lived once, they caught a tiger, one of the large leopards, and Rebekah went to the cage every day to feed it; she wanted to make it love her, but I was afraid of it ...' She paused as though she had lost the thread of her thought, then she said, remembering, 'And one day after dinner, when she was going to feed it, it nearly caught her hand and bit it off; my father just caught it in time and after that he sent it away to be sold.'

'Vell?'

She looked up. 'Oh, I'm frightened of him, like I was of the tiger, too. Rebekah, my sister, wasn't frightened. She never was frightened of anything.'

'Vhy are you frightened of him?' the Jew asked, looking down at her.

'I don't know,' she said slowly. 'I think it's his eyes – his teeth are so white when he eats.'

'He is no good,' the Jew said. 'I give him much money; I have sent him to ze University. He has always no money; it is ze pleasure, ze gamble, ze horse race, all ze bad zings he likes.'

Bertie looked passively at the fire. She seemed to have nothing more to say; and presently the Jew went down to finish his work and soon she went to bed.

During the next ten days the Jew's cousin called three times – once in the afternoon, when Isaac answered the door and told him the Jew was out; once in the evening just before dinner, when Martha opened the door for him and he exchanged a few words with her before she showed him into the Jew's room – the Jew did not ask him to stay and he soon went; the third time he came Bertie had been staying in bed all day, as she often did when the fog was bad. Martha and he had a long talk in the hall and he left a gold coin in her hand as he went out.

It was three days after that visit, on a heavy drizzly night, that he called again about nine o'clock. Bertie was sitting fast asleep before the fire upstairs; Isaac was in his little room; the Jew was in his den working; when there came the sound of a tap against the window in the area, and presently Martha, without a light, came out of the kitchen door, went up the area steps, unlocked the gate and led the Jew's cousin down into the kitchen where a candle was burning; she put her finger to her lips when he began to speak. 'The boy is in his room,' she said, 'but he may not yet be asleep; he is very sharp – be quiet!' She slipped off her own shoes. 'You had better take off yours.' He hesitated. 'You can get them again when you go.'

He sat down on the kitchen chair and removed them. 'There is no possibility of his returning tonight?'

'Not till tomorrow night.'

He rose and with his boots in one hand prepared to mount the carpeted stairs. Martha followed him. He looked back at her. 'You are sure she expects me?'

Martha nodded her head and pointed to the door under the stairs to signify Isaac was there; then she whispered to him, 'Remember, it's the door facing you on the first landing, the door at the side going into the bedroom.' As he passed the door of the Jew's room he glanced at it, but it was closed and the light from the hall lamp was too strong to allow any light to shine from beneath it. Martha, standing at the back of the hall behind the stairs, motioned with her hand for him to put his boots down by the hat stand, but he shook his head, hung his hat on it, and carrying the boots in his hand went softly up the thickly carpeted stairs. At the door of the drawing room he paused, drew on his boots, drew off his soiled gloves and removed his overcoat; then he knocked softly. Bertie, dozing before the fire with the kitten in her lap, was half roused by it and sleepily called an answer; she fancied it was the Jew bringing her wine and biscuits. He entered, hung his coat over a chair near the door, and walked with long light steps across the room to the fireplace. It was not till he stood beside her on the hearthrug that she turned her head and saw him. She started, partly raising herself. He held out his hand to her, but in her startled surprise she did not see it.

'I am afraid you will have thought me very late, but they wouldn't let me come before.' He bent a little towards her. 'It was very good of you to let me come.'

She turned her head to see if the Jew were coming; she thought the Jew must have asked him to spend the evening with them.

He noticed her glance at the door and said, 'I have shut it.' He turned and drew a chair onto the hearthrug, not two feet away from her, and sat down on it, carelessly leaning his elbow on his knee and bending a little towards her. She saw how spotless his black coat was and his white cuffs, and noticed his white hands with their long delicately rounded fingernails.

'I don't wonder you are very lonely here all by yourself,' he said softly. He put out his hand with its white fingers and nails and stroked the kittens sleeping in her lap. She was sitting upright with her right elbow resting on the arm of her chair; the wide sleeve of the crimson gown had fallen back; her left hand rested near the kittens; she moved it a little that his hand might not come near hers as he touched them.

'I suppose you are very fond of them,' he said, looking up into her face.

'Yes, I like them,' she said.

He thought his eyes had never been so near the face of a woman which had looked at him in a manner so absolutely passion-dead. 'It's a shame all your affections should be showered on them,' he said softly. 'One envies them their resting-place.'

He looked up into her face, then he withdrew his hand and raised himself a little. He looked down at her. 'How beautiful!' he said. 'You know, that was the first thing I noticed about you!' In a moment he had placed his full-curved lips upon her arm halfway between her elbow and her wrist.

With a half-suppressed cry Bertie rose; the kittens fell at her feet. 'How dare you! How dare you !' she cried, standing at her full height before him.

He also rose. 'I hope I have not been too hasty,' he said; his mouth drew back a little. 'After the kind message you sent me, I think,' – he put his hand out towards her – 'that perhaps ...' He smiled.

'Oh, I never sent a message to you; you are so terrible to me; I can't bear you! I can't bear you! Go, go, please go!'

He looked at her shrinking face with its wide-open eyes, and at that moment his quick ear caught the sound of steps on the stairs outside the door. In an instant the truth flashed on him. There was a sound at the door. In an instant his eye glanced round the room; then without a moment's hesitation he glided past her; the door that led into her bedroom stood open behind her; with two long steps he had entered it and closed it slowly behind him; as he did so the drawing room burst open and the Jew with Martha behind him stood there.

The Jew glanced wildly round the room. 'Vere is he?' he cried to Bertie, who stood before the fire. Before anyone could reach him he turned on Martha: 'You vitch, zere is no von; vhy did you lie to me?' He turned to the fireplace where Bertie stood crying, 'Oh, I'm so glad you've come, I'm so glad you've come!' But Martha took the overcoat from the chair beside the door and, holding it up high to her shoulders, called the Jew; he turned and looked at her. For a moment he stood transfixed; then he stepped near her, looking at the coat. Bertie had run up to him: 'Oh, he is horrible! Why did you let him come? Why did you let him come?' She put her two hands passionately on the Jew's arm; he was still staring at the coat. At that moment the street door closed loudly; the Jew's cousin had evidently made his way through the bedroom door on the landing. 'Oh, you must never let him come again! Never – never – never!'

The Jew turned an ashen grey face slowly to her. 'No, he will not come here again,' he said. A few drops of sweat stood out on his forehead; his face was shrunken; it was the face of a man of eighty. He looked at her. 'Come!' he said. He grasped her wrists, one in each hand, and drew her towards the door. 'Come!'

'Oh, you are hurting me!' she cried. 'What is it? What is it? Why do you look at me so?'

He had drawn her out of the door on to the landing; the kittens, suddenly awakened from their sleep, ran after her, climbing on to her train. On the landing he turned her round so that she was below him and he above, and pushed her slowly backwards down the first stair. It seemed impossible that the iron force with which he held her wrists resided in his little shrunken body.

'Oh, let me go!' she cried. 'What is the matter? Oh, what is it – what is it?'

He pressed her down step by step; the kittens, trying to hold to her dress, slipped down the stairs behind her. His eyes were fixed on hers. 'I ... I ...' he said from between his closed teeth, 'I took you ... you told me ... you had no home ... I ...' He grasped her wrists as he pushed her down.

'Oh, you are going to kill me! Oh, Martha, Martha, ask him to let me go, ask him to explain to me! Help me, help me, Martha!' They were halfway down the stairs now. Martha stood close behind the Jew with the man's overcoat over her arm. 'Oh, you are going to kill me!' she whispered. 'What is it? What have I done?' Then understanding something, she cried: 'It was not my fault that he came. You asked him! Oh, I hated him, I hated him so!'

Then something in the Jew's face silenced her; the only wish she had was to escape from him. They had reached the hall now. He pushed her towards the door; she offered no resistance. He loosened one of her wrists and, with the hand that had held it, he pulled from her fingers the three rings she wore, so roughly that the flesh of her fingers was torn. Then he turned and took from Martha the coat. He raised it and put it over Bertie's head and shoulders; quietly, almost gently, he opened the door and, taking both her wrists, pushed her out backwards. She offered no resistance; she gazed at his face in a kind of frozen horror.

'Go,' he said. 'Somevere he vaits for you.'

He shut the door.

For a while Bertie stood stupefied, with her face to the door and the man's coat thrown over her head and shoulders, on which the rain fell heavily. Then she felt dizzy and sat down on the step and leaned her face on her hands. It had happened so quickly it seemed dreamlike; only the pain in her wrists and fingers told her it was real. At last she rose and turned to the door as if to knock at it. She heard the sound of voices and steps in the hall, and a terror seized her. If the Jew had been alone she would have knocked till he opened and thrown herself at his feet, and, if he kicked her, have cried till he listened; but she feared Martha's face behind him. She walked down the steps, looking back to see that no one was following her, and then a little way down the street till she came to a place a few doors off where a short street opened from the long one and led into a square. She walked down it. The rain was falling softly and steadily on her head. There were a few lamps almost deadened by the rain, and in the centre of the square one saw dimly the outline of high iron railings and trees. At the corner of the square she stood still. Just beside her, in the first large house looking into the square, one of the blinds had not been pulled quite down. She stood close to the area railing and looked; it was a large dining room or sitting room; there was a great table;

at the other end, with his back turned to it as though sitting before a fire, was the head of an elderly man; at the table, near him, bending over her work, was the head of a woman with greyish hair and a white cap; two young girls and a boy were reading at it. There were books lying on it. The light inside was so intense and bright, seen from the dark outside, that she could see the pattern of the paper on the wall with a large gilt figure and the bottoms of the picture frames. She pressed close to the railing, looking in. Then from the other side of the quiet square someone came walking with long loud steps. She did not know it was a policeman, but she felt as if he noticed her, though on the other side of the square. She walked away a little distance and stood beside the railings shutting in the trees and plants in the centre of the square. She moved her arm in and out of the tall railing and rested her head on it. A shrub hung over the railing above her, but it did not shelter her; the rain fell on her back.

Suddenly a hand touched the sleeve of the man's coat; she started and looked around; someone brought his face close to hers. It was Isaac.

'I saw – all,' he said. 'I was behind the stairs. They think – I sleep.'

'Oh, Isaac, what have I done? Why did he do so?'

Isaac waited. 'She,' he said slowly, 'let him in at the kitchen – I saw – she took him up. She told *him*,' – he made the curious motion with his thumb with which he always signified the Jew – 'he came with his latch-key himself – she said he often came to see you.'

'Oh, but Isaac, it isn't true, it isn't true,' she said; 'if I go back and tell him all the truth won't he believe me, won't he let me in?'

Isaac shook his head strongly. 'He,' he said slowly, 'killed – all – the cats!'

Bertie shivered.

'It's – no – use,' he said slowly.

'But where can I go, Isaac? – I've no money.' She wound her arm about the railing again and rested her head on it.

'I know,' he said. He took a black bundle from under his arm.

'Put it on,' he said. It was a black lace shawl which she had left hanging in the hall, when last she went out driving, because it got wet.

'Put – it – on,' he said. He took the man's coat that covered her and held it for her to put her arms in and slowly buttoned it before; then he put the shawl over her head.

'Come!' he said. 'I know – a place. Come!' He opened the umbrella he had brought and held it over her head. He paused to pick up the train of her dress, which was hanging in the mud, and helped her to put it up. She was so faint and cold she asked him nothing. She walked close beside him.

The rain was pouring down heavier now. For a little while they walked through dimly lighted squares and streets; then they got to the fuller light of Oxford Street.

The shawl covering her head and shoulders prevented the strangeness of her coat from being very apparent. Isaac called the first cab he saw and put her in it and got in beside her. She sat very close to him, almost pressing to his side. She clung to him as a drowning man clings to a rope, frail and worn though it may be, but which is all that holds him to life. She felt faint and almost dizzy. When they got to a railway station he helped her out. When he had taken tickets he took her across a platform and got with her into a third-class carriage. She sat in a corner with her head thrown back into it. Only once she bent forward and said to Isaac: 'Don't you think he would ever believe me, and let me go back?' Isaac shook his head. 'No – no,' he said.

When the train stopped and they got out they were still in the suburbs of London, but the air felt fresher and lighter. A slight mizzle was yet falling.

Isaac walked close beside her with the umbrella. They went down a long rise among houses and then up, still among small houses closely packed together.

'Where are we going?' she said at last.

'To a woman,' he answered; then added, 'She – lodged in our house – I know her.'

As they passed the houses Isaac went up to one or two and peered at the numbers, which were hardly visible to his short-sighted eyes in the dimly lighted road. At last he stopped at one. Two or three steps led up to a little porch. He left Bertie standing on the pavement and went up and knocked. When he had knocked twice and waited for some time the door opened. In a very narrow passage the light of a dim gas lamp showed a woman of thirty in a shabby black dress, with a small, much worn and pinched face. She recognized Isaac and asked him what he had come for. He took her to the back part of the passage and talked in a low voice. The woman peered towards the figure of Bertie out in the street, and they had some discussion; he took out his little red purse and slipped two pounds into her hand, and then went down the steps and brought Bertie in.

The woman stared at the tall figure in its strangely cut overcoat, and the black shawl, so draped about the head and face that little was visible. Isaac pointed to the woman. 'She,' he said, 'will show you.' He put his head nearer to hers and whispered, 'I will come again – soon – when I can.' Then, without shaking hands or saying goodbye, he turned and shambled out at the front door, shutting it behind him.

The woman looked up at Bertie with her sharp pinched face. 'You've no luggage, I suppose?' Bertie shook her head.

The woman took up a bedroom candlestick from the little shabby hat-stand, lighted it and began to climb the very narrow flight of stairs, motioning Bertie to follow her up. Once Bertie's foot caught in a hole in the stair carpet. On the landing the woman stopped, opened a small door on the right and went in. Bertie followed her. She set the candlestick down on a chest of drawers with a soiled white cover. There was a single bed in the room, also with a white cover, and some other articles of furniture. She looked at Bertie as if expecting her to remove the shawl; then she went to see if there were water and a towel on the small wash-hand-stand.

'You don't want anything to eat, do you?' Bertie thanked her and said she did not;

and the woman turned to go out. 'You ring if you want anything,' she said, pointing to the bell, and went out.

When she had gone Bertie turned and, without removing any of her wraps, threw herself down on her face on the bed. After a little while she seemed to feel the wraps strike her damp, for she stood up and took off the overcoat and shawl and threw them over the foot of the bed; then she took off her small red satin shoes, soaked through with the rain, and threw herself down again with her arm over her head.

In twenty minutes the woman came again to the door and knocked and, getting no answer, opened it. She came in and stood at the bedside, but Bertie was fast asleep. She took up the light and looked down at her, afterwards not unkindly, but shook her head, and put the light down again on the drawers and laid near it an old calico nightdress she had brought to lend her.

Then she went out, but Bertie still slept on heavily without stirring. It was nine o'clock the next morning before she woke. For a little while she looked about her in surprise and then sat up on the bed. It was a small room, with a common wallpaper with a dull yellow-brown ground covered with diamonds of dull blue transverse lines. Besides the bed and drawers there was a small wooden washstand and a yet smaller chair; over the little unpolished fireplace was a yellow mantelshelf, and above it hung a picture in a yellow polished oak frame of Queen Victoria when she was a young girl. The paper on which it was engraved was yellow with age and under the glass were large swelled marks all over it as if at some time tears had fallen on it and blistered it; there was a little window with a green blind, and below it, through one round hole in it as big as a shilling, two streaks of sunshine came; both fell on the torn strip of carpet beside the bed and showed the dust and dirt which had almost caked it over and obliterated the faint pattern.

She sat for a moment, then she got slowly off the bed and went to the window. She raised the blind and looked out. It was a long curved street running up the side of a hill with little grey stucco houses built exactly alike and touching each other all the way along; each house had a little portico with mock pillars before the door and two or three steps leading up to it, and each had a little bow window on the right side of the steps. Some had a few pots of geraniums in the window, and some had none; that was all the difference between them; and one house far down had one tiny tree growing in its little area. The air of the suburb was clearer than it had ever been in Bloomsbury. The late autumn sunshine was brighter than any she had seen since she came to England, though it was December. She let the blind drop and sat down on the side of the bed.

Presently the door opened and her landlady came in carrying a small tray with some tea and bread and butter. 'I've been in twice already,' she said, 'but you were fast asleep.' She put the tray on the drawers.

'I haven't any money to pay you for it,' said Bertie slowly.

The woman looked at her. 'Oh, the young man who came with you gave me a couple of shillings' (she did not mention it was two sovereigns), 'and I said I'd do for you till he came again. – You'd better drink your tea before it gets cold.' She glanced down at Bertie's hands. 'You seem to have hurt yourself,' she said. There were blue marks round her wrists and the skin torn a little on two fingers where the Jew had torn the rings off.

Bertie said nothing, and the woman went out and closed the door. She had four children to support and four lodgers to attend to. When her husband lived they had hired the garret floor at the Jew's house in Bloomsbury, but he had died of drink a year before and left her with the children to support. Isaac had been sent with her when she moved into her new house, purely because she owed the Jew money and he wanted to know exactly where she was; and twice he had been sent again to collect the instalments, so he knew the place well. She had no time to think of other people's affairs, the pressure of life was too hard on her, but she fancied Bertie must have had a room in the Jew's house and been turned out because she had not paid rent, or perhaps some man had deserted her. Isaac had told her she had lived for six months in the house at Bloomsbury.

Bertie stood up and drank some of the tea, but the mouthful of bread she bit seemed to oppress her and she took no more; she sat down on the bed again with her arm across her eyes. She seemed to see the farm, the great dam in the flats by the willow trees, with the little ducks wading in and out among the weeds, and below, where it ran out, the Kaffir girls sitting in the sun and beating the clothes on the stones and laughing. She saw the orange trees before the door and the flower garden beyond and old Ayah working at the milk house and scolding the maids and Griet dancing about pretending to put the rooms neat. She saw all the thorn trees in the flats beginning to burst into their yellow blossoms ready for Xmas; she saw her father and her mother. Oh, she would go back to them, she would go back to them; it didn't matter what they said.

And then she saw, fleetingly, pressing it from her as quickly as she could, the little parlour in the bush, and John-Ferdinand's face with its great dark eyes, and Veronica's, and she saw the little face – she could not go back! She could never go back! Then she heard the voices of the women talking in the little back room at the dance and she had the feeling of running home through the avenue, and the suffocating tightness across her chest; and the people that looked at her as she came out of the church at her aunt's. No, no – she could never go back, never – never – never! Oh, what should she do? Where should she go?

She stood up and began pacing the room. Oh, if only the Jew had killed her, if she hadn't got away! 'If I were dead! If I were dead!' she cried, wringing her hands and pacing up and down. The wild uncontrollable weeping that had left her so long returned to her. 'If I were dead! If I were dead! O God! If I were dead!' All thought went from her as she paced, wringing her hands. 'Where shall I go? What shall I do? If I were dead!' By and by the woman came up and listened at the door. She had heard the pacing from below and fancied she heard cries. It was no affair of hers, so she went away again, and the pacing and crying went on.

At last Bertie stood still suddenly before the mantelpiece and leaned her head against it. Where was she?

What was she doing? Everything in her brain seemed to stand still and be a blank; she did not cry. She raised her head and looked about her; it seemed as if she suddenly saw again, after being quite blind, the little lodging-house bedroom with the streaks of sunlight coming in through the hole in the blind. It did not come from under the blind anymore. She leaned her elbows on the fireplace and looked at Queen Victoria as a girl. She noticed all the fly-blows on the frame and the large teardrops swelling on the yellow paper under the glass. Was it her wedding dress, or do queens wear those coronets and veils flung behind at any time? The 'Queen Victoria' and the date printed below were quite faded. It must be twenty-five years old. Then she suddenly began wringing her hands and crying again. She paced the room quickly. That little ray of sunshine shone right on a hole in the dirty little strip of carpet.

Then suddenly a barrel organ, which a man had drawn up before him, struck up *Polly is my sweetheart, Polly is my darling*. She stood quite still and listened to it. When it had finished it played *My Grandfather's Clock* – 'And it stopped short – Never to go again – When the old man – died!' It ate into her brain and made the pain at the top of her head worse. After a while it went away and played lower down the street, and then again lower down. And then it went away out of all hearing.

She lifted the blind and looked out into the street; it was perfectly empty and silent – not a thing moved there. All the houses were alike, so exactly alike. A horror of pain came on her, just as when she looked at Queen Victoria's picture or at the ray of light. She pulled the blind down. She went to lie down on the bed with her shawl wrapped right round her head and was quite still.

At one o'clock the woman brought her up a plate with some meat and cabbage, and Bertie got off the bed when she had gone and ate it all, and then lay down again. About three the woman came to fetch the plate. Bertie got up.

'I want to ask you something,' she said.

The woman stood still with the plate in her hand at the door.

'Couldn't you help me to get any work to do?'

'What can you do?'

'I could cook or sew, I could be a servant.'

'Well, you couldn't get a situation unless you had some reference. I don't know what they do in your country – the boy told me you came from some place far over the sea – but here no one takes people without references. You've never been a servant before, have you?'

'Oh no,' Bertie said slowly.

The woman looked keenly at her. 'Well, you'd get nothing to do in *those* clothes;

you'd have to get something quite different. Why don't you go home to your friends? It is much the best thing you can do.'

'I can't. I haven't any friends in this country.'

'Well, you know your own business best. I couldn't help you to work; I do all my own. The young man said he'd come again; and perhaps he'll help you.'

She looked at Bertie's curled hair, swollen baby-pretty face, and the red satin slippers, still wet from last night's soaking, which stood at the foot of the bed, and went out; and Bertie lay down: there was nothing else to do.

Just before dark she drew up the window blind and looked out again. There were more people in the street now; every now and then men passed up, principally clerks; and other men who had come home from the City walked up to one house or the other. The sky was dull and clouded over again as if it were going to rain and a wind was whirling down the road in gusts.

Then down the street from the top of the hill came a curious figure, a man who looked like a Chinaman. He lad a curious straw hat on his head with little bells all round tied onto it; on his head was a drum, which he hit with two sticks fastened to his shoulders; before his lips he had a curious wind instrument fastened, which he played with his lips by moving his head; in his hands he had bones and a pair of cymbals. He stopped before the window when he saw her standing there and played all his instruments together, making a kind of band. Seeing she had nothing to give him, he went on and the darkness gathered down.

Presently the woman brought her up a candle and some tea and bread and jam, but she said she wanted only the tea, and undressed and went to bed in the landlady's nightgown. But when the woman went upstairs to her bedroom at eleven o'clock, she heard the crying and sobbing going on in Bertie's room when she stood close to the door.

The next day it rained heavily and Bertie lay in bed all the morning; the woman brought her dinner up at one o'clock. 'You really must try to eat something,' she said; 'you've taken nothing since you came but that little bit of dinner yesterday.' She told Bertie she was going out on business in the afternoon, but that, if she rang the bell, her little daughter was at home and would bring her anything she wanted. Bertie took a few mouthfuls of the food and then turned on her shoulder again and slept till three o'clock. Then she was stiff with lying so long, and she got up and dressed, but soon lay down again. She had no wish to cry anymore; she was in a torpid state.

About four o'clock the landlady's little girl knocked at the door and opened it; she said a man had called and had asked to see Bertie.

Bertie rose quickly. So Isaac had not forgotten her. The little child said she had asked him into the front sitting room downstairs, and if Bertie went there she would find him. Without looking into the glass to arrange her tumbled hair, Bertie went down the stairs; to the right of the passage was a door opening into the little sitting room, which was unlet just then, as there was no lodger who could afford to take it. It

653

was a very small room, with a few geranium pots in the window and a discoloured pair of lace curtains, keeping out the little light that came in from the dull rainy world outside. In one corner was a little whatnot with a few China pigs and other animals upon it. There was a low horsehair sofa; four horsehair chairs stood about the room and an armchair with a broken spring in the seat stood in the corner next to the window. Over the mantelpiece was a mirror with a fly-blown gilt frame and bits of green tissue paper pinned about it, and before it stood two vases with hanging cutglass ornaments, several of which were missing; a small Japanese umbrella was opened in the fireplace and the room was almost filled by a small square table that stood in the centre, covered with a faded red tapestry cloth. At first when Bertie slipped in she saw no one; then a figure rose from the broken horsehair armchair in the corner. It was not Isaac; Bertie started and looked at it. It was the Jew's cousin who rose lightly to his full height and stepped towards the table. He had another overcoat on, open in front, and she could see the points of his sharply curled moustache as he moved towards her and held out his hand. She stood silent on the other side of the table and did not take it.

'I am not surprised you are astonished to see me, and not at all surprised that you should be angry with me,' he said softly, still bending across the table, 'but I felt that I owed it to you as well as to myself to explain to you about all the terrible trouble I've got you into. I'm so very, very sorry.'

Bertie stood still, with her arms drooping impassively it her side.

'Please go away,' she said.

'Oh, don't ask me to do that! Don't be so unkind!' he said gently; 'I've taken such trouble to find you! I feel I must do something to put things right. Please sit down.' He put a chair round the corner of the table for her. Still she stood. 'It's all that terrible old woman and the damnable lies she told! You really must let me explain to you; it won't take long. – Please sit down!'

Bertie drew the chair he had set for her further, so that not only the corner of the table but the whole width was between them. He sat down also and leaned his elbow on the table and looked at her. The rather dim light was behind him but it faced her.

'I always knew she had a spite against me, but that she would do such a thing as this I didn't dream. I used to lodge in the first-floor rooms you had and she used to carry my cousin all sorts of tales about me – the hours I came home and the people I had; but I never dreamed she could do such a thing. One day, when I came to see my cousin, she met me in the hall and talked about you.' (He did not mention that he had called specially, knowing the Jew was out, to see the woman and find out who Bertie was and what her relation was to the Jew!) 'And she told me how lonely you were, no one coming to see you, and that you had come from another country. I told her how much I admired you, and she told me you had wished that my cousin should bring me upstairs, but he refused it. In fact,' – he bent forward a little more – 'she implied that you felt lonely and would be glad to meet me. I sent a message to you to tell you how delighted and honoured I should be if I could see you. The next

654

time I saw her she told me you would send me word the first time my cousin was away on business. Of course I quite understood how lonely you must be shut up there with no one but that old man to speak to ...'

'He was always very kind to me,' Bertie said slowly, drawing herself up a little.

'Oh, of course, of course! Who could have been otherwise!' He moved his head a little and looked at her; it was a little difficult to explain to a woman who spoke and showed herself so little. 'She came to my rooms and told me my cousin had gone to the country for twenty-four hours and you would be willing to receive me; naturally I came. She assured me he was away and would not be back till the next morning. Of course I never dreamed she was lying and that all the while he was sitting in his office downstairs. – Shall I shut the door?' He half rose.

'No,' Bertie said, putting out her hand to keep it open behind her.

'You really must forgive me!' he said in a low voice. 'I have suffered just as much as you have in a way. I am his only living relative, and it has always been supposed that when he died I should be remembered. That was just what the woman didn't like; she thought if I were out of the way it would be better for her and that boy. I've no doubt she was afraid of you too in the same way!'

'If I went to him and told him all, do you think he would let me go back?' she said slowly.

'Oh no; it would be quite useless. I made inquiries and I find that yesterday every stick of furniture went out of the house back to the dealers, and he's sold the lease. The new people take possession on Monday. I inquired at his office, and I find he sails for South America tonight. The boy and the old harridan are to go to Hamburg in a few days. It would be no use your trying to communicate with him; he's not a man who forgives.'

Bertie stood up and turned to the door.

'Oh, don't go! Please don't go yet! If you knew what trouble I had taken to find you.' He rose also. 'You didn't think I went off and left you without a thought that night! I waited about outside; I knew how violent he was. I saw you come out and go round into the square. I followed you, but you know I'd been so deceived – I didn't know what further plot there might be. I saw Isaac come to you, and I followed you all the way here. I could not lose sight of you.' He lowered his voice a little and bent his head towards her. 'You must let me help you a little; you must let me take care of you. She told me you had no friends in this country – you must ...' He put out his hand a little, almost as if he would have stretched it and touched hers.

Bertie, who had half turned and stood looking at him, shrank and drew herself together, and went out at the door.

He looked after her; under the red gown the sinuous movements of her body were visible and he noticed how beautifully the little head was set on the little neck. She beckoned to the little girl, who was sitting at the head of the kitchen stairs, to follow her, and went up to her room.

For a moment the man stood doubtful; then he rang the bell.

The landlady, who had just returned, answered it. She was astonished to find the tall handsome man, from his dress and voice evidently a gentleman of a type her house seldom saw, standing in her little front parlour. He told her he had come to call on the lady who was staying there, who was a friend of his; he hoped she would pay her every attention. He took from his pocket a card with his name and address upon it; under it he had slipped a sovereign. He placed both in her hand. He would call again soon, he said, but if by any possibility the lady should leave she would kindly communicate with him at once. At that moment the little girl came down carrying over her arm an overcoat which she said Bertie had told her to give the gentleman. He said he could not take it then, and asked them to hang it on the stand in the passage; he would fetch it when he called again the next day. He gave the little girl half a crown, asked the woman to order anything Bertie might need and charge it to him. Then he opened his umbrella and walked out. The woman stood on the step for a moment watching the fashionably dressed figure in its overcoat and silk hat, and then went to the kitchen to prepare a good supper for Bertie.

It was three days after that Isaac stood at the same doorstep and knocked. It was a Sunday afternoon, and a soft mizzly rain was falling. He stood on the doorstep in his overcoat. He had not been able to get away before. His mother had kept him constantly employed and near her while the furniture was moving. Now she had gone to make some arrangements for their leaving the next morning for the Continent, and he was free. In the pocket of his greatcoat he carried a little square parcel; in it was a very tiny leather bag with gold coins, about which were wrapped a tiny roll of five-pound notes; all were carefully wrapped up in a bit of thick cloth and tied with string. He had kept his left hand in his pocket and on the parcel ever since he had left the house. He had been collecting the sum ever since he was a little boy of five and the Jew gave him halfpence when he swept his office or cleaned his boots. Gradually the pence had become shillings and the shillings pounds, and at night, when his door was locked, he got out his little hoard from behind the loose plank in the wainscoting, where it was kept in the inner of two little iron boxes. He liked the rustle of the bank notes even better than the gold. He was going to say goodbye to Bertie, and then, just as he was going, he would take out the parcel and put it in her hand. After he was gone she would see what was in it. His money had never seemed so valuable to him before.

After some moments the woman opened the door and looked at Isaac with the raindrops dripping from his hat.

'I want – to – see – the lady,' he said slowly.

'She's not here.'

He waited. 'Has – she – gone – for a walk?'

'No, she's gone. She went away this morning.'

Isaac looked speechlessly at her. 'Where to?' he said at last.

'A gentleman who's been here three times to see her came this morning. They went away in a hansom cab.'

'Where – to?' asked Isaac.

But the woman said she did not know.

CHAPTER TWELVE

Fireflies in the Dark

It was a still, hot night. Outside among the roses and lilies of Rebekah's garden the fireflies glinted. In the large bed of carnations, where the white blooms shone out like dim stars in the half-dark, they flitted everywhere.

There was little change about the house or garden since that time five years before,[1] when her youngest boy was born. Only the window of her study was now a door; its inner door, that led into the children's bedroom, was walled up, so that you could reach it only from the garden; and, between the billiard room and the little rose hedge, a new square block of buildings had been raised, not connected with the house. It contained two rooms; the large front room looked out into the garden through windows and a wide glass door; in two of its corners were little white beds in which the two youngest boys slept; by day all the children played in it and at night learned their lessons there; in the room behind, Rebekah slept with Sartje – a little, yellow-brown, frizzly-haired girl she had adopted five years before as a little baby and treated in all ways as her own child, except that it was taught to call her mistress. The two elder boys slept in the main building in the room which had once been the nursery and which opened out of their father's bedroom.

Tonight the French windows and glass door of the large room stood open and the heavy scent from the flowers in the garden came in with almost cloying sweetness on the night air. In the centre of the room on a large square table a lamp burned; about it hovered a cloud of insects and little night flies and moths, and curious creatures with long hard wings, and little flying beetles. Some hung about the opal shade of the lamp, others had stuck fast to the transparent glass bowl, while others walked slowly about on the brown tablecloth.

At the farther end of the table the children were gathered. The eldest, a tall fair-haired lad, with delicate features and eyes that would exactly have repeated his mother's had they not been so pale, was bending over a drawing pad on which he was working with coloured pencils. On the table was his brother, a year younger than himself, but already as tall and very powerfully built, his face and figure repeating, with a curious exactness, his father's. He rested his elbows on the table, with his chin on his hands, and looked down from under his fair almost white

---

1 See the end of Chapter 8 for the birth of her youngest son, Bertie. The children, in order of birth, are Charles, Frank, Hughie and Bertie. Sartje, mentioned a few lines below, is her husband's daughter by the Coloured servant.

eyelashes at his brother's pencils as they moved. Close to the left elbow of the eldest boy stood the third – dark, round-headed, with straight, short-cropped hair and curiously alert, dark, very round eyes; he was standing on tiptoe, trying, with his elbows on the table, to raise himself high to see well what his brother was doing. At the other elbow stood Sartje, the adopted child, whose small head of woolly hair and glittering narrow eyes hardly showed above the edge of the table, but who also was trying to get a glimpse of the work. Only Bertie, the youngest of the boys, lay already in his little white bed in the corner, his cluster of brown curls spread out on the pillow, his delicate rosebud mouth and tinted cheek and round eyes shaded by long lashes recalling the aunt who had never seen him and whose name he bore; but there was a still dreaminess in the eyes that hers had never known. Before him on the white quilt lay one of the lesson books of the older children in which he had been looking at pictures; but now his little elbows rested on the quilt, and his small hands were raised, the finger tips of one hand playing softly with the other's, and he was whispering as he looked at them, as though telling them a story. Between the face on the pillow and the little dark wizen face of the girl, who stood trying to look at the picture, there was a likeness; her forehead was drawn up with wrinkles, like an old woman's, as if from some pre-natal and inherited anxiety, while his was smooth as a white tablet; but both had the same low, broad outline; in both the hair grew directly up from the forehead in a long, straight line; her lips were blue and pouting and her black eyes twinkled between narrow lids; but both had the same perfect oval outline of face and the same rounded chin indented by a dimple – the likeness between a figure carved delicately in alabaster and the same cast roughly in brown clay; but it was there.

'I say, man,' said Frank, the second boy, looking down at his brother's work over his hand and filling out his chest as he spoke, 'it's just wonderful how you do it all out of your head! When I am a man and rich, and you are an artist, I'll buy your pictures to hang all round my room.' He took one hand from under his chin to flick away a moth. 'Get away, Sartje! Get away! – I say, get away! – You are not to come too close to me, touching my arm. – Get round the corner.'

Sartje got back to her first position close to the eldest boy, and slipped her hand on to his knee.

'When you've done this,' said Frank, again resting his chin on his hand, looking down at the work, 'you must draw a picture with fellows playing cricket in a field, all the fellows we know. I want to show the boys that you make them out of your head. That Grey boy says you take them out of your books; he can't say that if it's fellows he knows.'

'And you'll make me catching the ball, won't you, eh?' said Hughie, laying his hand eagerly on his brother's arm.

'*You* catching a ball!' said Frank, biting a thumbnail as he spoke and without looking down at the small child. 'Why, you can't catch anything! You just pick up a ball when it rolls to your feet – and then you fancy you are a big boy and can field! Why, you can't even talk plain! You lisp worse than Sartje or Bertie – just like a baby.'

Hughie's face flushed and his eyes flashed over the top of the table. 'I – I ...' he cried; then, suddenly realising the undeniable truth of the accusation, he slunk down from his tiptoes and almost disappeared behind his side of the table. 'I thall be theven nexth birffday,' he said softly, after a moment's pause, but whether because he wished to change the subject or at least to prove that the charge of babyhood was unfounded, no one asked him.

'There won't be time to draw another picture tonight,' Charles said, moving his head back to look at the effect of his work; then he bent low over the pad to add the finishing touches. 'I want to write to grandmother tonight and tell her that mother thinks we shall be able to come and visit her at the farm the month after next,' he said, without raising his head.

'Oh Goy! Won't that be fine!' Frank slapped his legs with his left hand. 'Just the time the fruit's all ripe!'

'And you'll tell her to make muth peath thjam, eh?' said Hughie.

'Pugh! – you can't tell people when you are going to visit them what they must make before you come,' cried Frank, blowing out his lips. 'She'll think you are an awfully greedy boy.'

Hughie slunk down again till his head almost disappeared behind the eldest brother's arm.

At that moment a firefly, which had flitted in through the open door, settled down on the drawing pad. With a shout of delight the two elder boys stretched out their hands and, interlacing their fingers, raised over the firefly a small dome with their hands, leaving only one tiny opening between the fingers at the top.

'A peep show! A peep show!' shouted Frank. 'Does anyone want to pay a penny for looking in, and see a live candle walking about?' He put his own eye to the opening. 'She's just walking over the tree you made; I can see it quite plainly by the light.'

The elder boy put down his own eye to examine also, and Sartje and Hughie were both allowed to climb onto the table and peep in.

At that moment the door of the room behind opened and Rebekah stood in the doorway. She had changed little in the five years; but the drawn lines that had gathered about the eyes and mouth had grown faint, and there was a repose about the face that was perhaps not rest but calm.

She was dressed in the black dress covered with little silver stars which years before she had made after the fashion of Mrs Drummond's because she thought her husband would like it and which had always hung in her wardrobe. During the last five years she had not gone out in the evening; but tonight there was a concert in town given by artists said to be the best who had yet visited South Africa. As Frank had said he was going, she had taken a ticket for herself for the seat next his and was going with him.

Generally her hair was brushed down in smooth waves at each side of her forehead, but tonight she had fastened it back and bound it up high with a silver fillet, and she had a little silver belt about her waist. The children, who had never seen her in evening dress before, looked round at her as she came in.

'Oh, how beautiful! How beautiful!' Charles cried, raising himself slowly from his seat and standing before her; while Sartje and Hughie ran to her and began feeling with their hands the little silver stars upon her skirt; and Frank, climbing slowly down from the table, stood with his hands in his pockets looking approvingly at her: 'I say – but you *are* a swell!'

She laughed.

'You are like Titania, the Queen of the Fairies,' said Charles softly, twirling his pencil between his fingers. 'Where did you get it from, mother?'

'I made it when you were a baby,' she said, moving forward, while the two little ones clung about her.

He looked at her with his head a little on one side. 'I'd like to do you so – like that'; he moved his pencil round and round softly. 'Only you know, I couldn't. – Perhaps ...'

'Let *me* see too!' piped a small voice from the bed in he corner. Rebekah turned and threw the red silk cloak he carried on her arm (the same Bertie had worn the night she went to the dance) over the foot of the bed, and walked to the bedside.

Bertie hardly looked at the dress, but wove his small arms round her waist and drew her down to him. 'Tell me a story!' he whispered, creeping close to her.

'Ah yes, finish the one you were telling last night,' said Frank.

'I'm afraid there is no time,' she said, drawing out her watch.

'Oh yes, there is. I heard father just now calling for the hot water for his bath; he won't be ready soon.' She sat down on the side of the bed.

'Tell,' said Bertie.

Rebekah raised her little black-slippered feet on to the bed and leaned her head against its iron fretwork, while Bertie crept closer under her arm. The two elder boys sat own on the floor between the table and the bed with their knees crossed; Hugh clambered on to the bed's foot, while Sartje sat flat on the floor close to the side of the bed where Rebekah's train hung down so that she might count the stars upon it softly as her hand passed over them.

'You were just where the Robber Baron had put the two pilgrims in a dungeon and the young girl was coming down the stairs in the dark,' said Charles.

It did not take Rebekah very long to finish the story; to tell how the girl, finding her father was going to starve the prisoners to death, had taken his keys from him as he lay in a drunken sleep; and how, having opened the dungeon, she took the prisoners to a secret gate in the castle walls, gave them food for the journey and directed them to a path through the woods by which they might escape to freedom.

The children listened intently; there was a moment's silence when she had finished. Generally they asked questions and there was a free discussion of the story when it was done; but tonight Frank burst forth suddenly, 'Mother, I want to say something to you: I'm never going to walk with Sartje again; never, never! In the streets or anywhere!'

Rebekah glanced down at him without raising her head. 'Why?' she asked slowly.

He puffed out his full cheeks a little and pushed forward his red lips. 'Because, when we came back from singing lesson yesterday, the boys at the corner house came out and laughed at us. They said, "Walking with a nigger-girl! – Walking with a nigger-girl! – Walking with a black nigger!" I'll never walk with Sartje again; never, never, never!'

Rebekah lay quite silent for a moment; she seemed looking at the wall opposite; then she said, very slowly, 'It was very cruel and very evil to speak as they did, and it is also not true. Sartje is not a black nigger any more than she is a pure white child.'

'She *is* a nigger!' Frank burst forth, looking down glumly at his hands. 'Father calls her that. I heard him say it to a man the other day – a black nigger; and that she and Bertie have to have their meals here and only come to table when father is away. I know it!'

Rebekah started as he began to speak, then she lay back motionless, with her eyes fixed on the opposite wall as though she saw nothing.

'She's a black nigger,' Frank repeated, half under his breath, 'and I'll never walk with her again!'

Sartje, not understanding what was said but feeling she was being discussed in some way not wholly to her advantage, sat pressing the back of her head into the folds of Rebekah's skirts as they hung down from the bed, and looked out at the boys with her thick lips a little pursed.

Rebekah, still leaning her head back against the iron-work of the bed, had half closed her eyes and thrown one arm across her forehead; while Bertie, with his head tucked under the other, was softly stroking it where it was bare from the elbow to the wrist.

'Do you know, boys,' she said suddenly, after a pause, 'sometimes I have had a dream. I have dreamed that as we are living here in this old world, just as we have always lived, suddenly there has arrived among us a strange, terrible new race of people, coming from I know not where, perhaps from the nearest star.'

She waited.

'I have dreamed they were like us in body and mind, but with terrible white faces; our skins are tinted, but theirs were white as the driven snow, and their hair like thick threads of solid gold.

'They talked and laughed just as we. Mothers brought their little babies into the world and trained and cared for them, and men and women had friends and relations that they loved, and when they died as we die bitter tears were shed into the new graves. When they were struck their bodies felt pain, and when they were insulted they resented it; they lived, living and fearing and hating and hoping, and in the end their bodies turned to dust like ours. They were human; but there was this difference between them and us – that, of many things, they knew what we did not, and they could do things we could not.

'We, here on earth, have been so proud of our little cities and our little inventions, our ships and our books and our telescopes and our laws and our manners, and we have thought we were so wise and knew right from wrong, but, suddenly, when these terrible white-faced strangers came among us, all changed. The cities we had taken ages to build they shovelled away in a few days, and in their places raised palaces so large that our cathedrals went into their cellars. They had learned how to grasp the force of the tidal wave and of the very movements of the earth, and to use it as they would. Where we with difficulty dug holes a few hundred yards into the earth, they with their wonderful machines cut in miles, as though it had been cheese. They had machines that drew great currents of cold air down from the higher regions to cool the tropical plains, and they could send vast currents of warm air up to heat the mountain peaks. They sent currents of warmed air and water to the poles to make perpetual spring there, and cooled the equator with water from the poles. If they wished to speak to one a thousand miles off they spoke and were heard, how we could not tell; and when they wrote they did not use their hand, they set something against their brains and the thoughts registered themselves. To go to the other side of the earth they had no need to use our little trains and ships; they passed through the air, and the highest mountain peaks warmed by hot currents from the plains were their resting places. They had instruments so delicate you could see the blood beat in the leg of a gnat no bigger than a pin's point; and others so strong you could see a pebble no larger than a thimble lying on the moon's surface, just as we now with our telescopes see the extinct volcanoes. They laughed at our dirty habit of putting diseased matter into our veins to save us from disease and of pouring poisons into our stomachs to mend all parts of our bodies. They had found out what it means when you say a thing lives and grows; they knew what passed on in our bodies, and when anything went wrong they knew how to go back to the cause to put it right. They called us savages. In their laboratories they shaped the most rare and delicious foods from gases and primitive atoms – foods such as we can get only when they have been drawn from the earth and air and combined in the living laboratories of the plants and animals. In every mouthful of food they ate they knew just how much of each substance the body needs was in it, and what the effect would be; they did not eat in the dark whatever came, as we do. The bloody flesh of our fellow creatures which we feed on, the roots we dig out of the ground too, the milk drawn out of the bodies of other living beasts, they thought as horrible and unclean as we think the grubs and entrails on which the Bushmen feed. And our clothes – the skin of dead creatures which we fasten over our hands and feet, the jackals' and bears' and skunks' skins which we hang about our shoulders with the tails flying and think ourselves so grand in, the feathers of birds and the dead birds which we mix with grass straws and fasten on our heads, the shreds of hair and wool from animals' backs, the threads from the insides of little worms, the torn decayed fibre of plants that we beat into clothes and are so proud to carry about everywhere on our bodies and think others savages if they have not got them – they thought disgusting.

'They were so civilised they knew the body of a human being was more wonderful and beautiful than any covering matter made out of dead animals or decayed plants, and when they wore any covering it was only for warmth or to fasten on their wings. What they wore were beautiful scale-like things, woven as we weave glass out of sand, but soft and of many colours, fitting each human being's body as perfectly as their own skins; so that, when a man was fitted out for flight with wings on, he looked as a dragon-fly looks when it is hovering over a pool. They thought our clothes and the way we hid our bodies from light and air uncleanly; and they turned their heads from us, as we turn our heads from natives dressed in skins and rubbed with fats.'

The two elder boys were leaning forward with their arms upon their knees and their lips apart following each word, and Hughie had knelt straight up at the foot of the bed, his eyes fixed on his mother's lips as she still lay with her eyes shut and her arm across her forehead. Bertie had still one arm tightly about her waist; the hand of the other was softly stroking down her arm but moving more and more slowly; and Sartje on the floor had drawn the folds of the bead-net train about her shoulders and was holding it fast at her chin, pretending she was a lady sitting in church with a black lace shawl on. The children were all quite silent when Rebekah paused for a moment. Then she went on.

'But it was not only about such things as clothes and food and houses they knew more than we. They had beautiful and wonderful things we have not even dreamed of – musical instruments more wonderful and sweet than ours, as our organs and violins are better than the gorra-gorras which the Bushmen and Hottentots play on. If you listened to their music, it was as if all the stars were singing together; it filled the earth and sky.

'The pictures talked and moved.

'Also, because their knowledge was different from ours, their laws and their ways of life were different. Things we had thought right they called wrong. They laughed at the things we believed, and called us ignorant and superstitious savages. They jeered at us when we put water on the foreheads of little babies to save them, and laughed when some of us said bread and wine could be changed into blood and meat because a man spoke a few words over them, just as we laugh at the Kaffir witch doctors who mumble over bones and make charms. They didn't feel sorry for us because we were ignorant; they only laughed at our books and our pictures and all that we made and did. They thought our bodies uglier than theirs, though we thought we were just as beautiful. They would not ride in the same airships with us nor breathe the same currents of air; they called us "The Inferior Races".

'Perhaps we were. But, in the world that had been ours, in which we had tried to grow and learn and make things a little more beautiful, *they* said there was no place for us unless we could serve and be of use to them. They broke down our little countries and our little governments and our little laws; they took all the earth. They said, "Work for us; that is all you are good for; we will let you go on living if you are of use to us."

'Here and there one tried to teach us and help us to know what they knew; but while one tried others cried, "This is sentiment; you are taking them out of their place; they are an Inferior Race." They wondered why we lived in the world at all, or what we had been made for.'

'And we? What did we do then?' asked Charles softly, leaning farther forward as she lay still.

'We ought to have driven them right out into the sea! If I'd been there I'd have shown them!' said Frank. 'What business had they coming here when we were here first? It was our world!'

Rebekah lay still an instant. 'We could not really fight them,' she said slowly: 'we could die, but could not fight them. Sometimes thousands of us did gather together. We said, "It is better to die with arms in our hands than to lie here like dogs and be trodden into our graves." And we gathered together our little guns and our little cannons, the things we had once been so proud of, and we came on in thousands; but we could not really fight them. From high above in the air they saw us and poured down blasts of poisoned air upon us so that we died by hundreds and by thousands, as locusts die when you spray poison on them, without knowing where we were struck from. Sometimes they shot streams of liquid metal at us, and we fell as corn falls in the harvest. We could not fight them – we could only die. And sometimes, if by a strange chance we managed to take the life of one or two of their men, they called us murderers – but our dead lay in heaps.

'Thousands of the bravest of us fell so; whole nations were swept away from the earth and were forgotten. We could only fight to die.

'But to some of us a much more terrible thing happened. We did not try to fight and were not killed suddenly; a more awful fate overtook us.

'Because they despised *us*, we began to despise *ourselves*!

'If you pull up a tree suddenly by the roots and throw it down on the ground with all its roots exposed (the roots through which it has sucked its life for so many years), for a little while the leaves may keep green and the sap run up the stem; but by and by the leaves will wither, and the tree dies. Even if you try to transplant it and stick it up carelessly in a bit of ground, if you do not spread out the roots in the new earth and press down the ground carefully on them and give it much water for a time – it dies.

'So, when they took from us all our old laws and our old customs, when they told us all we had thought right was wrong and all we had known foolishness – and when they made us believe them; when they did nothing to teach us their wisdom and make us grasp their freedom – then we despised ourselves; and so we died.

'We did not die suddenly; we faded and faded, as the leaves fade on an uprooted tree and grow browner and browner till they drop off and are blown hither and thither by the wind, till you see them no more. So we died by millions. And the strange white people said, "See, they are an inferior race; they melt away before us!"'

'And we, did we all die so?' asked Charles, bending yet more forward, his eyes fixed on his mother's shaded face.'

'Not all,' she said, after a little while. 'Some of us, perhaps not always the bravest or the most beautiful, but the wisest of us, said, "We will not fight their weapons, only to die! Neither will we fade away. This world also is our home. We also are men. We will not die. We will grasp the new life, and live!"

'And we did not despair; and we did not despise ourselves. We learned all the terrible white-faced strangers had to teach, and we worked for them. We worked – and we worked – and we worked – and we waited – and we waited – and we waited ...'

'And then, what then?' asked the boys together, seeing she said no more.

She lay quiet for a moment. 'I do not know,' she said. 'The dream ends there.'

Then suddenly she moved her arm from her forehead and sat upright. Bertie, whose large eyes were slowly closing, drooped his head softly over into her lap. 'You see, boys,' she said quickly, glancing down at those on the floor, 'when we talk of the dark peoples and the inferior races, it has often seemed to me, it is as with those terrible white-faced strangers of my dream.

'But we have not the excuse they had when they scorned us and tried to set their heel upon us. They came from another planet, and might say, "Those earth men and women, what are they to us? Except that we are parts of the same Universe, what connects us with them?"

'But we cannot say so of any men or women living.

'Once, on this old Mother World of ours, there were no creatures living such as we see today. I do not know, but I think there was a great silence. Then the time came when there were living things in the seas and in the air. Fishes began to swim and shellfish fastened on the rocks near the shores and tiny living creatures by myriads moved everywhere.

'And then there came a time when there were four-footed beasts and great birdlike creatures – the old monsters whose bones we find now everywhere turned to stone in the rocks, but who are nowhere with us on the earth today.

'And then there came a time when on the earth walked beasts and in the sea were fishes and in the air were birds and on the trees climbed four-handed animals, many of them such as we know today; but still, there was no man!

'And the ages passed. And then a strange little creature began to lift itself up and look round on the world. It tried hard to set the sole of its hind-limb flat on the ground and to straighten out its hip, so that the fore-limb might be free to carry the helpless young, and to pick the fruits and dig out roots. And then at last the time came when between its thumb and forefinger it could pick up even a very little stick; but yet there was no man!

'And then the ages passed. And there came a time when the creature's foot stood firm and flat on the earth, and he could grasp the very smallest particle between his forefinger and thumb and hold it tight. He had found that if you rub two sticks together sparks will fall. And at night, when he and his fellows sat together over their fires, they made many sounds which each one understood; they talked! – and then, there was MAN!

'Perhaps not just man as we know him: not man of the many thoughts and the many words and the much possessing; but still, man – the man whose little arrowheads and tools of flint we still find everywhere from the north seas to the equator, whose bones lie mixed with the bones of the animals he killed and the shells of the fishes he ate in the caves where he took shelter – caves from which he went out with his little flint and stone tools to hunt and fish. And the woman, perhaps with just such ringed stones as those I picked up and have now in my study, went out to dig for roots and insects, with the stones fastened on to the end of her stick, and to look for grass seeds and berries, with her baby tied upon her shoulders and with a skin. And at night, in the firelight, as she sat waiting in the cave for the footsteps of the man who was to bring game, while her baby lay on the floor beside her or still hung on her back, she crooned to it the first little human love song; and perhaps, as she sat waiting, she took a bone from the heap from which they had eaten and, with a sharp stone, began to carve on it those pictures and patterns which we find on the bones today, pictures like those the Bushmen have left in their caves, and patterns like those the Kaffir women ornament their pots with. And when the man came in with the game and they had cooked it in the embers, they threw fragments to the lean long-legged creature who lay near the cave entrance. And when they had finished they lay down to sleep beside the blaze; and the creature kept watch at the cave door ready to bark as no wild thing ever barked if the steps of animals or men came near: – then there was man, and woman, and child, and dog – there was a home! Nowhere on the earth was the civilised man that we know – but there was *Man* and *Home!*'

The boys leaned forward watching her intently. She had again leaned back with her head against the iron fretwork, looking upwards, hardly seeming to think of them, but her hand was on Bertie's head.

'And then again, the ages passed; and here and there, in this old earth of ours, men learned something more. Somewhere women found that, if you shaped vessels of clay and baked them in fire, they would stand great heat, and they learned to work in them. Somewhere men found that, if you put some kinds of earth into a great heat, you could smelt it, and they made iron and no more used bones and stones for weapons. Somewhere men found, perhaps in many parts of the earth, that if you hollowed out trees and guided them with sticks you could move on water – and there were boats. Sometimes, when female creatures were killed and their young caught, the women brought them up, and in time these had young and there were flocks and herds; and the milk of asses or camels or cattle made it easy for men to live without that terrible search for food every day. And in time women learned it was better to plant grasses and roots, and water and tend them, than to seek for them every day, and then there were gardens. And the men did not always hunt; they tended the tame beasts and defended them, and the women built houses and wove the threads of grasses and fibres of leaves into coarse cloths, and then there were rough clothes. And in time men found it was better to gather into large bodies and build their houses near together and have their gardens joining, so that they might defend them and tend them together, and then there were villages. And, when they found it was best that strong wise men should lead them all, they chose chiefs, and there were tribes and a government. And at last in many parts of the world there were half-civilised men and women such as the Kaffirs were when we found them, with flocks and herds, and houses and gardens and lawns – but still not just the civilised men we know.

'And then, as the ages passed, in different parts of the earth men went further. Here and there on different parts of the earth men learned to do better than hollow out trees for boats; they made large vessels with sails. Instead of mud and straw or skin houses, men learned to build them of stone and baked bricks. Women learned to weave many kinds of clothing. Then men learned to set down their thoughts in writing, so that what one generation knew was passed on to another – and then there was civilised man! – man with his palaces and temples and laws and cities and books – books, sometimes written on stone tables, sometimes on mud tablets, sometimes on leaves or bark or skin, but still books where the thought and knowledge of mankind might be stored and each generation begin where the last left off – and there was civilisation.

'Now it has spread from country to country. There are civilised men all over the earth, and we are proud of belonging to them. We despise the men who have not the material things we have and who have not learned to read and write, who have not the command of the stored-up knowledge of the ages; we despise them as the half-civilised Kaffir and Hottentot despised the Bushman.

'And yet – and yet – Englishman and Frenchman, Chinaman and Greek, Hindu and German, Zulu and Japanese, Roman and Hottentot – if we go far enough back we all have to come together and stand before that cave door. The lady in her white satin with her jewels and broidered handkerchief, the king with his crown, the judge in his ermine, the poet and the thinker, the millionaire and the beggar, the warrior and the slave – we all stand huddled there; and, as we peep over one another's shoulders and bend to look in, we have still to whisper to what we see there – "Father! – Mother!"'

Her voice sank almost to a whisper.

'Perhaps you will say, "Yes, we know we were savages once, but what we are so proud of is that we are not now. We are right to despise the people who do not possess the things we possess and have not the knowledge we have. We are right to despise them and call them Inferior Peoples and to treat them as it would not be right they should treat us."

'But have we really any right to fill out our chests so proudly? Is it really our civilisation – yours and mine – made by us?'

She sat up. 'Look at this little book!' She took up from the quilt the little school book which Bertie had dropped there and held it up half-open with the leaves turned to them. '"It is our book," you will say, "written and printed in English by Englishmen"; and perhaps you feel a little proud that even small English boys of ten and eleven can read it and understand all that is in it when the great chiefs and leaders of many barbarous nations could not. But how much of it have we made? Look at these little black lines and dots!' She held the book more open towards them. 'You will say they are only the alphabet, something so simple that even babes like Bertie and Sartje can learn them. Yes, and any fool can learn a thing when once it has been invented and another teaches him how to use and understand it – but who made them? – not we!'

She dropped her hand with the book upon the bed. 'From the old cave days men made pictures of birds and beasts and men on cave walls and stones and trees and bones; and at last a time came when they found these pictures could be made to speak to others. Sometimes I think I see a man carving figures with a flint on the stem of a tree; the sunlight about him is the sunlight of a day scores of thousands of years ago. He is drawing the pictures there, so that the friends whom he has lost in the chase may know he has been there, and he is the first man writing. As the centuries passed some men went farther; they learned to give each picture a meaning: a raven meant death and a serpent meant life, and a circle meant time, for instance; and then they would write long sentences in pictures, saying what men feel and think as well as what they say. And then the time came when men found that, by turning the pictures into short signs, by leaving out many lines they could write quicker – and so men wrote thousands of years ago in Egypt and Assyria and China. Then a time came when somewhere men found out the greatest thing men had discovered since they found out how to make fire; some men found out that if you used the signs not to mean words but simply sounds and put them together you could express at once and easily everything the human brain could put into words and the human lips utter – then there was the alphabet as we know it. For thousands of years men in Asia and Africa and on the shores of the Mediterranean laboured; the Phoenicians passed it on to Greece and Rome; and so today we read and write with it. Look at these little lines!' She held the book up again, where in parallel columns were rows of Roman and Arabian numerals. 'You will say they are only figures that any simpleton can read and even calculate with. – Yes, but each one of them has a history thousands of years old, since that time when our little first fathers and mothers first began to count upon their fingers and were proud when at last they could reach five. Countless millions of men have counted and thought and invented that these little simple signs might exist; and if the Arabian figures had never come to us from Asia, some of the work we are most proud of doing could never have been done. Look at this!' She held open a page on which was a picture of the solar system. 'Perhaps you think it very clever that little lads like you can tell the names of all the planets and how far they are from the sun, and tell much about the movements of the stars; but thousands of years ago, on the great solitary plains in Asia, dark-faced men through long nights lay and watched the stars, and in solitary towers night after night they watched how the heavens shifted and what rose and what set, and how the seasons of the year were marked; and, but for the labour of these solitary watchers, whose names we shall never know and whose very nations have passed away, the telescopes and observatory and calculations of which we are so proud could never have come into existence; they laid the foundations down; we raise the walls! The very paper of which this book is made: – You will say, "At least that is ours made out of rags spun in English mills and beaten into paper in English factories." But, when I hold these paper leaves between my fingers, far off across the countless ages I hear the sound of women beating out the fibres of hemp and flax to shape the first garment, and, above the roar of the wheels and spinnies in the factory, I hear the whir of the world's first spinning wheel and the voice of the woman singing to herself as she sits beside it, and know that without the labour of those first women kneeling over the fibres and beating them swiftly out, and without the hum of those early spinning wheels, neither factory nor paper pulp would ever have come into existence. If I tear one sheet of paper out of this little book and there were some being wise enough to tell me its whole story, with all the lines and dots and marks upon it, and what they mean and how they came to be, and how the leaf itself came into being, the whole story of the human race on earth would have to be told me, from the time our little forefathers and mothers rubbed two sticks together and made light. This little book! – this little book! – it has got its roots down, down, deep in the life of man on earth; it grows from there. It is not your book, it is not my book, it is not the African's book, or the Asiatic's book, or the European's book; it is THE WORLD'S BOOK!'

She dropped it again softly on to the quilt and leaned forward with her elbows resting on her slightly raised knees, so that Bertie's head within her lap was entirely hidden.

'Do you know what a *parvenu* is, boys? He is a man who becomes suddenly very rich. Often he keeps horses and carriages and houses and lands, and he swells himself out, and tries to make people believe he has always had these things; he would like to make people believe that the grand old house he lives in was built by his own ancestors, that the pictures on the walls were of his relatives, and that the beautiful old library was collected by him. He is proud of the things with the existence of which he had nothing to do and which he only enjoys because a fortunate chance has given him money – and men call him "upstart" – and perhaps they are right, because the lowest and most foolish sort of creature is one who is proud of the things which reflect no sort of credit on himself.

'I sometimes think, boys, that we, people like you and me, have to be very careful, lest we also become *parvenus*.

'For this one thing we have always to remember, because the moment we forget it, and speak and act not remembering it, we shall act like fools. It is this: We must always remember that, only the other day, as we count days in the life of men on earth, not even so many centuries ago as a savage would count on the fingers of his two hands – so short a time ago that perhaps the lichens which are growing on the rocks that have fallen from Table Mountain were growing exactly as they are today – our forefathers, yours and mine, were savages wandering naked in their woods and on their steppes, staining their bodies with coloured juices, wearing as their only covering the skins of wild beasts, and building for themselves huts of mud and straw.

'There were civilised men on the earth then. The Hindu had already built his great palaces and written his great books; the Chinaman had long wrapped his body in soft silken robes, and in delicately furnished rooms was sipping his tea out of China cups so delicate we cannot even now imitate them. The Medes and the Persians and Egyptians and nations whose names we do not know had had their great empires and their civilisations and had passed away; but we all the while lived the life of naked savages.

'Even the Greeks had gathered their learning from Asia and Africa and had already written their great books and carved their great statues and reared their great temples, while our forefathers were dancing naked round their wood fires at night. The Romans had built roads and cities and made collections of laws; they looked upon our savage Northern forefathers as "*something hardly human*"; "*more like beasts than men*" one old writer called them. And if a Roman woman had married one of your ancestors and mine, the time was when they would have buried her alive as one who had eternally disgraced her race and people. And if they captured one of our ancestors and took him to Rome to follow one of their triumphal cars, he stared about him in the streets with the same stupefied wonder at all he saw, as a Zulu from the heart of Zululand, if he had never left his *kraal*, would stare if you set him down in the streets of London or Paris. Perhaps they were wrong to despise us so; there are ways in which a Zulu chief may be higher than a learned professor – but we were savages!

'For you see, it was not only with regard to clothes and food and houses and the material things of life that we knew less than some civilised peoples. When our forefathers were still sacrificing human beings to their gods under the oak trees, and their priests, like the Kaffir witchdoctors today, were "smelling out" the people who should be killed; and when our forefathers dreamed that heaven was a place where men forever drank mead out of the skulls of their enemies – already – long ages before – the great teacher of Asia had sat under his Bo-tree, and had sent out to the earth his message of love and peace. And when our poet sings today:

> "He prayeth well, who loveth well
> Both man and bird and beast …
> He prayeth best, who loveth best
> All things both great and small"

he is only seeing over again what the man in Asia saw thousands of years ago. And our great men today are only slowly finding out bit by bit, as they climb along that path which we call science, what men of Asia saw years ago when they cried, "All life is one!"'

Her voice sank into silence. She seemed dreaming to herself rather than talking. Then she said gently, 'You know there are people who, before they eat, bend their heads and say a thanks. But for me, when I read a beautiful book or a great poem or see lovely pictures – and even when I have been very happy walking along and thinking – then it comes to me that I want to raise my hand to my forehead and salute, as the soldiers do when their officers go past. I want to say – "To all the great dead, to all the men and women who have been before me whose names will never now be known, without whom I could never know what I know, or understand as I understand or think as I think – Be Thanks!"

'And sometimes even when I am walking in my garden and I see the peach tree covered with blossoms in the corner and the roses and lilies growing all round, and the grapes hanging from the gable, and all the small flowers sending out their scent, the feeling comes to me, and I want to say – "To all the gardeners that have been before me – to the little old first mother, who scratched earth and put in roots and grasses – to Chinaman and Persian and Egyptian and Babylonian and Indian, and men and women of races whose names I shall never know, without whom I should never have this beauty – Thanks!" And sometimes as I work there I feel as if they were working beside me and the garden belongs to them and me. And sometimes I think perhaps in years to come, when I have long ages been dust, some woman working in a garden more beautiful than any I can dream of now will stretch out her hand and say – "To all the gardeners that have been before me …" and I, so long dead in the dust, will live in her heart again.'

There was a moment's silence. You could hear Bertie's slow, even breathing from her lap.

'You know, up-country on the great plains, where the camel thorn trees grow, there are ant heaps as high almost as a man. Millions of ants have worked at them for years, and slowly and slowly they have grown a little and a little higher. Sometimes I have fancied, if a little ant should come on the top of one of these heaps, and should rear himself on his hind legs and wave his little antenna in the air, and should look around and say, "My ant heap, that I have made! My ant heap, from which I see so far! – My plains – my sky – my thorn trees – my earth!" and should wave his little antennae and cry, "I am at the centre of all!" – and that then suddenly a gust of wind should come! The ant heap would still be there, the ant heap on the top of which he chanced to be born; there would still be the trees and the plain and the sky; but he would be gone forever.

'I have sometimes wondered: isn't it a little bit so with us, when we walk about so proud on the top of our little heap of civilisation? Because the most that any man can hope for, and the most that any nation can hope for, is this: The man, that, in the one little hour of life that is given him, he may be able to add one tiny grain, so small perhaps that no eye will ever see it, to the heap of things good and beautiful which men have slowly been gathering together through the ages; – the nation, that, when its time to pass comes as it comes to all, it may have added to the things good and beautiful, which humanity lays up through the ages for the use of all, one layer, perhaps one thin layer, but that so well and truly laid that all coming after shall say – "It was nobly done!"'

'Mother, mother,' whispered Hughie, 'why are your eyes so big?' He was kneeling forward with his knuckles on the bed, staring intently into her face; but she did not seem to see him.

'You will hear people talking often of Inferior Races and of how superior we are – the people who may be speaking; but for me I know this, that, if you took from me bit by bit all I have gained and learned from other races and other peoples in whom my blood never flowed, I should go back and back, and you would find me at last only a little cave mother with her baby tied by a skin onto her back, peeping out at the door of the cave to see if the man with his bone hook or flint arrows was coming home with game, while a dog who was not yet quite able to bark howled at the door. And when I think of all I have and all I know, the only feeling I have is – "Pass it on! Pass it on!"'

She lapsed into silence and the boys sat watching her.

'When I was a little girl,' she said, stretching her arms out upon her knees, 'I could not bear black or brown people. I thought they were ugly and dirty and stupid; the little naked Kaffirs, with their dusty black skins, that played on the walls of the *kraal*, I hated. They seemed so different from me in my white pinafores and my little stiff starched pink skirts that rustled as I walked. I felt I was so clever and they so stupid; I could not bear them.

'I always played that I was Queen Victoria and that all Africa belonged to me, and I could do whatever I liked. It always puzzled me when I walked up and down thinking what I should do with the black people; I did not like to kill them, because I could not hurt anything, and yet I could not have them near me. At last I made a plan. I made believe I built a high wall right across Africa and put all the black people on the other side, and I said, "Stay there, and the day you put one foot over, you heads will be cut off."

'I was very pleased when I made this plan. I used to walk up and down and make believe there were no black people in South Africa; I had it all to myself.

'But one day – I must have been about seven years old then – there was a war going on against the Kaffirs near where we lived, and a white man who had just been to the front came to see us. He sat talking to my father and mother in the front room and drinking coffee, and I sat on my stool in the corner, by my mother's worktable, and listened. He told how many Black men had been killed and only two White men hurt, one by falling off his horse. I did not mind that so many black people had been killed – they were only Kaffirs! Then he told about a fight he had been in the day before. It was a big fight. The white men had their cannon and all their soldiers on the top of a hill, and the Kaffirs came out below from the bush; there were hundreds of them; they had hardly any clothes or guns, only assegais, and they came on naked up the slope; but before them walked a young Kaffir woman. Her arms were full of assegais. As the men threw their assegais she gave them new ones; she called on them to come on and not to be afraid to die. She walked up and down before the front row, and called on them to come on. The guns fired and the dead lay in heaps. When she got close up to the mouth of the cannon she was blown away too with the others. He said hardly any escaped, only a few got away into the bush again. But I felt I was suffocating. I ran out quickly to my pear tree in the garden and walked up and down. I couldn't bear any more. I saw the woman walking with her bare arms glistening in the sun and her red blanket tied across her as I had often seen Kaffir women, and, with the assegais in her arms, calling the men to come on and not to be afraid to die. I walked up and down; at last I lay down on the ground and cried. After that, often in the night when I lay awake I thought I was the young Kaffir woman, and I called the men to come on – and then the cannon fired.

'And once, when I was an older child, about nine, I was sitting at the kitchen door on the lowest step feeding my chickens, and my mother and old Ayah were standing at the top, talking. I don't think they noticed me: they were talking of a Kaffir woman who used to live on the farm before I was born. I didn't quite understand everything they said – you know children often don't when grown-up people talk, and yet in a way I did understand everything. They were talking of a trouble which had come to her – I know now it was the greatest trouble that could come to any person – and they said, when she couldn't bear it any more, she took her two little children and climbed the mountain to the very top where the precipice stands so high. And when she came to the place where it curves out, she tied her two children under her arms and jumped down. They talked of how all the morning they looked for her and wondered she did not come to work, and then another Kaffir woman said she had told her what she was going to do. Your grandfather and all the men went up, and there they found her, just where the precipice curves out, with the two children tied to her, quite dead.

'They did not know I knew what they said; but the next Saturday, when I had no lessons, when breakfast was done I went up into the bush. I told no one I was going and I climbed up past where the tiger traps were; and then on where there was no path. And when it was nearly midday I got to the foot of the precipice where it curved out. The trees were all about and at the foot of the precipice were rocks that had fallen down with lichens on them and black ground between. I sat down on one of the stones. I knew that was where she fell. I thought perhaps if she knew it she would have liked to think that, so many years after she was dead, a little white child came and sat there and felt sorry for her. I had made up a little poem about how beautiful the world was, and how sad she must have been when she went away from it. And I sang it when I sat there. It was all I could do. And twice after that I came there, and often when I saw a Kaffir woman walking past I used to wonder if perhaps her husband was going to bring home a new wife, and if she felt as sad as that other woman did; and once I ran far down the road after a travelling woman I saw going by with her baby on her back, and gave her my slice of bread and jam, because I didn't know what might happen to her some day.

'And so you see,' she said, 'as I grew older and older I got to see that it wasn't the colour or the shape of the jaw or the cleverness that mattered; that if men and women could love very much and feel such great pain that their hearts broke, and if when they thought they were wronged they were glad to die, and that for others they could face death without a fear, as that young Kaffir woman with the assegais did, then they were mine and I was theirs, and the wall I had built across Africa had slowly to fall down.

'It's natural,' Rebekah said, 'that we should love those who are like ourselves. A little child feels very lonely if it has not another child of its own age and size to play with. And perhaps the greatest longing a human being can have is to find another being who feels and thinks as they do; and when they meet they are like two drops of water that run into one as soon as they touch. But, even if people aren't like us at all, deep down there is something that joins us together; and if you shrink from them at first, if you are very kind to them and try to help them, it's wonderful how you get to love them.'

She had dropped her right arm at her side, and the fingers of the hand were moving softly among the frizzled curls of Sartje's head which she had pressed back deep into her mistress's skirts, her drowsy eyes already full of sleep and dreams.

'And so, when I hear people talking of superior races and inferior peoples, and of keeping other races and peoples down, I hardly understand. Because, if I find people who seem to know a little less or to see a little less than I do, I always feel I want to say to them, "Oh little earth-brother and -sister, climbing with me that long climb out of the dark, through the cave doors and on we do not know up where, – if it should happen that I have climbed on to a step a little bit higher than the one you stand on and can see a little farther – here is my hand – let me help you up."'

For a moment she sat silent, her eyes looking straight forward almost as full of dreams as Sartje's. 'Out there in my garden,' she said softly, 'there are flowers of all kinds growing – tall queen-lilies and roses and pinks and violets and little brown ranunculas – and I love them all. But if the tall queen-lilies were to say, "We must reign here alone, all the others must die to give place to us," I do not know, but I think I may say, "Is it not perhaps then best *you* should go?"

'And perhaps the next day there might come a blighting frost; the rose bushes would live on and the little violets hidden at their roots, and even the little brown ranunculas sheltered by higher branches, would be alive; but the lilies – the tall white queen-lilies would all be dead!

'I am glad there are all kinds of men and animals living on the earth where I live, that I and men like me are not the only creatures. If the time should come when there was only one kind of creature left, then the blooming time of the gods' garden would be done, and I would be glad to creep away under the dust and sleep.'

She put Bertie's head down softly on the pillow, and slipping down herself, stood on the floor beside the bed, rousing Sartje from her half-waking slumber and causing her to sit upright on the floor.

'One thing I tell you, lads,' she said quickly, in a changed voice, looking at the two boys who themselves were now rising from their curved-knee position on the floor: 'it is this – I hope, I believe, I know, the day will come when you will regret utterly every slighting, every unkind word or act, that you have ever given place to towards Sartje, and when you will be deeply grateful for every kind or generous thing you have done towards her. Sartje is not a black child any more than she is pure white. It is not her fault that she is not white, any more than it is your virtue that you are not half-black. Sartje is alone in the world. Her mother does not want her; her father does not know that he has even such a daughter in the world. She has no one but us to take care of her. I shall not ever ask one of you to walk with her again. She shall walk with me.'

'Mother, mother,' said Hughie, sliding down from the bed and catching hold of her skirt, glad that the conversation had suddenly taken a turn in which he could find a part, 'I will walk with Sartje! And,' he cried, filling out his little chest and striking his fist against it, 'I will walk with her in the big street; and if the boys laugh at her, I fthrow them wifth stones!'

Rebekah put her hand on his short, dark hair. 'No, you wouldn't; you'd just be like Rover; when little dogs come out and bark he goes past, he doesn't see them. You'll be mother's big Rover!'

For a moment his face fell; then he said approvingly, 'Yesth, yesth, I *am* big Yover!'

'Well, and I'm sure,' said Frank, pursing out his lips and pressing his double-chin against his white collar as he looked downward at his hands, 'I don't mind walking with Sartje, if it's in the pine woods or somewhere people can't see. But I'm not going to walk with her in the main road or on the road to the station.' He pursed out his lips yet further.

Sartje, now wide awake, was paying no attention to anything that was said, as she was busy spreading out Rebekah's train in a great wide circle on the floor.

'You mustn't think I don't understand, laddie,' she said, putting her hand for an instant on his shoulder; 'I am your mother and three times older than you, and I ought to be much wiser; but when I go down the Government Avenue, and the Coloured girls sitting there laugh because they see I don't wear stays as other women do, it's as if a knife ran into me under my ribs. I know I'm right; that in years to come people will wonder women could be so mad and foolish as to deform themselves. And yet, when these women laugh at me, I am so full of pain I can hardly walk down to the station; and when I come home I feel I want to creep onto the bed and cry. I've tried to like Coloured women and do all I can to help them and then they jeer at me! I don't want for days to go out again. If I, your mother, who should be so much stronger and wiser, feel these things so, what right have I to expect that little boys like you can bear them? You would be heroes if you could.'

Frank had raised his chin from his collar and both boys were looking her full in the face. She looked at them a little wistfully.

'You know, laddies,' she said softly, 'you are always talking of being *men*, and how fine it will be when you are grown up. It is a finer thing to be a "man" than either of you can know now. But it's not being able to lift a great weight or strike a great blow or crush things beneath you that can ever make you that. The thing that really matters is this: that when that day comes, as it must come to you at last, when your bodies lie still and dead, whether it be in a palace or a poor man's hut, on a solitary Karoo plain or in a crowded city, whether you have been rich and famous or poor and unknown – what matters is this, that if one should stand beside you and look down at you knowing all the story of your life, they should be able to say, "This strong man's hand was always stretched out to cover those feebler; this great man's body never sought good or pleasure for itself at the price of something weaker." Then, though no eye could see it, you would lie there, crowned – the noblest thing on earth, the body of a dead man who had lived the life of a man! No strength and no size and no beauty of body can ever give you that.'

The two boys stood with their eyes fixed on her face; but Hughie, who stood close beside her, pulled down her arm and peered anxiously up into her face; but there were not tears there.

At that moment, through the window, came the sound of the opening of the front door of the large house and there was sound of a step on the gravel. Rebekah turned quickly and took from the foot of the bed the red silk cloak which Bertie had worn to the dance five years before. She put it on and drew the hood over her hair.

'Oh, little Yed Yiding Hood! Little Yed Yiding Hood,' cried Hughie, clapping his hands. Then, throwing himself on all fours on the ground – 'Now I'll be the wolf! – Boo-hue-hue!' He careered round her while Sartje, pretending to be greatly appalled, leaped on the bed and buried her face by Bertie's, who still slept on. Rebekah whisked her train out of his hands in affected fear, and stooped to pin up the skirt under her cloak. There was the pleasant scent of a good cigar, and in the open doorway the children's father stood.

He wore a grey cap and his overcoat, hanging open, showed a large expanse of white shirt front. He had grown stouter in the last five years, his face somewhat redder and the flesh stiffer. One passing him now in the street would hardly have noted him as a handsome man, but he had still a fine fully developed presence. But the latent vigour which had given him charm as a young man was lapsing into a placid self-content which made almost an impression of sluggishness.

'Well, what's the row about?' he said good-humouredly, taking the cigar from his lips as he looked down at Hughie, who was still on all fours. 'I'm afraid I've kept you waiting,' he said to Rebekah; 'but when I'd had my bath I found unless we hurried we'd miss that train; so I took things leisurely. We should have been half an hour early if we'd gone by that, and now we shall be three-quarters of an hour late' – he took out his watch; 'but it's such a long programme, it's rather an advantage.'

'I didn't at all mind being kept,' Rebekah said; 'I will be with you in a minute.'

He put the cigar back in his mouth and blew a long whiff of smoke. 'Well, I'll wait for you at the gate. We've still twenty minutes to get to the station.' He called goodnight to the children and went down the steps.

Rebekah turned to Sartje: 'There is a candle burning in my room; go in and go to bed at once. There are three peppermints on the mantelpiece which you can take to go to sleep with. And you two big boys, go and get your mattresses and bedding from your own room and spread them here on the floor, so that if the young ones wake and cry before I come back you can be here to hear them.'

'Oh, a bivouac! a bivouac!' shouted Frank. 'We'll be Red Indians sleeping in a wood.'

'We'll have a make-believe fire with twisted papers, and sit round it,' said Charles.

'Yes, and you can go and find the box of chocolates in my top drawer, and put them on the fire for chops,' said Rebekah; 'but mind you give the little ones some – Sartje too. You must all be in bed by nine o'clock. I'll kiss you and tuck you all in when I come back.'

Hughie ran to fetch the chocolates, and the two elder boys prepared to rush off to fetch the bedding. As Charles passed her he laid his hand softly on her arm. 'Mother,' he whispered quickly, 'you know I will never mind walking with Sartje?'

'Yes, I know, dear,' she said softly, 'but for her own sake I will not let her. Thank you.' They exchanged a swift glance; then he ran out and she turned to the bed. For an instant she put her lips on Bertie's forehead and spread his curls on the pillow; then she went out through the glass door.

She stood on the top step for a moment, drawing on her glove. The night was very dark now and absolutely still; the scent from the flowerbeds rose up almost overpoweringly, and the fireflies seemed to flit by in dozens among them as she walked slowly past the beds to the gate. In after years the sight of a firefly brought always back that night to her, with a sense of the coming dawn after the dark.

Frank stood outside the gate smoking. He pushed it open and closed it. He was always polite to her now, sometimes almost attentive. When they had walked a few steps they passed Mrs Drummond's gate.

'I met her today,' he said, inclining his head in the dark to the house, 'sailing out of the booking office, as I went in to get our tickets. Hadn't seen her for months. She says her husband's come. Goes away in a week on a long journey into the interior – rather a short visit after twelve years' absence!' He laughed. 'He must have found her much younger than he left her; the story goes now that she goes to bed three days in each month ostensibly for her health; really, to have her face enamelled.'

'I think it is going to rain tonight,' Rebekah said quickly, looking up at the sky.

'Why didn't you say so sooner, and I could have told the boy to come with the trap and fetch us?'

'Oh, it may not,' she said, looking up again, 'but it's so still and there were so many insects out tonight.'

Here they turned out of the main avenue into the short cut through the woods. The footpath was narrow, and he walked before, she following, holding tight her skirts.

'By the way,' he said, 'you don't want to buy that grey horse of mine, do you? He's too broken winded for hunting any more, but he'd do well to draw that milk cart, or fruit cart, or whatever it is, on that wonderful farm of yours.'

'No,' she said, 'that old horse I bought from the Malay for ten shillings because he was going to shoot him has turned out wonderfully. We feed him on warm bran and meal and give him two raw eggs a day, which he can eat without teeth, and he's got as fat as a young horse and takes the cart to the station twice a day.'

'Philanthropy turned out well this time, eh? I really must go and see this wonderful farm of yours. Growing quite a millionaire, I suppose! Sixpence for cabbages, sixpence for grapes, mounts up!'

'Well, it pays all my expenses and Sartje's, and keeps the man and woman at the farm, and we owe nothing.'

'Oh, I'll give you credit for making it pay,' he laughed. 'By the way,' he said, when they had gone a few steps further, 'I think I shan't put off my trip to the Eastern Province till you and the children return. I've practically made up my mind to go tomorrow. I know the captain going with this boat and there are some people I know going, so I might as well go now and perhaps have a week's shooting when I've done my business; it'll be the close season if I wait till you come back.'

Rebekah fell to no speculation as to why he had suddenly changed his plans since the morning; she had long ceased to look for the real reasons of his obviously superficial explanations or to have instinctive perceptions about anything that concerned him.

'Yes,' she said, 'and it will be cooler now than later. I suppose you will take the black trunk and your small portmanteau.'

'Yes,' he said, 'you might see about packing them tomorrow, as the boat will not leave later than four.'

The path here got so intricate and uneven, that they walked in silence till they got out into the road at the station. When they got to the hall in town where the concert was given they found it far advanced. Their own seats were in the front row but one, and the place seemed crowded. No place seemed vacant but the chair on Rebekah's left.

Rebekah felt very tired. She had been up and at work since six that morning, and she almost wished she had not come. Then four men on four violins began to render a passage by Beethoven. In a few moments she was leaning forward breathless and motionless like a little child who goes to the pantomime for the first time. It was the first music belonging to her own world she had ever heard: she did not see the men or the instruments, but had the joy one feels as one rides alone across a solitary Karoo plain in the sun and hears nothing but the rhythmic beat of the horse's feet.

Then it ended; and a woman, the great singer of the troupe, in a tight white silk dress, wearing many bracelets, stood on the platform; she shook out her dress and bangles, and bowed to the audience, and unfolded her music and began to sing. A wild burst of applause shook the hall when she finished, and again she bowed and smirked towards the audience and sang. Rebekah leaned back wearily, speculating why it was that one woman, with her song and her tight silk dress, should at once be able to produce an atmosphere as trivial and suffocating as an afternoon tea where women are discussing their neighbours' dresses and concerns.

And she fell to planning a new kind of concert room – quite round, with seats rising tier above tier and the music coming from the centre or one end, but all so arranged you could not see the players or the audience, high partitions shutting you off from your neighbours, and each seat so long that it was a couch on which you could lie down and lose every consciousness but that of sound; a dim soft light coming from veiled lights in the roof. She was a little distressed as to arranging the lights for the performers, so that while the sound was not impeded the light was not visible, and she was lost in this when her husband touched her to say he was going out.

The interval had come; almost all the men streamed out to the refreshment bar and the hall was left almost entirely to women. As she glanced back to look at the clock her eye fell on a man who had not gone out and sat in the seat beyond the empty one next to her. But beyond the fact that he had a closed music book upon his knees from which he had evidently been following the music, and that he was a stranger and not South African, he left no mark upon her thought. She sat back still trying to arrange the lights in the concert hall. As she sat dreaming her eye fell unseeingly on the hand which rested on the music book on the man's knee beside her. She started and looked at it consciously. She knew it; it was strangely familiar. It called back sensations of her childhood and of her past life; she looked up curiously into his face to see who he might be. But he was a man she had never seen before. His skin was bronzed like that of one long habituated to the open air; his beard was dark and close-clipped; his dark hair curled close to his head, and, though he did not seem more than thirty-five, was slightly tinged with grey. She knew no such man. She glanced back at the hand again, and the same strange sense of familiarity came back to her, only it seemed to have been a hand smaller and softer. Long afterwards she knew that the hand it reminded her of was her own.

She sat back in her seat again, looking at the empty stage and continuing her plan, till the people who had gone out for the interval came streaming back again. Frank, when he came back again, spent the rest of the interval in looking round and telling her who of their acquaintances were or were not there.

'So Mrs Drummond didn't come after all,' he said in a low voice, fixing himself back in his seat.

'Perhaps she is in the gallery,' Rebekah said indifferently.

'Hush – no! That empty chair next you is hers; that's her husband sitting beyond you.'

Rebekah looked round quickly. So, he was the man whose little statue had stood for ten years in the corner of her room, whose notes on the margin of the book she had read and re-read with the text, and whose comments she had herself put notes to – this was Mrs Drummond's husband!

The time was long past when any mention of Mrs Drummond affected her as rough matter touching a naked nerve-point; she had no living interest in her. But no creature which has ever crept into the core of our life, and fed on the bleeding macerated tissue it has created there, ever becomes for us again a matter of complete indifference. Anything connected with them makes in us a faint adumbration of pain.

Then the music began again, and she forgot him or was only faintly conscious of his presence.

Just before the concert ended, as the woman in white satin was for the last time raising her voice on the stage, there came the sound of pouring rain on the roof. It fell in torrents that almost drowned the woman's voice. People looked round anxiously, those who had not ordered carriages questioning how they were to reach the station or their homes in town. And before the last notes of the woman's song had died, everyone rose and crushed towards the doors, eager to capture any stray cabs that might be waiting outside. From their seats in the front row it was long before Rebekah and Frank reached the entrance hall. By that time many of the audience had left in some conveyance, or had walked away in the rain. But the hall was still crowded with people waiting for the chance of a returning cab or a diminution of the rain.

Rebekah made her way to the front door and looked out. The rain still fell in torrents, and, except a couple of private and pre-engaged carriages, whose owners, knowing they were secure, were leisurely making their way out, there were no conveyances in the street.

To the left of the hall, where a veranda jutted out, the motley crowd which gathers outside the doors of places of amusement when the hour of departure arrives – Coloured men and boys, white loafers, Coloured and white women in gaudy finery or squalor – had taken refuge from the rain and were standing under it, laughing or swearing as they tried to force their way to inside places for shelter. She turned back into the hall.

'I suppose,' said Frank, who stood buttoning his coat, 'we had better wait till the worst is over.'

'I can't,' she said; 'the children are alone, and I shall miss the last train. I will run down quickly to the station at once.'

'Well, I shall stay in town tonight. I'll have plenty to do in the morning if I'm to be off at four. You'll probably find someone at the other end who's going the same way as you are.'

She was trying to twist her dress about her to start, when someone, who stood pressed close behind them, accosted Frank. The hall was dimly lighted by one small lamp; she could not see that when Frank, in replying, held out his hand, the speaker seemed not to notice it.

'Let me introduce you to my wife. This is Mrs Drummond's husband,' he said rather hurriedly.

The man who stood close beside her bowed, without holding out his hand. 'You will excuse the liberty I am taking,' he said, 'but in these close quarters I could not avoid hearing that you were not going out to the suburbs tonight. I have a closed carriage waiting here; if your wife would do me the honour, I should be glad to put her down at her door. I believe the house is next to the one in which I stay.'

Before Rebekah could speak Frank had accepted the offer; the man pushed his way out to call the carriage to the curb stone, and Frank, seizing her by the arm, hurried her towards the door: 'Of course you must go. It's no favour – you'll get soaking wet before you get to the station.' He hurried her across the pavement.

The man stood holding the door of the carriage open; when she had taken her seat, he stepped in and took the seat opposite to her; Frank closed the door and was about to pull up the window, when from the crowd under the veranda there rang out a long, reckless, gurgling laugh. It was unmistakably a woman's. In an instant Rebekah sprang forward and stretched her arm through the window, trying to turn the handle of the door.

'Let me out! – Let me out!' she cried, shaking the door with her left hand as the handle refused to turn. Then the door burst open and she leaped out.

'Rebekah, what are you doing?' Frank stretched out his hand to detain her.

'It's Bertie!' she said hoarsely, evading his hand, and ran across the sidewalk, now deep in water, towards the veranda, her long train and cloak fluttering out behind her. The man inside looked out. Frank drew up the collar of his coat and drew the lappet of his cap closer over his ears and leaned in at the door, gaining shelter from the rain.

'I must really ask you to excuse my wife,' he said. 'She's really a most sensible and practical person generally, but there's one thing about which she's unhinged – a sister of hers who cleared off to England some years ago with a Jew; she and her people spent a small fortune trying to find her. Sent someone all the way to South America to look for her – found she'd never been there, been in London – stayed with the Jew for some time, then gone off with another man. The last they heard of her she'd landed in a brothel in Soho – never been able to hear of her since. My wife's possessed with the idea she'll turn up here some day. It's insanity. I've known her to leap up at three o'clock in the morning and rush out in the avenue because she thought she heard her step. She's fancied she heard her laugh now in that crowd, and has gone to see. Of course you won't mention what I've told you to anyone, but since you saw what passed I thought it was best to give you an explanation.'

The man pushed past him and got out. 'Are you going to help her look?' he asked shortly.

'Oh no; she'll find out her mistake in a few moments and be back.' They stood looking towards the dark little crowd under the veranda. 'It wasn't her, of course,' said Frank, 'though the laugh did sound a little like her. What I can't get my wife to see is how much better it is for everyone she shouldn't turn up!' He drew the collar of his coat yet higher, but did not like to shelter himself in the cab while the man was standing in the rain.

'I don't believe there's a disreputable place in Cape Town or Simon's Town where my wife hasn't had her looked for. She was a very pretty girl; the prettiest woman I've seen yet; but she wasn't much good, I'm afraid.' Frank stood with his back closer to the carriage. 'Won't you get in again? You're getting awfully wet.'

The man appeared not to hear him; his face was turned towards the veranda.

'Of course,' Frank said, moving a step nearer him, 'I need not ask you not to mention to anyone what has happened tonight, or repeat anything I have said; having seen so much, I thought it was better to be frank. People know, of course, that there was some sort of a scandal when she went away, but, as far as I know, nothing definite and things get so soon forgotten, if they're not talked of.'

The man turned his shoulder towards him.

Then they saw Rebekah coming through the rain. She was walking slowly; her train dragged behind her in the mud, and the light from the carriage lamps made the water glisten on her red cloak and hood as she came near.

'I am too wet to get in,' she said slowly; 'I will walk down to the station.'

She turned to go.

'Don't be ridiculous, Rebekah!' said Frank. The water from his cap was running into his neck. 'If you walked you would probably miss the train and have to stay in town all night.' He seized her arm and half lifted her towards the step; the man was holding the door open. 'Don't,' Frank whispered, 'don't let us make any further public exhibition of ourselves.' He raised her into the carriage, and she dropped on to the back seat. The man got in and Frank closed the door. He put his head in at the window, 'I shall likely not get out till half past two tomorrow; but if you have the black trunk and the portmanteau ready, I shall be in time to get on board by four. Goodnight!' He withdrew his head and told the driver to move on, and then turned to hail a cab which was fortunately passing at the moment.

Rebekah sat drawn into the corner of the carriage, her head leaning back. The man opposite her drew up the window and sat silent till they passed the station. Then he took off his coat and leaned forward towards her.

'Your cloak is very damp,' he said. 'Will you not take it off and put my coat round you? It is hardly damp.'

She shook her head and declined almost inaudibly. The reaction from the few moments of intense excitement and the long tiring day had left her almost exhausted. She leaned her head farther into the corner; she was not conscious of the pressure of her damp clothes or anything but the soothing motion of the carriage.

Presently, without speaking, he folded his coat and laid it down on the floor. 'Set your feet on it: put them into the folds,' he said shortly and quickly. He bent for an instant and moved the long wet train of her skirt farther from her.

'I have always found,' he said in a short sharp business tone, as he raised himself, 'in twelve years of travel and roughing it, that the secret of health lies in always keeping damp material from the feet, and, where that cannot be, in covering them. When we are civilised we shall wear no covering for the feet in warm climates.' His tone was markedly short and businesslike, precluding an answer, and he turned his face to the window. Little could be seen through the rain-speckled glass, and, as they got out into the suburbs, lights were few and far, and the landscape was dark outside, but he still appeared absorbed in watching it. For nearly three-quarters of an hour they drove on slowly, the carriage moving through the mud of the drenched roads. Rebekah sat motionless, as if she were asleep.

After a time they got more completely into the country, where the trees grew higher and thicker, and later turned into the avenue that led to Rebekah's house.

Then, for the first time, he turned from the window and leaned back in his place. They were almost within a stone's throw of her gate when he leaned forward.

'You will forgive my intrusion,' he said slowly and distinctly, 'but, when you had left the carriage, your husband told me you had gone to look for a friend whom you had long lost and hoped to find.' He paused. 'I should be intruding unforgivably,' he said, bending a little more forward and speaking yet more slowly and distinctly, 'but that once in my life I found that which to the world seemed lost and worthless, and which, to me, became the good of life. If,' – he paused, and then spoke a little more dryly – 'I could be of use to you in helping you to seek, I should feel it an honour. I have a week to spend here; and I have nothing to do. Unfortunately, as the world is today, a man has facilities of search in some directions that a woman has not. If you could make use of me, I should be glad. There is no house, however bad, which I could not enter to seek.'

Then he drew himself up quickly and the carriage stopped at Rebekah's gate. Again he leaned forward slightly before opening the door and said in a short whisper, 'If, thinking the matter over, you come to the conclusion I can be of use, will you set down on paper details that may be a guide to me? Send me a photograph, anything that would help me to identify. What you enclose in an envelope and address to the house next door will find me.'

He opened the door quickly and got out. Then he turned to help her. It seemed to her afterwards he had almost lifted her out and stood her on the ground. Then he turned sharply and opened the gate. She passed through it: he closed it, said shortly, 'Goodnight' without extending his hand, and turned and got into the carriage. She walked slowly up the path, and, when she got to the top step before the door of the new rooms, turned round and stood still. Then it struck her she had not thanked him for his offer or for driving her home. She still stood on the step. She heard the carriage, which had stopped before the gate of the next house, drive away; and there were steps going up to the house.

Then she turned and went in. The two boys lay in their beds on the floor; a few moths were still hovering round the lamp or lying dead on the table, and on the two little beds in the corners the small boys slept. She walked past them to her own room. She took the lamp from the drawers and set it down on the dressing table; then she dropped her wet cloak and dress upon the floor. Without removing any other article of her damp clothing she sat down before the dressing table. Out of the drawer she took the notebook and pencil with which she kept her household accounts and opened it on the table. She leaned her naked elbows on the edge and rested her face in her hands, thinking for a little while; then she began to write. Slowly she put down the items, numbering each one – colour of hair, height, walk, size of hands and feet. Sometimes she paused to think: then she took from her neck the gold chain and locket. There was a picture of Bertie as she was just before she left. She closed it and folded it in paper, and tore out the leaf of the pocketbook on which she had written and folded it and laid it beside it. Then she sat still, looking at them; after a time she folded her arms on the edge of the table and leaned her head on them. When she raised it she unfolded the locket and put it away in the drawer, and tore up the page she had written and left the fragments on the toilet cover. Then she got up almost stiffly and removed her damp clothing; and when she had her nightgown on went round to tuck in each of the sleeping children.

CHAPTER THIRTEEN

The Veranda

The next day Frank left, and four days passed; on the fifth Rebekah went to the farm to work all day and took Sartje with her.

When she returned at five o'clock she expected to find the boys home from school, playing cricket in the yard; but it was empty. She walked round to the front garden. Then she heard the sound of voices and the high ring of Hughie's laugh. She walked to the rose hedge and looked across.

Croquet had gone out of fashion and what used to be Mrs Drummond's lawn was now a tangle of long grass, with here and there a yellow flower; the late afternoon sunshine shining across it made it an intense green, the oak trees casting flickering shadows in some parts. Under the largest of the oak trees was a collection of heads bending down over something among the grass. The children were forbidden to go in without invitation, but she recognized the heads. She walked quickly to the little gate. It moved stiffly on its hinges now; the little path that had once been so deeply worn was now almost imperceptible. Frank seldom used it, nor did anyone come from Mrs Drummond's but now and then a servant to borrow something.

Rebekah stepped over the knee-deep grass. Lying at full length on his back under the oak tree, with his hands clasped under his head, was Mrs Drummond's husband. Little Bertie in his white embroidered dress sat at his head, bending over it, dividing with his tiny fingers the short stiff curls along the top and stroking them; Hughie knelt on the left, his fingers planted on the man's chest and his eyes fixed on his face; the elder boys sat close to him on the right with their backs turned to her. He was speaking, and all were so intently listening they did not hear her steps.

Hughie saw her first, just as her shadow fell across them. 'Mofther, mofther, it's about a baby chimpanzee was sticking fast, and the man ...'

'He asked us to come, mother,' said Charles, standing up; 'our ball came over from the yard, and he said we could come and look for it.'

The man raised his head and rose quickly to his feet: 'I hope I have not tempted them to break bounds,' he said; 'they have been entertaining me so well.'

'Mofther,' cried Hughie, running close up to her and trying to touch her chin with his hand, 'justh when he was going to take the baby chimpanzee the big mofther ...'

'He's been in a real big island,' said Frank, 'for more than two years, with no white people, and he dressed like a nigger with only a cotton cloth about him, and once he went down a river on a log ...'

Rebekah loosened Hughie's fingers, that were still trying to attract her attention by holding her chin. 'I'm afraid if you once began telling them stories, you did not find them very easy to get rid of.'

'Oh, I haven't done all the entertaining. Charles here,' he rested his head on the boy's shoulder, 'has been telling me things that interested me more than my stories did him.'

A delicate pink flush came into Charles's face. 'I didn't think you'd mind, mother,' he said quickly. 'I tried to tell him about the ant heap and the dark people. He's been in Central Africa himself and seen the great ant heaps and the camel thorns ...'

'Mother,' broke in Frank, 'he says we can come again tomorrow and he'll tell us a story about a war they had in Africa, and how he found a little boy with three Bushmen arrows sticking in him!'

Only Bertie was silent. He had risen gently and had caught hold of the man's forefinger, which he stood holding tightly.

'My fear is Mr Drummond will feel as the Britons did when they invited the Picts and Scots to come over the wall and couldn't get free of them,' Rebekah said.

'Oh no, he won't,' said Frank. 'What time shall we come tomorrow?'

'I shall be here about four; then I shall whistle for you, if your mother will let you come.'

'Oh yes, like the Lap did for the reindeer you said; and we'll all come trooping like a lot of reindeer.'

'Do not let them trouble you, please,' she said; 'send them back when they tire you.'

'Children and animals do not easily do that,' he said.

Rebekah turned to the children. 'You must come home for your tea now.' She held out her hand to Bertie. He loosened his hold of the finger, but turned to the man and stood looking up at him.

'Don't you seeth, he wanth to kissth you?' said Hughie.

The man stooped and lifted the child up and pressed his moustached lips softly against his; when he set him down Bertie walked to Rebekah and took her hand, but looked back as he walked. All the children shouted, 'Goodbye.' The man replied, 'Till tomorrow!' Rebekah said, 'Good night,' and they walked away to the gate in the rose hedge, Bertie holding her hand and stumbling over the grass as he walked with his head half-twisted round to look at the man who was standing under the tree and watching them.

When they had gone he lay down in the same position as before and was completely lost among the grasses.

At tea all the children talked at once. Hughie said when he was grown up he was going to travel all over the world with the man. Frank said he had promised to show him a real boomerang and explain how the savages used it. Charles said he had invited them to go to his room on the other side of the big house where all his things were, which he was packing away to send to the museums in Europe – fossils and dried plants and photographs and collections of insects and savages' implements. Sartje whispered to Rebekah to know if they went whether she might go too. Only Bertie sat silent in his highchair, eating his bread and milk with large intent eyes.

The next afternoon the children heard the whistle and went. In the evening they came back full of the stories they had heard and the things they had seen.

'And, mother,' said Charles, twisting his arm about her, 'he makes up stories like you. He has a little white box all full of manuscripts, and he let me read a little bit of one. It was beautiful. I could quite understand it.' But she did not question him about it.

The next day the children waited in the front garden; but there was no whistle calling them, or the next day either. Rebekah thought, as the week was nearly ended, perhaps he had left. On the third day they had gone to school at their governess's down the avenue, and Rebekah was at home alone with Sartje, who was dressing her dolls on the back *stoep*. Rebekah went into the pantry to put the shelves neat. She was dressed in a blue cotton dress with a dark blue cotton overall pinafore that she always wore at her work in the morning. She resolved to turn out the whole pantry. It was not really necessary; there was sewing that needed even more to be done; but she felt she did not wish to sit still. She stood on a chair before the dresser taking down piles of plates and dishes and dusting them one by one, before she put fresh paper on the shelves. It all looked so bald; the sunshine coming in through the pantry window and dancing on the yellow-washed walls and yellow-white shelves. She counted the plates in piles of eight and put them up again; was it worth doing, was anything worth doing? She began taking down the jugs from the next shelf.

Then there was the sound of a knock at the front door.

Often the carts with ferns and greenery to sell came up the front avenue at that hour and knocked at the front door. She called to the girl in the kitchen to go and see who it was. The girl came back and said it was the gentleman she had sometimes seen next door, who had called and wished to see her mistress for a moment. The girl handed up his card. She said he had declined to come in and was standing on the veranda waiting. Rebekah stepped quickly down from the chair, waited a moment, then hurried out through the kitchen and went round to her bedroom in the new building. Quickly she tore off the dark blue pinafore, and before she took off the dress went to the wardrobe and took down the white embroidered gown she often wore in the afternoon. She turned to the glass; her hair, brushed down at either side of her head and coiled in braids at the back, was a little ruffled in front with her morning's work. She caught up the brush and began to smooth it, making the dark waves show undulating and glossy. Then she paused and laid down the brush. If it had been an ordinary tradesman who had called, she would have gone just as she was; if it had been a formal caller, she would have dressed carefully. She hesitated. Why should she try to show herself to this man looking better than she often looked? Why should he not see her at her worst? For anyone else she would have dressed, but not for him. She turned to the chair and put on the blue pinafore and walked slowly back by the way she had come. In the front passage the door stood open; the man was standing with his back to it, looking out across the garden from the top of the veranda steps. As she came out he turned and raised his hat; he looked down very fully at her as she stood beside him.

'I hope I have not disturbed you by calling so early?' he said. She answered quickly that he had not. He looked again across the garden.

'What an astonishing blaze of colour!'

'There's a pleasure,' she said, 'if you have a very small space, in seeing how much will live in it.'

'Yes,' he said, looking somewhat abstractedly at the garden. 'I've sometimes thought that a life itself might be lived more satisfactorily a little hedged about with narrow conditions which compelled one to expand oneself in that circle – there's such a thing as being dissipated with too large an horizon and too much liberty to expand in it.'

'If the hedges are too close round, they may kill the plants,' she said quickly.

'Yes, that is so! – The reason why I called,' he said, glancing down at her again and then looking back across the garden, 'is that, though you did not write to me nor give me permission, I thought perhaps you would forgive me if I tried to go on with the search you made the first night we met. I got a photograph and the information I needed next door, without mentioning your name. – I have been to all the places, places where I don't think you could easily have entered, where there seemed possibility of news. The last two days I have spent at Simon's Town. Once it seemed to me there I was upon a track; but it disappeared again.'

'Thank you,' she said; 'but I have no hope really.'

'Do not say that,' he said, glancing down at her and speaking as one would to a little child. 'When we fix all our desires in one direction, I think one is almost bound to find what one hungers for at last. I have always had that feeling. I will not detain you longer; if I hear anything I will let you know.'

He touched his hat and began to descend the steps. But she walked down with him. He stopped as they passed a tall pink rose bush. 'How strange that is,' he said; 'one quite white rose where all the rest are pink.'

'That bush has always done so,' she said.

He bent down over it. 'That's rather strange. I thought it might be some injury or growth that caused it. May I take it home to examine it?' Rebekah cut it with her scissors that hung from her belt. He held it, examining the stem and the back of the flower. 'It's particularly healthy and perfect,' he said, as he walked to the gate, still looking down at it.

'You said you would be leaving in a week,' she said. 'Your stay is almost ended, is it not?'

'No,' he said, 'I shall be here for three weeks.' He opened the front gate and went out, hasping it on the inside.

'Thank you for what you have done,' she said. 'Oh, it's my concern now, as much as yours.' He bowed and turned down the avenue.

Rebekah turned and walked up the garden path. The roses had never been so red before – and the lilies and carnations so white. The sky above was a dazzling radiant blue, and the light poured down over the flowers and drew their scent. She stood by the pink rose tree; it had the most delicate scent. In the pantry she put the jugs and dishes quickly back on the shelves, then she went through the garden again to her study and sat down in the armchair.

After a while she laid her arm across her forehead and half closed her eyes. The arm slid lower till it quite covered them; her breathing became as soft and even as a little child's sleep. But she was not asleep.

She fancied one day she went into the garden and the man said quite frankly, 'I have come to see you.' And she went up to him just as one little child goes up to another who has come to play with it. She said, 'Come and I'll show you all my things!' And she took him into her study. She led him to the corner where her statue stood on the little bracket. She told him what she felt about it; and he told her about where he got it, and what exactly it was. Then she took him to the glass cupboard and showed him the fossils. They took out each one and she told him where she had found them and how. She told him especially all about the large dicynodont's head she had dug out in the *krans* in the river bed, how she had felt when, bathed in perspiration in the streaming sunshine one day, the last stone broke away and she held in her hand the old head that so many million years had lain under the sand, come out to see the sunshine it once loved, the same old sun shining, the same old life beating in her hand that had once beat in the old sightless head; she showed him the beautiful winged reptile fossil, that had played so large a part in her system of thought for so many years, being the first thing that had forced on her the knowledge how much of beauty and good has been killed out forever on earth by the brute struggle of animal power to kill; she explained to him all she felt about that, and he argued it with her; and then they went to her bookshelf and he held in his hand the little handbook of physiology which she had bought with her hoarded pence when a little child, and he understood how she had loved it; and she showed him his own old copy of *Plants and Animals* and his own notes in it, and hers written against them; and they argued over many things she'd wanted to argue with him for years; and she showed him great piles of notes and writing on Woman; and they sat discussing – when the girl from the kitchen came to the study to say the water was boiling and it was time to make the pudding.

Rebekah dropped her arm from her eyes and started up. The drawers of the desk were all shut, and no manuscripts were about and no voices sounded. She rose and followed the maid to make the pudding.

The next day and the next she heard no more of him. On the morning of the third day, just after the children had started for school, Hughie rushed back into the kitchen.

'Mofther, mofther,' he cried, 'he sayth he wanth to thee you. I've tooked him to your sthudy!' And without waiting to explain he rushed off to join the other boys, who were already going down the avenue.

In her study Rebekah found him standing before her glass case of fossils. He turned quickly.

'I hope the little son has made no mistake in showing me in here!' He glanced round the room at the desk and single chair, showing it was not meant for reception. 'He led me in here when I asked for you and planted me before the case, I suppose because I told him I should like to see your stones. They told me you had some.'

'Oh, it's quite right,' Rebekah said quickly.

'I came,' he said, 'to ask a favour – whether you would allow your Coloured boy to come over for a few minutes and help me to cord some of the heavier boxes I am packing to send to Europe.'

'I will send him at once,' Rebekah said, and made a movement as though she would have moved to the door.

But he had turned to the case. 'You seem to have some very interesting things here,' he said. 'That's a fine head. I got three of the same kind when I was in Africa before, but yours is larger and more perfect.'

She took the key down from the corner of the hanging bookshelf and unlocked the glass case quickly. He took down the head and asked where it was found. She said on a farm in the Midlands.

'Mine came from that part. May I look at the rest?'

She opened the other door wide and he took them out one after the other: bits of great leg bone and huge claws and prints of footmarks. Then he took up the small square slate with her winged reptile upon it. 'This is very curious, very valuable,' he said. He turned, walked a step nearer the door to get more light on it. 'Where was it found?'

'About two hundred feet from the head in the same bed of a mountain stream.'

He looked at it closely.

'What is it?' she said.

'I don't know. I have never seen anything quite like it. Did you find it yourself?'

'Yes,' she said.

He walked another step towards the door to look at it, then turned to return it to the case.

'Won't you take it?' she said. 'I don't need it.'

'Oh, I could not. It's the crown of your collection,' he said quickly.

'I'd like you to,' she said.

He hesitated: 'I don't collect for myself, you know. I send all my collections to a friend of mine at Vienna, and he puts them in his private museum or distributes them in public collections where others can make use of them. They are a kind of blood money with me, you see. One must, I suppose, contribute something to the world's scot and lot. So I do this and then I feel I'm free to do what I like with the rest of my life with a clear conscience.' He laughed, still holding the stone in his hand.

'It's better so,' she said. 'Someone might make use of it. I never will.'

He looked down at it, hesitating for a moment; then, 'Thank you, I will take it,' he said. 'Have you noticed how beautifully clear the veinings in the wings are?' He was moving towards the door. 'I will not interrupt you any more: I am sure you are busy. Any time today will do for the boy to come over.'

At the door he turned and wished her good morning and went down the steps with the stone in his hand. She stood before the case. She closed it and began to pace up and down. He had been there; she had shown him nothing. All the things she had to tell him she had not said! She walked to the corner and looked at the statue he had bought, and to the shelf, and looked at his Darwin with the notes in it.

That night at eight, when the smaller children had been put to bed and the two elder boys were amusing themselves in the large room, she sat on the veranda of the house. A tin lamp with a reflector was fastened on the wall behind her and threw its light down over her as she sat in the rocking chair under it, darning the week's stockings. A cloud of little night flies and moths fluttered round the lamp, so thick they seemed to make a halo about it.

Suddenly the front gate opened and Mrs Drummond's husband came up the path. He did not go to the steps, but stood below her at the side of the veranda.

'Good evening!' he said. 'I have not come on any business; I have merely come to see you. May I sit down?'

She half rose to draw a chair forward for him.

'No, I would rather sit here,' he said, seating himself on the side of the *stoep*, which rose about two feet from the ground. 'One likes all the air one can get tonight.'

She pushed a little mat towards him, saying that the stones were cool.

'Oh, I shall take no harm: I am an old traveller,' he said, but he drew it to him and reseated himself. He sat about five feet from her with his back against the veranda post. He looked out across the garden, the darkness of which was partly lit by the light from the lamp's reflector.

'Would you mind my smoking?' he said. 'I don't think the smoke would reach you from here.' When she assented he took out his pipe and slowly filled and lit it. 'You should learn to smoke,' he said after a pause, turning to her again; 'persons who lead a very intense life too quickly, at too great a tension, should smoke to slow down; lymphatic people never should.' He put the pipe back to his lips and drew a few long whiffs; then he took it out.

'Of course you will say, trivial and insignificant as it is, the man had no right to have even that little picture to himself. Instead of jumping up and lurching out of the wagon and making his coffee and going off to seek for fossils, he should at once have seized writing pad and scribbled it down on it, and spent a day in writing it out in proper form and he should have sent it home to a publisher and said, "How much will you pay me, one pound or two pounds or three pounds a page, what is it worth to you?" – bargain and chaffer over it, and in the end he loses and the publisher makes everything. A man might as well take a child and put her up to auction – Yes, she is very pretty but her nose is a little too long, her hair doesn't curl quite enough; her arms are nice and firm – he ought to have cut her hair shorter in front.' He drew some more short draughts at his pipe. 'Pugh! Their blame and their praise are alike an insult. Who thinks a man begets children for them? Of course, if he's starving, he may have to put her up, but it's rather like eating your own flesh!'

By this time he had discovered his pipe was dead, and knocked it out vigorously against the brickwork of the *stoep* and began refilling it.

'I did publish a thing once,' he said; 'it was many years ago when I was a student. That friend I told you of needed money; the doctor thought they could perform an operation and cure him of his deformity, and he hadn't funds. I gave him a thing I'd written, a little thing, but I cared for it; and I said he could publish it without my name and use what he got for it. I hadn't means at that time. He arranged with a publisher, but he didn't have the papers properly signed; they promised him so much a copy; in the end he got £50, and the publisher made hundreds. The publisher said he could give him one-third of what he had arranged for. A lawyer friend said we had better go to law. That would have been the ultimate prostitution: you have got my daughter, you have used her, and now you don't pay me properly. I got hundreds of letters from people all over the world'; he laughed a little inward laugh. 'They thought it must have been written to do them good or give them pleasure! I wonder how often, when a man begets a boy, he is thinking of the various instruction of the race it may undertake. One woman wrote me a love letter and said she didn't know my name, but she was sure we were made for each other, and she had four thousand a year. One man, an American, sent me a printed copy which he had had gloriously printed on thick paper in vellum binding, and told me I was please to write my name and an inscription in it, and he could assure me it would be placed in his library in company with the best writers of the day, Tom and Jack and Harry! I threw it into the fire.' He put his pipe back in his mouth and pulled. 'They think you write it for them! I suppose they think Newton struck on his great thoughts to please humanity, and Milton wrote *Paradise Lost* for the sake of the ten pounds he got: and so, of course, the small ephemera must do the same! They can't understand that their praise is as insolent as their blame, that there's no virtue or vice about the whole thing! It is because it had to be!' He puffed away for a good time in silence, and Rebekah's face was still bent over her work.

Then suddenly he bent nearer her, taking his pipe from his lips.

'There is something I want to ask you,' he said. 'I wasn't quite sincere in saying I only wanted to come and see you. I've a little thing I wrote ten years ago; would you read it if I sent it over with my Chinaman tomorrow? It took me two days copying it out; I've done it in my best round schoolboy hand twice, so it won't be difficult to read. I've had it ready for some days, but I haven't ventured to send it. You needn't say anything about it. I just want you to read it.'

'I shall,' she said. 'Is it a story?'

'Well yes – and yet – no. Hardly quite that. There are characters, men and women, in it, but you'll see it's Africa.' He smoked a little. 'Ten years or so ago I travelled there for a year and a half all over the country in my wagon. I went on towards the Kalahari and away to Lake Ngami. I had gone through a time of some stress before, and somehow the country appealed to me greatly. It's strange that ever since, though I've lived longer in so many countries, yet when anything comes to me, it's nearly always Africa, – Africa that sets it. I've a curious feeling for the country as if it had a personal connection with myself; perhaps because I travelled through it when I was particularly open to the influences of nature, as one is when one's mind has been perturbed. I've always thought I should rather like to be buried there at last. I never wrote about it while I was there; one doesn't about things that are present, you know. It was when I'd gone home to England for four months. I was in a little seaside lodging, busy arranging my specimens and cataloguing them to send to my friend before I started on my journey through Russia to the East. It was a drizzly rainy day and I was sitting at my desk writing out a description of Bushmen, and their habits as I'd seen them, to go with some curios; I was just setting down the exact measurement of some skulls I'd taken and was feeling rather depressed and heavy, when suddenly, in a moment, the whole of this little thing flashed on me. You know those folded-up views of seaside places and cities that you buy in a sort of little book, and as you pull them open they flash out one after the other in a moment. Well, it was so; in an instant, all the pictures in the thing ran out before me with a flash one after the other. I threw down my pen. It was exactly as though someone quite external to myself had shown them me suddenly. I wrote them all out that night, and the next day, when I came to read them, I saw it was Africa, the scenery – but you'll see, I put it away in a box with the other scribbles, and I haven't looked at it since; but I've always liked it best of all. It took me only one night to write the rough, but it's taken me three days and the best part of the night to revise and write fair. I hope you'll like it!' He leaned forward a little and glanced up gently at her, almost like a little child seeking sympathy. Then he drew himself up and relit his pipe and leaned back against the veranda post.

'I sometimes think,' she said, 'that that curious sense of weight and depression, often appearing quite causeless, which one feels before some sudden flash of perception, is because some part of one's brain we are not conscious of has been working intensely, so that the part we are conscious of is ill supplied with blood; then something bursts and it comes into consciousness. So it is with intuition; I think it's what Socrates felt when he talked of his Demon. We feel so entirely as if it were a flash from something beyond ourselves. I noticed it when I was a little child.'

'But is it the brain at all?' he said, leaning back against the post. 'I have a conviction, possibly quite wrong but from which I cannot shake myself, that it isn't the brain at all, or not nearly so much as people suppose, with which any kind of imaginary work is done or any unwilled mental process takes place, that it's far more spinal and visceral than people think and that results are simply flashed up to the brain – anyhow, if it is the brain, it's the back part above the spine and the whole body, especially the trunk, that is concerned; why else, if you've been making stories for six hours, should it never be the front of the brain that was weary, as if you'd been calculating miserable figures or learning lists of words, but always the small of one's back and one's body that is tired? I suppose science will work the matter out someday. Why, at first waking, do pictures and things, entirely uncalled for by the will, rush full-fledged into the brain, which they tell us is so ill-fed with blood during sleep? Why, when one lies half-dozing on one's back, does one start up with such a rush of ideas that by no power of will could one have evoked?'

He smoked on for a while in silence. 'I suppose,' he said at last, 'it's the spontaneous nature of imaginative work that makes one so impervious to criticism? If a man tells you pronounce a word wrong, or don't hold your fork right, you feel pained and try to reform yourself – as to the other things, they are as they are and be damned to him!'

'And yet one can, to a certain extent, determine their coming,' she said. 'One can put oneself into the condition in which they may come. When, as a little girl, I wanted to be happy, I used to go and lie under a pear tree in the garden or walk up and down, and they nearly always came.'

'Yes, that's just it,' he said. 'You may put yourself into the condition in which they *may* come, but you cannot determine they shall come, or what they shall be within certain limits! Suppose, in some city of Greece, say, a crown of wild olives or a prize of many talents had been offered for a Winged Victory and there were three artists of power. The first might keep his mind and body, especially the body, so absorbed in gymnastics or business or politics, that no picture comes to him, and he has either not to compete or to make up something he never saw, copied from others, and a complete failure. The second turns all his mind towards it and meditates over an ideal of victory, but there come to him only lovely Venuses and ripe cupids that he can wing and call Victories, though they are not so, because in his soft nature lies nothing Victory can shape itself from. But the third, deep in whose nature is something of hope, virility, strength – to him, when he turns his dreams towards it, a hundred Winged Victories leap out; he could not say just how they come, but he would recognise one as the best, and he would seize it, he would embody it in marble; and then, through the ages, without a head, without an arm, smitten and ill-treated, it would still stand the embodiment of Victory, calling men and women to struggle and conquer, though only through its broken fragment; it would do it because it was in the man, because nothing can come out of the man that was not first in him; he must have felt all the Victory speaks before he could make it; it is his soul.' He sat looking out at the garden with the pipe in his hand. 'All that a man has seen and known and felt, all that lies within him, is, so to speak, the substance out of which his imagination has to work, the bricks laid before it from which it can select for its work. The small man may be an artist; only the great man can be a great artist. A boy might write a song of yearning unrequited love, because youth knows vague yearnings of love at sixteen, but no boy of sixteen could have written *Paradise Lost* or the *Iliad*; the dream-power might be there, but the matter for it to work on could not be there. And yet, you know,' he said, 'that is not all! Why is art prophetic? Why does a man dream and hear and see things and faces which, as far as he can judge, are suggested to him by nothing he has seen or known? – and yet, long years afterwards, the faces and the people and the incidents, the very characters and actions, which seemed almost impossible and unlikely to him when he first saw them, come out and look at him from real life? Why is it that he can paint the actions and emotions of characters in complex conditions in which he never was and of which he knew nothing – and yet life as it passes verifies his work? I believe that a European man with imagination, lost among savages from his birth, would be haunted by an ideal of a living European face which he had never seen and perhaps never would see!'

'Is it not,' she said, 'because no individual is an isolated nomad? He may be one minute growth of the life of his race, of humanity, of living things on earth. Is an artist not simply a man in whom some of the accumulated life of his race, of the millions of human creatures who have been his ancestors in the ages past, is stored? Is not much of his work, if it be true artistic work, like the work of the bee who makes her perfect polygonal cell in the first year of her life? Is not the curious confidence of the artist that he is right due to the fact that he is working by a curious inborn necessity? You argue with the bee in vain, a four-sided cell is better; she builds it six; and, if you ask her why, she says she must – it is so, that's all! Her whole cell is meaningless unless you realise the storing of the honey and the bees that have yet to be born whom she has never seen and who will feed on the honey – but she builds.'

'Yes,' he said, 'but it's more than mere hereditary racial instinct; an artist sees that which his race has never seen. Take the matter of wings. Age after age the artists of every race have seen them on their gods and great spiritual beings – on their Winged Victory, on their angels and devils, on their very bull gods: "And with twain they covered their face and with twain did fly." It is useless for the superficial onlooker to say those wings wouldn't carry them, that their pectoral muscles are not strong enough to carry them. The artist says, "I see them." In after ages, men will have wings; how they will get the force to move them, or so to fasten them on that they will move freely, we cannot say. One day the man of science will realise the poet's dream, that dream – "So it is!" – which he would not and could not be shaken out of. The creative artist does not so much recall the life of the race; he paints its future, just as he often does his own. It can't be explained!'

'Yes,' she said, after a pause, 'but, isn't the answer something the same? The life and movement in a single finger is quite incomprehensible unless you know that it belongs to a hand and acts as part of it, and a whole hand with all its functions and movements is quite incomprehensible unless you know it as part of a complex body with a life bound to it. We know the man, and we know a little the race and the life on earth which that expresses; but the life of which it is only part – of that we know nothing; and that is the moving power.'

'Oh yes,' he said, 'the life of which we know nothing – that is it!'

'I wish they gave it a larger name,' she said.

'Yes,' he said, 'the name circumscribes it.'

She had left off working and was leaning forward with her elbows on her knees. The little moths, who hovered in a cloud about the tin lamp above her, made a little halo round her head, and sometimes settled on her brown hair with its smooth parting.

'I often think,' she said after a few seconds, 'that why men so misunderstand the nature of art is because there are three distinct processes to be gone through before it is given to the world; and men confuse them, though they are really wholly distinct. The first, the all-important element, without which there can be no art and no creation, is the sudden flash, or the slowly growing and intensified perception, over which, as you say, the man has and can have no control; it shapes itself in him; it is here as clearly and as actually as the outer world, though he knows it to have no connection with it. It can, as you say, be large only in an individual who is large; but it may be as complete, though smaller, in a smaller individuality. It is perfectly spontaneous, made of the man's substance, himself-of-himself; yet he feels in a way that it is something not himself but shown to him, while yet he feels also it belongs to him more than anything else in the world ever can. That is the first stage. When once he has perceived it clearly, it exists absolutely, perfectly and entirely – but within himself. He has no power to unmake it or to make it other than it is. It is this first stage, the really creative stage of the things, which I think people misunderstand so, because they confuse it with the second stage.

'In the second stage, of course, the artist's will does come into play, though only within certain limits. He must will, consciously or unconsciously, to create it as an external image, or it would remain forever only in his mind. He must seek for the knowledge and the materials and the leisure or other conditions without which it cannot be incarnated. If he is a sculptor, for instance, he must find the marble, the tools, the spot to work in, and the leisure to work. So far his will is acting, but, even in this stage, only within limits. He can determine whether he will work at all, or with what tool or what shade of marble; and he can determine the amount of sacrifice of other labours and interests and passions which he shall give up to his work; but what the work shall be, beyond a certain limit, he cannot determine without artistic adultery, which means the giving of a spurious art to the work. Always, as he works, he must be looking at the copy within, which is his only guarantee of truth and right. He must not reason and question; he must look. He may change, alter, break and try again, but always in the manner of following his copy. Afterwards, when the work is done or when any part is done, he may question it as to meaning and turn a fierce, unblind criticism on it, sterner than that he would throw on the work of any other man; but, while he works actually, there must be only one thought – the vision and the attempts to incarnate it. If the vision fails, the work should cease. Not only is his will bound in this way, but, I think, even in the undertaking, if there is generally (and the truer the artist the more certainly) a sort of restless pressure which *forces* him, or appears to him to force him, to his work. Of course literally he could resist it: the desire for sensual or other pleasures, the desire for wealth and the attempt to gain it, a sense of duty to others whose immediate service he believes must come first – all these may make a man resist it; but I believe with all true artists the desire to incarnate is instinctive; it may defy their reason; it is almost like the necessity of a woman to give birth to her child when the full time has come; she might kill it, as she might herself; but it is rather nature who compels her to give birth.

'Then comes the third stage. Now the work is completed as far as ever it can be. Seldom, probably never, has a great artist looked at any work that has proceeded from him with the infinite satisfaction and certitude of the dream-god of the Semitics, when he looked at his work and saw that it was good and rested. Perhaps that which he alone knows of remains always to him of a completeness and beauty which nothing he can create in the poor medium of words or paint or marble can show; perhaps that is why, to the true artist, no criticism of outsiders makes any difference in *his* estimate of the work; if they blame it, he knows that they have not seen the original which came to him and was not wilfully made by him; if they praise it, he knows how much better the original was. But the time comes when, as far as he can or will, the work is done. It is now severed from him; the cord is cut; it has now its organic existence quite apart from himself. As time passes he can turn upon it exactly the same objective criticism which he would on another man's creation. The child is weaned. Then comes the question, what shall he do with it? Here, in this last stage, his will is supreme; the question is one entirely of motive. He can burn or destroy it, he can sell it or keep it, publish or exhibit it, save it to be given to the world after his death, show it to one human being or to the world, as he wishes. I think it is because it is this phase of the giving of art to the world, which alone the ignorant person sees clearly, that makes him think so strangely of it. He supposes that, because a man can decide whether he will publish the book or exhibit the picture, his will was equally independent in determining what it should be; even with the highest work of art, ignorant people are probably of the opinion it came into existence only for them to see. That is perhaps why they are so generous with their advice – "You ought to have done so!" "Why didn't you make it so?" – not simply "I like it" or "I don't like it" – which is quite justified, if their opinion is asked.'

He was still leaning back with his arms folded against the veranda post; he glanced round at her and laughed: 'And the author says, "Damn you, take it or leave it, as you like!"'

'Yes,' she laughed, 'or something stronger if he knows it!' Then she leaned further forward: 'I think all kinds of motives may make him give his work to the world – the feeling that makes a little child, when it finds a pretty flower, always run to its nurse or its mother that they may see it too – perhaps in some cases the idea of helping or comforting others – perhaps in some cases the mere love of fame and notoriety, though I think the art given out for such a cause would have something fraudulent in its very nature and not be true art – very often there is absolute necessity, such that, if a man is to go on producing art, he must live by it, and cannot so live unless he gives it out.'

'Often not then! It's the middleman gets it, whether it's a picture or a cradle!' he interjected softly between his teeth, still looking out at the flower beds, which near the veranda were made visible amid the surrounding darkness by the light from the tin reflector of the lamp.

She paused to listen to him, and then said, 'I think, with the true artist, whatever other motive there may be, there must always be this, consciously or unconsciously – not to let the thing die! As he has striven and laboured to give it a perfect concrete form, that it may exist outside of his own mind, so there is in him a longing that it should live on – completely reflected in another mind as once it lived in his: "Shall I call to the birth and not cause to bring forth? saith the Lord" – I think it's something like that!'

'Yes,' he said, still leaning back and staring away at the flowerbeds.

'I have never seen any great sculptor's art,' she said; 'but in my study is a little statue nine inches high; it's a Hercules or a Bacchus (it doesn't matter what it's called) with some vine leaves about its forehead; the man's nude body, with all its gigantic power of muscle, holds in its arms an infant, and the bearded face smiles down at it. I think it was once yours; I bought it for a silk dress. Perhaps you, who have seen so much great art, might think nothing of it; it may be only a copy of some great work. But to me the glory is that – after all these hundreds, perhaps almost thousands, of years it has lain buried, while the man, whose being it first lived in, has for ages been Italian dust or rooted trees and plants on a Greek island – it has sprung out into life again – here, on the opposite side of the earth, after all those ages; with the joy, the comprehension of it, that throbbed in his brain when he saw it, beating here again in mine – the same, alive; it is *not* dead. When I finger it and feel its beauty, the throb in him lives, across all the centuries, as an actual throb in me. It's something like the feeling when you break off the last flake of stone and out comes the head of the creature that was an actual living being, having his day, as you are having yours, and as real; and it comes out into the sunshine, the very sunshine it loved and lived in millions of years ago. You feel and touch it – your fellow life – from across all the countless ages; and all life seems to be knit together even across boundless time.' She was speaking quickly, but stopped suddenly.

Then as though her thoughts had been wandering, she said after a few moments, 'I can fancy that, if a man were shut for years in some lonely castle by a lake, with no human companion and no hope of escape, he yet might find life tolerable if he found in his prison an old block and carved it year after year; and that, when the time came for him to be led out to execution, rather than that his captor should see it, rather than that they should possess it who could not understand it, he might take out his knife and utterly destroy it; but I have fancied also how he would have clambered up and dropped it out of the small window into the lake below, in the hope, as they led him to death, that someday it might be found and might fall into the hands of one who would understand it, and that all the agony and all the hope and despair graven into the block in those long years would find an answer in another heart. They would never know who had carved it, but the thing would live in another soul; and so I have fancied death would be easier to him. I think no artist need fear to give his work to the world because there are none who can understand. No human soul is so lonely as it feels itself, because no man is merely an individual but is part of the great body of life; the thoughts he thinks are part of humanity's thoughts, the visions he sees are part of humanity's visions; the artist is only an eye in the great human body, seeing for those who share his life: somewhere, sometime, his own exist.'

She was softly rumpling a tiny rumple in her little black silk apron between her thumb and forefinger. 'I have sometimes thought,' she said, 'that ages ago in Ancient Chaldea there might have been some thinker whose thought seemed to have no relation to the men about him, whose vision seemed for himself alone; yet, recorded on a mud tablet and preserved through the years and coming to the light today, it might be found most closely connected with our needs and new life, might find its own here today and live again, though the man who made it might be forgotten. I cannot feel there is anything ignoble in the wish that, when we pass, the thing we love should live on its own life. Even a woman feels that when she gives birth to a child; though, if she has not loved the man she lived with, she has not conceived it for the good it might do or the beauty it might show – yet, even then, when she is in the agony of childbirth, the thought will flash in her with sudden joy, "Perhaps it will live on when I am gone and be the beautiful and the good to others"; and the thought gives her joy, though those who win good and beauty from the child may never know it had a mother or who she was. I think there is nothing ignoble in this wish – that the thing we have loved, that has been so beautiful to us, should live on a little in the love of other souls, though we gain nothing by it and our names are not even known.'

'Yes,' he said, 'that is true.'

She had gathered up her darning again and was beginning to work. He laughed a little soft internal laugh, such as people do who live much alone, conversing only with themselves.

Then turning to her and looking up at her, he said, 'You know, turning from the worldwide discussion of art and creation to a very trivial and insignificant thing, if you will allow me – what you say is true. Even with my own insignificant little scribblings, which might never be of the slightest value to anyone but myself, I always have deep down a curious feeling that I don't want *them* to die. Somewhere deep down in my mind I've always had a feeling that, when I grow old and have lived enough and seen enough and am wearying, then will be the time to settle down peacefully somewhere and throw them into such form that they could live for others. Ever since I was a boy,' he said, bending towards her and leaning the palm of one hand on the floor of the veranda, 'I've had an old deal box with a slipping lid that came to me from Germany full of wooden bricks, and ever since all or nearly all I've written has gone in there. I believe why I haven't written so much lately is because it's nearly full,' he laughed; 'but someday, I'm always conscious deep down in my heart I'm going to make it fair and square. They can publish them after I die; it won't hurt me.'

She had dropped her work again. 'But life is so short,' she said.

He moved quickly. 'Yes!'

Then he laughed again and sat upright. 'I am forty; I have another forty years to live. I've had only one serious illness in my life, and then I was too small to remember it. I'm good for eighty! May I smoke again?' He took out his pipe.

She was passing the needle evenly in and out in her darning. 'I have sometimes thought,' she said, 'it would be a terrible thing if, when death came to a man or woman, there stood about his bed, reproaching him, not for his sins, not for his crimes of commission and omission toward his fellow men, but for the thoughts and the visions that had come to him, and which he, not for the sake of sensuous pleasure or gain, had thrust always into the background, saying, "Because of my art, my love and my relations to my fellow men shall never suffer; there shall be no loaf of bread less baked, no sick left untended, no present human creature's need of me left unsatisfied because of it." And then, when he is dying, they gather round him, the things he might have incarnated and given life to – and would not. All that might have lived, and now must never live forever, look at him with their large reproachful eyes – his own dead visions reproaching him; as the children a woman has aborted and refused to give life to might gather about her at last, saying, "We came to you; you, only you, could have given us life. Now we are dead forever. Was it worth it? All the sense of duty you satisfied, the sense of necessity you laboured under: should you not have violated it and given us birth?" It has come upon me so vividly sometimes,' she said, 'that I have almost leaped out of bed to gain air – that suffocating sense that all his life long a man or a woman might live striving to do his duty and then at the end find it all wrong.' She had stopped in her work again and was breathing quickly.

'Yes,' he said slowly, as he smoked with his face turned to the garden and almost his back towards her, 'but remember this – that no art, no creative thought can be greater all round than the creature from whom it takes its birth. If the man or the woman dwarf himself for the sake of art, in devotion to thought, the art and the thought are both shorn. Is a lovely life also nothing? Is it not the highest ideal to realise it? Many a man has shorn his life of all devotion to any aims except his art and thought, and in the end they have died starved out and weaklings.'

She had taken up her work again.

'I see that,' she said; 'but life is so terribly difficult. Men say it is so hard to do the right. I have never found that. The moment one knows what is right, I do it; it is easy to do it; the difficulty is to find what *is* right! There are such absolutely conflicting ideals; the ideal of absolute submission and endurance of wrong towards oneself – the ideal of noble resistance to all injustice and wrong, even when done to oneself – the ideal of the absolute devotion to the smaller, always present, call of life – and the ideal of a devotion to the larger aims sweeping all before it – all are beautiful. The agony of life is not the choice between good and evil, but between two evils or two goods!'

'Why don't you follow your demon? I do,' he said.

'I used to,' she replied. 'Long ago I always knew with absolute certainty, not what was the right course for another man, but for me – and I took it. But life grows so terribly complex as you grow older; there comes always the thought, "if I should be choosing the wrong."'

'Life doesn't become more complex to me,' he said; 'it lies right ahead. I know which path you would always choose,' he added.

'Which?' she asked.

'Whichever gave you most pain or least pleasure. You would always think that was the right one.'

At that moment the great clock in the hall struck half-past nine and the two elder boys, whose bedtime it was, came rushing out from the new room to their bedroom in the large house. As they saw Drummond they raised the war shout, which was their appointed mode of greeting him. They begged to be allowed to sit up just ten minutes more to sit and talk to him, and sat down beside him on the edge of the *stoep*, Charles on his right hand and Frank, who was generally demonstrative, on his left with his arm across his shoulder.

'Put your watch on your knee, so we can see exactly how the time's going.'

'I have been trying to paint reindeer like the one you told us the story of, standing by her young when it was wounded. I can manage the reindeer and the blue, but I can't make the snow glitter; does it ...'

'Oh, don't talk about your old picture; let him tell us an adventure instead; the time's half gone already.'

They talked till the ten minutes were over and then trooped away to bed, and Rebekah rose to go to the rooms to see if the three young ones were all right.

He rose. 'I also must go,' he said.

'It's very early,' she said. 'I shall be back again in an instant.'

'Then if you will allow me I will smoke this pipe out.' He relit it and sat down again.

When she returned he was still sitting absorbed in smoking and she took up her work, but neither spoke till the pipe was empty. Then as he took it from his lips and knocked it out carefully against the side of the veranda, he said, 'It was a nice old custom of the Indians for a man to hand his pipe to another in token of amity and union. We lose much in modern life by doing away with these old symbols of deeper things.' He put the pipe away in his breast pocket as he stood up. He stood below the veranda, looking at her as she darned. 'Should I be trespassing too much if I asked you to allow me to see your fossils again? I did not half examine them, and some, I think, will be quite new to me.'

'You can come and see them at any time you like,' Rebekah said; 'the door of the room is hardly ever shut; if it is, you will find the key on the ledge above the door; and the little key of the cabinet is in the top left-hand drawer of the desk. Please come at any time you like.'

'Thank you. Goodnight.'

Without offering his hand he turned down the path towards the front gate; when he had almost reached it he turned back and stood just within the circle of light the lamp shed.

'Wouldn't you care to come and see my fossils? I have not finished packing them yet. I could easily show them you.'

She hesitated a moment. 'No, thank you,' she said.

'They are in an outer room on the other side of the house; I have two rooms there; you would interfere with no one.'

'No, thank you,' she said.

'All right. Goodnight!' He turned and walked quickly down to the gate.

THE END

Subscribers to the collector's edition of *Karoo Moon*

Else Alma
MRD Anderson
Andy & Sally Argent

Clare Barnes-Webb
Dr & Mrs GG Barnett
Dr Nicolas Etner Baumann
R Bertram
Bobby & Tish Bertrand
Karin Beyleveldt
T L Bouwer
Marja Bremer
David H M Bridgman
Murray J M Bridgman
Tim & Sue Brukman
Tony & Gail Brukman
Anna Butler
Ashley Butler

Adv P Coetsee SC
John D Cook
Hugh Corder
Mike Crowe
John Currie

Caren E Dalhuysen
Adriana Darula
Dr & Mrs M de Kock
Dennis & Dorothy Delahunt
JCMD du Plessis

Anne Emslie
Clare Emslie

David Emslie
Denis Emslie, *in memoriam*
James Emslie
Stephen Emslie
Trevor Emslie

Alan Fergus
John & Vifi Franklin
I Franzen
Glenda Freitag
Ronald & Suzanne Fuller

Stefano & Tizi Gabba
Dick & Myrtle Goss
Lynne Greeff

Alan McA Harvey
Annelize Hennop
Janet Horn
Robin & Clare Horn

Darryl & Sylvia Jones
Gavin Charles Jones

Dr Jenni Karlsson
Johannes Zacharias Kriek

The Hon Mr Justice L E Leach
Yvonne Leibman
Mr & Mrs T T Long
Brenda Louw
Charles Louw, *in memoriam*
Nicola Louw

SUBSCRIBERS

Alison Lowry

Nikki Malcomess
Sharron Marco-Thyse
H A Molteno Library, Diocesan College
Beth Murray
Paul Murray

Carel A Nolte

Gavin Michael Oconnor
Johannes J Oosthuizen
Kate O'Regan
Lesley Osler

Jane & Haydn Parry
Peter N Pentz
Michael Pettit
Hendrik Frederik Prinsloo

DDR Rawdon
Gordon Reid
Freda Rens
Bruce & Kate Robertson
Ella Robertson
Jim & Elaine Russell
Saxe-Coburg Lodge, Prince Albert
　(023-541-1267) www.saxecoburg.co.za

Gunna Schmeer
Simon Sephton
Alice, Frances & Elsie Sholto-Douglas
Lisa Smith, P O Box 62, Prince Albert,
　5930 (023-541-1380)
　lisass@intekom.co.za

Francois Smuts
Barry Streek

Chris Theron
Lawrence Tucker

François J van der Merwe
Alastair & Janita van Huyssteen
Rudi van Rooyen
André van der Veen
Marie Viljoen

John & Alex Watson
Philien Webster
Gavin Woodland
Babe & Kathy Woods
David & Bridget Woods
Dr Ian Woods
Steve & Debbie Woods

Dr Suzanne Zlotowski

The publisher thanks the above subscribers,
as well as those who preferred not to be named,
for their support.

706